PATRICIA E ... d and travel and the coauthor of a guidebook on Spain. She has written many articles about the country for *Travel & Leisure* and *Bon Appetit* magazines, and visits it frequently. She is the editorial consultant for this guidebook.

TOM BURNS, a resident of Madrid since 1974, has been the Spain correspondent for *Newsweek* magazine and the *Washington Post* as well as a regular contributor to the *London Financial Times.* He is also the associate editor of *Lookout,* an English-language travel and leisure magazine published in Spain.

GERRY DAWES lived in Spain for eight years after studying at the University of Seville. He now lives in New York, where he is a restaurant wine specialist. He is the author of *The Wines of Spain Guide 1988,* and travels frequently throughout the wine areas of Spain.

ELLEN HOFFMAN is a freelance writer whose work has appeared in the *Washington Post* and the *Los Angeles Times,* among other publications. Hoffman received a prize from the Spanish government for her writing about the country. She spends several months each year on the island of Minorca.

CARLA HUNT is a freelance writer and contributor of articles to North American and international newspapers and magazines. Her family has lived in Portugal since 1970, and she travels regularly to the Iberian Peninsula.

ROBERT LEVINE, a New York–based music and travel writer, has contributed to the travel sections of the *San Francisco Examiner* and the *Denver Post,* and to *Ovation, Fanfare,* and *Opera Quarterly* magazines, among others. He visits Spain several times each year.

STEPHEN O'SHEA is a Canadian writer who also translates French fiction and screenplays into English. O'Shea has lived in Paris since 1981 and often travels to Spain. He is a contributor to *The Penguin Guide to France.*

ROBERT PACKARD has written many articles about Spain. His work has been published in the travel section of the *New York Times* and the *Philadelphia Inquirer* and in *Connoisseur* and *Travel & Leisure* magazines. A resident of New York City and Maine, he visits Spain frequently.

FRANK SHIELL is a freelance writer who lives in New York. He has attended the University of Madrid, is fluent in Spanish, and travels throughout Spain several times a year.

THE PENGUIN TRAVEL GUIDES

AUSTRALIA

CANADA

THE CARIBBEAN

ENGLAND & WALES

FRANCE

GERMANY

GREECE

HAWAII

IRELAND

ITALY

MEXICO

NEW YORK CITY

PORTUGAL

SPAIN

THE PENGUIN GUIDE TO SPAIN 1990

ALAN TUCKER
General Editor

PENGUIN BOOKS

PENGUIN BOOKS

Published by the Penguin Group
Viking Penguin, a division of Penguin Books USA, Inc.,
40 West 23rd Street, New York, New York 10010, U.S.A.
Penguin Books Ltd, 27 Wrights Lane,
London W8 5TZ, England
Penguin Books Australia Ltd, Ringwood,
Victoria, Australia
Penguin Books Canada Ltd, 2801 John Street,
Markham, Ontario, Canada L3R 1B4
Penguin Books (N.Z.) Ltd, 182-190 Wairau Road,
Auckland 10, New Zealand

Penguin Books Ltd, Registered Offices:
Harmondsworth, Middlesex, England

First published in Penguin Books 1990

1 3 5 7 9 10 8 6 4 2

ISBN 0 14 019.915 2
ISSN 1043-4593

Printed in the United States of America

Set in ITC Garamond Light
Designed by Beth Tondreau Design
Maps by Diane McCaffery
Fact-checked by Leslie Berke
Editorial services by John Berseth,
Patricia Fogarty, and Cynthia Sophiea

THIS GUIDEBOOK

The Penguin Travel Guides are designed for people who are experienced travellers in search of exceptional information that will help them sharpen and deepen their enjoyment of the trips they take.

Where, for example, are the interesting, isolated, fun, charming, or romantic places to stay that are within your budget? The hotels and resorts described by our writers (each of whom is an experienced travel writer who either lives in or regularly tours the city or region of Spain he or she covers) are some of the special places, in all price ranges except for the lowest—not the run-of-the-mill, heavily marketed places on every travel agent's CRT display and in advertised airline and travel-agency packages. We indicate the approximate price level of each accommodation in our description of it (no indication means it is moderate), and at the end of every chapter we supply contact information so that you can get precise, up-to-the-minute rates and make reservations.

The Penguin Guide to Spain 1990 highlights the more rewarding parts of Spain so that you can quickly and efficiently home in on a good itinerary.

Of course, the guides do far more than just help you choose a hotel and plan your trip. *The Penguin Guide to Spain 1990* is designed for use *in* Spain. Our Penguin Spain writers tell you what you really need to know, as well as what you can't find out so easily on your own. They identify and describe the truly out-of-the-ordinary restaurants, shops and crafts, activities, sights, and beaches, and tell you the best way to "do" your destination.

Our writers are highly selective. They bring out the significance of the places they cover, capturing the personality and underlying cultural resonances of a town or region—making clear its special appeal. For exhaustive, detailed coverage of local attractions, we suggest that you also use a reference-type guidebook, such as the Michelin Green Guide, along with the Penguin Guide.

The Penguin Guide to Spain 1990 is full of reliable and timely information, revised each year. We would like to know if you think we've left out some very special place.

ALAN TUCKER
General Editor
Penguin Travel Guides

40 West 23rd Street
New York, New York 10010
or
27 Wrights Lane
London W8 5TZ

CONTENTS

MAPS

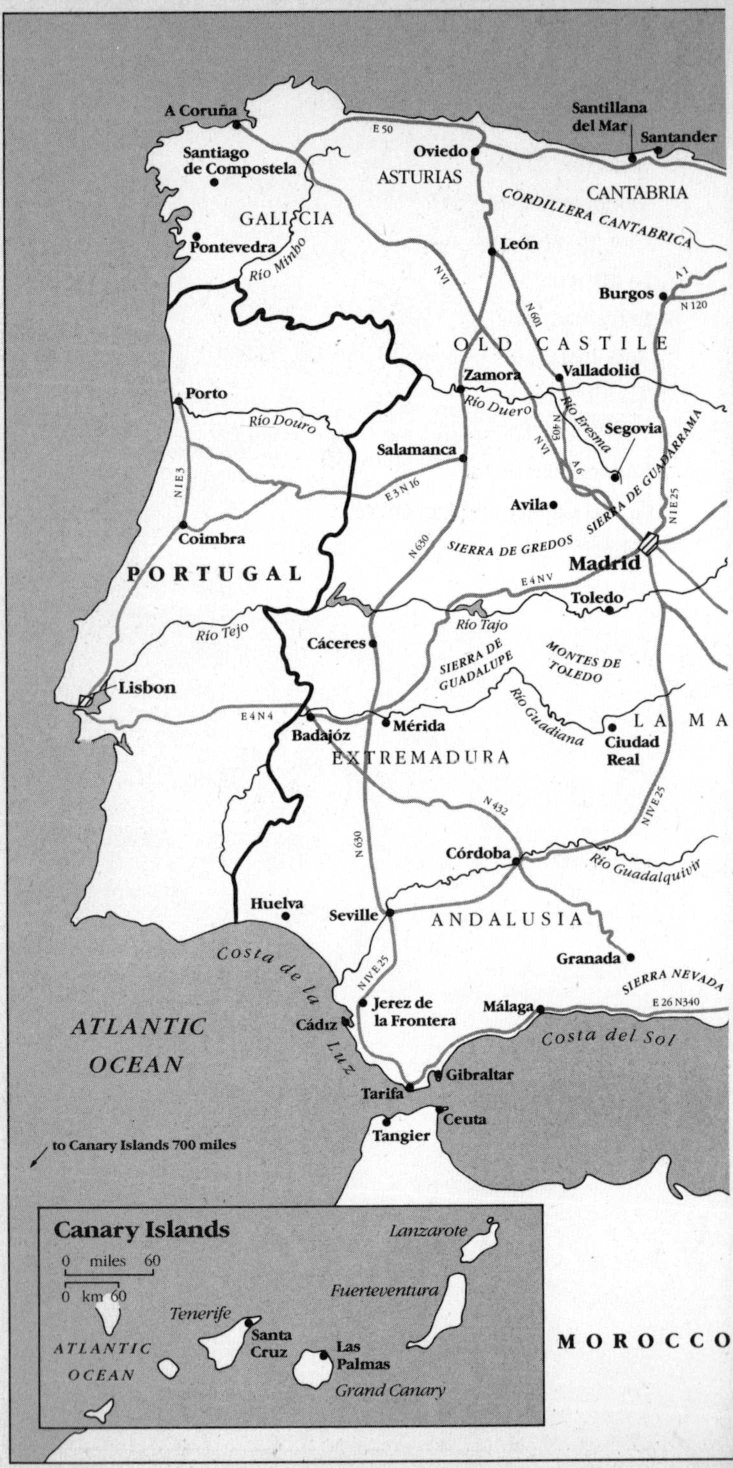
A Coruña
Santiago de Compostela
Pontevedra
GALICIA
Río Minho
E 50
Oviedo
ASTURIAS
Santillana del Mar
Santander
CANTABRIA
CORDILLERA CANTABRICA
León
Burgos
A1
N 120
NVI
N 601
OLD CASTILE
Zamora
Valladolid
Porto
Río Douro
Río Duero
Río Eresma
N 403
Segovia
Salamanca
NIE3
E3 N 16
A6
SIERRA DE GUADARRAMA
Avila
NIE25
Coimbra
N 630
SIERRA DE GREDOS
Madrid
PORTUGAL
E4NV
Toledo
Río Tejo
Río Tajo
Cáceres
SIERRA DE GUADALUPE
MONTES DE TOLEDO
Lisbon
E4N4
Badajóz
Mérida
Río Guadiana
LA MA
Ciudad Real
EXTREMADURA
N 432
NIVE25
Córdoba
Río Guadalquivir
Huelva
Seville
ANDALUSIA
Costa de la Luz
Granada
SIERRA NEVADA
Jerez de la Frontera
Málaga
E 26 N340
Cádiz
ATLANTIC OCEAN
Costa del Sol
Gibraltar
Tarifa
Tangier
Ceuta
to Canary Islands 700 miles
Canary Islands
0 miles 60
0 km 60
Lanzarote
Fuerteventura
Tenerife
Santa Cruz
Las Palmas
Grand Canary
ATLANTIC OCEAN
MOROCCO

Spain
0 miles 60
0 km 60
Bay of Biscay
FRANCE
San Sebastián
Bilbao
Biarritz
Toulouse
E 72
A 8
PYRENEES
PAIS VASCO
Vitoria
Pamplona
Logroño
NAVARRA
ANDORRA
Perpignan
LA RIOJA
ARAGON
CATALONIA
Girona
Costa Brava
A 68
Zaragoza
Lérida
N II
A 2
Río Ebro
Barcelona
Tarragona
N 330
Teruel
A 7
Cuenca
E 101
N III
COMMUNIDAD
VALENCIA
N 301
N C H A
Valencia
Minorca
Majorca
Palma
Ibiza
Balearic Islands
Alicante
Eiche
Murcia
Costa Blanca
MEDITERRANEAN SEA
Almería
Algiers
ALGERIA
N

OVERVIEW

By Patricia Brooks

Patricia Brooks is the author of 12 books on food and travel, and the coauthor of a guidebook on Spain. She has written many articles about the country for Travel & Leisure, Bon Appetit, *and other magazines, and visits it frequently. She is the editorial consultant for this guidebook.*

Spain is a country that evokes strong emotions.

The landscape—ranging within short distances from mountain highs to sea level, from tableland to marshland, with dramatic visual changes, often within a single mile—demands it. Few visitors who travel the country's length and breadth are unmoved by the experience, the scale, the scope, and, yes, the grandeur of the terrain and the effect it has had on the people who inhabit it.

Writers and artists are among those with the strongest proprietary feelings about Spain. Ernest Hemingway's fascination with the country is well known; yet Virginia Woolf, a writer of very dissimilar sensibilities, wrote this about Spain in one of her essays:

"It is the light of course; a million razor-blades have shaved off the bark and the dust, and out pours pure colour: whiteness from fig trees, red and green and again white from the enormous, the humped, the ever-lasting landscape."

If ever a landscape affected its inhabitants and shaped their character, their lives, their destiny, that landscape is Spain's. One of the pleasures awaiting a visitor to Spain is the opportunity to discover its many regions, personalities, and distinctive cultures.

Spain is not a single, ethnically unified country, but a *zarzuela* of many ethnic groups sharing what is the third largest landmass in Europe, after the USSR and France (if you include the Balearic and Canary islands). It is the diversity of all these regions, the fresh experiences and encounters as you move from one to another, that may turn you from a onetime visitor to Spain into a lifelong pilgrim and aficionado. A visit to Spain is like eating peanuts; it is almost impossible to stop with just one.

This is why those of us who have been nibbling at Spain for decades recommend that you do the same, savoring the country a region at a time. While a once-over-lightly tour may show you specific sights—the Alhambra in Granada, the Prado in Madrid, the Giralda in Seville—it barely touches the cultural, physical, and political differences that exist from region to region, sometimes even from town to town.

Every region has its proponents. Those who love the languid air and matching lifestyle of Andalusia, with its gentle rolling fields and sunstruck all-white villages, look askance at others equally enamored of the craggy, dry terrain and fierce, clear light of Castile, of the apple-green Galician northwest, or of the Pyrenean villages of Catalonia, where Romanesque church towers always surprise you, looming suddenly into sight around a tortuous turn of a mountain road.

To understand Spain, turn back to the land. The Pyrenees, Spain's natural Maginot Line in the north, have separated the country from much, but not all, of the savaging that has beset the rest of Europe for centuries. As Harold Livermore wrote in *A History of Spain:* "The Pyrenees rose like a wall to mark it off from the rest of the continent, and its coast was clear and economical. In early times men were struck by the sharpness of its outline: Strabo compared it to a stretched ox-hide, and the metaphor of a rough, tawny surface lying taut and dry in the strong sun is an apt one."

At its southern extreme Spain is farther south than Greece, and just nine miles from the tip of Africa, another geographic accident with cataclysmic effects on the country's history and cultural and political life. Spain's western edge, Extremadura, melts into eastern Portugal, and the history of the two countries that share what is called the Iberian Peninsula has often intersected through the centuries. Spain's eastern coast, from the edge of France south to Gibraltar, has endured the same seafaring conquerors, traders, and adventurers as other lands washed by the Mediterranean.

Next to Switzerland, Spain has the highest average land altitude in Europe. The Meseta, a massive plateau that dominates the country's interior, with Madrid at its center, has an average height of 2,000 feet and is crisscrossed by several mountain ranges. Dominating the northwest corner of the country is the Cantabrian Cordillera, which joins the westernmost Pyrenees, whose highest peaks, at 8,688 feet, are the Picos de Europa. Between the Meseta in central Spain and the Pyrenees are the plains of Aragón, drained by the río Ebro. Three western rivers flowing from Portugal—the Duero in the northwest, the Tagus (Tajo) and Guadiana farther south—have etched deep valleys into the Meseta. Between the Duero and the Tagus are the stark ridges, some over 8,000 feet high, of the Sierra de Gredos and Sierra de Guadarrama mountains, and between the Tagus and Guadiana rise the peaks of the lower Sierra de Guadalupe and the Montes de Toledo.

Farther south, flowing through Andalusia from near Córdoba, through Seville, and emptying into the Golfo de Cádiz at Sanlúcar de Barrameda, is the Guadalquivir, along which many of the caravels and galleons sailed into Seville heavy with gold and silver from the New World. Spain's highest mountain, Mulhacen, at 11,411 feet, crowns the Sierra Nevada range, which crests east of Granada.

The varied terrain accounts for sharp climatic changes from region to region as well, with the provinces of Galicia, Asturias, Cantabria, and the País Vasco bordering the Atlantic Ocean on the north being green and fertile, while the central Meseta—Madrid and Castile—is swept by frigid winds in winter and suffers a dry, scorching, airless heat in summer. Andalusia in the south and the east coast of Catalonia share the humidity common to areas bordering the Mediterranean.

History and Culture

Although Spain's protected, peninsular location shielded it from many sweeping invasions and petty territorial border wars, that doesn't mean that all was perennially tranquil south of the Pyrenean border; to the contrary, as we shall see.

The earliest known settlers were Paleolithic men who left their colorful graffiti in the cave paintings of the Altamira caves near Santillana del Mar on the north coast and in eerie, dressed-stone monuments on Minorca in the Balearics. Much later, Celtic tribes arrived in the north and west, and the so-called Iberians, a people believed to have originated in North Africa, settled in the south and east. Greek writers of the third century B.C. called inhabitants of the Meseta Celtiberians. Their most famous lasting monument is *La*

Dama de Elche, the mysterious stone portrait found in Elche on the southeast coast, now in the Museo Arqueológico Nacional in Madrid. Phoenicians established colonies (most prominently at Cádiz), as did the Greeks, but it was Carthage, an African colony itself established by the Phoenicians, that subdued most of the peninsula by the third century B.C.

Romanization came after the end of the second Punic War with Carthage (201 B.C.) and lasted through the fifth century A.D., during which time the country, like Gaul, was divided into three parts: the provinces of Tarraconensis (north, northwest, and central), Baetica (mostly southern Spain), and Lusitania (principally Portugal). Testaments to the endurance of Roman building skills exist most dramatically in the aqueduct in Segovia, the Roman bridge at Córdoba, the amphitheater and the aqueduct in Tarragona, and the theater and amphitheater in Mérida. But Roman calling cards—ruins—are almost commonplace throughout Spain, with notable excavations in Mérida in Extremadura, Empúries north of Barcelona, Itálica outside Seville (where two Roman emperors, Trajan and Hadrian, were born), and Baelo Claudio near Tarifa at Spain's southern tip.

The origin of Christianity in Spain is undocumented but is believed to date back to the first century A.D. Records of the time indicate Christian communities in Almería, Granada, and elsewhere in Andalusia. Later, as Christianity became an official faith of the Roman Empire, it spread north to Galicia and Asturias.

The collapse of the Roman Empire in Spain was followed by invasions by the Germanic Suevi (Swabians), Vandals (who gave their name to Andalusia), and Visigoths. Those last, who assumed control of part of the land around A.D. 484, were a mere 250,000 or so in a population of some six to nine million. Their legacy was small, most evident today in the Iglesia San Román in Toledo, which was their capital. Visigothic influence there was almost erased by the first Moorish invasion of 711, when a Moslem army, under Tariq, marched up Roman roads to defeat Roderick, the last Visigothic king, near Arcos de la Frontera in Andalusia.

The surviving Visigoths fled north to their strongholds in Asturias and the Pyrenees, skirting Basque territory, which even then was fiercely independent. It was Pelayo, a local Asturian hero, who led the charge against a Moslem invasion of the Picos de Europa at Covadonga in 722. From then on the Moors steered clear of this mountainous area with its perilously narrow valleys, and the neo-Gothic kingdom of

Asturias was left alone to survive, prosper, and join forces with Galicia in the west and Cantabria in the east.

For centuries thereafter, Spain's history is checkered by big battles and little wars between various Moslem caliphates and Christian kingdoms. The Moors touched every region of Spain, but their biggest impact was in Andalusia, where they brought a more advanced (for the time and place) culture and technology. Centers of Arabic learning flourished in Córdoba, Seville, and, farther north, Toledo.

Moorish architecture and art had enormous influence in Spain, as in the use of glazed *azulejos* (decorative ceramic tiles), calligraphy, carved plaster work, ornamental brickwork, mosaics, pierced marble screens, fretted woodwork, and wooden inlaid ceilings (*artesonado*). The legacy can be seen all over Andalusia, even in the smallest white town, and, sometimes surprisingly, throughout Castile, most dominantly in Toledo, Segovia, and Tordesillas. One can't imagine Spain today without its great Moorish monuments—Córdoba's Mezquita (mosque), Seville's Giralda tower and La Lonja, the Alhambra of Granada, and horseshoe Arabic arches in evidence throughout Andalusia, Castile, and parts of Catalonia.

As politics became more complex, with Moors subduing Christians, Christians subduing Moors, in territorial games of musical chairs that lasted centuries, the artistic legacies blurred. That is why there are artistic terms unique to Spain, where Mudejar art refers to Moslem work produced by Moslems living under Christian rule, such as in the Gothic-Mudejar cathedral of Teruel and the Alcázar of Seville. Mozarabic, conversely, signifies Moslem-influenced work by Christians living in Moslem-dominated areas.

As for the literary and philosophical culture of the Moslem world: Its importance to the development of Medieval philosophy and theology (especially Scholasticism) in the Christian world of Western Europe—via Spain in particular—cannot be overestimated, least of all in its transmission of the thought of ancient Greece and especially the works of Aristotle.

Meanwhile, on the Christian side of the frontier, the Catholic Church was the torchbearer of the arts as well as thought, as churches, monasteries, convents, and hermitages were built and embellished with paintings, sculpture, and interior decorations.

The eighth- and ninth-century pre-Romanesque style of Asturian churches, such as Santa María del Naranco near Oviedo, led in time to the Romanesque, which was introduced first in Catalonia, through that region's link with France and Italy, and then in the north by French religious orders and pilgrims following the renowned Camino de Santiago, the pilgrims' route along Spain's northern tier from France west to Galicia. It was epitomized by the inner façade and Pórtico de la Gloria of the cathedral at Santiago de Compostela, the pilgrims' goal.

Romanesque slowly gave way to Gothic, another French innovation, in such major Gothic triumphs as the cathedrals of Burgos, León, Toledo, and, much later, Seville. Gothic acquired a particular Spanish coloration in a unique style of ornate stone ornamentation known as Isabelline, introduced during the reign of Isabella la Católica (1474–1504) and shown at its most beautiful in the façade and patio of the Colegio de San Gregorio, now the Museo Nacional de Escultura in Valladolid. Isabelline evolved into Plateresque (from the word *platero,* "silversmith"), a lace-like carving of entire façades, so intricate they are reminiscent of silver filigree. The finest Plateresque work can be seen in the Patio de las Escuelas in Salamanca.

The Renaissance in Spain left many monuments, most prominently the Escorial and the Palace of Charles V at the Alhambra in Granada. When Baroque appeared in the 17th and 18th centuries, it too added an indigenous element: the exuberant flourishes known as Churrigueresque (named after the three Churriguera brothers of Salamanca), which is visible all over Spain. Salamanca's Convento de San Estebán and the Palacio de Dos Aguas in Valencia are two prime examples.

It was not until the rulers of two powerful Christian kingdoms, Ferdinand of Aragón and Isabella of Castile, joined forces (in matrimony and battle) that the Moors were finally and forever banished from the peninsula. The last battle, over Granada, was in 1492, a significant date in Spain for two other reasons: the expulsion of the Jews from Spain and Columbus's discovery of the New World.

The farsightedness, resourcefulness, and perhaps just plain luck of Isabella in financing Columbus's expedition to the Indies led to Spain's unusual new role as one of the prominent players on the world stage and to a long period of cultural and artistic flowering known as Spain's Golden Age. This era began during the reigns of Holy Roman Emperor Charles V, Ferdinand and Isabella's grandson, and his son, Philip II. As Queen Elizabeth's reign in England fused conquest with culture, much the same occurred in Spain during the 16th and 17th centuries with the written works of Fray León, Saint Teresa, Saint John of the Cross, Cervantes, Lope de Vega, Tirso de Molina, Calderón de la Barca, Quevedo, and others; the architectural achievements of Pedro Machuca, Juan de Herrera, Alonso de Covarrubias, Bartolomé Bustamante, Rodrigo Gil de Hontañón, Enrique de Egas, Andrés de Vandaelvira, and the Churrigueras; the paintings of Pedro Berruguete, El Greco, Zurbarán, Murillo, Valdés Leal, José Ribera, and Velázquez; and sculpture by Alonso Berruguete, Diego de Siloé, Rodrigo Alemán, Juan de Juni, Alonso Cano, Pedro de Mena, Gil de Siloé, Juan Martínez Montañés, and others.

In 1519 the Hapsburg Charles V was elected emperor of the Holy Roman Empire and annexed Milan and Naples, then added Burgundy and the Netherlands as Spanish provinces, biting off far more than his successors could chew. For a while, Spain was the dominant country in Europe, successful, expansionist, and extravagant, living overconfidently on the riches that spouted like La Granja's fountains from the Spanish colonies in the Americas. Under Philip II Portugal became a part of Spain, for example, losing its independence for the first time since the 12th century. The Battle of Lepanto against the Turks gave Spain control of the Mediterranean.

Eventually the bills came due. The Netherlands bubbled with political unrest and won its freedom. The Inquisition, having reached a nadir with the expulsion of Jews and Moors, continued to fester, isolating Spain intellectually from much of Europe. With the brilliance of hindsight, historians date the beginning of Spain's decline to the defeat by the British of the Armada in 1588, which demolished the Spanish navy and led to Spain's decline as a major maritime power. But in many ways Spain spent the next few centuries being nibbled to death by minnows: the Thirty Years War here, the War of the Spanish Succession there, the loss of a profitable colony here, there, and everywhere.

Spain's decline was helped along by a series of inadequate, ill-trained, spendthrift rulers. When Carlos II, the last Hapsburg, died in 1700 without an heir, the throne went to Philip, duke of Anjou, grandson of Louis XIV of France and María Teresa. This was the beginning of the reign of the Bourbons, and led immediately, from 1701 to 1714, to the War of the Spanish Succession, primarily a power struggle between Bourbon France and Hapsburg Austria, with a little help from their various friends and enemies. The final result was that Philip V was formally recognized as king of Spain. He and succeeding Bourbons seemed intent on making the

Spanish court as much a Frenchified home away from home as possible and proved ineffectual in leading the country that remained forever alien to them.

The 19th century began ignominiously for Spain, with the weak Carlos IV on the throne, and his domineering, dissolute wife, María Luisa, and her adviser, Manuel de Godoy, behind it. A series of misadventures followed: the Aranjuez Revolt, Napoleon's installation of his brother, Joseph, as king of Spain, and finally the War of Independence (or Peninsular War), in which the British under the duke of Wellington helped the Spanish repel the French. France's occupation was the first by a foreign power since the Moors had left in 1492. When the French departed, they carried off as much booty as possible, stripping churches and cathedrals of innumerable treasures. The wonder is that there is still so much left. Francisco Goya's etchings *Disasters of War,* displayed in the Prado, evoke the horrors of the period more effectively than any words. And his Prado paintings of the supercilious king, his foolish wife, and Godoy are as revealing of their frivolities as today's merciless television cameras can be.

The Peninsular War left Spain in control of its own destiny, but only in a manner of speaking. Actually, Spain's American colonies used the war to their own advantage, and by 1825 most of them had gained their independence. For the remainder of the 19th century Spain underwent a series of tumultuous revolts, uprisings, and civil wars, fueled by the spirit of liberty that fanned much of Europe and also by the weaknesses of an inept, self-indulgent monarchy. The coup de grace to Spain's image as a colonial power came in the Spanish-American War of 1898 when Cuba, Puerto Rico, and the Philippines were irrevocably lost. What followed was a long period during which much of the literary and intellectual energy in Spain was directed toward somehow coming to grips with the clear reality of the country's decline from eminence; Miguel de Unamuno's *The Tragic Sense of Life in Men and Nations* was an example, as was his emphasis on the Quixotic elements in the Spanish character. This national crisis of spirit, as so often happens, produced a cultural renaissance, if not a political one. In one respect, though, Spain was fortunate: It remained neutral during the carnage of World War I.

Much of the 20th century has nonetheless been unkind to Spain. General Miguel Primo de Rivera's dictatorship (1923–1930) and Alfonso XIII's abdication in 1931 led to a republic: A Popular Front government of Republicans, Socialists, Syndicalists, and Communists was elected in 1936. Then the assassination of Monarchist leader Calvo Sotelo triggered a military revolt led by Francisco Franco in Spanish Morocco, which quickly spread to the Spanish mainland. There Franco joined with the forces of the Movimiento Nacional, and the Civil War began. After three bloody years in which family fought family from region to region, the war ended with the Republican loss of its last three strongholds: Barcelona, Valencia, and Madrid. Franco's forces, much assisted by the Axis powers of Germany and Italy, were victorious and he became head of state. Considering the decimated, impoverished condition of the country, it might be said nobody won—but Spain lost.

The Franco years (1939 to 1975) were tranquil on the surface. As the old saying goes, the trains ran on time (and still do) and the streets were safe for wandering till 3:00 A.M. (no such guarantees today). Though the government of Spain was sympathetic to the Axis during World War II, the country remained nonbelligerent.

Franco died in 1975, and the grandson of Alfonso XIII, Don Juan Carlos de Bourbon, Franco's designated successor, became king. Three years later a new democratic constitution was passed establishing Spain as a constitutional monarchy; the country is now actually governed by an elected parliament, the Congreso de Diputados (commonly called the Cortes) and a prime minister. In 1981 Juan Carlos proved himself a hero and solidified his popularity by helping to undercut an attempted military coup.

In 1986 the country became a member of the European Community and anticipates full economic participation in 1992. That year represents an apotheosis of sorts for 20th-century Spain on several levels: In addition to the full fruits of European Community membership, the country expects to pull out all the stops in celebrating the 500th anniversary of Columbus's discovery of the Americas, with major celebrations planned in Seville and Barcelona. For Barcelona, 1992 also means playing host to the Summer Olympics. Spain perseveres.

Socially, today's Spain is not the place a visitor in the 1950s or 1960s would recognize. Freedom has brought its excesses, as elsewhere: pornography, drugs, disruption of family life, and street crime in the larger cities. It is no longer advisable to leave your car unlocked, even in smaller cities, or to keep anything of value in it even if it is locked.

But for the most part democracy is alive and well here, and most Spaniards revel in it. Economically, Spain has leapfrogged in a couple of decades from one of the more nies of Europe to one of the most robust. You rive through Extremadura now and compare it what it was 20 years ago, steeped in feudal poverty, when donkeys laden with fagots were more common on the roads than cars. Historically Spain's poorest province, from which so many conquistadores escaped to make their fortune (or so they hoped) in the New World, even Extremadura now boasts wide new highways and new factories.

Actually, Spain no longer merely perseveres. Nowadays it prospers, relatively speaking. An ever-expanding middle class has created a demand for better clothes and shops, new restaurants, and a better lifestyle. Life in Spain's largest cities is increasingly similar to life in other major capitals of the world. The difference from some is that Spaniards seem to have a knack for enjoying it.

Yet the amazing thing is that despite the prosperity and the desire to catch up with the 20th century after decades of isolation, so much of Spain retains its sense of place and of history.

For the visitor this means that, once outside the major cities, you can experience a Spain that is in many ways little changed from the post–World War I years, when Laurie Lee wandered by foot through the *barrios* and villages of Andalusia.

Spain for Travellers

For most visitors in this age of the jumbo jet, Spain begins in Madrid. In truth, all roads (and most air and rail routes) lead from the capital, whether you head north, south, east, or west. However, here we ignore the logistic realities and begin our discussion in the north and, while tending to move in brushstrokes from east to west, work our way south to Andalusia and then up along the Mediterranean coast to Barcelona—followed by the Balearic Islands in the Mediterranean and the Canaries in the Atlantic off Africa.

The first thing to keep in mind about Spain is not to be greedy. Resign yourself to the fact that in a country as vast as this one you can't see it all, learn it all, or understand more than a bit of it in the usual time frame of a short vacation. Relax, choose a landscape, a climate, a region—and experience *it.* Next time, try another.

What can help give a framework to your exploration of Spain is a marvelous network of government-run hostelries known as **paradores**. Back in 1928, in an effort to promote tourism in Spain, the government opened its first parador in the Gredos mountains west of Madrid. The idea was to preserve historic buildings—castles, palaces, monasteries—and in the process provide attractive accommodations for travellers in remote places and offbeat locales that they might not otherwise visit because of a dearth of adequate facilities. The subsequent popularity of the paradores is one of Spain's major touristic success stories. Today there are more than 80, with five more near completion. In many regions you can actually plan a trip using paradores as the overnight framework of your journey.

Paradores are no longer just installed in historic buildings; many are new, built in traditional regional style to blend with their landscape. A few are even located in popular tourist places, such as Córdoba, Toledo, and Pontevedra, where other decent accommodations do exist. For most travellers a parador serves as a recognizable beacon of civility in what is often a difficult landscape. In some places, Trujillo in Extremadura and Vic in the Catalan Pyrenees, for instance, it is the reasonable alternative to several characterless hotels; in small towns like Almagro and Chinchón it is virtually the only recommendable place to say.

In all the paradores, whether old and historic or new, regional cuisine, antiques, and indigenous crafts are the common threads. In the parador in Granada, for instance, the traditional Granada weaving is much in evidence in draperies and bedspreads, and the blue-and-green pomegranate motif of Grenadine pottery can be seen in decorative fruit bowls and flowerpots. Local lacework and the distinctive multicolored ceramics of nearby Talavera de la Reina and El Puente del Arzobispo are in evidence in the parador at Oropesa. The stunningly modern parador at Segovia retains its "Spanishness" through dramatic abstract paintings by contemporary Spanish artists and stylized terracotta pots rooted in the Castilian tradition.

Just over the northern border from France is **País Vasco**, Basque Country, for many visitors the first encounter with Spain. The Basques, with their rosy cheeks, high cheekbones, dark hair, and enigmatic language (thought to be a pre-Indo-European tongue, unique in Europe), are known as the gastronomes of Spain. Whether in the little fishing villages in the inlets below the steep cliffs facing the Bahía Biscay or in the fashionable coastal resort of San Sebastián, you will eat well in País Vasco, where tables are set with such dishes as *bacalao al pil-pil* (cod with garlic and red pepper), *el marmitako* (a tuna and potato stew), roasted fresh sardines, grilled *besugo* (sea bream), *merluza con salsa verde* (hake in an herb sauce), and the Basque goat cheese *idiazabal,* washed down with the refreshing white wine of the region, *chacolí.* For gastronomes, **San Sebastián** is the center of culinary gravity, and much time can be spent sampling the city's numerous award-winning restaurants.

San Sebastián is graced by one of the most beautiful beaches in Spain, Bahía de la Concha, strung like a half-moon between Monte Igueldo to the west and Monte Urgull on the east, and edged by a handsome beachfront promenade, paseo de la Concha. Military hobbyists might climb Monte Urgull to the old fort, Castillo de Santa Cruz de la Mota, where Napoleon's troops were holed up during a British-Portuguese attack in the Peninsular War.

Just east of San Sebastián are the delightful little towns of Pasajes de San Juan, where Victor Hugo lived briefly, and Fuenterrabía, with a comfortable parador ensconced in an old castle and a peekaboo view right into France.

Following the coast west will lead you to the Basque Country's major industrial center, Bilbao, which is of considerable importance to Spain's well-being. It also has its notable Museo de Bellas Artes and numerous restaurants. Vitoria (now called Basque Gasteiz) is another modern industrial mammoth, but its old section, the Campillo, is a worthwhile stop for its old mansions, narrow streets, and several exceptional churches.

Just to the west is **Cantabria** and its main city, **Santander**, which is also a smart and popular Atlantic resort in a prize location on the U-shaped Bahía de Santander. The city is distinguished by its many glass-fronted balconies, wide boulevards, plazas, flower-dotted parks, and a grand beach, El Sardinero. Several fine hotels, stylish shops and art galleries, and good restaurants add vivacity to city life. Cantabria's kitchen relies on the sea and the charms of *rabas* (fried chopped squid), anchovy pie, fresh tuna, sea bream, hake, and salmon, the last served often as *arroz santanderino* (salmon, rice, and milk). Desserts, especially pastries made of milk and eggs, are a regional strong suit—*los sobaos pasiegos* (a rich egg-and-butter pastry) and *quesada pasiego* (made with honey, cheese, and butter), *leche frita* (fried milk), and *arroz con leche* (rice pudding).

Cantabria is a sweet land of sailors, and also of shepherds, whose flocks can be seen chewing up the steep emerald-green hillsides. Near Santander is the Medieval village of **Santillana del Mar**, with tawny houses roofed with red tiles, rows of manorial houses with imposing stone crests on their façades, a first-rate parador, and a gem of a 12th-century Romanesque church, the Colegiata. Just a mile from the village are the **Cuevas de Altamira**, with their extraordinarily vivid paintings done more than 10,000 years ago by Cro-Magnon man.

Continuing west on the coast brings you to two beautiful little coastal villages with fine beaches, Comillas, with a hilltop location and a pavilion designed by Antoni Gaudí, and San Vicente de la Barquera, a small port with a photogenic castle ruin and notable church. Moving inland you will come to La Liebana and the rugged **Picos de Europa**, some of the most spectacular mountain scenery to be found in Spain.

Still farther west along Spain's northern tier is the province of Principado de **Asturias**. This is a terrain that combines a cliff-hung coastline with inland valleys bursting with apple orchards, rough mountain passes, mines, and an industrial base—all of which is of less interest to visitors than most of the rest of Spain. There are worthy sights, though, especially in the history-rich capital, **Oviedo**, with its Flamboyant Gothic cathedral, and in the scenic seaport of Gijón. Covadonga, known as the cradle of the Spanish monarchy, is as mist-layered in its awesome Picos de Europa site as it is mythic in its historic significance. Asturian food is highlighted by *fabada* (a uniquely Asturian stew of white beans, ham, pork, bacon, *longaniza* sausage, and *morcilla,* or blood sausage); a regional light, sour, hard cider known as *sidra; cabrales* (goat cheese); and *chorizo* (sausage) or *merluza* (hake) cooked in *sidra.*

Spain's northwest corner belongs to **Galicia**, one of the most beautiful provinces, and certainly the greenest, flagged by vineyards and tiered fields dotted with granaries and stone crosses. Galicia hugs the coast and descends south as far as northern Portugal. The coast is scored by a series of *rías* (firths), lagoons, gorgeous beaches and rock formations, sandy coves, and picturesque marinas. Proximity to the sea has formed Galicia's cuisine, which dotes on *angullas* (baby eels), *vieiras* (scallops), oysters, *percebes* (goose barnacles—an expensive delicacy), and lobster, but other dishes prevail as well, most notably *caldo gallego* (a stew of cabbage, potatoes, beans, *chorizo,* and ham) (*gallego* means "Galician"), *empanada* (pie filled with a variety of succulent ingredients), a delicate almond cake called Santiago, *filloas* (sweet pancakes), and *rosquillas* (biscuits). The best-known Galician wine is Ribeiro, which doesn't travel well, so enjoy it in its natural habitat.

Galicia's star is **Santiago de Compostela**, a Medieval town studded with churches, monasteries, university buildings, a stunning, historical parador, one of the most splendid cathedrals in Spain, and a monumental square, the plaza del Obradoiro. The city is a feast of Romanesque and Gothic architecture, a textured tapestry of sand-hued limestone buildings and terra-cotta-tiled rooftops.

You may choose to travel to Santiago along the pilgrims' ancient **Camino de Santiago**, and we will discuss some places along that route in a minute. But there are other points of interest as well as Santiago in Galicia: Pontevedra is a coastal city of quiet charm and many monuments; Lugo is a fortress of stone, with splendid walls, gates, and watch towers; La Coruña (A Coruña) boasts a fine harbor and the only Roman lighthouse still in use; peaceful Túy faces Portugal across the río Minho.

If you follow the Camino de Santiago—and such a plan provides an excellent raison d'être for a northern journey—you will begin in the eastern province of **Navarra**, in the border town of Roncesvalles, site of one of the most celebrated ambushes of Medieval times. The major Navarrese city is **Pamplona**, which has a cathedral, boulevards, parks, and a notable ayuntamiento (town hall) to recommend it, though its main fame comes from its annual Encierro, the running of the bulls at the fiestas of San Fermín, July 6 to 20.

Navarra stretches from the País Vasco and the French border in the north, south to **Tudela**, a city laced with Moorish, Jewish, and Medieval memories, west to Logroño, the beginning of La Rioja, and east to Aragón. Navarra's vast plains and mountains are a playground for quail, partridge, and rabbit, which, along with trout from the sparkling clear mountain streams, anchor the Navarrese cuisine. Puente la Reina, Los Arcos, and Torres del Río highlight the pilgrims' route here with their fine Romanesque churches and monasteries.

Logroño, major city of the wine region of **La Rioja** (and a good home base for winery hopping), is braced along a plain on the south bank of the río Ebro. You might combine a sampling tour of the complex and fine Rioja wines and the robust regional cooking with exploring such Camino de Santiago towns and villages as Laguardia, Nájera (with its monastery of Santa María la Real), and Santo Domingo de la Calzada. Visiting Romanesque and Gothic churches and monasteries, followed by wine-tastings and meals of roasted lamb chops and stuffed peppers, can make for a rewarding day.

An irregular stretch of vast plains, steep mountains, and valleys west of La Rioja, pierced by the río Duero and dappled with castles guarding hilltops, is the large province of **Castilla y León**, a rough-hewn playing field for many major episodes in Spanish history, and which we call Old Castile. Leading sites are **Burgos** and, farther west on the main east-west road that was part of the Camino de Santiago, **León**, both cities deserving considerable attention from a visitor. Both have splendid Gothic cathedrals, but Burgos rings with echoes of El Cid, while León is the most conspicuously French of all Spanish cities.

Castilian cities, each showing proud, stern hilltop profiles against the cloudless blue skies, share the same amber limestone in their sturdy, fortress-like buildings, but each city differs, too. **Zamora**, on the Duero, reveals its treasures slowly. The most spectacular are the elaborate, well-preserved 15th-century tapestries in the cathedral museum. **Salamanca** basks in a glow of golden lights, its two cathedrals serving as beacons in this comfortable university center. Underappreciated **Valladolid**, noisy and confusing at first acquaintance, deserves the effort you must make to find its core, and rewards with its wonderful Museo Nacional de Escultura. **Segovia**, rising above a hillside surrounded by ríos Eresma and Clamores, quickly reveals its treasures: its highly visible Roman aqueduct, its cathedral, and the turreted Alcázar.

Castile's smaller towns sometimes surprise the most: Tordesillas, where Juana la Loca was imprisoned much of her life; Ciudad Rodrigo, a bastion for centuries, its Medieval ramparts intact; Pedraza, a classic, fortified Castilian hill town. **Soria,** south of Logroño and not covered in this book, reveals a blend of Moorish, Romanesque, and Gothic influences.

And sitting majestically in the center of the Spanish universe is **Madrid**, the capital and a relatively new city, by Spain's standards, existing in its own orbit. It takes the magic of evening, when the city's café life begins to unfold, fountains are lighted, and lights twinkle throughout the old city, for most first-time visitors to begin to understand Madrid's lure.

Circling Madrid are its satellites, easily visited on short excursions from the city. **San Lorenzo de El Escorial** to the west suggests the most stern and forbidding elements of the Spanish soul, an austerity echoed in the forbidding walled city of **Avila**, while **Aranjuez**, south of Madrid, reveals the Bourbons' pleasure-loving ways. In **Chinchón** you will find one of Spain's innumerable surprises, a bull-fighting ring that doubles as the town's central plaza.

East of Castilla y León is **Aragón**, a harsh and forbidding land at first sight, until you become acquainted with its major cities, proud **Zaragoza** with its eclectic but fascinating Seo (cathedral), and Moorish-accented Teruel.

Spain's largest, most diverse, and most geographically puzzling province is **Castilla–La Mancha**, which sweeps in a band to the south of Madrid from fortress-like Oropesa on the west to Cuenca on the east, northeast to the hill town of Sigüenza, and as far southeast as Albacete. Towns as disparate as the touristic "must," **Toledo**, with its abundance of Moslem, Jewish, and Christian monuments and memories, and the harmoniously Medieval but "undiscovered" **Almagro**, with its gem-like 16th-century theater, are just two of the treasures to be uncovered throughout this windmill-marked land of Don Quixote. **Ciudad Real**, once a major thoroughfare, may not be quite the "dull, one-horse little place" Gerald Brenan has called it, but we have nonetheless not included it in our coverage of the region.

Your thoughts invariably turn to the conquistadores when exploring little-traveled **Extremadura**, whose parched land was home to so many of those gutsy adventurers. From Madrid, your route should lead you southwest to the austerely beautiful towns of Trujillo and **Cáceres**, enhanced by palaces and churches built with some of the treasure of the Andes. A detour is recommended to the imposing shrine of Guadalupe, with its lode of Zurbarán paintings. Farther south is **Mérida**, whose Roman past seems omnipresent, and finally there is Zafra, one of Cortés's last stops on his way to the New World.

Another broad sweep of territory encompasses **Andalusia**, whose profile has formed so many foreigners' images of Spain. Most visibly charming and seductive is that golden triangle of cities, **Granada**, **Córdoba**, and **Seville**, with their imagery of flamenco, gypsies, bullfights, and a languid lifestyle. Food and Sherry are a big part of Andalusian life, and you'll want to try the flavorful *jamón Jabugo,* which many consider the best ham in Spain, the famous *pescaito frito* (deep-fried fish), and, of course, the many versions of gazpacho.

But Andalusia in itself is too large and diverse to consume in a single gulp, including as it does **Málaga** and the lotus-eating playgrounds of Torremolinos and Marbella on the development-saturated **Costa del Sol**, the dazzling white interior hill town of Ronda, the Renaissance and Gothic gem that is Ubeda at the region's northern tip, and the pleasure-loving bodegas of Sherry-producing **Jerez de la Frontera** and its neighbor Sanlúcar de Barrameda, both near the major port of Cádiz.

We have paid scant attention to **Almería**, at the eastern end of the Costa del Sol, which Gerald Brenan called "the dead little town, so charming in its animated immobility," or to Gibraltar at its western end.

You might choose to follow in Columbus's footsteps, leaving Seville to trace a route to Andalusia's southwestern extremes, to the gleaming whiteness of Moguer and Palos de la Frontera, just above the nature reserve of Coto Doñana. A few miles west is Huelva, an industrial city to be passed through quickly en route to the Portuguese border.

A tiny bite out of the Andalusian landscape along the Mediterranean coast east of the Costa del Sol has been taken by the Región de **Murcia**, which we do not cover in these pages. Its capital, Murcia, has long been one of Spain's most neglected, impoverished cities.

Valencia is the capital of the Costa del Azahar, north of Murcia on the Mediterranean, and the region called Comunidad Valenciana, which shows us still another Spanish persona—level marshland, voluminously productive. This is the land of *paella valenciana* and other rice dishes, *horchata* (the refreshing milkshake-like drink), artichokes, almonds, and oranges. The city of Valencia takes most of our time here; don't rush it. Just outside Valencia is Manises, where a special blue-and-white pottery has been made for centuries. To the south of Valencia is **Alicante**, with its palm-lined Explanada and easygoing air. Side trips from Alicante will lead you to Elche, Alcoy, and Jijona, famous for its nougat-like *turrón*.

Continuing up the Mediterranean coast north of Valencia brings you to still another Spain, **Catalonia**. This triangular-shaped area is, like most other places in Spain, full of contradictions. What this means for a visitor is the possibility of several different itineraries.

For the wine traveller, one trip might center on Tarragona and the southernmost area of Catalonia, where the vineyards and wineries of the Penedès vie for attention with the coastal charms of the town of **Tarragona** itself and the resorts along the Costa Daurada, as well as sightseeing the monasteries of Poblet and Santes Creus. In this edition we haven't gone into much detail on the road farther west to Lérida (Lleida), an industrial city whose monumental cathedral is currently being restored.

Our major focal point in this area is **Barcelona**, capital of the region, and the city from which excursions flow. Barcelona's signatures—creative food, first-rate music, a rich museum life, and avant-garde art and design—are there to be enjoyed in a setting graced with lingering fin-de-siècle architectural landmarks that look as fresh as new. Don't let the Catalan reputation for business and commerce and the hustle and bustle on the streets fool you; when they aren't working, Barcelonans know how to enjoy life to the brim. Catalan food is among the best and most imaginative in Spain; its white wines and sparkling *cavas* are superb. You'll discover this in such dishes as *escudella* (a Catalan stew), *butifarra* (sausage), *suquet* (a fish soup), and the famous dessert *crema catalan* (a richer version of flan).

Barcelona is currently in the midst of a building boom, expanding hotel space and tidying up for the 1992 Olympics and the 500th anniversary of Columbus's discovery of the Americas, during which the city expects to share honors and touristic hordes with Seville.

From Barcelona you can move northeast up the rugged **Costa Brava,** with its many irresistible seaside villages, some of them arty, and its scalloped, rough-cut coastline, darting inland to visit the ancient cities of Girona, with its Roman, Arabic, and Jewish echoes, and Figueres near the French border, home to the unusual Salvador Dalí museum and two notable restaurants. From the latter two cities or Barcelona itself, art and architecture fans might make a foray into the Catalan Pyrenees to visit the many tiny, remote mountain villages, as locked in time as their landmark Romanesque churches are.

The Catalan coast is the springboard to the **Balearic Islands.** You will probably choose just one of the Balearics for a visit, and temperament often dictates choice. Those intrigued by history, botanical variety, and the romance of the George Sand–Chopin dalliance in **Majorca** will perhaps be lured there; **Ibiza**'s visual beauty, its stark whiteness, and its go-go international community seem to attract the artistically inclined; **Minorca**'s appeal, apart from its English connections, is as a getaway.

Spain's other island group, the **Canary Islands**, is just as diverse, with considerable topographical variety. Relatively few North Americans find their way to Tenerife, Grand Canary, or Lanzarote, the major sunny islands off the Atlantic coast of Africa that are magnets for European sun-seekers, especially in winter. Beachophiles may head for the profligately long stretches of sand on Fuerteventura, and solitude-seekers may wish to discover the reclusive islands of Gomera, Hierro, or La Palma.

"Where did you go?" a first-time visitor who had spent ten days in Spain was asked. "Everywhere!" was the exuberant reply. In Spain? Ten days? Everywhere? Impossible! Think of a first trip as an introduction. Then expect to spend a lifetime going back for more.

USEFUL FACTS

When to Go

There is no single season that is ideal all over the country; Spain is too large and topographically diverse for that. Generally speaking, late spring and fall are excellent almost everywhere and there are fewer tourists then to obstruct your view of *Las Meninas* in the Prado. You can expect rain in Galicia in the northwest in spring (indeed, throughout much of the year), but elsewhere the weather is usually well behaved, with sunny days and refreshingly cool nights. In spring the fields of Castile, Andalusia, Extremadura, and Catalonia are smothered in colorful wildflowers, and the hillsides are dappled with new lambs. The pageantry of Semana Santa (Holy Week) makes spring a compelling time for a visit, although in cities known for their spectacular processions (Seville, Málaga, Cuenca) hotels are booked as much as a year ahead. Barcelona and the Costa Brava are at their most tranquil then, before the French tourists arrive, and the weather is warm and breezy, as it is in the Balearics.

Fall lingers lovingly in Spain, especially on the coasts, turning grape leaves golden in the ubiquitous vineyards. The dry, merciless heat of Madrid and Castile and the humidity of Valencia and other southern cities can be suffocating in July and August, and in August many of Madrid's best restaurants close. Yet summer is the best time for the Cantabrian and Basque beaches of the north, and also, if you can tolerate the mobs of European sun seekers, for swimming along the Mediterranean's Costa del Sol. It is also the season, especially during August, to hear the very best flamenco in that musical triangle of cities: Seville, Jerez de la Frontera, and Cádiz.

Winter in Spain, especially in Castile and the northern regions, can be bone-chillingly cold, but it is the time when skiers head happily for the Catalan Pyrenees resorts and the Picos de Europa in Asturias and Cantabria. Winter is meant for Canary Islands sunshine (and swimming) and for Barcelona, which, of all major Spanish cities, usually manages to be balmy throughout most of the chilly season, warmed by its coastal waters. In fall, winter, and spring, cultural life in

Barcelona and Madrid blossoms, and the theater, music, and art scenes there are at their liveliest. While the Christmas holidays are quiet family times throughout Spain, January 6, Three Kings Day (the Epiphany), is celebrated with parades, fireworks, and pageantry almost everywhere. Fiestas know no seasonal restraints in Spain, so whatever the time of your visit *something* lively and interesting is almost guaranteed to be happening somewhere.

Entry Documents

All that is needed is a valid British, Canadian, Australian, or U.S. passport. Visas are required only if you stay longer than six months. Customs procedures are usually quick and easy.

Arrival at Major Gateways by Air

From London, British Airways flies four times a day to Madrid, once a day to Barcelona (twice a day Monday, Thursday, and Sunday), and once daily to Bilbao and Málaga (with an extra flight Thursday and Saturday to Málaga). Iberia flies from London three times daily to Madrid, three times a day to Barcelona, and once to Málaga.

From the United States, Iberia has daily flights from New York to Madrid and nonstop flights six days a week to Barcelona (not on Sunday). There are flights from Miami to Madrid three times a week, and from Chicago and Los Angeles, two times a week each.

From Canada, Iberia flies nonstop from Montreal to Madrid four times a week and to Barcelona twice a week. Air Canada has flights to Madrid four times a week from Toronto and Montreal.

In Madrid, planes touch down at Barajas airport, which is 16 km (10 miles) northeast of the city. You can reach the city by airport bus, which picks you up in front of the terminal and deposits you at plaza Colón, for 250 pesetas. From the plaza you can taxi to your hotel, or you can taxi directly from the airport for about 960 to 1,800 pesetas, depending on the traffic. The half-hour drive can take 50 minutes during peak traffic hours.

Arrival by Train

There is fast, comfortable, direct train service to Madrid from both Paris and Lisbon. From Paris, the excellent, modern Paris–Madrid Talgo (Tren Articulado Ligero Goicoechea y Oriol—the light articulated train of St. Oriol) leaves Austerlitz station about 8:00 P.M., arriving next morning around 8:30 A.M. at Chamartín station, Madrid. The Puerta del Sol overnight express, an older, more old-fashioned train, leaves around 5:45 P.M., arriving in Madrid at 9:55 A.M. The Barcelona Talgo leaves Paris about 9:00 P.M. nightly, arriving in Barcelona at 8:30 A.M. at Sants station.

From Lisbon, the Lusitania Express leaves around 9:25 P.M. and arrives in Madrid's Chamartín station the next morning at 8:55 A.M. The daytime train, Luiz de Camões, is about two hours faster.

Arrival by Sea

From Britain, there is a twice-weekly Brittany car ferry service from Plymouth to Santander; alternatives are available from Sealink Car Ferry Centre, Grosvenor Gardens, London SW1. From France, the Algerienne car-ferry line runs from Marseille to Palma de Majorca; other possibilities are available through French Railways, 179 Piccadilly, London, W1. From Portugal, it takes ten minutes to ferry across the río Guadiana from Vila Real de Santo António to Ayamonte in southwestern Spain. Ferries from Morocco leave Tangier, Ceuta, and Melilla for Algeciras in the south of Spain near Gibraltar.

Arrival by Car

You can drive into Spain from France, Portugal, and Gibraltar. There are 14 border crossings from France, but the most commonly used are between Perpignan and Girona/Barcelona and between Bayonne and the Basque provinces. From Portugal there are more than 12 crossing points, but the most travelled routes are from Valença to Túy (Galicia) in the north and from Elvas to Badajoz in Extremadura. From Gibraltar there is just one road through the checkpoint at La Línea de la Concepción. Except for La Línea de la Concepción, which can be slow and choked with heavy traffic, most other crossings are painless, quick, and easy.

Around Spain by Train

Spain's well-developed rail network is operated by a state railway, RENFE (Red Nacional de los Ferrocarriles Españoles), and generally excellent trains link the entire country. Train travel is clean, comfortable, and reliable and, depending on the type of service and destination, can be the least expensive means of transportation available, except for the bus. Round-trip fares on many routes have discounts of 25 percent; children ages three to seven travel for half-fare; a special kilometric card offers 20 percent discounts, a Gold Card for people over 60, 50 percent; there are also excursion fares and other special discounts. RENFE's calendar of discount days tells you the days each year when you can travel at reduced rates.

The Talgo's diesel trains are speedy, deluxe, and air-conditioned, and they provide express service between Madrid and other major cities: Barcelona, Bilbao, Cádiz, Málaga, Seville, Valencia, and Zaragoza. The diesel Ter and Electrotren, also with first-rate accommodations, make more stops, are a bit slower, and serve various parts of the country. Sleepers, couchettes, and coach seats are available in both first and second class, depending on the destination.

Trains are convenient for day trips from Madrid, with many trains a day leaving from Atocha station for Aranjuez, Avila, El Escorial, Segovia, and Toledo, none more than two hours away.

In addition, RENFE now offers a number of special excursions from May through October on a beautifully refurbished 1920s luxury train, the *gran luxe* Al-Andalus Express, which accommodates a maximum of 80 passengers. During May/June and September/October the train's two-day, one-night itineraries are in southern Spain, between Seville and Málaga; in July/August the itineraries are two-day, two-night through northern Spain, between Barcelona and Santiago de Compostela. There are also two extra Madrid–Seville itineraries: a four-day, three-night Holy Week excursion April 11 to 14, 1990; and a four-day, three-night Feria de Abril excursion April 24 to 27. At other times of year the train is available for charter.

RENFE schedules, fares, and supplements are complicated. For instance, you can purchase a Spain Rail Pass, similar in concept to the Eurail Pass, in advance, outside Spain. This pass (called the Tarjeta Turistica) is available in six different combinations in increments of 8, 15, and 22 days, for either first or second class, and is good for unlimited train travel on any RENFE train inside Spain (beginning with the day the first train ride begins). Such a pass represents good value for someone planning frequent and/or extensive travel. It is not necessarily a bargain if your plans include only a single trip from Madrid, say, to Barcelona.

The Spain Rail Pass and all Al-Andalus Express excursions are available in North America through travel agents (as they are in Britain), or through Donna Brunstad Associates, 25 Sylvan Road South, Westport, Connecticut; Tel: (203) 454-8916.

Available at RENFE offices *within Spain only* are several other cost-saving options:

- Youth Pass, available between May 1 and December 31 to anyone between the ages 12 and 26, for half the price of the regular ticket if you travel on certain designated Blue Days (specific days each year when you can travel at reduced rates) at least 100 km inside Spain;
- Round-Trip Pass, a 20 percent discount for travel on Blue Days for distances of 200 km or more;
- Family Pass (minimum of three persons), which provides one full fare, one 50 percent discount for a spouse, and a 75 percent discount for children ages 4 to 11, for travel on Blue Days;
- Children's Pass, a 50 percent discount for children over 4 and under 12 years.

It is advisable, if you plan much train travel, to write for a copy of *Como Viajar Borato en España,* a 52-page booklet published by the Secretaria de Estado de Turismo, Ministerio de Transportes, Turism y Comunicaciones, 50 María de Molina, Madrid. This booklet, which is also available at RENFE ticket offices, is full of information about special discounts and rates on Spanish railroads, airlines, and ships, and provides a calendar of Blue Days, when reduced rates pertain.

Around Spain by Air

Spain's two domestic airlines, Iberia and Aviaco, have offices in all major cities and serve more than 36 cities and towns. Flights from Madrid to many Spanish cities are usually one hour or less. One problem is the "you can't get there from here" syndrome, in which to go from city A to city B you often have to return first to Madrid and depart from there. And while many domestic airports are only a few miles from town, the airports at Málaga and Murcia, to cite two of the extremes, are 32 miles away; if your time is limited, this can be a problem.

Around Spain by Bus

Spain's cities and towns are linked by numerous small bus companies; there is no national bus company. While buses in general are inexpensive, much time can be wasted waiting for connections from town to town. For schedules and information check the telephone directory, or inquire at a travel agency or the local tourist office.

Renting a Car and Driving

Driving in Spain is the best way to see the smaller towns, villages, and countryside. If your visit is limited to large cities, it is much better to get there by air or train, then rely on local transportation. Fast traffic, a surfeit of one-way streets, and narrow, labyrinthine passageways make city driving hazardous. Parking is a problem, too, and tickets and tow-aways are standard operating procedures for city police.

If you plan to drive in Spain, you will need to be 18 years old and have a valid U.S., Canadian, British, or international driver's license. There are major car-rental agencies such as Avis, Hertz, Godfrey Davis, Budget, Europcar (National), and Atesa (the least expensive) in all large cities and airports. Rental fee includes basic public liability and property-damage insurance, oil, and maintenance. Full vehicle-damage insurance adds an extra daily charge. The high cost of gasoline in Spain and the narrow streets in many small cities are strong arguments for choosing a small car, and security concerns suggest one with a closed trunk, not a hatchback.

Spanish roads range from *autopistas* (superhighways), which often charge high pay-by-distance fees, to pockmarked, weathered country lanes. But the norm is a two- or three-lane asphalt road, well maintained and surfaced, with well-posted international highway symbols. Gas stations are few and far between in the countryside, so plan ahead. Spanish drivers are generally courteous, and truckers are known for signaling you to pass when the road ahead is clear.

A few caveats: Seat belts are mandatory outside city limits; even on a country road you might be stopped, ticketed, and fined if you are "unhitched." Also, radar zones shouldn't be taken lightly; you may receive a ticket forwarded to your home address, if you aren't tagged on the spot. Parking places even in small cities can be difficult to find; head for the big blue signs marked with a large white "P" for parking.

Telephoning

The country code for Spain is 34. Area codes for major cities are: Madrid 91, Barcelona 93, Seville 95, Valencia 96; when calling from outside Spain, drop the 9 in the area code.

Local Time

Mainland Spain is six hours ahead of New York, Toronto, and other areas on eastern standard time (five hours ahead from April to October during daylight saving time), one hour ahead of Greenwich mean time, and eight hours behind

Sydney, Australia. The Canary Islands are five hours ahead of eastern standard time (four hours during daylight saving time).

Currency

The peseta, the basic monetary unit, consists of 100 céntimos. Peseta bank notes are issued in 100, 200, 500, 1,000, 2,000 and 5,000 denominations. Coins are 10 and 50 céntimos; 1, 2½, 5, 25, 50, and 100 pesetas. Caution: The 100-peseta coin is similar in size to the 25-peseta coin, so inspect each carefully before disbursing. Money can be exchanged at banks, *cambios* (exchange offices), and hotels; the best rate is at banks, second best at hotels. Rates change almost daily nowadays, so check listings at major banks or in the *International Herald Tribune* or other daily newspapers.

Major traveller's checks are accepted widely throughout Spain, as are credit cards such as American Express, MasterCard, Visa, Diners Club, and Carte Blanche. Many hotels, restaurants, and shops have decals on their front windows indicating which cards are accepted; the Eurocard is equivalent to MasterCard. Some shops will add an extra charge for credit-card payments. Relatively few hotels and restaurants will accept personal checks.

Electric Current

Common voltage is 220, but in some places, especially newer hotels, 110 is in use in the bathrooms. Even so, the 110-volt outlets customarily require a Continental two-pin round-prong plug, not the usual North American flat-blade plug. The best solution is to carry an adapter. If you take a North American standard radio or cassette player with you, be sure it is battery-operated, as many hotels have electric outlets only in the bathroom, and the 50-cycle Spanish current won't match 60-cycle equipment.

Business Hours

Banking hours are from 9:00 A.M. to 2:00 P.M. weekdays, 9:00 A.M. to 1:00 P.M. Saturday. Most other businesses, shops, and boutiques are open from 9:00 A.M. to 1:00 P.M., then from 4:00 or 4:30 to 8:00 P.M., Monday through Friday. Many shops and businesses are open Saturday as well from 9:00 A.M. to 1:00 P.M. Department store hours are 9:30 or 10:00 A.M. to 8:00 P.M., Monday through Saturday. Restaurant hours are generally from 1:00 to 4:00 P.M. for lunch, 9:00 or 9:30 to 11:30 P.M. or midnight for dinner. Many restaurants and other businesses close for vacation part or all of the month of August.

Museums, monuments, and churches open to the public often operate on schedules that in some cases seem to be known only to themselves. This is especially true in smaller towns and villages. In general, the hours are from 10:00 A.M. to 1:00 or 2:00 P.M. Tuesday through Sunday, with certain institutions open weekday afternoons from 4:00 to 7:00 P.M. as well. To further complicate the picture, there are summer and winter hours at many museums, and most are closed Mondays and on certain holidays.

Hours for theaters and movies are usually 7:00 and 10:00 or 10:30 P.M. week nights and Saturdays, and about 4:30 P.M. on Sundays and holidays. Bullfights begin around 5:00 P.M. Sunday afternoons from March through mid-October. Soccer matches begin around 5:00 P.M. in smaller cities and towns, a little later in major cities, September through June.

Holidays

On the 14 official national holidays observed throughout Spain banks, offices, shops, and some restaurants are closed. These holidays include January 1 (New Year's Day), January 6 (Epiphany or Three Kings Day), March 19 (Saint Joseph's feast day), Holy (or Maundy) Thursday, Good Friday, Easter Monday, May 1 (May Day), Corpus Christi (a movable feast, usually in late June), July 25 (feast of Saint James, Spain's patron saint), August 15 (Assumption of the Virgin), October 12 (National Day), November 1 (All Saints' Day), December 8 (Immaculate Conception), and December 25 (Christmas).

Easter weekend is a *five-day* holiday, the major one in Spain, with many restaurants, shops, and museums closed. In addition, in many towns and cities the feast day of Saint Peter and Saint Paul (June 29) is celebrated, and the day honoring the local patron saint is also a local holiday, with many shops, offices, and museums closed.

Safety

The careful precautions you would take in a large city in the United States, Canada, or Britain should be applied in Spain's major cities as well. Lock your car when you leave it and do not leave anything visible inside. In fact, it is often unwise to leave luggage and other valuables even in the trunk, and *never* overnight. As a precaution against pickpockets and the current motorbike thieves who snatch and ride away, do not carry a camera on a strap around your neck or a shoulder-strap handbag; the straps are too easy to cut. Some experienced travellers wear a money belt around the waist; others wear jackets with zipper or inside pockets, in which they can carry a minimal amount of essential cash.

Madrid, Barcelona, and especially Seville, along with coastal tourist centers like Málaga and Torremolinos, are the cities where thieves operate most freely. In Seville, it is wise to leave passports and any unnecessary valuables safely locked up in your hotel and to avoid empty streets during the siesta hours. A current big-city scam is for someone to brush against a traveller on a crowded street and smear something on his coat. A colleague then stops and offers to help the victim rub out the smear. In doing so, he lifts the wallet from the jacket he is helping to "clean." Smaller cities, towns, and villages are relatively crime free, though a prudent traveller always safeguards wallet, passport, and other valuables.

For Further Information

The National Tourist Office of Spain (NTOS) has offices in London, Toronto, New York, Chicago, Miami, and Beverly Hills, with many brochures available to anyone planning a trip to Spain. There is no office in Australia; see a travel agent if you are planning a visit. The addresses of the major offices are: 57–58 St. James's Street, *London* SW1 A1LD, Tel: (01) 499-1169; 60 Bloor Street West, Suite 201, *Toronto,* Ontario M4W 3B8, Tel: (416) 961-3131; 665 Fifth Avenue, *New York,* New York 10022, Tel: (212) 759-8822; 845 N. Michigan Avenue, *Chicago,* Illinois 60611, Tel: (312) 642-1992; 1221 Brickell Avenue, Suite 1850, *Miami,* Florida 33131, Tel: (305) 358-1992; San Vicente Plaza Building, 8383 Wilshire Boulevard, Suite 960, *Beverly Hills,* California 90211, Tel: (213) 658-7188.

—*Patricia Brooks*

BIBLIOGRAPHY

MARCEL ACIER, *From Spanish Trenches* (1937). Letters, newspaper accounts, and journal entries from participants and observers in Spain's Civil War.

DAWN ADES, *Dali and Surrealism* (1982). A detailed study of Dalí's work in context with the main currents of 20th-century art, enhanced by photographs.

FRANCISCO AYALA, *Usurpers* (1987). Seven tales on the corrupting force of power, recalling different historical events of Medieval and Golden Age Spain, by a master of Spanish prose who won the National Prize for Literature in 1983.

PETER BESAS, *Behind the Spanish Lens: Spanish Cinema Under Fascism and Democracy* (1985). The history of Spanish films through the early 1980s.

BERNARD BEVAN, *Spanish Architecture.* A survey of Spanish architecture that includes styles indigenous to Spain, such as early-16th-century Plateresque and 18th-century Churrigueresque.

ANTHONY BLUNT, *Picasso's Guernica* (1969). An art expert's view of Picasso's controversial painting.

JOSÉ CABELLERO BONALD, *Andalusian Dances.* A standard text, with photographs, that examines the origins and development of "jondo" and flamenco dances. This historical survey of song and dance in Andalusia traces the gypsy and Arabic influences to their earliest sources.

GEORGE BORROW, *The Bible in Spain* (1843). After a century and a half, still an English-language classic on travel in Spain. Spirited, opinionated, engaging. "Unlike most books acclaimed by contemporary critics as unmistakable works of genius, *The Bible in Spain* is as impressive today as when it left the publisher's hands," writes Peter Quennell in the Introduction.

YVES BOTTINEAU, *The Wonders of Spain.* A collection of photographs that provides a sense of Spain's geographic and cultural range.

CLAUDE G. BOWERS, *The Spanish Adventures of Washington Irving.* A former American ambassador to Spain writes knowledgeably and sympathetically of Irving's two decades in Spain.

GERALD BRENAN, *The Face of Spain.* Memorable, especially for his account of his search for the burial place of Federico García Lorca.

———, *The Literature of the Spanish People.* A thorough, scholarly, yet eminently readable discussion of Spanish literature from Roman times to the present. Admirable in its scope and engrossing analysis.

———, *South From Granada.* A close and informed look at Andalusia's wild Alpujarras range.

———, *The Spanish Labyrinth.* An examination of the social and political background of the Civil War, as well as a searching look at the war itself.

VINCENT BROME, *The International Brigades: Spain 1936–1939.* A historical assessment of 40,000 men, a "modern crusade," who came from other countries to fight in the Spanish Civil War.

JONATHAN BROWN, *Diego de Velázquez, Painter and Courtier* (1986). An exceptional biography of the painter's remarkable life by a professor of fine arts at New York University.

WILLIAM CULLEN BRYANT, *Letters of a Traveler.* Somewhat stodgy and dated but often insightful.

TITUS BURCKHARDT, *Moorish Culture in Spain* (1972). An almost indispensable analysis of the culture of the Moors in Spain, with line drawings and photographs. Readable, scholarly, and something of a classic.

PEDRO CALDERÓN DE LA BARCA, *Life Is a Dream.* The prolific 17th-century dramatist's most frequently produced comedy, with tragic overtones, that advocates the necessity of order, however painful, against the terror of chaos: Life is a dream, but it must not be lived irresponsibly.

A. C. CALVERT, *Southern Spain* (1908). A book that centers on Andalusia and takes a particularly critical view of the Alhambra.

PENELOPE CASAS, *The Foods and Wines of Spain* (1982). That rare cookbook that is informative, literate, entertaining, and decidedly practical, by an expert on Spanish cuisine.

———, *Tapas* (1985). A definitive look at "the little dishes of Spain." Recipes, menus, and recommended *tapas* bars in Spain. Her high standards in writing and research prevail.

AMERICO CASTRO, *The Structure of Spanish History.* Perhaps the best scholarly analysis of Spanish thought and history.

MIGUEL DE CERVANTES, *Don Quixote* (1605). La Mancha's Don Quixote and Sancho Panza ride forth in one of the world's great novels.

GILBERT CHASE, *The Music of Spain.* A survey of Spanish music emphasizing its diversity of cultural influences and the qualities that make it unique.

J. M. COHEN, *The Penguin Book of Spanish Verse.* A splendid chronological anthology of Spanish poetry, with biographical notes and Cohen's prose translation of each poem.

VALENTINE CUNNINGHAM, *Spanish Front: Writers on the Civil War* (1986). An anthology of famous writers' letters, essays, and poetry on the Spanish Civil War. Includes much hitherto unfamiliar (and fascinating) material by Simone Weil, Stephen Spender, Herbert Read, Virginia Woolf, and Evelyn Waugh, among others.

REINHART DOZY, *Spanish Islam* (1972). A history of the Moslems in Spain through the 11th century. Translated by Francis Griffin Stokes.

HUBRECHT DUIJKER, *The Wines of Rioja.* A lively and informative work on the greatest red-wine region of Spain.

J. H. ELLIOTT, *Spain and Its World 1506–1700: Selected Essays.* An anthology that centers on the apparent paradox of a golden age of the arts coinciding with "an iron age of political and economic disaster."

HAVELOCK ELLIS, *The Soul of Spain* (1908). The eminent psychologist chooses Spain as an analysand.

EBERHARD FISCH, *Guernica by Picasso* (1988). A short, clear, explicit historical and critical look at this seminal painting of Picasso.

JAMES FITZMAURICE-KELLY, *Lope de Vega and the Spanish Drama* (1902). A survey that follows the course of Spanish theater up to 1900.

RICHARD FORD, *A Hand-book for Travellers in Spain* (1845). A classic that ". . . takes its place among the best books of travel, humor and history—social, literary, political, and artistic, in the English language," writes Sir William Sterling-Maxwell.

WALDO FRANK, *Virgin Spain.* The author claims that the world "nurses" two myths concerning Spain: that she is decadent, and that she is romantic. He attempts to dispel both of them.

FEDERICO GARCÍA LORCA, *The House of Bernarda Alba* (1936). In what is perhaps his most famous play, Lorca fuses powerful imagery and an almost surrealistic design in a theme of sterility and frustrated love. Many critics consider him Spain's finest poet-playwright since Lope de Vega.

IAN GIBSON, *Federico García Lorca: A Life* (1989). After 20 years of research, Gibson, now a Spanish citizen, offers what seems likely to be the definitive treatment of the life and art of García Lorca.

DAVID C. GOODMAN, *Power and Penury* (1988). Government, technology, and science in Philip II's Spain, a subject consistently overlooked until now by historians of science.

CLIVE GRIFFIN, *The Crombergers of Seville: The History of a Printing and Merchant Dynasty.* An account of an entrepreneurial 16th-century German family in Spain whose commercial interests in printing, mines, and ranches encompassed both Spain and Mexico.

JOSÉ GUIDOL, *Goya.* The text and illustrations illuminate Goya's chronological development in becoming what many believe to be Spain's greatest artist.

MARIANNE HARASZTI-TAKACS, *Spanish Masters.* A surprising look, through text and reproductions of rarely exhibited Spanish paintings in the collection of the Budapest Museum of Fine Art. El Greco, Zurbarán, Ribera, Murillo, Velázquez, and Goya are among the artists.

RICHARD J. HARRISON, *Spain at the Dawn of History: Iberians, Phoenicians and Greeks* (1988). A prehistorian's view of recent excavations in Spain, with emphasis on the Iberians between 1000 and 200 B.C.

ERNEST HEMINGWAY, *The Dangerous Summer.* An account (with an introduction by James A. Michener) of a visit to Spain in the summer of 1959 that highlights the rivalry between the bullfighters Antonio Ordóñez and Luis Miguel Dominguin.

———, *Death in the Afternoon* (1932). Many consider this the definitive book on bullfighting, written by an aficionado.

———, *The Sun Also Rises* (1926). His first and, many critics think, his best novel. Pamplona, Madrid, and a Spain that is more heterodox than historical.

THOMAS HINDE, *Spain.* Quotations from a wide variety of writers on various aspects of Spanish life, tied together by the author's observations. Photographs.

JOHN HOOPER, *The Spaniards: A Portrait of the New Spain* (1986). An excellent account by a British journalist of the changes in Spain after Franco, with insights into sociological, political, economic, and regional aspects.

DAVID HOWARTH, *The Voyage of the Armada* (1981). An account of the Armada's ill-fated voyage to England, told from the Spanish perspective. Draws on 16th-century documents and letters discovered in the royal archives.

PIERRE IRVING, *The Life and Letters of Washington Irving* (1973). Irving's nephew devotes much of this detailed biography to his uncle's stay in Spain. Many hitherto unpublished letters.

WASHINGTON IRVING, *Tales of the Alhambra* (1832). The book that many think is responsible for both the recognition and the condition of the Alhambra today.

GOTTHARD JEDLICKA, *Spanish Painting.* A critical study with excellent reproductions of seven great Spanish painters: Valdés Leal, Goya, Ribera, Zurbarán, Murillo, Velázquez, and El Greco.

JULIAN JEFFS, *Sherry* (1970). The authoritative work on Sherry and how it is made.

HUGH JOHNSON, *Hugh Johnson's Modern Encyclopedia of Wine* (1987). Sections on La Rioja, Jerez, and Catalonia are a must for anyone with a keen interest in the wines of these regions.

SIMON J. KEAY, *Roman Spain.* A thorough account, plus excellent pictures and maps, of the six-hundred-year Roman occupation of Spain, with an emphasis on archaeology.

GEORGIANA GODDARD KING, *Heart of Spain.* A Bryn Mawr professor examines the art, architecture, and literature of "Old and New Castile."

DAVID LOTH, *Philip II of Spain.* The history of the man who ruled Spain at the height of her power and prosperity, and at the beginning of her downfall.

NICHOLAS LUARD, *Andalucia: A Portrait of Southern Spain.* An English writer and naturalist's account of the eight years he spent with his young family living in Tarifa.

PAUL MACKENDRICK, *The Iberian Stones Speak.* A reconstruction of cultural history from archaeological remains in the Iberian Peninsula from 12,000 B.C. to A.D. 350.

GARRETT MATTINGLY, *The Armada.* An engaging and informative report of Spain's naval encounter with the British fleet in 1588.

THOMAS A. MCGANN, *Portrait of Spain.* A collage of British and American accounts of Spain in the 19th and 20th centuries.

JOAN MELLEN, editor, *The World of Luis Buñuel* (1978). Forty essays by international writers and film critics on Buñuel's films and career.

ROGER B. MERRIMAN, *The Rise of the Spanish Empire in the Old World and in the New.* A history that covers the period from Ferdinand and Isabella to Philip II.

JAMES A. MICHENER, *Iberia* (1968). The author gives Spain his usual exhaustive, often rewarding treatment.

SAMUEL ELIOT MORISON, *Admiral of the Ocean Sea* (1942). Morison's classic two-volume history of the events and adventures surrounding Columbus and his voyages.

JAMES MORRIS, *The Presence of Spain* (1964). The culture, history, and people of Spain as seen by possibly the best travel writer of our time. Photographs by Evelyn Hofer.

———, *Spain* (1979). A revised, updated text of the previously listed book by the author as Jan Morris. Now without photographs, this contemporary edition has a darkened tone.

H. V. MORTON, *A Stranger in Spain* (1986). A very personal look at Spain through sympathetic and perceptive eyes.

HENRY MYHILL, *The Spanish Pyrenees.* A thorough and engrossing discussion of the Basque, Aragonese, and Catalan Pyrenees, with maps and photographs.

MARTIN NOZICK, *Miguel de Unamuno: The Agony of Belief* (1982). A penetrating critical and biographical study of Unamuno, highlighted by the "Myth of Don Quixote" analysis.

JOSÉ ORTEGA Y GASSET, *Revolt of the Masses* (1932). A critique of modern society by a writer whom many regard as the foremost Spanish thinker of the 20th century.

GEORGE ORWELL, *Homage to Catalonia* (1937). Orwell describes his experiences fighting on the side of the Republicans in the Spanish Civil War.

ELLIOT PAUL, *The Life and Death of a Spanish Town* (1939). An expatriate resident in Santa Eulalia del Río on Ibiza describes how the onset of the Spanish Civil War tears the town apart.

ROBERT PAYNE, *The Civil War in Spain, 1936–1939.* Some 50 first-hand accounts by journalists, letter-writers, soldiers, and observers of the war that tore apart the Spanish nation.

F. ALLISON PEERS, *Catalonia Infelix.* The political and cultural history of Catalonia from the 12th century through the Civil War.

JOSEPH PLA AND CHRISTIAN SARRAMON, *Seeing Catalonia.* Text and photographs tell the story of Catalonia, its history, its culture, and its attractions for the traveller.

D. E. POHREN, *Adventures in Taste: The Wines and Folk Food of Spain.* This idiosyncratic, privately published classic describes encounters with artisan winemakers.

WILLIAM H. PRESCOTT, *History of the Reign of Ferdinand and Isabella the Catholic* (1838). After a century and a half, Prescott's three-volume history of the Catholic monarchs, Columbus, and the dawn of the Golden Age remains one of the fullest and most readable accounts in English.

SAMUEL PRIME, *The Alhambra and the Kremlin* (1873). Thoroughly astute, subjective, and, despite its age, informative.

V. S. PRITCHETT, *Marching Spain* (1928). A 300-mile walk in 1927 from Badajoz to León in a Spain that no longer exists but is instantly recognizable. Pritchett later described this book as "juvenile," but it offers the reader an invigorating ride high in the rhetorical saddle.

———, *The Spanish Temper* (1954). Pritchett once again proves himself a masterly writer on Spain, this time in the early 1950s, when the country was "poor in body, stunned in mind, but not . . . fundamentally changed."

JAN READ, *The Moors in Spain and Portugal* (1975). A broad historical narrative incorporating accounts of cultural and sociological development over the eight hundred years the Moors were in the Iberian Peninsula.

———, *The Wines of Spain* (1986). This book, or any of the four others by the reigning English-language authority on Spanish wines, is informative and engaging.

JAMES REYNOLDS, *Fabulous Spain.* Somewhat dated, and lacking a necessary index, this enthusiastic look at Spain is somehow contagious.

ARTHUR STANLEY RIGGS, *The Spanish Pageant.* A search for the "real Spain . . . somewhere between the spattery sunshine of two-weeks tourists and the gray textures of historians."

CEDRIC SALTER, *Try-Out in Spain.* A history of the Spanish Civil War based on the theory that it was in fact the beginning of World War II.

GEORGE SAND, *Winter in Majorca.* Her account of a less-than-idyllic winter sojourn with Chopin in Valldemosa, a Majorcan town that has never quite recovered. Robert Graves, who spent much of his life in nearby Deya, translated.

SACHEVERELL SITWELL, *Spain.* A rather eccentric and often perceptive view of Spain 50 years ago.

RHEA MARCH SMITH, *Spain.* A detailed but occasionally plodding history that ends with World War II.

JAMES JOSEPH SWEENEY AND JOSEP LLUIS SERT, *Antoni Gaudí.* A comprehensive study of Gaudí's art and architecture, supplemented by hundreds of photographs and drawings.

A. W. TAYLOR, *Wild Flowers in Spain and Portugal.* A definitive guide to Spain's wildflowers, from mountainous regions to the Meseta.

F. JAY TAYLOR, *The United States and the Spanish Civil War.* American attitudes toward, and participation in, Spain's Civil War, with an analysis of domestic political considerations.

TERESA OF AVILA, *The Life of Saint Teresa* (1611). The autobiography of Avila's Carmelite Renaissance nun, said to be the most widely read prose classic in Spain.

HUGH THOMAS, *The Spanish Civil War.* A thorough, penetrating account of the Civil War, with appendices on its economics, casualties, and foreign intervention.

MARIMAR TORRES, *The Spanish Table: The Cuisines and Wines of Spain* (1980). Useful basic information on wines by a member of one of Spain's most successful wine families.

MIGUEL DE UNAMUNO, *The Tragic Sense of Life* (1913). The philosopher Unamuno's passionate advocacy of his view of existentialism.

W. WALTON, *The Revolutions of Spain* (1837). A contemporary account of the Peninsular War, "with biographical sketches of the most distinguished personages."

F. J. WISEMAN, *Roman Spain.* A comprehensive study of Roman antiquities in Spain and Portugal.

—Robert Packard

MADRID

By Tom Burns

Tom Burns was born in London and read modern history at Oxford University. He was posted to Madrid in 1974 by Reuters and is currently a director of Spanish Trends, *a Madrid-based business monthly, and an associate editor of* Lookout, *a magazine for English-speaking residents in Spain. He contributes frequently to London's* Financial Times.

All main roads in Spain lead to Madrid. Wherever you are on the national highways, the red-topped kilometer markings will tell you how far you are from the Spanish capital. Madrid was designated Spain's capital city more than 400 years ago because it was as near the center of the peninsula as it was possible to be; at the **puerta del Sol**, the Spanish version of Piccadilly Circus in the heart of Madrid, you can stand on the flagstone that marks kilometer 0.

George Borrow, who was the Bible Society's agent in Spain midway through the last century and who earned fame with his account of his Peninsular exploits in *The Bible in Spain,* travelled every one of the Spanish highways several times, and most of the byways as well. He never quite got over his first impressions of Madrid. "I have visited most of the principal capitals of the world," wrote the engaging Borrow, "but upon the whole none has ever interested me as this city of Madrid, in which I now find myself."

Borrow had certainly been around, in Spain and well beyond it. He conceded that St. Petersburg had finer streets than Madrid, and that Paris and Edinburgh had more stately edifices. London, he wrote, had far nobler squares, and Shiraz, in Persia, could boast "more costly fountains, though not cooler waters." What was it then that enchanted Borrow about Madrid?

He understood exactly what the city is all—or at least

mostly—about. What amazed the much-travelled though never world-weary author and Bible agent was Madrid's people: "Within a mud wall scarcely one league and a half in circuit, are contained two hundred thousand human beings, certainly forming the most extraordinary vital mass to be found in the entire world."

With a current population of just over three million, Madrid has grown 15-fold since Borrow's time, and the mud wall has long since vanished. But the zest for life remains. Madrid, where all the national highways converge, remains the teeming melting pot of Spain. It draws all the peninsula's vitality toward it and shakes the peoples of Spain up into a sparkling cocktail.

MAJOR INTEREST

Museo del Prado
Dürer and Bosch
Titian
El Greco and Zurbarán
Velázquez
Goya
Picasso's *Guernica*

Hapsburg Madrid
The plaza Mayor
Capilla del Obispo
Real Monasterio de las Descalzas Reales
Convento de la Encarnación

Bourbon Madrid
The Palacio Real and the armory
Real Academia de Bellas Artes de San Fernando (Goya)
Museo Ceralbo (El Greco, Zurbarán)

Museo Arqueológico Nacional (*La Dama de Elche*)
Museo de Lázaro Galdiano (El Greco, Zurbarán, Velázquez, Goya)

Taverns and *tapas* bars around the plaza Mayor
Café terrazas on paseo de la Castellana
Fine dining, especially the Basque seafood restaurants
Shopping for antiques, crafts, and custom-made items off the Castellana and on calle de Serrano

Madrid's fizz can hit you head on. The city sits on Spain's central tableland in the shelter of the Guadarrama Sierra.

Being nearly 700 meters (2,300 feet) above sea level, the city's altitude may help create the effervescence. In *Death in the Afternoon,* Hemingway described the Madrid of the 1930s as a "mountain city with a mountain climate." This was, of course, pre-smog—the city began to acquire a large industrial belt in the 1950s—and Hemingway waxed lyrical about Madrid's environment: "It has the high cloudless Spanish sky that makes the Italian sky seem sentimental and it has air that is actively pleasurable to breathe."

There are many days, however—more than you might expect—when the skies that Velázquez loved to paint still make you gasp in admiration, and there are mornings when you gratefully gulp the gusts of air that sweep down from the Sierra. If you time it right, as you walk up the Gran Vía from the plaza de la Cibeles you can see the sun, looking every inch the fiery red ball it is supposed to be, dip over the brow of the busy thoroughfare. Madrid has not changed that much.

Certainly the joyousness, the boisterousness of Madrid that entranced Hemingway every bit as much as they did Borrow remain in place. "Nobody goes to bed in Madrid until they have killed the night," noted Hemingway. "In no other town I have lived in, except Constantinople during the period of Allied occupation, is there less going to bed for sleeping purposes."

Coming from the author who lauded Paris as a moveable feast, such observations are praise indeed. They are also relevant. Madrid today has appalling traffic problems, a good number of hideous buildings that have replaced elegant palaces and mansions, and a sprawl of unsightly suburbs—but fun it undeniably remains.

The Madrileños

Madrid, as befits the capital city of an old nation, has its fair share of places of historical interest. If you know where to look you will be virtually touching a Medieval world, smelling its odors and hearing its sounds. You will certainly come across the Madrid that the Hapsburgs built and also the one that the succeeding Bourbon dynasty created. There are palaces, churches, and convents, triumphal arches, ornamental gardens, and sturdy bridges. As the home of Velázquez, whose patrons were the Hapsburgs, and of Goya, who painted the Bourbons, Madrid is assured its place in the cultural firmament, and the Prado is its high temple.

There should nevertheless be a specific reference first to

its inhabitants: to the *ambiente* (ambience) and the *alegría* (joy), to the atmosphere and the joie de vivre that the Madrileños can, and do, create. You will only partly understand Madrid by its monuments and treasures.

To gain the full picture you must experience the terrazas of paseo de la Castellana from June to September, when they are in full swing long after the midnight hour. Stroll the Retiro on any Sunday morning, when the gardens are crammed with musicians, puppeteers, and mimes. Join the bullfight throng of the San Isidro *feria* (festival) in May. Dress up at Carnival time. Dance along at the neighborhood street parties during August and September.

Be part of the crowd that shops at Christmastime for nativity figures from the street vendors in the plaza Mayor. Form part of the tidal wave of humanity that invades the Rastro flea market on weekends. Have long lunches and longer dinners; go *tapas* hopping from old bar to older tavern, nibbling a wealth of snacks and drinking cold beer, served in the small, narrow glasses called *cañas,* and Valdepeñas wine, served in the smaller, stumpier glasses called *chatos.*

The Madrileños have a lot of swaggering style to them. Bumper stickers proclaim that Madrid is the "Gateway to Heaven." But the assertiveness is tempered by a self-deprecating, street-smart humor. Ramón Gómez de la Serna, a witty between-the-wars chronicler of the city's virtues and vices, said that Madrid was "putting your hands in your pocket better than anywhere else in the world." This would imply insolence were it not for the innate decency and humanity of the Madrileño.

Madrid has, when all is said and done, been it all and seen it all. It became the capital of Spain overnight because Philip II decided to make it so at a time when the Spanish might was at its 16-century zenith. But 100 years later Madrid's extravagantly Baroque exterior could scarcely mask the fact that it was the headquarters of a fast-decaying empire. Home of the court and of the bureaucracy, Madrid spent much of its time battling to hold Spain together and trying to make ends meet.

Francisco Goya, in the late 18th and early 19th centuries, and the novelist Benito Pérez Galdós many years later, depicted a city of heroism and intrigue that was graceful and bawdy by turns—and scarcely knew the difference between the two. The atrocious behavior of Napoleon's troops, the turmoils of the 19th century, the fierce siege the city endured during the Spanish Civil War, and the hungry years that followed its surrender to Franco—nothing succeeded in dampening Madrid's spirit.

Madrid's pace can be an exhausting one. The streets appear permanently crowded and the stranger may well wonder when anyone ever works—or sleeps. Cafés are crowded between 10:30 A.M. and noon, when office workers take a midmorning break for a late breakfast, and they fill up again from 1:30 P.M. onward for prelunch aperitifs. Lunch itself can start as late as 3:00 P.M. and normally lasts a generous two hours. Bars begin to fill up after 7:30 P.M., but few Spaniards ever sit down to dinner before 10:00. In summer downtown Madrid has traffic jams until well after midnight.

You can take Madrid in an orderly way, progressing from one specific interest point to another. That way of approaching it is by no means to be sneered at. Be warned, however, that Madrid is neither obviously grand, nor stylish, nor historical in the way that London, Paris, and Rome are. Another approach is just to let Madrid rush at you and to take you over, to let it infect you with its peculiar pace.

The second approach may not work for everyone. The historian Hugh Thomas rightly cautions in *Madrid, A Travellers Companion* that "the charm of Madrid is elusive." Richard Ford, a contemporary of Borrow and author of the classic *Handbook for Travellers in Spain,* never had time for the city—"the more Madrid is known, the less it will be liked"—and even Hemingway, who was to become such an aficionado of Madrid, conceded: "I do not believe anyone likes it much when he first goes there."

Madrid does not have obvious identity marks like the mix of Modernism and the Mediterranean that you find in Barcelona. It does not have the southern sensuality of a Seville, nor does it offer breathtaking silhouettes of ages past as Salamanca, Segovia, and Toledo do. That said, a visitor to Madrid is honor bound to give the city a chance to produce the kaleidoscope of sensations that it has evolved over the centuries.

The people of Madrid, Spaniards to the hilt as they are, have undoubted flair. There is no English equivalent for the Spanish verb *estrenar,* which means to use or to show off for the first time, much in the sense of "to premiere." Consumption-conscious Spaniards, and in particular Madrileños, are constantly *estrenando,* or premiering, everything from their new clothes to their new cars. Nor is there an exact Spanish equivalent to English words such as to eavesdrop or to overhear. In Spain it is impossible to eavesdrop in the usual sly sense of the word because people simply speak too loudly. The noise level in Madrid, as in all of Spain, is several points above what might be acceptable elsewhere. Everything is convivial and loud, and that applies to acquaintances meeting on a street corner as well as to groups gathered in a bar and to drivers honking their horns in gridlocked traffic.

Madrid's Origins

Back in prehistory a river ran down what is today's paseo de la Castellana, modern Madrid's main north-south axis, and mammoths grazed on its banks. Stone Age people grunted their way along the grassy edges of the river; evidence of their Paleolithic settlements has been found deep below the present-day sewers. The Romans and the Visigoths also came and went (traces of their fleeting presence in the Madrid area are exhibited in the city's Museo Arqueológico Nacional).

The founder of the city is nevertheless generally agreed to be Omeya, the fifth emir of the independent caliphate of Córdoba, who in the middle of the ninth century raised a watchtower near where the Palacio Real now stands. He named the location Mayrit ("running waters").

The Moorish occupation was to last some 200 years, but no real vestige of it remains today. In 1085 Alfonso VI, monarch of the kingdoms of Castile and León, razed Omeya's watchtower and established Christian control over Mayrit's 12,000-or-so souls. Alfonso was not particularly interested in the new property he had added to his domain, and his troops marched quickly on that year to take the far bigger prize of Toledo, a city soon to achieve the status of capital of the two kingdoms.

Madrid had to wait until 1202 and the reign of Alfonso VIII before it was granted a *fuero* (charter of rights), and it was not until 1346 and the reign of Peter the Cruel that it acquired that other status symbol of the Middle Ages, a proper castle. Peter's alcázar, or fortress, was built on the same original watchtower spot, overlooking río Manzanares, that is now occupied by the Palacio Real. The city failed, however, to acquire a lasting Medieval accolade by way of a decent cathedral. It was not then important enough for that.

British author Alastair Boyd (*A Companion Guide to Madrid and Central Spain*) makes the point that Madrid kept backing the losing side every time that Medieval Spain erupted into civil wars. The people of Madrid vainly supported Peter when he was murdered by his half-brother Henry II, the founder of the new dynasty of Trastamara.

More than a century and a half passed before the city was back in royal favor: under Henry IV, who resided occasionally in Peter's alcázar and died there.

Henry IV was known as the Impotent, and on his death the city unwisely decided to back the claims to the throne of his purported daughter Juana, a young girl who was popularly known as La Beltraneja (because her real father was reckoned to be the royal favorite Don Alvaro Beltrán de la Cueva). Ranged against little Juana were the ultimately victorious claims of her aunt, Henry's sister, the redoubtable Isabella—who was crowned queen of Castile in Segovia in 1474 and who was to go down in history as La Reina Católica.

There is a monument to Isabella set in pleasant gardens that look out on paseo de la Castellana, at the foot of a small hill that leads up to the Museo de Ciencias Naturales (natural history museum). But in fact Los Reyes Católicos, Isabella and her no less formidable husband Ferdinand of Aragón, effectively bypassed Madrid during an epoch-making reign that saw the conquest of Granada, the creation of modern-day Spain, and Columbus's voyage to the New World. Such were the follies of backing the wrong side. It was Philip II, Isabella's great-grandson, who finally put Madrid on the map.

The Two Old Madrids

Madrid is not an old European capital in the sense that London and Paris are, and compared with Spain's historical cities it is very much a newcomer. It was not until 1561 that Philip II had the court moved permanently to Madrid; it was then a small town of some 20,000 inhabitants. Toledo and Seville at that time had four times Madrid's population, and even Valladolid's was more than double that. It was an odd move given Madrid's insignificance in the 16th century, but the monarch had his reasons.

Philip disliked the powerful clergy of Toledo, which was where his father, the Emperor Charles V, had set down the court, and he was also worried about heresy in Valladolid, which had served as Spain's capital in the reign of his great-grandparents Ferdinand and Isabella. Another important factor was that Philip wanted to be near the Escorial, the monastery-cum-palace-cum-royal pantheon he had ordered to be built at the foot of the Guadarrama mountains, and yet another was that the monarch enjoyed the good boar hunting to be found in the woods that surrounded Madrid. But most of all Philip liked Madrid because it was central. The monarch thought it right that "so great a monarchy should have a city fulfilling the function of a heart located in the middle of the body," wrote his biographer Luis Cabrera de Córdoba, as cited by Hugh Thomas. Madrid thus finally came into its own through this royal decision, and it never looked back.

The all-powerful ruler whose beard Francis Drake boasted he had singed after successfully attacking the Invincible Armada when it was being assembled in Cádiz, Philip II is known to Spaniards as the Prudent King. Madrileños know the monarch as their *first* mayor.

A distant descendant, Carlos III, was in the 18th century to be known as the city's *best* mayor, because he worked hard to bring Madrid up to the architectural standards of rival European capitals of the time.

Both Philip, who belonged to the Spanish branch of the Hapsburg imperial family, and Carlos, who was a member of the Spanish branch of the Bourbons, the royal household of France, have a special place in Madrileño lore. The best of the city is owed to the two dynasties.

Hapsburg Madrid

The immediate consequence of Philip's move to Madrid was the rapid growth of the population. By 1597, less than 40 years after the king's decision, the number of the city's inhabitants had more than tripled, growing from around 20,000 to 65,000. Over the next 40 years the population almost tripled again; in 1630, during the reign of Philip's grandson, Philip IV, it stood at 175,000, making Madrid the fifth-largest city in Europe after Constantinople, Naples, London, and Paris.

The population boom was the direct result of the installation in Madrid of the massive bureaucracy—the chanceries, the councils, the secretariats, and the law courts—that was created by the Spanish Hapsburgs. Along with the army of bureaucrats came an even greater multitude of camp followers. The new capital attracted, according to Federico Sainz de Robles's *Brief History of Madrid,* "litigators, eternal students, sophists, retired soldiers, friars founding branches of their order, people looking for official jobs and contracts, bawds with their whores, fairground and market tricksters, purveyors of potions and the occult arts, strumpets who hang about the corners and under the arcades, back door smugglers here today and gone tomorrow."

Philip II ordered the building of the first stone bridge

across the río Manzanares, the **Puente de Segovia**, which stands south of the Palacio Real at the end of calle de Segovia. It is still in use today and not much changed, which is a testimony to the talents of Juan de Herrera, the architect who was to achieve fame and glory with the royal commission to finish the massive Escorial. The **Casa de las Siete Chimeneas** (house of seven chimneys) in the plaza del Rey, close to the plaza de la Cibeles just off the start of Gran Vía, also dates from Philip's reign. Occupied first by the British ambassador to the Hapsburg court, this building is typical of the private palaces that were built near calle de Alcalá during the city's rapid expansion (it currently houses the ministry of culture).

Herrera stamped his personality so clearly on the period that the Spanish Hapsburg architectural style has come to be known as the *estilo Herreriano.* (The many examples of the Hapsburg legacy that can be seen in Madrid today are covered in the Around Hapsburg Madrid section below.) For a rapid acquaintance with the period's architectural style you should head for the **plaza Mayor**, built according to Herrera's designs by his pupil Juan Gómez de Mora. The obvious feature of Herrera's style is its sobriety: The buildings are solid and somber to the point of being gaunt. Granite and red brick are used on the façades, and the roofs are usually covered with slate. Herrera favored dormer windows and spires.

Bourbon Madrid

Philip IV's son, the impotent and half-mad Carlos II, known as Carlos the Bewitched, represented a sad, freakish end product of the Hapsburg intermarriage policy. His death plunged Europe into the War of the Spanish Succession, which led to the arrival in Spain in 1700 of the Bourbon dynasty in the person of Philip V, the grandson of Louis XIV, the Sun King. The Bourbons soon stamped their personality on Madrid. The *estilo Herreriano* meant little to them, nor did the new dynasty favor the cautious drift toward Baroque ornateness that was favored by some late-17th-century Spanish architects, notably by the Churriguera brothers, Alberto and Joaquín, whose main achievement was the town square, the plaza Mayor, of Salamanca. With the Bourbons came a pronounced Classical style with all its columns and cupolas. Italian architects were much in vogue due to the good offices of Philip V's two Italian wives, María Luisa of Savoy and Isabella Farnese, and they continued to be in the forefront during the reign of Carlos III, son of Philip and Isabella

Farnese, who was king of Naples before he was crowned king of Spain.

Spanish Baroque, often referred to as Churrigueresque, was short-lived, and particularly so in Madrid, for the severe Herrera influence stretched long into the 17th century. Just as the florid, extravagant style began to hit its stride, fashion, sponsored by the Bourbons, dictated the return to the Classical. There are nevertheless some notable Baroque examples in Madrid, and, if you are interested in this exuberant style, examine the main façade of the Museo Municipal, which was built to serve as a hospice by Pedro Ribera, a contemporary of the Churriguera brothers, in 1720. It stands on calle Fuencarral, a street that leads north off Gran Vía, at number 78. Another example of Spanish Baroque, the Iglesia de San José, likewise built by Ribera, is at Alcalá 43, not far from the plaza de la Cibeles.

A fire that burned down Peter the Cruel's original alcázar in 1734 (the building had been much restored and extended in the intervening centuries) provided the Bourbon Philip with the perfect excuse to build a wholly new palace according to the new taste. The Italian architect Filippo Juvarra and his pupil Giovanni Sacchetti accordingly designed the massive present-day building that is known as the **Palacio Real** (royal palace) and also as the Palacio de Oriente. The Doric columns and the general sumptuousness of the palace mark a distinct break with the severe brickwork and the slate tiling that were favored by the Hapsburg architectural pacesetter Juan de Herrera and his pupil Gómez de Mora.

Philip V sponsored other major landmarks in Madrid, such as the domed Iglesia de San Francisco el Grande on calle Bailén not far from the Palacio Real, but it was left to his son, Carlos III, the monarch known as Madrid's best mayor, to promote the finest of the 18th-century Bourbon buildings in the city. Carlos, an enlightened ruler who assembled a talented and efficient government, is a readily recognizable figure: He posed frequently for Goya.

The **puerta de Alcalá**, the triumphal archway near the Parque del Retiro, is one magnificent legacy of Carlos's reign, and the building that now houses the Prado (it was originally intended to serve as a natural history museum) is another. Francesco Sabatini, yet another Italian architect, built the wonderfully measured Alcalá arch, and he also designed the present-day treasury, just off the puerta del Sol on calle de Alcalá. Juan de Villanueva, a Spaniard who was also much favored by Carlos and who successfully adopted the Classical style, built the Prado and the nearby pavilions of the Jardín

Botánico. (For a fuller discussion of the period's legacy, see the Around Bourbon Madrid section below.)

If you want to recapture in your mind's eye late-18th-century Madrid you need look no further than the Goya canvases that hang in the Prado and in other city museums such as the Real Academia de San Fernando (fine arts academy). There could be no more explicit diarist of a period's foibles and fantasies, its decorum and its disasters. The best fun was to be had at the *ferias* and fiestas in honor of Madrid's patron saints, marked by picnics and dancing on the banks of the río Manzanares. Goya attended them and enjoyed them to the fullest. The aristocracy was wont to dress up and pose for the famous artist in the broad-hatted and long-cloaked garb of the popular classes.

The royal court itself was a somewhat similar mix of grandeur and decadence. In 1788, the year before the storming of the Bastille in Paris, Carlos IV succeeded his father, Carlos III, but unfortunately had inherited none of his parent's intelligence. The façade of royal power remained, but the edifice was crumbling. A handsome young guards captain, Manuel de Godoy, became the royal favorite (and the queen's lover), and the cuckolded Carlos showered him with honors. Godoy, who became prime minister and was awarded the title of Prince of Peace, polarized opinions both in and out of the court; Goya was clearly conscious that a storm was gathering. When really bad times came and Napoleon's troops took over the city, the Madrileños rose up heroically against the invaders, and Goya faithfully recorded the change, the valor, and the tragedy of the patriotic populace.

Modern Madrid

By the mid-19th century the city was expanding as rapidly as it had 200 years earlier. The **paseo de la Castellana** had marked Madrid's easternmost limits in the time of Carlos III, and now it became the city's north-south axis as a whole new Madrid, which adopted the grid system following the Parisian fashion, evolved on its eastern "bank." This is the residential and shopping area called the Barrio de Salamanca, after the marqués de Salamanca, the real-estate tycoon who developed it.

Calle de Serrano, also running north-south parallel to and east of the Castellana, is the emblem of Barrio de Salamanca elegance and serves as modern Madrid's Bond Street.

The Castellana, a broad boulevard shaded by acacia trees, is in particular a first-class reference point for every newly

Madrid
0 yards 500
0 meters 500
to Escorial
AVENIDA GENERAL
CALLE DE DULCINEA
C. DE REINA MERCEDES
CUATRO
CALLE RAIMUNDO
CIUDAD UNIVERSITARIA
AV. DE PUERTA DE HIERRO
CALLE DEL ARQUITECO
AVENIDA JUAN DE HERRERA
Museo de América
AVENIDA REYES CATOLICOS
C. BRETON DE
CALLE JOSE
CALLE GARCIA DE
CALLE GAZTAMBIDE
CALLE ANDRES MELLADO
FERNANDO EL CATOLICO
AV. DE VALLADOLID
Parque del Oeste
CALLE ARAPILES
Glorieta de Quevedo
CALLE DE SAN BERNARDO
CALLE FERRAZ
CALLE DE AGUILERA
C. DE CARRANZA
Glorieta de Bilbao
C. DE SAGASTA
CALLE QUINTANA
Palacio de Liria
Museo Municipal
Río Manzanares
Ermita de San Antonio de la Florida
CALLE SAN VINCENTE FERRER
SAN MATEO
Museo Romántico
PASEO DE LA FLORIDA
RODRIGUEZ
CALLE DE LA PRINCESA
CALLE FUENCARRAL
ALMIRANTE
HORTALEZA
Puente de Reina Victoria
Plaza de España
CASA DE CAMPO
Estación del Norte
Plaza del Callao
GRAN VIA
Puente del Rey
Palacio Real
Plaza de Oriente
CALLE DE
CALLE DE ALCALA
Campo del Moro
Puerta del Sol
C. DE SA JERONIM
CALLE MAYOR
Plaza Mayor
CALLE JERONIMA
CALLE DEL LEON
CALLE DE SEGOVIA
CALLE DE BAILEN
PASEO DEL MARQUES DE MONISTROL
AV. DE PORTUGAL
Plaza del Angel
Puente de Segovia
RIBERA DE CURTIDORES
San Francisco el Grande
CALLE DE VALENCIA
Puerta de Toledo
RONDA DE TOLEDO
Glorieta de Embajadores
PASEO DE LAS ACACIAS
PASEO DE SANTA MAR
Puente de Heroes Alcáza de Toledo
to Toledo

to Chamartin Estación
CALLE PADRE DAMIAN
PERON
Plaza de Lima
CALLE ORENSE
CAMINOS
FERNANDEZ VILLAVERDE
CALLE PRINCIPE DE VERGARA
CALLE DE JOAQUIN COSTA
to airport, Barcelona
AV. DE AMERICA
LOS HERREROS
ALVAREZ DE BAENA
ABASCAL
Plaza del Dr. Marañon
CALLE DE MARIA DE MOLINA
PAREDES
Museo de Lázaro Galdiano
Museo Sorolla
MIGUEL ANGEL
GRAL. MARTINEZ CAMPOS
CALLE CLAUDIO COELLO
CALLE DE LAGASCA
CALLE DE VELASQUEZ
CALLE NUNEZ DE BALBOA
CALLE CASTELLO
C. ZURBANO
CALLE PADILLA
PASEO DE LA CASTELLANA
Plaza de Alonso Martinez
MARQUEZ DE RISCAL
CALLE DE SERRANO
CALLE DE ORTEGA Y GASSET
CALLE DE ALCANTARA
CALLE MONTESA
CALLE DE ALCALA
C. LUCHANA
AMADOR DE LOS RIOS
BARRIO DE SALAMANCA
CALLE AYALA
CONDE DE PENALVER
AV. DE LA PAZ
ALCALA GALIANO
CALLE HERMOSILLA
C. DE GENOVA
ARGENSOLA
ENSENADA
Plaza de Colón
CALLE DE GOYA
CALLE FUNDADORES
BRAGANZA
PUIGCERDA
CALLE DE JORGE JUAN
PIAMONTE
PASEO DE RECOLETOS
C. DE VILLANUEVA
XIQUENA
Plaza de la Independencia
CALLE DEL DR. ESQUERDO
AV. DE GUADALAJARA
Plaza de la Cibeles
Puerta de Alcalá
CALLE DE ALFONSO XII
Cortes
Museo del Prado
Parque del Retiro
PASEO DEL PRADO
CALLE ATOCHA
CALLE DE SANTA ISABEL
Centro de Arte Reina Sofía
AV. DEL MEDITERRANEO
Atocha (train station)
E LA CABEZA
to Valencia
N
Antigua Estación de Delicas

arrived visitor to Madrid. The boulevard takes on the role that a river does in certain cities, such as the Seine in Paris; like a river, the Castellana has a right "bank," its east side, and a left "bank" on the west. A second reference point is the long calle de Alcalá, which runs east-west and crosses the Castellana at the plaza de la Cibeles. The latter is the site of the fountains and statue honoring Cibeles, a mythological queen of the sea. A gorgeous monument built in the reign of Carlos III, Cibeles is Madrid's best-loved landmark. Calle de Alcalá effectively divides Madrid into an uptown, as the Castellana stretches north into the modern city, and a downtown, as Castellana runs south toward the Prado.

(Madrid's *real* river, the Manzanares, is of little interest, and has been unkindly talked about. It was put in its place by no less an authority than Miguel de Cervantes, who termed it an "apprentice river." Until recent channeling improved the situation, it used to dry up in summer. It has been said that Madrid either ought to sell its fine bridges or buy itself a proper river. Lope de Vega remarked that Philip II's Puente de Segovia was "hoping for a river.")

The Barrio de Salamanca and calle de Serrano glamour on the right "bank" of the Castellana is ritzy east-side Madrid. Across on the left "bank," the west side, the city moves into the older world of the original Hapsburg capital, with its center point in the **plaza Mayor**. You won't find the effervescent old-Madrid mix of bohemianism, trendiness, and classless popularity on the east side, nor will you stumble across old palaces and convents there. As a rule of thumb, this division between upscale and old works.

Uptown on the Castellana lies fast-paced North Madrid, of whose increasingly Manhattan-like skyline Madrileños are proud. This is where the city, and in particular its business area, has grown in the past 20 years. Downtown to the south, the boulevard echoes with the elegance of earlier ages of true leisure: From the plaza de la Cibeles down to the Museo de Prado and its adjoining botanical gardens, the boulevard becomes leafier and more sedate.

The **plaza de la Cibeles** itself is probably the best place of all from which to take your bearings. The square is flanked by the Palacio de Comunicaciones, a fantastic edifice built in 1904 that serves as Spain's main post office, by the Banco de España (bank of Spain), a large, Neoclassical mid-19th-century building and, in the midst of its own gardens and guarded by soldiers, the Spanish army's general staff headquarters, known as the Palacio de Vistahermosa. Surrounding the lovely Cibeles and her lion-borne chariot, you have three centers of modern might: communications, cash, and, that ultimate powerbroker, the military.

West from Cibeles, Alcalá climbs up to its starting point at the puerta del Sol. At the puerta del Sol you are within two blocks of the plaza Mayor and old Hapsburg Madrid. But as it climbs the hill from Cibeles, Alcalá gives birth to a no less grand city thoroughfare, **Gran Vía**. There is a lot of style, albeit of the fading kind, to this street. It was the pride of the city in the interwar years.

Once Madrid's main business center, Gran Vía remains its show-business territory—its Broadway, its West End. This is the home of the big movie houses awaiting the next film premiere. Between the cinemas there are touristy shops, fast-food restaurants, and, still, the occasional big bank and merchant house. Leading off Gran Vía's side streets are areas that in most cities in the world are loosely called a Chinatown, meaning tacky and seedy. To the northwest, Gran Vía ends up in the large plaza de España, home of an equally massive monument to Cervantes, overlooking the rolling expanse of Madrid's main leisure park, the Casa de Campo, home of a well-equipped funfair and of a scenic, well-stocked city zoo.

Back at Cibeles, directly south of the plaza is the **paseo del Prado**. Carlos III was especially interested in building up this downtown area, and in the last century, when it acquired its present-day name, it became the fashionable walkabout area where Madrid's well-to-do gathered to show themselves off to one another. (The Hotel Ritz is along here, for example.)

Théophile Gautier, who helped create the romantic image of Spain with his *Voyage en Espagne* (1845), marveled at the spectacle: "A glimpse of the Prado is in fact one of the most animated sights that can be seen and it is one of the most beautiful promenades in the world, not because of the site, which is most ordinary (in spite of all the efforts of Carlos III to correct the defects) but because of the astonishing assembly which gathers there every evening, from 7:30 until 10:00."

Today's paseo del Prado, with its summer sidewalk terrazas, is just as packed with look-at-me people, and it has inspired current chroniclers of Spanish mores to write up Madrid as a vibrant capital that throbs with the unexpected and is every bit as astonishing as it was during its most glorious periods. And it is, of course, the location of the Prado museum.

MUSEO DEL PRADO

Originally conceived by Carlos III and his architect Juan de Villanueva as a museum of natural history, the Prado was inaugurated as a museum of painting and sculpture by Ferdinand VII, Carlos's grandson, in 1819. It is ironic that Ferdinand, an arrogant and small-minded individual who has had rough treatment from historians and from artists (Goya painted him looking incredibly oafish), should have been responsible for this high temple of culture. The Prado alone makes a visit to Madrid worthwhile, or, put more exactly, the Prado is far and away the main reason for visiting Madrid. A visitor to Madrid, to gain his or her full money's worth from the trip, should spend much more time in the Prado than in all of the city's other cultural venues put together. This is why we devote a relatively large amount of space to it here.

The Prado opened as a museum shortly after the Louvre and before London's National Gallery. Clearly it has strengths, such as the displays of Velázquez and of Goya, that put it well ahead of its two peers, in the same way that it has deficiencies. It is, however, different from either in one curious respect: Everything in the Prado was either paid for or acquired through donations; there is not a single example of artistic war booty.

A second general point is that it is primarily a royal collection. In this sense the Prado reflects the tastes of the Spanish monarchs. While their standards of taste were generally high, in certain cases, notably that of Philip IV, the sensibility toward art was peerless. In addition, the ramifications of the Hapsburg family power being what they were, the Spanish royal collection, as it was built up in the 16th and 17th centuries, was able to draw on the Flemish, German, and Italian schools that flourished, as it were, in the backyards of the Madrid court.

The collection of the Prado is probably best approached chronologically, moving from the early Flemish and German masters on to the Italians and finally on to the museum's tour-de-force troika: El Greco, Velázquez, and Goya. The effect of the collection, as is true of all really first-class galleries, is normally exhausting, and the museum's pleasant cafeteria is the ideal place to take a break. Classier refreshments after you leave are near at hand at the Ritz and the Palace hotels, the former lying across the road from the museum's side entrance and the latter on the other side of the Castellana and

100 yards uptown toward the plaza de la Cibeles. If you need to gulp fresh air after the visit go to the botanical gardens, which lie alongside the Prado, or go to El Retiro park, two blocks away behind the museum. The latter route takes you past San Jerónimo el Real, a much-restored 16th-century church that is the scene of many society weddings, royal ones included.

The Prado's hours are 9:00 A.M. to 6:30 P.M. in winter, 9:00 A.M. to 7:00 P.M. from April 1 to October 1, 9:00 A.M. to 2:00 P.M. Sundays and holidays; closed Mondays.

Plans for the Future

As Madrid enters the 1990s great plans are afoot for the Prado, and it will, it is hoped, be able to extend its exhibition space considerably. The museum is an extreme case of *embarras de richesses,* for more than half of its 5,000-piece collection is either in storage or on loan elsewhere. Space is urgently needed at present because Madrid, under the umbrella of the Prado, is due shortly to receive the added artistic bonus of the fabulous **Thyssen collection,** which will be housed, for an initial ten-year period, in the **Palacio de Villahermosa,** on the other side of the Castellana and opposite the Palace hotel. The collection, built up by the aristocratic German steel-producing family, is reputedly the most important one in private hands in the world, and ranges from old masters to Picasso.

Villahermosa, used until now for temporary exhibitions, had once been thought of as a possible home for the Prado's Goya collection, which would have become a self-contained unit. Following the Thyssen windfall the idea now is for the museum to take over the nearby Museo del Ejército (army museum), which was once part of the Hapsburg Palacio del Buen Retiro, and place the Goyas there. The Prado also has its eye on the Palacio de Vistahermosa, which lies set in its own gardens by the plaza de la Cibeles. Once owned by the dukes of Alba and now serving as the army general staff headquarters, this large palace would cope with the Prado's overflow and also be home to special exhibitions.

Finally, the Prado annex, called the Casón del Buen Retiro, which is near the Museo del Ejército and was formerly part of the Palacio del Buen Retiro, is also due for an overhaul. It currently exhibits the museum's collection of 19th-century Spanish paintings as well as Picasso's *Guernica* with its accompanying large collection of preliminary sketches. *Guernica* is, under current plans, due to be rehoused in the Centro de Arte Reina Sofía, a large, recently refurbished museum near the Atocha railway station at the start of paseo del Prado, and it will be the centerpiece of a new Museo Español de Arte Contemporaneo that will replace the existing one, which is located on the university campus on Madrid's northwestern outskirts.

Early Flemish and Renaissance Painters

A host of paintings in the Prado have been familiar companions for years. This is certainly the case with Dürer's astonishingly contemporary self-portrait, which bears the legend: "I was 26 years old and I painted this picture of my face." The picture used to belong to Charles I of England; it was acquired—after his execution—by the discriminating Philip IV. Dürer's portraits of Adam and of Eve were presented to Philip by Queen Christina of Sweden. Tradition has it that Carlos III would have had them burned for indecency had Rafael Mengs, one of his court painters, not taken them away from the royal collection and hidden them in the Real Academia de San Fernando, where they remained until late last century.

Rogier Van der Weyden's showpiece in the Prado, *The Descent from the Cross,* is arguably one of the greatest Gothic paintings. It belonged to Queen María of Hungary, the sister of Emperor Charles V, and it was so admired by her nephew Philip II that he commissioned Michel Croxie to reproduce it. The copy, which is remarkable, now hangs in the Escorial; the original eventually came into Philip's possession after his aunt died. Critic Juan Gómez Soubrier compares it to the Christian message of peace and hope in Fra Angelico's *Annunciation,* which is yet another of the Prado's treasures.

The Garden of Earthly Delights by Hieronymus Bosch, known in Spain as El Bosco, is another of the highly familiar paintings in this section. It was bought by Philip II in 1593, five years before his death, and he kept it in his private apartments in the Escorial. Philip's final days, gout ridden and disease wracked, were frightful, and few ventured near him on account of the stench. Bosch's extraordinary evocation of short-lived sensual pleasures may have suited his mood.

The Italian Painters

One of the highlights of this section, Andrea Mantegna's *Death of the Virgin,* also belonged to Charles I, and was bought by the judicious Philip IV when Cromwell auctioned off the beheaded monarch's pictures. Other paintings here that once belonged to Charles include Veronese's *Jesus Disputing with the Doctors* and Tintoretto's huge *Lavatorio.* At least two other Tintorettos, *The Medianite Virgins* and the *Episode in a Battle between Christians and Turks,* were bought by Velázquez, who toured Italy scouting for art works for Philip IV—and picking up brush stroke and lighting skills in the process.

Raphael's *The Cardinal* is an arresting canvas. Art historian Alfonso Pérez Sánchez, the Prado's director, recommends it for prolonged viewing: "All the scornful intelligence, the implacable coldness and the refined sensuality which we imagine in the Renaissance prototype, bloom with an amazing intensity in this profound, sober portrait." Fra Angelico also hangs in this section, as do Botticelli, illustrating a grisly tale from *The Decameron,* Andrea del Sarto, and Giorgione.

Close attention is also demanded by Titian's fabulous equestrian portrait of Charles V, *Emperor at the Battle of Mühlberg.* The suit of armor that Charles wore in the picture, and in the actual battle, is exhibited in the Palacio Real's Armería (see Around Bourbon Madrid, below). The full range of Titian's astonishing output, from religious commissions to outpourings of pagan sensuality such as *Bacchanal,* is superbly represented in the Prado, topped off by his magnificent self-portrait, painted when he was in his 80s after a life of good living. One historically interesting Titian picture is his portrait of a dashing young Philip II, which was packed off to London where it won the heart, as was the intention, of Mary Tudor. Philip, who was then a prince and heir to his father, Charles V, disliked the picture and wrote to his aunt, María of Austria, "If there were more time I would have him [Titian] do it again," but the diplomatic advantages of marriage to the English queen outweighed his vanity.

Mary's return portrait to Philip, painted by Anton Van Dashorst, who was known as Sir Anthony More in England and as Antonio Moro in Spain, hangs among the Prado's Flemish pictures. It shows her looking distinctly shrewish and spinsterish. At 38 she was 11 years older than Philip, and he cannot have been enraptured by her likeness. Mary was the second of Philip's four wives; their marriage lasted from 1554 until her death in 1558.

El Greco and Zurbarán

Domenikos Theotokopoulos, El Greco, can best be appreciated in Toledo, which is an essential side trip for every serious visitor to Madrid. The Prado's collection of El Grecos, however, is far greater than that possessed by any other national art collection and, more than being merely an appetizer for the Toledo trip, it is essential viewing.

The great religious themes that El Greco perfected and devoted his art to—the Nativity, the Crucifixion, and the Resurrection—are all well represented in the Prado. So are all the elongated figures, the purples and the greens, the zigzags and the whole Mannerist bag of tricks that the Cretan-born genius evolved. *The Adoration of the Shepherds* is compelling because of the power that emerges from the absurdly tiny child. As the dead Christ in *The Trinity,* the same Savior is huge and heavy, suspended by a compassionate, painstricken father and weighted down toward earth. The Prado also boasts the intriguing portrait called *The Cavalier,* the subject of which has his hand on his chest. The gesture that El Greco painted and the searching eyes that he gave his subject are haunting in the extreme. Professor Diego Angulo suggests that this unknown *cabellero,* who shows only his right arm, is Miguel de Cervantes, who lost his left arm in the battle of Lepanto.

The best introduction to the Prado's strong Zurbarán collection is to examine first his canvas of Saint Luke as a painter before Christ on the cross, because Francisco Zurbarán painted himself, palette in hand, as the saint. Zurbarán is evidently both resolute and reflective, not at all flashy but quite aware of his value as an artist. From here you move on to the religious works that kept Zurbarán gainfully employed, to the series depicting the life of Hercules that he painted for the Palacio del Buen Retiro and that gained him royal recognition, and to the still life, or *bodegón,* that shows a collection of pots and that assured him enduring fame.

Zurbarán is worth taking some trouble over for he hands you over straight to Velázquez. "[Zurbarán's] work, while excellent, is still slightly claustrophobic," notes British author Alastair Boyd. "There is no air round his figures; they are substantial but they do not breathe—that comes with Velázquez."

Velázquez

It is hard to decide whether the Prado belongs more to Diego de Silva Velázquez than it does to Francisco de Goya Lucientes. Goya means more to contemporary man, but perhaps Velázquez wins by a hair's breadth because he was, as well as every bit a consummate artist, the court painter of Philip IV, who was the museum's greatest patron. The Prado is, without a doubt, the only place in the world where you will gain a close acquaintanceship with Velázquez, and the same is true in Goya's case.

Philip doted on the Sevillian-born Velázquez, just as his great-grandfather Charles V did on Titian. You should compare the portrait of the great-grandson with Titian's rendering of the victor of Mühlberg. Velázquez's Philip IV is sober in the extreme, bereft of armor, spurs, and lances; a shy, sensitive, and questioning man who had a special relationship with his painter. Tradition has it that the king himself painted the red cross of the order of Santiago on the breast of the artist in his self-portrait *Las Meninas.*

Las Meninas, a giant canvas with a room all to itself, has been termed a "theology of painting," and you can spend hours—quite a number of people do—working out its spatial depth and the influxes of light. The hall dedicated to the royal portraits, and the adjoining one dedicated to the buffoons, gives you the whole world picture that surrounds *Las Meninas.* For Velázquez at work on depth and on light you should pay close attention to *Las Hilanderas;* it was in this canvas that he solved the problems that he had set himself and applied later to his masterpiece.

The Surrender of Breda is another of the hugely famous Velázquez paintings; what is most remarkable about it, seeing it close up, is not so much the civility and courtesy of the surrender itself but the humor and the laid-back attitudes, picaresque in the extreme and typical of 17th-century Madrid, that are painted into the lance-bearers of the immediate foreground.

Velázquez knew all about decorum, for he was every inch a court painter and, as displayed in the astonishing equestrian portrait of the conde duque de Olivares, Philip IV's strongman, he knew all about political ambition and power too. But he also knew everything there was to know about real people, such as the ones in *The Drunkards.* His god Mars is not a fierce and proud warrior but an old soldier who has had a drink too many. There is nothing mythological either about the workers in his *Vulcan's Forge.*

17th-Century Spanish and Flemish Painters

Bartolomé Esteban Murillo, a sugary Sevillian contemporary of Velázquez, suffers by being so close to the master. His work is nevertheless highly indicative of the popular Catholicism of 17th-century Spain just as much as it marks general Hapsburg exhaustion and a decline in Spanish taste that was not to be properly righted until Goya appeared on the scene. Juan Carreño, who became court painter after Velázquez's death in 1660, offers a good insight into the Hapsburg decline with his portrait of Philip IV's aging widow, Mariana of Austria, and of the unfortunate product of that marriage, Carlos II (the Bewitched). Mariana was never attractive, as Velázquez's portrait of her when she was 19 and newly married shows all too well.

The Spanish Hapsburgs by no means confined themselves to the domestic art scene, for they were nothing if not a multinational royal family. Jan Brueghel and Rubens became known to Philip II by way of their patron the archduke Albert of Austria, who married the monarch's beloved daughter, the infanta Isabella Clara Eugenia. The two, together with other late Flemish school painters, are more than well represented in the Prado—too well, perhaps, in the case of Rubens; there is almost an overexposure of his fat matrons posing as nymphs.

The section's real highlights are the excellent oval portrait that Van Dyck painted of himself with Sir Endymion Porter, and a very revealing Rembrandt self-portrait that displays, as Alastair Boyd notes, "a frankly lascivious nature." There is also a Rembrandt rendering of Artemis in which the artist used his new wife, Saskia, as the model. You may compare this canvas to his portrait of Saskia that hangs in the city's Museo Lázaro Galdiano. Both the Prado Rembrandts were added to the royal collection by Carlos III.

Goya

Goya's genius lays bare his life and times. You move from the delightful cartoons, painted for tapestry weavers, which show a people at peace, at work, and at play, to the horrors of the Napoleonic invasion. The etchings of the *Desastres de la Guerra* (disasters of war) are like an album of war photography and constitute a searing antiwar manifesto. You are treated to his women—the nude and the dressed maja, who legend has it was the duchess of Alba—and, in the series known as the *Disparates* and the *Caprichos,* you share the keen, critical intelligence of a man of the Enlightenment. But Goya is much more than a magnificent recorder. In the *Milkmaid from Bordeaux,* for example, which he painted when he was 80, Velázquez and Renoir are present in the same canvas.

The Third of May, 1808, a giant canvas also called *Shootings in Moncloa,* is either the greatest of all protest pictures or it shares that honor with Picasso's *Guernica.* (The latter hangs in the Casón del Buen Retiro, the Prado's annex, so you can spend the morning with one picture and the afternoon with the other and make up your own mind.) There are other terrifying Goyas in the Prado. You can just about cope with the "black" paintings of sabbaths and witches, but the strange picture of a dog buried up to its neck in sand, and the beastliness of the two men, up to their knees in a bog, who are flaying themselves to death, the *Duelo a Garrotazos,* continue to disturb you long after you have seen them.

You also meet a very uninspiring court presided over by the cuckold Carlos IV and his toothless and brainless queen María Luisa. The whole royal group in the *Family of Carlos IV,* according to Goya expert Javier Sánchez Canton, is "looking at [Manuel de] Godoy who, from the royal guard, had come through the royal bedchamber to control the destiny of Spain." The young prince whose hand the queen holds is the spitting image of Godoy, who was reputed to be his father. Goya lost his job as court painter as a result of this group canvas.

Goya can overpower the Prado's visitors. "Velázquez, Rembrandt, and Nature are my only masters," he once stated. In his self-portrait, Goya, open-necked and tough-looking, appears arrogant and sure of himself, but his eyes are troubled and reveal a very complex mind.

Casón del Buen Retiro

This annex of the main Prado, five minutes' walk away, looks over the Parque del Retiro. The building's Retiro façade has an entrance that leads directly to the *Guernica* exhibit, which consists of Picasso's masterpiece and a good number of accompanying preliminary sketches. The collection was originally housed in New York's Museum of Modern Art; it finally arrived in Spain, after considerable haggling with curators and members of the Picasso family, in 1981. The artist had bequeathed his *Guernica* to the Prado, but he had stipulated that it could not come to Madrid unless democracy were restored to Spain.

It is somewhat ironic that this symbol of pacifism should hang in a building that flanks a museum dedicated to military memorabilia, the **Museo del Ejército** (army museum). Plans are nevertheless afoot to move the cannons that surround this second edifice and the warlike collection within to Toledo's Alcázar to create more space for the Prado's collection.

The Casón's other entrance, which faces the royal academy of letters, leads to a collection of 19th-century Spanish painting. It is an eclectic gathering of canvases ranging from Goya imitators, notably Eugenio Lucas, to French-influenced Catalan modernists such as Isidro Nonell, who will come as a pleasant surprise.

The museum's structure formed part of the Real Sitio del Buen Retiro, built in 1638 by Alonso Carbonell and used as their palace by the later Hapsburgs and by the early Bourbons until Carlos III moved into the Palacio Real in 1764. The main hall, which has a frescoed ceiling painted by Luca Giordano, known in Spain as Lucas Jordán, was the palace's ballroom. The fresco's theme is the Order of the Golden Fleece, a chivalric order created by the Spanish monarchy that in antiquity rivals England's Order of the Garter.

AROUND HAPSBURG MADRID

Orientation

Hapsburg Madrid is best appreciated in the neighborhood of the plaza Mayor. Juan de Herrera drew up the original plans for the square, and it was completed in the subsequent reign of Philip III, Philip II's son, by Herrera's pupil Juan Gómez de Mora.

The main axis of Hapsburg Madrid is **calle Mayor**, which starts at the puerta del Sol and ends at calle Bailén, near the Palacio Real. The plaza Mayor lies off calle Mayor on the left as you move out of the puerta del Sol toward calle Bailén; the Casa de la Villa (city hall) gives onto calle Mayor, also on the left, about halfway along it; and the **Palacio del Duques de Uceda**, the military headquarters, is again on the left of the street, farther on and close to calle Bailén.

The third major Hapsburg edifice in the area, the **Palacio de Santa Cruz**, housing the foreign ministry, lies one block east of the plaza Mayor, and you reach it either by crossing the plaza or by walking up calle de Esparteros, the first left exit as you leave puerta del Sol along calle Mayor. South of the plaza Mayor, calle de Toledo leads to the cathedral of San Isidro. Past the cathedral and continuing south along calle de Toledo you come to a square set off by La Latina Metro station. If you turn right, westward, here, you reach puerta de Moros and the Capilla del Obispo, and if you turn left, eastward, you enter the plaza de Cascorro and El Rastro (the flea-market area).

A series of narrow streets that leads off the right-hand side of calle Mayor as you walk west along it out of puerta del Sol takes you into a pleasant old quarter with a 17th-century flavor that properly belongs to Hapsburg Madrid. These streets lead to calle Arenal, an old artery similar to calle Mayor that also starts at puerta del Sol and leads to the plaza de Isabel II, a square flanked by the Teatro Real (the opera house) and which leads directly to the plaza de Oriente and the Palacio Real. Northeast of the palace is the Convento de la Encarnación, and the Real Monasterio de las Descalzas Reales is north of calle Arenal off San Martín; these two great Hapsburg convents are now museums.

Before you start on any exploration of Hapsburg Madrid, it is a good idea to check out **calle Victoria**, a small street close to the entrance of puerta del Sol along carrera de San Jerónimo, the street directly opposite the calle Mayor exit. Calle Victoria, and the alleyways leading off it, are lined with bars, and this block constitutes what is arguably the best *tapas*-hopping area in the city. Calle Victoria has always been favored by the bullfight crowd, and you can buy bullfight tickets here. There are good bars and restaurants around the plaza Mayor as well.

If you want to combine modern-day shopping with cultural touring, look in on **calle de Preciados**, a pedestrian precinct leading out of puerta del Sol and linking the latter with Gran Vía. Two branches of Spain's rival department-store chains, El Corte Inglés and Galerías Preciados, stand conveniently close to each other on this street. Walking around Hapsburg Madrid also puts you close to El Rastro (it's jam-packed weekends) and a newly opened design and boutique shopping mall, **Mercado de la Puerta de Toledo**, at the very end of calle de Toledo, at ronda de Toledo 1, the site of what used to be Madrid's main fish market.

To capture the atmosphere of the city 300 and more years ago as it bulged with a rapidly increasing population, you should wind your way southward from the Catedral de San Isidro toward the flea-market area, **El Rastro**, and its adjoin-

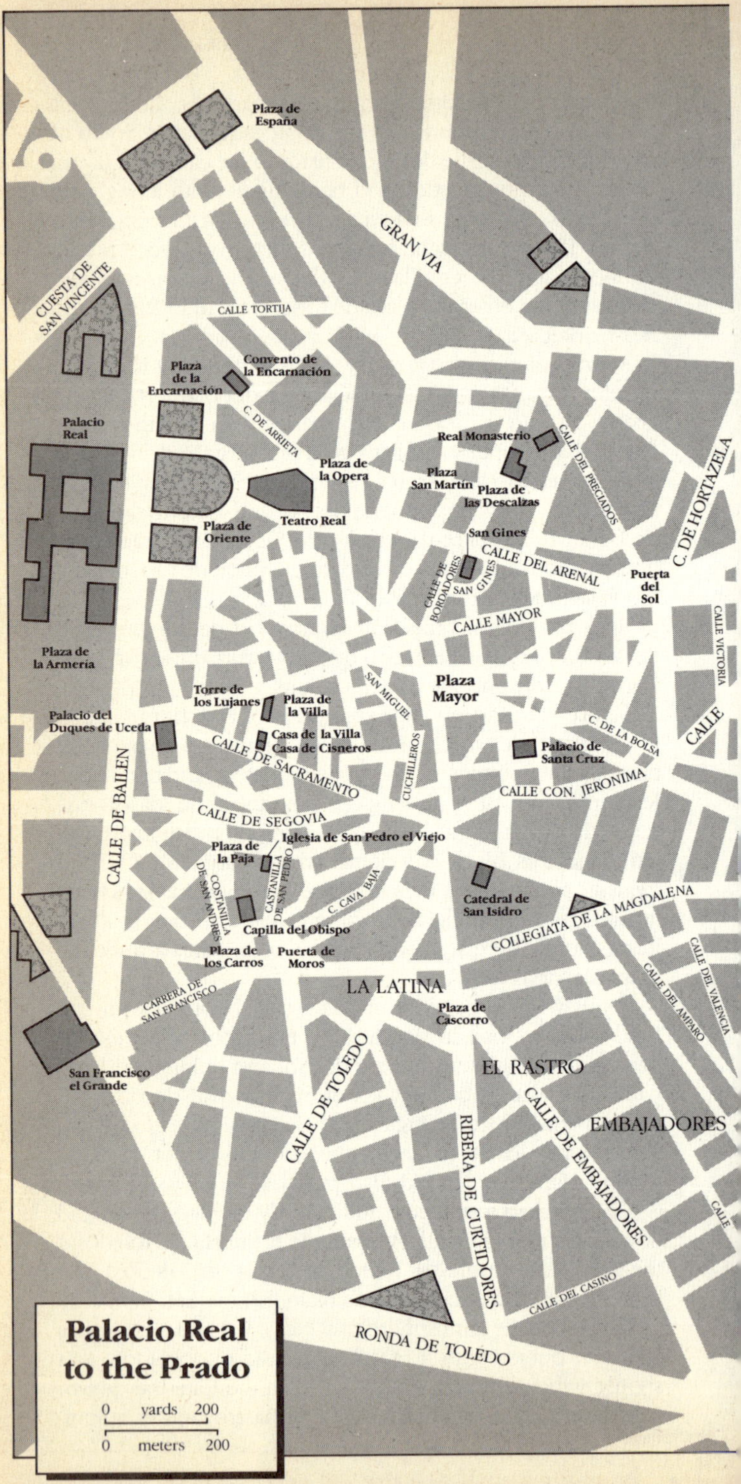
Plaza de España
GRAN VIA
CUESTA DE SAN VINCENTE
CALLE TORTIJA
Convento de la Encarnación
Plaza de la Encarnación
Palacio Real
C. DE ARRIETA
Plaza de la Opera
Real Monasterio
CALLE DEL PRECIADOS
Plaza San Martín
Plaza de las Descalzas
C. DE HORTAZELA
Plaza de Oriente
Teatro Real
San Gines
CALLE DEL ARENAL
CALLE DE BORDADORES
SAN GINES
Puerta del Sol
CALLE MAYOR
CALLE VICTORIA
Plaza de la Armería
SAN MIGUEL
Plaza Mayor
Torre de los Lujanes
Plaza de la Villa
Palacio del Duques de Uceda
Casa de la Villa
Casa de Cisneros
C. DE LA BOLSA
CALLE
CALLE DE SACRAMENTO
CUCHILLEROS
Palacio de Santa Cruz
CALLE CON. JERONIMA
CALLE DE BAILEN
CALLE DE SEGOVIA
Plaza de la Paja
Iglesia de San Pedro el Viejo
COSTANILLA DE SAN ANDRES
CASTANILLA DE SAN PEDRO
C. CAVA BAJA
Catedral de San Isidro
COLLEGIATA DE LA MAGDALENA
Capilla del Obispo
Plaza de los Carros
Puerta de Moros
LA LATINA
CALLE DEL VALENCIA
CALLE DEL AMPARO
CARRERA DE SAN FRANCISCO
Plaza de Cascorro
CALLE DE TOLEDO
EL RASTRO
San Francisco el Grande
CALLE DE EMBAJADORES
RIBERA DE CURTIDORES
EMBAJADORES
CALLE
CALLE DEL CASINO
RONDA DE TOLEDO
Palacio Real to the Prado
0 yards 200
0 meters 200

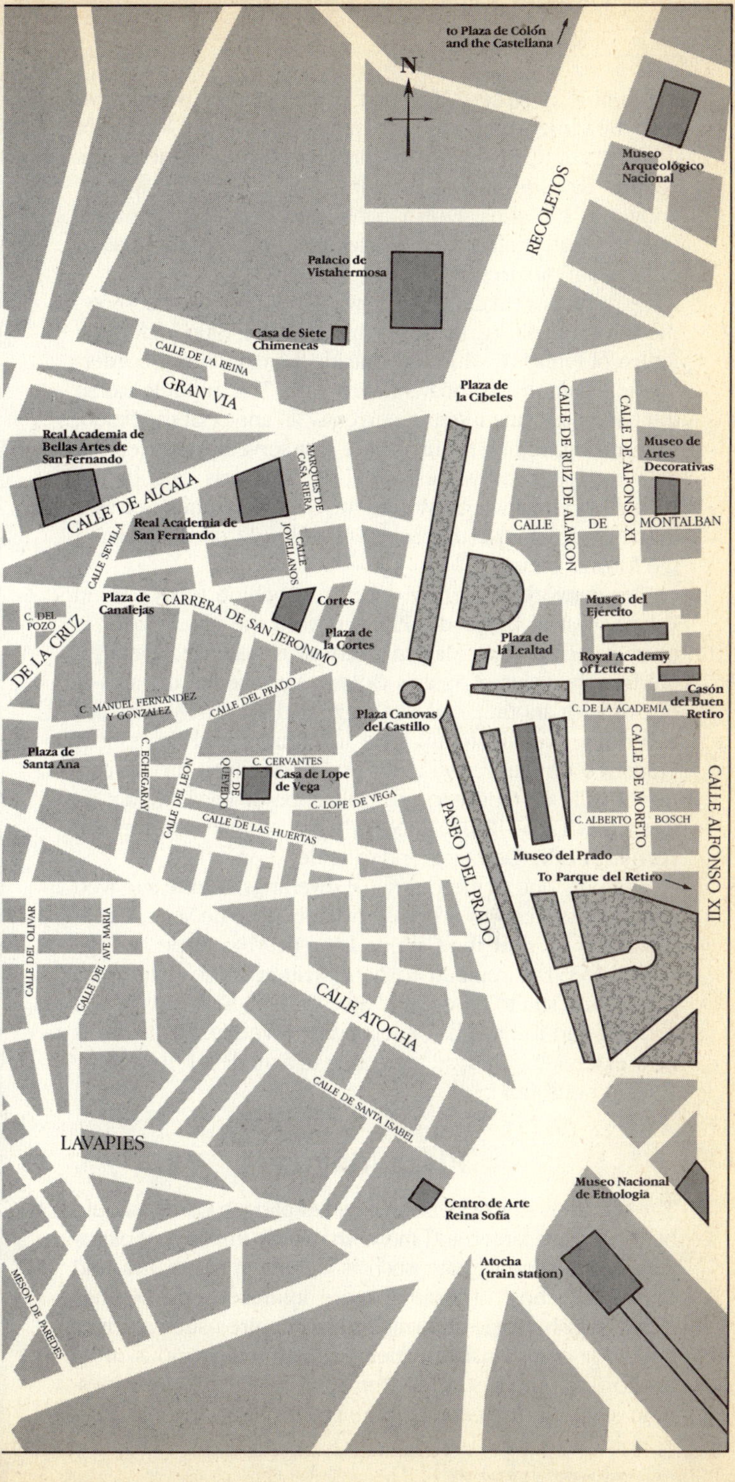

to Plaza de Colón and the Castellana
N
Museo Arqueológico Nacional
RECOLETOS
Palacio de Vistahermosa
Casa de Siete Chimeneas
CALLE DE LA REINA
GRAN VIA
Plaza de la Cibeles
Real Academia de Bellas Artes de San Fernando
MARQUES DE CASA RIERA
CALLE DE RUIZ DE ALARCON
CALLE DE ALFONSO XI
Museo de Artes Decorativas
CALLE DE ALCALA
Real Academia de San Fernando
CALLE JOVELLANOS
CALLE DE MONTALBAN
CALLE SEVILLA
Plaza de Canalejas
CARRERA DE SAN JERONIMO
Cortes
Museo del Ejército
C. DEL POZO
DE LA CRUZ
Plaza de la Cortes
Plaza de la Lealtad
Royal Academy of Letters
Casón del Buen Retiro
C. MANUEL FERNANDEZ Y GONZALEZ
CALLE DEL PRADO
Plaza Canovas del Castillo
C. DE LA ACADEMIA
Plaza de Santa Ana
C. ECHEGARAY
CALLE DEL LEON
C. DE QUEVEDO
C. CERVANTES
Casa de Lope de Vega
CALLE DE MORETO
CALLE ALFONSO XII
C. LOPE DE VEGA
CALLE DE LAS HUERTAS
PASEO DEL PRADO
C. ALBERTO BOSCH
Museo del Prado
To Parque del Retiro
CALLE DEL OLIVAR
CALLE DEL AVE MARIA
CALLE ATOCHA
CALLE DE SANTA ISABEL
LAVAPIES
Museo Nacional de Etnologia
Centro de Arte Reina Sofía
Atocha (train station)
MESON DE PAREDES

ing jumble of streets. This part of Old Madrid is still alive with the same "camp-follower" humanity as in the Madrid of the 17th century, which gave birth to the picaresque genre. To this day the somewhat slummy areas of Old Madrid, known as La Latina, Embajadores, and Lavapiés, with their taverns, stall holders, and tricksters, remain picaresque rather than picturesque.

Only hints remain of what was undoubtedly the showpiece of Hapsburg Madrid. This was the Sitio del Buen Retiro of Philip IV, which lay outside the city's limits bordering an estate that is today's Retiro park. The building called the Casón del Buen Retiro, currently an annex of the Prado, was an outbuilding of this palace that served as a reception hall; today's nearby Museo del Ejército was one of the palace's original wings. Most of the large Velázquez canvases in the Prado, such as the *Surrender of Breda,* used to hang in the former palace.

The network of narrow streets just behind today's Hotel Palace west of paseo del Prado toward the plaza Mayor is often referred to as Madrid's Parnassus because several of the literary giants of Spain's Golden Age lived in the area at one time or another. Luis de Gongora (1561–1627), who put a flowing, lyrical literary style in fashion, and the satirist Francisco de Quevedo (1580–1645) both lived on the corner of calle de Quevedo and calle Lope de Vega. Miguel de Cervantes (1547–1616) died in a house that stood at the corner of calle Cervantes and calle del León.

The only one of these original dwellings to have survived is the house that was occupied by Félix Lope de Vega at calle Cervantes 11, now the **Casa de Lope de Vega.** Lope de Vega (1562–1635) is reputed to have written more than 1,800 plays—and still to have found time to serve in the Invincible Armada and to have had a legendary love life. His home is now essentially a period recreation of a modest 17th-century Madrid household.

Plaza Mayor

The square is exactly what an arcaded plaza in Castile should be. There are larger and more artistically impressive plazas mayores in central Spain, such as the one in Salamanca, and there are a host of smaller, more intimate ones, because every largish village and small town required such a center point for communal activities. Perfectly harmonious in its proportions and in its 17th-century style—the bronze equestrian statue in the center of the square honors Philip III—

Madrid's plaza Mayor is, however, not only well up to the best architectural standards, but it is more historic than any other.

Important executions were held here, bloodcurdling autos-da-fé were organized with operatic grandeur by the Inquisition, and on major holidays the whole square was converted into a giant bullring. Edward Hyde, the first Earl of Clarendon, saw a bullfight here in 1650. The spectacle was then very different from today's corrida, and Clarendon described, with evident pride, how when the bull became too unruly "The King [Philip IV] calls, as a last resort, for the English mastives." The royal family used to occupy the balconies of the stuccoed Casa de la Panadería, on the north side of the square, during such spectacles.

The plaza Mayor, which is home to several restaurants that have tables out on the plaza as well as inside, is a pedestrian-only precinct and is within comfortable walking distance of most of Hapsburg Madrid's other major landmarks. Leaving the square by its southeast corner, through the **Arco de Cuchilleros**, you enter Madrid's oldest quarter. This area is ideal for those who like simply to "lose" themselves among taverns and artisan shops. You should aim for the Catedral de San Isidro to the south and then amble westward to the Capilla del Obispo in the plaza de la Paja and from there to El Rastro. (First to the west, however, to the plaza de la Villa.)

La Casa de la Villa

Situated in the plaza de la Villa, a square that lies just west of the plaza Mayor and opens on calle Mayor, the Casa de la Villa, Madrid's city hall, occupies the western façade of the plaza. Designed in 1644 by Gómez de Mora, who was responsible as well for the plaza Mayor, the Casa de la Villa originally imitated the severe lines of what is called the Herreriano style introduced by Gómez's teacher Juan de Herrera in the Escorial. The severity was later toned down and the building was extended by the Bourbon architects Teodoro Ardemáns, who built La Granja near Segovia for Philip V, and Juan de Villanueva.

The building located at the far end of the plaza and linked to the Casa de la Villa by a covered bridge is the **Casa de Cisneros**, built in the 1530s by a nephew of the famous 15th-century churchman Cardinal Cisneros. Its chief interest lies in the plateresque façade at the rear of the building, on calle de Sacramento; this is one of the very few examples in Madrid of that ornate Spanish Renaissance style that is so common in Salamanca and Toledo. The building facing the Casa de la Villa is the **Torre de los Lujanes**, which though much restored dates from the mid-15th century—a rare survivor of pre-Hapsburg Madrid. Francis I of France was imprisoned briefly in the tower in 1525 after he was defeated and captured by Emperor Charles V at the battle of Pavia.

From the plaza de la Villa a short walk east along calle Mayor leads to the busy puerta del Sol plaza that is the location of the famous kilometer 0. Walking west takes you to calle Bailén and the neighborhood of the Palacio Real.

Catedral de San Isidro and the Capilla del Obispo

San Isidro is only temporarily Madrid's cathedral; the proper one is still being built alongside the Palacio Real on calle Bailén. One of the curiosities about Madrid is that it does not have a magnificent church headquarters. When the court finally set up its home in the city, the great age of cathedral building had passed.

Standing on calle de Toledo south of the plaza Mayor, San Isidro is chiefly important for being the home of the uncorrupted remains of Madrid's patron saint, Isidro, an amiable and pious Medieval farm laborer. Tradition has it that angels descended to drive his plough when he was either having a siesta or attending mass. The basilica, completed in a low-key Baroque style in 1661 to serve as a Jesuit college, and converted into a cathedral when the Jesuits were expelled from Spain the following century, was modeled after Rome's Gesù church.

Far more interesting is the **Capilla del Obispo** (bishop's chapel), on the corner of the plaza de la Paja and costanilla de San Andrés, a short distance west of San Isidro near the end of the picturesque street cava Baja (see below). The chapel was built in the 1520s, and its combination of Gothic vaulting and Renaissance, or, more exactly, Plateresque decorations shows off the transition between the two styles. The altarpiece, by Francisco Giralta, a pupil of Berruguete, deserves close inspection. The domed Capilla de San Andrés next door contained the remains of San Isidro until they were transferred to the cathedral. A third old church in the immediate vicinity (a short walk from San Andrés up costanilla de San Pedro) is the **Iglesia de San Pedro el Viejo**. Built in 1354 over an old mosque, the brick Mudejar-style tower is all that remains of the original church; the main building, which has a Renaissance air to it, dates from 1525.

The plaza de Carros, south of the plaza de la Paja, is the site of puerta de Moros, one of the original entry points to the old Medieval city of Madrid. (The plaza's name is derived from *carros,* which means carts, and this square is where they were parked.) From the plaza de Carros the broad carrera de San Francisco leads southwest to the large basilica of the same name that belongs to the Bourbon period (see Bourbon Madrid, below) and stands at the end of calle Bailén. Leaving the plaza in the southern direction, and crossing calle de Toledo, you will be heading to the nearby plaza de Cascorro, home of **El Rastro**, Madrid's flea market. (If you follow costanilla de San Andrés northward where it meets calle de Segovia and then follow this large street eastward up the hill, you will be walking back toward the plaza Mayor.)

To get a more or less accurate picture of who was where in Hapsburg Madrid you should keep in mind that the court and the wealthy occupied the area near calle Mayor. This street was suitably close to the Palacio Real, or rather to the alcázar, which was what existed in that period on the site now occupied by the 18th-century Bourbon palace. The solid buildings around the plaza de la Villa and between calle Mayor and calle de Sacramento were the 16th-century's prime sites.

Calle de Sacramento meets calle Mayor by the Palacio del Duques de Uceda, the military headquarters, which looks out on calle Bailén. Sacramento then extends eastward to run into calle de San Justo. It is below this line, formed by Sacramento and San Justo, where the more popular classes lived. Artisan Madrid, the popular Madrid of the picaresque genre, extended from here southward to puerta de Moros, which in early Hapsburg times marked the southern limits of the city.

The taverns and restaurants in this area between Sacramento/San Justo and puerta de Moros still maintain the ambience of that period. **Cava Baja**, the narrow street that links puerta Cerrada (a small square at the end of calle de San Justo) and puerta de Moros, has two excellent eating houses: **El Schotis**, at cava Baja 11, and **Casa Lucio**, a bit farther on at cava Baja 35. At puerta Cerrada (if you are in the plaza Mayor, you reach this busy little square by leaving the plaza through the Arco de Cuchilleros exit) there is a third superb tavern: **Casa Paco**, at puerta Cerrada 1.

The area occupied now by El Rastro was built up in the

late 18th century as the city continued to expand southward, but it still exhibits the bustle of Madrid's popular quarters as recorded by Hapsburg writers. On Saturdays and Sundays a huge crowd assembles around the stalls that occupy both sides of the broad ribera de Curtidores, which runs down from the plaza de Cascorro. It is a noisy, boisterous scene as people haggle for bargains, tout all kinds of products, and fill the bars. All humanity is on this particular stage—including pickpockets and drug pushers.

Real Monasterio de las Descalzas Reales

Madrid is a busy city where the hustle and bustle is occasionally tempered by unexpected places where you can retreat into silence and contemplation. This convent-museum of the royal "barefoot" nuns, set between puerta del Sol and Gran Vía, is one such place.

If you are in the plaza de la Villa, cross calle Mayor, and walk north on the old calle de Bordadores, which crosses calle Arenal and leads to the plaza de las Descalzas, where the convent occupies the whole façade of the square. At the corner of calle Arenal (a street linking puerta del Sol and the Palacio Real) you will pass the 17th-century Iglesia de San Ginés, which was where Lope de Vega was married and where the satirist Francisco de Quevedo was baptized. Quevedo tore into the later Hapsburgs with much the same effect Alexander Pope and Jonathan Swift had against the Hanoverians.

The Real Monasterio is as good as the Prado, and considerably more intimate, for a close glimpse of the relatives of Emperor Charles V and King Philip II. It was founded by Juana, Charles V's youngest daughter, the widow of Prince Henry of Portugal and the mother of Portugal's ill-fated king Sebastian, who died campaigning in North Africa. Juana was later joined in the convent by her sister María, widow of the emperor Maximilian, and the institution was even more richly endowed by Isabella Clara Eugenia, Philip II's daughter. Hapsburg family portraits are as numerous in the museum part of the Real Monasterio as religious artworks are in the chapels of the convent area.

The building, which still houses a small community of nuns, is in the stern, austere mold that was favored by Philip II. A former mansion that housed Charles V's treasurer, Alonso Gutiérrez, it was adapted to serve as a monastery by

Juan Bautista de Toledo, the architect who began designing the Escorial before Juan de Herrera took over the monumental work. The convent and museum is owned by the Patrimonio Nacional, Spain's national trust, which is in charge of most royal foundations, and accordingly visitors have to join conducted tours that are herded through the different apartments. Some of the guides speak English.

Convento de la Encarnación

On calle Bailén, just off the north side of the plaza de Oriente, the large square that looks onto the Palacio Real, the Convento de la Encarnación, built in 1611, constitutes a little presence of the Hapsburg world near the giant orbit that the Spanish Bourbons created around their palace. It lies quite close to the Descalzas Reales, from which you reach it by returning to calle Arenal and walking west down it, away from puerta del Sol, to the plaza de Isabel II, a square dominated by the back of the Teatro Real, Madrid's opera house, the front of which is on the plaza de Oriente. From the back of the plaza de Isabel II walk up calle Arrieta, which is at its northeast corner; this street leads directly to the plaza de la Encarnación and its convent. The plaza de la Encarnación itself, graced by a statue honoring Golden Age playwright Lope de Vega, is a pleasant spot. **Alambique**, an interesting culinary-equipment store, which also runs a cooking school, stands across from the convent, and **La Bola**, a popular Madrileño bistro, is on calle de la Bola, a street leading off the square, at number 5. For a drink alfresco, walk down to the plaza de Oriente and over to the terrace of the **Café de Oriente** on the far side of the Teatro Real.

The Convento de la Encarnación was founded by Margaret of Austria, wife of Philip III, and built by the ubiquitous Gómez de Mora, who created the plaza Mayor for her husband. It has a museum attached to it, also run by the Patrimonio Nacional, which contains 17th-century artwork (Pacheco, Carreño, and Ribera, among others) that is somewhat less impressive than the collection in the Descalzas Reales. The church's exterior is suitably severe, but it is somewhat overdone within due perhaps to excessive royal patronage. The organ, which is played at 10:30 A.M. during Sunday mass, is arguably its best feature. A few of the convent's private rooms (La Encarnación remains a cloistered institution) are open to view; they preserve intact the atmosphere of the 17th century.

AROUND BOURBON MADRID

Orientation

The Bourbon dynasty, which arrived in Spain at the beginning of the 18th century when the Spanish Hapsburgs died out, oversaw the expansion of Madrid beyond the immediate confines of the plaza Mayor and the calle Mayor axis. The Bourbon mark on the city therefore tends to envelop the original 16th- and 17th-century center, most notably on the west side of the city along calle Bailén and on the east side at the southern, downtown, end of the Castellana.

Along calle Bailén stands the Palacio Real, the impressive plaza de Oriente, and the Iglesia de San Francisco el Grande. Also on the west side of the city, but some distance from calle Bailén, the Ermita de San Antonio de la Florida, also of the same period, stands close to the río Manzanares. This hermitage was decorated by Goya, then the Bourbon court painter, and is his burial place. Over on the east side of the city, the fountains—such as Cibeles and the one in honor of Neptune—that stand on the Castellana were built during the reign of the late-18th-century Bourbon monarch Carlos III in an ambitious attempt to beautify the city. Work on the building that houses the Prado was started during Carlos's reign, and the Jardín Botánico, alongside the art gallery, was laid out during those same years.

The Bourbons, specifically Carlos III, were also responsible for developing today's east-side calle de Alcalá, which runs from the puerta del Sol in Hapsburg Madrid down to the Castellana at the plaza de la Cibeles and then continues on to meet the Parque del Retiro at the triumphal puerta de Alcalá, one of the most impressive of the monuments built during Carlos III's reign. The academy of fine arts museum, Real Academia de San Fernando, yet another Carlos III initiative, stands on Alcalá close to the beginning of the puerta del Sol.

Palacio Real

The eastern façade of the royal palace, all 460 feet of it, looks out on the plaza de Oriente and the Teatro Real opera house on the western side of central Madrid. The more imposing façade, however, is the western one, which looms over the río Manzanares and beyond to the parklands of the Casa de Campo. Walk down the cuesta de San Vicente hill from the plaza de España toward the Manzanares to gain entry into the Campo del Moro royal gardens, which provide the best views of the palace.

The impeccably kept avenues of the Campo del Moro, the decorative fountains, the yew trees, cedars, and poplars—the **Museo de Carrozas** (museum of royal carriages) is also here—are in themselves worth visiting. The admirable Bourbon king Carlos III had his apartments on the western façade; he obviously wanted the view of the Casa de Campo, where he went hunting virtually every day. Goya painted engaging portraits of the weather-beaten monarch, musket in hand among the oaks of the Casa de Campo, with the Guadarrama Sierra on the horizon.

What you have, with whichever façade you look at, is a grand 18th-century palace, rectangular in shape and built around an internal courtyard. Building commenced in 1738, in the reign of Philip V and under the direction of Felipe Juvara, four years after the old alcázar that stood on the same site burned to the ground in a fortuitous fire. Juvara had intended a palace that would have been four times bigger than the one that was finally completed. Juan Sachetti, who succeeded Juvara as chief architect, rescaled the plans and the palace was finally completed in 1764, five years after Carlos III, Philip V's son, had ascended the throne.

The two monarchs whose presence is most felt in the palace are Carlos III, the first king to occupy it, who died in the palace in 1788, and Alfonso XIII, the last monarch to use it as a permanent home. Alfonso was forced to leave the palace for exile in 1931 when the Spanish republic was proclaimed. Alfonso, his wife, Victoria Eugenie, a great-grandaughter of Queen Victoria, and his mother, María Cristina, who reigned as regent during his infancy, all occupied the apartments that look out onto the plaza de Oriente.

The palace is now used only for official receptions, because the present monarch, Juan Carlos, Alfonso's grandson, prefers the intimacy of the Palacio de la Zarzuela, a former hunting lodge that lies beyond the Casa de Campo in the middle of a large deer park.

Entrance to the Palacio Real is gained through the parade ground called the plaza de la Armería that lies on the left of the palace as you look at it from the plaza de Oriente, between the palace and the Madrid cathedral, the Catedral de la Almudena, still under construction. Because the palace is run by the Patrimonio Nacional, you can only visit it as part of a conducted tour. These leave every quarter of an hour or so from the parade-ground entry lobby; there are English-speaking guides. The tour, taking you through more than 50 rooms, some of them huge and all of them overflowing with objets d'art, lasts about two hours. You may end up fairly weary of tapestries, chandeliers, and porcelains.

The guides rush you from room to room as they ply you with statistics about what you are seeing. Were you able to linger longer in the rooms you are shown, you would probably opt for the sumptuous Sala de Gasparini, so as to examine more closely the chinoiserie stucco ceiling, and the Sala de Porcelana, the china chamber. Both rooms are part of Carlos III's chambers and are visited in the early part of the tour. The state dining room is also impressive, with its ceilings painted by Francisco Bayeu, Goya's father-in-law, and by Rafael Mengs, Goya's rival as court painter. The music room has a magnificent clock collection that was started by Carlos III, and the private rooms of Alfonso XIII give interesting insights into the personality of the failed monarch of the interwar years—he favored the club atmosphere of a regimental officers' mess room, and he had the hooves of his favorite horses turned into paperweights.

The **Armería Real** (royal armory), adjoining the Palacio Real and also entered by the plaza de la Armería, is great fun. When you have viewed the 44 suits of armor made for and worn by Charles V—one of the greatest figures in the history of Europe—you feel you know quite a bit about the man who battled his way across the Continent to keep hold of both the Holy Roman Empire and the Spanish one. It seems all the odder that such a warrior should have chosen to abdicate in favor of his son Philip II in 1556 and to have retired to the Monasterio de Yuste, hidden away in the wilds of western Spain (northern Extremadura). Among the wealth of historic military hardware here are the swords that belonged to conquistadores Hernán Cortés and Francisco Pizarro.

San Francisco el Grande

South along calle Bailén from the Palacio Real, past the crossroads where the street meets calle Mayor and across the towering viaduct that looks down on the calle de Segovia, you eventually come to the large domed Iglesia de San Francisco el Grande. The church bears the stamp of Carlos III's Neoclassical ambitions for Madrid. He commissioned Sabatini to create the main façade in that style in 1776, at a time when work that had begun on the church 15 years earlier was at a standstill. Joseph Bonaparte, Napoleon's brother, who was briefly king of Spain during the

French occupation, wanted to turn the church into a parliament, and midway through the 19th century it became a military barracks. Nowadays it is a museum, housing an early work by Goya, a set of apostles by Ribera, and a host of mostly nondescript paintings by minor 19th-century artists. The Renaissance choir stalls stood originally in the monastery of El Paular, which nestles in the Guadarrama Sierra.

A short walk south from San Francisco brings you to the **puerta de Toledo**, a Bourbon landmark surrounded by an architectural wasteland. The triumphal arch lacks the grace, and the surroundings, of the puerta de Alcalá, but it is an interesting reminder of Madrid's—and Spain's—ups and downs. It was originally designed in honor of Napoleon, then it was hoped that it would be inaugurated by the patriotic liberal members of the Cádiz parliament, and it finally served to mark the arrival of the returning Bourbon, Fernando VII, who tore up the liberal constitution and exiled those who framed it.

Ermita de San Antonio de la Florida

This late-18th-century hermitage dedicated to Saint Anthony of Padua, northwest up paseo de la Florida from the Palacio Real and the Campo de Moro, is hallowed Goya ground. He is buried here—or, more exactly, the trunk of his body is, because mystery surrounds the whereabouts of his head. It is a suitable place of repose; the domed roof, which Carlos IV commissioned Goya to decorate in 1798, shows the artist in top form. What was intended to be a religious fresco depicting the appearance of the saint before the people of Lisbon becomes, with Goya, a bold and very secular celebration of the Madrid of his time. The little church lies close to the Manzanares, but unfortunately the river banks where Goya's Madrileños used to picnic have long been built up.

Museo Cerralbo

This mansion, standing just off the plaza de España at its northeastern edge on the corner of calle Ventura Rodríguez and calle Ferraz, was the 19th-century town house of the aristocratic Cerralbo family and houses an impressive art collection built up by the 17th marqués of Cerralbo, who donated it to the nation in 1924. The collection includes works by El Greco, Ribera, and Zurbarán, and there are also extensive archaeological exhibits thanks to the numerous digs that the marqués financed in Rome, Greece, and the

Middle East. The mansion itself is decorated in the grand style; the visitor is swept into a world of stuccoed ceilings, chandeliers, and mirrors.

Palacio de Liria

Occupying a whole block on calle de Princesa, the street that leads out of the plaza de España's northwest corner, and hidden behind its extensive gardens, the 18th-century Palacio de Liria is the Madrid home of the dukes of Alba and contains one of the best private collections of old masters in the world. It is very much a private residence but *occasionally,* and by prior appointment, groups of visitors are allowed in for conducted tours. Ask at the gatehouse—you may just be lucky.

Real Academia de Bellas Artes de San Fernando

Back on the eastern side of central Madrid, near the start of calle de Alcalá (at number 13), east of the puerta del Sol toward paseo del Prado and the Cibeles fountain, Madrid's academy of fine arts is a quiet place to pursue the study of Goya. There is the bright side of the artist in his canvas of the carnival called *Burial of the Sardine,* and there is the tormented side in his study of a madhouse. The critical, politically committed Goya emerges in his scenes of the Inquisition, an institution that he also lampooned brilliantly in a series of etchings that hang in the Prado.

The collection here includes a good number of old masters confiscated from the Jesuits when the order was expelled from Spain by Carlos III, but Goya, who was for a time the academy's director, provides the highlights. There are portraits of people he liked and admired, such as the liberal literary lion Moratín and the architect Villanueva, who redesigned the academy building along Neoclassical lines. And there are portraits of people he did not like at all, such as Godoy, the guardsman turned prime minister, and Ferdinand VII, the despotic son of Carlos IV. Goya's true feelings toward the woman known as La Tirana, whose large portrait also hangs here, are less clear. She was a well-known courtesan who was allegedly exceptionally severe to her admirers. To round out its Goya collection, the academy possesses a self-portrait similar to the Prado one.

The academy's shop is well worth a browse; it sells

reasonably priced prints by Goya and others from original plates.

The Fuente de la Cibeles and the Paseo del Prado

Madrid's best-known city landmark is the monument in honor of Cibeles, a mythical queen of the sea, that stands at the intersection of the Castellana and calle de Alcalá in the plaza de la Cibeles, one of the most traffic-laden areas of the city. Cibeles herself looks extremely relaxed in her chariot, lazily eyeing the lions that are dragging it along and constantly refreshed by the surrounding fountains.

Cibeles's companion is the statue of Neptune that stands farther south on the Castellana and is flanked, at opposite ends of the square, by the Ritz and Palace hotels. Both these fountain-bedecked, Classical-style monuments were inaugurated in 1790 during the reign of Carlos III and were part of his plan to create a refined paseo along which Madrid's fashionable society could stroll at their leisure or show off their carriages. This part of the Castellana is properly called paseo del Prado, and it extends beyond Neptune's statue to the Prado and the Jardín Botánico.

EL PARQUE DEL RETIRO

El Parque del Retiro is a people's park. On Sunday morning it is teeming with quick-portrait artists, musicians, and fortune-tellers. There is normally a puppet show and a concert (the theater and the bandstand are close to the plaza de Independencia entrance by puerta de Alcalá) on Sunday, and all-year-round art exhibitions are staged at the Palacio de Cristal and the Palacio de Velázquez, which lie close to each other in the middle of the park.

This is a big park—300 acres—and it has a very beautiful rose garden, a lake for boating, scores of sensational trees, gorgeous leafy avenues, areas that are countrified and others that have carefully laid out flower beds and box hedgerows according to the French ornamental garden tradition. It is well stocked with kiosks on whose terraces you can sip aperitifs, and there are a number of hansom cabs to take you around it in comfort. If you are so inclined you can take advantage of the park's jogging course.

The Retiro was originally a 17th-century Hapsburg hunting park and formed the private estate of what was known as the Palacio del Buen Retiro. All that remains now of that leisure palace is the Casón del Buen Retiro—the Prado annex housing Picasso's *Guernica*—on calle Alfonso XII, which runs along the park's western limits, and the Museo del Ejército, which lies behind the Casón. During the 17th-century reign of Philip IV, masked balls, concerts, fireworks displays, and even mock sea battles on the boating lake were staged in the park. In 1868 the gardens were opened to the general public.

Of all the park's landmarks, the Monumento al Angel Caído (monument to the fallen angel) deserves special mention. Standing near the rose garden and erected in 1878, it depicts Satan as an athletic, good-looking youth, crashing down to earth.

Museums near El Retiro

Originally part of the Palacio del Buen Retiro complex and just behind the Casón del Buen Retiro (for more on this, see the earlier section on the Museo del Prado), the **Museo del Ejército** (army museum) on calle Méndez Núñez has a series of menacing cannons and field guns occupying its terrace. Inside there is an astonishing array of weapons of the ages. There is case upon case of crossbows, muskets, swords, rifles, and every other conceivable war implement. The Spaniards are second to none when it comes to fighting and conquering, and the latter-day exhibits deal with the Spanish Civil War when they set upon each other.

Just off calle Alfonso XII on the park's western limits on calle de Montalban, which leads down to the Castellana, the **Museo de Artes Decorativas** (museum of decorative arts) at number 12 contains a pleasing collection of Spanish furniture and handiworks of the past 400 years. There are three floors of well-planned exhibits of lace- and leatherwork, jewelry, ceramics, and glass. One of the most charming areas of the museum is its collection of little Nativity figures. These elaborate Bethlehems have a place of honor in Spanish households during Christmas; if you happen to be in Madrid in December, you will find such figures on sale at special stalls set up in the plaza Mayor.

The **Museo Nacional de Etnología** (national ethnology museum) is a minor anthropological and ethnological collection occupying the ground floor of a late-19th-century building at the southern end of calle Alfonso XII (number 68). Inaugurated in 1875, the museum is in a somewhat dilapidated state, but its library is highly regarded by specialists.

Museo Arqueológico Nacional

Forming part of the huge national library building that occupies an entire block next to the plaza del Descubrimiento on paseo de la Castellana north of Fuente de la Cibeles, the Museo Arqueológico Nacional (archaeological museum) is at calle de Serrano 13. Its showpiece is the mysterious bust, possibly representing a Carthaginian goddess, called **La Dama de Elche**. The *Dama* (lady), unearthed in the southeastern town of Elche, is exhibited in the Iberian art section. Few remain unmoved in her presence; she has astonishingly modern looks and a distinctly strong, attractive personality.

After the Prado, this is Madrid's most important museum, and it contains by far the most comprehensive archaeological collection in Spain. Here is where an interested student and visitor will best understand the tapestry of cultures that make up Spain. There is a better exhibition on the Roman Empire in Mérida; Granada and Córdoba display more Islamic treasures; and there are astounding Romanesque art exhibits in Barcelona—but Madrid's museum has examples of all three influences, with a broad collection stretching well back into the Bronze Age. In the gardens a special exhibit reproduces that treasure of the dawn of Western art, the Altamira cave drawings.

OTHER MADRID MUSEUMS

The Museo Romántico and the Museo Municipal lie close to each other in an area of small, narrow, and often labyrinthine streets west of the Castellana between plazas de Colón and de la Cibeles. A good way to reach these two museums—and enjoy a slice of the city as well—would be to start at the plaza de Colón by the twin skyscraper office towers (Las Torres de Jerez) and walk up the busy calle Génova to the plaza de Alonso Martínez. Cross the street here to enter the adjoining rectangular square called the plaza de Santa Bárbara, where you might like to stop for a beer and a ration of prawns at the **Cervecería Santa Bárbara**. One of Madrid's best beer halls, it is very popular with students. At the far end of this rectangular plaza take calle San Mateo, which is where the Museo Romántico lies. Then for the next stop continue on to where the street ends at the junction with calle Fuencarral, and turn right for the Museo Municipal.

The **Museo Romántico** is a charming but undervisited museum at calle San Mateo 13 that contains the private collection left to the nation in 1920 by the marqués de la Vega Inclán, a cultured and energetic aristocrat, whose initiatives at the turn of the century included the creation of the Casa del Greco museum in Toledo and the opening of a parador in the Gredos Sierra, the first of today's large network of state-run hotels. The museum is housed in Vega Inclán's late-18th-century mansion.

The strength of the museum is the atmosphere it creates of the Madrid, or at least of the upper-class Madrid, of 100 years ago. It is a jumble of paintings, furniture, and assorted objects that run the gamut from duelling pistols to dollhouses. Nothing is particularly outstanding, but the whole is extremely pleasing and even . . . romantic.

The not very interesting 19th-century building (the Hospicio de San Fernando) that houses the **Museo Municipal** is made special by an amazing and original Baroque extravaganza encasing its main entrance (at calle Fuencarral 78) that was carved by Pedro de Ribera in the early 18th century. The museum within is worth a visit because its prints and models will give you a very clear idea of the growth of Madrid and the city's changing styles. There is a detailed town plan dating from 1656, the earliest extant, and a charming model of the city that was constructed in 1830. This being a Madrid museum, Goya could not be absent, and his *Dos de Mayo* canvas has pride of place.

After visiting the Museo Municipal, retrace your steps along calle Fuencarral and continue heading south (Fuencarral eventually meets Gran Vía) until you come to calle Agusto Figueroa. Turn right onto Agusto Figueroa and continue until you run into calle Almirante, a very upwardly mobile street, packed with fashion shops. Calle Almirante will take you back to the Castellana, close to Cibeles and right by the **Café Gijón**, the fabled temple of Madrid's café society.

Calle de Serrano, the fashionable street parallel to and east of the Castellana, is not all window shopping. The **Museo de Lázaro Galdiano**, at number 122, a large turn-of-the-century mansion close to where northern Serrano crosses calle María de Molina, the city's main access to the airport and to the N II (Barcelona) highway, houses a very rich art collection amassed by financier Lázaro Galdiano and bequeathed to the nation on his death in 1947.

Galdiano was an astonishing collector who cast his discriminating net very widely indeed. The collection of ivories and enamels is very inclusive, with, for example, magnificent Limoges exhibits. The religious plate gold and silver work, the glassware treasures, and the array of bronze work that goes all the way from early Iberian clasps and buckles to Renaissance candlesticks is also outstanding. There is even a collection of ladies' fans through the ages.

Pictorial art here is just as all-embracing, ranging from anonymous primitive triptychs to a Constable landscape with Salisbury Cathedral's spire in the distance. Rembrandt's portrait of his wife, Saskia, as herself instead of as a model for Artemis, as in the Prado, hangs here, and there is a good representation of the Spanish greats: El Greco, Zurbarán, Velázquez, and Goya.

Also standing in the grid-system, elegant, late-19th-century part of Madrid near the Lázaro Galdiano, although on the other side of the Castellana and just off calle Miguel Angel, at Martínez Campos 37, the **Museo Sorolla** was the home and studio of Joaquín Sorolla (1863 to 1923), a highly successful society painter. It houses a mix of the artist's belongings, which included a collection of baptismal fonts, which now stand in the garden, and of his output—a nostalgic celebration of sunny holidays, happy harvests, ruddy peasants, and fashionable young ladies wearing big hats.

Standing at present on the N VI exit from Madrid in far northwest Madrid, in the campus area that is called the Ciudad Universitaria (university city), the **Museo Español de Arte Contemporaneo** is to be moved in the near future to the Centro de Arte Reina Sofía close to the start of the paseo del Prado, and will therefore be much more accessible than its present location at avenida Juan de Herrera 2.

Pablo Picasso, Salvador Dalí, Juan Gris, and Joan Miró, an illustrious foursome of Spaniards, are well represented here, but perhaps more interesting, because they are less well known outside Spain, are the turn-of-the-century Catalan Modernist exhibits, notably the work of Isidro Nonell, Santiago Rusiñol, and José Gutiérrez Solana, who were members of the between-the-wars Madrid school of Expressionist Realism. The works of contemporary Spanish painters such as Antonio Saura, Antoni Tapiés, and Rafael Canogar indicate that much continues to happen on the Spanish art scene.

The **Museo de América** at avenida Reyes Católicos, a bit west of the Museo Español de Arte Contemporaneo in Ciudad Universitaria, is currently closed and undergoing extensive restoration. It has a strong collection of pre-Columbian art, including the gold hoard called the Treasure of the Quimbayas that was presented to Spain in the last century by the government of Colombia. The museum stands near a large and pretentious arch that was erected by Franco to mark his Spanish Civil War victory.

Special Exhibitions

In addition to these museums with permanent collections there are a number of galleries and art centers in Madrid that stage special exhibitions. Check in the local press or ask at your hotel or at the tourist office, and keep in mind the following venues that stage important cultural shows year-round.

The **Fundación Caja de Pensiones**, calle de Serrano 60, an art gallery financed by a bank, lies midway along Madrid's Bond Street/Fifth Avenue. Its exhibitions generally deal with 20th-century art and are usually outstanding. Not far away, the **Fundación Juan March**, calle Castelló 77, lies on a street running parallel to and five blocks east of calle de Serrano in the heart of the prestigious residential and shopping quarter known as the Barrio de Salamanca. Standing at the intersection of calles Padilla and Castelló, this cultural center is named after the founder of one of Spain's wealthiest banking families. The temporary home of some of the world's top contemporary picture collections, the Fundación Juan March also stages free lunchtime concerts and evening lectures. It boasts a good art shop on the premises selling reasonably priced prints.

The **Centro Cultural de la Villa**, the city hall's arts center, on plaza de Colón, is fun getting into—it lies under the huge gardens that form the plaza de Colón on the Castellana (the first intersection north from Cibeles), and you enter it behind the long waterfall that lines the Castellana side of the plaza. In addition to art exhibitions, the center has several venues for concerts, plays, and lectures as well as a good coffee shop. The bus station serving the airport is also under this square, and the massive building flanking the gardens on the south is the home of the national library, which you can enter from the Castellana, and the Museo Arqueológico Nacional, whose entrance is on the calle de Serrano side.

The **Centro de Arte Reina Sofía**, at Santa Isabel 52, lies at the south end of the Castellana, beyond the Prado and facing the Atocha railway station. Originally a hospital and transformed into an arts center at the beginning of the 1980s, the Reina Sofía has a book, print, and poster shop that alone is worth a visit. Temporary modern-art exhibitions are held here now, but the center is due to become the Museo Español de Arte Contemporaneo's new home in the near future.

You should also make a point of checking with the tourist office or in the local press to see what might be on at El Retiro's two exhibition halls, the **Palacio de Cristal** and the **Palacio de Velázquez**. Run by the ministry of culture, they were both built in the 1880s and lie very close to each other in the center of the park near a lovely, weeping-willow-rimmed pond. The Palacio de Cristal is a reproduction, on a smaller scale, of the Crystal Palace that was erected in London for the Great Exhibition of 1851.

GETTING AROUND

Most international travellers arrive at Barajas airport, 7.5 miles northeast of town and just off highway N II to Barcelona. If the traffic is flowing easily—most times it's not—the trip to downtown Madrid takes about half an hour. If you are catching or meeting a plane early in the morning, at lunchtime, or in the early evening, give yourself a good hour to reach Barajas.

There is an airport bus service that takes you to the airport terminal from the plaza de Colón on the Castellana, the next big intersection north of Cibeles. An alternative is to take a taxi, which will have a fixed extra charge for trips to and from the airport. Check on the extra charge when you take the cab (it is printed on a sheet that ought to be visible to the passenger), and make sure that the taxi driver has his meter running as he drives off. A normal run into town should cost under 1,500 pesetas.

Madrid's two main railway stations are Chamartín and Atocha, but Atocha is presently being extensively overhauled and all trains, except certain commuter lines, arrive and depart from Chamartín. When fully modernized, Atocha will once again serve southern and southeastern Spain, Andalusia, and the Levant coastline, while Chamartín will handle Barcelona, San Sebastián, and all other rail traffic north of Madrid.

Chamartín stands in the north of the city, off the northern limits of the Castellana, and Atocha is at the very southern end of the same boulevard. An underground rail line that runs all the way along the Castellana links the two stations and has intermediary stations at Nuevos Ministerios, in the northern zone of the Castellana, and at Recoletos, close to the plaza de Colón and the airport bus depot.

Both Atocha and Chamartín are on the Metro line, but travellers arriving at either station should opt for taxis. Again, there is a fixed extra fee for such pickups, so check the meter. There are extra charges for night service and for luggage, and these again are on the printed form that every cab driver possesses. Every taxi carries a complaint book and has its driver's license number clearly displayed; trouble should be reported to the nearest municipal policeman or to the Turismo office in the plaza Mayor.

Taxis are a sure way of getting around Madrid. They are relatively cheap, and the cabbies are normally pleasant. Tip 25 pesetas, as a rule, for a normal ride. Traffic can be frightful in Madrid, and buses, which have special lanes on thoroughfares such as the Castellana, are usually a faster means of transportation. The Madrid Metro, the subway, is even faster, and is clean, safe, and easy to use.

City buses have a fixed rate; buy your ticket from the driver as you board. You can also obtain a discount voucher for ten rides from the major bus stations, such as the one on the Castellana close to the Prado and also from most newspaper kiosks. You insert the voucher, a cardboard strip, into a punching machine near the driver. There are helpful signs at every bus stop indicating the route and the stops of each bus. There is also a flat fee as well as a discount voucher for the Metro. Bus route and Metro maps are available from travel agencies and from the Madrid Tourist Authority Office in the plaza Mayor. The subway maps are particularly well laid out and easy to use.

The area around the historic center of Madrid, the plaza Mayor and its Hapsburg offshoots, should be explored on foot. Distances here are comparatively short, and taxis a waste of time.

Roads out of Madrid

The national highways fan out of Madrid like the spokes from a wheel's hub. They are the symbol of the Spanish capital's exalted heliocentric status; the rest of the nation should—or at least that is the theory—revolve around the Madrileño sun. The highway network was built up methodically in the 18th and 19th centuries by the elite corps of state road engineers; its job was to transform into reality a royal policy that sought uniformity throughout the unruly patchwork of provinces, regions, and nationalities that together made up Spain, and to extend royal power to the farthest corners of the kingdom.

The Carretera Nacional I (N I) leads north across Castile to Burgos, on to San Sebastián, and to the French border at Irun-Hendaye. N II travels northeast to Zaragoza, to Barcelona, and to the French border at Perpignan. East out of the city, the N III reaches the Mediterranean at Valencia, and the N IV travels south through the La Mancha tableland to Córdoba, Seville, and Cádiz, near the Straits of Gibraltar separating Spain from North Africa. The N V leads directly west to the conquistador country of Extremadura and to Badajoz on the frontier with Portugal. The final spoke, N VI, travels to La Coruña (A Coruña) in the misty, Celtic northwestern corner of Galicia.

The Castellana axis serves N I at its northern end and N III and N IV at its southern one. Halfway down the Castellana, at the plaza del Dr. Marañón intersection, N II, which also leads to Barajas airport, enters Madrid along calle de María de Molina, and N VI enters through calle Abascal. To get onto N V west toward Extremadura from the city center, take calle de Alcalá and Gran Vía from the plaza de la Cibeles to the plaza de España. Madrid's ring road, M 30, encircles the city from its north entry points to the western ones and feeds traffic onto N I, N II, N III, N IV, and N V.

ACCOMMODATIONS

Most Madrid hotels are situated either on or very close to the Castellana, the main north-south boulevard that slices through Madrid and acts as its main reference point. The modern north end of the Castellana is now Madrid's main business area; the south, closer to the historic sites and the Prado, is considerably more casual. The farther away from the Castellana, the cheaper the accommodation is likely to be.

Cut-price accommodations for backpack travellers means resorting on the whole to *pensiones,* and the best of this bunch are to be found on the Castellana's downtown "west bank," off Gran Vía, on the calle de Alcalá as it moves into puerta del Sol, and off carrera de San Jerónimo, a parallel thoroughfare that likewise heads toward the puerta del Sol.

Madrid's area code for telephoning from within Spain is 91. When calling from outside the country, drop the 9.

Downtown Castellana

Madrid's utterly sumptuous **Hotel Ritz** is a splendid belle-epoque building on the plaza de Neptuno, a stone's throw north of the Prado. Across the square, facing it almost like a mirror image, stands the Hotel Palace, another wedding-cake slab of turn-of-the-century elegance. The Ritz oozes gentility and is stiff on protocol: It has a tradition of turning away film actors, and no one without a tie gets through its revolving doors. You sink into the carpets as you enter, and you'll feel obliged to speak in hushed tones, aware that you are paying exorbitantly for every breath you take. Exquisite chamber orchestra concerts are staged beneath its chandeliers, and, in summer, candlelit dinners are served in its gardens. Among its numerous extras, the Ritz has a special long-weekend program during the partridge shooting season—sportsmen are ferried to a shooting estate, and their nonsporty companions are indulged in a cultural tour.

Plaza de la Lealtad 5, 28014 Madrid; Tel: 521-2857.

The **Hotel Palace** is no poor relation of the Ritz. A recent face-lift has created a dazzling, mural-encased lobby: Trompe l'oeil walls and ceilings make you believe you are entering a Florentine villa where Giotto has stayed as a houseguest. The Palace also costs a pretty penny, but it has a considerably more relaxed atmosphere than its rival across the square. Stockbrokers make their presentations at the Ritz, and publishers launch their books at the Palace: It's a question of what sort of company you prefer. The Palace bar, which is where Jake and Lady Brett drank a lot of martinis together in the closing stages of Hemingway's *The Sun Also Rises,* has changed considerably, but it remains the chatty rendezvous for politicians (the parliament building, the Cortes, lies just across the road) and journalists. "How did you know about the plot?" a young right-winger was asked by a judge in the aftermath of a failed putsch attempt during the time of the Spanish Republic of the 1930s. "I heard about it in the bar of the Palace," he replied, and was acquitted without more ado.

Plaza de las Cortes 7, 28014 Madrid; Tel: 429-7551.

Calle del Prado leads west from the Hotel Palace up a hill lined with antiques shops to the boisterous plaza de Santa Ana and the **Gran Hotel Victoria**, a switch from the first establishment's grande luxe to the latter's homeliness. The hotel's pleasantly decadent atmosphere masks efficient service. Manuel Rodríguez ("Manolete"), the legendary matador who was gored to death by a Miura bull in 1947, used to patronize the Victoria, and the plaza de Santa Ana boasts a good beer hall that attracts the bullfighting crowd. The whole area is packed with taverns and flamenco joints, revelers and actors (the Teatro Español, Madrid's national theater, is also on the plaza de Santa Ana).

Plaza del Angel 7, 28012 Madrid; Tel: 231-4500.

Locked in between calle de Alcalá and the carrera de San Jerónimo where the Gran Vía begins, the **Hotel Suecia** is quiet, sedate, and popular among Madrid's culture connoisseurs. It backs on the **Círculo de Bellas Artes**, a turn-of-the-century arts center on calle de Alacalá that welcomes everyone to its exhibitions, poetry recitals, and bars, and lies close to the Teatro de la Zarzuela, the home of the Zarzuela operetta genre. Perhaps this is why literary travellers tend to patronize it. The only *sueco* (Swedish) element to the hotel is its smorgasbord.

Marqués de Casa Riera 4, 28014 Madrid; Tel: 231-6900.

Midtown Castellana

The **Villa Magna**, at the intersection of the Castellana and calle Ortega y Gasset is, like the Ritz and the Palace, one of Madrid's genuinely deluxe hotels. It hosts international bankers and upper-bracket business travellers who value first-class communications more than antique carpets, chandeliers, and murals. Movie stars are also welcome. You'll pay a lot for discreet and ultra-efficient service, but you get your money's worth. The hotel is extremely handy for calle de Serrano shopping—you can afford everything in the street's classy boutiques if you can afford to stay at the Villa Magna—and its rear door leads straight to a department store that has recently been acquired by Marks & Spencer. (For its excellent restaurant, see Dining, below.)

Paseo de la Castellana 22, 28046 Madrid; Tel: 261-4900.

The **Hotel Wellington** has a period charm to it. It is also the place to be during the mid-May to mid-June San Isidro bullfight *feria,* because this is where the top matadors change into the suit of lights before the *corrida,* and where the top aficionados gather for the postmortems when the fight is over. At the intersection of calle Velázquez and calle Jorge Juan, three blocks up from calle de Serrano and close to El Retiro, the hotel is strategically placed in the center of Madrid's grid-patterned residential and shopping quarter, the Barrio de Salamanca.

Calle Velázquez 8, 28001 Madrid; Tel: 275-4400.

The Castellana Inter-Continental, on the corner of calle Garcia de Paredes and the Castellana, close to the plaza del Dr. Marañón, was Madrid's Hilton until it was absorbed by the present chain. It has the sort of service you would expect, with the added bonus of a lot of style accrued over the years. Once the most modern of Madrid's hotels, in the three decades and more of its existence it has become almost part of the city's antique furniture. It is odd to think that when it was built it was virtually on Madrid's northern outskirts. American expatriates and embassy staff patronize the bar.

Paseo de la Castellana 49, 28046 Madrid; Tel: 410-0200.

The **Hotel Miguel Angel**, just off the Castellana's plaza del Dr. Marañón at the intersection of calle Abascal and calle Miguel Angel, is functional, yet retains a certain classiness. Older and cheaper than the Villa Magna, younger and more expensive than the Hilton-turned-Inter-Continental, it has good facilities for business travellers as well as an indoor swimming pool.

Calle Miguel Angel 31, 28010 Madrid; Tel: 442-8199.

On the street of the same name, at its intersection with calle Bretón de los Herreros, the smallish **Hotel Zurbano** offers extremely good services and doesn't burn holes in your credit-card statement. It lies just west of the Castellana, also near the plaza del Dr. Marañón, in a quiet residential area. The Zurbano belongs to a Spanish-owned chain of moderately priced hotels, with several other strategically placed establishments in Madrid; if the Zurbano cannot fit you in, the chain, NH Hoteles, should find you a room at another of its properties.

Calle Zurbano 79, 28010 Madrid; Tel: 441-4500.

Uptown Castellana

Up in the northern high-rise stretch of Castellana off the plaza de Cuzco intersection, the **Hotel Eurobuilding** stands on the corner of calle Padre Damián and calle Alberto Alcocer. It has its own mini–shopping mall, several bars, coffee shops, and restaurants. It offers a full range of services, and has an open-air swimming pool. This business rendezvous of modern Madrid is permanently busy.

Padre Damián 23, 28036 Madrid; Tel: 457-1700.

The **Hotel Meliá Castilla** is another huge, modern hotel complex catering essentially to the expense-account executive and built with the convention market in mind. It stands on calle Capitán Haya, an uptown street that runs one block west of and parallel to Castellana, at its intersection with calle Rosario del Pino. This area, just off Castellana's intersections with plaza de Cuzco and plaza de Castilla, has a fast-paced nightlife. People cruise around its clubs and discotheques until the wee hours.

Capitán Haya 43, 28020 Madrid; Tel: 270-8400.

One of the newer of the city's hotels, the **Holiday Inn Madrid** was launched in 1985 and offers the usual standards and facilities of the U.S. chain. It stands just to the west of the

Castellana's intersection with plaza de Lima among the towering office blocks that have changed Madrid's skyline during the 1980s.

Plaza Carlos Trias Bertran 4, 28020 Madrid; Tel: 456-7014.

Cheaper Hotels at Puerta del Sol and Gran Vía

The large lobby and the high hallways of the **Hotel Asturias** are a reminder of better times. No longer grand, the hotel represents value for money. It stands a block away from the puerta del Sol on a short but busy street that links calle de Alcalá with carrera de San Jerónimo.

Calle Sevilla 2, 28931 Madrid; Tel: 429-6676.

On the corner of puerta del Sol and calle de Alcalá, the **Hotel Paris** has a fading air to it.

Calle de Alcalá 2, 28014 Madrid; Tel: 521-6496.

The **Hostal Delfina**, two blocks up from Gran Vía's start at its intersection with calle de Alcalá, is typical of the cheap but mostly clean boarding houses that are either on or just off Madrid's "Broadway." If they cannot accommodate you, take their advice on the next-best choice.

Gran Vía 12, 28013 Madrid; Tel: 521-2151.

—*Tom Burns*

DINING

Back in the frugal 1950s there were just two premier restaurants in Madrid, the Jockey Club and Horcher, both specializing in Continental cuisine. Now there are more than 3,000 Madrid restaurants in all, with a wide range of cooking styles including *nueva cocina española* (a *nouvelle* approach to Spanish cooking), traditional Spanish, and regional Spanish as well as French, Middle Eastern, Oriental, even American—a sign of how Madrid has changed, prospered, and expanded its gastronomic horizons.

Predominant here are the regional cuisines of Spain itself. The center of Spain geographically, Madrid is also the country's psychic center. Here you'll find restaurants from every region guaranteed to assuage any provincial Spaniard's homesickness. Most ubiquitous of the regional cuisines in Madrid, aside from Castilian, is Basque. So respected is Basque cuisine here that it is sometimes said, only half facetiously, that behind every successful restaurant, no matter what the cuisine, stands a Basque chef.

On every menu in almost every restaurant, seafood occupies center stage. In many countries you might hesitate about ordering fish hundreds of miles inland, but in Spain geography has nothing to do with the freshness of the seafood. Truck drivers race by night to rush the day's bounty from the Atlantic and the Mediterranean to Madrid's markets. You have only to visit the Mercado de San Miguel, near the plaza Mayor, early in the morning to see the freshness and diversity of the seafood.

The variety boggles: shrimp, oysters, clams, scallops, sole, turbot, cod, and fish unknown to most North Americans, such as *besugo* (sea bream), *merluza* (hake), *salmoneta* (red mullet), and *rape* (anglerfish). Then there are *angulas* (baby eels), a Spanish favorite called *percebes* (edible goose barnacles that look like prehistoric denizens of the deep), *berberechos* (tiny clams), *necoras* (small crabs), *bigaros* (minuscule black snails), *navajas* (reed-like shellfish), and such variations of shrimp as *gambas, langostinos, carabineros, cigalas, santiaguinos,* and other fish and shellfish unknown elsewhere.

Madrileños thrive on eating out. In fact, they probably spend more time at meals away from home than most Europeans. Although Madrid authorities have tried to shorten lunch hours and eliminate the siesta, centuries-old habits die hard. While the siesta itself may be dying, the custom of preprandial drinks and the long lunch hour persists. As most tourist attractions and many stores (except department stores) are closed during the lengthy afternoon break (from 1:30 to 4:30 or 5:00), *la comida* (the midday or main meal) is a long repast. Relax and enjoy it: It's the wise foreigner who follows the crowd and makes lunch the main meal of the day, then has *la cena* (a light dinner) at 10:00 P.M. or later.

After work, which for most people ends at 8:00 P.M., Madrid really comes alive. In warm weather the sidewalk cafés throb with life and high-decibel conversation. Even in chilly weather people are on the streets and avenues, enjoying a *paseo* or dropping by a favorite bar to nibble *tapas* (tidbits or appetizers) with Sherry or wine before dinner. It's not until 10:00 or 10:30 P.M. that thoughts finally turn to the evening meal.

Where to eat depends on how fancy or trendy you want to be. The fashionable new restaurants, mostly located in the Barrio de Salamanca and even farther uptown, are expensive by Madrid standards (6,500–9,500 pesetas per person), but not when compared to their chic counterparts in New York or London. Many rustic and simple old-time restaurants serve hearty, unsophisticated fare for approximately 1,100 to 1,700 pesetas per person, and neighborhood *tascas* (small cafés) and roughcut *tabernas* charge even less. Madrid also has its share of inexpensive fast-food places where savings are even greater. Still another alternative is to go "*tapas* hopping"—an informal meal of a variety of appetizers and a few glasses of house wine can be had for under 1,000 pesetas. Several department stores have inexpensive dining rooms that make convenient lunch stops, especially since you can then shop while everything else in town is closed.

Some things to keep in mind about dining in Madrid: Reservations are expected at all the fashionable restaurants, and many places are closed on Saturday and/or Sunday and for the entire month of August, so it's wise to call ahead. The telephone area code for Madrid is 91 (drop the 9 if you are dialing from outside the country). Some restaurants do not accept credit cards, and most add a service charge to the bill, though a 5 to 10 percent additional tip is considered proper.

—*Patricia Brooks*

The Wines of Madrid

Every type of regional Spanish cuisine is represented in Madrid's restaurants and *tascas,* whose bars are lined with *tapas.* And there is also a variety of good Riojas to go along. Here *tapas* hopping is the province of the wine drinker as well as the gourmet. Each *tasca* specializes in several dishes: Tripe, pickled anchovies, *tortilla española* (Spanish omelet), potato salad, grilled prawns, steamed clams, and any of hundreds of other dishes are taken with small glasses of wine, some of which comes from the wine-growing area of the autonomous community of Madrid, a specific denomination.

Three areas south of Madrid—Navalcarnero, San Martín de Valdeiglesias, and Arganda—form the *denominación específica* (DE) Madrid, which produces over 13 million gallons of wine per year. From the white grape known locally as Malvar, Madrid produces some very nice white wines—young, fresh, fruity, and medium bodied. Local vintners also make good *rosados* (rosés) and some excellent red wines from Tempranillo and Tinto de Madrid grapes, especially in the charming Arganda towns of Colmenar de Oreja and Chinchón. If you visit the picturesque town of Chinchón, which is also famous for one of Spain's best liqueurs, *anis,* don't fail to try the excellent red wines of Jesús Díaz from Colmenar de Oreja.

—*Gerry Dawes*

Old Madrid

The area around the plaza Mayor is where you'll find most of the old Castilian *mesónes* (rustic inns or taverns) and *tascas,* many of them very inexpensive.

Prevalent throughout Castile, *tascas* are very much a part of the Madrid dining scene. They began in the 19th century as simple taverns, so rough-edged that the heavy wine of La Mancha would be served from the goat skins in which it was stored. Before long, some taverns began serving plain, homespun meals. Roast suckling pig and baby lamb were the mainstays, as well as, on specified days, a typical Madrid boiled dinner known as *cocido*. Traditionally, *tascas* have been egalitarian places where workers and aristocrats rub elbows at the bar. Today, as Spain becomes increasingly Europeanized, *tascas* are more popular with Madrileños than ever—nostalgia, no doubt, for an identifiable but disappearing past.

High on most visitors' agenda is a visit to **Antigua Casa Sobrino de Botín**, better known as just Botín's, located at calle de Cuchilleros 17, on one of the oldest streets in Madrid, just below the southwest corner of the plaza Mayor, which has several *tascas* and considerable character of its own. Popularized for English speakers by Hemingway ("We lunched upstairs at Botin's . . . we had roast young suckling pig and drank rioja alta."), Botín's has actually been going strong since 1725. The *Guinness Book of World Records* calls it the oldest restaurant in the world. Surprisingly, despite its long run and a massive overdose of tourists, its food remains excellent and a fine value; it would be hard to find better roast suckling pig anywhere in town. It and the roast baby lamb are prepared in *hornos* (ovens) fired with *encina* (oak), then shoveled with wooden ladles onto big wooden platters. Enjoy your roast with a big ceramic pitcher of the house wine, a red Valdepeñas. Although Botín's is always busy, for both lunch and dinner, it avoids the feel of herd feeding because its five cozy dining rooms—decorated with blue-and-white tiles, small windows with mullioned glass panes, and low ceilings with rustic exposed beams—are spread out over three floors. You can't miss Botín's from the outside: It's the place with all the pink, uncooked whole baby piglets in the window. Tel: 266-4217.

Unusually chic for a Castilian *tasca,* and perennially popular with upscale Madrileños, is **Casa Lucio**, at cava Baja 35, a continuation (southward) of calle de Cuchilleros. Even King Juan Carlos is a regular (more or less incognito), and the tables at dinner look like a Who's Who of local politicos, actors, and other celebrities. Located below the plaza Mayor in the oldest part of the city, the restaurant looks from the outside like an ordinary *tasca.* Don't be deceived. Inside, past a bar where rows of *jamón Jabugo* (cured hams) hang from exposed beams, there are two floors of whitewashed dining rooms with ceramic floors, wood-beamed ceilings, and brick arches. The menu is classic Castilian: Begin with a starter of razor-thin slivers of ham, followed by shrimp in garlic sauce, then baby lamb chops or *churrasco de la casa,* a thick one-pound steak served on a sizzling platter. Tel: 265-3252.

Another Castilian classic, **Posada de la Villa,** just down from Lucio's at cava Baja 9, has even more atmosphere. An old inn restored and converted to a new restaurant in 1982, the Posada has the air of a country *mesón,* with an arched vaulted ceiling and a huge rounded beehive oven and open hearth. You can watch the suckling pigs and baby lambs being removed from the oven and savor the wood scent at the same time. A long bar, featuring a wide display of *tapas* to whet your appetite and round loaves of excellent hearth bread add to the dining pleasure here. Tel: 266-1880.

Casa Ciriaco, calle Mayor 84, off the southwestern edge of puerta del Sol, is a favorite of Madrid artists, writers, and celebrities. The old-style food is nothing special, but it's always reliable, especially the chicken dishes. Tel: 248-0620.

Light-years away in style from Ciriaco is **Café de Oriente**, in a fin-de-siècle setting, at the edge of the peaceful plaza de Oriente (at number 2), across from the Palacio Real. The cuisine here is a mix of classic Spanish and *haute* French, with *haute* prices to match. Fresh Rascafría trout and roast suckling pig are among the many specialties. This is a pleasant place to drop by for afternoon tea or coffee or for a less expensive meal in the basement grill, **Horno de San Gil**. Tel: 247-1564.

Just east of the puerta del Sol at carrera de San Jerónimo 8, is **Lhardy**, an important Madrid tradition, though not in the *tasca* mode. Lhardy's opened in 1839 and was going strong as the city's only temple of *haute cuisine* by the time Dumas dropped by in 1846. It is still a Madrid custom, especially among the over-50s, to stop by Lhardy's ground floor for a pick-me-up cup of consommé served from a massive silver samovar, paper-thin tea sandwiches, *tapas,* and/or Sherry before lunchtime. Meals in three high-ceilinged, aged belle-epoque upstairs dining rooms, with well-polished parquet floors and burnished, tooled-leather wall coverings, still yield gustatory if pricey dividends, but you must choose carefully to avoid the mundane. A hearty *cocido madrileño* (chickpea stew), tripe in a succulent garlicky tomato and onion wine sauce, and a *soufflé sorpresa* (baked Alaska) are among Lhardy's strong suits. Tel: 521-3385.

About four blocks east of Lhardy is **Luarques**, at Ventura de la Vega 16 (between San Jerónimo and calle del Prado, but much closer to Prado). This unobtrusive, minimally decorated place is one of the best values in Madrid and is extremely convenient for visitors staying at the Hotel Palace (it's just three blocks away), yet few seem to find it. Local businessmen flock here for grilled salmon and other fish, *setas y angulas, arroz con leche, fabada asturiana,* and other Asturian dishes. Portions are huge, prices low. Unfortunately, Luarques does not take reservations, so it is smart to go early (about 1:30 P.M.) for lunch. Tel: 429-6174.

Regional and Seafood Restaurants

Seafood is fresh and wonderful, if expensive, in almost any Madrid restaurant, but at **La Dorada**, Orense 64, it is often a work of art. This Andalusian restaurant, located in a residential, uptown, high-rise neighborhood two long blocks west of the Castellana, just south of avenida General Perón near the Urbanización Azca, is a branch of a similar and equally fashionable restaurant in Seville. It specializes in authentic Andalusian dishes such as *fritura especial malagueña* (a mix of tiny Mediterranean fish lightly and crisply fried), *coquinas* (tiny clams) in a parsley and wine sauce, and *dorada* (literally giltfish, similar to red snapper) *a la sal.* The fish is baked in a heavy overcoat of rock salt that retains the juices but that leaves no saltiness on the moist, flavorful fish once it is chipped off. Seafood is flown in to La Dorada from Andalusia by private plane daily. Tel: 270-2002.

Fish also gets star treatment at **Cabo Mayor**, downstairs on Juan Hurtado de Mendoza (just east of the Castellana, a block north of the plaza de Cuzco in a smart post–World War II neighborhood), whose late owner, Victor Merino, from Santander, was a pioneer in the new Spanish kitchen. A *nueva cocina* flair for lightness, creative dishes, and pleasing presentations of seafood prepared the northern, Cantabrian way characterize this charming nautical-themed establishment. The stylized ship-like interior of one dining room even has portholes, allowing diners, most of them too sophisticated to bother, to peer into the pristine kitchen, where such delights as *besugo estofado al tomillo* (sea bream stewed with thyme), red mullet sautéed with mint, and a salad of oyster and sea bass drizzled with lemon, olive oil, and fresh dill are being prepared. Tel: 250-8776.

Also on Hurtado de Mendoza, at number 11, is **Sacha**, a very "in" Parisian-style bistro with good Galician fish dishes and a fine house Rioja. Try the *filloas,* dessert pancakes filled with jam, a typical Galician dessert. Tel: 457-5152.

While some restaurants overwhelm you with their decor, the extravagances at the Galician restaurant **O'Pazo** come in the live seafood displays, the *joyerías* (jewelry windows). The lavish piles of expensive shellfish invite conspicuous consumption (and heart failure when the bill is presented). The variety is mouth watering, with lobsters, king crab, scallops, oysters, shrimp, and prawns as stellar attractions. You're best off here ordering your fish grilled or sautéed and your shellfish steamed or grilled, and avoiding dishes with more elaborate sauces, which are sometimes prepared with a heavy hand. Located uptown at calle Reina Mercedes 20 (a short street between Orense and calle de Dulcinea, one block south of avenida General Perón), O'Pazo's slightly glitzy *moderne* decor shouldn't distract you from the superb seafood. Tel: 234-3748.

El Pescador, José Ortega y Gasset 75 (between calle de Alcántara and Montesa), with the same ownership as O'Pazo, has a smart address in the Salamanca district, and prices to match. The setting is rustic and simple, yet savvy locals head here for the stunning abundance of fresh fish and shellfish. On any given day as many as 30 varieties of seafood (many flown in from Galicia) are on view in the glass cases. It's best to order your fish here *a la plancha* (grilled) with a slice of lemon. The delicious house fish soup is also a good choice. Tel: 402-1290.

Finding a good Valencian restaurant in Madrid wasn't easy until **L'Albufera** opened uptown at the Meliá Castilla hotel, Capitán Haya 43 (on the corner of calle de Rosario Pino, one block west of the Castellana). The specialty here, as you might expect, is paella, prepared in a variety of ways. The most notable is the *paella de mariscos* (with shellfish). Tel: 279-6374.

Stylish Dining

Nueva cocina española, the new Spanish cuisine, has been especially well interpreted by the Basques, perhaps because their traditional cuisine has a light touch and relies on fresh, light sauces. Basque chefs are acknowledged, even by rival Catalans, as creative masters.

Be that as it may, many of the fashionable *nueva cocina* restaurants that have sprouted like wild *setas* in recent years in uptown Madrid have Basque origins. A case in point is the city's premier gastronomic temple, **Zalacaín**.

Aficionados have known for years that this Basque-owned restaurant, located at Alvarez de Baena 4 (a quiet, fashionable street off bustling calle de María de Molina, just a block east of the Castellana), is the best in the city—in fact, in most views, the best in the country. What makes it so is absolutely seamless perfection, from the polished brass nameplate by the front steps to the warm farewell by staffers as you leave. The salmon-hued walls, fresh flowers, paintings, and the elegant china and silver service plates are a backdrop for intriguing variations on Basque-Navarrese classics and original creations by the Basque chef Benjamin Urdain. Owner Jesús María Oyarbide describes the food as "modern *haute* cuisine with a Spanish flavor." It is all that and more. Fresh foods, mostly from Spain, such as fish and game, Guadalajara truffles, and olive oils are augmented by a vast cellar of mostly Spanish wines. Since Oyarbide opened his doors in 1973, Zalacaín has set new standards and spawned imitators all over Spain. For a first visit, the *menu de degustación* (tasting menu) is recommended for a sense of the breadth and depth of the restaurant's capabilities. Expensive but memorable. Tel: 261-4840.

Oyarbide's first Madrid restaurant, now run by his son, is **Príncipe de Viana**, at Manuel de Falla 5, a short street off Castellana just north of Bernabeu stadium. It is as popular with chic Madrileños as ever, but its mystique eludes many nonregulars. Certainly you can't fault the service or the comfortably luxurious decor, but while most dishes look elegant and are skillfully prepared, many lack intensity, and few are done with the flair of Zalacaín, although prices are almost comparable. Tel: 259-1448.

The food is very good at **El Amparo**, but it's the restaurant's romantic ambience that makes it so popular with Madrid trendsetters. Tucked into an alley, at callejón de Puigcerdá, near the corner of calle Jorge Juan (even taxi drivers have trouble finding it), the Basque-accented restaurant looks like an abandoned warehouse from the outside. The inside has three levels and resembles a loft, with huge rough-hewn beams, posts, and a skylight. Beige, fabric-covered walls complement the elegant pink linen and oversized china. If the food doesn't always live up to the dramatic decor, it is usually interesting, occasionally inspired, often worth the rarefied prices charged. Among some of the better dishes here are *bisque de marisco armagnac,* duck with vinegar and honey, lobster salad, mango and apricot sorbets, and a superlative dessert of poached pear in puff pastry with *crème anglaise* laced with Pear William eau de vie. The tasting menu is usually a good option for a first visit. Tel: 431-6456.

Relatively new and trendy, attracting Madrid's most elegant diners, is **El Cenadór del Prado**, one of the few *nueva* *cocina* restaurants located in Old Madrid, at calle del Prado 4, near the plaza de Santa Ana. Among the prettiest, most romantic restaurants in Madrid, it has two tiny dining rooms, one a study in shades of apricot, the other in tones of yellow. Chef Tomás Herranz worked for years in New York, and his menu is a Spanish interpretation of nouvelle cooking with many imaginative variations. While some dishes are bland, many are winners, such as cream of eggplant soup with a flan of basil-accented tomato floating in the center, cheese-flavored gnocchi semolina with brains over a spinach purée, and duck leg in a caramelized prune sauce. Tel: 429-1549.

A newcomer—and among the most promising of Madrid's *nueva cocina* restaurants—is **La Gamella** (the feeding trough). Chef-owner Richard Stephens, a friendly American expatriate from Peoria, came to Madrid as a choreographer 25 years ago and fell for the lifestyle. There's nothing Peorian about La Gamella's food or decor, which uses adaptations from Matisse prints on tablecloths and banquette covers. The location could hardly be better: the ground floor of a 19th-century mansion in which philosopher José Ortega y Gasset was born (calle Alfonso XII 4, next door to Sotheby's and directly across from El Retiro). After a lunch of creamy almond-garlic soup, red mullet stuffed with Spanish blue cheese in olive sauce, or sea bream filet encrusted with toasted garlic and hazelnuts, a brisk stroll through the park is more than just a good idea; it's almost a necessity. Tel: 542-1331.

A favorite of the culinary cognoscenti, though almost unknown to others, is **Irizar-Jatetxea**, a Basque restaurant where chefs dine on their evenings off. Irizar is hardly hidden—it's directly across the street from the Teatro de la Zarzuela, at Jovellanos 3, a tiny street behind the northwest corner of the Cortes (which faces San Jerónimo) in the central part of town. But its brass sign is small and discreet, and the sparkling, all-white dining room is upstairs. Crepes of *bacalao* (cod) with pimiento sauce is just one of Irizar's innovations. Such creativity does not come cheap. Tel: 231-4569.

So many new restaurants have opened in recent years that it's easy to forget the classic **Jockey**, Amador de los Ríos 6, just northwest of the plaza de Colón, off Alcalá Galiano. Yet this longtime favorite of local movers and shakers has been serving consistently fine food year in, year out ever since it opened in 1945. The background is understated, with wood paneling, banquettes, and soft lights. The Continental specialties are predictable—Chateaubriand with Béarnaise sauce, veal kidneys tarragon flambée, and the like—but nobody does them better. There are a few surprises, such as an appetizer of smoked eel mousse and turbot flambée with Pernod. To avoid the fate that occasionally befalls the first-time foreign visitor, ask for a corner table when making a reservation. Otherwise you may find yourself at the apex of a whirlpool of waiters hurrying to and from the kitchen. Tel: 419-2435.

In the same general neighborhood, and just as centrally located as Jockey, is the new and noteworthy **Lúculo**, calle de Génova 19, off the west side of the plaza de Colón. The chef is Catalan (a rarity in Madrid), and the food is *nouvelle* French with an inventive Spanish flair. The sleekly modern chrome-and-glass setting is pleasant any time, but an open courtyard makes summer dining even more so. Be prepared for a heady bill. Tel: 419-4029.

Viridiána, calle Fundadores 23, in the eastern part of Madrid, is another stylish newcomer, with an enthusiastic clientele and a very inventive approach to *nueva cocina,* all managed in tiny quarters. About a mile south of the plaza de Toros, the restaurant is off the beaten path for tourists. Tel: 256-7773.

Two worthy places to eat are in the heart of the new avant-garde fashion district, where you're likely to see the rising stars (or those already risen) of this scene at nearby tables. This is especially true at the well-named **El Mentidero de la Villa** (the gossiping place), Santo Tomé 6, a block from the Palacio de Justicia on calle Bárbara de Braganza. The decor in the two tiny dining rooms revolves around large wooden horses (like those seen on carousels, but stripped to the natural wood), and the menu is exquisite *nueva cocina* with a delicate Japanese accent and presentation. Ken Sato, the chef and co-owner, is Japanese and once had a restaurant in London (the Secret Garden on Old Brompton Road). Tel: 419-5506.

The tab will be lower at **Apriori**, Argensola 7, off calle Fernando VI. This low-key, chef-owned place, in sunny lemon and orange with a vaguely Neoclassical decor, offers fine value and some creative dishes. Moroccan lamb with cilantro and *merluza* in white wine sauce are standouts. Tel: 410-3671.

Horcher, handily located at calle Alfonso XII 6, across from El Retiro, is one of Madrid's oldest shining stars (founded in Berlin in 1903, it moved to Madrid in 1943 to escape the Allied bombings). While it has lost a bit of its luster in recent up-and-down years, it still maintains fine service (with such details as an embroidered cushion placed under each female diner's feet) and offers, on the whole, an excellent classic German menu strong on game. Venison is a longtime favorite, and the Viennese desserts are luscious. Tel: 522-0731.

The dining rooms at both the **Hotel Ritz** and **Hotel Palace** have been rejuvenated, and both have become, once again, exemplary, if expensive (the Ritz especially so), places to dine. The Ritz, now under the guidance of French chef du cuisine Patrick Buret, has been particularly successful, diversifying its French menu with Spanish classics such as smoked Asturian salmon, Galician mussels simmered in saffron, and Aragonese lamb roasted with thyme.

Making even more of an effort since its sale to the British company Bass and its subsequent 1988 refurbishing is the **Hotel Villa Magna**. Its three adjoining downstairs dining rooms, decorated in cool green with a creamy lattice trim, feature elegant *nueva cocina* dishes such as exceptional grilled scallops with caviar in basil sauce and baby lamb chops in a subtle Sherry vinegar sauce. Tel: 261-4900.

Most of the restaurants located in the Barrio de Salamanca and farther uptown are more expensive than those in and around Old Madrid, but there are some moderately priced establishments, as well as reasonably priced coffee shops, cafeterias (more like cafés than what we think of as self-serve cafeterias), fast-food places, and department store restaurants. One old reliable is **Alkalde**, Jorge Juan 10 (between Lagasca and Velázquez), where Basque dishes are served in agreeable, rustic, barrel-vaulted rooms. You can also make a meal out of the enticing selection of *tapas* in the large bar, which is hung with cured hams. Tel: 276-3359.

An even better buy than Alkalde is **Casa Ricardo**, Fernando el Católico 31 (between calles Gaztambide and Andrés Mellado, three blocks east of Parque del Oeste on the west side of the city). More than 100 years old, this standby *taberna* was redecorated not long ago and now sports new glazed tiles, marble, and a bullfighting motif. Solid, nothing-fancy offerings, such as *calamares en su tinta* and *rabo de toro,* are among the many home-style dishes served here. Tel: 447-6119.

Foreign

Another sign of changing times is the recent popularity of restaurants serving foreign cuisine. A mainstay for some years has been **Al-Mounia**, at paseo de Recoletos 5, north of puerta de Alcalá just west of Serrano. Related to restaurants with the same name in Casablanca and Paris, Madrid's Al-Mounia is a fiesta of Moorish tiles, fabric-covered banquettes, horseshoe arches, and Moroccan accoutrements. Service is excellent, from the ewer brought to your couch for hand washing before dinner to the mint tea poured into your glass at meal's end. Big brass trays deliver a first-rate couscous, *tajine aux amandes* (lamb with almonds), and other authentic Moroccan delicacies—all an excellent value. A dessert cart, wheeled to your table, carries wonderful pastries, especially the *cigarillos* filled with marzipan and sprinkled with sesame seeds. Tel: 435-0828.

De Funy, on the corner of Serrano 213 at Infanta Mariá Teresa, specializes in Lebanese dishes and has live piano music and belly dancing in the late evenings. Be sure to order the *mezze,* with ten different appetizer tidbits, eaten with chunks of pita bread. Squash stuffed with rice and lamb is an unusual, tasty specialty; so too is *kharous-ousi* (lamb with rice, almonds, and spices). Tel: 259-7225.

Another well-established Middle Eastern restaurant, not too pricey but out of the way for most visitors, is **Sayat Nova**, calle Costa Rica 13 (an extension of calle Alberto Alcocer) off the plaza de Cuzco, in the northeast commercial section of the city. Well-seasoned shish kebab is a signature dish. Tel: 250-8755.

Among the newer foreign restaurants is a very good Indian restaurant, **Annapurna**, centrally situated at calle Zurbarán 5, a few blocks west of the Villa Magna Hotel on paseo de la Castellana in a residential area full of art galleries and boutiques. The carpet and walls, painted a terra-cotta color, and the Mogul arches, brassware, and a tease of a garden create a tranquil Eastern ambience for such delicious dishes as the lamb-based *rogan josh, pulao arasta, murgh karabi,* and other Indian and Pakistani specialties. The only complaint: a certain timidity in letting the traditional incendiary spices loose. Tel: 410-7727.

On calle Jovellanos, a short street behind the Cortes and opposite Teatro de la Zarzuela, are several restaurants, including the aforementioned Irizar-Jatetxea and the longtime favorite **Edelweiss** at number 7, where the moderately priced food has a German accent, but you'll find a few nods to Spain in such dishes as paella; Tel: 521-0326. A recent arrival here is the English-owned-and-run **Armstrong** at number 5, where a beautiful, spacious decor makes an elegant if incongruous backdrop for what might be called "homesick food" for North Americans and British: club sandwiches, baked potato stuffed with tuna salad, and the like. Sunday brunch, a new Madrid custom, is very popular here. Tel: 522-4230.

Churros, Snacks, and Tea

Churros con chocolate is a Madrid institution. Squiggles of "raked" dough the size of breadsticks, deep-fried and served hot, *churros* (and the thicker *porras*) are eaten sprinkled with granulated sugar and/or dunked into a cup of thick and rich hot chocolate. Dunking is de rigueur at a *churrería.* The most popular place in Madrid for *churros* is **Churrería de San Ginés**, located along the alley-like pasadizo de San Ginés (easily missed unless you are looking for it) next to the walls of old Iglesia de San Ginés between calles Arenal and Mayor in the heart of Old Madrid. This century-old *churrería* is pipe-rack plain and totally unprepossessing—and that's the way Madrileños like it. Catch it as they do, in the early morning hours (it opens around 4:00 A.M. and closes at 10:30 A.M., reopening later in the afternoon, from 5:00 to 10:00 P.M.), when it jumps with people. Stopping by a *churrería* after a nightlong revel of *tasca* hopping is the Madrid equivalent of having a predawn bowl of onion soup in the old Les Halles in Paris.

Afternoon tea isn't a strong Spanish custom, though you can find it at the Ritz and the Palace. Tea and pastries, usually served between 6:00 and 7:00 P.M., are also a tradition at **La Mallorquina**, an old-fashioned tea salon on the puerta del Sol. A longtime favorite stop for foreign residents and locals for tea and cakes, a snack, or a light meal is **Embassy**, handily located for shoppers at Castellana 12 (corner of Ayala). Half of the space is devoted to a first-rate food shop where you can buy delicious cookies or sweet rolls (to nibble on back in your room) as well as picnic items. The tearoom is in the rear, with the entrance on Ayala. Tel: 225-9480.

Another tea or coffee stop might be at the **Círculo de la Belles Artes**, a new arts center at calle de Alcalá 42, where Alcalá intersects Gran Vía. On the ground floor in a grand high-ceilinged *sala* hung with crystal chandeliers is a bustling bar, a hangout for artists and students. You can watch the action on the avenue from huge windows while sipping thick hot chocolate, *café con leche,* or tea.

Tapas

A unique Spanish custom is *el tapeo* (indulging in *tapas*), and it is at its liveliest in Madrid, though Sevillanos claim they invented the custom. Originally named from the verb *tapar* (to cover), a *tapa* is a small, saucer-sized dish containing an appetizer—as simple as ripe olives, salted almonds, a few chunks of *queso manchego,* a slice of *tortilla española,* or slivers of *jamón Serrano*—served along with a *chato* (small glass) of *tinto* (red) house wine, *fino* (pale dry Sherry), or *cana* (glass of draft beer).

The concept of *tapas* hopping—moving from bar to bar, usually within a single neighborhood, to have a drink and sample the bar's special *tapas*—is ingrained in Madrid. It takes place daily from about noon to 2:00 P.M. before lunch, then from 8:00 to 10:00 P.M. before dinner. Because of the *tapas* tradition, most Spaniards are ready to order dinner immediately, without a preliminary cocktail, when they finally sit down at a restaurant table.

Each *tapas* bar has its specialties, running the gamut from marinated mussels to grilled *setas* (mushrooms) to sautéed squid, to boiled shrimp in their shells. Today *tapas*, reflecting Spain's new prosperity, have become more elaborate: béchamel-coated mussels with cured ham, small servings of casserole dishes, bits of pickled quail, lobster salad, creamed kidney and onions. *Tapas* hopping is an enjoyable and inexpensive way to dine, the Spanish equivalent of "grazing." Never mind dinner later. With enough *tapas*, you won't need it.

Some of the coziest, most typical bars for *tapas* are on the tiny streets of Old Madrid off the plaza Mayor and puerta del Sol (especially along calle Victoria just off San Jerónimo) and around the plaza de Santa Ana (especially calle Echegaray, a zigzag northeast of the plaza). Many of these *tapas* places also have full-fledged, if casual, restaurants—often in the rear or upstairs.

At **El Gallego**, adjacent to the plaza Mayor, the businessmen who crowd in after work find 25 or more varieties of *tapas* to choose from, including shellfish pie and sliced octopus marinated in olive oil. (A restaurant with "Gallego" in its name is almost a guarantee of the fresh seafood that is a trademark of Galician cooking.)

La Toja, outside an arch leading from calle Mayor into the plaza Mayor, serves the classic *gambas al ajillo* (shrimp in garlic and hot oil) in a terra-cotta dish and an elegant *salpicón de mariscos* (a mélange of seafood with a vinaigrette of onions and green peppers), among other delicacies. Outside the Botoneras arch, across the plaza, is **Mesón los Gallegos**, where *chopitos* (fried baby squid) is a specialty; consider staying for a dinner of Galician seafood. Nearby cava de San Miguel is lined with wonderful *tapas* bars, such as **Rincón de la Cava**, **Mesón de la Guitarra**, and **Mesón de Champinon** (devoted to mushrooms). At **Bar Gallego** on the plaza de puerta Cerrada you'll find Galician specialties such as steamed mussels (best eaten with Ribeira, a Galician white wine). Calle Cuchilleros is also wall-to-wall *tapas* bars, each with a single specialty. At **La Chata**, farther along on cava Baja, a specialty is *jamón de bellota* (cured ham from acorn-fed pigs).

A great favorite with local *toreros* is **Vista Alegre**, calle del Pozo 2, a tiny street just east of Victoria, parallel with carrera de San Jerónimo. A one-time Hemingway wateringhole was **Cervecería Alemana**, plaza de Santa Ana 6, and it's still going strong, its stand-up *tapas* crowd spilling out on the street on warm evenings. *Cerveza* (beer) is the drink of choice here. Nearby, just northeast of the plaza de Santa Ana on calle Manuel Fernández y Gonzáles 7, is the popular **Café Viva Madrid**, easy to find because of the colorful tilework on its façade. **La Trucha** at number 3 is also a local favorite.

One of the pleasures of *tapas* hopping is that you'll make your own discoveries. That's the Madrid way.

—*Patricia Brooks*

NIGHTLIFE

Bars and Cafés

The **Café Gijón**, which stands at number 12 on the strip of the Castellana called paseo de Recoletos, is the most famous of Madrid's old-style bars and cafés; you will find people here from breakfast time until very late at night. It is the home of the *tertulia,* an old Spanish ritual that consists of regular meetings among like-minded friends to exchange news and discuss everything under the sun. You are likely to find a famous author holding court here. Meals are served at lunchtime on the marble-topped tables, and in summer the Gijón's outside terrace is one of the most popular on the Castellana.

The **Café Comercial** is another *tertulia* haunt with marble-topped tables and wood-paneled walls. It lies on Glorieta de Bilbao, a plaza at the intersection of calle Carranza and calle de Sagasta beyond the plaza de Alonso Martínez. You can reach it by going west from the Castellana's plaza de Colón up calle Génova. The Comercial is nowadays particularly popular with younger people, who meet there to map out their evening: There are lots of cinemas and cheap restaurants on and around calle Luchana, which leads into the Glorieta de Bilbao from the north, and immediately south of the plaza lies the narrow-streeted neighborhood of Malasaña, which is packed with discobars. Malasaña can be rough late at night as police search out drug pushers.

Different sorts drink in different parts of town. There is a very distinct crowd of people—literati, theater people, hangers-on, and poseurs—who congregate at the **Círculo de Bellas Artes**, at calle de Alcalá 42, just up from the plaza de la Cibeles and moving west toward puerta del Sol. The Círculo stages experimental drama and photography exhibitions, and it has a very lively bar, **La Pecera**, where this crowd ends up in the evening. Later on these same people tend to cross over calle de Alcalá to Gran Vía and to a narrow street, calle Reina, that runs parallel and north of Gran Vía. At **Cock**, calle Reina 16, drinking and chatting continue until the early hours.

The yuppie crowd and the fashion models follow their own evening itinerary. You will find them at the **Hispano**, the Castellana 78, just north of the plaza del Dr. Marañón intersection, or farther uptown east of the Castellana's plaza de Cuzco intersection. Favored spots in this area are **El Balneario**, calle Juan Ramón Jiménez 37, which is full of potted plants, and **El Sur**, calle Alberto Bosch 14, which is similar. Both of these bars lie a few blocks north of the Hotel Eurobuilding.

Totally unpretentious people, students both of the real and of the eternal kind, flock to the plaza de Santa Ana in the evening and stay in that area most of the night. The plaza, flanked by the Teatro Español and the Gran Hotel Victoria, lies close to the Hotel Palace, up calle del Prado. There is a group of bullfighting aficionados in the **Cervecería Alemana** beer hall, on the plaza de Santa Ana, that acts as if Hemingway had just walked out of the door (he did often drink there) and there is also a big crowd at **Café Viva Madrid**, another beer tavern that lies on calle Manuel Fernández y González at calle Príncipe leading into the plaza.

For serious drinkers there is nothing to beat **Balmoral** except perhaps the bar of the Hotel Palace, which is where the Balmoral's chief barman learned to shake cocktails. The Balmoral has an English club atmosphere—hushed conversation, oak panels, and hunting trophies—and it is located on calle Hermosilla 10, between calle de Serrano and the Castellana, just north of the plaza de Colón intersection. On the corner of calle Ayala, the next street north, and the Castellana, the **Embassy** bar serves superlative Champagne cocktails and also extremely good English teas with wafer-thin sandwiches. The Embassy's founder, a Mrs. Taylor, set up the business after she grew tired of being a governess.

Nightclubs

The recently opened **Archy**, in an elegant mansion west of the Castellana at Marqués de Riscal 11, is the current "in" spot. Although it is essentially a discotheque where celebrities like to be seen, it also serves lunch and has a bar open from midday on. **Joy Eslava**, between puerta del Sol and the plaza de Oriente at calle Arenal 11, which used to be a theater, and the rather more sedate **Mau Mau** (part of the Hotel Eurobuilding, with an entrance at José Lázaro Galdiano 3), were the top spots until Archy came along, and they still retain a faithful following.

The best jazz is usually to be heard at the **Café Central**, plaza del Angel 10, just alongside the plaza de Santa Ana's drinking venues and by the main entrance of the Gran Hotel Victoria. There is a good cabaret at the **Café Maravillas**, calle San Vicente Ferrer 33, four blocks south of Glorieta de Bilbao, in the heart of the Malasaña neighborhood, and folk music at **Eligeme**, down the street at number 23.

For big international-type shows you have to go to **Scala Meliá**, at Capitán Haya 43, which is part of the Meliá Castilla hotel complex. Flamenco is performed very professionally at the **Café de Chinitas**, on calle Tortija, a small, narrow street south of Gran Vía and close to the Convento de la Encarnación and the Palacio Real, at number 7 (it also has a restaurant; Tel: 248-5135), and at **Zambra**, at calle Velázquez 8, in the same Salamanca quarter and close to El Retiro. Most visitors have more fun at flamenco clubs where you can participate as well as watch, and if you want to join in, try **Al Andalus**, at Capitán Haya 19, one block west of the Castellana, just after its intersection with the plaza del Lima.

—*Tom Burns*

SHOPS AND SHOPPING

You might expect to find everything made in Spain available in Madrid, and you probably would—if you had the time, interest, and energy to search for it. After all, there are more than 50,000 shops in the city to choose among. But it's far better, if your travels take you elsewhere in Spain, to buy the locally made products in their natural habitat. If that isn't possible and if Madrid is your only Spanish stop, there are special things to look for and certain places to find them. In general, the best shopping is concentrated in two general areas of the city, both easy to cover on foot.

Madrid's most fashionable shopping is in the **Barrio de Salamanca** (Salamanca district), along the 15 blocks of calle de Serrano that stretch from plaza de la Independencia and calle de Alcalá at the south end north to calle de María de Molina. Cross streets, such as Jorge Juan, José Ortega y Gasset, and Diego de León, form a grid in between, and parallel streets—Claudio Coello, Lagasca, and Velázquez in particular—are lined with boutiques, clothing and shoe shops, bookstores, *perfumerías,* art galleries, and restaurants favored by Madrid's chic and fashionable. In this area you'll find many customary international names—Yves Saint Laurent, Giorgio Armani, Hermès, Jaeger, Ted Lapidus, and Christian Dior, among others.

A second prime area for shopping runs from carrera de San Jerónimo near the Hotel Palace to the streets between Gran Vía and puerta del Sol, as well as a honeycomb of streets around the plaza Mayor. There you'll find custom crafts, antiques, and specialty shops, as well as two of Madrid's major department stores.

A number of hot new fashion boutiques are clustered in a new shopping area west of the plaza de Colón and south of Génova. Look for them in calle Almirante (just west of Recoletos) and nearby Conde de Xiquena (perpendicular to Almirante), Piamonte (west of Xiquena), and Argensola (several blocks north of Xiquena).

In general, Madrid offers good buys in crafts, custom-made items, leather goods, high fashion, art, and antiques. Certain French perfumes and liqueurs are also actually made in Spain, and cost less here than if bought elsewhere in Europe.

Shop hours are generally 10:00 A.M. to 1:30 P.M. and 3:30 to 8:00 P.M. weekdays, and Saturday mornings. Department stores are open 9:00 A.M. to 8:00 P.M. Monday through Saturday.

Crafts

For a good selection of Spanish crafts and made-in-Spain household accessories, try the government-run **Artespaña** shops. Prices are competitive, and the range of goods is extensive, displaying the finest workmanship from all over Spain. Furthermore, the shops will ship overseas.

There are four Artespaña shops in Madrid: at plaza de las Cortes 3, Hermosillas 14 (east of the Castellana, one block north of the plaza de Colón), D. Ramón de la Cruz 33 (west of plaza de Roma at the corner of calle Castelló in the Barrio de Salamanca), and in La Vaguada shopping center in the north part of Madrid. The largest, at Hermosillas 14, specializes in furniture. For many visitors the plaza de las Cortes shop, directly across from the Hotel Palace, is the most convenient. It has a wide selection of pottery from all over Spain; handsome, contemporary Garrido wall hangings; rugs; country furniture; tapestries; chests; mirrors; and many small, one-of-a-kind items.

If you can't visit the town of Talavera de la Reina, you'll find the famous decorated Talavera ceramics at **La Cerámica de Talavera**, Lagasca 44 (two blocks east of Serrano, near Goya). **La Tierra**, at calle Almirante 28 just west of paseo de Recoletos, specializes in antique and modern ceramics, as well as some other crafts. The much-collected Lladró porcelain figures may be seen and bought at **Lladró**, the company's Madrid showroom at calle Quintana 2, just west of calle de Princesa (an extension of the Gran Vía). Lladró figures are also available at the department store Galerías Preciados (see the section on department stores below).

BD Ediciones de Diseño, calle Villanueva 5 just east of Serrano, three blocks north of Alcalá, a branch of a famous Barcelona furniture-design showroom, features top-quality, well-priced contemporary furniture and classic reproductions of pieces by Gaudí, Le Corbusier, Mackintosh, and others.

Custom-made Clothes and Objects

Time was when Madrid was a center for custom-made clothes, shoes, linens, furniture, and accessories of various kinds. That era is passing, but it is still possible to find exquisite handmade goods in Old Madrid, on streets radiating from the plaza Mayor.

For fine made-to-order leather boots, all kinds of people—from Franklin Roosevelt, Ernest Hemingway, and Anthony Quinn to horsemen from Argentina to Zambia—have made the trek to the minuscule workshop of **Hijos de García Tenorio** at calle de la Bolsa 9. Carrying on a 150-year-old tradition, the García brothers make every boot by hand from a pattern drawn to the purchaser's foot. Each pair takes about three months to make and may last forever.

If you fancy a dashing Spanish cape, the place to have it made is **Seseña Capas**, calle de la Cruz 23. They've been selling their seductively warm wool capes to the rich, famous, and beautiful since 1901.

Fans have become popular again in Spain with women *and* men, and **Casa de Diego**, puerta del Sol 12, is the place to buy them, as well as gentlemen's walking sticks. Nearby at **Casa Yustas**, plaza Mayor 30, you'll find every imaginable kind of men's hat or cap, even the Royalist red beret. **Ramírez**, Concepción Jerónima 2, sells top-quality classical and flamenco guitars.

Fine leatherwork is a Spanish tradition, and it is almost synonymous with the name **Loewe.** Loewe suede and leather coats, suits, jackets, handbags, gloves, wallets, and accessories can be bought at three main shops in Madrid: numbers 8 and 26 on Serrano, and Gran Vía 8, as well as in 15 branches throughout the rest of Spain. Another much-respected place for leather and suede, clothes, handbags, and the like is **Herrera y Ollero**, Almirante 9.

Bookbinder **Antolin Palomino Olalla**, at calle de Conde Duque 11 (northwest of the plaza de España), does beautiful work.

Spanish couturiers have been turning out elegant clothes for generations. Among today's hot names are three in the Barrio de Salamanca: Purificación García, Velázquez 55; Adolfo Dominguez, at calle Ayala 24, calle José Ortega y Gasset 4, and calle de Serrano 96; and Sybilla, Jorge Juan 12. Francis Montesinos, calle Argensola 8; and Agata Ruiz de la Prada, Marqués de Riscal 8, are west of the Castellana. Longtime favorites include Manuel Pertegaz, Matias Montero 8, just east of the Castellana; Elio Berhanyer, G. Mena 25 (boutique), and calle Ayala 124 (atelier); and Antonio Nieto, calle del Prado 22 in central Madrid. Many consider **Angél Collado**, Almirante 21, the best men's tailor in town, a view reputedly shared by King Juan Carlos.

Antiques and Art

Two streets on which numerous antiques shops are clustered are carrera de San Jerónimo and nearby calle del Prado (which leads off from San Jerónimo). One of the oldest and largest shops, **Abelardo Linares**, plaza de las Cortes 11 at the corner of San Jerónimo, sells age-burnished Talavera plates, gilded Baroque wooden angels, *santos,* and vintage furniture.

Many visitors do their antiquing on a Sunday visit to El Rastro (see Markets, below), but keep in mind that 40 percent of the antiques shops in the Rastro area are open daily. Serious buyers should visit them on weekdays, when they are far less frenzied. Three galleries—modified malls with 30 or so shops in each—are located on ribera de Curtidores: **Nuevas Galerías** at number 12, **Galerías Ribera** at number 15, and **Galerías Piquer** at number 20.

More than 50 antiques and art galleries fill the **Centro de**

Arte y Antiqüedades, housed in a handsomely restored building from the 1850s at Serrano 5. **Centro de Anticuarios Lagasca**, Lagasca 36, is an "umbrella" for 11 or so dealers under a single roof.

Bargaining or negotiating the price is as much a practice in Madrid antiques shops as anywhere else, unless an object is marked P.V.P. (*precio venta público,* or fixed price).

Antique jewelry is still underpriced in Spain. In Madrid, look for it at **Sala Faberge** (which doubles as an auction house) on Gran Vía; **L'Ermitage**, Villanueva 27 (in the Salamanca district); and at **Monte de Piedad**, plaza de Celenque 2, where there are monthly auctions.

Rare books can be found at **Luis Bardon Mesa**, at plaza San Martín 3, and also at **Ramón Montero**, callejon de Preciados 4, both near puerta del Sol in the old city.

Contemporary Spanish art, especially paintings and graphics, has been an excellent value since the late 1960s. Most Madrid galleries are located on small streets east and west of paseo de la Castellana. A few of special interest are Galería Theo, Marqués de la Ensenada 2; Galería Celini, Bárbara de Braganza 8; Fernando Vijande, Núñez de Balboa 65; and the galleries along Villaneuva, such as Juana Mordó (number 7) and Galería Egam (number 29). For good prices on original prints, try the **Fundación March**, calle Castelló 77 near the corner of Juan Bravo.

A helpful booklet, *Arte y Exposiciones,* is available free at most art galleries. Published three times a year, it lists all Madrid galleries and exhibitions and has an invaluable artist index, telling where each artist exhibits on a regular basis.

Department Stores

Travellers in a hurry can solve many of their gift problems with one stop at one of Madrid's numerous department stores. The three major stores and their main locations are **Galerías Preciados**, plaza Callao off Gran Vía; **El Corte Inglés**, calle Preciados, off puerta del Sol; and **Celso García**, calle de Serrano 52 (at the corner of Ayala). El Corte Inglés has the widest selection of high-quality goods, and its best branch store is at calle Raimundo Fernández Villaverde 63, where it crosses Orense (just off the Castellana). Its other Madrid branches are at Goya 76 and Princesa 56 (near the corner of Alberto Aguilera). Galerías Preciados has four branches in Madrid: Goya 87, Serrano 47, Arapiles 10 and 11 (near the Glorieta de Quevedo intersection), and La Vaguada (see Markets). Celso García, smallest of the Big Three, has nine Madrid branches, including at puerta del Sol 11, Castellana 83 (in the Urbanización Azca shopping center), a ladies' store at Serrano 32 (near Goya), and a men's store at number 62 (near calle Don Ramón de la Cruz).

Markets

Madrid's famous flea market, operating only on Sundays, is **El Rastro**, with stalls that sprawl along ribera de Curtidores, (below the Catedral de San Isidro) from the north end of the plaza de Cascorro south to ronda de Toledo. Morning is the time to visit; by noon you can barely move through the crush of people, and by 2:00 P.M. the crowd thins out to head for *tapas* or lunch. El Rastro is made to order for pickpockets, so be careful. There's more trash than treasure, but the panorama of people makes a visit a must.

A stamp-and-coin market is held each Sunday from 10:00 A.M. to 2:00 P.M. under the covered arcades of the plaza Mayor. Even if you're not a collector it's worth going for the people-watching. **Filatería Castellana**, plaza Mayor 28, is a stamp and coin shop in the same area.

New in 1989, the **Mercado de la Puerta de Toledo**, located below the plaza Mayor in the southwesternmost area of Madrid, is a modern four-story brick complex built on the site of the old central fish market, using the market's cyclops-eye tower as a symbol. The new market is home to some 150 mostly stylish shops, two *tapas* bars, and a bistro, the **Café del Mercado**, which has live jazz in the evenings. For the visitor with limited time, the market is a précis of Madrid antiques, crafts, books, boutique clothes, and shoes. The most imaginative one-of-a-kind items are on the top floor. Especially noteworthy are Tafetán Taller Textil, with unusual hand-woven stoles, rugs, and towels; Jesús Riano for witty, original adult toys; Cristina de J'osh for vintage and modern dolls; and L. Sierra Anticuarios for Spanish country antiques.

Shopping complexes were latecomers here, but they are now a fact of Madrid life. César Manrique, an artist from Lanzarote in the Canary Islands, designed the most unusual one: **La Vaguada** (sometimes called Madrid-2), at Barrio del Pilár in the north end of the city, reachable by the Metro line. It's a three-story complex almost two blocks long, with some 300 shops, an Artespaña, a branch of Galerías Preciados, several inexpensive restaurants, nine cinemas, a bowling alley, and an open-air park on the roof. It's out of the way for most visitors, but worth seeing if you're in the neighborhood.

Food and Culinary Shops

The subbasement of El Corte Inglés's main store on Preciados has an impressive *supermercado* (supermarket) and is an excellent stop for anyone contemplating a picnic in El Retiro or a drive to the country, taking home food gifts, or just searching for Spanish specialty foods. The cheese, pâté, and sausage sections are especially impressive.

The most complete selection of the many wonderful Spanish cheeses is at **Cuenllas**, at Ferraz 3, an extension of calle Bailén (north of the Palacio Real, across from the plaza de España). Even handier is **Ferpal**, Arenal 7, one block west of puerta del Sol, where you will find great cheeses, Spain's excellent regional hams, sausages, *turrón* (nougat), and other foods. If you're hungry and don't want to take time for a proper lunch, buy a *bocadíllo* (small sandwich) and glass of beer and eat stand-up style as the regulars do.

Casa Mira, circa 1855, at carrera de San Jerónimo 30, behind its handsome wood-paneled exterior has the best *turrón* in Spain. You can buy it (as well as many other candies and sugared almonds) by the slab, cut to order on a marble countertop. Up the street is **La Violeta**, plaza Canalejas 6, a tiny shop known for its violet candies and other *bombónes*.

Madrid's best-known cookware shop, **Alambique**, plaza de la Encarnación 2 near the Palacio Real, sells all kinds of kitchen accessories, cookware, and china. Alambique also offers cooking classes, sometimes in English.

—*Patricia Brooks*

SIDE TRIPS FROM MADRID

AVILA, EL ESCORIAL, SEGOVIA, ARANJUEZ

By Patricia Brooks

Few capitals are as well situated as Madrid for visitors who want to see as much of a country as they can in a limited amount of time.

Madrid's geographic location dead-center in Spain helps, but it is enhanced by the fact that the towns nearby are at least as laden with historic and cultural sights as the capital itself; many of the Castilian cities encircling Madrid are far older and richer than it in monuments and memorabilia.

An occasional day trip from Madrid can lead you to such Castilian treasure towns as Avila, Segovia, El Escorial, Alcalá de Henares, and Aranjuez. Alcalá and Aranjuez are easy day trips. But ideally you should bunch together El Escorial, Avila, and Segovia, spending a full day in the first, and driving to Avila for the first night. Then enjoy a day there and drive on, via N 110, to Segovia for a *minimum* of two nights, but preferably three or four, using Segovia as your base for the daily excursions mentioned below. In so doing, you will enjoy a hearty helping of Castilian art, history, cultural life, and cuisine. You will also discover the crosscurrents of Moorish, Jewish, Castilian, and Germanic cultures that have enriched Spain over the centuries. And you will experience some soul-stirring scenery that takes you from scraggy, rock-encrusted, surreal landscapes to pine forests and soaring mountaintops (north and west of Madrid are the Guadarrama mountains, popular with hunters, fishermen, and skiers).

Toledo, south of Madrid, is another good day trip from Madrid; we cover it in the La Mancha chapter later in the book.

MAJOR INTEREST

Castles, Gothic cathedrals, and Romanesque churches
Castilian food
Moorish architectural elements
Castilian art and architecture

Avila
City walls
Basílica de San Vicente
Romanesque churches
Cathedral
Real Monasterio de Santo Tomás

El Escorial
Valle de los Caídos

Segovia
Acueducto Romano
Casa de los Picos
Cathedral
Alcázar
La Vera Cruz
Monasterio del Parral

Near Segovia
Riofrío
La Granja
Rascafría
Pedraza de la Sierra

Alcalá de Henares
Colegio Mayor de San Ildefonso

Aranjuez
Palacio Real
Casa del Labrador
Jardín del Príncipe

Chinchón
Plaza Mayor

Castile

For centuries Castile was a battlefield, fought over by competing armies: Visigoths versus Moors, Moors versus Christians, Christian kings against one another. From the death of Fernando III in 1252 until the reign of Los Reyes Católicos Ferdinand and Isabella (always called the Catholic Kings, even though one of the "kings" was a queen) in the early 16th century, the region was in almost continuous turmoil. It was hard on the inhabitants of the towns caught in the endless tug-of-war, but it probably built character. That may explain why even today Castilians are known to be tough, stoical, wryly independent, indomitable. They've had a lot of experience.

The very name "Castile" derives from those centuries of interminable warfare. It signifies *castillo*—castle—the mountainous landscape having been stippled with castle-fortresses that served as lookout posts and garrisons for various rulers. Mile for mile there are probably more castles or shells of castles in Castile than anywhere else in Spain.

In this guidebook we cover the part of Castile to the north and west of Madrid, beyond Segovia and Avila, in a separate chapter, later in the book, called Old Castile.

Castilian Food

Castile's robust cuisine, reflecting its rugged, mountainous terrain, is strong on game, such as partridge, hare, and rabbit, and on fresh river trout and *trucha plateada* (silver trout). Its dishes are as hearty and straightforward as the favorite *queso manchego* (ewe's milk cheese).

This is the land of *cochinillo asado* (roast suckling pig) and *cordero asado* (roast lamb), roasted in wood-burning ovens to a perfection rarely experienced elsewhere, with crackling skin and juicy, succulent meat that can be cut with a fork.

Cocido madrileño, a well-simmered stew of beef, pork, fowl, *chorizo* (sausage), garbanzos (chick-peas), potatoes, onions, carrots, and cabbage, with other ingredients added at the whim of the cook, is Castile's most famous dish. Traditionally, it is a complete meal, its constituents served in three consecutive courses: first the soup, then the vegetables, and finally the meats.

Other standbys to be found throughout the area are *sopa de ajo* (garlic soup), *tortilla español* (Spanish omelet, which is made with potatoes, not tomatoes, and often served cold on picnics and in cubes as *tapas* with cocktails), and *leche flan,* the rich caramel-enveloped custard that is popular throughout Spain.

For the wines of the area, see the Dining section in Madrid.

AVILA

At 3,711 feet above sea level, Avila, 111 km (68 miles) west of Madrid on the way to Salamanca, is Spain's highest provincial capital and has a population of 33,500. It is also the coldest—fair warning if you're planning a winter visit. The city's most memorable and significant sight, its encircling **Medieval walls**, accentuate Avila's closed-in-upon-itself austerity. Even in summer, this sense of gravity or sobriety is almost tangible, though in warm weather the walls are lighted at night, giving them a luminosity not evident in daylight.

The walls are unusual in Europe for their completeness, and are the oldest and best-preserved circumferential walls in Spain. Ten feet thick and an average of 33 feet high, they make a bold, dramatic statement from any direction. Depending on the time of day and amount of sunlight, they can reflect gold, gray, lavender, or deep purple.

Avila's walls would be a remarkable engineering feat in any era. In 1088, when Count Raymond of Burgundy, son-in-law of the ruler Alfonso VI, undertook construction, the project must have seemed superhuman. It took three years to encircle the city. Completed with 88 cylindrical towers and bastions and nine gateways into town, the walls gave Avila, well-situated as it was on a wide ridge that slopes west to the Adaja River, a commanding view of the approach to the pass across the Central Sierras, between the Sierra de Gredos and Sierra de Guadarrama, and the junction of two major roads. Small wonder that from the time the walls were completed, the city remained a Christian stronghold, keeping the Moors at bay. Later, in the 12th century, the crenellated apse of the transitional Romanesque-to-Gothic cathedral was incorporated into the walls.

The best view of the walls is from a *mirador* (scenic lookout) at Los Cuatro Postes on the road to Salamanca. You can pause for a drink and the vista at **Hotel Cuatro Postes**. Returning to Avila on avenida de Madrid, you must decide where to park. Avila, inside the walls, is a Medieval hill town of narrow, cobbled streets and passageways, difficult for driving but very walkable (if you don't mind steep inclines).

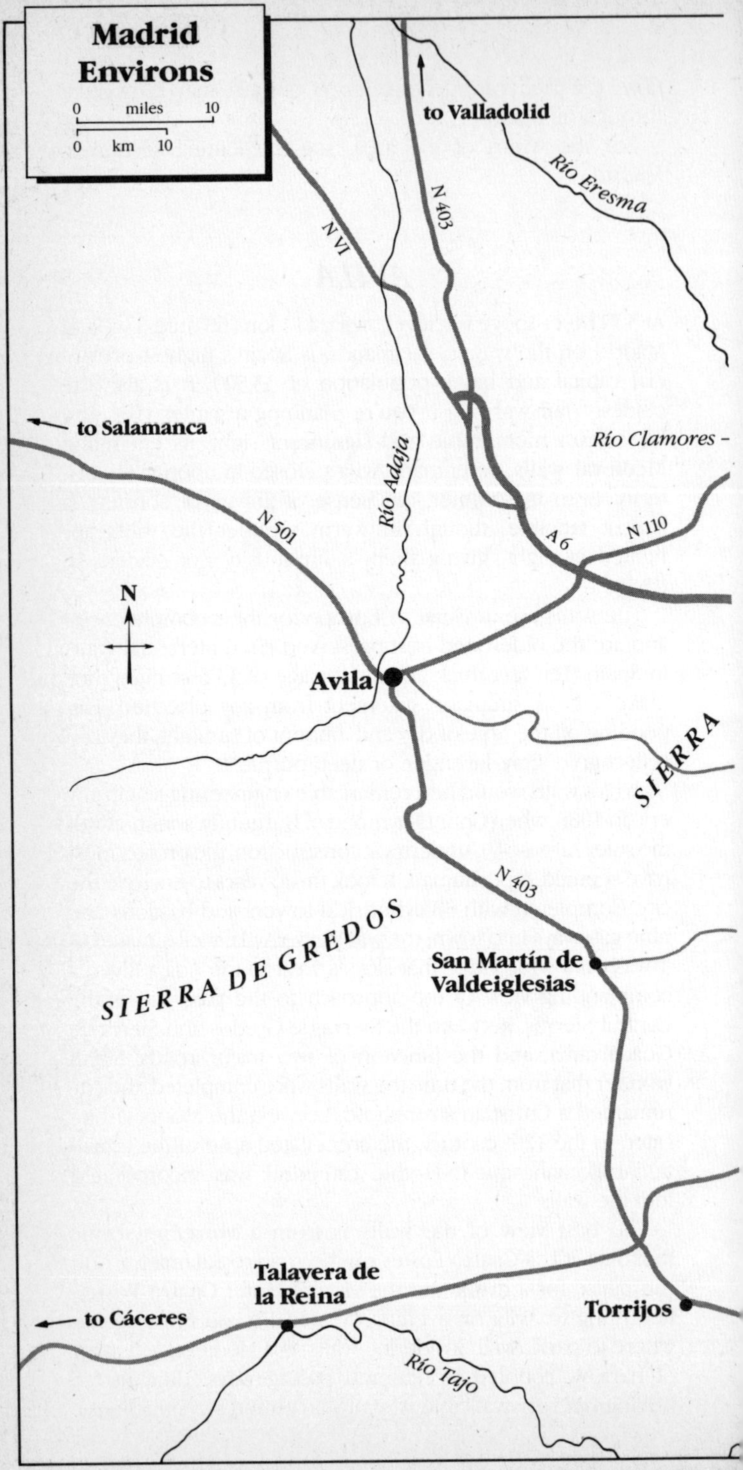

Madrid Environs
0 miles 10
0 km 10
to Valladolid
Río Eresma
N 403
N VI
to Salamanca
Río Clamores -
Río Adaja
N 501
A 6
N 110
N
Avila
SIERRA
N 403
SIERRA DE GREDOS
San Martín de Valdeiglesias
Talavera de la Reina
Torrijos
to Cáceres
Río Tajo

to Burgos
SG 233
Pedraza de la Sierra
N 110
GUADARRAMA
Segovia
La Granja de San Ildefonso
C 604
Rascafría
Riofrío
N 601
N 603
SIERRA DE NAVACERRADA
DE
Río Jarama
Guadarrama
Valle de los Caídos
El Escorial
to Guadalajara
M 505
A 6
N I E 25
Alcalá de Henares
Río Henares
N II
Madrid
N 501
N III E 101
M 302
N IV
E 4 N V
C 300
C 404
Chincón
N 401
Aranjuez
N 403
Río Tajo
N 400
to Cuenca
Toledo
to Ciudad Real

If you are spending the night, park at your hotel and take off on foot from there. A good overnight choice is the **Parador Raimundo de Borgoña**, a modernized, government-run, somewhat glum version of a 15th-century palace, built right near the north walls. There is a pretty garden in the rear, from which you can climb the city walls for exhilarating views of the city and the rolling countryside. (In fact, it's the *only* entry point for walking around the walls.) "Parador" signs will lead you through a gate right to it. Another accommodations choice, more expensive but even more convenient, is the Palacio de Valderrábanos (see below).

Avila's major sights are mostly in the north, east, and south of the city, hugging the walls inside or sprawled a few blocks east and north outside. For the sights inside the walls, a car is only a handicap, but outside the walls parking is easier, and you can make faster time driving.

For fanciers of Romanesque art and architecture, Avila is a diminutive feast. The Romanesque churches are all outside the walls, forming a wide arc from south to west to north. **San Nicolás**, near the road to Toledo, a few blocks south of puerta de Rastro, and **Santiago**, six blocks or so to its east, are both restored but still appealing. Going clockwise to the northwest corner, just below the ramparts, you come to the hermitage of **San Segundo**, with well-carved capitals in the apse, though the interior was much altered in 1579. Note the 16th-century statue-tomb by Juan de Juni of Segundo, Avila's first bishop, who achieved fame by flinging a Moorish chief from the ramparts above the church. **San Andrés**, just north of the major gate into the city, has a 12th-century apse and fine south and west doorways.

But if you have time for just one Romanesque church, it should be the **Basílica de San Vicente**, founded in 1307 on the site where Saint Vincent and his sisters, Cristeta and Sabina, were martyred around 304. The saint's ornately carved sarcophagus (about 1180) has graphic renderings of the three martyrs stretched on the rack, with their skulls being crushed by boulders. The church's style evolved from 12th-century Romanesque to 14th-century Gothic before it was finished. The most notable elements are the well-carved south portico and a west façade, with a double doorway bordered by superbly sculpted Romanesque figures, reminiscent of the Portico de la Gloria in Santiago de Compostela.

The church is diagonally across from the puerta de San Vicente, one of Avila's oldest gates, and the main entrance point to the city. Once inside the gate, you will want to head for the major sight within the walls, the **cathedral**. An immediate left turn will lead you along calle del Tostado ("the swarthy," named for a 15th-century bishop) to the cathedral, attached to the eastern wall. The cathedral's interior is far more graceful than its formidable fortress-like exterior suggests. Especially notable are the retables depicting events in Christ's life painted by Pedro Berruguete, a 15th-century Castilian master, Juan de Borgoña, his successor, and Santos Cruz; a silver monstrance by Juan de Arfe, a Renaissance artisan, in the museum; and the *sillería* (choir stalls).

The **Palacio de Valderrábanos**, on the plaza de la Catedral at number 9, is a four-star hotel built inside a 15th-century bishop's palace and decorated with Spanish provincial furnishings and handicrafts, yet it has the desired modern accoutrements. Its location across from the cathedral is very convenient.

Saint Teresa of Avila

Avila, or Avila de los Caballeros, to state its full, if rarely used, name, is a city of churches. Its focused asceticism has long been attributed to a single resident, a remarkable woman known as Santa Teresa de Jesús or Saint Teresa of Avila, one of the great mystics of the Catholic Church. Much of your sightseeing in Avila, other than that mentioned above, will be to follow Teresa's trail throughout the city, both inside and outside the walls.

The daughter of an affluent Avila family, Teresa Sánchez de Cepeda y Ahumanda became a Carmelite nun at 18, in 1534. This was a time of turmoil in Europe. The new Reformation was gaining ground and the Catholic Church was increasingly criticized for the laxity and softness of its monastic orders. Teresa was in her forties before she found her mission in life, reforming a religious order that had grown rich with time but lazy and dissolute. She managed to convert many nuns to a back-to-basics spartan life in a new order called the Descalzas Carmelitas (barefoot Carmelites). She personally founded 17 convents, preached throughout Spain, and wrote extensively. Somerset Maugham called her autobiography one of the greatest ever written. Her letters to her spiritual advisor, Saint John of the Cross, himself a poet of stature who also lived in Avila, became famous. Unlike Teresa, he left few traces—except for his writings.

Teresa's life in her native city is well documented: in the Baroque Convento de Santa Teresa, built on the site of her family home near the puerta de Santa Teresa, in the south of the city; San Juan on the plaza Mayor, where she was baptized (and which contains the tomb of Sancho Davila, Philip II's brilliant commander); the Convento de Nuestra Señora de Gracia, just outside the southeastern wall, where she was educated; the **Convento de la Encarnación**, to the north of town, her first convent (where she lived 20 years before beginning her reforms), which contains the kitchen and typical nuns' cells as they were during her stay; and the **Convento de las Madres**, east of the puerta del Peso, the first convent she founded (1562), and now a museum of her artifacts and her relics.

As befits a place devoted to spiritual matters, Avila lays no special claim to the pleasures of the table. **El Torreón**, calle del Tostado 1, is a reliable, moderately priced restaurant known for roast lamb, veal, and pork, accompanied by the robust regional red wine, Cebreros. **Palacio de Valderrábanos**, besides being a luxury hotel, serves the best food in town, and with some flair, but it is pricier. Also convenient, if a bit mundane, is the dining room of the **Parador Raimundo de Borgoña**, which emphasizes regional dishes. This is a good place to try the local sweet, *yemas de Santa Teresa,* made with lots of egg yolks.

If you go south from the cathedral, on calle Cruz Vieja, you'll come quickly to puerta del Alcázar, the southeast gate, which leads into the **plaza de Santa Teresa**, large enough for you to visualize the autos-da-fé once held here. Facing the plaza is the **church of San Pedro**, an 11th- to 13th-century gem with a lovely rose window, a Romanesque apse, and a retable in the Berruguete tradition. Two long blocks to the northeast is the aforementioned Convento de las Madres (sometimes called San José).

If you walk about 15 minutes southeast (downhill getting there, but a tiresome uphill return) from behind San Pedro's along calle de Santo Tomás, you'll soon arrive at the late-15th-century Gothic **Real Monasterio de Santo Tomás** (1482–1493), which Ferdinand and Isabella founded. In front of the main altar, their only son, Prince Juan, who died at 19, is buried inside an imposing white marble tomb. Another tomb is no longer in the convent: Grand Inquisitor Tomás de Torquemada was buried in the chapter room, but 19th-century revolutionaries destroyed his tomb. Torquemada reportedly condemned some 8,000 Castilians to death from 1485 to 1498. A simple slab now marks his burial site in the sacristy. The convent also contains a masterly retable by Berruguete depicting the life of Saint Thomas Aquinas; three richly decorated Gothic cloisters; the royal quarters where

Los Reyes Católicos stayed on their frequent visits; and a modest display of Asian art collected by the missionary monks.

Any additional time available in Avila should be spent strolling up and down the hilly side streets, enjoying the façades of some of the 15th- and 16th-century Renaissance palaces. A number of them, notably the palace of the Dávilas and the mansions of the Polentinos and Núñez Vela families, are snuggled close to the south walls, near the convent of Saint Teresa.

Don't look here for the sparkling café life of Andalusia; Avila, after all, is a Castilian town, and an unusually reserved one at that. Experience it for what it is: a chance to step back, at least in atmosphere, to the spirit of the Middle Ages.

EL ESCORIAL

Whether you make a special day trip to El Escorial (which is about 50 km/31 miles northwest of Madrid on A 6) or see it en route to Avila or Segovia, you might pay a brief visit to **Valle de los Caídos** (valley of the fallen), some 9 km (5.5 miles) north of El Escorial, near the village of Guadarrama. This grandiose memorial to the Civil War dead of both sides may be interpreted by the cynical as Francisco Franco's monument to himself and to Falangist martyr José Antonio Primo de Rivera. Unquestionably, Franco chose a glorious site, a stark and awesome mountain-ringed valley. Marking the spot is an enormous reinforced-concrete cross faced with stone. The stated intention was to erase the scars of the devastating 1936–1939 struggle (though political prisoners were used to work on the memorial); the result, with its pompous theatricality, may have the opposite effect. Franco himself is buried behind the main altar of the Capilla del Sepulcro, and José Antonio is under the cupola of the overblown, subterranean basilica.

Juxtaposed with the monastery of **El Escorial**, Franco's monument seems almost trivial, massive though it is. Few edifices evoke the presence of past rulers as tangibly as does El Escorial in speaking of Philip II, son of the Hapsburg emperor Charles V and great-grandson of Ferdinand and Isabella. Among them, these four rulers were responsible for the creation of Spain as a nation and as the international power that dominated Europe for decades—decades that shaped the country's image for centuries. It is no small legacy.

Philip II, the most complex and least understood of this great foursome, has fared poorly in recorded history, especially in Anglo-American history. A proud, publicly austere, formal man (who was privately jolly, amusing, and warm-hearted), he presided over Spain's Golden Age in the second half of the 16th century and also, because of the misadventures and misfortunes of the Armada, the beginning of his country's long decline.

You can understand how the remote (at that time) setting must have appealed to this ascetic monarch, who from 1563 lavished 20 years on a building project that included a royal palace, a monastery, a church, a library, and the Panteón de los Reyes (royal mausoleum). Philip's first architect, Juan Bautista de Toledo, had worked with Michelangelo on St. Peter's in Rome, but died while work on the Escorial was in progress; an assistant, Juan de Herrera, completed it.

All the while, Philip fussed over the plans, altering and blue-penciling, climbing over scaffolding to view the progress. Much of the final look should be credited to him. In his orders to Herrera, the king requested "simplicity in the construction, severity in the whole, nobility without arrogance, majesty without ostentation." Ultimately that was translated into a massive gray granite rectangular parallelogram, with slate roofs and turrets, towers at each of the four corners (reminiscent of those in Madrid's plaza Mayor), and an elevated central section in the form of an inverted grid with higher towers and the church dome. There are simple Doric elements in the courtyards (16 in all), doorways, and architectural detailing, developed as a reaction against the Plateresque flourishes of the preceding period. As you approach from a distance, the complex looks more like a fortress—some say a prison—than a palace, with its rows of windows overshadowed by the somber gray walls. Of the four elements the king desired, severity seems to have won out.

In its day, El Escorial was rivaled in size and complexity only by St. Peter's. Not every visitor has been impressed. Théophile Gautier, in the 19th century, called it "the dullest and most wearisome edifice that a morose and suspicious tyrant could ever conceive for the mortification of his fellow creatures."

El Escorial owes its existence to two vows Philip made: one to his father to build a royal mausoleum, and the second to Saint Lawrence just before Spanish troops launched an attack on the French at Saint Quentin in Flanders. It was

August 10, 1557, Saint Lawrence's Day, and Philip pledged to the saint that if the Spaniards won, a monastery would be built in thanks. They did and it was. The king chose as his site a small, isolated, scruffy village on a foothill between ridges of the Sierra de Guadarrama and called the complex he built there El Real Sitio (the royal seat) de San Lorenzo el Real del Escorial.

Philip was so satisfied with the buildings that he spent the last 14 years of his life at El Escorial, boasting that from the foot of a mountain he ruled the world. His intention was to keep things simple, as royalty went. He dwelled in relative austerity in the palace, which was attached to the monastery where 50 Hieronymite monks lived (it is home now to Augustinians). But simple here is as royalty does: Philip hired artists from Italy and northern Europe to do paintings and frescoes for the walls, amassed one of the world's great collections of rare manuscripts and books for the library, and provided the church with paintings and gold and silver vessels. Later rulers carried the decoration and enlargement of the place even further, though fire (in 1671) and plunder (by French troops in 1808) created some havoc, both inside and outside. After the death of Ferdinand VII in 1833 most of the finest art was taken to Madrid, and in 1861 El Escorial ceased to be a royal residence altogether.

Your first surprise at El Escorial is seeing how vast the complex is. The second surprise may be the discovery that it doesn't exist in a vacuum in the middle of nowhere but is in the center of a flat but lively, bustling provincial town, in the shadow of Mount Abantos. During your lunch break (when the palace complex shuts down), you can enjoy a leisurely meal (see below) and still enjoy a walk around a bit of the town, which developed as a resort for Madrid aristocrats during the period when the palace was still used as a residence. Today, Madrileños enjoy driving here for a Sunday outing.

The complex consists of the royal apartments, the church (built in the shape of a Greek cross), the royal pantheon (where all but two of the Spanish rulers from Charles V on have been buried, in 26 identical Baroque sarcophagi), the new museums, chapter houses, library, monastery, and King's courtyard. A single ticket, obtained at either the north or west entrance, admits you to all sections except the monastery and, in addition, to the Casita del Príncipe and Casita de Arriba, two 18th-century royal lodges outside the grounds. Connoisseurs of fine woodworking can also purchase an extra ticket to the Habitaciones de Maderas Finas (apartment of fine woods), a small, choice suite in the Palacio Real with exquisite marquetry on furniture, doors, windows, and floors, dating from the reign of Carlos IV at around the turn of the 19th century. You can visit the church without a ticket.

As you will soon discover, all this is too much to see in a single day, except in the most superficial way. To compound the problem, you lose a little time waiting for the requisite conducted tour. This tour leads you, almost in lockstep, through the royal apartments and then, mercifully, pretty much leaves you on your own for the more compelling (at least to art lovers) new museums, where you can wander at your leisure. In doing so, though, keep in mind the other aforementioned treats still to be seen along the way. Still, the new museums have to be a top priority.

Considering the monumental size of this grid-like complex and its formidable exterior, the interior is on a more human scale than you would expect, as royal palaces go. Some of the most pleasing rooms of the royal apartments are the small ones that you enter first, hung with tapestries made from cartoons by Goya, Teniers, Bayeu, and others. Especially evocative is Philip II's cell-like bedroom, which contains the litter on which he was carried on his last, painful, gout-ridden journey from Madrid. This room adjoins his simple audience room, with white-washed walls, Talavera tiling, and two 16th-century Brussels tapestries.

Much of El Escorial's extraordinary art collection was collected by Philip himself. In the series of connecting vaulted galleries called the **new museums**, followed by several subsidiary galleries, you are left to your own pace to savor Gerard David's *Descent from the Cross,* Velázquez's luminous *Joseph's Tunic,* Hieronymus Bosch's satiric *Los Improperios,* and works by Titian, Veronese, Tintoretto, Dürer, Rembrandt, Van der Weyden, El Greco, and many others.

In the remainder of your Escorial tour, you will want to notice especially Benvenuto Cellini's white marble Christ sculpture and Herrera's tabernacle and massive marble-jasper-onyx retable above the main altar in the church; the curious *pudridero* (rotting place), a vault outside the royal pantheon where the regal bodies were preserved for ten years before being placed in the royal pantheon; the paintings by Ribera, Daniel Seghers, and others in the chapter houses; and the remarkable **library**, with vaulted ceiling, marble floor, Herrera's gracefully designed Doric bookcases, Philip II's globe, and some 40,000 books, including Saint Teresa's diary and prayer books belonging to Charles V, Ferdinand and Isabella, and Philip II.

A simple but zesty lunch, washed down with a house wine from Cebreros, can be had at **Fonda Genera**, inside the Real Coliseo, near El Escorial at plaza de San Lorenzo 2. The food is good, but star billing goes to the place itself, part of a skillfully restored, beautifully decorated 18th-century royal theater built for Carlos III. Scores of distinguished guests have visited the theater, including Goya, Godoy, and, most recently, Queen Sofía.

Also handy (and in a similar upscale price range) is **Charoles**, Floridablanca 24 (around the corner from the plaza), a favorite with Madrileños who come out on weekends for the grilled meats and steaks and the terrace views of the palace rooftops. (In winter you can lunch just as amply indoors.) A runner-up lunch choice is the dining room of the **Victoria Palace Hotel**, just a short walk also, on the main thoroughfare, calle Juan de Toledo 4, the road that leads out of town toward Valle de los Caídos. You might also sit in the sunshine on the hotel terrace and admire El Escorial's towers rising above the trees. If you opt for spending the night, the Victoria Palace is the place to do it. As its name implies, this is a huge, old-fashioned establishment, comfortable but not fancy, with big rooms, wide porches, terraces, gardens, ample grounds, swimming pool, and a central location. Next door at number 6 is another choice for overnight, **Hostal Cristina**, a small villa with a cheerful garden.

The **Casita del Príncipe** is nearby in the Jardines del Príncipe, just east of the Escorial complex. Its finest paintings have been removed to the Prado, but you'll still be able to enjoy all the 18th-century French and Spanish furniture, carpets, clocks, and *objets.* This miniature palace, designed by Juan de Villanueva, was built in 1772 for Carlos IV as a prince, in the style of the Casa del Labrador at Aranjuez. Villanueva's even more petite and slightly less ornate palace, **Casita de Arriba**, is 3 km (2 miles) southwest of town on the Avila road. It was home to Prince Juan Carlos before he became king.

SEGOVIA

The drive from Madrid 88 km (55 miles) northwest through the Guadarramas to Segovia is a beauty, passing through hunting and fishing country, with grand vistas on both sides of the road and an ever-escalating landscape dotted with pines and brilliant yellow gorse.

Like other Castilian hill towns, Segovia surprises the first-time viewer with its dramatic profile of golden buildings with red-tile roofs, roosting on a rocky spur some 325 feet high, with two little rivers, the Eresma and the Clamores, forming a necklace, or natural moat, around the base. The land is shaped like a ship, with the stern on the east, the aqueduct at its feet, and the prow, where the Alcázar commands the view, facing west, with deep valleys on either side. Unlike most towns its size (more than 50,000 inhabitants), Segovia isn't content with one major attraction. There are three, each part of the stunning Segovia skyline and each a testament to a different period in the city's history.

Most spectacular, because it is so surprising, is the **Acueducto Romano**, whose 165 gray granite arches extend almost half a mile southeast from the city, marching like rows of massive stone soldiers between two hills. In the plaza del Azoguejo in the lower, more level part of town, the arches rise to 96 feet, but elsewhere, depending on the contours of the land, they are as high as 422 feet. All the massive, cut stones were carefully fitted together without cement, lifted into place by huge pincers (you can still see the slots in each stone where the pincers gripped). The Romans came to this area on the northern slope of the Sierra de Guadarrama in 80 B.C. and renamed the small existing Iberian village Segobriga, but it wasn't until Trajan's reign (first and second centuries A.D.) that the aqueduct was built. Considered the finest Roman structure extant in Spain, this masterpiece of engineering was used steadily, *más o menos,* until a few decades ago. Despite the rush of religiosity in 1520 that substituted statues of the Madonna and Saint Sebastian for Hercules in the highest niches, the aqueduct is almost surreal in the timeless way it dominates the landscape.

After the Romans came the Visigoths, followed in the eighth century by the Moors, who stayed in this region only until 1085 or so, but left many traces here in doors, gates, archways, foundations, and façades decorated with Mudejar designs, which a walking tour of the **old city** will reveal.

Walking is really the *only* way to savor Segovia, a truism that applies to the old part of every Castilian city. If you arrive here by bus, or even by car, the natural place to park is around the plaza del Azoguejo. From there you can stroll up calle de Cervantes, past the **Casa de los Picos**, a 14th-century mansion whose unusual façade is armored with protruding pointed stones (*picos*), to calle Real, the main street. This is the place to catch your breath from the steep ascent with a *café con leche* or aperitif in the first square you come upon, plaza de San Juan. At the tiny **El Ojo Bar** you can look out on the bronze statue of Juan Bravo, a local hero, and the old 16th-century Lozoya tower with its fine Renaissance galleries. Then walk west along calle Juan Bravo to the 12th-century Romanesque **Iglesia de San Martín**, with sculptured porticos and a Mozarabic tower, one of numerous Romanesque churches in town, all heavily restored. Another Moorish legacy that adds to Segovia's interest can be seen in the pastel (pink, lemon, avocado, and pale blue) buildings with decorative designs incised into their façades.

Behind San Martín is calle de Infanta Isabella, lined with pastry shops and bars, which leads within minutes to the plaza Mayor, a big, bustling square (with the tourist office located at the southeast corner), full of sidewalk cafés and small hotels, facing the **cathedral**, the highest point in town.

Segovia's is the last Gothic cathedral built in Spain, completed in 1590. It was the work of Juan Gil de Hontañón and his son Rodrigo, who followed up their success at Salamanca by repeating a similar design here, using the stellar vaulting learned in Germany and beautiful golden stones that give the exterior a tawny glow. Like most Spanish cathedrals and churches, Segovia's is packed with treasures; unlike some, it is well lighted inside (except for some of the rear chapels), and its wide aisles and richly detailed vaulting give it a sense of space and elegance. Look particularly for the 16th-century Flemish stained glass by Pierre de Chiberry, the 1571 retable by Juan de Juni in the **Capilla de la Piedad**, and the graceful 15th-century Gothic **cloister** transported from an earlier, demolished cathedral. In the **Sala Capitular** are 17th-century Flemish tapestries from Rubens's cartoons and an *artesonado* (wooden-coffered) ceiling.

Segovia's third major sight is the **Alcázar**, on the western edge of the old town, dominating its hilltop as a well-planned fortress-castle should. Turrets, towers, and slate roofs crown the golden-hued stone walls: a fortress straight out of the *Arabian Nights.* The Alcázar is so perfect, so much a fairy-tale castle, that it comes as a surprise to discover that it isn't all it seems. The Alcázar's origins are obscure; the roots might have been Roman, but it later became a fortified Moorish palace. The word itself is Arabic, meaning fortress, castle, or royal palace. By the mid-14th century, when the Christians got around to building their own fortress, there weren't many Moorish elements left here, only the foundation, parts of some walls, and the name—all of which they co-opted, adding Gothic elements and Mudejar decorations. Extensive additions were made in the first half of the

15th century by Catherine of Lancaster and her son Juan II. Isabella was crowned queen here in 1474. England's Charles I, as a prince, dined here in 1623 on "certain trouts of extraordinary greatness." A fire gutted the building in 1862 (when it was being used as an artillery school), and the 1882 rebuilding added the present Romantic arabesques.

If you climb the 162 steps of the circular staircase inside the building to the top of the crenellated Mudejar tower, your reward will be some spectacular views of the city, the *meseta* (plateau), and the verdant valley across the twists of both the Eresma and Clamores rivers. Inside, you'll also want to note the **royal chapel**, with a fine wooden Mudejar ceiling inlaid with "stars," and the **hall of armor**, with much Medieval weaponry.

Architectural aficionados should take a ten-minute hike (or drive) downhill from the Alcázar, across the Eresma and just west of town, to see **La Vera Cruz**, a tiny Romanesque gem of a 13th-century chapel, 12-sided, with three apses, built of tawny limestone by the Knights Templar. If you climb the 52 steps up the tower, you'll have thrilling views upward of the Alcázar and a Segovia profile.

Just east of Vera Cruz, still north of the city, off the Ronda (the circular road around Segovia), is the 15th-century **Monasterio del Parral**, once a mammoth monastery, now the still-splendid but deteriorating home to a mere ten monks. It harbors many treasures: a splendid Flamboyant Gothic portal at the entrance, 15th-century stained-glass windows in the apse, Gothic and Plateresque tombs, and a fine 16th-century retable by Juan Rodríguez. In the tranquil garden there is a grand view across the river of the Alcázar, and this is a good place from which to photograph it without including the telephone wires that spoil so many pictures.

If you have extra time, return to the lower part of Segovia to see the tenth-century **Iglesia de San Millán**, which is just off avenida Fernández Ladreda, a southeast diagonal road from the plaza del Azoguejo. Though much restored, San Millán is a visual delight, with its triple apse, exterior arcades, and carved capitals.

Dining and Staying in Segovia

Two restaurants outshine all others in Segovia. Both are historic, have similar menus that encompass the best of Castilian cooking, and are within walking distance of the major sights. **Mesón de Cándido**, plaza del Azoguejo 5, in fact, is in the shadow of the aqueduct, in a three-story 15th-century building, though the restaurant has "only" been in the same family since 1860. The colorful atmosphere, with smoked hams hanging overhead, fireplaces, and many cheerful white-washed rooms with exposed beamed ceilings, can sometimes get cloying, chiefly at lunch when the place is crammed with tourists. Nevertheless, even King Juan Carlos dines here on occasion. With reason: The robust Castilian specialties are fairly consistent (after all these decades, they should know what they're doing), and the roast suckling pig and lamb are especially satisfying, washed down with a sturdy red house wine from La Mancha. Try the Segovian dessert *tarta de ponche,* a marzipan-rum-egg yolk concoction.

At **Duque**, Cervantes 12, just up the hill from the aqueduct, the decor is even more overwhelming, but it's all in good fun, and the *asados* (roast pork, lamb, and chicken) are very tasty indeed. As a grand finale you'll be offered a monster-size (ten inches in diameter) brandy snifter with the house escutcheon on it. The waiter warms it with hot water, empties it, then fills it with brandy sufficient for twice the number at your table.

If you're surfeited with folklore, the more restrained, modern dining room in the **Parador de Segovia**, 3 km (2 miles) northeast of town, on the *carretera* (highway) to Valladolid, might be more appealing. The succulent *cochinillo asado* here almost measures up to the exhilarating views of the city across the river, especially at dinner, when Segovia's major monuments are lighted. This is one of the most modern paradores in the country, furnished in contemporary style and with Spanish paintings on the walls. All the rooms have balconies and stunning city views, and there are heated swimming pools indoors and outdoors.

Side Trips from Segovia

Riofrío (cold river), just 11 km (7 miles) south of Segovia, is the least known of the many *real sitios* (royal seats) near Madrid. What makes it different from the others is that part of it houses a **hunting museum**, a deceptive title for an opulent Italianate palace built in 1752 for King Philip V's Italian-born wife, Isabel Farnese. Used for years as a royal hunting lodge, it was less rustic than most—with a Classical courtyard and staircase, luxurious furnishings, tapestries, and paintings by Goya, Velázquez, and others illustrating the history of the hunt.

About 11 km (7 miles) southeast of Segovia is **La Granja de San Ildefonso** (the farm of Saint Ildefonso), usually called just

La Granja. More of a *petit palais* than the farm Philip V dubbed it, La Granja must have reminded the king of his French roots. A sweeping carriageway lined with chestnut trees leads to a French-style palace (which 19th-century English traveller Richard Ford called "a theatrical French château, the antithesis of the proud, gloomy Escorial, on which it turns its back") and formal French gardens. La Granja's furnishings are sparse because of a disastrous 1918 fire that gutted most of the royal apartments, but don't miss the splendid tapestry collection, which includes some brought from Brussels by Emperor Charles V and others made from Goya cartoons.

What truly distinguishes La Granja, however, is its tiered fountains, some 26 of them, spouting from various levels along floral walkways, designed in a Classical Versailles-like plan—but even more elaborate. The water isn't a "given," but three times a year (May 30, July 25, and August 25) there's a maximum effort, and the resulting cascades, sprays, spurts, spirals, and waterfalls are a sight to behold. The village of La Granja itself is a quiet, understated summer resort where Ernest Hemingway set some of his action in *For Whom the Bell Tolls.*

For a small place, La Granja has had more than its share of historic events, from the day in January 1724 when Philip V abdicated (only to return the following August) to the time in 1795 when Queen María Luisa's inept advisor, Manuel de Godoy, signed the treaty that effectively put Spain into France's pocket, thus opening the door to the Napoleonic invasion. Perhaps even more dramatic was the day in 1836 when another hapless Bourbon, Queen Regent Cristina, deferred to mutinous soldiers and agreed to restore the 1812 constitution.

Farther afield, tucked into the curves of the Navacerrada mountains between Segovia and Madrid, off C 604 (94 km/58 miles north of Madrid), is **Rascafría.** Its claim to fame is the **Monasterio del Paular,** a Carthusian monastery that began life in 1390. The monks were expelled in 1836 and their buildings confiscated by the government in a burst of anticlericalism. In 1954 Benedictines were invited to take over the property, and since then a comfortable détente has existed between church and state. (There is a small irony in the fact that filmmaker Luis Buñuel once spent a peaceful month here writing his virulently anticlerical movie *Viridiana.*)

The government has built a modern hotel within the monastery, but the few monks still in residence go about their business making and selling their Pau Gor cheese (in a shop next to the church), cultivating their trout ponds, and giving tours of **San Bruno**, a tiny jewel of a church on the grounds.

San Bruno is a fantasia of Flamboyant Gothic (with a restful Gothic courtyard), exalted Baroque, and a dash of the Churrigueresque. Like a small bandbox, it contains some lovely things: a lavish 15th-century Gothic retable with Last Supper and Resurrection scenes; a 1500 *reja* (grille) by Juan Francés, as delicate and intricate as embroidery; and an exuberant Baroque chapel of the tabernacle created in 1719–1724 by Francisco de Hurtado.

Lunch or dinner in the monastery's restaurant, **Mesón Trasta María**, which overlooks a cobblestone patio, can be a delight. Choose the hearty *cocido* (garlic soup) and grilled sea bream—or trout from the pond on the grounds—and, for dessert, almond ring filled with a creamy custard. A solid wine list, strong in Riojas, features several well-priced house brands. The government-owned **Hostal Santa María del Paular**, installed in the monastery structure, is thoroughly modern, with tennis, a heated pool, an equestrian center, winter sports facilities—and mountain views.

PEDRAZA DE LA SIERRA

A favorite day trip for Madrileños, who love any excursion that combines a small bit of sightseeing with a larger helping of lunch, is north of the city 75 km or so (47 miles) via superfast E 05 to Pedraza de la Sierra, one of the most pristine Medieval hill towns in Castile, a designated treasure town, preserved "as is." Pedraza is also a pleasant trip from Segovia, which is about 19 km (12 miles) to its southwest.

As you approach Pedraza, the castle guarding the hilltop seems welded to solid rock. Inside the town gate, the beige stone buildings with red-tile rooftops are typically Castilian. It is best to park near the gate and then wander on foot through the twisting Medieval lanes, most of which eventually end up in the **plaza Mayor**. This is one of Castile's most charming main squares, ringed with arcaded stone and wood buildings, many with heraldic crests. Since the days when the painter Ignacio Zuloaga (1870–1945) had a studio in the castle (which once held as prisoners the sons of France's Renaissance king Francis I), Pedraza has become something of an artists' colony, and part of the fun of a visit is to stop by various pottery workshops and studios.

In fact, the two main draws in the town, aside from its feudal countenance and harmonious architecture, are the artisan ateliers and the restaurants, with signs proclaiming *hornos de asar* (roasting ovens) to tempt you inside for traditional Castilian dishes, especially *cordero asado* and *cochinillo asado*. One of the best places to lunch is **El Yantar de Pedraza**, whose windows overlook the plaza Mayor. This cozy restaurant features some of the best Castilian food in town. Roast lamb is also the specialty at **Hostería Pintor Zuloaga**, Matadero 1, a parador-like hilltop building, the former Casa de la Inquisición, with a toasty fireplace on chilly days and sweeping views of the valley below.

A few steps down the same street is **De Natura**, one of the most attractive shops in Castile, three floors in an ample country house filled with handmade accessories you may find nowhere else in Spain: baskets, mirrors, glassware, candles, and pottery, as well as sophisticated country furniture.

ALCALA DE HENARES

Just 31 km (20 miles) east of Madrid on E 90 heading into the northeastern part of Castilla–La Mancha is the lively once-and-future university city of Alcalá, on the north bank of the río Henares. In many ways the town is more interesting for what it *was* than what it is.

What it was, for three centuries, was the intellectual heart of Spain, until the university was moved to Madrid and became the University of Madrid. Queen Isabella's confessor and later regent of Spain, the ambitious Cardinal Francisco Jiménez de Cisneros, founded the university in 1508, dedicating it to humanistic studies. The Complutensian Polyglot Bible, a masterwork in Hebrew, Greek, Chaldean, and Latin, was produced here in the early years of the 16th century. Don Juan of Austria studied here, and during Spain's Golden Age Lope de Vega and other poets were in residence for a time, as were assorted philosophers, humanists, scholars, and, in the university's heyday, 10,000 students.

Miguel de Cervantes y Saavedra was born in Alcalá in 1547, and his bronze statue, with sword and pen, dominates the tree-sheltered **plaza de Cervantes**, the central square (really a rectangle) of the old quarter. Catherine of Aragón, Ferdinand and Isabella's daughter and England's Henry VIII's first wife, was also born in Alcalá, but no traces of her time here remain.

Alcalá is once again a university town, with a branch of the University of Madrid, though now it is also a bustling industrial center. The tree-shaded streets in the old university area are usually crowded with students. The most imposing of the many fine old buildings centered in this area is the **Colegio Mayor de San Ildefonso**, facing pretty little plaza de San Diego (just east of the plaza de Cervantes, via calle Bustamante), with its statue of the all-powerful Cisneros modestly garbed as a friar. The Colegio was the major building of the old university, begun in 1498 by Pedro Gumiel and augmented in 1543–1583 by Rodrigo Gil de Hontañón. Extensive bombing during the 1936–1939 Civil War played havoc with it, as with many of Alcalá's finest architectural treasures, but much of the building has been restored. A beautiful Plateresque façade embroidered with stone *cisnes* (swans, Cisneros's emblem) opens onto a series of splendid patios, each unfolding episodically like a picaresque novel. First and most spectacular is the three-story Renaissance Patio Mayor, bordered by 96 Neoclassical columns. All four sides of the stone well in the center bear a swan in bas-relief. From the third patio, El Trilingüe ("three languages")—in whose surrounding rooms were the schools of Greek, Hebrew, and Latin—you enter the Paraninfo (great hall), now being restored, with delicate Plateresque galleries and a colorful red, blue, and gold *artesonado* ceiling decorated with six-pointed stars.

El Trilingüe also leads into the bar of **Hostería Nacional del Estudiante**, located in the old college of Saint Jerome. Now a rusticated *restaurante* decorated with vintage Castilian furniture, it is the best lunch stop in town (try the cream of asparagus and clam soup, the *pisto manchego,* or the *cochinillo asada*). The restaurant's main entrance is at Colegios 3. Also, remember that most of Alcalá's public monuments are closed Mondays.

ARANJUEZ AND CHINCHON

Foreigners visit Aranjuez (Ah-RAN-weth), just 46 km (29 miles) south of Madrid on superhighway N IV down into La Mancha, any time of year, but to Spaniards the best times to go are late spring, when the prized white asparagus is in season, and midsummer, for the tiny pea-size wild strawberries (*fresas*) that are sold with cream at roadside stands on the way. (Toledo—see the La Mancha chapter—is only about 44 km/27 miles southwest of Aranjuez.)

It was Queen Isabella II, ever the hedonist, who began the custom of the Trena de la Fresa (strawberry train) in 1851, leaving sweltering Madrid for a weekend of cool river breezes and emerald greenness at the royal seat in Aranjuez. Other Madrileños followed suit, and the strawberry train soon became a regular summer happening. (The custom has recently been revived, with a special excursion train, complete with attendants in Victorian costumes serving baskets of berries en route, making the 75-minute trip every Saturday, Sunday, and holiday from midsummer to mid-September, excluding August.) Actually, however, it is in spring and summer that the royal palace's gardens are at their best, and the gardens are the primary reason for a visit. Off-season, especially in winter, the flat chessboard of a town seems lifeless, and the palace and grounds are bleak.

Although the town was the site of a summer residence in Ferdinand and Isabella's day, and was a shooting preserve for Charles V, it was Philip II who ordered his Escorial architects to create a true palace. Two catastrophic fires, in 1660 and in 1665, led to an 18th-century reconstruction by Philip V, grandson of France's Louis XIV, and by subsequent Bourbon kings, that became something of an exercise in nostalgia for the glories of France. Its proximity to Madrid and its oasis-like greenness, a rarity on the Castilian plains, make it seem like nirvana in summer to sweltering Madrileños.

When Spaniards think of Aranjuez, other than for the seasonal foods, their thoughts may turn to March 1808, the time of the infamous Motín (revolt) de Aranjuez. The less-than-regal family of Carlos IV and María Luisa (captured so well in Goya's purse-lipped portraits) were in the summer palace, planning their escape to America, a decision that had been made on the advice of their foolish and venal prime minister, Manuel de Godoy (Goya got him right, too). The people, angered at the Godoy "neutrality" that gave the French army free passage to Portugal through Spain, attacked Godoy's palace. Carlos panicked and abdicated in favor of his son, Ferdinand VII, for all the good it did; Napoleon soon named his own brother, Joseph, king of Spain.

The somewhat listless **Palacio Real** here is a rather sterile showcase of 18th-century opulence, left much as it was at the end of the last century, with a plethora of Brussels tapestries, porcelains, mirrors, and *regalos* (gifts) from other monarchs to the Bourbons. One wing, the central section and the first floor, are open to view. In addition, you can stroll the many walks and avenues of the Parterre, the formal French garden, with its heroic statuary, magnolia trees, boxwood hedges, and ornamental fountains along the willow-shaded Tagus (the mouth of which is at Lisbon). The informal island garden is at the west end. Listen for the nightingales, permanent residents of Aranjuez.

In an extensive park, Jardín del Príncipe, between the Tagus and the calle de la Reina, is the **Casa del Labrador** (house of the worker), built (1803–1805) in the Petit Trianon style. Here Carlos IV and entourage played farmer amid frescoed Pompeian ceilings, embroidered silk hangings, and furniture such as a green malachite table and chair (a gift from Prince Demidoff of Russia).

If you want to sample the local asparagus and strawberries in season, **Casa Pablo**, Almíbar 20, nearby in the tree-shaded town, is the place of choice; also try its roast suckling pig, local pheasant, and excellent wine cellar.

Chinchón

It is possible on the same day trip to Aranjuez to visit Chinchón, nearby to the northeast, and from there it is just 52 km (32 miles) back to Madrid. The contrast between the two towns of Aranjuez and Chinchón is dramatic, as you drive from the languid riverside greenery of Aranjuez over the dusty La Mancha hills and plains to Chinchón, a study in ochre and red-tiled roofs nestled against a hillside. With an early start from Madrid to Aranjuez, you can arrive in Chinchón in time for a late lunch at the handsomely restored **Parador de Chinchón**, one of the most appealing and sprightly paradores in Spain. Then sample the local anise-scented *aguardiente* (an eau-de-vie) called Chinchón, which is distilled in the old castle atop the town, and enjoy the parador's restful garden, with its towering cypress trees and tinkling fountain. You might even have a refreshing dip in the pool.

There should still be plenty of time for a look at Chinchón's chief attraction, the colonnaded **plaza Mayor**. This prettified and much restored half-oval, half-rectangular plaza is ringed with bright-green wooden balconies, from which spectators watch bullfights when the plaza doubles as a bullring on summer weekends. If the plaza looks familiar, it probably is: It has been used as a background in innumerable movies. On the balcony of **Mesón de la Virreina**, number 29, right on the plaza, you can dine on *perdiz escabechada* (marinated partridge), *judías con chorizo* (beans with sausage), and other Castilian and Manchego specialties, and if there's a bullfight in progress you'll have a ringside seat. The plaza is the most level part of a town that spirals upward with a number of steep streets and inclines. The parador also offers accommodations, if you should decide to spend the night. This old brick convent was impeccably restored in 1982, and the guest rooms are simple—but a total delight, with hand-painted alcoves, modern tapestries, and hangings that tie in with the building's religious heritage.

GETTING AROUND

Buses (from Metro América, avenida América 18) and trains (from Atocha or Chamartín stations) run every few minutes each day from Madrid to Alcalá de Henares, which is practically a suburb. There are 15 trains daily to Avila, via El Escorial, and 20 or more trains (from Atocha or Chamartín) and four buses (Metro Moncloa or Herranz, paseo Moret 7) directly to El Escorial.

Aranjuez is a major railroad junction, and trains from Madrid's Atocha depart for it every 15 minutes daily. From Madrid to Segovia there are 12 trains daily (from Atocha) and four buses (Metro Norte or La Sepúlvedana, paseo de la Florida 11).

RENFE (the Spanish national railway system) offers a number of special tours by train from Madrid to major sights. The one-day **strawberry train** to Aranjuez departs spring and summer on Saturdays, Sundays, and holidays, except in August; the one-day trip to Avila, called Murallas de Avila (walls of Avila), departs Sundays only. Information is available from RENFE ticket offices or travel agents.

Still, the most recommended way to visit all these towns is by rental car. The roads range from good to excellent, with *autopistas* (superhighways) from Madrid going almost all the way to El Escorial, much of the way to Avila and Segovia (A 6), and directly to Alcalá de Henares (N II) and Aranjuez (A 4).

ACCOMMODATIONS REFERENCE

When dialing telephone numbers in Spain from outside the country, drop the 9 in the area code.

▸ **Parador de Chinchón.** Avenida Generalíssimo 1, **Chinchón**, 28370 Madrid. Tel: (91) 894-0836.

▸ **Hostal Cristina.** Calle Juan de Toledo 6, **San Lorenzo del Escorial**, 28200 Madrid. Tel: (91) 890-1961.

▸ **Palacio de Valderrábanos.** Plaza de la Catedral 9, 05000 **Avila.** Tel: (918) 21-10-23.

▸ **Parador Raimundo de Borgoña.** Marqués de Canales y Chozas 16, 05001 **Avila.** Tel: (918) 21-13-40; Fax: (918) 22-61-66.

► **Hostal Santa María del Paular.** El Paular, **Rascafría,** 28741 Madrid. Tel: (91) 869-1011; Telex: 23222 HPRM E.

► **Parador de Segovia.** On the carretera to Valladolid, 40000 **Segovia.** Tel: (911) 43-04-62.

► **Victoria Palace Hotel.** Calle Juan de Toledo 4, **San Lorenzo del Escorial,** 28200 Madrid. Tel: (91) 890-1511.

OLD CASTILE

By Robert Levine and Gerry Dawes

Robert Levine, who has contributed the introduction and the sections on Salamanca, Zamora, and León for this chapter, is also the contributor for the subsequent chapters on Asturias and Galicia and on Cantabria.

Gerry Dawes, the contributor for the sections here on Valladolid, Palencia, and Burgos, has also done the chapters on the Basque Country, Navarra, and La Rioja, and the sections on regional wines throughout the book.

Old Castile per se no longer exists as an area, and even at its peak seems to have been more in the minds of the Spanish occupying—and fighting for—its provinces than on the plans of cartographers. Its regions lie generally north and west of Madrid. In 957 Castile comprised Avila, Segovia, Valladolid, Burgos, Logroño (the capital of La Rioja), Palencia, and Soria. Later, the territory west of this area—Salamanca, Zamora, and the province of León (which made up the Kingdom of León)—united with Castile. But borders were blurred and reblurred as provinces were conquered or joined forces with others. The most northern and eastern areas dropped out, either becoming autonomous or joining with other regions.

What we are calling here Old Castile—Valladolid, Segovia, Salamanca, Zamora, Avila, Soria, Burgos, Palencia, and León—is today known as the Castile–León region. (Toledo, Madrid, Cuenca, Albacete, Ciudad Real, and Guadalajara make up today's Madrid–Castile–La Mancha region.) In this guidebook, certain of the Old Castile cities have been covered elsewhere. Segovia and Avila, for instance, because of their proximity to the capital, can be found in the chapter on side trips from Madrid.

MAJOR INTEREST

The heart of old Christian Spain as it used to be
Roman and Medieval Castilian cities
Romanesque and Gothic churches and monasteries
Major wine-producing areas

Salamanca
The Roman bridge
The Renaissance and Baroque buildings of the University of Salamanca and life in the student quarter
Plaza Mayor's 16th-century buildings
The two cathedrals

Cathedral and fortress-parador at Ciudad Rodrigo
Well-preserved traditional mountain town of La Alberca
Tomb and cell of Saint Theresa at Medieval town of Alba de Tormes

Zamora
Romanesque churches and cathedral

León
Gothic cathedral
Romanesque Basílica de San Isidoro and its treasury
Gaudí's Casa de Botines
The city's fountains
San Martín quarter's taverns and artisans' shops

Around León
Medieval towns and monasteries

Valladolid
Herreran cathedral
The Plateresque university building
Pre-Plateresque Colegio de San Gregorio (and national museum of sculpture)
Museo Oriental
Cervantes house

Medieval former palace at Convento de Santa Clara in Tordesillas
The Rueda–Peñafiel Ribera del Duero wine country
Castles

The Palencia Area
Palencia City's cathedral and Romanesque churches
Seldom-visited Medieval towns and churches on the Camino de Santiago

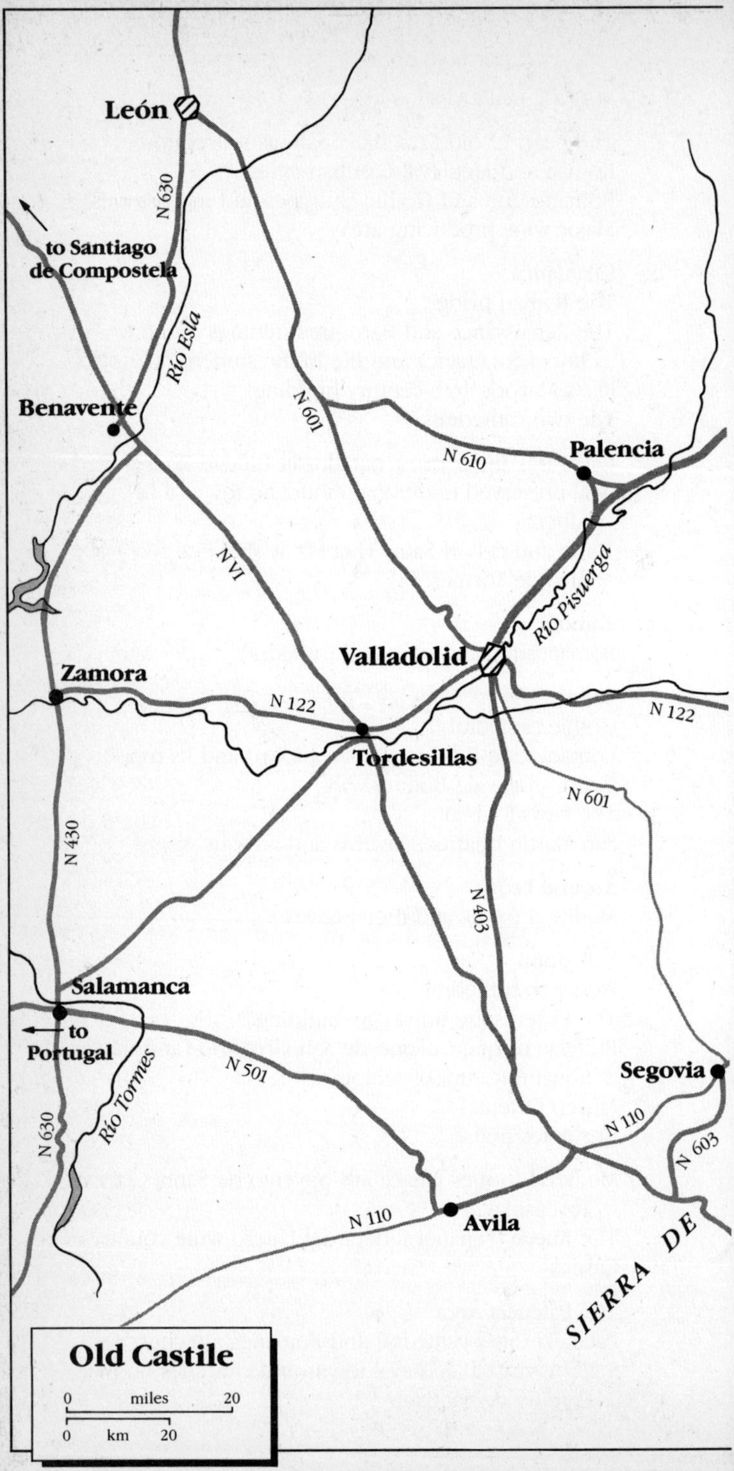
León
N 630
to Santiago
de Compostela
Río Esla
Benavente
N 601
N 610
Palencia
N VI
Río Pisuerga
Valladolid
Zamora
N 122
N 122
Tordesillas
N 601
N 430
N 403
Salamanca
to
Portugal
Río Tormes
N 501
Segovia
N 630
N 110
N 603
N 110
Avila
SIERRA DE
Old Castile
0 miles 20
0 km 20

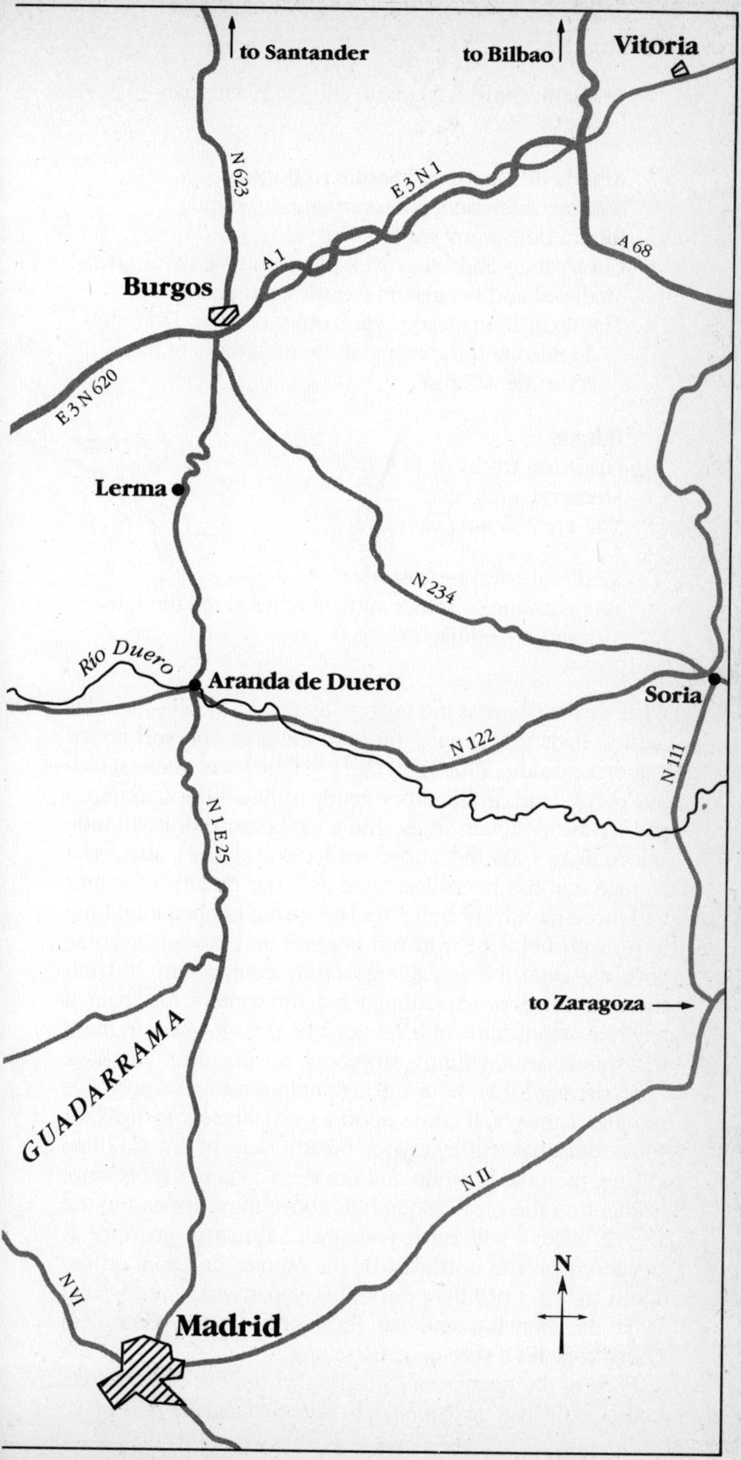

to Santander
to Bilbao
Vitoria
N 623
E 3 N 1
A 68
A 1
Burgos
E 3 N 620
Lerma
N 234
Río Duero
Aranda de Duero
Soria
N 122
N 111
N 1 E 25
to Zaragoza
GUADARRAMA
N II
N VI
N
Madrid

Seventh-century Visigothic church of San Juan de Baños

Aranda de Duero and Southern Burgos
Asador restaurants for roast lamb in Aranda
Ribera de Burgos wine country
Covarrubias and other well-preserved Medieval towns
Medieval and Renaissance castles and palaces
The great Romanesque monastery of Santo Domingo de Silos and the ruins of the monastery of San Pedro de Arlanza

Burgos
Historical traces of El Cid
Medieval ambience
The great Gothic cathedral

Medieval royal monasteries
Romanesque hospices and churches along the Camino de Santiago

What we have here is the heart of Spain, the Meseta (literally, "table," flatland). Driving through the area you will notice that on one side of the road there will be bare, treeless, red-soil mesas, and on the other gently rolling hills often tiered and landscaped with trees. The area, because of its altitude (more than 3,000 feet above sea level in places), also has a climate that has been described as "nine months of winter and three months of hell." Yet late spring is a beautiful time here, with fields of wild red poppies and broom or gorse covering even the scraggling, scruffy countryside. In truth these summers *are* appallingly hot; the winters, for Spain at any rate, windy and cold. Yet don't be put off—bear in mind that this is castle country, storybook Spain, and if you have been driving for an hour through uninteresting scenery, five minutes later you'll come upon a town, ancient fortress, or *something* that will take your breath away. In any Castilian village, the golden stone and the terra-cotta tile roofs—not to mention the picturesque hills above those located in the Duero valley—will catch your eye. Salamanca province is bordered on the northeast by the Montes de León, on the south by the Cordillera Central (Guadarrama, Gredos, and Peña de Francia), and on the north by the Cordillera Cantabrica: It's a very majestic setting.

Each of the many small villages that dot the Old Castilian countryside has an oversized church, normally 400 or so years old, at its center. The people are simple, friendly workers who would be uncomfortable in Spain's large metropolises. The entire region's population does not equal that of Madrid. The population in some of these towns has declined radically because life has been hard, and young people flee to the cities and greener pastures. However, these hardships have not affected the temperament of the natives. The visitor dropping in at a roadside restaurant in a town of 300 people will be received graciously, without suspicion. And if you speak Spanish, you will be family.

The Food of Old Castile

The food in the region is hearty, as befits the land. Old Castile is as far from major bodies of water as you can get in Spain, and so the fare relies heavily on very earthbound staples, such as lamb and suckling pig. The *sopa castellano* is a specialty; its other name is *sopa de ajo* (garlic soup)—and it's well named. In Burgos you can also try the fabulous *queso de Burgos*—ewe's-milk cheese—almost nonexistent outside the general vicinity. Other dishes native to the area include *gazpacho serrano,* a cold soup of boiled eggs, onions, garlic, parsley, vinegar, oil, and bread; *picadillo,* tasty beef or pork cooked with vegetables, garlic, and beaten eggs; and two general favorites—*chanfaina,* a rice dish with diced chicken and sausage, and *cordero asado,* seasoned lamb roasted in a wood-oven fire. Those who worry about their cholesterol levels should stay away from the *hornazo,* a pie filled with sausage, pork loin, ham, and boiled eggs.

The Wines of Castile-León

The valley of the Duero (which in Portugal becomes the Douro, the fabled Port river) is the home of Spain's most expensive wine, Vega Sicilia, which was once the only winery of note in the **Ribera del Duero** (Burgos, Valladolid). In 1982 the Ribera del Duero was granted DO (*denominación de origen,* or classified region) status, and a number of new wineries—notably Pesquera, Mauro, Viña Pedrosa, and Victor Balbás—have begun to receive justly deserved critical acclaim. The Tinto del País grape (Tempranillo in La Rioja) reigns supreme here, but Garnacha is also authorized, as well as limited plantings of Cabernet Sauvignon, Merlot, and Malbec. The best red wines from Ribera del Duero are a beautiful black raspberry color, have nice perfumed noses laced with oak, are well-balanced, and age beautifully.

In the past decade, **Rueda** (Valladolid, Avila, Segovia), located northwest of Madrid between Medina del Campo and Tordesillas, has begun producing excellent dry white wines from the Verdejo grape by cold-fermenting the musts and giving them little or no time in wood. The permitted grape varietals are Verdejo, Palomino Fino (the main grape of Jerez), and Viura. The wines labelled Rueda Superior (12.5 percent alcohol) are crisp, fresh, balanced, and medium-bodied, with good fruit and texture. Marqués de Griñon, Marqués de Riscal, and the exceptional Martinsancho are three of the best Ruedas.

Toro (Zamora, Valladolid) is one of Spain's newest official *denominaciones. Toro* literally means "bull" in Spanish, and most Toro wines live up to their name, attaining alcohol levels of 15 percent, but the trend is toward a more modern style—still big, rich concentrated wines, but with more finesse and less alcohol. Several Toro wines, notably the excellent Colegiata from Bodegas Farina and Tió Babu and Valdevi from Bodegas Luis Mateos, reflect this style. (Toro wines should not be confused with Torres Sangre de Toro, a wine from Penedès.)

A new *denominación,* El Bierzo, officially became DO number 34 in early 1989. The red wines show promise, especially the well-made Valdeobispo 1987, which uses the highly prized local grape Mencia.

—*Gerry Dawes*

We cover Old Castile in two segments. The first begins at the *western* side of Old Castile, closer to Portugal, and picks up where the Side Trips from Madrid chapter leaves off northwest of the capital (which is at Segovia and Avila), with Salamanca, farther to the northwest. From Salamanca we move north to Zamora and then to the Camino de Santiago city of León—the last city in Old Castile before the green northwest corner of Spain: Asturias and Galicia.

The second segment also begins just beyond Avila and Segovia, but covers the half of Old Castile *east* of the first half, the part due north of Avila and Segovia. From Valladolid and the wine country around it we move north to Palencia, then east to Aranda de Duero and its wine country, and finally north up to the great Camino de Santiago city of Burgos, the gateway to the Basque Country to the northeast and to Cantabria on the Spanish north coast.

SALAMANCA

England has Cambridge; the United States has Boston. Spain has Salamanca.

This is a college town. From the ancient sandstone university towers rubbed to a delicate gold by time and history to the tunas—bands of student minstrels costumed in black doublets—most of Salamanca will take you back to its erudite past. As in all Spanish cities there's an Old Town and a New Town, but here in Salamanca the visitor need be concerned only with the former. One-tenth of Salamanca's population is students (about 16,000)—it only seems like more. The student population has dominated the city since the university's founding in 1218, and the young tend to dictate a great deal of Salamanca's present, as they have done in the past.

But Salamanca, 212 km (133 miles) northwest of Madrid, like Avila (see Side Trips from Madrid), isn't only about students. Right outside this city of learning—to the southwest, en route to Ciudad Rodrigo, especially around the town of Robliza de Cojos—are the cattle ranches that produce some of Spain's finest bulls. During fiesta time in September Salamanca is overrun with cattle barons in their ancient native dress. (If you are planning to visit in September, it would be wise to book your hotel early.) And if you wander down the city's side streets, away from the center of the Old Town, you may catch a glimpse of farmers and gypsies tending their sheep in the shadow of the many towers that make up Salamanca's golden skyscape. But, in general, Salamanca is a seat of learning and religion (the two are hard to separate in Spain).

Sitting on a hill above the río Tormes, Salamanca looks from a distance like a patchwork of ancient towers (mostly Gothic and Plateresque) and modern architecture. Located on an ancient trade route linking Spain and Portugal—the Vía de la Plata—Salamanca played an important role during Roman times.

The plaza Mayor is the hub of city life, with the cathedrals and university buildings arrayed west and south from the plaza to the riverbank. Salamanca is a great town for walking. You need never worry about public transportation or a car—neither would help. A good walking tour would begin at the Roman bridge, continue uphill to the cathedrals, then to the Universidad, Colegio Anaya, Casa de las Conchas, plaza Mayor, Palacio de Monterrey, and Colegio de los Irlandeses.

The Roman Bridge

You can cross the río Tormes, which runs alongside the city, by walking over the Roman bridge, which probably isn't Roman. The construction date of the 1,300-foot bridge is as uncertain as its builder. Some say the bridge was built by Emperor Vespasian; others claim it was Hannibal. To confuse the issue more, the structure was rebuilt several times, most recently in the 16th century during the reign of Charles V and during the 1660s under Philip IV. Amazingly, 15 of the 26 arches are the originals. And even if the Romans did not build the bridge, the remains of the walls that surround the city and the stone Vía de la Plata are certainly testament to the Roman domination of the region.

You can reach the bridge from the center of town via Arco de Anibal. The question is, do you want to cross it? The only reason would be to sleep or eat, either of which could be done at the very comfortable **Parador Nacional de Salamanca**, a large, modern, vaguely out-of-place building with good-size rooms, a restaurant, spacious public areas, and spectacular views across the river to the Old Town proper. Make sure to ask for a room facing the Tormes; Salamanca is lit up at night, and the view from the parador's glassed-in terraces facing it is part of the appeal.

The Universidad

The main part of the university is located south of the plaza Mayor and just behind (northeast of) the cathedral complex, centered around the Patio de las Escuelas, although many other buildings sprinkled throughout the city house schools of the Universidad. King Alfonso IX of León founded the university in 1218, but most of the buildings date from the 14th century on. This was *the* place of learning during Spain's Golden Age. Columbus came here to present his proposed trip around the world to the department of theology and to consult the astronomy professors. About the same time, the first woman professor in the world, Beatriz de Galindo, was teaching Latin here. Cervantes is thought to have studied in Salamanca; so did the conquistador Hernán Cortés, Saint Ignatius Loyola (founder of the Jesuits), and Lope de Vega. The Copernican system was taught here before it was accepted anywhere else.

The fame of the university reached its height during the reigns of Charles V and Philip II (during the 16th century), when the institution had about 70 different departments and

12,000 students. In scholarly reputation it ranked ahead of Oxford (just 50 years its senior) and was second only to the University of Paris.

The university's standards lagged through the 18th century because of political upheaval, war, and student rebellions. There was one brief modern moment of rebirth when the Spanish philosopher-novelist Miguel de Unamuno became university rector. Unamuno, one of Spain's and the world's most distinguished writers and philosophers, was named rector in 1911 and, excluding a period of political exile in the 1920s, remained at the post until his death in 1936. His office, bedroom, and library, off the Patio de las Escuelas on calle de Libreros, next to the main university building, have been preserved and can be visited. The Civil War and Franco's reign delivered the coup de grace to the preeminence of Salamanca's university (as well as all the other Spanish schools), and it may take centuries for the school to awaken again.

Still, the Universidad is glorious to walk through and experience. The structure is basically a series of lecture halls off an interior courtyard. The entrance is in the Patio de las Escuelas. The formation of patios, or levels, was common in 13th-century Spain, and the traveller will see it often in Salamanca. The façade of the university can be best viewed from this level. The original university building, rebuilt in the 16th century, is the prime example of Salamanca Plateresque. It appears as nothing less than tapestry in stone.

Plateresque refers to a style of decoration as detailed and fine as silver work. It grew out of the Isabelline style (1470–1500), a transition between the Gothic and Renaissance styles in Spain. The Plateresque is characterized by heavy ornamentation and façades carved in relief, and was strongly influenced by the Italian half-pointed arch and decorative medallions, pilasters, and cornices. Salamanca pioneered this style as a result of a nationalist mood that led it to combine native styles with Italian influences. A study of the university façade reveals even more: Medallions of Ferdinand and Isabella, as well as likenesses of other monarchs, have been carved into the stone. These likenesses are then surrounded by a whole company of figures—pagan, literary, religious. All manner of symbols adorn the entrance. If you have a little time, stop to find the frog "hidden" in the stone.

If you are as interested in scholars as in architecture, step into the **Escuelas Mayores** and downstairs into the lecture hall that was the domain of Frater Luis de León (1527–1591), a theologian and humanist who started the School of Poetry. He did the majority of his writing in Salamanca. The hall where de León taught is still furnished with the original pre-Inquisition wooden desks and dais. It is said that the Hebrew scholar began the first lecture after his five-year imprisonment on trumped-up charges during the Inquisition with the words, "As we were saying yesterday. . . ." The scholar's ashes rest inside the chapel of the university.

There are many treasures in this ancient house of learning. On the same level as the original lecture hall is the Salinas music room, in which hang two panel paintings by the Spanish artist Juan de Flandés. The original building also houses a portrait of Charles IV by Goya, which hangs amid Baroque tapestries in Paraninfo Hall. The old library, in the upper cloister, holds more than 50,000 volumes bound in parchment and leather. The Universidad's modern library is next door.

Near the entrance to the Universidad is **Escuelas Menores**, a kind of prep school. The night before their exams, candidates for the university were locked inside the school's lecture room with only their books. To this day, students who pass leave their marks in oil and bull's blood on the wall of the cloistered courtyard. One of the classrooms of this 16th-century school has been painted with signs of the zodiac, a reminder that the school once had a department of astrology.

The Universidad has schools of philosophy, law, natural history, and medicine. Other colleges you can visit include the Colegio de los Irlandeses, Colegio de Calatrava, and Colegio de Anaya. The **Colegio de los Irlandeses** (also known as the archbishop's college or palace) on calle Fonseca was founded in 1521 by Alonso de Fonseca, archbishop of Salamanca. It housed Irish (*irlandeses*) students at the university and is presently a residence for university lecturers. It is Plateresque for the most part, and the patio is one of the most beautiful examples of Spanish Renaissance architecture. Note the capitals and medallions.

The **Colegio de Calatrava**, located on calle de Escoto and plaza del Rosario, is currently the School for Theological Studies. It was originally the College for the Military Order of Calatrava, founded by Charles V in 1522. The Baroque building (1717) was designed by Joaquín Churriguera; many of the original decorative figures of the façade were ordered removed in 1790.

The **Colegio de Anaya** was founded in 1411, but the building standing now dates from the 1760s. Located on the plaza de Anaya, the school was named after Diego de Anaya Maldonado, owner of the building and a cleric who was active in politics. Currently, philology, geography, and history are taught there. The building is Neoclassical in style. The lobby has on display four Roman tablets that were found during the building's construction—the three on the top are fake, the bottom one is genuine. In the courtyard, on the staircase landing, there is an imposing bust of Unamuno by Victor Macho. The upper floor has the Aula Magna (great lecture hall) with carved wooden medallions and portraits of Spain's kings and queens. The old chapel, by Alberto Churriguera, dates to 1731 and is presently known as the Iglesia de San Sebastián.

The Churriguera name has been mentioned a number of times in reference to the design of these colleges. There is a certain style associated with these designers, one that can best be called exuberant Baroque. "Churrigueresque" architecture is characterized by the use of sculptured lines and curves, exaggerated reliefs, and motifs drawn from nature and blended with the architecture to decorate façades, altarpieces, and so forth. Alberto (1676–1750) and Joaquín (1674–1724) Churriguera initiated this style, which can be seen at its most magnificent in Salamanca.

Learning aside, as you might expect there's another side of student life: East of the plaza Mayor, in the plaza del Mercado, are many student bars serving strong red wine and a sausage called *farinato* as well as regional cheeses. And, of course, listen for la tuna, a band of young men called tuneros—traditionally, students who dress in 17th-century costumes complete with ruffled collars, velvet suits, black berets, and capes covered with ribbons corresponding to their school colors and pattern. Tuneros sing in public squares and serenade young women with songs about the college, the city, and love. La tuna is popular today in the universities of northern Spain, principally Castile. Don't be shy: If it's evening, and the wine is strong enough, join in—if you know the words.

Plaza Mayor

The cathedral used to be the center of city life, but around the 15th century the hub shifted to the plaza San Martín. As craftsmen and tradesmen opened their shops and as noble families built their houses in the area, it was decided that a new square was needed. In 1728 Philip V granted permission. The project was enthusiastically supported by the citizens of Salamanca. The east and north sides were funded by local authorities, and the west and south sides were funded by private initiative, beginning with the Pabellon Real (royal pavilion). The plaza Mayor took 30 years to complete. Salamancans claim this is the most beautiful square in Spain, and most Spaniards would agree. Part of it was designed by Alberto Churriguera. The square isn't a square, making it all the more interesting: It is a trapezoid, and from it you can see just about all the major sights. If you lose your bearings when sightseeing, just return here and start over again.

Other than the parador mentioned earlier, which is a 10- to 15-minute stroll across the Roman bridge, most of Salamanca's major hotels are within easy walking distance of this central square. The **Hotel Monterrey** is not only elegant but also very conveniently located at calle Azafranal 21, northeast of the plaza Mayor. Its sister, the **Gran Hotel**, is a good spot to stay if you want to be near the plaza Mayor. For something a little less grand, there's the **Hotel El Zaguan**, located on Ventura Ruiz Aguilera (also known as La Calleja), a small street right off the plaza.

Students gravitate to this pleasant central square to pass the time between classes or for other comings and goings, but, unlike in many university towns around the world, adults have not been intimidated: As is true everywhere in Spain, all age groups and social strata mix and mingle in the same bars, restaurants, and squares.

Around the plaza are a number of sights worth seeing. The **Palacio de Monterrey**, located at the intersection of plaza de Monterrey and plaza de Agustinas, is a fine example of a 16th-century Spanish Renaissance mansion, though what you see today, one side of the quadrilateral and two towers, is only one-quarter of the building originally designed in 1539. Another palace you might want to see is **La Salina**, also located near the plaza, on calle de San Pablo, between calle Felipe Espina Minagustin and calle del Jesus. Built in 1519, it now houses the provincial government, and has the most harmonious façade of all the 16th-century buildings in the city. A bit farther away is the 15th-century **Torre de Clavero**, surrounded by eight smaller towers. If you don't feel like walking the few blocks, just stand inside the square and look to the southeast.

A favorite building in Salamanca is the **Casa de las Conchas** (house of shells), built by Dr. Talavera Maldonado, a knight of Santiago and counselor to Queen Isabella. The outside of the house is decorated with 400 scallop shells, the religious symbol of pilgrims on their way to Santiago de Compostela during the Middle Ages. It has recently undergone a thorough, well-needed cleaning and renovation.

The Cathedrals

In the center of town, south of the square and just a block or two up from río Tormes, are the old and new cathedrals of Salamanca. The first view of them can be quite confusing because the two cathedrals are attached to each other. One building simply extends on to the next; their very different styles and towers give the cathedrals a sort of mix-and-match look. They are surrounded by a complex of cloisters and chapels. Most visitors still have trouble figuring out where one cathedral ends and the other begins.

Don't take their names too seriously. The so-called **Catedral Nueva** (new cathedral) was begun in 1513 and took 200 years to complete. Its architects were Juan Gil de Hontañón, Juan de Alava, Juan Gil de Mozo, and Rodrigo Gil de Hontañón. After 1550, Juan de Ribera (architect of León's cathedral) took over; the finishing touches were added in 1714 and 1725 by the Churriguera brothers. The years taken to build it are reflected in its complicated mix of styles. The Catedral Nueva is basically a Gothic-style building, although Renaissance and Baroque elements, such as the choir stalls by Joaquín Churriguera, are visible. The **Catedral Vieja** (old cathedral), dedicated to Santa María, dates back to the 12th century and has very simple Romanesque and Gothic lines. It was built on the site of an earlier church that marked the Christians' defeat of the Moors in A.D. 722. One side of that cathedral was simply removed and the Catedral Nueva was added on, so that you walk directly from one to the next.

You can spend days in this complex or, if you wish, minutes. If there is one thing in the Catedral Vieja that is a "must see," it is the statue of the patron saint of Salamanca, the Virgen de la Vega. The statue, located in the center of the cathedral, is made of bronze-plated wood and adorned with Limoges enamel. It has been said to be the finest work of art in Spain. Two chapels that surround the cloister of the Catedral Vieja are worth mentioning, and visiting: the chapels of Santa Barbara and San Bartolomé. The former was founded by Bishop Lucero in 1314 and contains his tomb. The university faculty used this chapel as a meeting place until they had their own buildings. The latter was donated by Diego de Anaya in 1422, and it houses his sepulcher. San Bartolomé's altarpiece, by Nicolás Florentino, is a vast painting that was completed in the cathedral itself in 1445. It consists of 53 ornately carved and painted panels depicting the life of Christ and the Virgin Mary. It's frequently so poorly lit that commercial photographs almost do it better justiçe.

A short walk from the cathedrals is the **Convento de San Esteban.** This 16th-century, Plateresque-style Dominican monastery houses one of the most intimate churches anywhere. From a distance, the sandstone façade looks as if it was carved from marzipan. Inside, golden columns support altars topped by arches of gold. Its wood-layered floors serve as a nice contrast and give it warmth.

Dining in Salamanca

Salamanca is nontouristy Spain. Because it is not in one of the coastal regions, its fare tends toward meat rather than fish. The traditional roast suckling pig and lamb are staples of the local restaurants. Greasy sausages such as *farinato* are found more commonly at *tapas* bars than as a part of a full-fledged meal, but if you have a sensitive stomach, watch out. Although you will find regional wines on the menu, they are generally not as good as the standard Riojas.

Try **Nuevo Candil**, at plaza de la Reina 1; Tel: 21-90-27. This 25-year-old restaurant is the offspring of **El Candil**, located at calle Ventura Ruiz Aguilera 10 (Tel: 21-72-39), which is 100 yards from the "nuevo" Candil. El Candil is known as the *old* Candil; it was founded in 1940. It is wise to make reservations. The decor and cuisine are typically Castilian, with such dishes as *tostón* and *lechazo pierna asado* (two variations of suckling pig), *truchas del Tormes* (trout from río Tormes), and *sopa de rabo de buey* (oxtail soup).

A smaller, charming, and somewhat less pricey choice is the **Río de la Plata**, located a block southeast of the plaza Mayor, at plaza Peso 1. The menu features seafood as well as traditional Castilian fare.

The most raved-about restaurant in town is not Spanish at all; it is French. **Chez Victor** is expensive, but worth it. The cuisine changes depending on what's in season, so ask owner-chef Victoriano or his wife Marguerite for a recommendation. The restaurant is at Espoz y Mina 26; Tel: 21-31-23.

Shopping in Salamanca

Salamanca is set in excellent hunting and fishing territory. Shops that sell such equipment are **Esterra**, located at calle Consuelo 16, for guns and camping equipment, and **Sky**, located at avenida Portugal 48, where you can purchase mountaineering, skiing, camping, and angling gear.

Salamanca has a strong tradition of leathercraft and garment making. Its importance is reflected in the existence of a tanners' guild, which supplies the province's numerous craftsmen, some of them immensely skilled. The surrounding area is interesting as well: In Béjar, you can buy leather gloves made in the traditional method; if riding is your fancy, the best saddles are made in Alba, Fuenteguinaldo, Lumbrales, and Villavieja as well as in Salamanca. You can have beautiful Spanish boots made to measure in Alarez, La Bouza, Macotera, Martín de Yeltes, Mogarraz, and Villar de Ciervo. Some shops in Salamanca itself that carry leather and fur goods are: **Abolengo**, plaza Mayor 24, **Armino**, calle Corral de Villaverde 4, and **Campero**, plaza Corrillo 5.

You can also find beautiful jewelry in Salamanca. Metal craftsmanship reaches its height here with the delicate gold and silver filigree work that features as part of the traditional Salamancan costume. Rings, earrings, and key rings are readily available in jewelers' and souvenir shops. The most important workshops are those in Ciudad Rodrigo, Mogarraz, Sequeros, and Tamames. Jewelers and other shops can also be found in the **Multiplaza**, a general shopping mall located off the plaza Mayor.

AROUND SALAMANCA

If you have a car there is lots you can see right outside Salamanca. One great excursion is to go from Salamanca along the road toward Portugal (Guarda). Take N 620 west from Salamanca for 87 km (58 miles) to **Ciudad Rodrigo**, named after the Spanish liberator Count Rodrigo González Girón. (Incidentally, every duke of Wellington is also the duke of Ciudad Rodrigo since the Iron Duke of Britain defeated Napoleon here in 1808.) The old fortress is now the handsome **Parador Enrique II**, with 28 rooms, lavish gardens, and an excellent restaurant.

The town itself is lovely and its **cathedral** is magnificent. It was begun by Ferdinand II and was built in the 12th, 13th, and 14th centuries. The present apse was done by Gil de Hontañón in the 16th century. The Renaissance altar features a breathtaking alabaster *Descent from the Cross.* And make certain to note the choir stalls by Rodrigo de Aleman, who is best known for dotting the Spanish countryside with parish churches whose choir stalls are covered with pagan-inspired designs like the ones you'll find here. The Capilla de

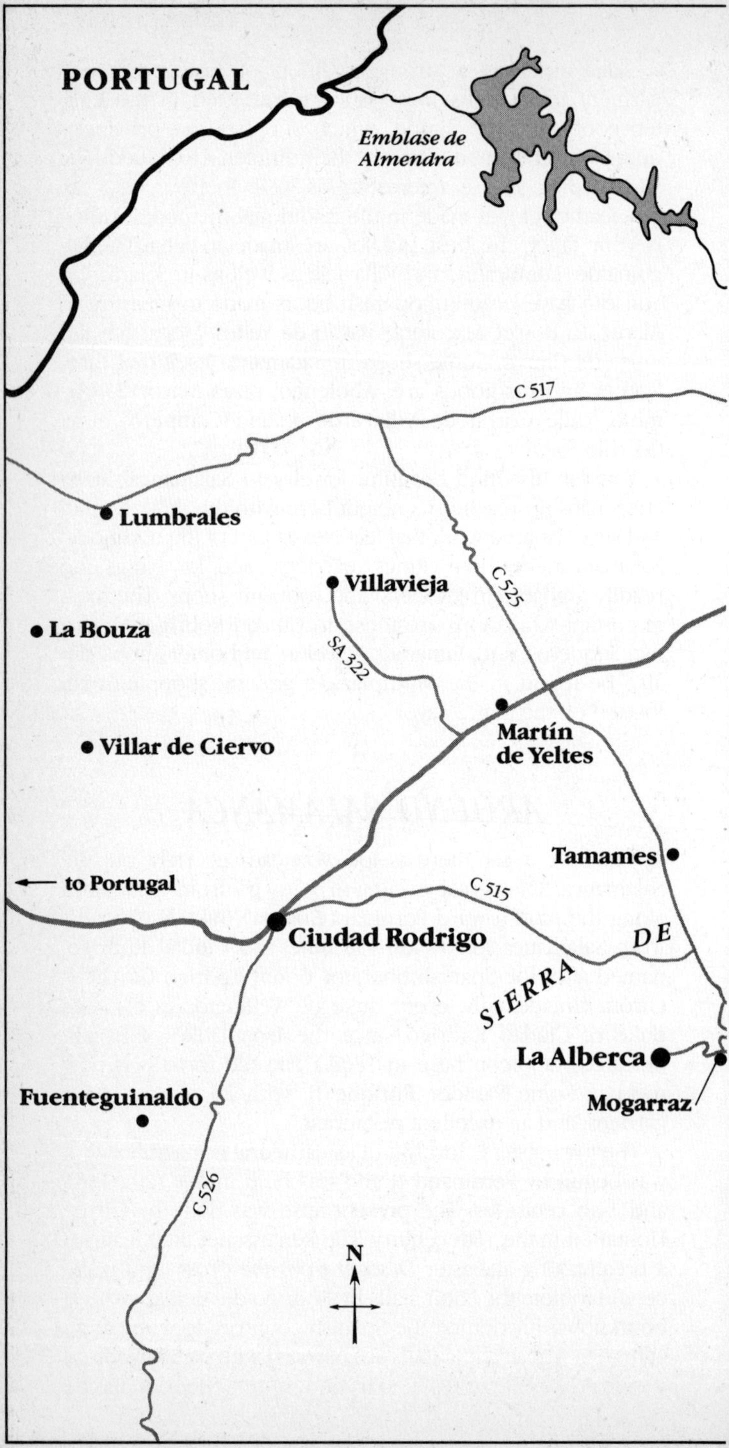
PORTUGAL
Emblase de Almendra
C 517
Lumbrales
Villavieja
C 525
La Bouza
SA 322
Martín de Yeltes
Villar de Ciervo
Tamames
to Portugal
C 515
Ciudad Rodrigo
SIERRA DE
La Alberca
Mogarraz
Fuenteguinaldo
C 526
N

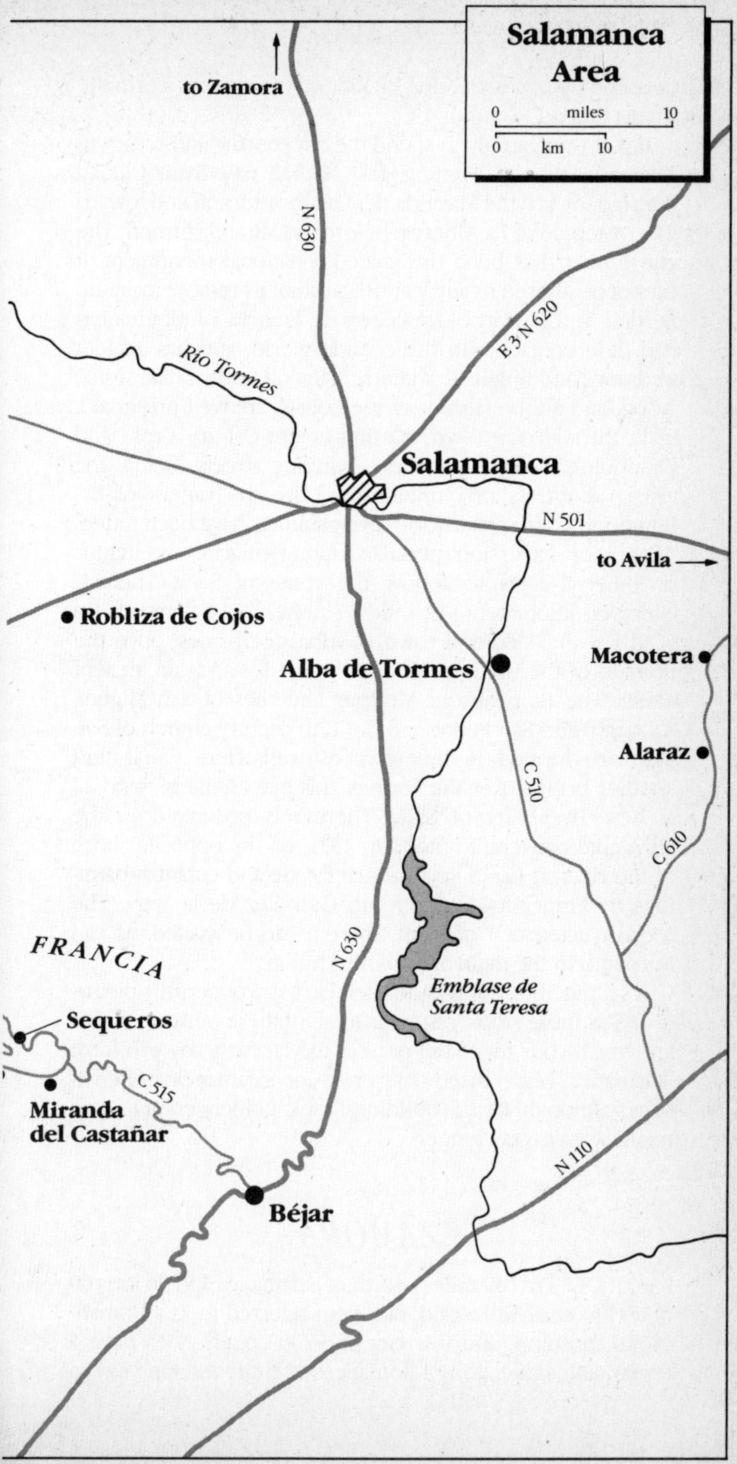
Salamanca Area
0 miles 10
0 km 10
to Zamora
N 630
E 3 N 620
Río Tormes
Salamanca
N 501
to Avila
Robliza de Cojos
Alba de Tormes
Macotera
Alaraz
C 510
C 610
FRANCIA
N 630
Emblase de Santa Teresa
Sequeros
C 515
Miranda del Castañar
N 110
Béjar

Cerralbo houses a painting by Ribera that alone is worth the trip to Ciudad Rodrigo.

If you want simply to spend the day touring and return to Salamanca in the evening, take C 515 east from Ciudad Rodrigo toward the Miranda del Castanor turnoff and toward Béjar. Stop off at **La Alberca**, before the Miranda turnoff. The entire town has been designated a national monument; it cannot be altered in any way. Because of its remote location, nestled in the heart of the Sierra de Francia, La Alberca has had little contact with the outside world, and has ancient traditions and linguistic characteristics all its own. The stone, wood, and adobe façades of the houses are well preserved. Walk through the town, starting at the Calvary Cross and continuing along the ancient, winding streets. Below the town (about 8 km/5 miles away) are the valleys of Las Batuecas, where prehistoric cave paintings have been found.

Another excursion popular among pilgrims—religious or otherwise—is to follow the route of Saint Theresa. Nineteen kilometers (12 miles) southeast of Salamanca on C 510 is the Medieval town of **Alba de Tormes**, once the domain of the duke of Alba, over which stands an ancient castle. The Romanesque-Mudejar churches of San Miguel, Santiago, and San Pedro and the 12th-century church of San Juan are located in the town as well. Here you'll find another bridge over the Tormes, this one Medieval, with 22 arches. The body of Saint Theresa is preserved in the Carmelite convent, founded in 1571, on the opposite shore of the river. It has a Renaissance façade and contains paintings by Francisco de Ricci and González de la Vega. The reconstructed cell of Saint Theresa can be visited, as can her tomb in the main altar of the church.

It's a pity the countryside itself isn't as wonderfully picturesque as these stops, but visits to all of these outlying places are worth your time, and none is too far for a day trip from Salamanca. Leave three days or so for Salamanca and environs, although if the buildings look golden enough you might want to stay longer.

ZAMORA

Zamora, 65 km (40 miles) north of Salamanca and 96 km (60 miles) west of Valladolid, has been referred to as a Romanesque museum, and this city of 55,000 really does have a remarkable collection of Romanesque churches. One day in

Zamora is normally enough to see what there is to see—and the churches are definitely worth a visit.

Also worth dropping in on, for both artistic and practical reasons, is the city's parador, the **Condes de Alba y Aliste.** Located right in the middle of town on the plaza de Cánovas and a five-minute walk to all the other sights, this 54-bed parador is a real treasure. The building is a restored Renaissance palace, with beamed ceilings, hardwood floors, and a grand staircase (watched over by a knight and horse in armor)—a stunning example of Leonese/Castilian architecture. And the patio is magnificent: Each of its columns has a crowning medallion depicting a historical or mythological figure, and you can also find the family tree of the original owners of the palace. The accommodations themselves are charming as well.

Just next door, on calle Ramos Carrión, is the **Iglesia de San Cipriano**, which was begun in 1025. It is a rather squat building with fine exterior carvings, and inside is a handsome 15th-century Madonna. A block farther west (on rua de los Notarios) is the **Iglesia de la Magdalena**. This 13th-century church has only one aisle, rose windows worthy of note, an arched doorway carved with flora and fauna, and a pair of canopied tombs within. Diagonally across the street from La Magdalena is the **Iglesia de San Ildefonso.** Built in the 11th century and rebuilt several times since, this church boasts a tower from 1719 by the flashy Joaquín Churriguera. Inside, behind seven locks, are the relics of the town's patron saints, as well as a fine triptych by an unidentified master.

Another five-minute walk west, at the end of the Old City, will win the visitor Zamora's prize—the surprising **cathedral**, still partially surrounded by the town's ancient walls and looked over by the ruins of a 12th-century castle. The first thing you notice is its great dome. While it is properly Romanesque, having been completed in 1174, its style is decidedly Byzantine, unlike anything anywhere else in Spain (although within Zamora province you can find a sprinkling of other examples of this style). The dome is surrounded by four smaller, rounded towers with points, and the whole effect, with flat, overlapping stones, is truly Turkish in flavor and just a little bizarre. The entire structure is gigantic, and its square tower only adds to the architecturally entertaining hodgepodge. Within are great doors, huge columns, and painted, twisted ribs supporting the grand dome.

Architecture aside, there are treasures to be found in the

cathedral. The choir stalls, behind an exquisitely intricate wrought-iron grille (there are several such grilles worth seeing here), are each different, each intriguing. Most are carved with figures of saints and biblical personages, each with a sympathetic face. On the seat bottoms and armrests are carved dragons and other beasts in odd positions, and comparably zany scenes from the lives of monks—these last were meant as satires, and during the 16th century the seats were nailed down by church officials so they couldn't be seen. In a side altar on the left you can see the sculpted 13th-century *Virgen de la Calva.* Note that it was "colorized" only in the 16th century. A silver monstrance from 1515 is also on display.

The cathedral's cloister is unexceptional, but leading off it, up a small staircase, is a museum with a fine collection of Flemish tapestries given to the church by the sixth count of Alba y Aliste in 1608. The ones depicting the Trojan War are particularly vivid.

All over the old city of Zamora are churches with something to offer; it's a pity there isn't terribly much more to the town.

An excursion worth taking if time permits is to the **Iglesia de San Pedro de la Nave,** 20 km (12 miles) northwest of the city. Take N 122 to Venta del Puerto and take a right after 12 km (7.5 miles) onto a small, almost-dirt road leading to San Pedro—follow signs to **El Campanillo.** This simple church dates from the end of the seventh century and contains some marvelous examples of pre-Moorish Christian carvings, mostly of scenes from the Old Testament, but many with Christian symbols—doves and the like. (As you enter the town of El Campanillo, ask about how to get to see the church; it isn't always open, but someone will be glad to show you around.) Pilgrims on the way to Santiago invariably stopped here; if you're in the area, it's an interesting side trip.

LEON

León is a city and a province whose landscape and history are a study in highs and lows. Situated on a gently rolling, triangular slope formed by the confluence of the Bernesga and Torio rivers, in the geographical area known as the Meseta Norte, it is 320 km (200 miles) northwest of Madrid. The city center lies on the western bank of the Bernesga.

León was founded by the Seventh Legion of Rome. To this

day, many of the most important treasures of León are Roman. Having defended itself against Castile on one side and Portugal on the other, this dignified and hardy country ultimately relinquished its independence and joined with Spain in the 13th century.

The city and its environs flourished through the early Middle Ages. León became the capital of the Kingdom of León (encompassing an area that would be the modern-day provinces of León, Palencia, Valladolid, Zamora, Salamanca, and the regions of Asturias, Galicia, and even Portugal before that country achieved its independence in 1140) in the tenth century, when García I transferred his court here from Oviedo in order to improve Christian Spain's position in the Reconquest from the Moors. Religious pilgrims trekking through the great Medieval city on their way to Santiago de Compostela made León known around the ancient world as a hospitable stopover.

The city was at its zenith during the tenth to the 13th centuries. But then history happened to León. Pedro the Cruel moved his court to Seville in the 14th century, and León would not be memorable again as an international force until the industrial age. From the 15th to the early 20th centuries, as if someone ripped the section devoted to León out of a Western Civilization text, both city and province floundered.

The architectural movement begun by Antoni Gaudí led to a small renaissance for León in the early 1900s. The modern city and the ancient city lie side by side. The old district, characterized by the plaza Mayor and nearby small ancient streets (and still, essentially, surrounded by walls), is nestled right beside modern buildings along ample streets and thoroughfares. The effect is, oddly, not jarring—but it is very noticeable.

As though shaped by history, too, the land of the province is known for its highs and lows—literally, its peaks and valleys. The city itself exists high above sea level, and a number of excursions discussed later will take you out to where four rivers come together to create flat, fertile agricultural lands. The Picos de Europa (see Cantabria), found at the northeastern edge of the province, offer some of the highest, most beautiful peaks in Spain to devotees of mountain climbing and the sheer majesty of nature.

Allow a fair amount of time to visit León. You'll want to travel here by car if possible in order to cover both the city and the outlying provinces. (If you only have a day in León, we suggest you drive to the Hostal de San Marcos, leave your car, and walk to all the crucial sights: the cathedral, the Basílica Real de San Isidoro, and the hostal itself.) Many travellers enjoy tracing the pilgrims' trek from León to Santiago de Compostela, moving west through Astorga, Ponferrada, and Lugo before reaching their destination.

The Cathedral

The "Jewel of León," the cathedral, is located in the east end of the city, on calle Puerta Obispo. It is, arguably, the finest Spanish Gothic cathedral. Some have termed it a symphony in light and stone. Begun in 1258 and finished in the 14th century, the church is most recognizable by its shape and sheen, seeming to be a cross erected from golden sandstone.

The stained glass is the light component of the "symphony." There are 125 stained-glass windows, 57 oculi, and three giant rose windows in this church; some of the windows are 39 feet high. In all, there's about 13,000 square feet of stained glass. The rose window above the south portal is, especially, an astounding work of art. The rose theme is repeated three times above the portals of the church. The glass art, spanning from the 13th to the 20th centuries, is arranged in three themes: The lowest level represents all the flora of León; the next level is based on heraldic themes; and the upper windows represent saints, prophets, martyrs, monarchs, and other important figures. On a bright day it's like being in a giant kaleidoscope.

"The windows *are* the cathedral," the locals say, but while the stained glass is by far the most startling feature of the cathedral, it certainly is not the only one. For example, the doorjambs in many areas display figures from legend. And then there is the Locus Appelation, the place where the supreme court of justice in ancient León met to settle disputes; it is dominated by a statue representing justice.

Opposite the church is the Seminario Mayor, which houses the **diocesan museum** comprising three separate galleries. The first houses a collection of paintings, including *The Adoration of the Three Kings,* by Pedro Campana, and *La Inmaculada,* by Eugenio de Cajes. There is also a Mozarabic Bible, considered to be the oldest document in the Romance language existing in Spain. The second room of the museum houses a cupboard in the Mudejar style, a style very evident in León. The third gallery of the museum houses many old stone tables and statues of Roman origin.

Basílica de San Isidoro

If you exit through the main door of the cathedral and take calle Damasco Merino, making a right on calle Cervantes and walking past the plaza Omana, you'll come to the Real Basílica de San Isidoro within five minutes. This Romanesque structure is built on the ruins of an ancient temple, subsequently dedicated to Saint John the Baptist, that was destroyed by Almanzor's troops in the tenth century. Alfonso V built a modest church here shortly thereafter. Ferdinand I, the first king of León and Castile, began to build a new church in honor of San Isidoro on the site in 1063 when he ordered the saint's remains transferred to León from southern Spain. Ferdinand died in the structure five days after the remains arrived. Only the pantheon remains from Ferdinand's reign. His daughter, Queen Urraca, had the building expanded from the pantheon later that century, and Alfonso VIII completed the right nave in the second half of the 12th century. This is the structure we see today.

The basilica reflects the history of the early monarchs of Spain. In the **royal pantheon** are buried the remains of 11 kings, 12 queens, 21 princes, and assorted nobles. The crypt is adorned with many fine Romanesque works. The ceiling of the mausoleum has earned the basilica the name "the Sistine Chapel of Romanesque Art" because it is decorated with magnificent, almost completely preserved Romanesque frescoes dating from the reign of Ferdinand II (1157–1188). They depict Christ enthroned, biblical figures, themes from the Apocalypse, the first complete Nativity scene in all of Spain, the constellations, and themes from everyday life—all in ochers, violets, blues, yellows, and grays.

The route through the basilica to the royal crypt takes you through the library, museum, and the treasury. The **library** includes a Bible that dates from 960. The museum is located in a spacious hallway and houses many interesting Roman pieces, including stone tablets, found during excavations in the garden outside the kitchen of the old monastery, that bear the seal of the Seventh Legion of Rome.

But it is the **treasury** that could very well take your breath away. First, there is the reliquary of San Isidoro himself. Born in 570, Isidoro was an important figure in early Spanish history, when the country was undergoing the transition from Roman rule to the autonomy of individual regions. He was known as Doctor de las Españas (note the plural). As the bishop of Seville, in 619 he presided over the second Council of Seville and in 636 (the year of his death) the fourth Council of Toledo, at which ecclesiastical laws were reviewed and rewritten to strengthen the Church in its dealings with the changing political scene. His remains are enclosed in an 11th-century wood-and-silver casket. Another important item in the treasury collection is an ivory piece carved in the shape of a coiled dragon, which dates from the tenth century. There is also a casket containing the remains of San Pelayo and Saint John the Baptist, a gift from Ferdinand and his queen, Doña Sancha, inlaid with 26 pieces of ivory. Another casket is a 12th-century enamelled piece from Limoges. There is a chalice made of onyx mounted on gold and surrounded by precious gems. The treasury also contains a priceless collection of Medieval tapestries, including two 12th-century stoles said to have been designed by the noblewoman Leonore Plantagenet.

While you're in the area, be sure to look at the city's well-preserved ancient walls from the second and third centuries, which stretch from the rear of the cathedral almost to San Isidoro. The huge turrets are particularly impressive.

Hostal de San Marcos

What is a church, cloister, museum, and opulent parador all in one? In León, the answer is San Marcos. Located on the banks of the Bernesga, overlooking the Medieval San Marcos bridge, it was founded in the 12th century by Doña Sancha. It was her idea to build a church and hospital near the bridge, which carried the main road out of León to Santiago. Shortly thereafter the canons and friars of San Loyo, a military order, took over. Under the auspices of Ferdinand I, they formed the Military Order of Santiago of the Sword in 1173, with the purpose of protecting pilgrims en route to Santiago from highwaymen and bandits, providing lodging in their inns, medical care in their hospitals, and, when necessary, burial in their cemeteries. Nothing of that original building remains. In 1513 the Order of Santiago began the construction of a new building to house their ever-growing activities and staff. Construction was supervised over the centuries by Pedro de Larrea, Juan de Orozco, Juan de Rivero, and other important Spanish figures in art and architecture. At that time, 300 *maravedies* per year were granted for its construction, quite an extravagant sum, and every bit of money poured into the structure shows. Construction went on and on, finally ending in the 18th century, when another section was added to the main façade.

When you are facing the complex, the parador entrance is on the left and the church is on the right. Cloisters are in the rear of the church and can be reached via the north end of the transept (the cloisters are frequently closed but can be seen through enormous glass windows from the hostal). The Museo Arqueológico—small but important—can be reached either through the hotel lobby or the right end of the transept; it occupies the sacristy designed by Juan de Badajoz in 1549 and two adjacent rooms.

The structure itself is remarkable. The exterior of the building contains an enormous Plateresque façade extravagant in its statues, pillars, medallions, scallop shells, and visages of famous Spaniards. There is a figure of Santiago on horseback. The top of this section is in the shape of a Spanish ladies' coiffure or hat.

The church is a fine piece of work, with extraordinary choir stalls on the upper level. The intricate wood carvings depict the apostles in the upper row and biblical characters in the lower. The cloister was built in three stages during the 16th, 17th, and 18th centuries. If you can, stop to see the large relief by Juan de Juni depicting the Nativity.

The **Museo Arqueológico** is notable for its Romanesque capitals, Iberian artifacts, and Roman mosaics and sarcophagi, but its real treasures are two crosses: There is an 11th-century ivory crucifix known as *Cristo de Carrizo,* which is unforgettable for its penetrating gaze, braided hair, and tunic, which suggest Byzantine influences, and the tenth-century Mozarabic *Cruz de Penalba.* Your visit to this museum will take only a half hour, and it's worth it.

More treasures are to be found in the **Parador San Marcos** itself. Built as they were, within the old monastery, the walls of the parador rooms are three feet thick, offering plenty of privacy. Many of the rooms are decorated with works of art dating back as far as 1027. Tapestries cover the walls in some rooms, or you might find your bed bedecked with a hand-carved headboard. Antiques abound. Other rooms have four-poster beds or handwoven rugs. The parador even offers a bridal suite if you're interested. Or you might prefer a suite in the tower, where the ceilings are 20 feet high. Some suites have canopied beds and marble bathtubs. This is a place for people who want to feel the ambience of centuries of history—all in comfort, with television and minibar, of course. (Some people find it a bit too museum-like; there's no accounting for taste.) There is, by the way, a modern wing; while it is nothing to sneer at, make certain you specify that you want the original building. The rooms range from moderate to expensive, and parking is available.

The parador is an easy ten-block walk to the other sights in town, and staying in it really is an experience (unequaled by anything other than Los Reyes Católicos in Santiago de Compostela). Its restaurant, the **Rey Sancho**, is excellent, and the grilled trout is a regional specialty. If for some reason you can't stay at the parador, at least visit the grand, Moorish bar in the lobby—everyone in León, dressed up or dressed down, eventually stops by for a drink.

Another good bet in hotels, but in a different league, of course, is the **Hotel Riosol**. It is on avenida de Palencia on the other side of the river and can be reached by crossing the Glorieta de Guzmán bridge. The hotel has recently been renovated. And the **Conde Luna**, a modern hotel in the town's center (on avenida de la Independencia) boasts a pool, garage, and terrific location at very reasonable prices.

Also worth seeing is the old Ayuntamiento (city hall) on the east end of the plaza de San Marcelo. It was begun in 1585 and is handsomely Renaissance. The imperial coat of arms of León crowns the façade, and the building houses historical documents as well as a collection of full-length portraits of all of León's monarchs, from the beginning to the 20th century.

Stop also to see **Palacio de los Guzmanes** (the Guzmáns were wealthy noblemen), at the corner of calle Generalísimo Franco and calle del Cid, now the official Diputación (county council). Begun in 1559, this old building has stone tablets in front that display the family arms; note the beautifully preserved Renaissance patio inside with Doric columns and oculi punctuating the arcade. The building also has the distinction of having a doorway located off-center, making the entire façade appear a bit wobbly.

Casa de Botines

As though you've been transported from the antiquity of places like San Marcos to the first third of the 20th century in the twinkling of an eye, the cityscape offers the house that Gaudí built. Antoni Gaudí was more than an architect; he was a movement unto himself. His buildings looked away from Spain's past into her future and foretold the end of royalty. A freethinker, Gaudí was definitely a 20th-century man, though with Gothic-inspired underpinnings.

Directly opposite the Palacio de los Guzmanes on the

plaza San Marcelo is Gaudí's Casa de Botines. Begun at the end of the 19th century, the building is Neo-Gothic, nearly square with four simple towers around its boundaries. It is one his more understated edifices, but it still makes quite an impression.

Gaudí influenced other builders, who then erected other modern buildings near the plaza Santo Domingo, such as the post office, built in 1910 across from the cathedral by Leonese architect Manuel de Cardenas.

These and other early-20th-century buildings are now surrounded by supermodern designs, such as the plaza de la Inmaculada and the plaza de Calvo Sotelo, making León appear to be an instantaneous time trip between antiquity and the future. And, for some reason, this is never disconcerting.

The Fountains of León

Like Madrid, León loves its fountains, and they come in all shapes and sizes. You might want to stop and enjoy the famous Neptune's statue created by Mariano Salvatierra located in the San Francisco gardens, at the intersection of avenida de la Independencia and avenida de Madrid, in the south end of town, just outside the old walls. The fountain in the plaza de San Isidoro, just outside the basilica, an obelisk with carefully carved lions, is also worth seeing. For something of a laugh, visit the fountain in the plaza del Mercado (three blocks southeast of the plaza Mayor, just behind the Iglesia de Nuestra Señora del Mercado): It's in exaggerated Baroque style with two angels embracing a column representing the Bernesga and Torio rivers and the seal of León. There's another fountain, a Neoclassical one, in calle de la Plegaria, located between the Iglesia de San Martín and the rear of the Ayuntamiento, reachable via the calle Escalleria.

There is also a fountain in the plaza San Marcelo, across from the Casa de Botines. You may want to stop near the plaza and eat at the **Casa Pozo**. Its peasant bread, Rioja wine, and fine desserts make it a good bet. The brother of the owner of this restaurant has his own establishment, **Adonias**, at Santa Nonia 16. This moderately priced restaurant features terrific food, is decorated with Spanish ceramics, and has friendlier service than Casa Pozo. Or, if you're in the mood to explore, take C 623 about 5 km (3 miles) northwest of the city to the **Casa Teo** (Tel: 22-30-05) in San Andrés de Rabanedo. The restaurant is known for its homemade meat stews and is worth the short trip. There's outdoor seating in the warmer months.

San Martín and Other Quarters

León is divided into different areas or quarters, each with its own special flavor. **Santa Marina**, for example, is known for its stately homes and mansions.

San Martín is known affectionately as Barrio Humido (the wet quarter) because there are many taverns and inns here, each with its own flavor and ambience. The street names of San Martín refer to the craftspeople who were the area's original inhabitants. There is a Platería (silversmith) street, a Zapatería (shoemaker), an Ollería (pots and pans), and a Frenería (bridle maker), among others.

Santa Ana, another quarter, has been inhabited over the centuries by people of peasant stock, so it is more of a mixed bag of sights and sounds, and almost seems like an international melting pot. It isn't quite poor, but it's definitely earthy—and another side of León.

EXCURSIONS FROM LEON

El Bierzo

The El Bierzo region (northwest of the city, toward Galicia) is quite mountainous: the Picos de Ancares, the Sierras de Caurel, the Montes Aquilianos, the Sierra de Pobladura, and the Sierra de Jistredo. The geography here makes it possible to see snowcapped mountains while you are in a valley surrounded by Mediterranean crops. The valley was also a milestone on the pilgrims' route, so the countryside is strewn with remnants of monasteries, abbeys, and old churches.

There are many interesting villages along this route. The tiny town of **Compludo** (it's so small that you practically have to come upon it accidentally) has a Medieval blacksmith forge still in operation. The town was a great ironworking center, and has its own parish church, dating from the 16th century. Just two miles north of León, on the banks of the río Torio, is **Navatejera**, where the ruins of a Roman villa have been discovered. The villa dates to approximately the fourth century; some mosaics from that period still survive here.

Directly west of León, nearby Carrizo has as its main attraction the **Convento de Santa María**. The figure of the Christ of Carrizo, which is found in the archaeological museum attached to Hostal de San Marcos in the city, comes from the Santa María convent. This 12th-century building, still occupied by Cistercian nuns, houses interesting sculptures.

In another direction, 51 km (32 miles) east of the city on LE 211, is **Almanza**, whose Arabic name means lookout. Located on the río Cea on the boundary between the kingdoms of Castile and León, Almanza was fortified in the 13th century. Take note of the old gate, the Arco de la Villa, that was the portal to the old walled quarter.

If you take N 601, 14 km (9 miles) southeast of the city, near the town of Villarente, you'll come to the **Monasterio Santa María de Sandoval**, founded in 1167 by Cistercian monks. Much of this building is in the Mozarabic style, particularly the entrance to the church on the left side. And the setting is lovely, too—the monastery sits where the Porma and Esla rivers flow together.

Sahagún

A worthwhile whole-day trip would be to Sahagún, an outstanding provincial city and one of the most important in León province, at least from a historical point of view (it was an important stop on the pilgrims' trek to Santiago; and it's a natural stop if you're coming from or going to Burgos). From León take N 601 south 67 km (42 miles) and then take highway N 120 for about 25 km (15.5 miles) east into the city itself. Sahagún is also due south of Almanza on route C 611.

The Moorish influence is evident here; Sahagún was the center of Mudejarism, and there are many 12th- and 13th-century churches here in this style. On calle San Francisco (probably the first main street you'll spot) are the remains of a **Benedictine monastery**. This was the richest monastery in León province in the 12th century; it was destroyed late in the 19th century, but what is left of the main façade can be seen as an entry arch.

Directly across the street is the 12th-century **Iglesia de San Tirso**, one of the first and most notable examples of Romanesque-Mudejar style in Spain. The church has three naves, a transept, a trapezoidal main chapel with half-circle apses, and a magnificent tower over the main chapel. Farther southeast, across this small town (five minutes on foot), on the plaza de San Lorenzo, is the church of the same name. Dating from the 13th century, the **Iglesia de San Lorenzo** is flawless Romanesque. It is made of brick, and has three naves and three beautifully decorated apses. The tower over the main chapel is worth a close look.

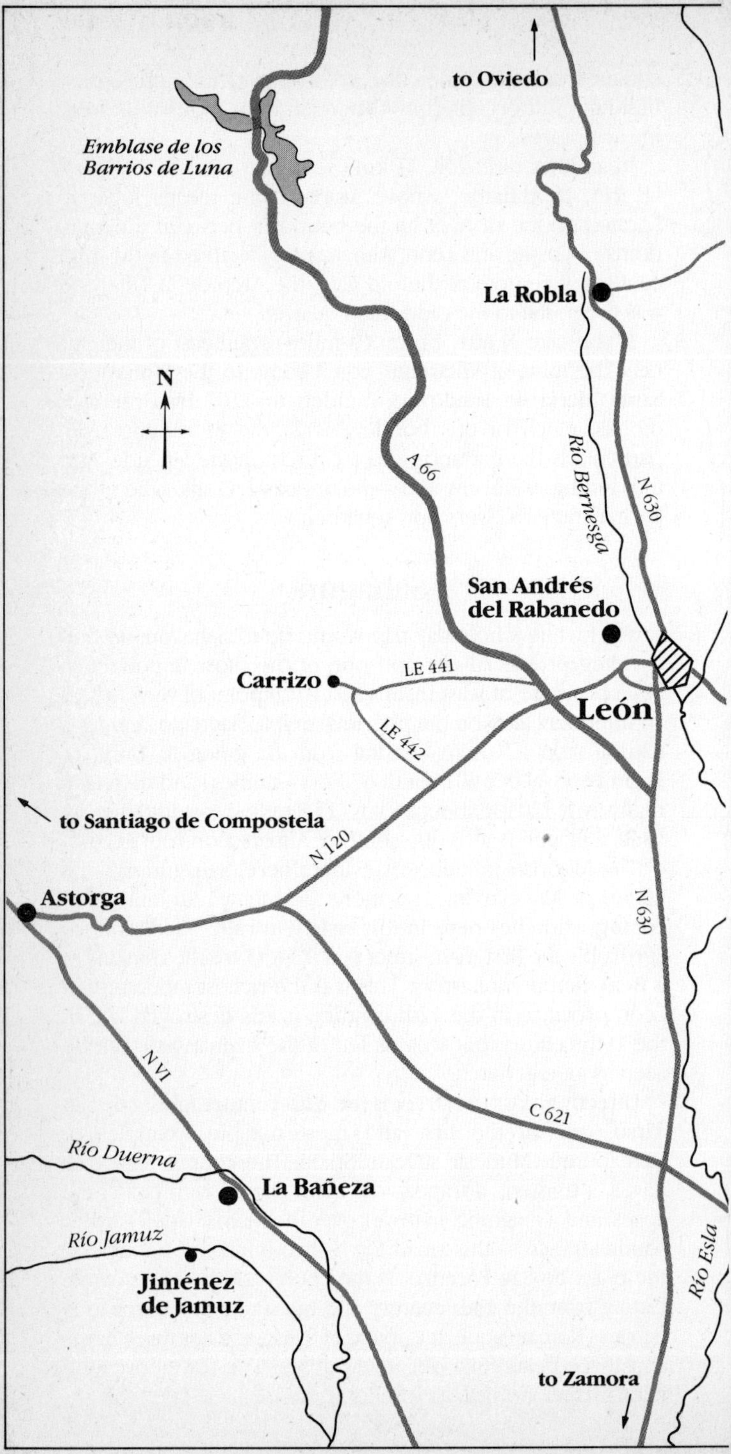
to Oviedo
Emblase de los
Barrios de Luna
La Robla
N
Río Bernesga
N 630
A 66
San Andrés
del Rabanedo
Carrizo
LE 441
León
LE 442
to Santiago de Compostela
N 120
Astorga
N 630
N VI
C 621
Río Duerna
La Bañeza
Río Jamuz
Jiménez
de Jamuz
Río Esla
to Zamora

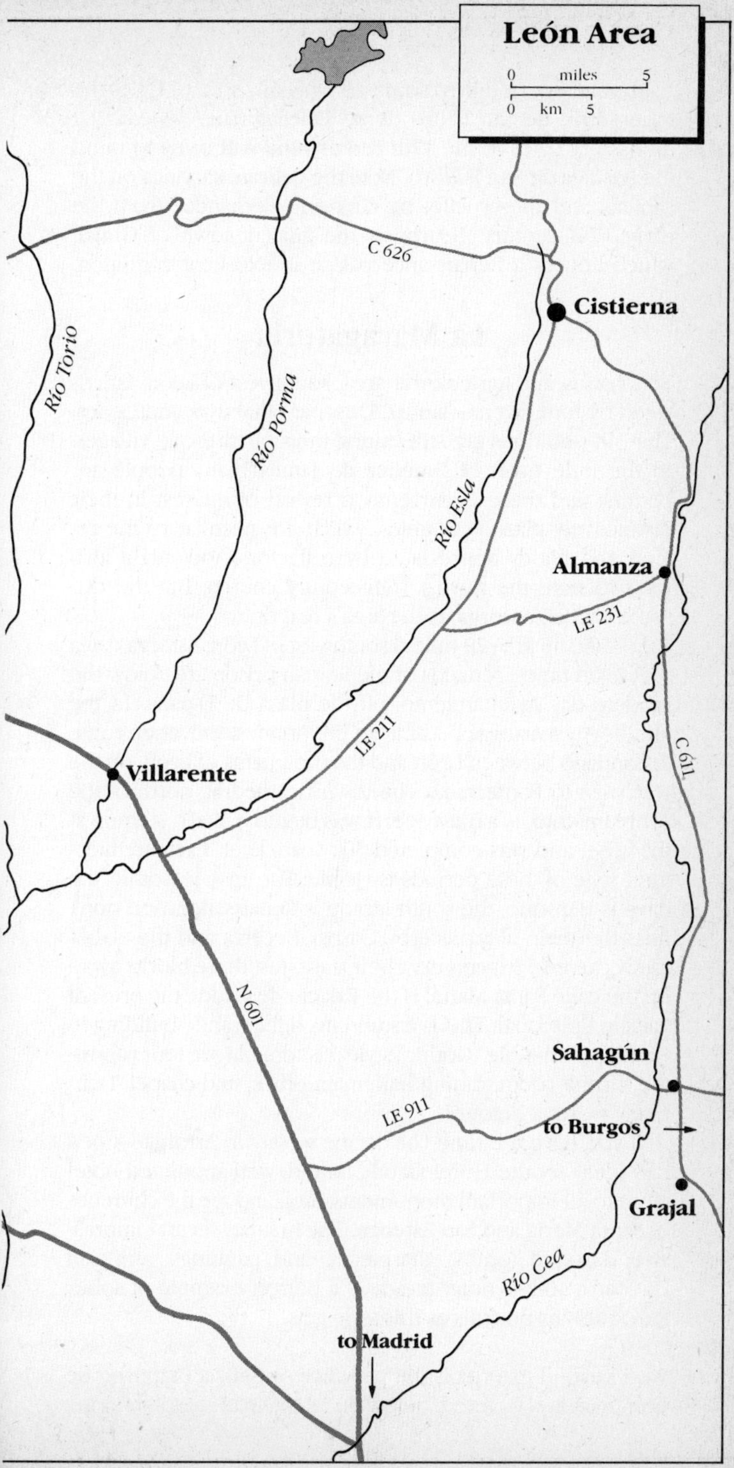

León Area
0 miles 5
0 km 5
C 626
Cistierna
Río Torio
Río Porma
Río Esla
Almanza
LE 231
LE 211
C 611
Villarente
N 601
Sahagún
LE 911
to Burgos
Grajal
Río Cea
to Madrid

About 6 km (4 miles) south of Sahagún, on C 611, lies the **Monasterio de San Pedro de las Dueñas.** This Benedictine monastery dates to the 12th century and will bring to mind the Basílica de San Isidoro. Note the delicate carvings on the capitals and the crucifix by Gregorio Fernández from the early 17th century. Nearby is the ancient town of **Grajal,** which houses a Renaissance palace in excellent condition.

La Maragatería

This handsome agricultural area, southwest of León, is irrigated by four rivers—Jamuz, Duerna, Valtabuyo, and Codes. The old traditions are still valued in its picturesque villages. In the little town of **Jiménez de Jamuz** many people are potters, and there is currently a revival of interest in their distinctively glazed ceramics, which are peculiar to the region and highly appreciated by collectors. You might also want to note the town's 16th-century church. But the district's capital, **Astorga,** is the area's real draw.

Located 46 km (29 miles) southwest of León, Astorga dates to Roman times; remains of the Roman prison are below the modern-day Ayuntamiento, off the plaza de España. In the Middle Ages Astorga became an important stopover en route to Santiago between León and the mountains of León, on the way west to Ponferrada. The town's **cathedral,** north of the Ayuntamiento, is a must-see. It was begun in 1471, starting at the apse, and was completed 300 years later. Each architectural style of these periods is visible: The apse is Gothic, the nave is Baroque, the south façade is Renaissance. And don't miss the main altarpiece by Gaspar Beçerra and the elaborately carved 15th-century choir stalls. Just three blocks away, on the calle Santa Marta, is the **Palacio de Gaudí,** the present Palacio Episcopal. This is a stunning, light-granite building in Gaudí's inimitable "Gothic" style. Visitors can see four rooms: the throne room, dining hall, main office, and chapel. Definitely worth a detour.

If you have the time (or decide to stay in Astorga—not a bad idea) try the **Hotel Gaudí,** an old, well-appointed hotel close to all important monuments. Stop and see the churches of **Santa María** and **San Esteban.** The first has several impressive Baroque tombs, altarpieces, and paintings, and San Esteban's 16th-century façade is a perfect example of sober Baroque—as no-frills as this style gets.

West beyond Astorga is the province of Galicia (Santiago de Compostela), covered below in a separate chapter along with Asturias. East of the entire León region (Salamanca–Zamora–León) is the Valladolid–Burgos segment of Old Castile. We begin our coverage of that segment with Valladolid, which is east of Zamora, and move generally northeast to Burgos.

VALLADOLID

Valladolid (from the Arabic Belad-Walid, land of the governor), located 193 km (120 miles) northwest of Madrid and 90 km (55 miles) east of Zamora, is a large provincial capital with a population of about 330,000. The city sits surrounded by wheat fields on a high plain (over 2,100 feet above sea level) at the confluence of the Pisuerga and Esgueva rivers. The area is in the middle of the famous Castilian plateau, the Meseta Central, which means that the climate of Valladolid is subject to the same extremes—bitterly cold in winter, blazing hot in summer—as the rest of Castile.

Compared to many other Spanish and even Old Castilian cities, Valladolid, founded by Count Pedro de Ansurez in 1084, one year before Toledo was recaptured from the Moors, is a latecomer. For centuries this area, including the valley of the Duero, was a no-man's-land, a buffer between the warring Moorish and Christian forces. But this former capital of Old Castile was the site of a number of important events in Spanish history, including the wedding of Ferdinand and Isabella; the death of Christopher Columbus; the births of Philip II, Philip IV, and Anne of Austria (mother of Louis XIV of France); and a three-year sojourn by Cervantes. It had the unfortunate distinction of having Napoleon use it as his headquarters during the Peninsular War. During its greatest period, in the 15th and 16th centuries, Valladolid proved fertile ground for a number of Spain's most important artists and architects.

In addition to being the center of Castile's vital agricultural region—the breadbasket and wine pitcher of this part of Spain—and a major university town, in recent years Valladolid has become highly industrialized. As new factories such as the giant Renault plant have been built, the population of the city has grown apace.

Valladolid today is crowded, and its less-than-visionary traffic patterns can make it a very difficult city to get around in, but even before the unbridled growth of the last decade or so Valladolid was no favorite of travellers. William Byron, author of a splendid biography of Cervantes, tells of a 16th-century

Dutchman who claimed that the city was full of "*picaros, putas, pleytos, polvos, piedras, puercos, perros, piojos, pulgas*—rogues, whores, lawsuits, dust, stones, swine, dogs, lice, and fleas." And 20th-century wayfarers have not upgraded the city's reputation much. Nikos Kazantzakis wrote that the city, the correct pronunciation of which is a test of proper Castilian (Vye-yah-DOH-leeth), "is like a fallen princess whose lovers all have died, and so she has had to take to industry and commerce in order to survive."

Alastair Boyd, who wrote a book detailing the artistic and cultural treasures of Castile, confessed to being "prejudiced against Valladolid for years," but pointed out that there are few places in Spain without some redeeming qualities, Valladolid included. Still, he said, "it is difficult to give a coherent account of a no longer coherent city." In many Spanish cities, the great tourist treasures are set like jewels in a necklace of old and restored buildings that accentuate an overall atmosphere of antiquity. In Valladolid the necklace is broken by modern high-rises; incongruity and incoherence reign, and the jewels—many of them less than crown jewels at that—are scattered around. Be aware, too, that the majority of the sights here are architectural; during the Peninsular War Napoleon's troops stole, burned, or wantonly hacked up a great number of artworks in the interiors of churches and other buildings. But if you are seriously interested in Spanish history, architecture, art, and culture, many of Valladolid's remaining treasures are well worth searching out.

The old quarter, the core of Valladolid where most of the city's attractions are located, is a warren of narrow streets that twist and turn and change names every couple of blocks. Consequently, it's best to walk to the many historical and architectural monuments in this town—the Museo Nacional de Escultura in the remarkable "Plateresque" Colegio de San Gregorio, the Isabelline-Gothic façade of the Iglesia de San Pablo, the Romanesque-and-Gothic Iglesia de Santa María la Antigua, the unfinished Herreran cathedral, Columbus's house, Cervantes's house, and the multitude of low-priority sights considered important enough to be listed by the Valladolid tourist office. Leave your car at your hotel, or, if you are staying outside the city and driving in for the day, put your car in one of the car parks on the west side (one in the plaza Mayor, and two more north of plaza del Poniente near río Pisuerga). Explore the old quarter on foot, and use a taxi, if you are not up for the trek, to get to the Museo Oriental in the southern part of town. Valladolid is also well served by train and bus service from Madrid and other major cities; both the train and bus stations are located south of Campo Grande park near the Museo Oriental.

We recommend staying in Tordesillas (see the next section), 30 km (19 miles) southwest, to enjoy the quiet peace of the countryside, and for easy access to the considerable backcountry attractions of Valladolid province, but if you choose to stay in the city, the most practical choice is the **Olid Meliá**, a modern hotel (renovated in 1982) with a parking garage. Besides providing perhaps the city's most comfortable accommodations, the Olid Meliá is located in the heart of the old city on the plaza San Miguel, within walking distance of most of Valladolid's major attractions. The other two hotel choices are the **Felipe IV** and the **Meliá Parque**; both are located in the southern part of Valladolid near the large Campo Grande park, the bus and train stations, and the Museo Oriental—a substantial hike from the main points of interest.

Seeing Valladolid

To find your way around this convoluted city, it is important to choose the proper maps. The tourist-office brochure map has río Pisuerga on the top of the page; a popular commercial Spanish guidebook series, *Editorial Everest,* whose map is handy because it has more streets labeled, has the Pisuerga on the bottom of the page; and the *Michelin Guide* has it correctly shown on the left, or western, side of town, where it should be.

Most entrances into Valladolid cross the Pisuerga from the west. After crossing the river you should follow paseo de Isabel la Católica and look for the car parks north of the plaza del Poniente, or if you are going to the Olid Meliá, continue to calle San Quirce, then turn right and drive four blocks to calle de León, where you turn right again, and drive two blocks southwest to the plaza de San Miguel, where the Olid Meliá and its parking garage are located.

Beginning in the morning and using the 16th-century arcaded plaza Mayor—facing a rather undistinguished city hall—as a reference point on your map, you can then decide which of the monuments you want to visit, perhaps starting with the cathedral to the east; then detouring past a number of buildings of primarily architectural interest near the cathedral; going on to visit the Museo Nacional de Escultura in the Colegio de San Gregorio and nearby San Pablo; and finishing at the Iglesia de San Benito before returning to the plaza Mayor and the many *tapas* bars in the area.

The Cathedral/University Area

From the south side of the plaza Mayor, walk east for a few blocks until you come to the **cathedral**, which was originally intended to be one of the largest churches in the world. Construction started on this still-unfinished edifice in the early 16th century, but over 50 years passed before Juan de Herrera, the famous architect of the Escorial and many other outstanding buildings in Spain, got the project going in earnest, and put the Herreran stamp on it. But Herrera's design was only partially completed—the west front and the tower—before construction languished again, this time until the 18th century, when Alberto Churriguera, with his unique vision of Baroque, added the portion of the façade above the main portal, a touch that, strangely enough, meshed very well with Herrera's austere style. This church sorely needs at least one more tower (out of the four originally planned) for symmetry, and the interior was never finished; for instance, the Latin Cross floor plan never even reached the crossing. The high altar, by Juan de Juni, who is well represented in the Museo Nacional de Escultura, was originally carved in 1572 for the Iglesia de Santa María la Antigua.

Because work on the cathedral was stopped, several sections of the existing collegiate church from early periods were saved. The fine **diocesan museum** is installed here; you can see Mudejar designs, Romanesque tombs, and Gothic doors in the chapel of San Llorent. The sacristy contains one of Toledan silversmith Juan de Arfe's major pieces, a huge four-tiered silver monstrance from the late 16th century.

Southeast from the cathedral is the **Universidad**, whose Baroque façade surrounding the main portal was done by Narciso Tomé in 1715. As Alastair Boyd points out, during this period Spanish architects such as Tomé, who did the Transparente in Toledo, and the Churrigueras, with their wildly extravagant altarpieces, were still relatively sober in their decoration of exteriors. Artists such as Tomé were in transition, still restrained by the power, weight, and conservatism of Herrera's influence, but in the end, just as florid Gothic gave way in Spain to Plateresque, what was once confined to altarpieces, as Boyd puts it, "moved cheerfully outwards from the *retablos* to the façades." Spanish decoration would eventually degenerate into Rococo, but not yet. The façade of the Universidad de Valladolid would like to take off, but it is anchored firmly by four unadorned columns, set on square pedestals, to the no-nonsense conservative building it decorates.

Around the corner to the southeast of the Universidad, the Colegio de Santa Cruz represents the late-15th-century Renaissance style of Enrique de Egás, and just northeast, along calle del Cardenal Mendoza, which becomes calle Colón, is Christopher Columbus's house.

In 1506 Columbus died in Valladolid, a broken man; "If I had stolen the Indies and given them to the Moors, Spain could not have shown me greater enmity." The house where he died was demolished in the 1960s, then completely rebuilt to house the **Columbus museum**, whose most interesting displays are the wall plans of the great admiral's three voyages, and some artifacts from his New World discoveries.

Just behind the cathedral to the north is the early-14th-century Gothic **Iglesia de Santa María la Antigua**, with a Romanesque portico and an exceptional 11th-century Romanesque tower. This *conjunto* works beautifully; Santa María la Antigua is one of the finest buildings in the city. A block northwest is the early-17th-century Iglesia de Nuestra Señora de las Angustias (anguish), which contains Juan de Juni's celebrated *Virgen de los Cuchillos* (Virgin of the knives), a polychrome statue of the Virgin Mary clutching her breast, into which enough silver daggers have been plunged to cause anguish indeed.

The Colegio de San Gregorio

Located northeast of the plaza Mayor, and just two blocks northeast of the Olid Meliá, are two of Valladolid's main attractions: the Colegio de San Gregorio, the remarkable, incredibly ornate (Jan Morris called it "almost edible"), late-15th-century Isabelline-Gothic building in which the Museo Nacional de Escultura is housed, and, next to it, the equally ornate Isabelline Iglesia de San Pablo.

Both these pre-Renaissance buildings are often called Plateresque, but they are not. They preceded Plateresque and obviously contributed to its development, but they were executed by foreign architects and stonemasons inspired—according to Professor Denning of Trinity College in Dublin—by the kind of decoration then commonly used on the title pages of books and by the woodcarvings done for the altarpieces of the period. It is to this, not to the silversmiths who inspired Plateresque decoration, that we owe the remarkable style in these two structures.

The 15th-century **Iglesia de San Pablo**, which preceded San Gregorio and is even more detailed (if that is possible), was added to in the early 17th century by the duke of Lerma, whose coat of arms can be seen on the façade. The French looted and destroyed the original interior during the Peninsular War, but a striking pair of Isabelline doorways remains in the since-restored church.

The Colegio de San Gregorio, commissioned by the prelate of Palencia, Bishop Alonso de Burgos, confessor to Queen Isabella, was built between 1488 and 1496. The façade, like that of San Pablo, looks like a giant florid Gothic altarpiece, except that the figures, including the huge heraldic emblems of Castile and León, are largely secular. The delicacy and intricacy of much of the stonework, obviously an exceptionally laborious accomplishment, is amazing. San Gregorio's architect was Juan Güas, but the decoration of the façade has been attributed variously to others: to Enrique de Egás; to Simón de Colonia, who planned the splendid La Cartuja de Miraflores and Capilla de los Condestables in Burgos, and did the façade on the Iglesia de San Pablo, which preceded San Gregorio by a few years; and to the great Gil de Siloé, believed to have been a native of Antwerp, who worked on both Miraflores and the cathedral in Burgos with Simón, and is believed to have worked on the church at Aranda de Duero with him as well. Many experts opt for a collaboration among these foreign artists, for whom, as Sacheverell Sitwell describes, "It is the 'Espagnolade' of a foreigner, as much so as the drawings of Gustave Doré or the music of *Carmen*."

The great patio of San Gregorio is exceptionally rich. Beautifully turned barley-sugar columns support a second-floor gallery of archways filled with profusely decorated, intricately carved stone balconies, each with three short columns supporting a double-arched, heavily decorated panel. Running below the gargoyle-studded roofline is a frieze decorated with a repetitive yoke-and-arrows (the symbol of Isabella and Ferdinand) motif that is broken at each corner by the coat of arms of the unified kingdoms of Castilla, León, and Aragón.

The **Museo Nacional de Escultura** (national museum of sculpture) in San Gregorio is filled with polychrome wood statues (many with meticulously detailed bleeding wounds); complete tableaux representing biblical scenes; Holy Week processional *pasos* (floats); entire altarpieces; paintings; and even an entire set of carved wooden choir stalls, done by Gil de Siloé, Alonso Berruguete, Juan de Juni, Gregorio Fernández, Pedro de Mena, and others. The museum is to Valladolid, as one book put it, "what the Prado is to Madrid."

One of the masterpieces in the museum's collection is the early-16th-century altarpiece by Alonso Berruguete, who,

Alastair Boyd claims, was "the only inspired artist of the Spanish Renaissance." Berruguete spent five years working in Florence and was greatly influenced by Michelangelo (he was mentioned in the master's letters), Leonardo da Vinci (he was in Florence when Leonardo was painting the *Mona Lisa*), and Raphael; he returned to Spain to become the greatest Spanish sculptor of the 16th century.

Originally built for Valladolid's Iglesia de San Benito, Berruguete's retable, now dismantled and displayed in three rooms on the ground floor of the museum, measured over 50 feet high. The museum also displays another exceptional altarpiece taken from the Convento de la Mejorada in Olmedo, several first-rate pieces including the superb statues *San Sebastián* and *The Sacrifice of Isaac,* and a fine *Nativity* painting, all by Berruguete, whose talents did not stop here: He also did part of the woodcarving on the upper parts of the magnificent choir stalls in the Toledo cathedral.

The Frenchman from Champagne, Juan de Juni, whose work can also be seen in the cathedral and in the Iglesia de Nuestra Señora de las Angustias here, is represented in this museum by one of his most highly regarded works, the *Entombment of Christ,* and by a good *John the Baptist.* Gregorio Fernández, who in the early 17th century carried Juni's Illusionism even further by using human teeth, glass eyes, and graphically depicted bleeding wounds to get his point across, is very well represented here, but a little bit of Fernández goes a long way. His *Cristo Yacente* (Christ reclining) here is just one of a number of profusely bleeding Cristos—shown reclining, in Pietà tableaux, and hanging from the Cross—done by this prolific artist and scattered throughout Valladolid.

Other notable works in this museum, where the pieces are beautifully displayed and well lighted, are Pedro de Mena's fine 17th-century statue of Mary Magdalene; the bronze statues of the duke and duchess of Lerma kneeling, whose models were done by Pompeo Leoni and cast by Juan de Arfe; and the richly detailed, carved wooden choir stalls by Diego de Siloé, son of Gil de Siloé and creator of the great golden staircase in the Burgos cathedral. There are also two fine Hispano-Flemish paintings from the 15th century: one of San Jerónimo, which was in the Convento de la Mejorada in Olmedo, and the other of Santiago, dressed as a pilgrim with his staff and a scallop shell on his hat, and San Andrés, with an X-shaped Saint Andrew's cross.

Also facing the plaza de San Pablo, besides the San Pablo church and San Gregorio, is the Palacio de Pimentel, where

Philip II was born. Around the corner, northeast of San Gregorio, is the Casa del Sol, which has a 16th-century minor Plateresque façade. Also in this area, but not worth detours unless you are a very serious student, are the Palacio de Vivero (rebuilt in the 16th century), where Ferdinand and Isabella were married in 1469; the home of the 19th-century poet and playwright José Zorilla, author of *Don Juan Tenorio;* and, farther west past the plaza de San Miguel, the massive façade of the 15th-century Iglesia de San Benito. This church is only a couple of blocks from the plaza de Poniente to the west, and the plaza Mayor to the south.

South of the Plaza Mayor

South of the plaza Mayor is calle de Santiago, the major shopping street of Valladolid, with its own special twist, a place called **Centro Commercial las Francesas**, which has a number of shops surrounding the cloister of an old nunnery. The Iglesia de Santiago on this street contains a fine retable by Alonso Berruguete. At the southern end of calle Santiago is the plaza de Zorilla, which forms the northern tip of the triangular-shaped **Campo Grande** park, an oasis of trees, fountains, flower gardens, and pleasant walks. Located at the southern end of the park, the convent of the Order of the Philippines houses an interesting **Museo Oriental**, which has a fine collection put together by Augustinian missionaries stationed in the Far East.

Valladolid was the capital of Spain for five years (1601–1606) under Philip III after the city bribed the duke of Lerma, the royal favorite, with 400,000 ducats to move the court from Madrid. Miguel de Cervantes Saavedra spent three years in Valladolid during this period in a house on calle del Rastro. William Byron, author of the definitive biography of Cervantes, describes what the building was like in those days: ". . . one of five new houses jerry built by a small-bore speculator hoping to cash in on an influx of riffraff into the city. It was an instant slum." Cervantes, along with more than 20 of his relatives, friends, and perhaps a down-at-the-heels servant or two, crowded into 13 rooms above an old tavern that was the hangout for butchers from the nearby slaughterhouse.

The **Casa de Cervantes** is located two-and-a-half blocks southeast of plaza de Zorilla at calle del Rastro 7. Don't expect to be moved by the spirit of the great writer in today's contrived surroundings, however; the house is more interesting as a refurbished 17th-century dwelling, certainly in better shape now than it was in those days, than as a Cervantes museum. Besides, by the time Cervantes moved here, *Don Quixote* was already finished and in the hands of his publisher, Francisco de Robles, who had moved to Valladolid from Madrid to be close to the real money—in this epoque certainly—around the supremely corrupt duke of Lerma and the court of Philip III. Cervantes was arrested in this house, though, after the mysterious death of a nobleman wounded in the dangerous streets of this quarter. Cervantes and his family helped the man into their apartments, where he died two days later, and when no one could put a finger on the man's assailant, Cervantes and several members of his family were arrested, albeit briefly, thus adding Valladolid to the list of jails—Algiers, Castro del Río, and Seville—that the great writer had graced with his presence—most unjustly.

Dining in Valladolid

Next door to Casa de Cervantes is **Mesón Cervantes**, Rastro 6, for over two decades a good Castilian restaurant serving typical dishes to the *Vallisoletanos,* as the people of Valladolid are called, and to those who come looking for the spirit of the author of *Don Quixote.* Besides classic Castilian dishes such as roast suckling pig, lamb dishes, *pisto, menestra,* and traditional stews of the region (a house specialty), you can get game dishes—rabbit, partridge, venison, and wild boar—and fresh fish and shellfish from the Cantabrian coast.

Just around the corner from Mesón Cervantes, one block to the southwest, is **Mesón Panero**, Marina Escobar 1, where traditional Castilian and Leonese cuisine reigns supreme, especially during the gastronomic festival run by this restaurant each February. Artfully prepared dishes such as beans with pigeon, lamb sweetbreads with clams, stuffed pheasant, rabbit with thyme, and Castilian stew, accompanied by a fine white wine from nearby Rueda, a local Cigales *rosado,* or a superb Ribera del Duero red from Mauro, Pesquera, or Vega Sicilia, will reward hearty appetites.

La Fragua, paseo de Zorilla 10 (just west of Campo Grande), considered the best restaurant in the province, strikes a balance between refined versions of authentic Castilian dishes and modern cuisine, all served in a beautifully, and expensively, decorated Castilian atmosphere. Here you can get impeccably prepared standards such as *lechazo asado* and *cochinillo asado,* as well as fresh Cantabrian fish, "grandma's" veal *morcilla,* leeks stuffed with shellfish, and oxtail cooked with *aguardiente.* Homemade tarts, chocolate truffles, and figs stuffed with nuts beckon from the dessert menu. From one of the best wine lists in Castile you can try the marvelous new wines of the up-and-coming Ribera del Duero, or, if you have a well-upholstered wallet, you can select an older vintage of Vega Sicilia, Spain's rarest and most expensive wine, a distinguished red once praised by Winston Churchill.

Santy, Manzano 4 (just north of the plaza Mayor on a street running along the east side of city hall), with only nine tables, is an old-style tavern-restaurant decorated with tiles. It serves a very hearty version of Castilian home cooking, with dishes such as oxtail with potatoes, hake in batter, and *solomillo* (steak).

Harry Debelius, a veteran journalist who has lived in Madrid for many years, succinctly describes Valladolid as "Dullsville," but you may find the lively evening *tapas*-bar scene around the plaza Mayor to your liking. Try **Taberna Pan con Tomate** on the plaza or **Caballo da Troya,** a typical Castilian tavern, at calle Correo 1, northwest of city hall and near the post office. Surprisingly, there are often good flamenco festivals in Valladolid, partly due to a heightened national interest in this colorful Andalusian folk art and partly due, possibly, to an influx of Andalusians escaping to Valladolid's factories from their home region's high unemployment rate. Look for posters around town and newspaper announcements of upcoming performances. The **Casino de Castilla y León,** featuring blackjack, roulette, *chemin de fer,* and so on, is in Boecillo, 12 km (7.5 miles) south of town on N 403, the highway to Madrid. The casino has a restaurant and a nightclub.

Semana Santa (Holy Week) is a very big attraction in Valladolid, and the processions, during which many of the pieces in the Museo Nacional de Escultura are carried through the streets, are much more somber and serious even than those of Andalusia. The big fiesta in Valladolid is San Mateo in September, featuring major bullfights.

VALLADOLID PROVINCE

One of the best ways to approach the province (and the city) of Valladolid, which has a number of historical sites and castles, is to make your base at the **Parador Nacional de Tordesillas,** a modern, comfortable building with Castilian furnishings and a swimming pool, located 30 km (18.5

Valladolid Area
0 miles 10
0 km 10
N 120
Carrión de los Condes
980
Villalcazar de Sirga
Frómista
Castrojeriz
Río Carrión
N 611
E 3 N 620
to Burgos
Monzón de Campos
N 610
Palencia
Autilla del Pino
to León
Baños de Cerrato
Medina de Rioseco
Dueñas
to Aranda de Duero
N 601
E 3 N 620
Río Pisuegra
Cigales
Río Esgueva
C 611
Fuensaldaña
San Bernardo
Wamba
Valbuena de Duero
Pesquera de Duero
VA 514
Torrelobatón
Valladolid
Simancas
N 122
Quintanilla de Onésimo
to Zamora
Tudela de Duero
Río Duero
Tordesillas
Peñafiel
Río Duraton
N 403
Serrada
to Salamanca
La Seca
N 601
Rueda
C 610
Nava del Rey
Medina del Campo
Olmedo
N VI
N
Segovia
to Madrid

miles) southwest of Valladolid, just outside of the town of Tordesillas on N 620, the road to Salamanca. There is nothing to do here at night except have dinner and read, but that is often a blessing after traversing the broad expanses of Castile all day. Townsend Miller's entertaining novelesque history *The Castles and the Crown,* which chronicles in *Dynasty* soap-opera fashion the incredibly rich history of the events that occurred in this region during the 15th and 16th centuries, is an excellent scene-setter for the next day's outing. For dinner, there is the dining room of the parador, which serves typical regional cuisine, or the only decent restaurant in town, **El Torreon**, in the center of town at the junction of the Valladolid and Zamora roads, where you can get a good salad, lamb chops cooked on an open-hearth grill in the dining room, and a fine bottle of Ribera del Duero or Rioja.

Fortified by one of the parador's huge buffet breakfasts, you can set out in practically any direction and find a castle or historic town that figured prominently in the epoch of Ferdinand and Isabella and Charles V. **Tordesillas**, itself one of the most historic towns in the region, stands on the banks of the Duero. Several crucial events in the history of Spain took place here, including the signing of the treaty of Tordesillas (the Line of Demarcation) in 1494, arbitrated by Pope Alexander VI, which caused South America to be split between Spain and Portugal. Juana la Loca, the mad daughter of Isabella and Ferdinand, and heir to the throne, who carried her husband Philip the Fair's lime-covered corpse all over Castile with her for years, was confined in the castle-palace (now destroyed) of Tordesillas for 46 years during the 16th century. The town was one of the centers of the *comuneros* revolt, and the leaders of the uprising came here to put Juana on the throne, but she was too out of touch to be of any use to them.

Back in the 14th century, Pedro the Cruel ("cruel and sensual, more a sultan than a Christian prince," as one Spanish writer described him)—to placate his mistress, María de Padilla, who pined for the warmth of Seville and the Moorish south—brought Moorish carpenters and masons from Seville and Toledo here to work on the palace (originally built by his father, Alfonso XI) that is now the **Convento de Santa Clara**. The craftsmen furnished the palace with a Mudejar façade and a spectacular ceiling that lives up to Townsend Miller's description: "a gorgeous dome of Moorish *artesonado* which burns and glitters like the star-strewn vault of some blazing Oriental night." The patio has Moorish horseshoe arches and

Moorish tiles and inscriptions; and, of course, there are the Moorish baths, so loved by María in Seville's Alcázar, of which this place is highly reminiscent. All of this remained hidden in the cloistered convent until the beginning of this century, when special authorization was obtained for a visit by King Alfonso XIII, which led to the discovery of its treasures by the outside world, and the subsequent restoration of Santa Clara. The convent sits on a hill above the río Duero and its multiarched Medieval bridge, and looks out over fields and vineyards to the south toward Medina del Campo and the Castillo de la Mota (see below). The guided tour of the convent, along with a brief walk through Tordesillas and a coffee in a bar in the arcaded plaza Mayor, from which you can admire the Herreran tower of the Iglesia de Santa María, can be handled in a pleasant hour in the morning before you set off to explore the Castilian countryside.

Castle Towns and Wine Villages

As Alastair Boyd wrote, "Our slavery to the industrial civilization we have created compels us to seek space, light, air and architecture that stands properly against the sky." All around Tordesillas is castle country, where the architecture does stand out against the sky. This is the Old Castile of the harsh, treeless landscape and austere spirit, a far cry from the jasmine-perfumed pleasure gardens of the south, but this austerity is crowned by a number of impressive castles, old churches, and other powerful evocations of an illustrious history.

Just south of Tordesillas is Rueda wine country, which was once known for its Sherry-like fortified wines but which, in the last decade, has become better known for its dry white table wines. Many of the wineries in Rueda and the Ribera del Duero, northeast of Tordesillas and southeast of Valladolid, are small family-run operations. They are not equipped for formal tours, nor do they have English-speaking public-relations directors, slick brochures, or pristine tasting rooms, but that is part of their charm and authenticity. Obviously, you will get more out of your winery visits here if you speak some Spanish.

The town of **Rueda**, a few miles south of Tordesillas on N VI (the road to Medina del Campo), and its satellite towns of La Seca, Serrada, and Nava del Rey form the heart of the Rueda wine district. You can drop in on one of several stores in Rueda or stop at a *bodega* (the best times for visitors are usually from 10:00 A.M. to 12:00 noon and from 4:00 A.M. to

6:00 P.M. on weekdays) to sample some of Spain's best white wines. At the north edge of town on N VI is a large modern *bodega,* **Vinos Blancos de Castilla**, where Marqués de Riscal, the famous Rioja producer, makes a good Rueda white. At the southern edge of town on the same highway is **Vinos Sanz**, where one of the region's most innovative winemen, Antonio Sanz, makes a wide range of white, rosé, red, and fortified wines, including his own Rueda Superior white, a good red called Almirante, and the highly rated Cabernet Sauvignon of Marqués de Griñon, whose grapes come from an estate near Toledo. Sanz has a tasting room where you can also buy wines.

If you speak Spanish, try to visit the winery of **Angel Rodríguez**, 6 km (4 miles) east of Rueda at La Seca. (In the center of Rueda there are clearly marked road signs to La Seca; once there you will have to ask someone to direct you to the winery.) It's advisable to call ahead; Tel: (983) 86-81-17. Don't be put off by the unassuming (and unmarked) entrance to the place. This an artisan family winery, not a slick commercial enterprise; the underground caves where Angel Rodríguez makes his excellent Martinsancho white wines are beautifully rustic, not the kind of place you often get a chance to see. To give you a taste of wine, Señor Rodríguez merely plucks a quill from a hole in one of the big barrels coopered down here many years ago, and catches the arching green-gold liquid in a glass.

South of Rueda on N VI lies the great Medieval market town of Castile, **Medina del Campo**, whose huge 15th-century Mudejar **Castillo de la Mota**, where Cesare Borgia was once imprisoned, and where Queen Isabella is popularly believed to have died (she actually died in Medina in a house next door to the Ayuntamiento on the plaza Mayor), is one of the most impressive castles in Spain.

East of Medina is the historic town of **Olmedo**, where several important battles were fought, including the pivotal battle of Olmedo in 1445 for control of Castile that pitted the armies of Juan II of Castile (father of Isabella I) and his powerful favorite, Alvaro de Luna, against the forces of the Infantes de Aragón. Castile's forces carried the day, insuring that Castile, not Catalan Aragón, would be the dominant force in Spain. The town still has sections of its old walls, the 13th-century churches of San Andrés and San Miguel, and the Convento de la Mejorada, where Isabella spent the last spring of her life in 1504, and where Berruguete did the fine altarpiece that is now in Valladolid.

North of Tordesillas, and within a few miles of Valladolid,

you can tour the castle towns of Simancas, Torrelobatón, and Fuensaldaña, all of which have their well-preserved castles standing "properly against the sky."

Simancas, 19 km (12 miles) northeast of Tordesillas and 11 km (7 miles) southeast of Valladolid on N 620, was a Roman town, and because of its strategic situation at the confluence of the Pisuerga and Duero rivers has seen a lot of history since. In 939 forces led by Ramiro II of León and Count Fernán González of Castile won a decisive battle over Abd ar-Rahman III here, even capturing the caliph's personal illuminated copy of the Koran. A superb, ancient 17-arch bridge, albeit a narrow one, still carries traffic over the Pisuerga. The watchtower on the bridge was the dividing line between the Christian and Moorish kingdoms for a while in the 11th century.

Originally built by the Moors in the ninth century, the historic **Castillo de Simancas**, reconstructed in the 13th century and again in the 15th, was set up by Philip II as the national archives and now houses over 30 million documents dating from the reigns of Ferdinand and Isabella through 1808, when Napoleon had many of them carted off to Paris. Most of the documents not destroyed (countless ones were used to build fires or merely thrown away) were returned a few years later, and the rest found their way back here in 1942, returned by Marshal Pétain. Here you can see the marriage contracts of Ferdinand and Isabella, and of Philip II and Mary Tudor, as well as the document appointing Columbus admiral, and an incredible wealth of documents bearing the signatures of many of Spain's greatest figures.

The 14th-century **Castillo de Torrelobatón**, north of Tordesillas on C 611 (the road to Medina de Rioseco), was the last stronghold of the *comuneros* before their defeat at Villalar, ten miles to the southeast. This castle, with its well-restored walls, square donjon, and round towers, is simple in design, dignified and stately. It can be seen for miles across the wheat fields, dominating the small village below its towers. A few miles northeast of Torrelobatón, on a secondary road that leads to Fuensaldaña, is Wamba, the site of the 13th-century **Iglesia de Santa María**, which contains the important remains of a tenth-century Mozarabic church with horseshoe arches. This church contains the tomb of Recceswinth, the Visigothic king of Spain who died here in 672 and was succeeded by Wamba, who took his oath on the dead king's tomb.

The beautiful 15th-century **Castillo de Fuensaldaña**, with its imposing keep, located 20 km (12.5 miles) northeast of

Wamba along this secondary road (and only 8 km/5 miles northwest of Valladolid), was built by Alfonso Pérez de Vivero, treasurer of Juan II of Castile, who so provoked the royal favorite, Alvaro de Luna, that Luna tossed him headfirst off a tower in Burgos. Luna was beheaded for the crime in Valladolid.

Fuensaldaña also has two restaurants, **Bodega la Nieta** and **Bodega la Sorbona**, both with dining rooms dug into caves in the hill, and both serving typical Castilian dishes such as *embutidos* (charcuterie), stews, lamb chops, and grilled steaks. You might want to range a few miles beyond Fuensaldaña to the northeast to **Cigales**, where you can sample the town's excellent rosé wines in a bar near the huge Renaissance church by Juan de Herrera.

Peñafiel and the Red-Wine Villages

Tudela de Duero, 14 km (9 miles) southeast of Valladolid just off N 122, has nothing of architectural interest except a 16th-century church, but it does have one of the great new wineries in Spain, **Bodegas Mauro**, located on the town's main street at calle Cervantes 12, at the western end of town not far from the river. The winery, which is unique in having both underground and second-floor aging rooms, is installed in an ancient house remodeled especially for the purpose by one of the winery's partners, Luciano Suárez. Suárez is an architect who specializes in restoring ancient buildings, and is so good at it that he has been entrusted with the restoration of some of Spain's greatest architectural treasures, including the splendid Monasterio de Santo Domingo de Silos (more on this later).

Mauro's red wines, while not technically from the *denominación de origen* Ribera del Duero (Tudela is just outside the boundary), are some of the best wines of this region. To arrange a visit to Bodegas Mauro in Tudela de Duero, it is best to call ahead; Tel: (983) 68-02-65. If you are coming from the east, stop at the *bodega*'s roadside sales office, just down the road from Vega Sicilia at Quintanilla de Onesimo, 20 km (12.5 miles) east of Tudela on N 122.

In Tudela de Duero there is an exceptional unheralded restaurant, simply called **Mesón 2,39** at Antonio Machado 39, Tel: (983) 52-07-34, which serves excellent regional cuisine. Start with superb home-cured olives; then, especially in springtime, try the *esparragos de Tudela* (these are even better than the exceptional asparagus of the other Tudela in Navarra); have *chuletillas de cordero* with potatoes and fried green peppers; and finish with Tudela strawberries followed by coffee and one of Mesón 2,39's house *aguardientes,* in which pineapple, cherries, peaches, or other fruits have been marinated. Try the excellent Mauro 1986 or a bottle of Vega Sicilia Valbuena with your meal.

Vega Sicilia (founded 1864), where Spain's most exotic and expensive wine is made, is officially in the municipality of Valbuena de Duero, but the winery itself is just east of Quintanilla de Onesimo, 40 km (25 miles) east of Valladolid on N 122. For decades Vega Sicilia has enjoyed a legendary niche in the pantheon of world wines (Winston Churchill is claimed to have thought it was a fine Bordeaux; it does have some Cabernet Sauvignon in it). Although it can be found on the wine lists of Spain's greatest restaurants, relatively few people have had much experience with the wine, because of its scarcity and its extraordinarily high price. Vega Sicilia makes three red wines: Valbuena third year, Valbuena fifth year, and Vega Sicilia "Unico," which has been known to spend up to 23 years in barrel. The wines are tremendous, powerful, and deeply colored; they finish with long, deep, spicy flavors that smooth out with food. Call ahead (Tel: 983-68-01-47), except in August when the winery is closed, to arrange a visit.

After Valbuena de Duero, just northeast and across the Duero from the Vega Sicilia winery on the river's north bank, a few miles to the east on N 122, next to the small modern farm village of San Bernardo, is the 12th-century Cistercian **Abadía de Santa María de Valbuena.** As you will see from its size, this abbey was once a very important church. It may also have been extremely important to the viticulture of this region; the Cistercians, who also founded the great Clos de Vougeot in Burgundy, may have brought cuttings of the supernal Burgundian red wine grape Pinot Noir to this region. The Pinot Noir may well have become acclimatized over the centuries into what is now the Tinto Fino, the main grape of the Ribera del Duero that is responsible for Vega Sicilia, Mauro, Pesquera, Pedrosa, and the other great red wines of this region.

Continuing a few miles east on this road, you will soon reach Pesquera de Duero, home of one of the brightest new stars on the Spanish wine scene, **Pesquera.** Since Robert Parker, an influential American wine writer, compared Pesquera's red wines to Château Petrus a few years ago, this modest winery has rocketed to fame, and the owner, Alejandro Fernández, now travels the world promoting his wines. He recently sold a large order of Pesquera to his old friend Julio Iglesias—not bad for a man who started out as a blacksmith. Ask Señor Fernández to show you the old Roman-style winepress, where his first vintages were made. To visit Pesquera, call (Tel: 983-88-10-27) or write ahead to Bodegas Alejandro Fernández, 47315 Pesquera de Duero (Valladolid) or, in the United States, write or call Pesquera's American agent, Classical Wines of Spain, 4000 Aurora Avenue North, Suite 118, Seattle, Washington 98103, Tel: (206) 547-0255, to arrange a visit to Pesquera or several other top Ribera del Duero wineries represented by this importer, who is a major discoverer of fine small producers in Spain. (Note: It is absolutely imperative that you confirm your visit to any of these wineries by telephone the day before.)

The town of **Peñafiel**, 56 km (35 miles) east of Valladolid on the way to Aranda de Duero and just a few miles south of Pesquera de Duero (note the ancient bridge over the Duero just north of Peñafiel), is the only town of real touristic merit on the way to Aranda (see below) from Valladolid. The long, narrow, white-gray, 14th-century **Castillo de Peñafiel** (castle of the faithful rock) on the hill above the town is like a battleship in the sky, plowing through the clouds instead of waves. The castle, whose origins date to the tenth century, is one of the best preserved and most impressive remnants of Spain's military power during the centuries-long drive to push the Moors out of the Iberian Peninsula. Try to see it in the evening, when the golden rays of the setting sun intensify the drama of the mighty fortress standing out against the sky, as a herd of sheep grazes across the hill beneath it.

Peñafiel itself is a fascinating and lively old market town with loads of atmosphere. In addition to the castle, the town has a number of impressive old churches (especially the 14th-century Iglesia de San Pablo, with a Mudejar apse) and ancient buildings scattered along its steep, narrow streets. The plaza del Coso, an unpaved square plaza—surrounded by three-story balconied houses with shuttered multipaned windows—still serves as the town bullring. Along río Duratón, which flows through town and meets the Duero here, there are inhabited millhouses, which generate electricity from the rushing waters and have their own little gardens and cherry trees along the river. The stone *zarceras* (ventilation chimneys) leading to undergound wine caves burrowed into the hill (see below, Ribera de Burgos Wine Country) are a prominent feature in Peñafiel. Here the *zarceras* dot the castle hill, which is a warren of undergound *bodegas,* and some even project from the steep streets.

Mesón Mauro (no relation to Bodegas Mauro), on calle Ataranzas (ask), one of the high streets leading to the castle, is one of the best *asadores* (roast houses) in the region. The brick oven is in the dining room, so you are right in the middle of the action, experiencing the sight, sound, and delicious smell of lamb as it is roasted for you. Salad, a plate of local cheese and *chorizo,* a quarter of roast baby lamb, a pitcher of Mesón Mauro's house wine—perhaps one of the best house wines in the world—from a local producer, and a clay pot of *cuajada* (a mild custard-like sheep's curd, sweetened to taste with wild honey) for dessert is the repast here, and the object of many a pilgrimage.

PALENCIA PROVINCE

The province of Palencia is one of the least visited in Spain. Ostensibly, there is little here of major historic and architectural interest except a few spots on the Camino de Santiago and the seventh-century Visigothic Iglesia de San Juan de Baños. However, to diligent travellers bent on discovering the undersung and little-explored, Palencia, with its tranquil back roads, ancient churches of the Campos Góticos (fields of the Goths), little-known Medieval towns, and sleepy brown villages, offers rewards of the spirit not always found in the more heavily touristed areas that command the most publicity.

Dueñas, north of Valladolid just off N 620, only 17 km (10.5 miles) south of Palencia, is a reasonably well-preserved village that retains some of its Medieval walls and gates. Although Isabella and Ferdinand first met in the Palacio de Vivero in Valladolid, the same place where they were married, the local tradition is that they were secretly married here in Dueñas—due to the lengths to which political enemies were willing to go to prevent their union—before the public ceremony in Valladolid. During the turbulent political period just after their marriage, they lived here for a short time, where they also held court and had their first child, Isabella. The 13th-century **Iglesia de Santa María de la Asunción** retains some vestiges of its Romanesque roots and contains late-15th-century Isabelline tombs, a 16th-century Gothic altarpiece, and a tower from the late 16th century.

A few miles north of Dueñas, and just south of Palencia, is **Baños de Cerrato** (look for signs on the eastern side of the road), whose little seventh-century **church of San Juan de Baños**, built by the same King Recceswinth whose tomb is at

Wamba, stands at the edge of a field (follow the signs, turn right after you cross the railway, and follow the road to the end of the village). San Juan de Baños is one of the most important Visigothic monuments in Spain; the modified horseshoe arches in the church may predate the arrival of the Moorish horseshoe arch in Spain. The arches rest on Roman columns taken, like much of the stone for the church, from an earlier Roman temple nearby. You will probably have to track down the priest who lives nearby to be let into the church.

The City of Palencia

Palencia, the capital city (population 76,000), located 47 km (29 miles) north of Valladolid on N 611, sits on the banks of the little río Carrión surrounded by the vast high plain and great wheat field, the Tierra de Campos, also shared by Valladolid, León, and Zamora (on clear days from a hill near Autilla del Pino, 11 miles southwest of Palencia, you can see over 30 miles in all directions out over the Tierra de Campos). Because most of the province *is* a plain, the buildings in this region, especially remarkable for church towers and castles, do not soar like buildings in other parts of Spain; perhaps they didn't need the height from which to detect the approach of an army. This is true even in the capital, which tends to have an odd overall horizontal feel that seems reflected in its earthbound, conservative inhabitants.

Palencia's Gothic **cathedral** was built during the 14th to 16th centuries and was decorated by some of the greatest artists and craftsmen working in Castile at the time. Like most cathedrals in Castile, this one incorporates a number of architectural and artistic styles: Visigothic, Romanesque, Gothic, Flamboyant Gothic, Isabelline, Renaissance, and Baroque all in the same place. The cathedral has an 11th-century Romanesque chapel—reached by an Isabelline stairway—housing a fine seventh-century Visigothic chamber that is all that remains of the original church that stood on this spot, and is believed to be the crypt of the martyred San Antolín, whose remains were brought here by King Wamba from Toulouse in 673.

The early-16th-century main altarpiece of gilded wood by the famous sculptor and woodcarver Felipe Vigarni, who did the carvings for this piece, and Juan de Flandés, who painted 12 truly exceptional Flemish-style panels, is quite spectacular. Vigarni carved more than two dozen separate figures to fill most of the golden-painted niches in the retable; then, for whatever reason, Juan de Flandés was commissioned to paint scenes from the life of Christ for the center niches on each side and along the bottom of the piece. The colorful Flemish paintings provide a counterpoint to all that gold and breathe life into what would have been an impressive, but monotonous, procession of polychrome figures. Among other treasures in the cathedral are the impressive *trascoro* by the great collaborators Simón de Colonia and Gil de Siloé; a great triptych by Juan de Flandés; works by Alonso Berruguete, Diego de Siloé, and El Greco; and a number of late-15th- and early-16th-century tapestries commissioned by Bishop Fonseca. Many parts of this cathedral, especially the side chapels, are very dimly lit; ask the custodian to light them for you.

Palencia has several other churches dating from the 11th to the 15th centuries, including the 11th- to 13th-century Romanesque **Iglesia de San Miguel**, whose handsome restored tower is crenellated like a castle tower and has handsome Gothic windows in the belfry; a lovely ancient **stone bridge** across the Carrión that is Roman in origin, and a bustling vehicle-free shopping street, the calle Mayor—but there is nothing more to detain you here for more than a few hours. Just off the plaza Mayor, where there is a modern monument to Alonso Berruguete, who was born in nearby Paredes de Nava, is the **Peña gourmet shop**, where you can buy the ingredients for a fine picnic. Señor Peña has an excellent selection of cheeses, including the rare Cabrales from Asturias; some superb *chorizo* sausages and mountain hams; a selection of pâtés and tinned delicacies from all over Spain; and a good selection of wines. Don't be surprised if you hear Señor Peña and his son in an animated discussion about Los Celticos y Los Jazz—not the people or the music, but American professional basketball teams, whose televised games are the rage in Spain.

Two of the best-regarded restaurants in Palencia, **Casa Damián**, Martínez de Azcoitia 9 (the street behind the Ayuntamiento, northeast of the plaza Mayor), and **Lorenzo**, avenida Casado del Alisal 10 (one block east and two blocks north of Damián), are owned by brothers, and both serve a limited menu offering conservative, old-style Castilian dishes such as *menestra* (vegetable soup), scrambled-egg dishes, and roast lamb.

North of Palencia City

On N 611, 12 km (7.5 miles) north of Palencia at Monzón de Campos, is a quiet, inexpensive, ten-room hotel in the tenth-century **Castillo de Monzón**, the property of the government of Palencia, which makes it a rare find—for it is essentially a provincial parador, a little-known category of hotels not listed in the national system of paradors. Write or phone ahead, though, because it is sometimes completely booked by Spanish tour groups.

Frómista, north of Monzón de Campos on N 611, and **Carrión de los Condes**, 20 km (12.5 miles) northwest of Frómista via a secondary road, are two major shrines on the Camino de Santiago, with important Romanesque churches (Carrión is just over 85 km/53 miles west of Burgos on N 120).

James A. Michener describes Spain's Romanesque monuments in *Iberia:* "There is something perpetually clean and honorable about the best Romanesque, and when I see it my whole being responds. . . ." And Edwin Mullins called them "squat brick churches rubbed by the wind." Frómista's 11th-century **Iglesia de San Martín** was founded by the widow of Sancho the Great of Navarra, and taken over by the monks of Cluny in the early 12th century. Although a little less wind-rubbed than some Romanesque churches on the Camino de Santiago because of its extensive restoration at the turn of the century, San Martín is nonetheless an impressive example of Romanesque architecture. An extraordinary feature of this church is its 300-odd corbels, each with a different stonecarving. Especially in the evening light, the church takes on a warm golden-brown color which, as Walter Starkie described it, "harmonizes with the golden wheat piled up on the threshing floors and the all-pervading brown immensity of Castile and Visigothic Tierra de Campos." Frómista also has a 15th-century Gothic church, **San Pedro**, and **Santa María del Castillo**, a late-Gothic church whose 16th-century retable contains 29 Hispano-Flemish panels.

Between Frómista and Carrión de los Condes is the village of **Villalcázar de Sirga**, also known as Villasirga, whose 13th-century Templar **Iglesia de Santa María la Blanca** contains an image of the Virgin that was celebrated in the Middle Ages as a faith-healer, purportedly curing pilgrims who were still ill even after a visit to Santiago de Compostela. Because of these miraculous cures, this simple brick-and-adobe village for a brief moment presumed to rival the fabled Galician destination, the tomb of Santiago Matamoros. But, even with the great Medieval king Alfonso X, El Sabio (the wise), trumpeting the miracles of this Virgin of Villalcázar de Sirga in the famous *Cantigas*—his collection of 400 poems written in *gallego,* or Galician—in the end pilgrims were not to trudge from all over Europe to stop short of their ultimate goal of Santiago de Compostela and exchange homage to the Saint and Moorslayer for that of the poet-king's Virgin. Alfonso X had good reason to sing the praises of this Virgin, since she watched over the remains of his dead brother Philip, whom he had killed, and Philip's second wife, Leonor Ruiz de Castro. Their painted Romanesque sarcophagi in this church are masterpieces of Medieval art.

Carrión de los Condes, 20 km (12.5 miles) northwest of Frómista, and just a few miles beyond Villasirga, was the home of the infamous Infantes de Carrión, who married El Cid's daughters, sponged off their famous father-in-law, then carried the girls off from Valencia, beat them, stripped them, and abandoned them in a forest. It was also the site of the annual tribute to the Moors of 100 virgins, which provoked the famous battle of Clavijo in Rioja. Carrión is now a properous town with several important Romanesque monuments, including the 12th-century **Iglesia de Santiago**, whose frieze of an earthly band of presumably local artisans (a cobbler, a potter, a cook), musicians, and knights is in refreshing contrast to the usual collection of apostles and angels found on such buildings, and is a match for the greatest Romanesque stone carvings along the entire Camino de Santiago. Other noteworthy churches in Carrión are **Santa María del Camino**, also 12th-century Romanesque, with a façade containing stone carvings of what Dr. Starkie says are Mithraic bulls, and the **Benedictine monastery of San Zoilo** (now a seminary), originally built in the 11th century, with a 16th-century Renaissance cloister whose vaulted ceilings in the arcades are decorated with some exceptional Plateresque stone carvings by Juan de Badajoz and his disciples.

ARANDA DE DUERO AND SOUTHERN BURGOS

Aranda de Duero

Aranda de Duero's importance stems from its crossroads location: It lies on N 1, 156 km (97 miles) north of Madrid, and is only 83 km (52 miles) from Burgos to the north. Aranda is also on the east-west Soria–Valladolid road (N 122), which runs down the Duero river valley for most of its length; Soria is 114 km (71 miles) to the east, and Valladolid lies 93 km (58 miles) to the west.

At first glance Aranda de Duero is a dull place, nearly bereft of monuments of interest—the superb 15th-century Isabelline façade of the **Iglesia de Santa María**, the narrow streets and charming **plaza Mayor** of the 15th- and 16th-century old quarter are the exceptions—but as a base for any extensive exploration of southern Burgos province and the Ribera del Duero it is a practical choice. And, for those who truly love lamb, Aranda has a half-dozen top *asadores* that have made the town a gastronomic legend.

"Aranda de Duero, Vino y Cordero," reads the sign at the entrance to the town, and what incredible *vino* and *cordero* (lamb) it is. Every *asador* in Aranda has a brick oven for roasting lamb and baking bread (of course, the bread oven came first), and every restaurant has its source of excellent Ribera del Duero house wine, which is served in pitchers (if you want to try a bottled wine from Aranda itself, Torremilanos is a very nice red). The *lechazo asado* (roast suckling lamb) comes out with a crackling crisp skin, and the meat is so tender and moist that it falls off the bone. Start with grilled *chorizo, morcilla con arroz* (blood sausage stuffed with rice), and *queso de Burgos* (cheese), all *para picar* (to "pick at"—as hors d'oeuvres), then have a salad before going on to the main event, the lamb.

Mesón de la Villa, plaza Mayor 1 (just through the archway, west of the río Duero bridge, in downtown Aranda), whose owners get some of their recipes from centuries-old texts; **Mesón El Roble**, plaza Primo de Rivera 7 (in the center of town just east of the avenida de Castilla), which spawned a whole chain of *asadores de Aranda* in Spain; and the restaurant at **Los Bronces Hotel** (north of town) are all *asadores* with good all-around menus for those who tire of a steady diet of lamb. But if you have time for only one meal in Aranda, **Rafael Corrales**, Obispo Velasco 2 (just off avenida de Castilla in the center of Aranda, where half-a-dozen taverns and *asadores* are located), a tiny, family-run *asador* founded at the turn of the century, is a must for homemade *chorizo* and roast quarter of lamb. The larger and more commercial **Casa Florencio**, Arias de Miranda 14 (on the other side of the main street, two blocks west of Corrales), is another good choice. Most of these *asadores* have their brick ovens near the entrance, where they exude irresistibly appetizing aromas as one crockery platter after another, laden with quarters of lamb, is pulled from the ovens on a wooden paddle.

Aranda's best hotels, including what is probably the best, the convenient **Los Bronces** (out past the bullring at the northern end of avenida de Castilla, Aranda's main street, just before the junction with N 1), are clean, have plenty of hot water, and are not expensive, but they win no prizes for tasteful decor or firm mattresses (ask for a *tabla*—a bedboard—if your bed is too soft). However, Aranda's central location and its *asadores* for the evening meal more than compensate for the lackluster hotels, so consider forgoing the ultimate in creature comforts for a couple of days and get into the spirit of Old Castile by making Aranda your base for excursions into the highly rewarding, little-known areas around this city. (If you are willing to drive the extra hour each way to and from Burgos, you can make your base in the capital for these excursions.)

Ribera de Burgos Wine Country

From Aranda you can easily explore the Ribera de Burgos wine villages (still Ribera del Duero *denominación*), located north and west of the city (areas discussed in this section can also be tied in with the Ribera del Duero wineries discussed above in Valladolid province). You will enjoy meandering through this strange, picturesque section of Castilian landscape, which is studded with small, unspoiled backcountry villages such as La Aguilera, Gumiel de Mercado, Sotillo de la Ribera, La Horra, Roa, and Pedrosa de Duero—places where tourists are practically unknown, and where you can taste the area's excellent wines in cooperatives, family wineries, and local bars. Beginning just west of Aranda and just north of the main road to Palencia (C 619), where a well-paved secondary road branches off, drive northwest following road signs toward La Aguilera, Gumiel de Mercado, and Sotillo de la Ribera, where you turn southwest to La Horra and Roa, then west to Pedrosa.

Two excellent wines to try are those of Victor Balbás (Tel: 54-10-52) in **La Horra** and Viña Pedrosa from Bodegas Hermanos Pérez Pascuas (Tel: 54-04-99), in **Pedrosa de Duero**. Victor Balbás and his son, Juanjo, are dedicated *cosecheros* (small grape growers who produce wines from their own grapes), making some of the Ribera's most delicious wines—dark, rich reds and beautiful ruby rosés. The Balbás recently built a new winery a few hundred yards from the southern edge of the village (down a side street off La Horra's main street—ask for Bodegas Balbás). If you visit Balbás, also ask to see the incredibly rustic man-made caves where they age their wines. Those strange chimney-like rock formations above the Balbás caves are man-made ventilation shafts called

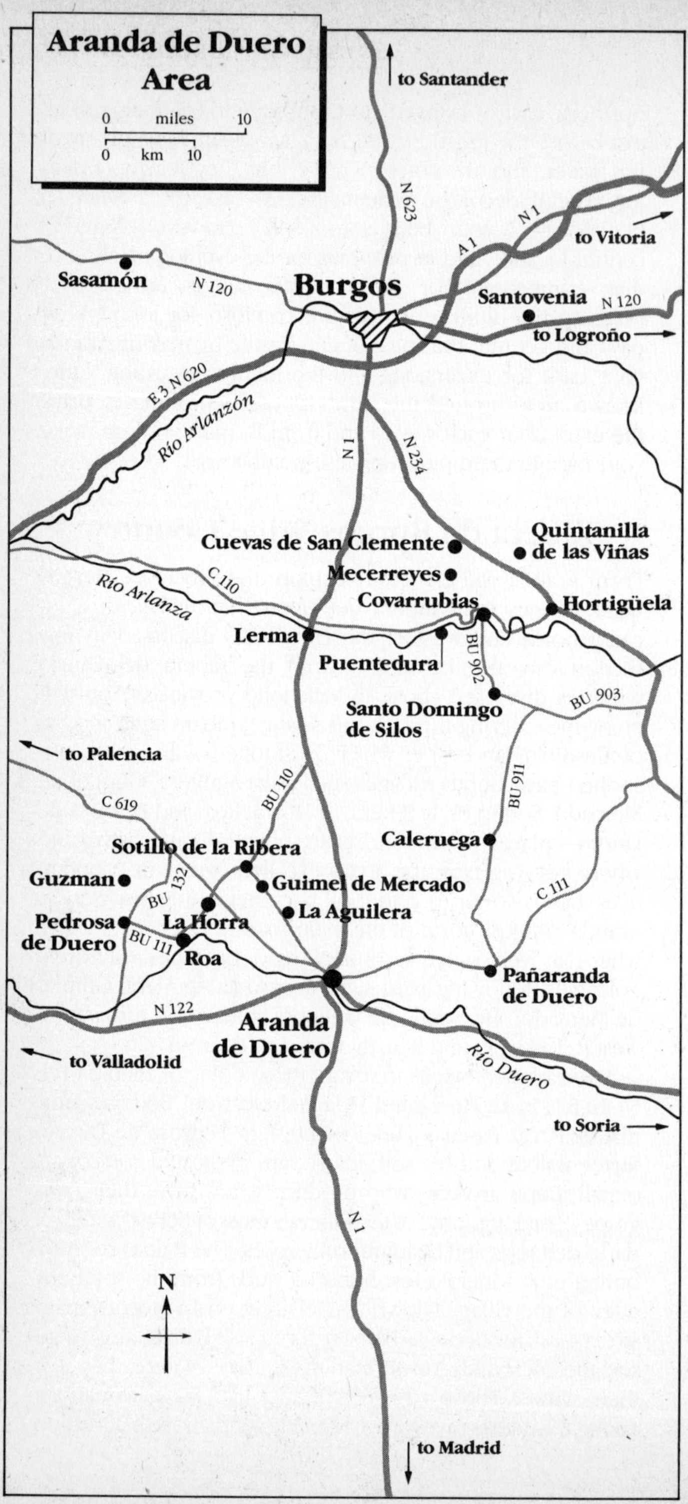
Aranda de Duero Area
0 miles 10
0 km 10
to Santander
N 623
N 1
A 1
to Vitoria
Sasamón
N 120
Burgos
Santovenia
N 120
to Logroño
E 3 N 620
Río Arlanzón
N 1
N 234
Cuevas de San Clemente
Quintanilla de las Viñas
Mecerreyes
C 110
Río Arlanza
Covarrubias
Hortigüela
Lerma
Puentedura
BU 902
BU 903
Santo Domingo de Silos
to Palencia
BU 110
BU 911
C 619
Caleruega
Sotillo de la Ribera
Guzman
BU 132
Guimel de Mercado
C 111
BU
La Aguilera
Pedrosa de Duero
La Horra
BU 111
Roa
Pañaranda de Duero
N 122
Aranda de Duero
to Valladolid
Río Duero
to Soria
N 1
N
to Madrid

zarceras. The villages in this region have hundreds of these *zarceras* sprouting from the hills, which are honeycombed with caves that were carved out for aging wines and, in some villages, cheeses.

The Pérez Pascuas brothers—Adolfo, Benjamin, and Manolo—run a clean, well-maintained winery, and they are also exceptionally dedicated viticulturists. Their wines are made of grapes grown almost entirely in their impeccably tended vineyards within the municipality of Pedrosa. In this cooler upland region the three brothers produce some of the Ribera del Duero's most beautifully balanced red wines, lighter in color and style than any of the wines from the warmer Valladolid district. Because of their tawny-edged color, soft fruit, and distinctive nose, these wines are more reminiscent of Burgundy than any in the valley.

In nearby Guzmán, Ambrosio Molinos, a close friend of the Pérez Pascuas brothers, makes an excellent *queso de Burgos* called Páramo de Guzmán, which he ages in caves at the edge of town. He also puts his cheeses in quality olive oil and packages them in tins, so that it is now possible to take home an authentic Spanish cheese. Look for them in round, gray one- and two-kilo tins in specialty food shops all around Castile.

There are two choices for lunch in this region. You can buy the food for a picnic at local stores or in morning markets (accompanied by a bottle of Ribera del Duero that you purchased at one of the *bodegas*). Or you can eat in **Roa** (about 8 km/5 miles north of N 122, about halfway between Aranda and Peñafiel), a picturesque village perched on a hill overlooking the Duero, where a locally esteemed restaurant, **El Chuleta**, General Varela 6, specializes in *lechazo asado,* grilled meats, and grilled fish. (There is also the option of going on toward Valladolid to Peñafiel to eat at Mesón Mauro, described earlier in the Valladolid Province section.)

Roa is the town where the powerful regent of Spain, Cardinal Cisneros, Queen Isabella's top adviser and the guiding light behind Toledo's cathedral, died in 1517, some think after he received a letter from Charles V relieving him—by then he was an ailing octogenarian—of the position he had filled so honorably and so well. Cisneros, borne on a heated litter with his frail body wrapped in furs, was on his way to Tordesillas to meet Charles, newly arrived from Brussels to take the crown of Spain (whose language he could barely speak) from his mad mother Juana la Loca. Roa has a fine 16th-century Plateresque church, La Colegiata, facing the town square.

The return east to Aranda de Duero from Roa is a short, easy, unhurried drive on good country roads. If you are instead continuing west to Valladolid and Tordesillas, the leisurely afternoon's drive down the Duero valley offers sightseeing, wine tasting (see the Peñafiel and Red-Wine Villages section), and coffee in a village bar as diversions along the way.

The best time to visit this region is in the spring, when the wheat fields are green and ablaze with flaming red poppies and the roads are trimmed with splendid wildflowers of just about every hue.

Another excellent day trip from Aranda (or driving down from Burgos, perhaps with a stop for lunch in Aranda) is the loop to the northeast through Peñaranda de Duero, Santo Domingo de Silos, Covarrubias, Lerma, and back to Aranda (or Burgos).

Peñaranda, a few miles east of Aranda on C 111, is a picturesque old walled town with a castle and a photogenic, arcaded plaza Mayor with timbered houses. Along the western side of the plaza is one of the greatest Renaissance palaces of Spain, the **Palacio de los Condes de Miranda**, which incorporates a number of architectural and decorative influences, including Moorish, Gothic, Plateresque, and Italian. Just across the square is the 16th-century **Iglesia de Santa Ana**, with an undistinguished 17th-century Italianate portal, and in the center of the plaza is a fine Gothic *rollo,* the spot where edicts were read. Ask for **La Botica**, the town pharmacy, the second oldest in Spain, which is still functioning and has been in the same family since the 18th century. It is run by Señor José Jimeno, who, for a small admission fee to his museum, will show you his collection of over 200 Talavera ceramic pharmaceuticals *botes* (canisters) dating from the 18th century. This lovely town is still unspoiled and is great for tarrying over a late-morning coffee at one of the little outdoor cafés just north of the plaza. The village priest will probably stop by to inquire about your nationality and ask what you think of his town.

Driving north on paved country roads, you pass the village and the Dominican monastery/school of **Caleruega**, the home town of the founder of the Dominican order, Santo Domingo de Guzmán, who was born here in the 12th century. (Santo Domingo de Guzmán, Santo Domingo de Silos—more on his eponymous cloister below—and Santo Domingo de la Calzada in the Rioja are three different saints.) Between Caleruega and Santo Domingo de Silos is some spectacular scenery, especially the **Paso de la Yecla**, a scary narrow gorge that is about a half-mile long, several hundred feet deep, and in some places little more than a yard wide. You can walk the length of the bottom of Yecla canyon on a narrow concrete walkway with a slender, barely adequate, steel-pipe handrail, which is all that keeps you from falling into the cold, clear pools of the tiny Mataviejas stream below. If you are careful, it is great fun.

The 11th-century cloister of the **Monasterio de Santo Domingo de Silos** is one of the great jewels of Romanesque art in Spain; more than one writer has described it as the most beautiful Romanesque cloister in the world. This building has two stories. On the lower level, exquisite 11th-century stone capitals crown rows of double columns. Carved by at least three different unknown, Eastern-inspired Medieval artists, each of whose work is distinguishable in style from the other, the capitals feature gryphons, winged horses, bird-like creatures with human faces, and strange other-worldly plants and flowers. Some experts believe the artists may have been Persians, because that Moslem sect permitted the depiction of the human form in art, something seldom found in Mudejar art.

The Doubt of Saint Thomas, one of eight magnificent Romanesque stone carvings depicting scenes from the life of Christ in relief on the cloister's corner piers, alone is worth the trip. Walter Starkie, whose writing drew great inspiration from Santo Domingo de Silos, summarizes the cloister and those eight great carvings as "a gigantic panorama of the 11th century, created by artists who had combined harmoniously the ornamental devices of Byzantium and the East with those of Visigothic Spain."

The monastery's other attractions are considerable: the upper cloister's capitals dating from the 12th century; the *artesonado* ceilings (painted in the 14th century); the 13th-century sepulcher of Santo Domingo, resting on the backs of three very Oriental-looking lions; the monastery **museum**, which has a beautiful small collection of religious artifacts such as a Mozarabic chalice and a walking stick that once belonged to the saint, a beautiful Limoges-like enamel reliquary believed to be from the 12th century, and a 10th- or 11th-century Mozarabic breviary made from some of the earliest paper in Spain; plus another old *botica* dating from 1705, with hundreds of fine ceramic jars like those in Peñaranda. In the evening, haunting Gregorian chant, rising and falling from the throats of the Benedictine brothers seated in the choir, carry throughout the candlelit church.

If you wish to stay overnight in Santo Domingo, there is a good hotel and restaurant here, **Tres Coronas de Silos**, in a fine 18th-century stone house located on the little plaza Mayor overlooking the monastery. Tres Coronas, decorated with rustic Castilian dark wood and wrought-iron trappings, and furnished with antiques and period furniture reproductions, is reminiscent of a parador. The hotel has a cozy bar and a restaurant serving house *tapas,* roast goat, baby lamb chops, and good Ribera del Duero wines.

A short distance northwest of Silos is **Covarrubias**, an almost perfectly preserved village with centuries-old half-timbered houses. Nestled in the Arlanza valley, and looking like an age-old settlement in perfect harmony with its natural surroundings, Covarrubias is a find.

In the early tenth century this small town was the powerful base of Count Fernán González, a figure even more important in Castile than El Cid, since by hook or by crook he managed to forge the nascent county of Castile by continually playing the Moors and the Kingdom of León off one another. As J. Vicens Vives wrote in *Approaches to the History of Spain,* this was "a transcendental moment in Peninsular affairs in which Castile actually made her appearance in history," and the period when "Castile forged her warrior temperament, her will to command, and her ambition to achieve a great destiny." The *Poema de Fernán González* is a famous 13th-century work, possibly written by a monk at the Monasterio de San Pedro de Arlanza, that glorifies the exploits of this storied knight of Castile.

The sights in Covarrubias include the tenth-century **Torre de Doña Urraca**, claimed by some to be haunted by the ghost of Urraca, who was imprisioned there by her father, the great Ferdinand; a 16th-century town gate; a superb plaza Mayor; and a number of churches of merit, including the **Colegiata**, which now houses the tomb of Fernán González, whose remains were brought here from the Monasterio de San Pedro de Arlanza. Built on the ruins of former Visigothic and Romanesque churches, the Colegiata we see now dates primarily from the 15th century, although the cloister is 16th century. Apart from the impressive tombs of Fernán González and his wife, there are some 40 other tombs in this church, including that of an abbot done by Juan de Colonia. The church also contains a sacrisity with some important documents from early Castile, a wooden pipe organ that is highly esteemed for its rich tone, and a superb piece by Gil de Siloé, the *Tríptico de Covarrubias,* whose centerpiece is a truly exceptional *Adoration of the Magi* in polychrome wood.

Covarrubias also has a good *parador colaborador* (an affiliate parador) and restaurant, the **Arlanza**, both decorated in old Castilian style. The restaurant serves typical regional cuisine, and on special occasions offers a Medieval menu. **Galin**, plaza Doña Urraca 4, a better choice than the hotel restaurant, serves inexpensive *comida casera* (home-cooked food) such as the famous *olla podrida* (rotten pot stew; Sundays only, not in summer), roast lamb, and stewed rabbit, plus their own homemade wine (there is a little-known wine area here, the Ribera de Arlanza).

To go to the extra effort to capture the true spirit of this corner of Castile—which incorporates Visigothic, Romanesque, and Renaissance architecture and has a pronounced feel of the old Spain of El Cid and Fernán González—an hour-long side trip from Covarrubias through the area's rugged juniper- and pine-covered hills before going on west to Lerma is recommended. Drive east from Covarrubias past the 11th-century Romanesque (rebuilt in the 15th century) **Monasterio de San Pedro de Arlanza**, whose dramatic ruins on the banks of the río Arlanza not only inspire contemplation but also offer an excellent site for a picnic. Eagles soar on the wind currents above this once-powerful abbey, whose roofless walls now provide, from the road above, a bird's-eye view of the floor plan of a Medieval monastery. San Pedro de Arlanza was the original resting place of Fernán González.

Turn north at Hortiguela and follow the Burgos–Soria highway a few miles until you see signs for **Quintanilla de las Viñas**. In the village is a house with a "Turismo" sign, where you have to pick up the official guide, who will accompany you to the village church with the keys to let you in.

The church at Quintanilla is claimed to be seventh-century Visigothic, but parts of it definitely date from at earliest the tenth century. Regardless of its imprecise lineage, Quintanilla's is still one of the oldest churches in Spain, and it has some exceptional rare stone carvings of bulls, lions, peacocks, pheasants, and other animals and birds, which decorate several rows of stone blocks high on the apse of the church. The simple block lines of the church contrast with the restrained but rich stone carvings, and evoke a spirituality so sadly missing in the huge, heavy buildings you will encounter in Lerma, the last stop before returning to Aranda or Burgos.

Travel a few miles farther north on N 234 to Cuevas de San Clemente, then turn left and head southwest following the road signs to Mecerreyes and to Puentedura, where you catch C 110 west along the north bank of río Arlanza to meet the N 1 highway at **Lerma**, a town that dates to at least the eighth century, though it is now dominated by buildings from a much later period.

From this northern approach especially, Lerma's massive 16th- and 17th-century Renaissance buildings brooding on the hill overlooking the Arlanza are impressive, and so is the ancient bridge east of the main road. Lerma's entrance is an archway guarded by two fortified 12th-century towers that are all that remain of its ancient fortifications. Once inside the town, though, many people find the dull Herreran-style buildings as oppressive architecturally as the man who built them, and his family, were politically. This was the virtual fiefdom of Philip III's corrupt *privado* (favorite) and the de facto ruler of Spain, the duke of Lerma. Alastair Boyd described the town of Lerma's attractions as "hollow grandeurs" and observed that "Lerma was built in all its essentials on the ill-gotten gains of one man and has had no real *raison d'être* since." However, Spaniards consider the duke's huge stone palace to be one of their most important pieces of 17th-century architecture.

The huge **Colegiata de San Pedro**, riding high on a hill overlooking the Arlanza, dates to 1606, and contains the impressive tomb of the duke's uncle, Archbishop Cristobal de Rojas, who, like many of Lerma's relatives and friends, was appointed to the highest and most lucrative posts in the land. This tomb was done by Pompeo Leoni and Juan de Arfe, the same pair who did Lerma's funerary monument, now in the Museo Nacional de Escultura in Valladolid. The Iglesia de San Blas, also at Lerma, is plastered with two huge coats of arms of the duke like the ones on the flanking faces of the church of San Pablo in Valladolid.

Because Lerma is roughly equidistant in travel time between Aranda, 44 km (27 miles) south, and Burgos, 37 km (23 miles) north on N 1, it is an easy return on N 1 to either city.

BURGOS

Culturally and historically, Burgos is an important city. Its strategic location at the junction of the north-south road from France to Madrid and the east-west Camino de Santiago virtually assured this old Castilian town of a prominent place in the history of the country. Spread out along a valley of the pretty little río Arlanzón, Burgos is located 80 km (50 miles) north of Aranda de Duero, and 240 km (149 miles) north of Madrid. It is also easily accessible on good roads (highway N 620) from Valladolid (122 km/76 miles) and Palencia (88 km/ 55 miles) to the southwest. Vitoria is 114 km (71 miles) northeast on A 1, and Santander and Bilbao lie on the coast to the north and the northeast.

Because of its location, its significance in the history of Spain, its grand Gothic cathedral, and its fame as the hometown of El Cid, Burgos has long been an essential stop for serious travellers in Spain. However, Alexandre Dumas, Hans Christian Andersen, James A. Michener, and almost every other writer who has ever set foot in the country—like most travellers—either paused at Burgos just long enough to see the cathedral, pay their respects to El Cid, and have lunch, or allowed a mere day or two here to satisfy stronger pangs of cultural curiosity. Hemingway would stop for a bullfight or to lunch on fresh trout, and he always had the "delicate Burgos cheese" that he so fondly remembered having brought back to Gertrude Stein in Paris ". . . when I'd come home from Spain in the old days third-class on the train."

It's a shame that most of those famous writers didn't stay longer, because Burgos is one of the finest cities in Spain, and its people are among the noblest of Spaniards. Even though you *can* see most of the sights in a couple of days, Burgos is a place where you could easily spend a week, or you could use it as a base for a month. Burgos's charm, its easy-paced life-style, and the beauty of its old city along the north bank of the Arlanzón are reminiscent of one of those fine small cities in the Loire valley, and its soul, albeit a distinctly Castilian and less outwardly demonstrative one, is on a par with that of Seville. With a population of just over 150,000, most of whom seem to still cling to conservative Castilian values, the town is not yet overrun by the impossible traffic, rampant crime, and drugs that have plagued other cities. (Of course, no place is immune to car break-ins, petty thievery, and occasional muggings, and even though there is less danger in Burgos than in most places, it is still wise to exercise normal precautions.)

Burgos does have, however, a reputation for extreme weather. The old Spanish adage "nine months of winter, three months of hell" has long been the standard descriptor for the area's weather, but it was winter in Burgos, not summer, that proved a veritable hell to a number of famous travellers.

Hans Christian Andersen almost died in Burgos. Attempting to keep warm in his icy hotel room, he and his travelling companion had a charcoal *brasero* lit. They fell asleep, and soon Andersen was dreaming that he was being transported to "where the Cid's ashes long have lain." The fumes from the brazier were asphyxiating him. Andersen awoke choking, barely able to open the doors to the balcony and fresh air.

In the early years of the 20th century, William Dean Howells searched the town in vain for a hotel with fireplaces in the rooms, only to return, hat in hand, to his original hotel, whose owner had proudly shown him the shiny radiators of a steam heating system that he apparently had no intention of firing up. Howells entitled a chapter in his *Familiar Spanish Travels,* "Burgos and the Bitter Cold." The modern traveller will find that Burgos now has plenty of well-heated hotels. The winter weather will be cold, brisk, and bracing, but no more so than New York or Edinburgh, and with less humidity.

Many writers have taken at face value the "three months of hell" portion of the old adage, but summer in Burgos is not as bad as often claimed. It is hot during the day, but the wonderful outdoor cafés under shade trees along the Espolón, the tree-lined *paseos* along the river, and the shade of buildings in the narrow streets diminish the effects of the heat. Burgos is some 2,900 feet above sea level, so many summer nights are lovely and cool; usually a jacket or sweater is needed for comfort as you join the lively parade of *Burgaleses* in their nightly *paseo,* even in July. Late June, when the Fiesta de San Pedro y San Pablo takes place, is an ideal time to visit, but May, September, and October are also very good months.

Burgos came into being in 882, some 160 years after the first invasion of the Moors, as one historian put it, "unhampered by a past of someone else's making." It became the first capital of nascent Castile, then but a county. Burgos was originally, and is today, uniquely Castilian. And in no figure is Burgos and the essence of Castile better personified than the 11th-century figure El Cid Campeador (from the Arabic for "lord," and from Spanish roughly meaning "champion among warriors"). On his legendary horse, Babieca, El Cid rides across the pages of Spanish history, at times a ruthless soldier of fortune but ultimately a great hero, a patriot, and one of the most exemplary family men in history. At Santa Agueda church, west of the cathedral, he made King Alfonso VI of Castile swear three times in front of the populace that he had had no part in the murder of his older brother, King Sancho.

El Cid then pledged his allegiance to Alfonso, but his fate was sealed. The king ultimately banished him from Castile, and the great warrior sold his services to Moor and Christian alike until, after years of battles, he tricked some moneylenders into giving him the money he needed to fund his assault on the great Moorish city of Valencia, which he conquered and held for a number of years. He redeemed his security, a locked chest of worthless stones and sand, from the moneylenders, and finally returned to his beloved Castile in death, his corpse dressed in battle gear and seated on the noble Babieca, so the legend goes. His exploits were the basis of the great anonymous epic poem of the 12th century, *El çantar de mio Cid,* and El Cid became the national hero of Spain.

Here in Burgos physical reminders of the real-life Cid, whose name was Rodrigo Díaz de Vivar, mingle with the air of romantic legend that surrounds his life. His image on the Arco de Santa María; the fine equestrian statue standing in a square just north of the Puente de San Pablo; the statues of his wife, Doña Jimena, and other notables of the epoch lining the San Pablo bridge; the repository of the bones of El Cid and Jimena beneath a plain stone in the cathedral; the line of measure, said to be the length of La Tizona (his famous sword), on a wall of the cathedral; and the coffer (also in the cathedral) with which he supposedly tricked the moneylenders—all infuse the city with a magical sense of his presence. You can also make an excursion into the nearby countryside to San Pedro de Cardeña, the monastery where Doña Jimena and her children resided during El Cid's long periods of exile from Castile. All these reminders of El Cid exist, for the most part not sentimental or contrived, but the Medieval ambience of Burgos that all these remnants combine to evoke will stay with you longer than the remembrance of the icons themselves.

Once you get past Burgos's cocoon of dingy industrial buildings and nondescript modern high-rise apartments, you will find the inner core of the city—beautifully restored and vibrant—to be one of the finest in Spain. The ruins of a once-mighty castle crown the hill above the city, and the airy, filigreed, steel-gray spires of the magnificent cathedral rise majestically to the sky. The sights of cultural and historic interest are easily visited because the historic core of Burgos is so compact and walkable. The great Gothic cathedral, the history-steeped Casa del Cordón, and many other sights are all linked in a relatively short semicircle just north of the river.

This historic-artistic *conjunto* (ensemble), the old center city, whose recent building code prevents construction of any structure over three stories, is full of charm. With the cathedral and the other historic buildings as backdrop, the old quarter has many nice little shops; the bustling alley-like market street, San Lorenzo; the plaza Mayor; a wonderful river (though the Arlanzón makes some modest trout streams look like raging torrents); and a splendid tree-shaded esplanade, the **paseo del Espolón**. Sidewalk cafés like the venerable Café Pinedo along the Espolón and those around the plaza Mayor are wonderful for watching the people parade while you sip coffee or a frosty glass of beer accompanied by a dish of fine green olives cured with anchovies in the brine.

Staying in Burgos

Before starting a tour of Burgos, you need to consider your accommodation options, since hotel location is vital for getting the most out of this city. Considering the charm of old Burgos, it is unfortunate that the town's best hotel—and one of the finest in Spain—the luxurious **Landa Palace**, which also has the best restaurant (see below), is a few kilometers south of town on the busy N 1 highway. The Landa Palace, a Relais et Châteaux hotel, is sumptuously decorated with period furniture, tapestries, and wrought-iron fixtures. It is incorporated into a 14th-century tower that was brought here stone by stone, reconstructed, and embellished with Gothic stonework. The Landa Palace also has a heated swimming pool with Gothic vaulting and other special touches such as marble baths. Of course, there is a hefty tariff for such opulence.

Old Burgos is such a special and romantic city that leisurely walks to and from a centrally located hotel really ought to be an integral part of the total experience, so you might prefer to drink in the atmosphere of old Burgos by staying in the city. The **Fernán González**, a charming hotel decorated in period furniture, is located on the south bank of the Arlanzón, directly across from the Espolón and the Medieval precincts of the old city. As you walk out from the Fernán González, you have the choice of heading either a block east along the river to the Puente de San Pablo or a block west to the Puente de Santa María. Either way, you will be able to contemplate the unfolding panorama of old Burgos. These short walks reinforce the notion that you are indeed in a very special town.

Other good hotel choices are the venerable **Almirante**

Bonifaz, just a few blocks west of the statue of El Cid, the nearby **Condestable**, which is comfortable now after its recent modernizations but sterile with its white marble floors and ultramodern furniture, and the relatively new, very pleasant, and friendly **Cordón**, on a side street a few doors west of the plaza Calvo Sotelo and the Casa del Cordón.

Around in Old Burgos

The great Gothic cathedral of Burgos (see below) will take at least half a day to see properly. If you are only going to be here for a day, we suggest you leave it for the afternoon, and dedicate your morning to exploring the outdoor sights of Burgos while the city is bustling with life.

Start at the Puente de San Pablo (also called the vía Cidiana, after El Cid), which is flanked with eight 20th-century stone statues of major figures in El Cid's life—including Doña Jimena, the Cid's son, and his Moorish friend. Just north of the bridge is the excellent statue—done in 1955 by the sculptor Juan Cristobal—of a luxuriantly bearded Cid dressed in chain-mail armor, his huge sword La Tizona pointing toward the enemy, and his cape flying behind him as he charges into battle astride his mighty horse.

Behind the statue of El Cid, less than a block to the north on the right, is a pedestrian street leading into the fine plaza de Calvo Sotelo, where the **Casa del Cordón** and three restaurants (see below) are located. The Casa del Cordón, a recently restored Renaissance building now occupied by a bank, is so called because of the thick Franciscan cord carved in stone above the portal. The coats of arms above the doorway belong to the palace's original owners, the high constable of Castile, Don Pedro Hernández de Velasco, and his wife, Doña Mencia, whose splendid tombs are in the equally splendid Capilla del Condestable that they had built in the cathedral.

Isabella and Ferdinand received Columbus in this house in 1497 after he returned from his second voyage to the New World, and a number of Spanish monarchs, including Charles V, lived here at one time or another. Perhaps the most important event that ever occurred in this house was the death of a foreign prince, Philip the Handsome, who was bent on usurping the throne of Spain from his supposedly mad wife, Juana, the daughter of Isabella and Ferdinand. After playing a hard game of *pelota* with a Basque guard, Philip caught a chill (though some say he was poisoned). Within a week "the dark angel of the house of Trastamara [Isabella's family] found him," as Townsend Miller put it. Juana then set out from here on a peripatetic journey across Castile with Philip's coffin, which she was to open a number of times before the handsome young libertine prince's body would finally end up in the royal chapel in Granada. Philip and Juana's son became the Emperor Charles V and King Charles I of Spain, and subsequently locked his mother up in Tordesillas, where she was to remain for 46 years.

Calle de la Puebla leads from the northeast corner of the plaza, past Hotel Cordón and down a few blocks to the 14th-century pilgrims' Capilla de St. Lesmes and, nearby, the old ruined **monastery of San Juan**. The Plateresque cloisters there now house the museum of Marceliano Santiago (1866–1952), a distinguished Burgos impressionist artist whose paintings are along the style of his contemporaries Sorolla and Zuloaga. But these are secondary destinations, for those who are here for more than a day.

In that category, too, are the fine 13th- and 14th-century Iglesia de San Gil, northwest of the Casa del Cordón; the 12th-century Moorish Arco de San Estebán and a section of old walls located just west of San Gil; the recently restored 13th-century Iglesia de San Estebán with its tiny 14th-century cloister, just south of the arch; and the early-15th-century Iglesia de San Nicolás with an exceptional early-16th-century reredos in alabaster by Simón de Colonia, just northwest of the cathedral in calle Fernán González. Southwest of the cathedral, and not to be missed by devotees of El Cid, is Iglesia de Santa Agueda, where the great Campeador made Alfonso VI swear his innocence.

From the ruined **castillo** (perhaps Castile owes its name to this one) crowning the hill above Burgos there are excellent views of the cathedral, the town, and the valley. There are several other historic landmarks flavoring the historic *olla* of Burgos, worthy of perhaps a snapshot and a cursory inspection as you stroll the streets of the old quarter. Just below the castle hill, along calle Doña Jimena, are the 16th-century Arco de Fernán González built under Philip II; the Solar del Cid, a monolithic trio of monuments marking the former site of El Cid's ancestral home; and the 14th-century Arco de San Martín, one of the original gates in the walls of the old city.

As you descend the steep streets from the San Martín gate along Santa Agueda you will come to the cathedral.

The Cathedral

Some who visit the great Gothic cathedral of Burgos find its exterior fine and its interior not so fine, because it is broken up too much by the choir, so you do not get the vistas of the cathedrals of Seville and Toledo. The cathedral is also hemmed in by the buildings that huddle around it, so views of this massive edifice are more encumbered than those of the cathedrals at Seville and Santiago. The rose window is lovely, but all of León's stained glass adds up to greater magnificence. Despite these shortcomings, this is still one of the greatest religious structures in Spain, and to those interested in religious art and history the cathedral of Burgos offers a wealth of both.

Work on the cathedral began in 1221 and continued for another 300 years, so like most Spanish churches it incorporates a number of architectural styles. Few, however, can match the sheer quantity of artistic detail in this building.

The cathedral's dominant exterior feature, the lacey Gothic spires that soar almost 300 feet into the Burgos sky and give the city a Germanic air, were built in the mid-15th century by Juan de Colonia (Johan of Cologne), father of Simón, and are believed to have been inspired by the original plans for the cathedral of Cologne. Because the cathedral's exterior is so rich in sculpture and decoration, and so that you can understand some of the peculiarities of its interior, you should walk the multilevel circuit of the exterior first. The cathedral is built against a hill, so a high street runs along its northern side, requiring portals on that side that would be halfway up the façade on the south side opposite. Here you will see the logic of the interior's Escalera Dorada (golden staircase), a stairway that seems to go nowhere.

Begin at the western door, the Puerta de Santa María, which is the main entrance. The lower third of the façade is pierced by three massive arched doorways, but it is rather plainly decorated as a result of a poorly handled 18th-century attempt at restoration that stripped it of much of its sculpture. The upper two-thirds of the façade, the florid Gothic masterpiece of Juan de Colonia, seems to gather its strength from the lower third to propel its lighter, airy towers into the sky. Ribbed pinnacles and ventilated filigreed bell towers flank a massive rose window topped by a twin-arched florid Gothic gallery with eight statues of the kings of Castile and a balustrade formed by stone letters spelling "Pulchra est et Decora."

A stairway to the left of the main door leads up past Iglesia San Nicolás to calle Fernán González and east along the north side of the cathedral to the 13th-century Puerta de la Coronería, also known as the Puerta Alta and once called the apostles' door, leading to the north arm of the transept. Like much of the stone carving on the exterior of this and other churches, Puerta de la Coronería is showing the ravages of modern-day pollution, which is melting away the delicate artistry in soft stone that withstood the pounding of rain and wind for centuries. The door is almost always closed to prevent people from using it as a shortcut to the lower part of town.

Walking east along Fernán González, to your right as you face the cathedral you can get excellent views of the multi-spired, three-story, octagonal **lantern tower**, richly decorated with balustrades, stained-glass windows, and stone carvings covering most of its surfaces. The original lantern, built by Juan de Colonia in the mid-15th century, collapsed and was replaced in the mid-16th century with this one by Juan de Vallejo. To the left of the lantern is the buttressed 13th-century apse, which is the oldest part of the church. And to the left of the apse, closest to the stairway entrance, is a third set of spires and tall stained-glass windows crowning the Capilla del Condestable, executed by the chapel's architect, Simón de Colonia, in the late 15th century. While profusely decorated with crocketed spires, balustrades, and florid Gothic trimmings, it is still almost subdued in comparison to Vallejo's wedding-cake style, which must have given the Churrigueras plenty of inspiration.

Next, down a flight of steps to the floor level of the cathedral, is the Puerta de la Pellejería, so named because it was the entrance from the old tanner's district once located here. This richly decorated 16th-century Plateresque doorway by Francisco de Colonia is also suffering from decay. Almost comical now is the figure of Saint John in a cauldron of boiling oil, the flames under which are fanned by a kneeling figure with a bellows.

Calle Diego Porcelos leads past the cloister on the east side of the church to calle de la Paloma, an arcaded walk that is a part of the cloister, and reaches the south face of the cathedral and the **Puerta del Sarmental**, considered the most exceptional of the great church's doorways. The Sarmental façade features the monumental doorway with a frieze of the 12 apostles, a multitude of carved figures decorating the archivolts, and a tympanum with Christ presiding over the four evangelists, who are each seated at desks taking down the word of the Lord. Above this is a huge rose window, then another florid Gothic screen guarded by 13 stone angels, topped with a balustrade and flanked by crocketed spires as on the western face.

If you enter at the Sarmental door, you will be in the center of the cathedral, so we recommend that you return to the west front and start your tour of the interior at the Puerta de Santa María. The cathedral has a wealth of artistic treasures, and you will need a specialized guidebook to get the most out of it. We will point out the highlights, but even many of them deserve a scrutiny beyond the scope of this book.

As you enter the Puerta de Santa María, look high up to your left for the cathedral's comical version of a cuckoo clock—the 16th-century mechanical torso, thought to be German, of Papamoscas (the flycatcher), whose mouth pops open to mark the hours. In the first chapel on the right is the famous **Cristo de Burgos**, a terrifyingly graphic depiction of Christ on the Cross with profusely bleeding wounds. Curiously, the statue is dressed in a skirt and its feet rest on a pile of ostrich eggs. It is claimed that the statue was the work of Nicodemus; reports of pilgrims date it to at least the 15th century.

The choir, as in many Spanish churches, breaks up the sweep of the nave, but it is a fine example consisting of 103 walnut stalls beautifully carved by Felipe Vigarny in the early 16th century. Enclosed by a huge early-17th-century *reja* (wrought-iron grille), the choir contains the tomb of the cathedral's founder, Bishop Mauricio. In the center of the transept, between the choir and the main chapel and below the lantern, is the plain stone that covers the remains of El Cid and Doña Jimena. Four huge, richly decorated columns support the lantern and its splendid dome, with an eight-pointed star superimposed on another eight-pointed star that is thought to have been inspired by the beautiful, intricate Mudejar ceilings seen in many parts of Spain. North of El Cid's tomb is the magnificent, gilded double staircase, the **Escalera Dorada**, done by Diego de Siloé in 1519, which leads to the Puerta de la Coronería, now covered by tapestries.

The **Capilla Mayor** (main chapel) has a massive, multi-niched 16th-century altar by Rodrigo de la Haya and his brother Martín. But here it is the *trasaltar,* the back wall in the ambulatory behind the main altar, that is worth your attention. In the early 16th century Felipe Vigarny carved three of the panels in stone, including his famous *Calvary.*

The great jewel of the cathedral's interior is the octagonal **Capilla de Condestable**, located behind the main altar. This exceptional chapel is the combined work of great German, Flemish, and Burgundian artists, and their acclimated sons, of the late 15th and early 16th centuries. It was begun in 1482 in florid Gothic style to house the tombs of Pedro Hernández de Velasco, the constable of Castile, and his wife (the same couple who owned the Casa del Cordón), and it was variously worked on by several consummate artists until well into the 16th century. Simón de Colonia, son of the cathedral's master builder, was the architect; Gil de Siloé, whom Alastair Boyd calls "the last great Gothic carver," did the stone carving of the figures in the balustraded, florid Gothic archways above and alongside the altar, and he probably also carved the two huge *escudos,* or coats of arms, on either side of the main altar; Felipe de Vigarny and Diego de Siloé did the superb main altarpiece and also collaborated on a Plateresque side altar; and Felipe de Vigarny carved the splendid tombs of the constable and his wife in Atapuerca marble. The superb grille guarding the entrance to the chapel was done by Cristobal Andino in 1523.

There is much more to see in the cathedral: the 13th-century **cloisters** of the original church; El Cofre del Cid, the coffer that the Cid gave to the moneylenders, in the Corpus Christi chapel; another fine retable by Gil de Siloé in the chapel of the Conception, which was built by Simón de Colonia; and the overblown chapel of Santa Tecla by Alberto de Churriguera, who presumably saw the decoration of Juan de Vallejo's fine lantern, decided to outdo Vallejo, and fell into a morass of vulgar excess instead.

The Plaza Mayor and the Espolón

East of the cathedral is the plaza Mayor, a pear-shaped area surrounded by an arcade surmounted by three- and four-story buildings with interesting, often beautiful façades. These buildings house cafés and pastry shops as well as all sorts of stores. Around the plaza Mayor is a network of lively, narrow shopping streets, such as **calle San Lorenzo** on the north side of the plaza. Colorful San Lorenzo is filled with specialty food shops offering a variety of regional foodstuffs. Fishmongers, butchers, greengrocers, bakers, *tapas*-bar waiters, street vendors, and street musicians vie for your attention, and if all this becomes a bit too much, you can step into the fine Baroque church of San Lorenzo for a respite. Many of the stores on the south side of the plaza Mayor have a front entrance on the Espolón as well, so that within an easy walk the traveller can select from a wide array of gifts.

On the south side of the plaza is the 18th-century Ayuntamiento by Ventura Rodríguez, the architect who built the façade of Pamplona's cathedral. Beneath the city hall are some archways leading to the Espolón. On the columns, note the high-water marks from floods of the normally tame Arlanzón.

The **Espolón** is the great pedestrian artery of Burgos, the communal living room of the city at leisure, and one of the greatest streets of Spain. Along the northeastern side of this white stone-paved concourse, sidewalk cafés are arrayed beneath a canopy of espaliered trees that run in multiple rows the length of the Espolón and provide shade for the entire walkway. During siesta and in the early evening the cafés are filled with Burgaleses catching up on the latest gossip and enjoying the peregrinations of their fellow citizens. Children play in the fine garden that occupies the southern portion of the Espolón, frolicking around the topiary, statues, fountains, and fine wrought-iron bandstand, while lovers stroll along the balcony overlooking the Arlanzón. The Espolón is not just Spain, but Europe, at its best and most civilized.

At the western end of the Espolón is the multiturreted, fairy-tale archway the **Arco de Santa María**, one of the most wonderful public monuments in Spain; it's even more wonderful when seen from the south bank of the Arlanzón at night when the archway and the spires of the cathedral rising dramatically behind it are lighted. Originally a gate in the 11th-century town walls—parts of which are still visible inside the current gate and were once covered with intricately carved Moorish inscriptions—the current façade dates to the 1530s, when it was constructed by the people of Burgos to appease Charles V for their part in the *comuneros* revolt. The six main figures on the façade just above the archway are Charles V and the great heroes of Castile: El Cid, Count Fernán González, the early Castilian magistrates Laín Calvo and Nuño Rasura, and Diego Porcelos, the man credited with founding Burgos. Porcelos, legend has it, got his name because he was born one of septuplets, just like *porcillos* (little pigs).

Walking along the esplanade on the south bank of the Arlanzón, you get fine views of the houses facing the Espolón, the Puerta de Santa María, and the spires of the cathedral, and you are near the Fernán González hotel just south across the avenue at the head of calle Calera. South of the Fernán

González, just around the corner on Miranda, is the 16th-century **Casa de Miranda**, which now houses a small museum of archaeology. Besides the interesting two-story Renaissance patio of the palace, items of interest in the museum include Roman sculpture and mosaics taken from the archaeological site at nearby Clunia, Visigothic sarcophagi, examples of Moorish and Mudejar art, and one of Gil de Siloé's finest pieces, the late-15th-century tomb of Juan de Padilla (one of Queen Isabella's favorite squires, who was killed during the siege of Granada; not the Juan de Padilla who led the *comuneros* revolt).

Dining in Burgos

Burgos has a wide range of restaurants, few of which are exceptional, but most of which offer good typical Castilian dishes such as *alubias con chorizo y morcilla, cordero asado, chuletillas de cordero, menestra,* and grilled fish.

The most highly rated restaurant in Burgos is the **Hostal Landa**, the very expensive, luxurious, and elegant dining room of the Landa Palace hotel a bit out of town, where you can eat first-rate versions of Castilian classics as well as dishes like asparagus in puff pastry, smoked salmon mousse, venison rib chops with stewed potatoes, and foie gras in Port sauce.

The hotel **Fernán González**'s restaurant is another serious new entry on the Burgos culinary scene. In recent years the owners of the hotel have built an elegant new restaurant next door. Classic dishes alternate with *nueva cocina* offerings such as green beans with foie gras and truffles, sole in prawn sauce, and baked apples with pistachio sauce. The proprietors also own wineries in the Rioja and the Ribera del Duero; try their Valduero rosé and *tinto.*

Mesón del Cid, plaza de Santa María 8, is located just west of the cathedral in a restored 15th-century house that was once the shop of one of Spain's earliest printers. Specialties here include *sopa de Doña Jimena* (a type of *sopa castellana*), *morcilla con arroz, berenjenas* (eggplant stuffed with codfish), and baby lamb stewed with mushrooms.

Casa Ojeda, Vitoria 5, just one block east of El Cid's statue, has been a Burgos institution for three-quarters of a century. A wood-fueled brick oven turns out classic *cordero asado* to go with dishes such as *alubias con chorizos y morcilla* and *merluza en salsa verde con kokotxas* (hake in a garlic and parsley sauce with glands from the cheek of the fish—a delicacy). On the ground floor of Ojeda is a gourmet shop and a popular bar frequented by tout Burgos. A pleasant sidewalk café at the rear entrance faces the Casa del Cordón on the plaza de Calvo Sotelo.

Also located on the plaza de Calvo Sotelo are two good, inexpensive restaurants. **Polvorilla** is a Burgos favorite, especially popular with the bullfight crowd, who flock here during the Fiesta de San Pablo y San Pedro in late June. After a cold glass of beer or *vino* at the downstairs bar, where Juanjo Santillana, one of the owners, holds court, you can climb the stairs to the second-floor dining room for a typical meal of *ensalada, alubias, chuletillas,* and *vino.* **Casa Alonso**, in the southeast corner of the plaza, has a good bar on the ground floor and cozy dining rooms on the second and third floors overlooking the square. This popular luncheon spot is good for salad, scrambled eggs, beans, lamb chops with potatoes, and *cuajada* for dessert.

Gaona, on Virgen de la Paloma east of the cathedral, offers a good selection of *mariscos,* excellent *chorizo de Burgos, alubias blancas* with clams, monkfish with *cigalas,* and pigeon. Don't ask for a no-smoking section here, though; the owner collects cigarette and cigar packages, which he displays in glass cases running along the top of the dining room walls.

The **Asador Ribera del Duero**, at plaza de Santo Domingo de Guzmán 18, just west of the plaza de Calvo Sotelo and a block north of Hotel España on the Espolón, is a new restaurant that took the place of the highly touted but short-lived La Becada. The Ribera del Duero emulates the great *asadores* of that region, and does it extremely well. If you stay long in Burgos, you will find yourself coming here often for superlative *chorizo cocido, jamón serrano,* Burgos cheese, salads, scrambled eggs with green garlic shoots, superb *chuletillas* with fine fried potatoes, roast lamb, and the terrific wines of Victor Balbás and Viña Pedrosa.

Another new place, just south of the Puente de San Pablo at San Pablo 3, is **Don Jamón**, which is packed every evening with Burgaleses sampling the place's exceptional *embutidos* (sausages)—*jamón, chorizo, morcilla,* and *lomo*—and the Páramo de Guzmán *queso de Burgos* of Ambrosio Molinos. You can also dine on sophisticated fare such as salmon and avocado salad, free-range chicken, and sweetbreads.

Outside the Center of Burgos

Three other religious monuments of extraordinary historical and artistic significance, and one of great interest to students of the Camino de Santiago, are located within a few miles of the center of Burgos: the Cistercian convent of Las Huelgas Reales; the Carthusian monastery called La Cartuja de Miraflores; the monastery of San Pedro de Cardeña; and the Hospital del Rey, a Santiago pilgrims' hospice.

The **Hospital del Rey**, 3 km (2 miles) west of the old quarter at the end of El Parral park, was founded in the 12th century by Alfonso VIII as a pilgrims' hospice, and was under the auspices of the powerful convent of Las Huelgas (see below). The nuns' largesse gave the hospice an exalted reputation among the tired, thirsty, and hungry pilgrims walking the Camino de Santiago. All pilgrims who could show some proof of their status were allowed to remain at the hospice for two days and were given an ample ration of bread, meat, chickpeas, and wine (16 oz.) each day. The main entrance to the hospice is the 16th-century Plateresque Puerta de Romeros (pilgrims' gate), decorated with scallop shells, coats of arms, and a seated *Virgin with Child.* The 16th-century Plateresque façade of the hospital shows another version of Santiago Matamoros wielding a sword, while his horse tramples the infidel underfoot. There is also a fine door with exceptional woodcarvings depicting pilgrims.

Las Huelgas Reales (literally "royal leisure time," from its origins as a royal retreat), located only a mile southwest of the center of Burgos, is another of Castile's great Medieval treasures. Las Huelgas was founded in 1187 by Alfonso VIII and his wife, Eleanor of Aquitaine, daughter of England's King Henry II and sister of Richard the Lion-Hearted. It became a Cistercian abbey and a pantheon for Alfonso and Eleanor and more than 50 members of the royal families of Castile. The fine 13th-century wooden statue of Santiago in the Mudejar chapel here has an articulated right arm that holds a sword. Manipulated from below a platform, the arm of Santiago moved to bestow knighthood on several kings of Castile, including Ferdinand III, who legend says had the statue made so that he would not have to be knighted by someone of lower station.

Under the protection of the royal families of Castile, Las Huelgas became one of the most powerful religious institutions in Spain. The predominant architecture of the convent is the austere transitional Gothic of the 12th- and 13th-century Cistercians that can be seen in other churches along the Camino de Santiago, with plenty of Romanesque touches as well. Among the attractions here are the 13th-century tower where Pedro the Cruel is thought to have been born, the 12th-century Romanesque *claustrillos* (small cloisters), and a 13th- to 15th-century Gothic cloister with Mudejar vaulting. The convent is rich in tapestries, woodcarvings, and royal tombs. What is claimed to be a Moorish standard captured at the battle of Las Navas de Tolosa in 1212, but in reality is probably one of the flaps of the caliph's tent—the tent itself was sent to Pope Innocent III in Rome—is also displayed here. Of particular interest at Las Huelgas is the **Museo de Telas**, with its collection of clothing worn during the 13th century, especially the cap, tunic, and belt found in the tomb of the Infante Don Fernando de la Cerda.

The 15th-century monastery of **La Cartuja de Miraflores**, 3 km (2 miles) east of Burgos on the road running along the south bank of the Arlanzón, was built by King Juan II, father of Queen Isabella, on the site of the former hunting lodge and palace of his father, Enrique III. This rather severe building, decorated only by some 16th-century Plateresque trim along the the roofline and a florid Gothic doorway, was begun in 1454 by Juan de Colonia, architect of the Burgos cathedral, and completed by his son Simón in 1488 under the direction of Isabella, for the purpose of housing the tombs of her father, mother, and brother.

These tombs and the superb retable of the main altar are masterworks of the great Flemish sculptor and woodcarver Gil de Siloé. Many experts consider Siloé's funeral monument of King Juan II and Isabella of Portugal, intricately and elaborately carved in exquisite detail, to be one of the finest tombs in existence, and that of Prince Alfonso not far behind. The former is of white marble, probably taken from the Atapuerca quarries located near Santovenia, east of Burgos, and is laid out in the pattern of an eight-pointed star thought to have been inspired by the wooden Mudejar doors at Las Huelgas convent, but the pattern is common in this area: It can be seen in the great dome of the Burgos cathedral, surrounding the *escudo* of Castile and León on the tomb of Princess Blanca of Portugal at Las Huelgas, and in many other places. The superb reclining statues of Juan and Isabella are surrounded by exceptional carved biblical figures, some of which have had their heads lopped off by vandals.

The funeral monument to a kneeling young Alfonso is done in alabaster so elaborately and intricately tooled that Alastair Boyd wrote that here "Gothic carving has reached its highest pitch of ripeness and, dabbling with the revival of pagan themes, trembles on the brink of decadence—from which it is just restrained in this case by the precision of the master." The master, Gil, has placed his own image in the lower left-hand portion of this tableau; he's the one wearing pince-nez glasses.

The altarpiece of polychrome wood done from 1496 to 1499 by Siloé and Diego de la Cruz departs from the traditional compartmentalized pattern for retables that dominates most altarpiece designs in Spain. Siloé used a series of round medallion shapes to set his scenes apart, including the great centerpiece featuring the Crucifixion. The artists' rendition of the Last Supper and of Santiago dressed as a pilgrim is particularly appealing, but most of the scenes in this magnificent work are worth studying. The gilt on the altar was supposedly crafted by Diego de la Cruz with the first gold brought by Columbus from the New World.

After the three stupendous Gil de Siloé monuments, the rest of the church is an anticlimax, but there is also a fine 17th-century statue of San Bruno by the Portuguese artist Manuel Perreira, the fine late-Gothic monk's choir stalls carved around 1489 by Martín Sanchez, some Plateresque choir stalls by Simón de Bueras, an Annunciation by Pedro Berruguete, and a triptych attributed to Juan de Flandés.

Except for patches of yellow broom, the last few miles to the **San Pedro de Cardeña monastery**, located 7 km (4 miles) southeast of the monastery of La Cartuja de Miraflores, are barren. There are no buildings or other obvious signs of modern life within a two-mile radius around the monastery, and even though the 11th-century Romanesque tower and part of the cloister of the martyrs from the same period are all that remains from the time of El Cid (most of the monastery is of the 15th century), the natural setting, a little oak- and ilex-covered valley, is just as El Cid saw it. To those steeped in the history of El Cid, there is a pervasive and powerful sense of his presence; you know that he crossed this same ground to say goodbye to Jimena and his children, who were staying at San Pedro. Then, as the bells tolled from the fine Romanesque tower, he rode off with heavy heart from his family and his beloved Castile into exile. Years later, after Valencia, Jimena brought El Cid's body back on his horse, Babieca, for interment here.

For centuries San Pedro de Cardeña was the resting place of El Cid and Jimena, and it still is for Babieca, who is even honored here with a stone monolith. After Bonaparte's troops profaned their tomb, which is still on display in a chapel here, and destroyed, defaced, or carried off many objects connected with El Cid, the bones of the couple were transported to Burgos by the French in 1808 and kept on the Espolón. In 1921, with the king of Spain as witness, the remains were moved to the cathedral. The walls of the monastery chapel where El Cid once lay are decorated with the coats of arms of 26 personages of El Cid's retinue.

The origins of San Pedro de Cardeña are believed to be Visigothic, but nothing of that epoque remains. Some 200 monks were said to have been massacred here by the Moors in 834, and it is to the memory of this event that the fine 11th-century cloister is dedicated. Ironically, though, the archways of this cloister are painted with alternating bands of red and white, calling to mind the striped archways of the Mezquita in Córdoba.

From juice purchased in the Rioja, the Cistercian monks at San Pedro make a white, a rosé, and a very good red wine, called Valdevegon, in a rustic old *bodega* on the premises, and they also make La Tizona, a chartreuse-like liqueur named after El Cid's famous sword. These can be purchased in the monastery's gift shop.

The Camino de Santiago around Burgos

Burgos together with León and Santiago itself are considered the greatest pilgrim cities on the Camino de Santiago. In addition, in Burgos province there are two major shrines: the **Iglesia de San Juan de Ortega**, located 21 km (13 miles) east of Burgos on N 120 just off the Logroño–Burgos road and through the village of Santovenia; and Castrojeriz, 45 km (28 miles) west of Burgos.

San Juan de Ortega, who lived from 1080 to 1163, was a disciple of Santo Domingo de la Calzada. San Juan built a Romanesque church to San Nicolás de Bari to serve pilgrims travelling through this desolate, bandit-infested stretch of the Camino de Santiago, thus providing a much-needed safe haven, the last stop before Burgos. San Juan's tomb is a superb Romanesque sarcophagus, and there are several fine Romanesque capitals here.

To reach Castrojeriz, take N 120 about 20 km (12.5 miles) west of Burgos to the Sasamón/Olmillos de Sasamón crossroads. You may want to go a mile or so north to see the 13th-century **church of Sasamón**, another pilgrims' church with a fine door and an exceptional doorway resembling the Puerta del Sarmental of the Burgos cathedral. Returning south to N 120 you will see Olmillos and its ruined, photogenic 15th-century castle. Follow N 120 west for 5 km (3 miles), turn south at Villasandino, and take the Palencia road about 15 km

(9 miles) to **Castrojeriz**, the place James A. Michener imagined as being, in Medieval times, "a magnificent settlement rising in the sky."

Castrojeriz is a decrepit old town now, with a ruined castle, the remains of the 14th-century monastery of San Antón, the 13th-century Colegiata de Santa María del Manzano, the church of Santo Domingo with some fine 16th-century tapestries, and the Romanesque church of San Juan. Castrojeriz needs a facelift, but its old buildings emit a sense of the past that lingers long after the image of many restored towns of tourist-poster quality have faded. Some 30 km (20 miles) west of Castrojeriz is Frómista (see the Palencia section, above), the next major stop westward on the Camino de Santiago.

GETTING AROUND

Salamanca–Zamora–León

To take in the countryside and the cities in this region travellers are well advised to rent a car. From Madrid take the A 6 *autopista* northwest to Villacain, then take the N 501 west through Avila to Salamanca. The 200-km (125-mile) trip takes about two hours. From Salamanca N 630 leads to Zamora, about 60 km (36 miles) north, and León, about 200 km (125 miles) farther along. Salamanca, Valladolid, and Burgos are linked by a major highway, the N 620/E 3. There is frequent bus service along these major highways, too, especially to Madrid, two and a half to three hours from Salamanca.

The closest airport to these cities is in Valladolid. Rail service is spotty in the region, but there are nine trains a day between Salamanca and Valladolid, with connections on to Burgos. From León there are trains to Burgos, Barcelona, Madrid (one *Talgo* express that takes about four hours), and Oviedo, to the north.

Valladolid–Palencia–Burgos

Burgos and Valladolid are fairly well served by trains and buses between each other and from Madrid, Salamanca, León, and other cities. Valladolid has a small airport, but unless you enjoy travelling in the provinces by buses that often run only once a day in each direction, the only practical way to explore this area is by car.

An excellent approach to this region is to head north from Madrid on N VI to Valladolid province, and either stay in Valladolid or Tordesillas, from which you can explore the recommended sights of the Duero river valley, then perhaps visit Palencia, Frómista, and Carrión de los Condes. This area can also be seen using Burgos as a base. The eastern Duero valley, Peñaranda, Santo Domingo de Silos, and the rest of southern Burgos province are most convenient from Aranda de Duero, but many people will prefer the more cosmopolitan attractions of Burgos as a base. For those with little time, this trip can be done in a few days, but this region's attractions really call for a week or more.

ACCOMMODATIONS REFERENCE

When dialing telephone numbers in Spain from outside the country, drop the 9 in the area code.

▶ **Almirante Bonifaz.** Vitoria 22–24, 09004 **Burgos.** Tel: (947) 20-69-43.

▶ **Arlanza.** Plaza Mayor 11, 09346 **Covarrubias**, Burgos. Tel: (947) 40-30-25.

▶ **Los Bronces.** Carretera de Madrid-Irún, km 160, 09400 **Aranda de Duero**, Burgos. Tel: (947) 50-08-50.

▶ **Castillo de Monzón.** 34410 **Monzón de Campos**, Palencia. Tel: (988) 80-80-75.

▶ **Hotel Conde Luna.** Avenida de la Independencia 7, 24003 **León.** Tel: (987) 20-65-12.

▶ **Condes de Alba y Aliste.** Plaza de Cánovas 1, 49014 **Zamora.** Tel: (988) 51-44-97.

▶ **Condestable.** Vitoria 8, 09004 **Burgos.** Tel: (947) 26-71-25.

▶ **Cordón.** La Puebla 6, 09004 **Burgos.** Tel: (947) 26-50-00.

▶ **Parador Enrique II.** Plaza del Castillo 1, 37500 **Ciudad Rodrigo.** Tel: (923) 46-01-50.

▶ **Felipe IV.** Gamazo 16, 47004 **Valladolid.** Tel: (983) 30-70-00; Telex: 26264; Fax: (983) 30-86-87.

▶ **Fernán González.** Calera 19, 09002 **Burgos.** Tel: (947) 20-94-41.

▶ **Hotel Gaudí.** Eduardo de Castro 6, 24700 **Astorga**, León. Tel: (987) 61-56-54.

▶ **Gran Hotel.** Poeta Iglesias 5, 37001 **Salamanca.** Tel: (923) 21-35-00.

▶ **Landa Palace.** Carretera de Madrid–Irún 236, 09000 **Burgos.** Tel: (947) 20-63-43.

▶ **Meliá Parque.** Joaquín García Morato 17, 47007 **Valladolid.** Tel: (983) 47-01-00; Telex: 26355; Fax: (983) 47-50-29.

▶ **Hotel Monterrey.** Calle Azafranal 21, 37001 **Salamanca.** Tel: (923) 21-44-00.

▶ **Olid Meliá.** Plaza San Miguel 10, 47003 **Valladolid.** Tel: (983) 35-72-00; Telex: 26312; Fax: (983) 33-68-28.

▶ **Hotel Riosol.** Avenida de Palencia 3, 24001 **León.** Tel: (987) 22-38-50.

▶ **Parador Nacional de Salamanca.** Teso de la Feria 2, 37008 **Salamanca.** Tel: (923) 22-87-00.

▶ **Parador San Marcos.** Plaza San Marcos 7, 24001 **León.** Tel: (987) 23-73-00.

▶ **Parador Nacional de Tordesillas.** Carretera de Salamanca, km 153, 47100 **Tordesillas,** Valladolid. Tel: (983) 77-00-51.

▶ **Tres Coronas de Silos.** Plaza Mayor, 09610 **Santo Domingo de Silos,** Burgos. Tel: (947) 38-07-28.

▶ **Hotel El Zaguan.** Calle Ventura Ruiz Aguilera 7–9, 37002 **Salamanca.** Tel: (923) 21-47-05.

ASTURIAS AND GALICIA

By Robert Levine

Robert Levine, a New York–based music and travel writer, has contributed to the travel sections of the San Francisco Examiner *and the* Denver Post, *and to* Fanfare *and* Opera Quarterly *magazines, among others. He visits Spain several times each year.*

This is green Spain. Those yearning for the whitewashed look of white-hot towns are bound to be disappointed. Those searching for the Arab influence in architecture or the cult of the bullfight will similarly be let down. However, for fine examples of Roman and Romanesque buildings, 8,000-foot-high mountains just 12 miles from the sea, lush greenery, and coastlines that range from rough to silky, those interested need look no farther than these two connecting regions, which occupy the northwest portion of the country. They could easily occupy ten days of a vacation.

Asturias, which is west of Cantabria along the north coast of Spain just above León, ends in the west at the río Eo; Galicia, to its west, is defined by the Atlantic Ocean on its western side and Portugal to the south. Asturias is known for its wonderfully heady cider, Galicia for its food and music played on a bagpipe-like instrument. Galicia was once a Celtic land, and some of that influence still shows there—it even *looks* like Ireland.

But both of these regions, whatever they may look like,

are most assuredly Spain: the festivals, the folklore, the food, the independent spirit. These were the people who fled the Moors and who kept their part of Spain almost entirely free of any influence other than Christian. And the two regions are as different from each other as they are from Andalusia.

Asturias's exquisite coastline is matched only by its inland region filled with apple trees, dense forests in which bears still roam, and the majestic mountains, the Picos de Europa. And at the foot of these mountains are tiny fishing villages that seem frozen in a time gone by. The region's capital, Oviedo, is a modern city whose ancient roots seem to lie beneath its Gothic cathedral.

Galicia's *rías*—fjord-like inlets on the Atlantic believed to have been formed when whole valleys caved in and were buried by the sea thousands of years ago—are quite an attraction, and not to be found anywhere else. And then there's the jewel in Galicia's crown, one of the reasons why this part of Spain—indeed, of the world—cannot be missed: Santiago de Compostela. A town, a shrine (one of the greatest in Christendom), a museum, and a place for great seafood and wine as well, this endpoint of pilgrims' journeys during the Middle Ages is one of the most memorable spots on earth.

The Asturias and Galicia area is wild, rugged Spain, a place with the cornerstones of Western civilization at its heart.

MAJOR INTEREST IN ASTURIAS

Oviedo's cathedral and old town
Hill country
Gijón's beach and restaurants
The picturesque fishing village of Luarca

MAJOR INTEREST IN GALICIA

The food of Galicia
Festivals
The Pilgrims' Way
The Roman and Medieval city of Lugo

Santiago de Compostela
The cathedral of Santiago
Hostal de los Reyes Católicos

A Coruña's marina and old town
The *rías* (fjords) on the Atlantic coast

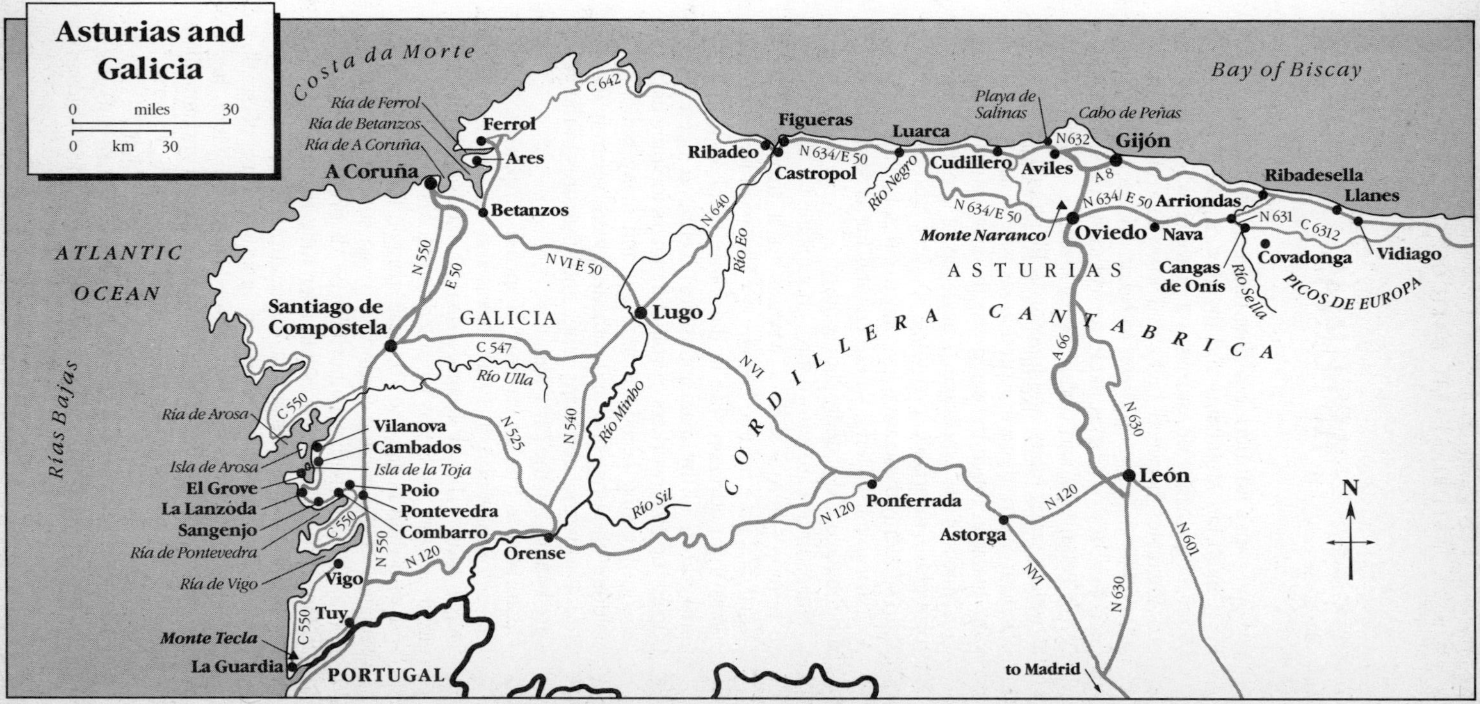

Asturias and Galicia
0 miles 30
0 km 30
Costa da Morte
Bay of Biscay
ATLANTIC OCEAN
Rías Bajas
Ría de Ferrol
Ría de Betanzos
Ría de A Coruña
Ferrol
Ares
A Coruña
Betanzos
C 642
Figueras
Ribadeo
Castropol
N 634/E 50
Luarca
Río Negro
Playa de Salinas
Cabo de Peñas
N 632
Gijón
Cudillero
Aviles
A 8
Ribadesella
Llanes
N 634/ E 50
Arriondas
N 634/E 50
Monte Naranco
Oviedo
Nava
N 631
C 6312
Covadonga
Vidiago
Cangas de Onís
Río Sella
PICOS DE EUROPA
ASTURIAS
CORDILLERA CANTABRICA
N 640
Río Eo
N VI E 50
N 550
E 50
Santiago de Compostela
GALICIA
Lugo
C 547
Río Ulla
NVI
A 66
N 630
C 550
Ría de Arosa
Vilanova
Cambados
Isla de Arosa
Isla de la Toja
El Grove
Poio
La Lanzóda
Pontevedra
Sangenjo
Combarro
Ría de Pontevedra
Ría de Vigo
N 525
N 540
Río Minho
Río Sil
León
Ponferrada
N 120
Astorga
N 601
Orense
Vigo
Tuy
Monte Tecla
La Guardia
PORTUGAL
to Madrid
N

ASTURIAS

Set on Spain's northern coastline between the highlands of the Cantabrian Mountains and the Bay of Biscay north of León, the province of Asturias is a province whose geography fluctuates between highs and lows. Here, high limestone cliffs may swoop down to broad and densely populated beaches or, just as likely, to secluded coves. Cabo de Peñas, Pendueles, and Gijón offer dramatic rock formations as well as sandy inlets. And in Asturias, like much of "green" northern Spain, there are rural areas where farmers make their living in much the same way their ancestors did long ago. Much of the landscape is made up of apple orchards, cornfields (invariably providing fodder), and pig farms. Then suddenly these areas give way to cities, like the cosmopolitan capital, Oviedo, where cultural life is sophisticated and the pace is decidedly 20th century.

The Asturians are known throughout Spain for their sense of humor—there's such a wryness to it that even the Madrileños have trouble keeping up. Like most humor, part comes from adversity; life in the mines (coal and copper mining are still the main industries) has never been easy. During the 1934 workers' revolt, the miners took the city of Oviedo. Fighting lasted for ten days and many buildings, including the university and cathedral, were severely damaged. Two years later, many other fine structures in the city were battered in the Civil War.

Asturias was the last territory of ancient Hispania to submit to Romanization, in 19 B.C. It was also the kingdom that fought most valiantly against Islam; it was settled in the eighth century by Goths who fled the Moors from Toledo, and who then began the 700-year struggle for reconquest. Remains of the ancient fortifications can still be seen. The region is filled with an unusual type of pre-Romanesque architecture called Ramiresque, after King Ramiro I (842–850). It is a style you might expect from a no-nonsense people: The buildings, made of limestone, are of small proportions, with completely vaulted interiors. When they are decorated, it is with simple reliefs of human and animal figures. There are about 60 of these structures dispersed throughout the region (a few will be discussed later).

Besides the contrasts in landscape and culture and the unusual architectural types, there are two other Asturian hallmarks to look for: the spectacular regional cheeses, such as *cabrales* (a ferocious blue cheese) and *amonedo* (mild, soft), and *sidra,* a not especially sweet apple cider served in taverns and restaurants throughout the province. It's a real thirst quencher and, even if you aren't interested in drinking it, just watching the waiters pour it from urns slung over their shoulders is enough to keep you entertained. The cuisine is nothing to skip over either. The *fabada* (stewed beans), *pote Asturiano* (beef and vegetable stew), *merluza a la sidra* (hake poached in cider), and *pulpo guisado* (stewed octopus) are all treats to be found nowhere else.

Asturias can be approached from the east along the coast, a spectacular, if necessarily leisurely drive, via **Ribadesella** (worth a stop for the "Tito Bustillo" cave containing prehistoric drawings and carvings) and Gijón, or from the southeast via the staggering Picos de Europa. Coming from Galicia, to the west, you can stop in the small fishing villages of Luarca and Cudillero, among others. The main road directly north of León in Old Castile will take you directly to Oviedo.

OVIEDO

Oviedo, the region's capital, is a city so diverse that its different aspects should clash, but for some reason they blend. Parts of the city are sleek and modern, with buildings in which the symphony orchestra and the state opera company perform. But much of it, particularly its most important structure, the cathedral, is ancient. The two worlds complement each other, and there are no barriers between them. The city center is compact and very easy to walk around. And while it isn't particularly pretty, it's a city-lover's city.

You might want to spend a couple of full days exploring this city on foot, which is more advisable than trying to crowd it all into a day. Start at the grand **Parque de San Francisco**—the "lungs" of the city—where all Oviedo goes for their *paseo* (stroll) among fountains, kiosks, and flowers. This is a great city park: clean, safe, and pretty, it's a good place for wandering, jogging, or sitting on a bench and watching the crowd—or the swans in the pond. From the park, stroll to Gil de Jaz and you're at the **Hotel de la Reconquista**, by far the finest place to stay in town. Formerly a royal building, it is a seemingly endless labyrinth of hallways and stairways. The 18th-century Reconquista is thoroughly deluxe, the rooms gracious yet modern. The hotel's restaurant is elegant, and the food never disappoints.

Walk south to calle de Uria, which leads to calle Fruela, and bear left down the narrow calle Jesus. You'll come to the rectangular plaza Mayor, dominated by the Ayuntamiento (City Hall), begun in 1622 and one of the city's most important meeting places. Groups of locals congregate below the arcade to bicker about current events, *fútbol,* and other aspects of daily life.

Continue north to the plaza de Riego. On your left will be the very Classical building of the old (1608) **university**, still functioning today. A walk into the handsome courtyard will allow you to see a statue of the university's founder, Fernando Valdes.

Keep going north to the plaza Porlier. Take note of the elegant façade of the 18th-century Palacio de los Campos Sagrados, today the seat of the region's Territorial Court. One block east you'll suddenly find yourself in the **plaza de Alfonso II**, the location of the always surprising cathedral (more on this later). If you can take your eyes from the cathedral, note the mostly 15th-century Casa de la Rúa, the city's oldest house, also on the plaza. Walking south around the cathedral you'll see the San Tirso window, all that remains of a ninth-century church of that name. Then note the monasteries of San Vicente and San Pelayo around the back of the cathedral. The **monasterio de San Vicente** was founded in 781, making it the city's oldest building. It was restored in many different centuries, most recently the 18th, although part of the original building is still visible; the **Museo Arqueológico** (the provincial archaeological museum) is housed here. The San Pelayo's Baroque façade is worthy of note. On the plaza de Santo Domingo, farther south, is the Teatro Campoamo, a 19th-century building now used as an opera house.

When you get back to the plaza de Alfonso II, return to the park and travel southeast, down calle Suarez de Riva to the plaza del Fontán for a visit to the **Palacio de San Felix** (a.k.a. the Palacio del Duque del Parque). Within is an impressive "Apostle" painting by El Greco, one of the last remaining of a series.

The Cathedral

The expansive cathedral, Sancta Ovetensis, on the plaza de Alfonso II, is in the heart of the city. It is a stunning Flamboyant Gothic building, but it is covered with soot—nothing has been done, apparently for centuries, to clean it. Destroyed by the Moors, the eighth-century church was begun to be rebuilt in the 14th century and finished 200 years later.

The cathedral has three entrances, each a different height, and a beautiful tower, which the 19th-century essayist Leopoldo Alas called a "poem in stone." The building's asymmetry is odd but intriguing. Directly inside, on the left, is the Saint Eulalia chapel from the 17th century; its Churrigueresque, ever-so-slightly kitsch shrine containing the saint's remains is definitely an offbeat introduction to the cathedral.

The cathedral's retable, or altarpiece, from the 16th century, is a masterpiece of carved intricacy, but it has been poorly touched up and repainted in an attempt at restoration. Still, it's worthy of close examination. Almost 40 feet by 40 feet, it's made up of five sections, each containing five carved scenes from the life of Christ. And there's the occasional anachronism to keep you guessing—one of the saints is wearing glasses. Off in the north corner of the church is the burial place of the Asturian kings. Their remains are housed in a 12th-century marble-lidded sarcophagus.

The Cámara Santa (Holy Chamber), whose entrance is on the right side of the transept, was built by Alfonso II to house Spain's Christian treasures (it was destroyed during the workers' revolt and later rebuilt) and consists of two rooms. Six double columns adorned with the heads of the Apostles are in the larger of the two, which dates from the 12th century. The other room, from the ninth century, contains, among other treasures, two important crosses: the Cruz de los Angeles (Cross of Angels), from 808, inlaid with gems and used in the ritual to open court, and the ornate Cruz de la Victoria (Cross of Victory), from 908, used to close court. A cedar chest covered in silver bas-relief houses the remains of Alfonso XI.

The cathedral is the focal point of the Festival of Saint Matthew, celebrated on September 21, when after mass the whole plaza fills with celebrating townfolk in traditional and not-so-traditional finery, and the famous Asturian cider flows.

Another church worth visiting is San Julián de los Prados. This important Asturian church/monument is a bit off the beaten track, in the center of a field a 15-minute walk northeast of the center of town. (Take calle Martinez Vigil to calle Marcelino Fernandez. The latter leads right into the plaza de Santullano.) Built in 814, the oddly constructed **Santullano**, as San Julián is known, contains murals, including one depicting the construction of the church itself. Beautiful windows let natural light into the sanctuary. (The church's dialect name is derived from "sant-u-llano," literally, "Saint of the Fields.") As long as you're in the neighborhood, stop at the nearby 12th-century Iglesia de Santa María de la Vega. What it lacks in art treasures it makes up for in elegant simplicity.

Eventually you'll have to stop to eat. Back downtown, **Casa Fermín** on calle de San Francisco is a treat, and it has a spectacular wine cellar. Try their *caldereta,* a stew made from fish that live among the rocks. If you're in the mood for meat, try *morcilla* (Asturian blood sausage), with beans or in a stew. Or for a meal that *seems* light, go to **Babilonia**, an exotic, Arabic-looking *fromagerie* on calle Asturias (and around the corner from the Reconquista). They serve an entire meal of local cheeses and pâtés. For the most "elite" meal in town (outside of the Reconquista's dining room), try **La Goleta**, serving regional specialties, such as *fabes con almejas* (clams with white beans).

Monte Naranco

A 3-km (1¾-mile) excursion northwest of town to Monte Naranco offers a variety of rewards. From the Parque de San Francisco take Marques de Pidal across Viaducto Marquina, turn left on avenida de Enol, and then right on avenida de los Monumentos, which leads to two fascinating buildings: the Iglesia de San Miguel de Lillo and the Iglesia de Santa María del Naranco. These two examples of Asturian pre-Romanesque architecture alone are worth the trip.

Santa María del Naranco, built in 848 at what is believed to have been the entrance hall of the palace of King Ramiro I, was a totally unorthodox structure for its time. The adornments were placed where they were needed for structure rather than simply for decorative value. The building was considered somber, its minimal decoration making it appear nearly Oriental to the Spanish. It defines Ramiresque architecture. The palace was converted to a church some time after the ninth century. Demolished in the 15th, it was put back together by, unfortunately, a rather blundering builder, so that it now seems haphazard. Inside, make sure to see the painting of the Holy Family and the angel playing a flute, very early representations of Spanish art.

San Miguel de Lillo may have been the palace's church. It was badly damaged in the 13th century, but what is left is intriguing: The grotesque carvings on the pillars and around the doors are unequaled in their peculiarity. From the top of the hill on which the church stands take in the breathtaking panorama.

Monte Naranco is also the home of an amphitheater cut right into the mountain. Every September the theater comes alive with all kinds of cultural events, from opera to bullfights. There's also the Día de las Américas (Americas Day) festival on September 19.

EASTERN HILL COUNTRY

Inland, Asturias is green country—an anthology of meadows, woods, and countryside surrounded by the snow-capped Picos de Europa at the far east, and the Cantabrian chain.

Before you begin your trek from Oviedo west to Galicia or north to Gijón, you may want to take an eastern detour to the most important hill town in the area, **Cangas de Onís**, 70 km (44 miles) east of Oviedo on N 634/E 50, turning right past Arriondas. Located on the banks of the río Sella in rugged, green countryside, this town is famous for its "Roman bridge" (it's actually Gothic, dating from the 13th century) across the Sella. This first capital of Spain is near an old Celtic burial ground, on top of which is built the **Capilla de Santa Cruz**, founded in 735.

But to get the real flavor of the hill towns, see **Covadonga**, the town most celebrated as the site where the Spanish halted the northward march of the Moors with a victory at the so-called Battle of Covadonga in 722. From Cangas de Onís take route C 6312 east; the road to Covadonga will turn off to the right after about 6.5 km (4 miles). You'll travel through apple orchards and past waterfalls on the river Deva. The village of Covadonga is positioned atop a mountain and, even farther up, in the Cave of Auseva atop a rocky cliff (no need for climbing gear; there are stairs), sits an altar to the Virgin, built in thanks for Prince Pelayo's victory over the Moors in 718. Because the prince and his wife are buried here, the place is practically a national shrine. You may also want to visit the Parque Nacional de Covadonga, a sanctuary for animals, birds, and flora. If you want to stay in the area, the **Ventura** in Cangas de Onís on avenida de Covadonga is recommended.

Near Vidiago, a village 8 km (5 miles) east of the coastal town of Llanes near Asturias's eastern border with Cantabria, stands the Celtic idol **Pena Tu**, a Bronze-Age monolith whose meaning has not yet been deciphered. (There are plenty of signs showing the way to Pena Tu; it's the main attraction in this area.)

COASTAL ASTURIAS

Gijón

The trip from Oviedo northeast to the central coastal city of Gijón is only about 30 km (19 miles). Gijón is on the Cantabrian coast, on a very large bay dominated by the Santa Catalina Rock, site of the original settlement. It is the largest city in Asturias (almost 300,000 inhabitants) and the most important industrial center, after Bilbao, in northern Spain. There's a fine parador here, the **El Molino Viejo** (which actually was an old mill, although it's been entirely redone), located in the beautiful, bird-filled, relaxing Parque Isabel la Católica: a fine place to relax as you're travelling through the province. (Or, if you want a hotel right on the bay, the **Príncipe de Asturias** is a good bet.)

Hardly anything is left here of the Roman, Visigothic, or Moorish cultures, which, at one point or another, have taken up residence in Gijón. In the eighth century the Asturian kings called this town home, and in 1588 what little was left of the Armada settled here. Until the 19th century Gijón was primarily a fishing town, but with the advent of increased commerce with South America and of the railroad lines, which were opened in 1860, the port became a major gateway for mineral export. Most of the activity in Gijón centers around the port. The city was practically demolished during the Civil War, but it has been rebuilt, and it is now almost entirely modern.

Gijón's modern aspect may strike you as heartless, but at the foot of the Santa Catalina cliff is the **plaza del Marqués**, flanked by the only two majestic old buildings in town: the Iglesia de San Juan Bautista (begun in the 15th and finished in the 18th century) and the 16th-century Palacio del Conde de Rivillagigedo. Both are in terrible condition and exude dreariness, but at least they're not modern. Directly behind the plaza, however, is the **Cimadevilla**, the picturesque old fishermen's quarter. It's confusingly laid out and takes some time to get used to, but the winding, narrow streets and vaguely tilting buildings have a charm, albeit a somewhat ominous one.

Nearby is the town's **San Lorenzo beach,** a large curve of sand that attracts thousands of mostly Spanish vacationers every year—mainly a crowd that has no interest, for one reason or another, in such better-known places as San Sebastian or Santander. The tides are gentle and the weather, at least in summer, reliable. There are bars and somewhat seedy nightclubs galore on the side streets facing the beach, and you get the impression that there's something decidedly down-market about the whole scene. Not so the cuisine, however: This is the heart of Asturian cooking, and in a restaurant such as **Casa Victor** the *pulpo* (octopus) and grilled salmon can't be beat, and neither can the wine list. **El Retiro** is another good bet; try the *merluza a la cazuela* (hake stew).

Literary buffs may want to know that Gaspar Melchor de Jovellanos, the poet, activist, and encyclopedist, was born here in 1744; in the center of town, on the plaza del 6 de Agosto, there's a monument to him. Just northeast, on plaza Jovellanos, there's a museum in the house in which he was born. The main reason for going there is to arrange to see what little is left of some **Roman baths**, to be found under the Cimadevilla barrio; ask the person in charge of the museum to arrange for your visit.

Gijón, in general, does not enchant, but it's a worthy overnight stopping-off point if you want a good dip in the ocean or if you're travelling either to or from Galicia or the Basque country across the northern coast. And the food is definitely worth a detour.

West to Galicia

West from Gijón, many little coastal villages line the way to the town of Luarca, once an important whaling capital at the mouth of the río Negro. Almost halfway there, for example, there's **Salinas**, a fir-lined beach. **Luarca** itself is built on several hills, and the whitewashed, slate-roofed houses are a charming sight, adding to the quaint, uncalculated appeal of this port town. Also here: a castle in ruins; a cemetery situated on a peninsula near town; a nearby lighthouse (at its best in the fog, which is most of the time); and seven bridges spanning the river.

The traveller on the way to Galicia will probably also go through **Figueras**, a fishing village overlooking the río Eo, and, across the river in Galicia, **Ribadeo** (the Parador de Ribadeo on Amador Fernandez has a fine restaurant and panoramic views). The reasonably priced **Peñalba** restaurant, on El Muelle in Figueras, serves excellent seafood from the river; the fish stew is particularly good.

GALICIA

Galicia, one of the least-known and least-travelled provinces in Spain, sits just above Portugal. Quite unlike the rest of Spain both in appearance and in attitude, Galicia looks like Ireland. The landscape is lush and green, and you will be hard put to find here the sun-drenched look of the villages to the south. The countryside is thick with pine and eucalyptus. The beaches, rough and often a bit cold, are noteworthy because of the famous *rías,* somewhat like the fjords of Norway. The rías make Galicia's beaches special, especially on the west coast.

And then there are the people. Galicians—*Gallegos,* as they're called in Spanish—are different from other Spaniards and seem a race apart. The rest of their countrymen sometimes see them as provincial, maybe a little backward. Their industriousness seems to lack the high-tech energy of the Catalans, and their nightlife definitely lacks the sophistication of Madrid or Seville. They love poetry, music, land, and family. They are fascinated with death, witchcraft, and superstition. They are thoughtful, maybe even a little evasive, yet they're willing to accept outsiders gracefully. They treat outsiders like family, yet they will fight each other brutally over a piece of land. Indeed, they worship land.

Perhaps many of these traits came from the Celts, who conquered the area in about 1000 B.C. and stayed in control until A.D. 137. This may explain why the people seem to have so much in common with the Irish and the Scots. They even play a bagpipe-like instrument called a *gaita.*

Galician, the dialect, which is close to Portuguese but with French overtones, is so beautiful that by the 13th century the great poets of Madrid dropped their short-syllabled Castilian and adopted Galician for the language of love. Over the years the Gallegos have had to fight to keep their language. Today, Galician is taught here as the primary language in the schools, and fairly recently road and street signs have begun to be converted from Castilian. The two look enough alike not to confuse visitors, however; for example, the Spanish *La Coruña,* becomes in Galician *A Coruña.*

The Food of Galicia

First of all, remember that this is a land of winegrowers. Talk to a local shopkeeper, or perhaps your tour guide, and you're apt to find he has his own vines and winery on the side. Galician wines are commonly characterized by their freshness—their alcohol content is low—and their purity (no preservatives are needed because they're consumed right here). *Aguardiente,* used as an after-dinner *digestif,* is a by-product of the wine-making process.

The vinegrowers of Galicia are also licensed to distill their product, which means that they can make brandy. And what brandy it is! Try the cherry.

There's another way in which the Gallegos like to tempt brandy lovers: *quiemada,* a local after-feast custom involving burning the brandy and adding sugar and lemon peel to it. Drink it fast; it's strong, but what a nice effect!

As for the food itself, there's fish, needless to say. *Merluza* (hake), *cigales* (prawns), *camarones* (small shrimp), *chipirones* (little squid), *langostinos* (baby lobsters—a bit hard to eat, but delicious), *almejas* (clams—very tiny and sweet and served in a broth) as well as trout and local fish of all kinds are prepared in casseroles or broiled or steamed. They are also rolled into delicious crepes, or "pies."

In the colder seasons, the meat served is local—and fabulous; game and rabbit are Galician specialties. One of the local dishes is ham with turnip tops; the ham is cooked with pork sausages and whole boiled potatoes and served en casserole. Local turnips and small peppers are especially good in season.

Gallegos, like Asturians, are cheese makers *par excellence.* You could eat an entire lunch here made from local cheese: cheese from goat's milk, sheep's milk, everything, it seems, but the more pedestrian cow's milk. There are varieties of soft, semi-soft, et cetera, all of it ripened naturally and without preservatives. Try the breast-shaped *tetilla*—it's mild and smooth. Some of the blue cheeses are ferocious, so go slowly. And to make all of these cheeses even more satisfying, eat them with homemade peasant bread.

For sweet desserts the locals make what they describe as a "humble" pancake pastry known as *filoa,* wonderful with custard. (By humble, they apparently mean it isn't one of those fancy French subtleties.) The Gallegos also make great almond and sponge cakes, not to be found in the rest of the country.

The Wines of Galicia

Of Galicia's four provinces—La Coruña, Lugo, Orense, and Pontevedra—only the last two are major wine producers, with three DOs (*denominaciones de origen*): Ribeiro, Valdeorras, and the newly created Rias Baixas (Pontevedra), where Albariño, Galicia's greatest white wine and certainly one of the best white wines of Spain, is made. The traditional growing area for Albariño is around the town of Cambados on the Atlantic coast in western Pontevedra province, and near Túy along the Miño (Minho) river bordering Portugal.

Albariño is a rare wine, dry and elegant, with a pretty, flowery nose reminiscent of fine Riesling, the German grape that many Galicians believe was the ancestor of Albariño. Traditionally it has been made in small lots by artisan producers, some of whom are local legends. Production has been limited, so most Albariño, usually not even bearing a label, never left its native province. Recently, however, a few firms have begun making Albariño on a larger scale, so it is now possible to find these superb wines outside Galicia. Albariño goes beautifully with the rich variety of Galician seafood. One particularly good Albariño is Martin Codax.

Since Galicia produces much less wine than it consumes, **Ribeiro** (Orense) is much in demand. Ribeiro's best wines are young, fresh, fruity, *petillant* white wines similar to the *vinhos verdes* of Portugal. The wines are made from Treixadura, Jerez (Palomino), Macabeo, Godello, and a host of other indigenous grapes. The vines are trained on wires supported by stone posts.

Valdeorras (Orense) is centered around El Barco de Valdeorras in the Sil river valley of mountainous eastern Orense. Although rainy like the rest of Galicia, the climate here is moderated by the weather of continental Spain, so that the vines get a good deal of sun. The picturesque trellised vineyards are terraced on steep slate hills, which provide good drainage. The Godello grape (related to the Verdejo of Rueda) makes the best Valdeorras white wines, which are fresh, medium to full-bodied, and quite aromatic. The reds—light, cherry-colored, fruity wines—are made from Garnacha and Mencia grapes. In 1983 only 5,000 bottles of Valdeorras were exported, but experts believe that Valdeorras has great potential.

—Gerry Dawes

Festivals in Galicia

There is strong religious feeling in Galicia. Ask a Gallego where he's from and he may very well tell you the name of his parish rather than his town. A visit to churches here will reveal mystical offerings and votives. There are some unusual practices too, such as the Puebla del Caraminal procession, where once a year those who have somehow been saved from dying go into their coffins.

Every parish church in Galicia holds an annual festival in honor of its patron saint. Because there are almost 4,000 parish churches, chances are you're going to come upon a festival no matter when you visit. After mass, the main town square, wherever you are, fills with townspeople and comes to resemble New York's Fifth Avenue on Easter Sunday. People stroll and show off finery and stop to gossip with their neighbors. There are live bands, frequently playing not very good but loud rock music. There may very well be a group of vendors selling crafts, giving you a fine opportunity to shop for gifts. And the prices will be negotiable.

Some well-known festivals are Los Maios, celebrated in May to honor the spring, and, on November 11, Magosto, when chestnuts are roasted and new wine is tasted. There's also La Rapa das Bestas, when wild horses are branded (check with a local travel agent or the National Tourist Office of Spain for details concerning date and locale). Carnival has been celebrated here as well since pre-Christian times. The very important Feast Day of Saint James (Santiago) is July 25, and when this day falls on a Sunday a Holy Year is designated. (The next one is 1993.) There are fireworks in the main square of Santiago de Compostela (more later), and it is only during the Holy Years that the cathedral's Puerta Santa (the rear door) is open.

The Pilgrims' Way

Other than the pull of the Gallegos themselves, their food, and their scenic province, there is something else that draws people to this part of Spain: Santiago de Compostela. The cathedral, the relics, and the town itself have attracted pilgrims from around the world since the very early Middle Ages. Galicia's role as a destination on the Medieval Pilgrims' Way—the **Camino de Santiago**—has shaped and colored the province's past and importance to the country and the Western world. Santiago de Compostela, for reasons discussed later, goes along with Rome and Jerusalem to make up the three great Christian destinations.

There are many routes to Santiago. The Medieval pilgrims came from France, Great Britain, Germany, Scandinavia, and elsewhere, walking great distances and resting in hospices that had been set up for them. Pilgrims invariably entered Spain from France via the Somport Pass or the Roncesvalles Pass in the Pyrenees. One of the most frequently taken routes was Pamplona–Santo Domingo de la Calzada–Burgos–Sahagún–León–Santiago, with stops in any number of towns along the way and at monasteries and shrines. Our book covers points along the Pilgrims' Way in several chapters, starting near France in the east with the Aragón and Basque Country/Navarra/La Rioja chapters, then, moving westward, in the Old Castile chapter (Burgos, León), and finally in Galicia (Lugo, followed by the goal, Santiago de Compostela).

The Medieval pilgrims' journeys took months or even years. The modern visitor can do it in 55 minutes by flying directly from Madrid. But then, of course, you would miss the rest of the north and the whole feel of the experience. And that would be a shame. There's a happy medium to be struck: A trip here by car or train is heartily recommended for the curious traveller with a week to spare in this region.

LUGO

One of the pilgrims' stops was Lugo, about 107 km (67 miles) due east of Santiago, and if you're coming from Asturias in the east, or from León in Old Castile, this might be your first big stop in Galicia. Pilgrims were happy to see its fortifications—it meant safety from the disagreeable elements they would encounter, both human and natural. Most people in this century prefer to see it as a day trip from Santiago, an hour and a half away on C 547.

Located in the province of the same name, Lugo seems a city of stones. The first glance is overwhelming—the walls are 20 feet thick and 35 feet high. You can walk a mile or so along the old **Roman walls** and get an almost precise idea of the size of the old Roman town. The plaza de España was the amphitheater and the plaza de Campo was the site of the forum. It's easy to imagine. There are 50 watchtowers and ten iron and wooden gates cut into the walls. The most interesting of these gates is the **Puerta de Miño**, one of the oldest, now known as the Puerta del Carmen, located on the western side of the city. The thickness of the walls and the size of the stones are testimony to the fact that this was one of the city's real strongholds. Again, you can, and should, mount the ramparts here or elsewhere and walk around the perimeter to get an overall feel of the city. Another of the ten gates, Santiago, the southern one, opens onto the plaza Pio XII and the **cathedral**.

The cathedral, built to imitate the one in Santiago de Compostela, is Romanesque-Gothic, having taken six centuries to build; it was completed only in 1768. The cathedral houses the relics of Saint Froilan, Lugo's patron saint. Visit the Capilla de Nuestra Señora de los Ojos Grandes in the east end of the cathedral. The sculpture of the Virgin there is polychrome alabaster, dating from the 12th century, when, it was believed, her intercession in many of the battles of the Reconquest were said to have made victory possible.

You should also pay a visit to the Iglesia de San Francisco and the **Provincial Museum** located next door, on the ground floor of the Provincial Palace on calle San Marcos. The collection of Roman coins, sarcophogi, and other ancient items here is impressive. The Iglesia de Santo Domingo, at the dead center of the old city, dates from the 13th century but nevertheless has a Romanesque-style façade.

Lugo gives you an opportunity to see a well-preserved Medieval city and the finest example of Roman military architecture in Spain, but it would be wise to ignore the modern, built-up sections outside the walls. If you should decide to stay overnight in Lugo, swimming-pool-equipped **Gran Hotel Lugo** will make you comfortable, although it's less than a bargain. It's located in the town's residential section, five minutes from the center. A good place to eat, and at reasonable prices, is **Verruga**, at Cruz 12. Another is **Mesón de Alberto**, at Cruz 4, where you'll find high prices for superb delicacies such as *revuelto de salmon con angulas* (salmon and baby eel omelette), and other fish dishes. The setting here is charmingly rustic.

SANTIAGO DE COMPOSTELA

This is the jewel of Galicia, and if you're coming from the east or southeast it will follow Lugo. After Rome, Santiago de Compostela was Western Europe's first tourist attraction, as it were. During the Middle Ages, Charlemagne, Louis VII, El Cid, Saint Francis of Assisi, and between 500,000 and two million others every year came to this town just 20 miles from the Atlantic Ocean, near what the Romans called *finisterre*—the end of the earth.

"Compostela" is a name derived from various sources. *Campus stellas* is Latin for "field of stars" (see the legend of the hermit Pelayo, discussed below), and while this poetic appellation has a certain charm, it is more widely held that the town was built over an old cemetery, or *campostela* (field of the dead). The city was officially named Santiago de Compostela by Pope Urban II in the late 11th century, when it was growing into a major pilgrimage destination.

Saint James (*Sant'Iago* in Spanish) was the apostle who carried Christ's doctrine to Spain. In the Book of Isaiah, Saint Jerome wrote that one apostle went to India, another to Greece, and Saint James to Spain. After his first visit to Spain, James was executed by Herod, in A.D. 44. His disciples, Teodoro and Atanasio, took his body back to Spain. The burial is legend; many stories exist about how the body ended up in Galicia, but nothing is certain. Nevertheless, Saint James and his disciples lay buried here for 800 years. Early Christians kept their whereabouts secret to protect them during Barbarian invasions. In the year 813, more legend has it, a hermit named Pelayo observed a shower of stars. He informed Bishop Teodomiro, who also saw the shower, and they followed the lights to a cave where the remains of a man in pontifical robes were discovered. The town has been the journey's end for pilgrims ever since. The remains were hidden again for centuries until Cardinal Miguel Paya y Rico organized a successful hunt for them. Later, Pope Leon XIII had them examined and declared them authentic in the Papal Bull of July 25, 1884. Known as "the Jerusalem of the West," Santiago de Compostela now stands as an exquisite, living monument—with a few worldly delights as well.

You'll be staying in the old town, but you'll have to pass through the new town to get to it. The new part of Santiago is like any modern city, with department stores, restaurants, and traffic problems. But when you arrive at the **plaza del Obradoiro**, the heart of the old town, you'll understand the reason for your pilgrimage.

The Cathedral of Santiago

This huge square, also known as the plaza de España or the Gran Plaza del Hospital, is flanked on all four sides by magnificent buildings. On its south side is **Colegio de San**

Jerónimo, which now houses the Institute of Galician Studies and the University Rectory. The building dates from the 17th century, but its handsome Romanesque-style door is from 1490. The west side of the square houses the former **Palacio de Rajoy** (Rajoy Palace), now the Town Hall. Its striking classical 18th-century façade is by Gambino y Ferreiro, but the building itself was designed by the French architect Charles Lemaur, and it is decidedly French-looking. The square's north side is occupied by the luxurious Hostal de los Reyes Católicos (more on this later).

You won't even notice these other buildings at first, for on the east side of the square is the wildly 17th- and 18th-century Baroque façade of the cathedral of Santiago, with its twin towers rising almost as high as the sky and looking like, as one writer has put it, "tongues of flame." The stunning building shines gold in the afternoon sun (*obradoiro,* the name of the cathedral plaza, means "work of gold"; it refers to the front of the cathedral). This look is the result of centuries of lichen reflecting the setting sun. People have been known to faint upon seeing it for the first time.

The rub is that the 18th-century façade is like a Hollywood set—it was constructed only to protect the building's *real* façade, the **Portico de la Gloria**, from erosion by time and weather. Although there is some Plateresque work on the church's actual façade, it is noteworthy how little this style is used in Galicia as a whole (the portal of the Hostal de los Reyes Católicos being a magnificent exception). The Gallegos are rugged individualists, and their stonecutters held stubbornly to the styles they knew. In fact, throughout the countryside in the province, Romanesque architecture dominates in the 500-or-so churches. The Plateresque style of architecture and ornament was considered alien to the local stonecutters.

The Portico de la Gloria is what the pilgrims of the Middle Ages saw first, and it is no exaggeration to say that it is one of the greatest achievements in Romanesque sculpture in the world. The portico, executed from 1168 to 1188 by a master known only as Mateo, is actually three doorways, with handsome statues carved out of stone. The faces are those of those of human beings who actually existed. Below, the tympanum is a carving of the prophet Daniel—don't miss his famous smile. On the central pillar you'll notice five indentations; your fingers will fit perfectly into them. This is where weary pilgrims first rested their hands after their arduous journey. There's something about putting your hand in the same place that Saint Francis did that sets the spine tingling. At the foot of the columns is Mateo's self-portrait, kneeling and facing the sepulcher, pointing to himself, perhaps indicating his responsibility for the work you're viewing.

The church's centerpiece is the statue of a seated Saint James, atop the main altar at the head of the central nave. It can be reached from behind by a staircase on either side—pilgrims go up to kiss his mantle. Beneath the altar is a crypt that is built into the foundation of a ninth-century church and that contains the saint's remains and those of his disciples. It, too, is accessible via stairs—rather garishly lit with fluorescent lights.

High-vaulted ceilings give the interior of the structure an otherworldly feel. On holidays a gigantic incensory called *botafumeiro* hangs over the center of the church in front of the altar. It scents the entire church, requiring eight men to swing it. Chapel after chapel line the aisles, each adorned with rich altars, tombs of Spanish kings, and various works of art. Make sure to see the **Puerta de las Platerias**, a handsome, double-arched Romanesque doorway, and note the carvings of King David and the creation of Adam and Eve. Four scenes from Christ's Passion decorate the right tympanum; the left, showing the Temptation and the Woman Taken in Adultery, dates from around 1100.

A visit to the **reliquary chapel**, located off the right nave just inside the cathedral and entered through a Plateresque door, is worth a visit. It contains valuable busts, urns, and statues. The **treasury**, entered the same way but a bit farther toward the church's center, contains gold, silver, and bronze crucifixes from various centuries, statues of Saint James, and jewelry. The bust of Santiago Alfeo, from the 14th century, is a must-see, encrusted with semiprecious stones, cameos, and engravings. The four-foot-high processional monstrance (carried during Holy Week), dating from 1546, is considered to be the first Plateresque work in silver. Upstairs, in the Sala Capitular (**chapterhouse**), you'll find 17th-century Flemish tapestries and later ones based on Goya cartoons. The view from the balcony here is matchless: A glimpse of the square below and the town's spires and the generally impressive, make-believe skyline will stay in your memory—but it's easier to photograph than to describe.

Walk downstairs to the **cloister**, built in a mixture of Renaissance and Gothic styles. Diagonally across the cloister is the entrance to the library, where the *botafumeiro* is displayed when it is not in use. Back outside, you'll find endless pleasure in the doors to the building itself; the squares surrounding the cathedral, too, are ancient and picturesque. Leave yourself more than a couple of hours just to see the cathedral and its surroundings, although you will probably return to it often during your stay.

Hostal de los Reyes Católicos

Churches, sanctuaries, inns, and hospitals sprang up along the pilgrims' route to Santiago. Many of them, like the Hostal de los Reyes Católicos, exist today in other forms, to welcome the modern-day traveller. The Hostal de los Reyes Católicos was built early in the 16th century by the Catholic monarchs Isabella and Ferdinand to lodge weary pilgrims. Later it served as a hospital for the monarchs and the nobility. Now it is an exquisite, finely furnished hotel, with four inner courtyards (named Matthew, Mark, Luke, and John) and its own chapel, in which concerts and exhibitions are held. The building is a combination of styles: Late Gothic, Renaissance, and Baroque. The Plateresque entrance is prodigiously carved and crowned by a frieze of bas-relief figures, which contrast with the bare, stone walls of the rest of the façade.

Stay at this magnificent hotel, which is right on the plaza del Obradoiro, if you possibly can. (Rooms are currently priced at a reasonable 17,000 pesetas a night for a double—outrageously inexpensive by Rome/London/New York standards, considering what you get here.) If you are planning on visiting in July, you might have to book a year ahead, because St. James's Day is July 25, and the celebrations, including fireworks in the square, normally bring thousands of pilgrims as well as just plain tourists. However, at other times of the year there are usually openings.

The rooms, all recently refurbished, are dignified and quiet. Paintings decorate the rooms and hallways. In many of the rooms, enormous casement windows open onto a courtyard. The lobby is filled with antiques, as are some of the bedrooms. There are two restaurants in the hotel; one is casual, the other is superb if pricey. The latter has vaulted ceilings and looks Medieval, and one of its specialties is *vieras* (Galician for *coquille Saint Jacques,* which got its name from the pilgrim's symbol, the scallop shell). And don't miss the buffet-style breakfast, whatever you do. The table is a true groaning board: fruit, fish, cheese (many varieties available only within the region), homemade peasant breads, cereal, eggs, pancakes, and on and on—but above all the heavenly, full-roasted Spanish coffee with steamed cream.

There is also a very pleasant bar in the hotel. Patrons sit in the antique-filled lobby/living room on fine couches and chairs and wait for their table in one of the hotel's two restaurants, or just enjoy a drink before seeking dinner elsewhere. It's difficult to feel anything but special in the Hostal de los Reyes Católicos—it's as important a stop as the San Marcos in León or either town's cathedral. If the Hostal de los Reyes Católicos is too rich for your blood (or you can't get a room), you might try the modern, swimming-pool-equipped **Peregrino** or the **Compostela**. They're both in the heart of the old town and quite nice—at about half the price of the first choice.

Around in Santiago de Compostela

Of course, Santiago has other churches and religious structures. There's the **Iglesia de San Felix de Solovio**, which dates back to the sixth century. It was rebuilt in the 12th, but the Romanesque façade remains. This structure and the **Monasterio de San Pelayo de Antealtares** share an ancient wall that closes off one side of the plaza de la Quintana to the right as you face the cathedral. An even more important structure is the huge **San Martin Pinario** (overlooking the plaza de la Immaculada, on the left as you face the cathedral), which was founded in 899 by Benedictine monks. For many hundreds of years it was the most powerful monastery in Galicia, with 39 other priorates dependent on it; it is now a seminary. Its façade is Compostela Baroque, and the main altar is a stunning Baroque creation; there are three cloisters, and a handsome Baroque fountain in the monastery.

The **Monasterio de San Francisco**, which is said to have been founded by Saint Francis of Assisi when he came to Santiago on his pilgrimage in 1214, is located on a long block north (left) from the front of the cathedral, and the atrium of the attached church has a 20th-century statue of Saint Francis, the work of Francisco Asdrey, a native of Santiago. The contrast is fascinating.

The rest of the old town, with its arcaded stone walkways, narrow streets, and ancient buildings, oozes atmosphere. The **rua Villar** and **rua Nueva** hold endless shops, bars, *tascas* (taverns), and restaurants. They're located southwest (to the right) of the cathedral, and walks down, through, and off them will delight and surprise. You can't get lost here, so wander aimlessly—a familiar fountain always pops up. **Don Gaiferos**, **Retablo**, and **Chiton**, three of the city's finest eateries, are all within two blocks of each other on the rua

Nueva, and a street away is **El Franco,** on calle Franco, a typical city *tasca* with plenty of local color and fine ambience. **Black**, the city's hippest disco, is located nearby as well, on the rua Rosalia de Castro; a more conservative dance club, not exclusively for a student crowd, is **Duque**, at Santiago de Chile 15.

Leave some time for shopping, either at sidewalk stalls or in the shops. There are crucifixes and scallop shells used in every conceivable way. Students spill out of bars until the wee hours in this area (remember, this is a university town, although the university itself has no center; its many buildings are spread out), and costumed musicians, also students, stroll about ready to serenade at the drop of a peseta.

A 20-minute walk from the cathedral (presuming you don't linger too long in the cafés or shops), at the southwestern tip of the old city, the handsomely landscaped horseshoe-shaped **paseo de la Herradura** is a perfect lookout point for the town. In the park is a statue of the late-19th-century poet Rosalia de Castro, a native of Galicia, whose works focus on human suffering, especially the departure of many Gallegos for the New World in the late 19th century. If you catch a glimpse of the city from the Herradura, you'll realize what a showplace it is; it will seem as if the city is ablaze as the sun catches on the sandstone spires. Santiago is a city with a spirit and a soul.

Less than a mile outside the city, in the middle of a very green valley, on the banks of the río Sar, is the 12th-century **Iglesia Santa María del Sar**. Although it seems that it is almost invariably closed when one wants to see it, take note that the sacristan lives in the house behind the church and if you look pious, interested, or generous enough he'll let you in. The columns of this tiny Romanesque jewel are visibly slanted and the effect is eerie. There's an ongoing debate as to whether shifts in the soil over the centuries have caused the peculiar angle of the columns or whether they were constructed that way. The lovely cloister has carvings that are by either Master Mateo or one of his students. The church can be reached by highway N 525 (known as the *Circunvalación*)—or, better yet, walk.

GALICIA OUTSIDE SANTIAGO

A good route farther into this lush region is to go north to the coast, to A Coruña, and then circle counterclockwise along the Atlantic coast, taking in the famous *rías,* arriving at Pontevedra and the islands, and following this with a last look at the region—practically in Portugal, at Túy and La Guardia.

Along the way you'll notice squat structures, granaries, each one of which will invariably have a cross on top; some of them also have pyramids or various symbols of luck or fertility. These *horreos,* also called *cabazas,* are peculiar to Galicia. No one quite knows where they came from. For the last few hundred years or so they have been used to store wheat and corn.

Some experts believe that the *horreos* were first built by Celts as dwelling places, but that they became storehouses for grain as man moved into more comfortable dwellings. In Orense province in southern Galicia the granaries are always rectangular and raised on stilts four feet off the ground. These are known as *cabeceiros;* many believe that they were built by the Swabians (or Suebi), a migratory tribe that briefly controlled Galicia (as well as northern Portugal) after the Romans.

Some *horreos* are very primitive. Others, located on the acreage of *pazos* (houses of noblemen), are grand enough to house a family of four. In the province of Lugo the granaries are always covered with slate; around Santiago they are covered with granite rubble. When you see them you will know you are definitely in Galicia.

A Coruña

What comes to mind immediately about this port city situated around a giant marina is the **Torre de Hércules** (Tower of Hercules). A Coruña, in the very northwestern corner of Spain, dates back to the second century, and surviving from that era is this stone lighthouse, the only Roman lighthouse still on active duty. The tower, built by a Portuguese architect, restored in 1652 and again in the 1790s, is more than 300 feet high; its beacon can be seen 40 miles out to sea.

There's much to see in this quaint, peaceful town, especially around the Old City. Begin by walking the avenida de la Marina past the anchored fishing boats. Stoneworkers were as prevalent in old Galicia as whalers were in Melville's New England, and you'll see their handiwork in the old arcade that still stands. There's a local fish "auction" at the fisherman's market (*muros*), but you have to arrive early in the morning to get its full impact. Jutting out into the harbor from the **San Carlos Gardens** is the 18th-century fort **Castillo de San Anton.**

When you're hungry, stop at the fanciest restaurant (and inn, if you're thinking of staying) in town: **Atlántico**, located at Jardines de Mendez 2. Make sure to get a seat looking out over the marina. Try the crepes, or, of course, any of the seafood.

The Rías

Rías, geological structures found only in Galicia, are fjord-like inlets through which the sea penetrates the land. They make for beautiful, warm beaches in the Galician southwest particularly, since the *rías* there are protected by islands such as Arosa. The *rías* also make for some interesting experiences sunbathing. When you stretch out at noon, you never know where the sea will shift by 2:00. So keep your eye on the water level, and protect your camera in case you have to wade back to your car.

The *rías* break down into those to the north and those to the south. The Rías Bajas, located in the south, are four firths, located south to north at Vigo, Pontevedra, the Firth of Arosa, and A Coruña. The southern *rías* are calm and warm. The northern firths are located on a fragment of coast ominously nicknamed Costa da Morte (coast of death). But don't be put off. It's your basic Galician flare for the mystical at work here. Despite the name of the coastline, these waters are never dangerous, just rougher than those in the south. The towns here are quiet, not resort-like, with single-dwelling houses, each with gardens and tilled lands. These beaches are much less populated than those in the south, and that makes for nice, solitary walks and places to hide.

Pontevedra

About 50 km (30 miles) south of Santiago on the Atlantic coast, Pontevedra is an inviting and lively town. The so-called Sailor's Basilica, located in the old part of town, where the fishermen used to live, looks out over the *ría* of Pontevedra, as though waiting for the fishermen to return from the sea. Built in the 16th century by the sailors' guild, the **Basilíca Menor de Santa María** boasts a stunning Plateresque door by Cornelius de Holanda, handsome Baroque altars, and finely sculpted statues. It has been declared a national monument and is well worth a visit.

The *zona antigua* (old town) is full of charm, very

walkable and compact (no map is needed), and filled with old mansions sporting coats of arms.

The **Provincial Museum** on the plaza de Leña is housed in two Baroque buildings. Within is a large collection of prehistoric gold and silver work, exhibits about local history, and paintings from Spain's Golden Age to the present. A bit north is the **Iglesia de La Peregrina**, a bizarre round building with even odder towers. Within is the statue of the town's patroness, the Virgen Peregrina. Behind the church, which dates from 1778, are modern apartment buildings that will make you want to leave town, but don't. There's more to see.

Near La Peregrina is the **Iglesia de San Francisco**, a 13th-century building with a fine rose window and interesting tombs in front of the apse. And a short walk away are the ruins of the **convent and church of Santo Domingo**, a highly evocative shell with a spooky collection of stone crosses, prehistoric objects, and Gothic crypts.

A welcoming place to stay in Pontevedra is the **Parador Casa del Barón**, which occupies an elegant 18th-century mansion in the center of town. It's very much in keeping with its antiquated surroundings but has every modern amenity. Around the corner on avenida del Buenos Aires is the restaurant **Jules II**, where all the fish specialties are recommended.

Excursions from Pontevedra

Excursions along the coast are a big draw for visitors to this area. The **Isla de Arosa**, reached by frequent ferry from Villanueva, northwest of Pontevedra, has some fine, sheltered beaches. It's the largest island in Galicia, close to the mainland beaches, with a population of 5,000, most of whom are fishermen. The sportfishing is excellent.

If all-in-one resorts are to your liking, the **Isla de la Toja** is also recommended. It's up the coast north from Pontevedra, just south of the Isla de Arosa. If you take C 550 you'll pass the Neoclassical monastery of San Juan de Poio, a series of beaches including the up-and-coming summer resorts of Sangenjo (Sanxento in Galician—all the signs will read that way) and El Grove. From El Grove there's a bridge to La Toja.

La Toja is an island resort paradise: There is golf, tennis, swimming, a spa, casino, exquisite landscaping, fine dining, and plenty of very modern atmosphere. Although there are other places to stay on the island, if you're going to do it, do it right and stay at the **Gran Hotel**. La Toja is known as "dream island" to the locals, but it sounds as if an ad agency thought up the name.

La Guardia and Túy

Finally, in Galicia, there are two towns that are practically not in Galicia. If your travels on C 550 should take you south along the coast from Pontevedra rather than north, you'll come to the mouth of the river Miño (Minho) and the town of La Guardia, practically in the Atlantic. A kilometer south is **Monte Tecla**, which, along with phenomenal views, offers a small museum with fascinating pre-Roman relics. Parts of walls, huts, possible cooking implements, and other oddities are practically a history of Galicia from the year 2000 B.C. onward. A worthwhile detour.

And then on around to the northeast to Túy, along the Miño. Túy is on the Portuguese border; it is here that you cross the 1000-foot-long bridge into Portugal (Valença). Túy is worth a visit for its overwhelming fortresslike, primitive cathedral dating from the 11th to the 13th centuries. The carvings on the choir stalls are fascinating, and the cloister, from the 15th century, is nicely atmospheric. Two other churches here, Santo Domingo and San Bartolomé, have been declared national monuments.

And the next thing you know, you're in Portugal.

GETTING AROUND

Travel within the region is most easily done by automobile. There is a good network of roads, from the *autopistas* that link Santiago de Compostela with A Coruña and Oviedo with Gijón to the charming, winding roads of the coastal regions. Santiago de Compostela is served by a major airport, 11 km (7 miles) east on N 547. There are many domestic flights as well as international service to London and other European cities. The trains to Madrid take up to 12 hours, but there's frequent and speedy service to A Coruña, about an hour away. In Asturias the hub is Oviedo, with train service to Madrid (7–8 hours), Barcelona (13 hours), and, most conveniently, frequent service to León, which takes 2–3 hours.

ACCOMMODATIONS REFERENCE

When dialing telephone numbers in Spain from outside the country, drop the 9 in the area code.

▶ **Hotel Atlántico.** Jardines de Mendez 2, 15006 **A Coruña.** Tel: (981) 22-65-00.

▶ **Parador Casa del Barón.** Calle Maceda, 36002 **Pontevedra.** Tel: (986) 85-58-00.

▶ **Compostela.** Calvo Sotelo 1, 15702 **Santiago de Compostela.** Tel: (981) 58-57-00.

▶ **Gran Hotel.** **Toja,** 36991 Pontevedra. Tel: (986) 73-00-25.

▶ **Gran Hotel Lugo.** Avenida Ramón Ferreiro 21, 27002 **Lugo.** Tel: (982) 22-41-52.

▶ **Parador El Molino Viejo.** Parque Isabel la Católica, 33204 **Gijón.** Tel: (985) 37-05-11.

▶ **Peregrino.** Avenida Rosalía de Castro, 15706 **Santiago de Compostela.** Tel: (981) 59-18-50.

▶ **Hotel Príncipe de Asturias.** Manso 2, 33203 **Gijón.** Tel: (985) 36-71-11.

▶ **Hotel de la Reconquista.** Gil de Jaz 16, 33004 **Oviedo.** Tel: (985) 24-11-00.

▶ **Hostal de los Reyes Católicos.** Plaza de España 1, 15705 **Santiago de Compostela.** Tel: (981) 58-22-00.

▶ **Hotel Ventura.** Avenida de Covadonga 3, 33550 **Cangas de Onís.** Tel: (985) 84-82-00.

CANTABRIA

By Robert Levine

Cantabria province, situated on the north-central Spanish coast—the Costa Verde—is traditionally called La Montaña (the mountain country). Covering an area of approximately 53,000 square kilometers, Cantabria stretches from the city of Castro-Urdiales and the neighboring Basque province of Vizcaya to the east to the region of Asturias and the Picos de Europa to the west, and from the provinces of Palencia and Burgos to the south to the Cantabrian Sea to the north. Travel through the province will take you from France and along the coastline west into Santiago, the famous destination of Medieval pilgrims. From modern Santander to Medieval Santillana del Mar, and all the lovely Cantabrian coastline in between, this is a perfect resort area for taking a break from heavy-duty sightseeing.

Many historians and visitors (and natives as well) think of this northern tier as the "real" old Spain because the Moors never gained much influence here. The seaside climate didn't agree with the desert dwellers, and so they tended not to settle on the coastline. Cantabrians are also proud of the fact that the Romans, too, never really settled in their region. (Augustus sent Agrippa's troops to Cantabria in A.D. 21 to conquer the local tribes, and, while they landed at Santander, they didn't stay longer than was necessary.) The Cantabrians retain an independent, unconquered, and uninfluenced nature, and the atmosphere in these environs tends to be similar to that in the countryside in the south of France around the time of the Middle Ages rather than, say, that of southern Spain or even Castile-León.

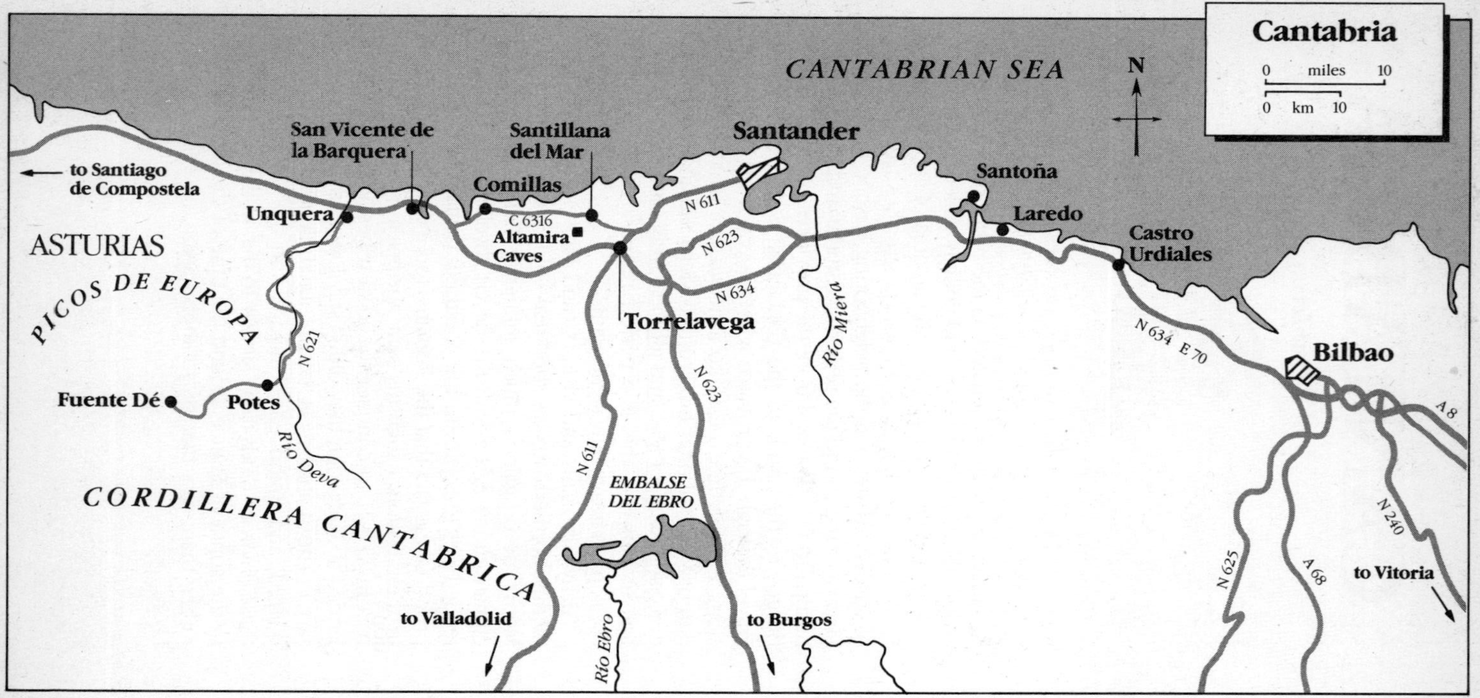
Cantabria
0 miles 10
0 km 10
N
CANTABRIAN SEA
Santander
San Vicente de la Barquera
Santillana del Mar
Comillas
Santoña
Laredo
Castro Urdiales
Bilbao
to Santiago de Compostela
Unquera
ASTURIAS
C 6316
Altamira Caves
Torrelavega
N 611
N 623
N 634
N 634 E 70
PICOS DE EUROPA
N 621
Potes
Fuente Dé
Río Deva
Río Miera
CORDILLERA CANTABRICA
EMBALSE DEL EBRO
Río Ebro
to Valladolid
to Burgos
N 625
A 68
N 240
A 8
to Vitoria

MAJOR INTEREST

Cantabrian coast fishing villages and beaches
Santander
Santillana del Mar
Altamira Caves
Picos de Europa

The East Coastline

Cantabria has several large ports and 72 long, narrow beaches punctuated by hills sloping down to the sea and by scattered fishing villages. Some of the beaches are large, some are protected by the bay of Santander, and some you have to travel to by boat, but any one of them is enveloped in history. You're as apt to see a Romanesque church or old fortress off in the distance here as you are to see a mountain in Switzerland.

The port town of **Castro-Urdiales**, just west of Bilbao on the eastern side of Cantabria, is a good place to start. The setting is fantastic. Here, glassed-in pavilions and balconies line the beach. Brazomar and Orinon are two scenic beaches to stop and relax on. Also stop to see the **Iglesia de Santa María**, a 14th-century structure situated on a rocky promontory almost entirely surrounded by water. This large, almost monolithic building with little exterior detail and unfinished towers is still the most important Gothic structure in the province. The church's harmonious interior is its glory, especially the apse, with large buttresses and handsome brasses.

The larger town of **Laredo**, to the west, was a commercial port in the Middle Ages. Now it is probably the most tourist-filled of the smaller coastal towns, with proliferating high-rises and vacation houses. Frequented in large part by German and French vacationers, Laredo grows from a population of 12,500 in the off-season to over 100,000 in summer. If you stop here, two spots to see are the lively Playa de Salve and the Iglesia de Nuestra Señora de la Asunción. The latter is 12th-century Romanesque-Gothic, the only building surviving from a 1638 invasion by French corsairs.

El Ancla hotel is close to the beach; **Risco**, slightly more elegant, is situated in the upper part of town overlooking the beaches. The main restaurant/nightlife area is in the Zona rua Mayor, around the rua de San Marcial. **El Jardín de Oporto** (Lopez Seña 16) is a good spot for local *tapas* as well as coffees from Jamaica and Brazil.

Santoña, on the other side of the bay and watched over by a fortress, is a fishing town with some nice, sandy beaches, but it has little to recommend it for an overnight stay. You may want to stop and see its 13th-century church, however. After Santoña, it might be more rewarding to leave the highway and take regional roads to travel west through the rest of the province. This may be a slower strategy than taking the larger route N 624, which runs you across the province most efficiently, but, after all, you want a vacation.

Santander

Charles V landed in Santander on his second trip to Spain, and Prince Charles (later Charles I) of England embarked for home from Santander after his visit to Madrid. Neither would recognize it today. On February 15, 1941, a fire fanned by the strong winds of a tornado destroyed more than 40 of Santander's blocks. The damaged area has been almost totally rebuilt, in line with reconstruction laws that stipulated a building of no more than five stories. Seeing such a modern town sitting along the coastline in ancient Spain is a very strange experience.

Santander is 395 km (245 miles) north of Madrid, at the northern end of the spacious Bahia de Santander and enclosed by the rocky peninsula of La Magdalena. The town itself is generally flat, but the hills behind it, to the south, make a nice change. The correct approach to Santander, with a small exception or two, is recreational—as a break from cultural or historical sightseeing. It's a summer resort, mostly for Spanish and French vacationers, and it makes no apologies for itself; indeed, it need not. Protected from the ocean as Santander is along its bay, it makes the perfect location for a holiday getaway. The weather, quite simply, is pleasant almost all the time.

The town is known for its wide boulevards and byways, modern in design. A stroll along the waterfront **paseo de Pereda**, which runs north-south along Santander bay, will give you an overview of the town and harbor.

Two kilometers (a mile or so) from the center of town arc the beaches—Playa del Promontorio, La Magdalena, Playa de Camello, and the Primera and Secunda playas. These last two make up the **El Sardinero** area—the most popular and trendy of the beaches—and are joined in one strip of sand at low tide. There is a handsome park on one side. The beach is close to the royal palace of Magdalena, built in 1912 by Queen Victoria Eugenia for her daughter, who was married to Alfonso XIII. The king and his English wife summered here in Santander. Nowadays, in summer, there are classes in Hispanic subjects in the old palace. On the other side of the beach is the Cabo Mayor lighthouse.

There's not too much to do in Santander, but it's hardly dull. People are fairly mellow and spend time drinking wine, having fun in the Art Nouveau casino at El Sardinero, and looking at the brightly colored beach tents that are used for both shade and as dressing rooms. Shopping is a pastime as well. Santander is a very fashionable resort and has the shops to match. If it's ceramics you're after, try **Al Fareria**, cuesta del Hospital 5. You'll find a nice selection of traditional Spanish and Cantabrian works.

And there's the marvelous Cantabrian cuisine. The **Bar del Puerto**, Hernán Cortés 63 (Tel: 21-30-01), serves excellent traditional Cantabrian cuisine with an emphasis on seafood. Diners can watch their dishes—ox cutlet with pimientos or clams with kidney beans, for instance—prepared on an open grill. **Rhin**, on the plaza de Italia (Tel: 27-30-34), on the Primera Playa in El Sardinero next to the casino, is another good (if pricey) bet. Their hake with scallops and cream of crab soup are recommended. And 12 km (7.5 miles) southwest of the city (take highway 611 to Torrelavega) is **El Molino**, on carretera Central in Puente Arce (Tel: 57-40-02). This restaurant weds nouvelle cuisine and traditional Cantabrian food. Hake with lemon and saffron mousse and sea bass with green pepper on grilled wild mushrooms are two of the specialties.

But still, this *is* Spain, and so there must be some culture and history to take in. The **cathedral** was built in the 13th century, then restored from the 16th to the 18th centuries. Some of it miraculously survived the 1941 catastrophe, and the rest was restored between 1942 and 1955. The bare, rustic exterior and austere interior permit you to savor the architectural lines, both Romanesque and Gothic. The crypt holds the remains of two saints, Celedonius and Emeterius, and there are some minor Roman ruins to be seen on the premises.

The **museum of fine arts** (calle Rubio 4) shares a building with the library bequeathed by the famous Spanish man of letters Marcelino Menéndez y Pelayo. When he died in 1912 his library of some 40,000 volumes and original manuscripts of Spanish writers passed to the town. He is buried in the cathedral's north transept. Pelayo memorabilia can also be found in his house, separated from the museum by a garden. The museum itself has the odd distinction of carrying portraits of disliked Spanish rulers: Ferdinand VII and Isabella II, the latter of whom was deposed as she was vacationing in the Basque Country. Of more general interest are four etchings by Goya from his *Disasters of War* series, which was suppressed by Carlos IV for its subversive nature.

Drop in, if you can, at the **Museo Provincial de Prehistoria y Arqueología** (calle Casimiro Sainz 4). Its collection of prehistoric objects, some as old as 15,000 years, is considered one of the most interesting of its kind in Europe. Note the El Pendo truncheon (cane), an object made of antler and carved with figures of a deer and a horse. A visit here is a good prelude to the Caves of Altamira (see below), where the pieces in the museum were discovered.

But you'll eventually return to the beaches. Across the bay from Santander are **Somo** and **El Puntal** beaches, which are well worth the 20-minute ferry trip. (The ferry dock is just off the calle de Antonio López). Or you can drive. The cafés there are fun, and the sunbathing is unhampered, particularly on Somo, a long, flat peninsula of beige sand stretching over four miles.

The finest place to stay in Santander is the **Hotel Real** (open only from June through September). Located in swank El Sardinero, this establishment is costly but worth it; the view of Santander bay from the terrace is unforgettable.

Each August Santander hosts a lively international festival of concerts, opera, dance, and other spectacles. If you're interested in attending, advance booking for both events and rooms is crucial.

Santillana del Mar

A confusion on the name Santa Juliana, Santillana del Mar is only 30 km (20 miles) west of Santander, on route N 611. You'll drive among deep-green hillocks and hillsides, with cows, goats, donkeys, and their stables specking the meadows. The word "bucolic" is unavoidable here. Many people prefer to stay in Santillana del Mar and commute to Santander's beaches and casino rather than the other way around.

Santillana is Medieval, not only in its history but also in its fabric. Each cobblestone and medallion rings of the past; each side street yields another pleasure. The town is one of the loveliest, best-preserved in Spain. In the eighth century it was the capital of eastern Asturias, and later it was an important stop on the pilgrims' path to Santiago de Compostela.

Nowadays, in the morning, you're apt to be awakened by the sound of roosters crowing. The farmers here have traditionally settled in town rather than in the countryside, living with their families between the animals stabled on the bottom floor and the chickens kept on the roof. You're liable to see a herdsman watering his cows at an ancient stone trough next to a pool where townswomen wash their laundry. Santillana has outlawed billboards and electric signs. Automobiles are banned as well, except for those belonging to residents. This ban is strictly enforced; you'll have to leave your car in a parking area at the edge of town and travel on foot. Even when you are checking into the local parador, one of the country's most charming, you will be allowed only to drop your luggage off before driving the car down to a special parking area. And frankly, since most streets are either too narrow or too steep for most automobiles, and it's impossible to get lost or tired here anyway, you're better off on foot in the middle of town.

Visit Santillana in the spring or fall if you can. The local population is only 4,000, but in summer it swells to the breaking point with French (and other) tourists on outings from Santander or on their way to the Altamira Caves, just over a mile outside of town.

If you can, get a reservation at the **Parador Nacional Gil Blas** (located at the end of calle Juan Infante, on the plaza Ramón Pelayo), one of the most popular in Spain. You'll find beamed ceilings, dark wood paneling, and some rooms that overlook a lush inner courtyard. The parador's 26 rooms are much in demand, so book early. Prices are reasonable, and the excellent restaurant is the best in town.

If you don't get a room in the parador, try the **Hotel Altamira** just around the corner on the calle Canton. This 17th-century stone mansion is inexpensive and clean, with 30 rooms, a garden, and parking. Another choice, the higher-rated **Los Infantes**, on the avenida Le Dorat at the entrance to town, is moderately priced and feels rather like a ski lodge.

The **Mesón de la Villa** on calle Santo Domingo is a good place for a light snack or breakfast (they serve hot chocolate and *churros*), and in the summertime they set up tables in their garden. Also, you might sample a local delicacy, *bizcochos,* a slightly eggier angel food cake. The **Casa Quevedo**, on the plaza de las Arenas, is a good place to find it. And if you're looking for local souvenirs and gifts, the pottery and ashtrays made of glass enclosing crushed glass as a base is not only a good bet, it's your only bet.

Once you're settled, there's plenty to see, and it's all easy to find. There's only one entrance to town—calle de Santo Domingo—and the town's two main streets radiate off it: calle del Río on the left, and calle de Juan Infante on the right.

The whole town is an historic monument. The houses, with their eaves and balconies, provide a glimpse into the past, and all the streets are cobblestone. Coats of arms have been carved out of stone above many doorways in Santillana, which in feudal times was a playground for the rich. Many wealthy Castilian and Basque families still own places in Santillana, the original money having come from fortunes made in the New World in the 16th and 17th centuries. (Santillana became particularly fashionable with the Madrid nobility when cholera swept San Sebastián a couple of hundred years ago.)

One of the mansions worth looking for is the Casa de Los Hombrones (house of giants), former home of a nouveau-riche dandy who must have wanted his coat of arms to make a statement. His mark is two oversized statues of knights flanking the coat of arms. The shield overpowers the house.

The **Iglesia Colegiata**, on the plaza de las Arenas, is hard to miss. This squat (it may be long, but it's oddly wide and low) Romanesque building from the end of the 12th and start of the 13th centuries is rather crude even compared to most other Romanesque churches, but its elaborate altar is decked out in silver from the 17th century. This work of art was created by a team of Spanish, Mexican, and Flemish silversmiths. If you ask the sacristan (*and* tip him), he'll remove the silver panel and show you a rare Romanesque stone panel on the altar with vividly carved portraits of Matthew, Mark, Luke, and John. Santa Juliana's sepulcher, carved in the 15th century, is located in the central nave, and there is a statue of her above the church's entrance in a niche. The church is protected in front by a metal grille, which looks like a piece of torture equipment but was actually designed to keep cows from wandering into the building.

The church opens onto a cloister whose garden is surrounded by columns that aren't uniform, as though each stoneworker had been encouraged to do his own thing in stone. When you examine the columns, you'll notice plant-like, abstract designs and allegorical scenes, such as Christ and six apostles, the Baptism, the decapitation of John the Baptist, and Daniel in the lion's den. You'll also see carvings of knights piercing demons and other nightmarish images.

Next to the collegiate church is the palace of the Archduchess Margaret of Austria. Diagonally across from it are the attached palaces of the Cossíos and Quevedos (on the calle del Río), two important Santillana families. See also the palace del Marqués de Santillana, a Gothic-style 15th-century structure. The marqués (1398–1458) was a soldier, politician, poet, and writer of the Spanish Renaissance who was greatly influenced by Dante, and the palace is the very soul of Spanish-Italian elegance.

The 16th-century convent of Regina Coeli, at the entrance of the town, houses the **diocesan museum**, chock full of religious art. This former Dominican convent now belongs to the Clarisa order, and nuns still live here. The museum is sophisticated and well-lit and contains some real treasures: a 14th-century bronze cross, some naïve Romanesque sculptures, a Norman cross, and a 14th-century polychrome wooden sepulcher. Most of the objects were collected throughout the Cantabrian region by the diocese, especially paintings and sculptures from abandoned churches.

Near the plaza Ramón Pelayo is the **Torre del Merino**, the tower of the magistrate. It was built at the start of the 14th century, and in the 18th century a spacious residence was added. It has a square foundation and large stones at the corners of the thick masonry walls. It has narrow shooting windows and windows with semi-circular peaks. During the early Middle Ages the towers were feudal houses. Later they came to form a part of new houses in which the servants lived on the lower floors and the lords on the upper levels.

Diagonally across the square from the Torre del Merino is a palace with an attached 16th-century tower that once belonged to a branch of the Spanish Borgias. The palace next door belonged to the daughter of Queen Isabella II. Together the two buildings now house an art center, the **Santillana foundation.** The buildings, recently renovated, are handsome, and the 16th-century patio is nice and restful. Though the foundation is open all year, the summer season finds the greatest number of changing exhibitions, mostly of the work of local painters.

It's impossible to have a bad time in Santillana del Mar. A day-and-a-half visit here is just right for an escape from the turmoil of the 20th century. When you're ready to leave, get back on the road and head for the Altamira Caves, just over a mile to the southwest: Signs lead the way out of town straight to the caves.

The Altamira Caves

In 1868 nine prehistoric caves in the area were identified, and five years later bona fide prehistoric paintings, probably from 12,000 B.C. but possibly twice that old, were found within. The most famous of these paintings is of a bison lying down, curled into the contour of the stone. This figure is so sophisticated that it made specialists consider whether or not the caves might be a hoax.

The ceilings of the caves are low, barely five feet high, and the figures are quite large, some over six feet. You'll find that the best way to view the polychrome paintings of animals is to lie on your back and look at the ceiling. There is just enough time to take a time-delayed, black-and-white picture, but you need permission to take photos, and it will cost you a few extra pesetas.

It is very important to book far ahead to get a tour of the caves. Since fissures were discovered in the cave walls, the number of visitors has been strictly limited. Write about three months ahead to Director, Centro de Investigación Museo de Altamira, 39330 Santillana del Mar, Santander, Spain. Request permission to visit the caves, and tell them how many are in your party (no more than five are permitted) and the date of your visit. The tours start at 10:45 A.M. daily except holidays. If you haven't written, stop at the museum office; they keep a standby list in case there are cancellations.

If you can't get into the Caves of Altamira, there is the nearby Cave of the Stalactites, where ice formations have dripped and preserved cave drawings. They may not be as impressive as the Altamira ones, but your chances of seeing them are far greater, and you need not make reservations.

The West Coastline

On the coast west of Santillana del Mar is **Comillas**, a resort town. This charming fishing village is the home of the pontifical university. There are two beaches, Comillas and, to the west, Oyambre. The town flourished in the 19th century because of the frequent visits of King Alfonso XII to the marqués de Comillas. The marqués's palace is now a museum containing paintings, ancient bronzes, and archaeological objects. But the real treasure is to be found in the palace garden: **El Capricho**, a beach house designed by Antoni Gaudí, stands out here like a fascinating sore thumb. Everything about this bizarre house is designed to intrigue. One of the nice details: When any window is raised, a bell located in the sash tinkles. The 1885 building, complete with green and yellow tiles in intricate sunflower motifs, Mudejar-style brickwork, and wrought-iron balconies, has recently opened as a high-priced restaurant. Even if the food happens to be second-rate compared with its cost, a visit will definitely be rewarding. (And if you prefer, just look at El Capricho and dine at the moderately priced, long-popular **Fonda Colasa** on Antonio López 9. Hearty, abundant homemade soups and stews are specialties; Tel: 72-00-01.)

Another town worth dropping in on is **San Vicente de la Barquera**, a fishing village 35 km (22 miles) west of Santillana, perched on the ridge of a promontory. Charles V stayed in the now-ruined castle in 1521 en route to suppress a rebellion in Castile. The **Iglesia de Nuestra Señora de los Angeles**, in the upper part of town, is a good example of the transition from Romanesque to Gothic: The south façade and west side are Romanesque, but the rest of the exterior and virtually the entire interior are pure Gothic. The lower (coastal) part of town is more heavily visited for its ample beach, seaside restaurants, and cafés. Give **Restaurant Maruja** a try for its local seafood. If it's overcrowded, try any of the others along the avenida Generalíssimo, near the port.

Picos de Europa

The Cordillera Cantábrica, the "Spanish Alps," begins in Cantabria and nearly covers Asturias to the west. It is made up of the Cornion, Urrieles, and Andorras. The Picos, the highest peaks, are at the western edge of Cantabria and partly in Asturias. On a sunny day you can see them from the beaches, the peaks snowcapped even in summer. The highest are Torre Cerredo, Pena Vieja, Santa Ana peak, Cortes peak, and Tesorero peak. The area is well known for big-game hunting, including deer, wolf, chamois, wild boar, and bear. To the south there is a national reserve for the protection of mountain goats, and some interesting mountain huts (in which you can stay if you're feeling outdoorsy) at Collado Jermoso and Vega Huertes. The mountains are truly majestic, some rising to almost 9,000 feet, just twenty-some miles from the sea.

To get to the heart of the Picos from San Vicente, take N 634. (From Comillas, you'll have to take the small C 6316 until you arrive at N 634.) Just past Unquera, turn south onto N 621, which runs along río Deva. The road divides at Potes; go west in the direction of Espinama to the town of **Fuente**

Dë, your destination (it's also where the road ends). The drive from Comillas is only 80 km (50 miles), but it takes quite a while on the twisting mountain roads. At Fuente Dë is the **Parador Río Deva**, a perfect hideaway located in a valley between massive slopes covered in meadows and forests. This three-star parador is more than 3,000 feet above sea level and affords views, peace, and an ideal location for hiking, fishing, or mountain climbing. A cable car a kilometer away from the parador will take you up 6,500 feet to a vista you won't soon forget. This is awe-inspiring Spain, unlike anything else you've seen in the country—and most assuredly worth a detour.

GETTING AROUND

Aviaco, the domestic network of Iberia, flies from Madrid to Santander several times a day, and from Barcelona to Santander once a day (but the flight is not direct).

You can get from Madrid to Santander by train—several departures a day—in six hours on the special Talgo. There is also an overnight train from Madrid to Santander that departs Madrid at 11:30 P.M. and arrives at Santander at 8:00 A.M. the next morning. It's *possible* to get from Barcelona to Santander by train, but the route is Byzantine and the trip involves lots of time, much of it waiting in stations.

The only effective way to see Cantabria once you're there is by car, which you can rent in Santander.

ACCOMMODATIONS REFERENCE

The telephone code for this area is 942. When calling from outside the country, drop the 9.

▸ **Hotel Altamira**. Calle Canton, 39330 **Santillana del Mar**. Tel: 81-80-25.

▸ **El Ancla**. Calle Gonzalez Gallego 10, 39770 **Laredo**. Tel: 60-55-00.

▸ **Parador Nacional Gil Blas**. Plaza Ramón Pelayo, 39330 **Santillana del Mar**. Tel: 81-80-00.

▸ **Los Infantes**. Avenida Le Dorat, 39330 **Santillana del Mar**. Tel: 81-81-00.

▸ **Hotel Real**. Paseo Pérez Galdos 28, 39330 **Santander**. Tel: 27-25-50.

▸ **Parador Río Deva**. 39588 **Fuente Dë**. Tel: 73-00-01.

▸ **Risco**. La Arenosa 2, Alto de Laredo, 39770 **Laredo**. Tel: 60-50-30.

THE BASQUE COUNTRY

By Gerry Dawes

After studying at the University of Seville, Gerry Dawes lived in Spain for eight years. He now resides in New York, where he is a restaurant wine specialist. The author of The Wines of Spain Guide 1988, *he tours Spain regularly.*

First, some travel strategy. The Basque Country, lying on Spain's northern coast between Cantabria on the west and Biarritz and France to the east, is arguably more likely to be a gateway to this part of Spain than are La Rioja, the province to its south, or Navarra, the one to its southeast toward Aragón and then Catalonia. For this reason we cover the Basque Country first, and the other two in following chapters. The entire area (except for San Sebastián and Pamplona), however, is one of the lesser known in Spain, and so for travellers who want to get off the beaten track it may be one of the most rewarding.

A good travel plan is necessary for getting the most out of these three regions, because many of the tough mountain roads discourage indiscriminate province-hopping here. In fact, with the exception of stopping off at San Sebastián on the way in or out of Spain from France, it is better to plan a trip to this region as a destination, not a quick drive-through.

These days the images most associated with the Basque Country, La Rioja, and Navarra are Basque terrorism, wine, and the running of the bulls at Pamplona, respectively. Except for Pamplona in July and San Sebastián in August, there is little here to draw the hordes of tourists who descend on other parts of Spain in summer. So much the better for serious travellers, who can find richly rewarding experiences in these historic and colorful regions, each of which retains its strong individual character.

In La Rioja, you will find some of Spain's greatest wines and most glorious *bodegas* (wine cellars) in picturesque, historic villages surrounded by terraced vineyards with a backdrop of awesomely beautiful mountains. Significant stretches of the Camino de Santiago cross the Rioja, so exploring the major sites associated with that wonderful Medieval pilgrimage route is reason enough to visit the region. The excellent country cuisine of the Rioja, accompanied by the region's splendid wines, is at its best in the colorful restaurants of Rioja's mountain villages. A *bodega* visit in the morning, followed by a long, leisurely lunch in a country restaurant and a slow-paced afternoon of exploring villages before returning to the region's major city of Logroño for an evening of *tapas* hopping in the bars along calle Laurel make a memorable day.

The former kingdom of Navarra, whose capital is Pamplona (of *The Sun Also Rises* fame), is a must for Hemingway fans and bullfight aficionados, but this province has more to recommend it: superb restaurants and excellent wines; colorful, raucous fiestas with splendid folk music; sites of great historical interest, including some of the greatest artistic and architectural treasures along the Camino de Santiago; trout streams; mountain villages; and one of the world's loveliest bridges at Puente la Reina. Perhaps because the eyes of the world focus on the running of the bulls at the Fiestas de San Fermín in early July, Navarra's other attractions get much less attention—another plus for travellers in search of the less trodden.

The Basque Country receives a lot of negative press because of the Basque separatist movement, in whose name appalling acts of terrorism have been committed. Thus far, little of this has ever been directed at tourists, but if you find yourself at a fiesta that suddenly begins to take on political overtones, or in the middle of a demonstration, get out of the way. Politics aside, El País Vasco has a number of beautiful villages hidden away in the fresh, verdant mountains; charming fishing villages along the Bay of Biscay; some of Spain's greatest restaurants; and one of the world's most elegant seaside resorts, San Sebastián.

There are several ways to approach this area by car. If you begin in France, you can enter at Irún, visit San Sebastián, then go southwest to Vitoria, and southeast down into the

Rioja via the *autopista,* then take the national routes and secondary roads northeast to Pamplona, then north back to your starting point at the French border.

If you are travelling in northern Spain and coming from Santander in Cantabria, you will have to do some backtracking to cover the loop of attractions in this region. If you plan to continue to Madrid after you visit this region, after Santander you should go to Bilbao and take the *autopista* to visit Vitoria, then drive down to La Rioja, on to Pamplona, north through the mountains to San Sebastián, then back by Bilbao and south again on the *autopista* to Burgos and Madrid.

If you are heading to Aragón and Catalonia, you can exit the area from either Pamplona or Logroño and go east on the *autopistas* to Zaragoza and Barcelona.

Entering the region from Madrid via Burgos, you might best take the *autopistas* north to Vitoria and on to San Sebastián via Bilbao. Then see Navarra, leaving the charming backcountry Rioja until last, before returning to Burgos and Madrid.

THE BASQUE COUNTRY

Have you ever heard of Bizkaia, Gipuzkoa, and Araba? Probably not, because they are names in Euskera, the Basque language. Some people will know these three provinces of El País Vasco (Euskadi—the Basque Country) as Vizcaya, Guipúzcoa (hard to pronounce even in Spanish), and Alava. But most people tend to think of each of the three as a city: elegant San Sebastián by the sea, industrial Bilbao to its west, and to the south Wellington's Vitoria, the capital of the Basque Country.

The Basque Country is small, and for touristic purposes the principal points of interest can be covered in a few days. Usually only seasoned Spain travellers, those spending a few days on the beach at San Sebastián, true fanciers of Spanish haute cuisine, or bullfight aficionados bound for Semana Grande in Bilbao, where bulls as big as buffaloes test Spain's gutsier matadors, will stretch their itineraries to include this region.

The Basque seacoast is a series of picturesque fishing villages nestled in coves, with crescent-shaped beaches interspersed with industrial towns and graffiti-marred suburbs, but many of these villages—Guetaria, Zumaya, Zarauz, Pasajes de San Juan, and Fuenterrabía, all near San Sebastián,

The Basque Country
0 miles 10
0 km 10
Deba
Motrico
Ondarroa
Leeketio
Bermeo
Mundaka
C 6313
C 6315
C 6212
N 634
to Santander
Guernica
VIZCAYA
Bilbao
N 634
A 1
CANTABRIA
Río Nervión
N 240
Río Urola
SERRA DE URQUILLA
A 68
ALAVA
Vitoria
Argomañiz
N 1
SIERRAS DE CANTABRIA
N 1
A 1
Miranda de Ebro
to Burgos
Laguardia
Logroño
N
A 68
N 111
LA RIOJA

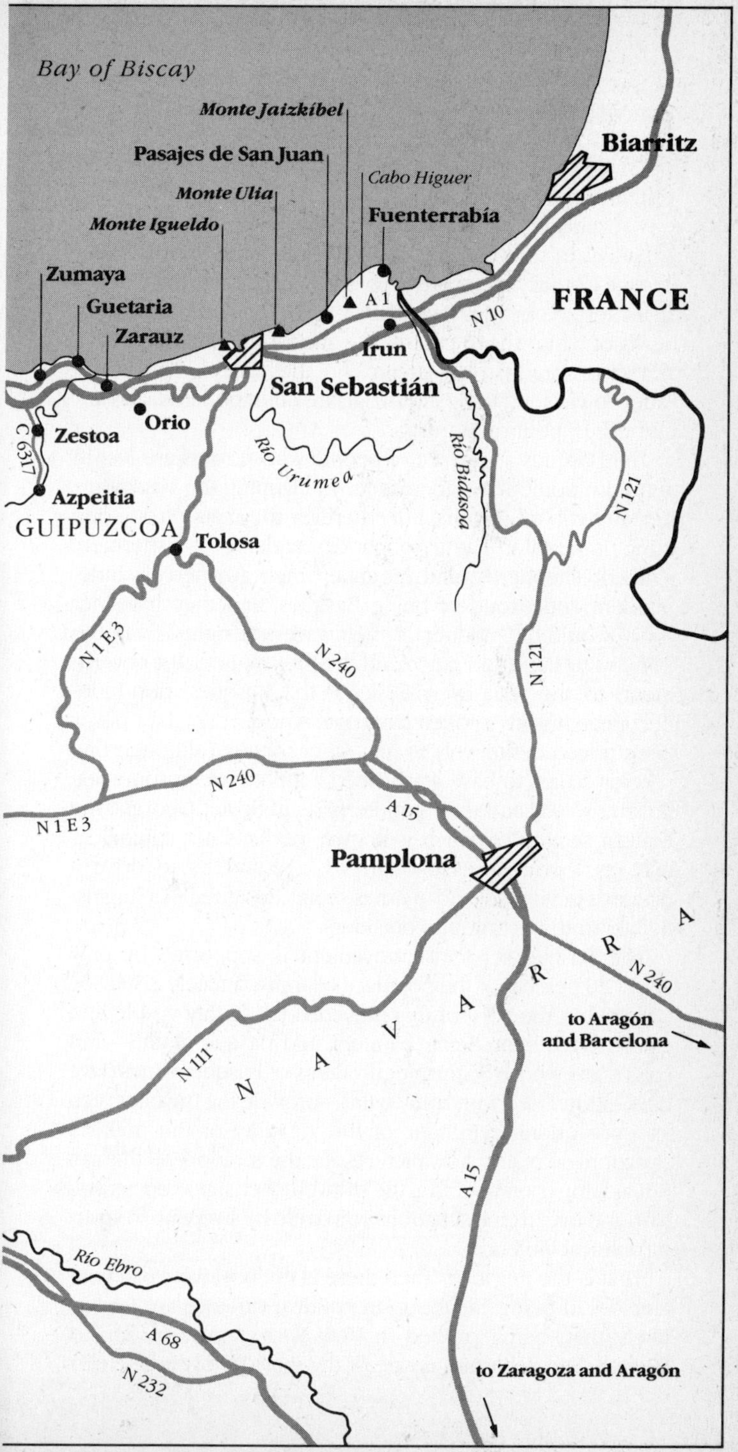

Bay of Biscay
Monte Jaizkibel
Pasajes de San Juan
Cabo Higuer
Monte Ulia
Monte Igueldo
Fuenterrabía
Biarritz
Zumaya
Guetaria
Zarauz
A 1
FRANCE
N 10
Irun
San Sebastián
Orio
Zestoa
C 6317
Río Urumea
Río Bidasoa
Azpeitia
GUIPUZCOA
Tolosa
N 121
N 1 E 3
N 240
N 121
N 240
N 1 E 3
A 15
Pamplona
N 240
to Aragón and Barcelona
N A V A R R A
N 111
A 15
Río Ebro
A 68
N 232
to Zaragoza and Aragón

and Bermeo near Bilbao, to name the most attractive ones—are well worth a visit, especially if you have time to laze away the afternoon at a dockside fishermen's restaurant over a lunch of salad, grilled fresh fish, and *txacoli,* the local petillant white wine.

A dramatic counterpoint to tawny Castile and dry Andalusia in summertime, the misty green hills of the inland Basque Country are scattered with small agricultural villages characterized by big-timbered stone houses called *caseríos,* herds of white sheep contrasting against the emerald fields, and fast-running trout streams in the valleys. The larger valley towns tend to be industrial, are often polluted, and are hotbeds of political unrest.

The Basques are a race of people whose roots are lost in antiquity. Some have gone as far as claiming the *Vascos* are the survivors of Atlantis, but wherever they came from, one thing is certain: These tough descendants of fishermen, whalers, shepherds, and mountain men are fiercely independent and proud of being Basques, and they have put every would-be subduer of their ancestral rights, from the Romans to General Franco and the present Socialist government, to the test. Even Euskera, the Basques' non-Indo-European, mostly spoken language, whose roots have never been traced definitively to any other tongue (although one scholar claims to have established a link between some 360 Basque words and their counterparts in Soviet Georgia, the eastern section of which is known, perhaps not coincidentally, as Iberia), uses enough k's, x's, and z's to drive a printer's devil mad, and at times seems designed as a linguistic labyrinth to confound outsiders.

The Basque separatist movement is supported by only about 20 percent of the populace of approximately 2,500,000 *Vascos,* but the core of this movement is highly visible and extremely violent. Signs, banners, and Basque graffiti—and road signs whose Spanish equivalents of Basque names have been obliterated with spray paint—provide the traveller with an ever-lurking reminder of the volatility of the political situation, no matter how picturesque the location. All this can put a damper on your fun, the sprayed-over signs can get you lost, and in extreme situations you could be swept up in an act of political violence.

That is the negative. Then there is the positive. First, your chances of being caught up in political violence are far less likely than being robbed in New York, Rome, or Seville. Second, San Sebastián is one of the world's loveliest, cleanest, and most elegant beach resorts. And, third, Basque cuisine is magnificent.

MAJOR INTEREST

The beach resort town of San Sebastián
Basque cuisine, especially restaurants in San Sebastián
The fortress town of Fuenterrabía
Bay of Biscay fishing villages
The Medieval quarter of Vitoria

Basque Cuisine

Basque cuisine is considered by all but the Catalans to be the best in Spain. It is at times supremely sophisticated; sometimes rustic, homey, and peasant-inspired; usually delicious; often served in trencherman portions; and in the best places frightfully expensive. A profusion of top-notch Basque restaurants have opened in the past decade in other regions, and the chefs at many of the best restaurants in Spain are Basques, even when the food itself is not.

Nueva cocina vasca (new Basque cuisine) began to evolve during the mid-1970s during the period when Spain's fledgling democracy was trying its wings, and, as much as in fashion, art, cinema, music, and a new morality, it is a symbol of new Spain's renaissance. Borrowing liberally from foreign influences (most notably Paul Bocuse of France), Juan Mari Arzak of the restaurant Arzak (San Sebastián), Pedro Subijana of Akelarre (San Sebastián), and Jesus María Oyarbide of Zalacaín (Madrid) caused a culinary revolution. During the first eight years (1974–1981) that Spain's national gastronomy prize for best chef was awarded, it was presented to four Basques, including Arzak, Subijana, Zalacaín's chef Benjamin Urdain, and a woman chef, Valentina Saralegui, at Oyarbide's other Madrid restaurant, Príncipe de Viana. Luís Irizar ran a cooking school in Zarauz, a few kilometers from San Sebastián, and turned out superstar chefs such as the brilliant Karlos Arguiñano. Ramón Roteta scored spectacular triumphs in the kitchen at El Amparo in Madrid, helping to catapult it into the ranks of Spain's top ten restaurants.

Jan Read and Maite Manjón, authors of *The Wine and Food of Spain,* quote Pedro Subijana describing *nueva cocina vasca:* "... the return to simple cookery and the respect for tradition and its rehabilitation. You therefore have on your menu: old dishes, some included more for nostalgic reasons than for their flavour; traditional dishes, but very carefully cooked; and finally some new ones."

The last line is where the rub comes in: "Some new ones" include everything from perfectly cooked seafood in lovely delicate sauces to a surfeit of rich dishes made with *foie gras,* truffles, or sea-urchin sauce, for example. Like the "new" cuisine of any other country, new Basque cuisine has its sublime practitioners and its ridiculous imitators. Perhaps the line in the *nueva cocina vasca* credo, "traditional dishes, but very carefully cooked" is where its ultimate genius lies.

The best of traditional Basque cuisine is based on seafood from the sparkling cold waters of the Bay of Biscay. Fresh fish—fabulous *rodaballo* (turbot), *besugo* (sea bream), *sardinas* (sardines), and *anchoas* (anchovies)—are sometimes sprinkled with oil and lemon, always with salt, and grilled over hot coals. The fish are delivered to the table whole and without sauces, all very fresh, natural, and sublimely delicious.

Angulas (baby eels), especially those from Aguiñaga, an estuary village a few kilometers west of San Sebastián, are sizzled briefly in olive oil laced with garlic and a bit of hot pepper, then served piping hot; you are provided with a bib and a wooden fork to avoid dry cleaning bills and burned lips. *Angulas,* which are only found in Spain and France in the Bay of Biscay, are a supernal Basque delicacy, an easily acquired taste for those with caviar budgets (at this writing they cost 15,000 pesetas per kilogram in La Brecha market, but you can usually get a 100-gram *ración* for 2,500–3,000 pesetas in a restaurant).

Other traditional Basque Country seafood preparations are *merluza* (hake), *kokotxas* (*cocochas;* hake glands from the cheek of the fish, a delicacy), and *almejas en salsa verde* (clams in a green sauce—garlic, parsley, and peas); *ajoarriero* (*bacalao,* salt cod, in tomato sauce, muleteer-style); *chipirones en su tinta* (squid cooked in a rich sauce made from its own ink); *txangurro* (*changurro,* spider-crabmeat, cooked with onions, tomatoes, Sherry, brandy, and breadcrumbs, then returned to the shell and baked), a superb dish that is often poorly done in many *típico* restaurants; and *marmitako,* a fisherman's casserole of tuna and potatoes.

Traditional inland contributions to Basque cuisine include lamb, *chistorra* (thin cheroot-like *chorizos*), *perrichicos* (tiny fingertip-size spring mushrooms), *pimientos de piquillo* (spicy peppers, usually stuffed with meat, crab, *bacalao,* or other fish), *alubias de Tolosa* (white beans cooked with *chorizo*), *truchas* (trout) and salmon from the Bidassoa river, *chuleton* (huge, thick steaks), and smoked Idiazabal ewe's cheese from the mountains. *Cuajada,* a mild, custard-like sheep's curd, sweetened to taste with wild honey, comes in a little brick-colored pot that never seems to hold enough.

A unique facet of the Basque Country is its all-male *sociedades gastronomicas* (gastronomic societies)—over 1,000 of them in Guipúzcoa alone, 100 in San Sebastián—each with its own *txoko* (*choko,* as they call their clubhouse) consisting of a kitchen, wine cellar, and dining room. Each member of a society, which may include anyone from a political dignitary to a bus driver, takes turns cooking his own specialties for the others. Members follow the honor system to pay for the food, condiments, and wine they use.

These societies date to the 19th century, and their existence goes far to explain the brilliance of Basque cuisine. As one Spanish gourmet publication puts it, "It is the cuisine of a race where everybody cooks." The *txokos*—where the constant challenge is to come up with new variations of classic dishes and creative new dishes, and then try them out on your peers, all of whom cook—are the proving grounds where many of the great dishes of Basque cuisine are born.

Membership in these eating and drinking societies, according to Penelope Casas, is "a constant cause of marital friction." So addicted are some to the art of cooking and the food, wine, and camaraderie of these clubs that they spend every evening with the boys. Recently, however, a few *sociedades gastronomicas* have opened their doors to women.

Basque Country Wines and Spirits

Technically speaking, the Basque Country is an important wine producer because of the Rioja Alavesa, a section of the Rioja wine district above the río Ebro, but, in reality, if it were not for political boundaries, this region would be considered a part of Castilian Rioja, because geographically and climatologically it is. (We will cover the Rioja Alavesa in the chapter on La Rioja.)

The other noteworthy wine district, and it is only noteworthy to the Basques, is the maritime district around Guetaria and Zarauz that produces the green, petillant, quaffable wine called *txacoli* (*chacoli*). In this rainy climate the grapes seldom get fully ripe, so *txacoli* is high in acid, which makes it a good wine to accompany oysters and other shellfish, but, like French Muscadet, it is an acquired taste for many people. It is low in alcohol, however, so it can be drunk with relative impunity. The Basques love *txacoli* and drink copious quantities in the bars and grilled fish restaurants of this region. The best *txacoli* is made by Txomin Echániz of Guetaria.

The Basques, like the Asturians, also drink huge quantities of *sidra* (cider), and you will see many *sidrerías* (cider bars) in the Basque Country. Sometimes a waiter or a patron will hold a bottle of *sidra* above his head in one hand and arc it into a wide-mouthed tall glass held below his waist in his other hand. This amusing and spectacular technique of pouring from a height into the glass causes the cider to splash and fizz, releasing some of the carbon dioxide trapped in the liquid. The *sidra* is then knocked back in one gulp and the glass is passed to the next drinker. You can order a bottle of cider, however, without feeling the obligation to imitate the dexterity of the Basques in this maneuver.

Spirits, often accompanied by the lighting of a *puro* or *habano* (cigar), are de rigueur after a substantial meal in the Basque Country. People drink *aguardiente de orujo* (marc or grape spirits), usually referred to only as *orujo; aguardientes* (literally, "firewater") made from apples and other fruits, and similar to eau-de-vie; *anis* (anisette); *pacharan* (sloeberry- and anis-flavored *aguardiente*) from Rioja, Navarra, and the Basque Country; and the native Basque liqueur, *Izarra* ("star" in Basque), made from up to 48 different mountain herbs, flowers, and plants. All these popular drinks are usually served ice-cold in short, cylindrical glasses.

SAN SEBASTIAN

Located on a sheltered crabshell-shaped bay of the Cantabrian Sea, with two extraordinary beaches, San Sebastián (Donostia, in Basque) is one of the most stunningly beautiful cities in Spain. Also, as the birthplace of *nueva cocina vasca* the city draws food epicures to its temples of gastronomy as the Camino de Santiago attracted religious pilgrims.

This elegant city plays the role of a grand fin-de-siècle resort as few others can. It first became fashionable in the mid-19th century, when Queen Isabella II came here in the summer to bathe in the sea. Isabella's court followed, and for the next century the Spanish government kept the custom of moving to San Sebastián for the summer, making it Spain's premier beach resort until the demise of *franquismo,* when most of the jet-set crowd drifted to warmer Marbella on the Costa del Sol. Still, in August, the influx of Spaniards and French families (the city is only 12.5 miles from the French border on a natural route into Spain from northern and western France) seems to double the normal population of 172,000. San Sebastián has managed to remain elegant, however, while the Costa del Sol, inundated with foreign and Spanish tourists, seems to fight a constant battle against being overwhelmed by the cheap and gaudy.

The sheltered La Concha bay, with its two beaches, is guarded by two hills, **Monte Igueldo** to the west and **Monte Urgull** to the east, and buffered from the wild Bay of Biscay by Isla de Santa Clara. Monte Igueldo is reachable by car or funicular and has an amusement park, and Monte Urgull has a walkway around its base and footpaths to the top, where the **Castillo de Santa Cruz de la Mota** has a marginally interesting military museum. Both offer superb views of the city, the bay, and the fishing port.

Most of old San Sebastián was destroyed by fire in the early 19th century, so don't expect to see many vestiges of the centuries-old buildings so characteristic of many other cities in Spain. San Sebastián has a few historical monuments, churches, architectural points of interest, and a noteworthy museum, but the reason you really come here is for the beach, the food, the street life. The raffish **Parte Vieja** (the old quarter, below Monte Urgull, rebuilt after the fire), with its lively narrow streets filled with bars, restaurants, markets, quaint (not usually touristy) shops, the fishermen's quarter, and a few older buildings of interest, more than compensates in atmosphere for what it lacks in antiquity. This area is the more typically Spanish area of San Sebastián, while the newer parts of town, especially on the isthmus between the Playa de la Concha and río Urumea—roughly the area between the Alameda del Boulevard (the southern limit of the old quarter) on the north and calle San Martín near the **Catedral del Buen Pastor** on the south—where most of the chic shops and cafés are located, are more reminiscent of France. The cathedral is a late 19th-century Neo-Gothic structure with a fine steeple.

As you stroll through the old quarter, you will see the 18th-century Baroque façade of the **Iglesia de Santa María** at the north end of calle Campanario. **San Vicente**, the city's oldest church, is located east of Santa María, along calle 31 de Agosto, the only street not burned during the disastrous fire set by Anglo-Portuguese forces on August 31, 1813, and now home to some of San Sebastián's best *tapas* bars. San Vicente is an austere early-16th-century building, in need of another tower to balance the main façade. The late-16th-century retable is the main attraction in its interior.

The municipal museum is located two blocks northwest of San Vicente in the 16th-century former **Convento de San Telmo**. The museum contains minor paintings by El Greco and Goya, portraits by Vicente López, works by Dario de Regoyos—a Spanish Impressionist much influenced by Van Gogh—and a room of Zuloaga's pictures. The museum also has a section devoted to Basque culture, another to the Carlist Wars, and the enclosed cloisters hold a display of Basque funeral steles found in the region. The convent's church is decorated with 17 huge paintings by Josep Maria Sert depicting heroic, historical, and cultural scenes of San Sebastián and the province of Guipúzcoa: whaling in the Cantabrian Sea, Juan Sebastián Elcano circumnavigating the globe, Saint Ignatius of Loyola, and so on. Sert was a Catalan artist who decorated the Palace of the League of Nations, the Catedral de Sant Pere in Vic (Catalonia), and the Waldorf-Astoria in New York.

The fine, arcaded **plaza de la Constitución**, located in the center of the old quarter, is the epicenter of social life in this district. In former days bullfights were held here, but now the plaza is used for anything from folkloric festivals and political demonstrations to flea markets. The former town hall here dates from the 1830s.

West of the plaza de la Constitución below Monte Urgull in the port is the fishermen's quarter, with its colorful fishing trawlers and arcaded buildings along the docks. The ground floor of almost every house along this row is dedicated to an al fresco restaurant serving grilled sardines and other typical fish dishes. These restaurants are unpretentious but somewhat touristy, and they are certainly a far cry from the temples of high cuisine mentioned earlier, but if you choose the restaurant carefully—look at what is being served to other patrons; if a dish looks good, try it—you can pass a delightful, long lunch over salad, grilled fish, and a bottle of *txacoli* while watching the comings and goings in the port.

At the western end of the row of sardine restaurants is an aquarium with a seafaring museum featuring some fascinating dioramas of different ocean-fishing techniques employed by Basque fishermen, sea fishing and boating paraphernalia, and a Basque fisherman's kitchen.

Boats leave every hour during the summer from the fishermen's quarter for the short trip to Isla de Santa Clara and sightseeing tours of the bay. Tickets can be purchased at a booth located at the southern end of the port next to the yacht club.

The city hall of San Sebastián, located on the bay next to the old quarter, is a huge belle-epoque palace built in 1897 as a casino rivaling Monte Carlo, Deauville, and Biarritz. The twin towers of this building can be seen from anywhere along the esplanade; they draw the eye to this dominant building that, more than anything else in San Sebastián except the Maria Cristina hotel, leaves you with an indelible impression of fin-de-siècle style. The beautiful Alderdi Eder park in front of the city hall is unusual because of its 200 tamarisks, small Mediterranean trees that need considerable coaxing to grow in this Atlantic climate. They were chosen for planting here because their dense foliage throws good shade and because they are short enough not to block the views of the sea from surrounding buildings.

San Sebastián's splendid **Esplanade**, with its beautiful wrought-iron railings and lampposts, borders the golden sands of two of the world's finest urban beaches, the crescent-moon-shaped **Playa de la Concha** and **Playa de Ondarreta**, separated only by a small rocky promontory. In summer the beaches are a sea of bodies, including those of women sunbathing topless. In peak season the beaches are very crowded but seem to absorb the mass of people until high tide, when the broad band of sand is cut so dramatically that you must either get off the beach or be prepared to emulate the proverbial tinned sardine. June, early July, and September are the best months for the beach if you want to avoid the heaviest crowds. (Note: Even in summer, you will encounter occasional rainy days and cool weather; the summer climate of the Basque Coast is not perpetually cloudless like that of southern Spain.)

San Sebastián hosts an excellent, internationally known jazz festival in late July, always after the one at Vitoria. In August Semana Grande is the big celebration, with regattas, spectacular fireworks, and general merrymaking, but since the mid-1970s no bullfights. The San Sebastián International Film Festival, a prestigious event à la Cannes, draws major international film stars to the splendid Maria Cristina hotel.

About 10 km (6 miles) south of San Sebastián on N 240 (the San Sebastián–Tolosa–Pamplona road) is the Hipodromo de Lasarte, a grass racetrack where some of the finest thoroughbred racing in Spain takes place in July, August, and September, and again on Sunday mornings from mid-December to the second Sunday in February.

The parking situation in San Sebastián is not good. All of the old and new sections of town on the isthmus are blue zones. To park in such areas, you must buy a paper parking permit, punch holes in it to show the time you parked, and place it on the dashboard so the parking police can check it. In some areas, such as the port, you can buy a permit from a machine; in other areas the concierges at most hotels will have them. At this writing the Hotel Niza and the Bataplan discotheque mark the western boundaries of the blue zones; beyond that you can park on the street, but unless you are fluent in Spanish and can decipher the street parking signs, and are willing to risk a break-in, we suggest you leave your car in one of the two underground car parks on the isthmus: at plaza Cervantes near the Hotel de Londres y de Inglaterra or at Reina Regente near the Maria Cristina hotel.

Doing the Chiquiteo

The Parte Vieja is a wonderful place to prowl in search of *tapas* (bar hopping for *tapas* in San Sebastián is called *el chiquiteo* after the short, wide-mouthed glasses known as *chiquitos;* in other Basque cities, *tapas* hopping is called *el tapeo*). Here, in the bars along these lively, colorful streets, you can rub elbows (literally—you have to vie for space at the bar) with the people of Donostia and sample many of the traditional dishes for which the Basques, and San Sebastián in particular, lay claim to the gastronomic crown of Spain.

If you wish to do your own *tapas* tour of the old quarter, we suggest you begin at **Bar Portaletas**, Puerto 8, for *banderillas* (*tapas* skewered with toothpicks) of *guindillas con anchoa y aceituna* (small piquant green peppers with anchovies and olives), *tortilla de patata* (Spanish omelette), *pimientos rellenos* (stuffed peppers), *serrano* ham, *bonito* (tuna) with mayonnaise on puff pastry, *hueva* (fish roe), *alcachofa con bonito* (artichokes with tuna), and cold beer or *clarete* (light red or rosé wine) served in *chiquitos.* **Tamboril**, calle Pescadería 2 (in a corner of the plaza de la Constitución), serves deep-fried *pimientos rellenos de carne, boquerónes* (fresh anchovies), *guindillas,* canapés of smoked salmon, and a *rosado* from Catalonia.

Follow Pescadería down to the best market in San Sebastián, **Mercado de la Brecha**, where you can peruse the wide variety of seafood that constitutes the catch of the day. This is a good way to scout the best choices for dinner. Just outside the fish market, **Bar José Mari** in Fermín Calbetón serves fine crab canapés, with a glass of *txacoli,* the Basque Country's answer to Muscadet. And along calle 31 de Agosto, between the churches of Santa María and San Vicente, you will find two of the best *tapas* bars in San Sebastián, **Martínez** at number 13 and **La Cepa** at number 9.

Another notable *tapas* bar, outside the old quarter and especially convenient for those staying in one of the hotels near the paseo de la Concha, is a friendly neighborhood bar, **Ostarte**, located two short blocks east of Hotel Niza on calle San Martín at the corner of Marinel. Joni, the friendly young woman who runs Ostarte, serves wonderful *tapas:* slices of excellent *tortillas* (Spanish omelettes) with potatoes, red peppers, and green garlic shoots, a three-layered affair with *chorizo,* spinach, and potatoes, and another with shrimp and garlic shoots; canapés of cheese, scallions, and anchovies, of smoked trout dressed with minced onion in lemon and olive oil, and of smooth, creamy *bacalao;* and stellar, fresh homemade *chorizos.* Get to Ostarte before 3:00 P.M., or the first round of *tapas* will be gone, or come back around 6:00 or 7:00 when the evening selection is laid out.

For early-evening aperitifs or for postprandials, try **Kabutzia** on the top floor of the Club Nautico overlooking the harbor, **Dionis** (formerly Maxim) behind city hall, or the **Bataplan Bar and Discotheque** next to Hotel Niza at the western end of paseo de la Concha overlooking the beach.

Nuevo Gran Casino de Kursaal, calle Zubieta 2, in the Hotel de Londres y de Inglaterra, is open from 6:00 P.M. to 2:00 A.M. (3:00 A.M. on holiday eves) for baccarat, blackjack, roulette (French and American), and other games of chance. The Kursaal also has a restaurant and bar.

Staying in San Sebastián

With the exception of the **Maria Cristina**, plaza de la Republica Argentina, San Sebastián's best hotel, a beautifully renovated belle-epoque jewel with glittering chandeliers and sumptuous furnishings, and **De Londres y de Inglaterra**, Zubieta 2, centrally located along the paseo de la Concha with fine views of the bay, convenient to the best shopping areas of the newer parts of town and housing the Kursaal Casino, San Sebastián is not a city of luxurious hotels. However, because space is at a premium in summer and not every traveller can afford the likes of the two top choices, we have selected several comfortable, if not opulent, medium-range choices in San Sebastián.

Every room at the **Orly**, located on plaza Zaragoza halfway between the de Londres y de Inglaterra and Hotel Niza, one block from the paseo de la Concha, faces the sea, but the higher floors have better views. The **Niza**, Zubieta 56, on the paseo de la Concha, facing the beach, still exudes Old World charm, complete with a rickety old elevator, in a fantastic location. Ask for a room *mirando al mar* (looking to the sea). The Niza needs renovation but is moderately comfortable. Avoid the crowded basement pizzeria serving the oddest pizzas and soupiest pasta sauces you would ever taste.

Costa Vasca, avenida Pio Baroja 15, near Playa Ondarreta in a quiet location; **San Sebastián**, avenida Zumalácarregui 20, near Ondarreta at the foot of Monte Igueldo, and one of the Aranzazu chain; and **Monte Igueldo**, 5 km (3 miles) from the center of town on Monte Igueldo, with stunning views of the bay: All are alternate, adequate lodgings if you can't get into any of the centrally located hotels.

Dining in San Sebastián

Some of the best restaurants in Spain can be found in San Sebastián, and several of them are worthy of a gastronomic pilgrimage. Most of these restaurants feature many of the traditional dishes on which the reputation of Basque cuisine is based, but many of them also emphasize the creative French-influenced style of *nueva cocina vasca* that often reaches the pinnacle of gastronomy but sometimes borders on wretched excess. In San Sebastián's top restaurants you will find dishes such as grilled fresh *foie gras* (from Spain, as are many of the truffles in jars marketed as "produce of France") served on a bed of julienned zucchini; crepes with duck confit in truffle sauce; sautéed loin of lamb and lamb brains with mint and lemon sauce; and a dazzling variety of other dishes, some sublime, others conceptually flawed and occasionally ridiculous.

Many of San Sebastián's best restaurants require reservations weeks in advance, and many close at different times of the year for up to a month for vacation, so write or call ahead. Most San Sebastián restaurants of all classes are closed on Sunday nights and often close one other night during the week.

Juan Mari Arzak, owner of **Arzak**, Alto de Miracruz 21 (Tel: 27-84-65), has established himself as one of the premier chefs of Spain with such dishes as oyster and green asparagus soup, crepes stuffed with *txangurro,* Bidasoa salmon in pastry, and desserts such as honey ice cream with caramelized pears, a light cheese soufflé with apricot cream, and a mousse of red fruit and white chocolate. More exotic palates may appreciate Arzak's veal tongue with green peppercorns, and sautéed prawns with prunes and sweet peppers. Arzak is located east of San Sebastián on N 1 on the road to Pasaias. It is closed in late June and early July and for the month of November.

Located 7.5 km (4.7 miles) west of town on Monte Igueldo, **Akelarre**, Barrio de Igueldo (Tel: 21-20-52), named for the *akelarre*—a mythological feast and orgy involving witches, sorcerers, and satyrs that Basque folklore says takes place about 19 miles east of San Sebastián in the mountains of Navarra—serves first-rate *nueva cocina* and offers fine views of the Basque coast. Afterward, below the restaurant, at the **Ku discotheque**, one of the city's top night spots, you can do your own version of the *akelarre* until the wee hours with *todo* San Sebastián.

Along with Arzak, Pedro Subijana, the chef-owner of **Akelarre**, is in the vanguard of *nueva cocina vasca* and continues to vie with the maestro for the honor of having the best restaurant in San Sebastián. The new cuisine is constantly changing, depending on fresh and seasonal ingredients and the creativity of the chef. A sampling of Akelarre's specialties from past menus includes: a salad of red cabbage and endive with warm, broiled tuna with coriander seeds in a mustard vinaigrette, turbot in sea urchin sauce, monkfish with rosemary and fresh tomatoes, gout-inducing sweetbreads in Port sauce, and a wild-strawberry tartlet. The restaurant closes from June 1 to 15 and for the month of December.

Casa Nicolasa, Aldamar 4 (Tel: 42-17-62), located across the street from the famous Mercado de la Brecha, is always among the finest and most elegant restaurants of Guipúzcoa, serving excellent renditions of more traditional northern dishes, such as *menestra, txangurro,* and hook-and-line-caught *chipirones en su tinta* (squid caught in nets exhaust their ink) as well as turbot with caviar, filet mignon with *foie gras,* seasonal game dishes, and a superb lineup of desserts, including something Juan José Castillo, the owner, calls *orgia de postres,* an orgy of desserts, for two or more people, of course. Closed for three weeks in March.

Panier Fleuri, paseo de Salamanca 1 (Tel: 42-42-05), located just around the corner from Nicolasa on a street running along río Urumea, has moved from its old digs in the industrial suburb of Renteria, where it had established a decades-old reputation for good food. It was recently awarded Spain's national prize for gastonomy. *Alta cocina* (haute cuisine) rules here, as reflected in such dishes as *cigalas* (langoustines) in puff pastry, pheasant with grapes, artichoke hearts filled with *txangurro,* and venison with chestnut puree and cranberries, any of which can be complemented by wines from one of the best cellars in Spain. Closed for three weeks in June and during the Christmas holidays.

West of San Sebastián on the road to the Barrio de (Monte) Igueldo, **Rekondo**, subida de Igueldo (Tel: 21-29-07), with a wine cellar holding over 100,000 bottles, has one of the greatest wine lists in Europe. Recondo, with a few deviations, sticks to a short menu featuring grilled meats and fish: thick steaks, lamb chops, turbot, sea bream, and so on. It is a perfect place to go when you want to drink a fabulous bottle and do not want elaborate sauces to combat your enjoyment of the wine. Closed from June 20 to June 30 and from November 1 to 20.

Patxiku Kintana, San Jerónimo 22 (Tel: 42-63-99), is located in the center of the old quarter, where ex-jai-alai star Patxi Kintana oversees the dining room, and his mother and wife cook excellent, traditional Basque cuisine with a personal touch: *albondigas de jabali con alubias* (wild boar meatballs with white beans), *txangurro* in puff pastry, and *merluza* with clams and *kokotxas.* Closed during Holy Week and for the Christmas holidays.

The menu at the very popular and up-and-coming **Urepel**, paseo de Salamanca 3 (Tel: 42-40-40), located next to Panier Fleuri on río Urumea, changes daily according to what is available in the nearby Mercado de la Brecha. **Chomin**, avenida Infanta Beatriz 14, started out as a small *tapas* bar, famous for its *merluza* with clams, in the industrial town of Eibar, where some of the world's finest shotguns are made. Now Chomin is in a pretty chalet near Playa Ondarreta and still serves the kind of down-to-earth, traditional dishes and homemade desserts that made it famous.

In addition to these fine restaurants there are three in the old quarter worthy of special mention: **Kokotxa**, Campanario 11 (Tel: 42-01-73), run by disciples of the famous Luis Irizar of Zarauz, one of the architects of *nueva cocina vasca,* whose cooking school produced Karlos Arguiñano and other culinary stars; the venerable **Salduba**, Pescadería 6 (Tel: 42-56-27), open for over 40 years, still serves traditional dishes such as *merluza Salduba* (hake with clams and *kokotxas*) and *pimientos rellenos de txangurro;* and **Casa**

Urbano, 31 de Agosto 17 (Tel: 42-04-34), where beautifully grilled fish, typical Basque seafood dishes, a good wine list, and reasonable prices have earned it a good following.

Those who like discoveries should try **Bretxa**, General Echagüe 5, just east of the Mercado de la Brecha, a popular, moderately priced restaurant specializing in grilled seafood.

THE FISHING VILLAGES OF THE BAY OF BISCAY

The Pasajes, or the Pasaias, as they are known in Basque—San Juan, San Pedro, and Ancho—are located a few miles east of San Sebastián in the best-sheltered deep-water harbor between Bilbao and Bordeaux. Most of San Sebastián's commercial shipping uses the port of Ancho; San Pedro and San Juan are among the most productive deep-sea fishing ports in Spain. **Pasajes de San Juan** (look for signs to Pasaia Donibane), a picturesque fishing village and former whaling port with only one street, is one of the most beautiful towns on the Basque coast. It has all the prerequisites: pretty fishing boats, timbered houses with flower-and-laundry-bedecked balconies and coats of arms, and quayside seafood restaurants. Victor Hugo lived here in 1843 at San Juan 59. The house is preserved as a museum; the second floor has a display of models of the best-known ships built in the shipyards of the Pasajes, where the *Mari Galant* (Columbus's *Santa María*) and several ships of the Spanish Armada were constructed.

Don't take a car to San Juan in summer. The one-lane street, which actually tunnels through what normally would be the ground floor of several houses, is a natural traffic jam, and there is only a small car park at the edge of town. Either go by bus from the center of San Sebastián (catch it on calle Aldamar near the Mercado de la Brecha) or drive to Ancho or San Pedro and take a ferry across the inlet. You can get great seafood in San Juan at **Casa Cámara**, San Juan 79, where you can choose *langosta* (rock lobster) or *centollo* (spider crab) from a tank in the floor, and at **Txulotxo**, San Juan 82, famous for its *txangurro,* with fine views of the beautiful harbor.

Fuenterrabía

Fuenterrabía (Hondarribia), 20 km (12.5 miles) east of San Sebastián, is one of the most historic and attractive towns on the Basque coast. Overlooking the mouth of río Bidasoa marking the border with France, Fuenterrabiá was a key fortress town for centuries, and it still retains substantial sections of its old ramparts. The historic **castle** was originally built in the tenth century and was reinforced six centuries later during the reign of Charles V. During a two-month siege by French forces in 1638 the people of Fuenterrabía put up a heroic defense in this castle, an event commemorated each year on September 8 with a fiesta in honor of the town's patroness, the Virgin of Guadalupe. The castle, with its thick fortress walls and *bovedas* (vaults), has been converted into the moderately priced 16-room **Parador El Emperador**, decorated with period furniture, antiques, suits of armor, heraldic banners, and other paraphernalia evoking a Medieval atmosphere. The terrace has beautiful views of the sea and neighboring France.

In 1660 Louis XIV of France was married by proxy to María Teresa, daughter of Philip IV, in the historic and imposing Gothic Iglesia de Santa María here, paving the way for the eventual introduction of the Bourbon dynasty into Spain.

Fuenterrabía itself is a picturesque town of steep, narrow streets lined with baronial houses embellished, like San Juan, with flower-covered balconies and coats of arms. The town has ten art galleries and a number of antiques shops. The fishermen's quarter, **La Marina**, is famous for its colorful fishing fleet, flower-bedecked houses, sidewalk seafood restaurants, and *la lonja* (fish auction).

Fuenterrabía has two fine restaurants: the luxurious and exceptional **Ramón Roteta**, on calle Irún in the Villa Ainara (Tel: 64-16-93), and **Arraunlari** (Tel: 64-15-81), located on paseo Butrón overlooking the mouth of río Bidasoa and the sea.

Ramón Roteta is one of the early stars of *nueva cocina vasca;* he was the chef at Madrid's brilliantly successful El Amparo. His restaurant, perhaps the most elegant in Guipúzcoa—a few years ago readers of Spain's best regarded gourmet publication voted it one of the three most elegant restaurants in the country—is in a stunningly beautiful old house with a beautiful flower garden, dining terrace, and porch. The tables are set with different patterns of tablecloths, silver, china, and glassware for each group of diners to suggest the atmosphere of a private home.

Roteta's kitchen regales the guests with such dishes as poached, country-fresh eggs with *foie gras* and truffles, sole poached in *txacoli* with *cangrejos del río* (river crayfish), and Bidasoa salmon filled with langoustine tails and mushrooms, and complements the menu with an excellent wine list, liqueur selection, and, important in Spain and totally acceptable in fine restaurants, a good selection of properly cared-for *habanos* (Cuban cigars).

Arraunlari, while not in the same league as Roteta (few are), excels at the fine Basque art of preparing fish, delivered directly to the restaurant by local fishermen each day. If you haven't already had *rodaballo* (turbot), which must be ordered for two or more people, try it here.

If you want to stay in Fuenterrabía at the parador, advance reservations are a must unless you luck into a last-minute cancellation. If you can't get into the parador, there is another exceptional hotel, the **Pampinot**, in a beautiful 15th-century palace in the center of old Fuenterrabía. It rivals the parador for atmosphere, but, alas, it has only eight rooms, so you may have to try a less-romantic but adequate alternative, the **Jauregui**, a modern, centrally located hotel with 53 rooms.

Several spots in the area from San Sebastián to the French border offer excellent views of the Basque coast. **Monte Ulía**, the third hill of San Sebastián, just east of río Urumea, has three fine *miradores* (vantage points), including the Mirador de Ballenero (whaler), where a lookout used to watch the sea for an approaching herd. Once whales were spotted, huge bonfires were lit to signal the whalers to launch their boats.

The drive on the road over the heights of **Monte Jaizkibel** between the Pasajes and Fuenterrabía provides the most spectacular views of the entire coast. Cabo Higuer, a few miles north of Fuenterrabiá, has fine views of the French coast.

West of San Sebastián

West of San Sebastián are three fishing and beach towns that can easily be visited in a half-day outing. Take the road along La Concha beach and follow the signs to the *autopista,* then follow it to the Zarauz exit. **Zarauz**, 17 km (10.5 miles) from San Sebastián, was once the summer residence of Isabella II. Here, in 1868, Isabella learned that she was no longer queen, so she left for exile in France. Although the town is still famous as a summer place for aristocrats, it's frustrating trying to get through the villa-lined blocks (with few places to park) that cover the approaches to Zarauz's beautiful mile-long beach, so you may not want to get tied up here.

Zarauz does have an exceptional restaurant, **Karlos Arguiñano**, Mendilauta 13 (Tel: 83-01-78), that offers first-rate traditional and modern Basque cuisine based primarily on seafood. Over a decade ago Karlos Arguiñano was a star pupil at the Zarauz cooking school run by Luís Irizar, one of the chefs responsible for the evolution of *nueva cocina vasca,* and over the years Arguiñano has become part of the vanguard of great Basque *cocina del autor,* signature cuisine. His kitchen is inventive, constantly creating new dishes from fresh, seasonal market products, redefining traditional Basque dishes, and putting a personal twist on others. Karlos Arguiñano's elegant restaurant is in a beautiful old summer house with a dining terrace and gardens facing the sea.

Guetaria, a fishing village 9 km (5.5 miles) from Zarauz along a twisting coastal road, is the most picturesque and interesting town on this part of the coast. The village sits on a hill facing the port, the sea, and Isla San Antón, known locally as El Ratón because its shape resembles a crouching mouse (San Antón is connected to the close-by mainland by a short, man-made isthmus). The 13th- to 15th-century **Iglesia de San Salvador** is, architecturally, one of the most important religious monuments in the province of Guipúzcoa. A curiosity of this church is the alleyway (leading to the port) that passes beneath the church. In the archway is an image of the Virgin worshipped especially by fishermen and their families.

Juan Sebastián Elcano, the man who brought back the battered remnants of Magellan's fleet and crew (one of five ships and fewer than 20 of the more than 240 men who originally began the voyage limped into Sanlucar de Barrameda three years later), thus becoming the first man to circumnavigate the globe, was from Guetaria. There is a fine statue of Elcano in the center of town across the street from the excellent seafood restaurant **Elkano** (Elcano in Basque).

If you want to dine in the port area, **Talai-Pe**, next to the isthmus and looking out over the harbor, is a good choice in cool weather. In good weather you can get a salad, a splendid *rodaballo* (turbot) sprinkled with lemon and oil and cooked on an outdoor *asador* (grill), and a bottle of Guetaria *txacoli* or *sidra*—both among the best in the Basque Country—at the unassuming dockside fishermen's bar **Itxas-Etke**, served at an open-air table under the arcade. If you are ever going to try *chipirones en su tinta,* well, Guetaria is the place that made this squid dish famous.

Zumaya, 5 km (3 miles) west of Guetaria, at the mouth of río Urola, is another picturesque fishing village. There is a small beach on the harbor, a larger beach along the sea, a lighthouse, a charming footbridge over the boat moorings of the Urola, and a good seafood restaurant, **Abegi-Leku**—but the main attraction here, just east of town, is the **Villa Zuloaga**, the home of Ignacio Zuloaga (1870–1945), the famous Basque painter. Built on the site of a Camino de Santiago (the old northern route) pilgrims' inn, **Santiago Echea**, of which a 12th-century chapel and portions of the cloister remain, Villa Zuloaga is now a museum containing the works of Zuloaga and works from the artist's personal collection, including several paintings by El Greco, Goya, Zurbarán, and Morales.

If you retrace your route back to San Sebastián through Zumaya, Guetaria, and Zarauz, you might skip the *autopista* entrance at Zarauz and follow the N 634 back to town. After Orio, whose oarsmen are the best rowers on the Basque coast, follow the picturesque road through the green hills and along the river for a pleasant re-entry into urban San Sebastián.

Those interested in Saint Ignatius of Loyola (1491–1556), founder of the Jesuits, can visit the huge sanctuary of Loyola at Azpeitia, 16 km (10 miles) south of Zumaya past the spa town of Cestona (Zestoa) (follow N 634 a few miles west from Zumaya, then take C 6317 south). Cestona, by the way, is famous for its mineral waters. The **Gran Hotel Balneario de Cestona** is a fin-de-siècle spa for taking the waters for the digestion.

The sanctuary of Loyola surrounds what is left of the former Loyola ancestral home, including a 14th-century tower where Saint Ignatius was born. Years later, while recuperating from the wounds he received as a soldier defending Pamplona from a French attempt to recover Spanish Navarre, he conceived the idea to form the Society of Jesus.

If instead of returning to San Sebastián you continue west along the coast road, you will pass two more typical, colorful fishing villages—**Deba**, whose **Iglesia de Santa María** has a noteworthy 13th-century Gothic portal and a 15th-century cloister, and Motrico—before entering the province of Vizcaya.

VIZCAYA PROVINCE

Vizcaya is a small province dominated by industrial Bilbao. Ondarroa, Lequeito, and Bermeo are the most picturesque fishing villages along the north coast of Vizcaya between Zumaya and Bilbao, but the big attraction is **Guernica**, the subject of Picasso's painting (in the Casón del Buen Retiro in Madrid). On a market day in April 1937, during the Spanish Civil War, Guernica was bombed (the world's first major air raid against civilians) by General Franco's German allies. Over 2,000 people died before the *Luftwaffe* was done, but the famous **Guernikako arbola**, the Tree of Guernica, long sacred to the Basques, still stood.

King Ferdinand the Catholic came here in 1476 and swore to uphold the Basque *fueros* (rights) beneath the tree, and four years later Queen Isabella did the same, even dressing in regional costume for the event. After that, all the kings of Castile and Spain made the trip to *jurar* (swear) beneath the venerated oak until 1876, when Vizcaya lost its *fueros* because it sided with the Carlists. Juan Carlos I, the current king of Spain, essentially renewed the custom by going to Guernica for a speech to the new Basque parliament in 1978. Grown from a sapling taken from the original oak, a descendant of the tree still stands. A piece of the old tree, said to be a thousand years old, is preserved at the Casa de Juntas (Vizcaya assembly hall).

Just a few miles southeast of colorful Bermeo (44 km/27 miles from Bilbao)—the most important fishing port on the Cantabrian Sea—on the road from Guernica (C 6315) is the pretty fishing village of Mundaka, with a charming, inexpensive 12-room hotel, **El Puerto**, ensconced in a renovated fisherman's house overlooking the port. There are great waves along this coast, too.

Bilbao

Bilbao, the capital of Vizcaya since 1300, is now a large (population 433,000), modern industrial city divided by the commercial, crane-lined río Nervión and surrounded by steep green hills. Bilbao's smoky factories account for its prosperity, but the city has been hit hard in recent years by high unemployment brought on by a steep recession, which in turn has been exacerbated by atrocious acts of terrorism, including the kidnapping and murder of a number of prominent businessmen and two directors of a proposed nuclear plant. Needless to say, potential investors are hesitant to bet on Bilbao.

The **Casco Viejo** (old quarter) of Bilbao, on the eastern bank of the Nervión, has been renovated—it needed it—

since a disastrous flood in 1983, and the results are impressive. Its narrow pedestrian-only streets are filled with bars offering the same kind of *tapas*-bar-prowling opportunities as in San Sebastián. Be aware, however, that, unlike in San Sebastián, many people here will speak to you only in Basque; they refuse to answer in Spanish.

The attractions of note in the old quarter are the much-restored **Catedral de Santiago**, originally built in the 14th century, with a Gothic cloister from 1404, and the arcaded plaza Nueva. The **Museo de Bellas Artes** (fine arts museum), in the Parque de Doña Casilda Iturriza in the new part of town, contains paintings by Velázquez, El Greco, Goya, Zurbarán, Regoyos, Sorolla, and others.

Semana Grande, beginning the first Saturday after August 15, when the biggest bulls in Spain are brought in to face Spain's bravest matadors, the majority of whom are from Andalusia or Castile, is a big event for bullfight aficionados. But if you want to see something truly frightening, try to get a ticket to see a soccer match in San Mames stadium when Atletico de Bilbao is playing one of the first-division teams from Madrid.

The big draw in Bilbao, however, if you are a lover of great food, has to be the restaurant scene. Bilbao has more than 20 highly rated restaurants. Although you may need a Basque interpreter to help you with some of the names—Gorrotxa, Machinventa, Goizeko Kabi, Zortzico, Jolastoky, and Estraunza, to list a few (Señor, Guría, Bermeo, Andra-Mari, and Begoña are excellent pronounceables)—you will have no trouble remembering the dining experience, for either the exceptional quality of the cuisine or the size of *la cuenta* (the check), where, at last, New York meets its match. Or both.

Bilbao's best hotels are the **Villa de Bilbao**, the top lodgings, a modern superluxury hotel centrally located on the Gran Vía in the newer part of town; the **Aranzazu**, a comfortable, modern, moderate-to-expensive hotel located near the Parque de Doña Casilda Iturriza in the western section of modern Bilbao, and owned by the quality Aranzazu group that owns the Villa de Bilbao and several top hotels in San Sebastián, Vitoria, and Haro; the centrally located **Ercilla**, the society epicenter of Bilbao, a favorite of seasoned travellers, the bullfight crowd, and journalists, and home to the excellent Bermeo restaurant; and, reasonably priced in an expensive town, the **Conde Duque**, which looks out on the river and is the best choice for those who want to be near the old quarter.

VITORIA

Vitoria, or, in Basque, Gasteiz (population approaching 200,000), the prosperous capital of both El País Vasco and the province of Alava, is located 64 km (40 miles) southwest of Bilbao off the A 68 *autopista* or on the difficult mountain route N 240. From the south (via Burgos), Vitoria is easy to reach on the A 1 *autopista* or on the heavily trafficked N I, both of which come through the spectacular pass of Pancorvo southwest of Mirando de Ebro.

Vitoria is divided into two parts, the new town and the Medieval quarter. The streets of the newer sections branch off like an irregular spider's web around the picturesque core city, the **Campillo**, or Ciudad Vieja (old city), which was founded in the 12th century by King Sancho the Wise of Navarra on the site of the Basque town of Gasteiz. Tightly wrapped around the highest point in Vitoria, much of this old quarter, including portions of its 12th- and 13th-century walls, is still intact. The Campillo quarter is well worth the day you might devote to Vitoria: Its pedestrian-only streets are fascinating to explore (wear good walking shoes; the steep streets, inclines, and stairways leading up the hill will give your legs a real workout).

Imagine the bulb of a small bermuda onion cross-sectioned lengthwise and you will have a good idea of the old quarter's oval layout. Wrapped in concentric lines around a core block of old buildings and tapering to a point at the north are streets with Medieval names such as Herrería (ironsmith shop), Zapatería (cobbler), Correría (strapmaker), Cuchillería (cutler), and Pintorería (painter). In these narrow streets you will find a number of distinguished old houses and mansions (among them the 16th-century Casa del Cordón and the 15th-century Palacio de Bendaña in Cuchillería), *tapas* bars, gift shops, antiques shops, horsemeat butchers, exotic spice and health-food stores, and student hangouts.

At the northern end of the Campillo (follow Correría or Cuchillería, which converge) within an area of two short blocks are the 14th-century Gothic **Catedral de Santa María** with an exceptional doorway; the interesting **Museo Arqueológico** in a balconied, brick-and-timber palace; the 16th-century Plateresque **Palacio de Escoriaza-Esquivel** (Fernán López de Escoriaza was physician to both Henry VIII of England and his Spanish wife, and to Holy Roman Emperor Charles V); and the 15th-century inn, now a restaurant-cum-museum, El Portalón.

El Portalón, Correría 151, Tel: 22-49-89, is expensive, but the food, based on traditional Basque specialties taken a step further (stuffed peppers *al gratin,* for example), is highly rated, and the antiques and old-time trappings in this spectacular house are quite special. El Portalón is known for its *menu de degustación,* a sampling of every dish on the menu.

If you are in the area of El Portalon at *tapas* time, try a *chorizo a la brasa* at **Tulipán de Oro**, Correría 157, near El Portalón. A sliced *chorizo* is presented to you on a most unusual grill: a small pottery pig with a belly full of flaming cooking alcohol. You grill your own *chorizo* to taste and eat it with chunks of bread, accompanied by bracing glasses of cold *clarete* or beer. You can even purchase a pig brazier to take home.

At the old quarter's southern end (the onion's root), you will find the 14th-century Gothic **Iglesia de San Miguel** perched above the **plaza de la Virgen Blanca**, named for Vitoria's patroness, represented by a polychrome Madonna and Child occupying a niche at the church entrance overlooking the plaza. Just east of San Miguel, an unusual arcaded set of stairways, the **Arquillos**, leads up to the **plaza del Machete**, where various outside administrators were made to swear on a *machete* (cutlass) to uphold the *fueros* (rights) of Vitoria, under pain of being beheaded.

The plaza de la Virgen Blanca is surrounded by shops and fine houses with balconies enclosed by the lovely multipaned windows characteristic of northern Spain. In the center of the plaza is the large monument built in 1923 to commemorate Wellington's decisive victory at Vitoria over Joseph Bonaparte's booty-laden troops. A good place to relax and contemplate the plaza is from a window table at the **Virgen Blanca Cafeteriá** (a coffee house and bar) in the northwest corner of the square.

Immediately east of the Wellington monument and the plaza de la Virgen Blanca is the late-18th-century Greco-Roman style **plaza de la Constitución** (formerly plaza de España), a symmetrical arcaded square with balconied apartments. Just southeast of this plaza is the post office, where you can get some amusing photographs of its patrons sticking their mail in the letter drops: the mouths of two well-polished bas-relief lions.

If you are in the area of la Virgen Blanca at lunchtime, just northeast of the plaza at Mateo B. de Moraza 9 is restaurante **Zabala**, a typical area restaurant, very popular with the people of Vitoria. *Alubias rojas, menestra, re-*

vueltos con ajos verdes y gambas, cordero, and the house wine, a typical young *cosechero* (grower) wine from the Rioja Alavesa, are all good here. With your *café,* sample a *licor de manzana verde* (green apple), a Basque *pacharán* (sloeberry-flavored anisette), or *aguardiente* (marc), delicious after-dinner drinks served superchilled (the current rage in Spain, but especially in the Basque Country).

Southwest of the plaza de la Virgen Blanca at the end of calle Prado, and next to the shady, flower-filled Parque de la Florida, is the new cathedral of María Inmaculada, a striking Neo-Gothic church (begun early in this century but consecrated only 20 years ago), whose apse resembles a giant crown.

The **provincial museum**, with its finely sculpted topiary gardens, is located south of the cathedral in the **Agusti palace** on the plaza de Fray Francisco. The museum has a pair of Riberas and a Cano. The museum of the diocese of Alava displays polychrome religious sculpture, custodials, ecclesiastical garments, some fine triptychs, and five exceptional, highly detailed, 16th-century reliquary busts of the Rhenish school.

Across from the provincial museum in the **Palacio de Ajuria-Enea** at Fray Francisco de Vitoria 3 is **La Armería**, (arms museum), which has a fine collection of suits of armor and weapons, some dating from prehistoric times. East of the two museums, along calle del Marqués de Urquijo, then south and east leading out of the plaza San Cristóbal (also two blocks southwest of the bullring), is calle Heraclio Fournier, where Casa Fournier at number 19 houses the **Museo de Naipes**, a museum of playing cards (Fournier is the foremost producer of playing cards in Spain) dating back to the 15th century.

The big fiesta of Vitoria, beginning the week of August 5, is called, not surprisingly, La Fiesta de la Virgen Blanca. At 6:00 P.M. on the eve of the fiesta, an effigy of Celedonio, a mythical bon vivant dressed in Basque costume and holding onto an umbrella, descends, à la Mary Poppins, from a cable attached to the tower of Iglesia de San Miguel across the plaza de la Virgen Blanca high above the heads of a throng of cheering fiesta-goers, who light up huge cigars to celebrate the moment. The rest is a tamer version of Pamplona, also with top bullfights. There is also a well-regarded jazz festival beginning the third week in July.

As most of the top restaurants in Vitoria—Dos Hermanas, Zaldiaran, Olarizu, and Ikea—are located in the newer sections west of the old town near avenida de Gasteiz, where most of Vitoria's best hotels are located, you will probably want to save any *alta cocina* experience for dinner.

Now a century old, although in a new locale, **Dos Hermanas**, Madre Vedruna 10 southwest of the plaza de Lovaina (Tel: 13-29-34), is still considered by most to be Vitoria's finest restaurant. Dos Hermanas excels with a menu based on typical Alavesa and regional specialties (Cantabrian fish, local mushrooms, Swiss chard, lamb, wild boar, and so on), and dishes enhanced with those ubiquitous stars of French and modern Basque cuisine: *foie gras,* magret of duck, vegetables in puff pastry, and others. The wine cellar is extensive, with a great list of Rioja *reservas* and a special selection of wines from the Rioja Alavesa.

Zaldiaran, avenida Gasteiz 21 (Tel: 13-48-22), and **Olarizu**, Beato Tomas de Zumarraga 54 (Tel: 24-77-52), located a few blocks north and west of Zaldiaran, are owned by the same person. Zaldiaran specializes in sophisticated *nueva cocina vasca,* and is the more expensive of the two. Olarizu tends to lean a little more toward classical cuisine but also serves dishes such as magret of duck in sweet-and-sour sauce, not exactly what you might call down-home Basque cooking.

Ikea, Paraguay 8 (Tel: 22-41-99), a rising star among Vitoria's restaurants, features fish dishes prepared in more traditional style, and thus is probably the best choice for those who have had enough of *nueva cocina vasca.* Ikea plans a move to a new location. Call first.

Vitoria's two top hotel choices are **Canciller Ayala**, Ramón y Cajal 5, located a few blocks southwest of the Campillo and looking out on Jardines de la Florida, downtown Vitoria's large park, and **Hotel Gasteiz**, avenida Gasteiz 45, one of the Aranzazu chain, located on the main avenue leading in from Bilbao and the airport.

If you don't mind a short drive from the city, you may choose the **Parador de Argomañiz**, located 13 km (8 miles) east of Vitoria off N I (Madrid–Irún highway) at km 361.7 (signs to parador). The parador has 54 rooms in a renovated 17th-century palace that is quiet and has fine views over the Alavesa plain. The parador restaurant, featuring regional specialties, is in an old granary.

ALAVA PROVINCE

In topography, climate, agriculture, and history, the province of Alava is part Basque, part Navarra, part Castile, and part Rioja. In the north are rainy, pine-clad mountains enveloped in Scotch mists; stretching to the southwest are the wheat fields and high plains of Castile; to the east, seldom-visited, craggy mountains border Navarra; and to the south the Sierras de Cantabria form a stunning, blue-gray backdrop for the terraced vineyards of Rioja Alavesa along the Ebro. Scattered throughout the province are a number of isolated mountain villages waiting to be discovered by the intrepid traveller who is undaunted by winding mountain roads.

The main attraction in Alava province outside of Vitoria is the Rioja Alavesa wine district, with its strikingly beautiful mountain scenery and not-to-be-missed wine town of Laguardia, which we will cover in the following chapter on La Rioja since, geographically, it is separated from La Rioja by only a couple of miles, while over 30 miles of twisting mountain roads separate it from the capital, Vitoria.

GETTING AROUND

The Basque Country is served by the *autopista* combination A 1, A 68, A 8, which is both expensive and indirect unless you are going straight to Bilbao, but given the alternative of the truck-clogged national and regional highways, with serpentine mountain passages that often become extremely dangerous in winter, it is your best bet. Coming from France to San Sebastián is nothing; going from San Sebastián to Vitoria or Pamplona is difficult. There are airports in Bilbao, Vitoria, and Fuenterrabía (for San Sebastián), with daily flights from Madrid. There is daily train and bus service linking all three major cities in the Basque Country to Madrid and other cities. Local bus service can get you to most of the villages in the region.

ACCOMMODATIONS REFERENCE

When dialing telephone numbers from outside the country, drop the 9 in the area code.

► **Aranzazu.** Rodriguez Arias 66, 48013 **Bilbao.** Tel: (94) 441-3100; Fax: (94) 441-6529; Telex: 32164.

► **Parador de Argomañiz.** Apartado (P. O. Box) 601, 01080 **Vitoria.** 13 km (8.25 miles) east of Vitoria on N I (Madrid–Irun highway). Tel: (945) 28-22-00.

► **Canciller Ayala.** Ramon y Cajal 5, 01007 **Vitoria** (Alava). Tel: (945) 13-00-00.

► **Conde Duque.** Campo Volantin 22, 48007 **Bilbao.** Tel: (94) 445-6000; Fax: (94) 445-6000; Telex: 31260.

► **Costa Vasca.** Avenida Pio Baroja 15, 20008 **San Sebastián.** Tel: (943) 21-10-11; Telex: 36551.

► **Parador El Emperador.** Plaza Armas del Castillo, 20280 **Fuenterrabía.** Tel: (943) 64-21-40.

► **Ercilla.** Ercilla 37, 48011 **Bilbao.** Tel: (94) 443-8800; Fax: (94) 443-9335; Telex: 32449.

► **Hotel Gasteiz.** Avenida Gasteiz 45, 01009 **Vitoria.** Tel: (945) 22-81-00; Fax: (945) 22-62-58; Telex: 35451.

► **Gran Hotel Balneario de Cestona.** Paseo San Juan, 20740 **Cestona** (Guipúzcoa). Tel: (943) 86-71-40. Closed December 15 to March 15.

► **Jauregui.** San Pedro 28, 20280 **Fuenterrabía.** Tel: (943) 64-14-00.

► **De Londres y de Inglaterra.** Zubieta 2, 20007 **San Sebastián.** Tel: (943) 42-69-89; Telex: 36378.

► **Maria Cristina.** Plaza de la Republica Argentina, 20004 **San Sebastián.** Tel: (943) 29-33-00; Telex: 38195.

► **Monte Igueldo.** Monte Igueldo, 20008 **San Sebastián.** Tel: (943) 21-02-11; Telex: 38096.

► **Niza.** Zubieta 56, 20007 **San Sebastián.** Tel: (943) 42-66-63; Telex: 38195.

► **Orly.** Plaza Zaragoza, 20007 **San Sebastián.** Tel: (943) 46-32-00; Fax: (943) 45-61-01; Telex: 38033.

► **Pampinot.** Nagusia (Mayor) 3, 20280 **Fuenterrabía.** Tel: (943) 64-06-00.

► **El Puerto.** Portu Kalea 1, 48360 **Mundaka.** Tel: (94) 687-6888.

► **San Sebastián.** Avenida Zumalacarregui 20, 20008 **San Sebastián.** Tel: (943) 21 44 00; Telex: 36302.

► **Villa de Bilbao.** Gran Vía 87, 48011 **Bilbao** (Vizcaya). Tel: (94) 441-6000; Fax: (94) 441-6529; Telex: 32449.

LA RIOJA

By Gerry Dawes

La Rioja, which takes its name from the río Oja, a small tributary of the Ebro, is located some 300 km (185 miles) northeast of Madrid. It lies south of the Basque Country—Bilbao, Vitoria, and San Sebastián—and west of Navarra. Its chief city, Logroño, is 113 km (70 miles) east of Old Castile's Burgos on N 120. The region's craggy, serrated mountains form a dramatic backdrop for a trough-shaped valley scored by thousands of terraced vineyards. The famous Rioja winemaking district stretches for 80 miles along the banks of the Ebro, which flows on southeast past Tudela through southern Navarra, past Zaragoza in Aragón, and finally empties into the Mediterranean between Tarragona and Valencia.

Besides the obvious attractions of visiting *bodegas,* which range from rustic, century-old, virtual working wine museums to dazzling state-of-the-art wineries rivaling those of California, this mountain enclave offers plenty of little-known, delightful attractions to the discerning traveller. The Rioja is dotted with picturesque old villages, castles, and monasteries rich in history. The great pilgrims' road of the Middle Ages, the Camino de Santiago, passes through the Rioja, and several of the famous sites connected with it here are prime attractions. The area is still largely unspoiled and peaceful, the scenery is spectacular, and the mountain air is wonderful. The climate is very pleasant even in summer, except in the Rioja Baja, the area around Calahorra, which is very hot—dry, but hot. From April through November are the best months to visit La Rioja (the grape harvest is usually in October).

MAJOR INTEREST

The wines of Rioja
Hunting and fishing

Logroño
Rioja country cuisine and restaurants

Haro, capital of the Rioja Alta wine district
Rioja Alta and Rioja Alavesa wine villages

The Camino de Santiago
Clavijo castle
Nájera
The monasteries of southern Rioja
Santo Domingo de la Calzada

Rioja Baja's Roman heritage

The Food of the Rioja

You will find some of the best country food in Spain in the Rioja—to go with the fine wines you will want to try. The cuisine of the Rioja is simplicity itself, so you will encounter little of the more elaborate food of the Basque Country, but chances are you will remember some Rioja classics long after you have forgotten the sophisticated dishes of Rioja's neighbors to the north. As to the wines, in general stick to the *reservas* and the "bottled in the 3rd, 4th, 5th year" *crianza* wines in restaurants, rather than house wines in the Rioja. The chances of getting an ersatz Rioja from a region (seemingly almost as big as Spain itself) calling itself "Alto Ebro" are greater than your chances of discovering a house treasure from "a little old *bodeguero*."

Trout, quail, and partridge are good in the Rioja and can be found on the menus of most restaurants, but they are overshadowed by two of the simplest but finest of all Spanish dishes, *pochas* (fat, tender white beans, often cooked with *chorizo* and/or quail), for which a craving bordering on addiction can quickly be acquired, and *chuletillas de cordero al sarmiento* (baby lamb chops grilled over grapevine cuttings). A delicious *ensalada de lechuga, tomate, y cebollas* (dressed with wine vinegar, olive oil, and sea salt), a plate of *pochas,* a brazier stacked with *chuletillas,* a pile of crisp fried potatoes, and a bottle of Rioja shared with friends is an unforgettable experience.

Other down-to-earth regional specialties are *pimientos a la riojana* (stuffed green peppers in tomato sauce); *espárragos con mahonesa* (succulent white asparagus with homemade mayonnaise); *menestra a la riojana* (a dish made of carrots, leeks, artichokes, green beans, peas, etc., cooked with ham); *patatas a la riojana* (potatoes cooked with *chorizo* sausage); as in many places in Castile, *cordero asado* (oven-roasted lamb) and *lechazo* (milk-fed baby lamb); and *revueltos con ajo* (scrambled eggs with young green garlic shoots). For dessert try *melocotones en almibar,* peaches preserved in syrup, but with a difference; they are large, whole yellow peaches with the stones left in.

The Wines of Rioja

Rioja's official *denominación de origen* is divided into three zones: La Rioja Alta, centered around the wine capital of Haro and the provincial capital, Logroño; La Rioja Alavesa, a tip of the Basque province of Alava above the Ebro between Haro and Logroño; and Rioja Baja, around the old Roman city of Calahorra southeast of Logroño and spilling over into southern Navarra.

Rioja produces traditional-style oak-aged *blancos,* which rely upon mellowed wood flavors, austerity, stony texture, and balance for their appeal, somewhat like the white wines of the Rhône. Modern cold-fermented Rioja whites, which spend little or no time in wood, are reminiscent of Loire Valley wines.

The Rioja produces some excellent *rosados* and *claretes,* (light red wines), but the *vinos tintos* (red wines) are the backbone of the Rioja's reputation. Some 50 firms here produce wines of such consistently high quality that many experts think that Rioja wines offer the best quality/value ratio of any red wines on earth.

The Tempranillo, a grape believed by some to be a long-acclimatized strain of Burgundy's Pinot Noir brought to the Rioja centuries ago by the monks of Cluny and Citeaux (who built the first monasteries to help establish the Camino de Santiago), generally accounts for 70 percent or more of a typical Rioja wine. The other authorized grape varietals, Garnacha, Mazuelo, Graciano, and the white Viura, also contribute to the overall balance, harmony, flavor, and aging potential of the wine. Riojas are aged in small oak casks and in bottle for several years before being released.

Rioja *reservas* and *gran reservas* are the glory of Spanish viniculture. In quality and aging potential perhaps their only peers are the great growths of Bordeaux and Burgundy, and a few special wines from Italy and California. *Reserva* wines are laid down in good years; *gran reservas* only in exceptional years. The years 1982, 1981, 1978, and 1975 are the top vintages you are likely to encounter on current wine lists, but because *reservas* are only made in good years you

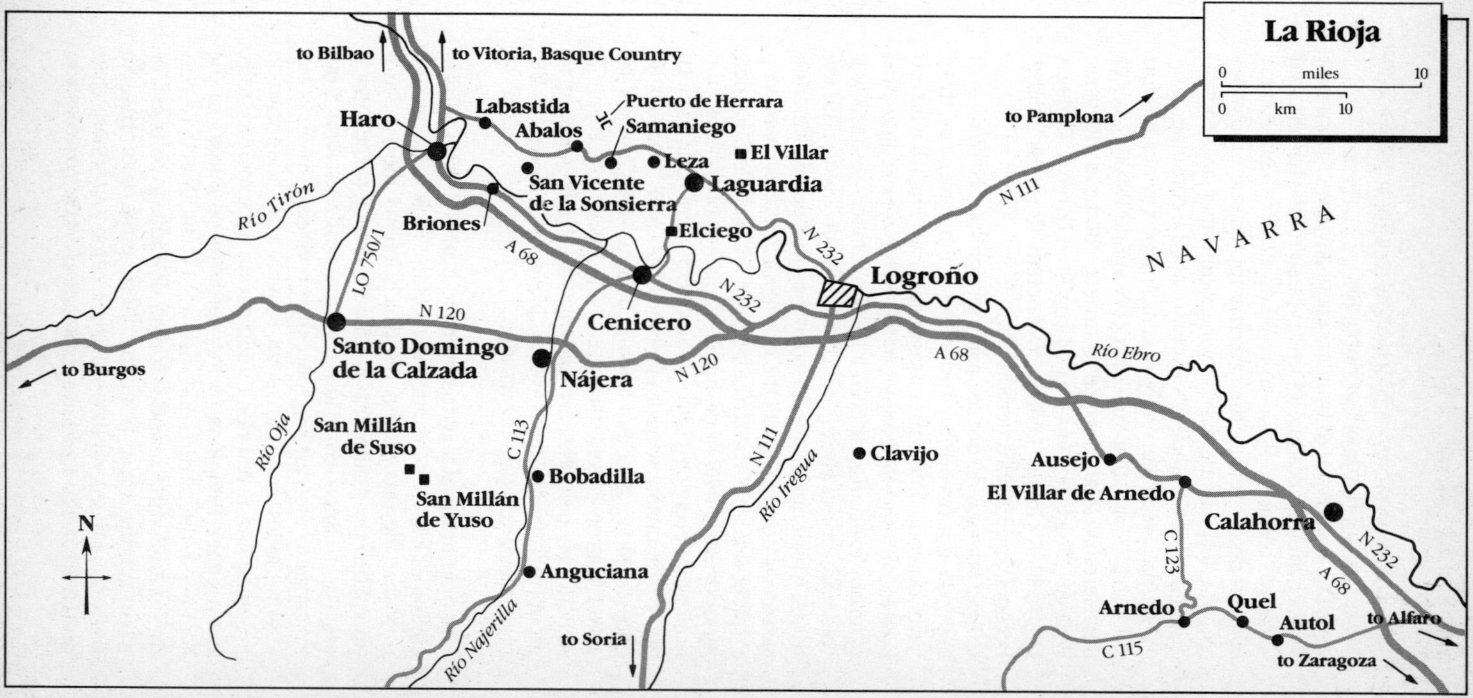
La Rioja
0 miles 10
0 km 10
to Bilbao
to Vitoria, Basque Country
Haro
Labastida
Abalos
Puerto de Herrara
Samaniego
Leza
El Villar
San Vicente de la Sonsierra
Laguardia
Briones
Elciego
Río Tirón
LO 750/1
A 68
N 232
N 111
to Pamplona
NAVARRA
Logroño
Cenicero
N 120
Santo Domingo de la Calzada
Nájera
to Burgos
Río Ebro
Río Oja
San Millán de Suso
San Millán de Yuso
C 113
Bobadilla
Anguciana
Río Najerilla
to Soria
Río Iregua
Clavijo
Ausejo
El Villar de Arnedo
Calahorra
C 123
Arnedo
Quel
Autol
C 115
to Alfaro
to Zaragoza
N

do not have to worry as much about getting an off year as you do in, say, Bordeaux or Burgundy.

Classic Rioja *reservas* from exceptional vintages are meant to reach their peak some 15 to 20 years after the harvest, and some will drink well for up to 30 or 40 years. Since many *bodegas* do not release their *reservas* for ten years, the wines are, in effect, cellared at the winery until they are ready to drink, aged at the *bodega*'s expense, not the consumer's.

The producers currently making the best wines of Rioja are CVNE (Compañía Vinicola del Norte de España), López de Heredia, Marqués de Murrieta, Bodegas Riojanas, Bodegas Muga, La Rioja Alta, Marqués de Cáceres, Bodegas Montecillo, Granja Remélluri, Contino, Bodegas Olarra, Beronia, and Palacios Remondo.

Rioja *bodegas* do not see many foreign visitors, so most of them do not have formal tours set up, but many of them have someone on the premises who speaks English who can take you around. Sometimes it will be the export director, a company executive, or even a family member—especially if you write or call ahead. Visitors will usually get to taste the wines, which can be purchased in most, but not all, wineries, at *bodega* prices. Consult the *Guía Práctica para Amantes y Professionales del Vinos de España* of the Club de Gourmets for addresses, telephone numbers, names of contacts, and hours for receiving visitors. The ARBOR group, an association of ten quality wineries that includes CVNE, Marqués de Cáceres, Montecillo, and Contino, is located at Gran Vía 43, 26002 Logroño; Tel: (941) 22-53-04; Fax: (941) 20-40-52. ARBOR can help you arrange visits to the *bodegas* in its group, except in August, when, like most wineries in Europe, they are closed for vacation.

The only practical way to cover the beautiful wine villages and other backcountry attractions of the Rioja is by car, and now that the *autopista* A 68, which follows the vineyard-lined Ebro river valley, has been built, getting to the Rioja is easy from Bilbao or Vitoria to the northwest and from Zaragoza to the east. Logroño, the provincial capital, is 468 km (291 miles) from Barcelona, roughly a five-hour drive on the *autopista,* if you don't mind paying the expensive tolls. From either Pamplona to the northeast or Burgos to the southwest, the picturesque roads (N 111 and N 120, respectively) follow the historic Camino de Santiago to Logroño.

To get the most from the Rioja, make your base in Logroño and accomplish your sightseeing and winery visits on day trips. For extensive exploration and winery visits in western Rioja, make Haro or Santo Domingo de la Calzada your base.

Every September, from the 16th to the 25th, Logroño celebrates its San Mateo Rioja Wine Harvest Festival, with a grape-treading contest, parades, bands, and bullfights. It's a major fiesta, and a fine one.

LOGRONO

Logroño, the capital of La Rioja, with a population of 116,000, is located on a river plain on the south bank of the Ebro, just south of the Basque Country. Except for its Medieval core, which evolved over the centuries from the Roman Juliobriga, Logroño is a modern city of broad avenues and affluent-looking apartment blocks rising a few stories above smart shops, cafés, and bars. At first look the city has nothing, other than wine, of compelling interest to merit a detour, but once you get to know this prosperous, efficient provincial capital it begins to grow on you. Logroño is an easy city to get in and out of, its old quarter bustles with life, and the absence of tourists is an attraction in itself.

You are not likely to suffer from acute attacks of visit-a-monumentitis in Logroño. Except for seeing Santa María la Redonda cathedral and the churches of Santiago el Real, Santa María del Palacio (a national monument), and San Bartolomé (all of which can be done in less than two hours), the main demands on your time in Logroño are winery visits, shopping, lazing over a drink in early evening in the plaza del Espolón, and searching out good *tapas* bars in the Casco Viejo, the old quarter.

The Casco Viejo, in the north-central part of town next to the river, contains all the main historical attractions, some of Logroño's most interesting shops, and most of the city's best *tapas* bars and restaurants. The area is eminently walkable and can be reached easily on foot from the major hotels.

A good place to start a walking tour of Logroño is on the fine shop-lined boulevard Gran Vía del Rey Juan Carlos I (known simply as the Gran Vía), in the vicinity of the comfortable, centrally located **Carlton Rioja**, the city's best hotel. Here Logroño's burghers and their wives gather in the evening for drinks at the bar on the second floor. Just east of the Carlton is the modern monument to the Labrador, the city's homage to agricultural workers, especially those who work the small vineyard plots so important to the economy of the region. Walking north on General Vara del Rey, you will soon reach the beautiful tree-shaded **plaza del Espolón**, which has a bandshell, fountains, kiosks, flower gardens, outdoor cafés, and a colossal equestrian statue of General Espartero, Logroño's favorite son.

Baldomero Espartero was a hero of the Carlist Wars in the 19th century, one-time regent of Spain until Isabella II assumed the throne, and a man much admired by Washington Irving. He married an heiress from Logroño, retired to the Rioja, and put a *bodega* and some vineyards that he owned at the disposal of Luciano Murrieta. Murrieta, who became the famous Marqués de Murrieta, himself an adopted son of Logroño, patterned the winery after the famous Bordeaux châteaux of the 1850s and is considered the father of the winemaking style that made Rioja famous.

From the northeast corner of the Espolón, walk north along Muro del Carmen to reach the first of two national monuments, **San Bartolomé**, a 12th- and 13th-century church with a fine Mudejar tower and an interesting, but deteriorated, early-14th-century portal depicting scenes from the life of Saint Bartholomew. A block north, on calle San Nicolás, is Logroño's major architectural monument, **Iglesia de Santa María de Palacio**, also a national monument. Santa María was originally a palace given to the Knights of the Order of the Holy Sepulchre by King Alfonso VII in the early 12th century. The main attraction is the unusual 13th-century ogival spire, known in Logroño as **La Aguja** (the steeple) or, colloquially, the needle. Walter Starkie claimed that the spire "is undoubtedly the most beautiful in Spain and has been compared with that of Salisbury Cathedral."

One block north of San Nicolás, turn left (west) on rua Vieja (all along the Camino de Santiago are towns with Medieval *ruas* that trace the old route, *rua* being a linguistic legacy of the dominant French influence in northern Spain during that epoch). Walk two blocks to calle Sagasta, which crosses the Ebro on the Puente de Hierro (iron bridge) and ends at the turn-of-the-century Franco-Españolas winery, now given over to producing some palatable but run-of-the-mill wines in a modern style. You can visit the *bodega* weekday mornings if you call ahead (Tel: 25-13-00).

The **Iglesia de Santiago el Real** and an old fountain used by Santiago pilgrims lie just northwest of Sagasta. High on the church's south façade is the most amazing statue of Santiago Matamoros (Saint James the Moorslayer) on the entire pilgrims' route. Wearing a plumed hat and dressed in a tunic and flowing robes more suitable to a bishop than a warrior, Santiago charges into the battle at Clavijo (see below) wielding a large saber in one hand and holding a streaming banner in the other. The saint's huge horse tramples a multitude of Moors under his feet and exhibits what Edwin Mullens described as "the most heroic genitalia in all Christendom, a sight to make any surviving Moor feel inadequate and run for cover." The statue is another unintentional example of Baroque excess, surpassing the statue of Fame on the city hall of Pamplona.

Return to calle Sagasta and walk uphill from the river. On the left you will find Felix Barbero's *bota* (wineskin) shop and the excellent roast house, La Chata (see Dining below). At calle Portales turn east and you will see the 15th- and 16th-century **cathedral of Santa María la Redonda**, whose stark lines contrast with its 18th-century main façade and fine Baroque twin towers, an overall effect that is pleasing. The plaza del Mercado in front of the cathedral and calle Portales, alongside, are both arcaded and bustle with shops that are among the most interesting in Logroño (see also Shopping in Logroño below).

West on Portales, back across Sagasta, are more shops and a plaza where the rather grandiose post office and **Espartero's palace**, now the provincial museum (combining archaeology, revolving shows of pieces from the national fine arts trust, and periodic art shows), are located. A few feet behind the post office down calle San Augustín is the **travesía Laurel**, where you can begin a tour of Logroño's famous *tapas* bars (see below), which can do for lunch. Halfway down the travesía Laurel is calle Laurel, a colorful, bustling pedestrian street, which you follow east for two blocks to Sagasta, where, a few feet to the south, you will return to the plaza del Espolón.

Dining in Logroño

Logroño has lots of good small, unpretentious restaurants and *tapas* bars, many of which are located in the old quarter. Just a block from the plaza del Espolón near the market is calle Laurel, where each bar usually has a different specialty. It seems that by 9:00 P.M. each evening half of Logroño's citizens descend on calle Laurel to eat *tapas,* drink wine and draft beer, and watch the peregrinations of their fellow citizens.

For a do-it-yourself *tapas* tour, start in calle Laurel with *champiñónes* (grilled mushrooms) or *riñones* (lamb kidneys) at **Bar Torrecilla.** At the end of Laurel, on the travesía Laurel, is **Bar Blanco y Negro**, which offers a variety of anchovy *tapas*—fried, freshly pickled in vinegar and oil, on toast, etc. **Bar Lorenzo**, a few doors north and across the narrow travesía, specializes in *pinchos morunos* (grilled lamb kebobs marinated with Moorish spices) and exceptional *pimientos de piquillo* (piquant red peppers stuffed with meat). **La Casita**, a new bar at the north end of the travesía, displays on colorful ceramics platters one of Logroño's best selections of *tapas*: Shrimp salad with capers, white asparagus, stuffed peppers, marinated octopus, olive salad, garlic shrimp, pork loin with pimientos, beet salad, and croquets are typical of the selections available here.

For dinner on calle Laurel try **El Cachetero**, a popular restaurant serving typical Rioja dishes and rated one of the best in Logroño. A Logroño institution for roast lamb and *cabrito asado* (roast goat) is **Asador La Chata**, just off Sagasta at calle Carnicerias 3. La Chata's oven, made from volcanic stone, is claimed to have special qualities. In any case the roasts here are excellent, and your chances of hearing someone at a nearby table spontaneously sing a lovely *jota* are good. The famous **Mesón de la Merced**, San Nicolás 109, is large, elegant, and very expensive, with several stunningly decorated dining rooms and a magnificent wine cellar. A recommended inexpensive new restaurant, much frequented by Logroño merchants and shopkeepers at lunchtime, is **Las Cubanas**, San Agustín 17, just steps from Espartero's palace and the post office.

Shopping in Logroño

Shopping at a leisurely pace in a provincial capital like Logroño is much more fun than running to a big department store in Madrid at the last minute to cover everyone on your gift list. Prices are often better. If the selection is not as varied here, the uniquely regional quality of the choices more than compensates.

You can visit Felix Barber's *bota* shop and factory, Sagasta 8, and pick up a real handmade wineskin, or explore the variety of shops under the arcades near the cathedral. There you can buy anything from baskets and books to ceramics, clothing, *alpargatas* (rope-soled shoes made in Rioja Baja), and regional culinary specialties ranging from *pimientos de piquillo, bacalao* (salt cod), and tinned white asparagus to local candies. You might want to buy a special Rioja *reserva* or two at the Palacio del Vino, avenida de Burgos 140 (at the western edge of Logroño), which has a huge stock, or at Rioja Selección, República Argentina 12, which has a good selection of wines and regional food delicacies.

EXCURSIONS INTO LA RIOJA

There are three immensely rewarding day-trip excursions from Logroño into the little-traveled Rioja countryside. The first is the round trip west to Haro, taking in wineries and discovering the unspoiled villages of the Rioja Alta and Rioja Alavesa; the second is to continue visiting important shrines on the Camino de Santiago, including the off-the-beaten-track monasteries in the mountains of southern Rioja; and the third is a trip southeast to Calahorra and the dusty, historic villages of the fertile Rioja Baja, on the way to southern Navarra and then to Zaragoza in Aragón.

Haro: Wineries and Villages

The first trip, to Haro, 48 km (30 miles) west of Logroño, should be set up by writing or calling ahead (see the Wines of Rioja section above) to arrange one or two winery visits in the morning. Plan to have lunch in Haro, and allow plenty of time for the lovely villages on the return trip north of the Ebro through the Rioja Alavesa, which, for reasons of geographical proximity, we include in the Rioja chapter instead of the chapter on the Basque Country.

Because you are apt to be caught on a wicked hill behind a long line of trucks if you take N 232, take the A 68 *autopista* from Logroño to **Cenicero**, where two important wineries, Marqués de Cáceres, one of Rioja's finest new *bodegas,* and Bodegas Riojanas, one of Rioja's great historic *bodegas,* are located. Notice the fine modern monument to Rioja's grape harvesters on the village's main thoroughfare. Cenicero, which means ashbin—or, in current use, ashtray—was reportedly the site of a Roman crematorium and burial ground. **Conchita**, a well-regarded local restaurant, serves excellent *pochas* and other regional dishes. Street addresses won't help much in villages this small, so just ask someone for directions. They may even lead you to the place you are looking for.

Continuing west on N 232, you will see the Davalillo castle (there are more than a hundred castles in the Rioja, but many of them, like this one, are not worth a detour) overlooking the Ebro in the distance to the north, and soon arrive at **Briones**, which has been declared of historic and artistic merit by the Spanish government. Briones, five minutes outside of Haro, is a picturesque town full of old houses emblazoned with coats of arms.

Haro is the capital of the Rioja Alta, the region's finest wine district. It is a charming town with a fine arcaded main square complete with an 18th-century town hall, a beautiful bandstand, the **Gonzalez Muga** wineshop (not to be confused with Bodegas Muga), where you can purchase most of the greatest wines of the Rioja, and the venerable **Café Suizo**, whose terrace provides a relaxing place to watch the meanderings of the *Jarrenos* (literally, "jugmakers"), as the people of Haro are known. The 16th-century **Santo Tomás church** in the old quarter has an exceptional Plateresque stone façade carved by Felipe de Vigarni to resemble the wood-carved altarpieces of the period.

Haro also has the greatest concentration of fine wineries in the Rioja, many over a century old. The best *bodegas* are clustered below the hill on which Haro is perched, just north of town near the convergence of the tiny río Oja and the Ebro. The area, which now calls itself the Costa del Vino (wine coast), is traditionally known as the Barrio de Cantaranas (singing frogs) or the Barrio de la Estación (railway station), for the railhead that was established here in 1880 to ship copious amounts of Rioja wine to France to be sold as Bordeaux (and other famous names) after French vineyards were devastated by *phylloxera,* the infamous vine louse. López de Heredia (founded 1877), CVNE (1879), La Rioja Alta (1890), Bodegas Bilbainas (1901), Rioja Santiago (1904), and Muga, a winery built in 1970 but using completely traditional methods (they use only wooden vessels for every stage of the winemaking process from fermentation through aging in small oak barrels), are all located here. López de Heredia, with its distinctive Art Nouveau tower and fabulous old *bodega,* should be declared a national monument, and CVNE is perhaps the best winery overall in Spain. La Rioja Alta and Muga would also be on anyone's short list of Rioja's finest wineries.

Haro has a new hotel (opened in spring of 1989) in a recently renovated, 600-year-old Augustinian convent called, appropriately, **Los Augustinos**. Like an upscale parador, Los Augustinos is decorated with antiques and period furniture reproductions. It is managed by the Aranzazu hotel chain, which runs a number of other hotels in the Basque Country. Not only for charm but also for comfort, Los Augustinos is now one of the top choices in the entire Rioja.

Terete, west of the Haro town square, is a must for *cordero asado* roasted in their baker's oven and for a great lineup of *reservas.* Everyone in the wine trade who has ever visited the Rioja has had at least one meal at the famous scrubbed-white picnic tables upstairs at Terete. Ask someone to show you the dining room in Terete's private *bodega* in the ancient cellars below the place. **Beethoven II**, Lucrecia Arana 17 (left of the town hall on the street leading to Santo Tómas church), with good Rioja regional dishes and a fine wine list, is also very popular, as is its sister establishment across the street, which has excellent *tapas.*

Another favorite is the small, inexpensive, and typical **La Kika** (open for lunch only), just up the street from Beethoven. La Kika has a few tables in a luncheonette-style dining room, no menu, and no price list. La Kika, the owner's wife, just cooks regional home dishes on a cast-iron stove in her tiny kitchen from whatever ingredients are available in the market that morning. A lunch might include a plate of salad with tuna, olives, and boiled eggs thrown in; plump, white asparagus with fresh mayonnaise; a platter of grilled shrimp; clams in a delicious garlic and parsley sauce; hake, cooked in batter; a pile of baby lamb chops with fried green peppers on the side; fresh *cangrejos del río* (river crayfish); a bottle of *rosado* from the San Vicente cooperative; and *cuajada* for dessert.

If you are a lover of fiestas you might want to schedule your trip to coincide with Haro's Semana del Vino (wine week), which begins June 24 and culminates early in the morning on June 29 with the Battle of Wine, one of the most colorful wine-related events in the world. Near the San Felices Hermitage in a glen on a mountain called Riscos de Bilibio, six kilometers northwest of Haro, the celebrants, backed by music from bands sponsored by various *bodegas,* proceed to pour, squirt, spray, and throw some 50,000 liters of young Rioja wine on, in, or around one another—while dancing the *jota.* By mid-morning they manage to turn the mountain purple (and did so even before someone got the bright idea in recent years to bring in a helicopter spraying wine to make sure everyone gets doused). The fiesta changes venue by midday, when the wine-soaked warriors parade through downtown Haro, have a daredevil amateur bullfight, and dance in the streets until dawn. There is also a top professional bullfight on June 29, and you can sample wines at displays set up by Haro's wineries in the main square.

The return trip to Logroño through the beautiful villages of the Rioja Alta and the Rioja Alavesa is best done in the afternoon with the sun at your back, when these fine old towns are beautifully illuminated in the golden light of evening. Leaving Haro via the Barrio de Cantaranas, follow the signs to **Labastida** (province of Alava), another town with heraldic emblems on many fine old houses, then take the clearly marked Logroño road (N 232, which also runs south of the Ebro from Logroño through Cenicero to Haro) 10 km (6 miles) east through scenic terrain to **San Vicente de la Sonsierra** (back in La Rioja province), one of the most picturesque mountain towns in the Rioja. Surrounded by vines, San Vicente's hilltop profile incorporates a 16th-century church, a former Camino de Santiago pilgrim hospice, the remains of the castle, and ramparts that offer stunning views of the Ebro, the mountains, and the terraced vineyards of the region.

San Vicente is a town of extraordinary character. During the War of Independence, when the local guerrillas caught some of Napoleon's troops who had raped several of the town's women, they drowned the invaders in huge vats of wine. To this day the locals will tell you that a good wine, like the one from the excellent San Vicente cooperative, has a French touch to it. The men of this town are so tough that, during Holy Week, they still practice the outlawed penance of self-flagellation with multithonged whips and wax embedded with broken glass.

In San Vicente de la Sonsierra, **Hostal Toni**, despite the video games in its entrance, has a good kitchen that turns out top-notch baby lamb chops *al sarmiento, pochas,* and *ensalada.* The house wine is also excellent here.

On the road to Abalos (also in La Rioja province), barely a couple of kilometers to the east of San Vicente, is a turn-off to the north marked Peciña. Perhaps 3 km (2 miles) along this road is the 12th-century Romanesque church **Santa María de la Piscina**, which was founded by Don Ramiro de Navarra, a son-in-law of El Cid. Other than the beauty of the landscape, with its rugged gray mountain walls and terraced vineyards along the way, and the picturesque quality of the two towns' settings, there isn't much to detain you in either Abalos or Samaniego, the next town to the east. (Note the sign Arabako Errioxa/Rioja Alavesa—Basque first, then Spanish, as you reenter the province of Alava.)

A few kilometers east of Samaniego, near Leza, is a sign for the road to Vitoria via Puerto de Herrera. A drive of 3 km (2 miles) north along this road will bring you to a spectacular *mirador* (lookout) called **El Balcón de la Rioja** (the balcony of the Rioja), where you can see the entire Rioja Alta, Rioja Alavesa, and farther off to the south the wild, beautiful, and sparsely populated Sierra de la Demanda, whose peaks are often snowcapped.

Back on the main road (N 232) at Leza, continuing east, a drive of 7 km (4 miles) will bring you to **Laguardia** (Biasteri in Basque), one of the most picturesque and unusual wine towns in the world. In its own way Laguardia rivals Riquewihr in Alsace, Bernkastel in the Mosel, and Chinon in the Loire, yet, unlike those three superb wine towns, Laguardia has not been exploited as a tourist destination. Perched on a hilltop some 1,200 feet above sea level, Laguardia is a completely walled village that can be entered only through its six Medieval gates. Vehicular traffic is prohibited in the narrow streets of the town, except for an occasional small truck making deliveries. Most of the bread, produce, and daily staples are delivered by pushcart.

Street life in Laguardia is particularly rich because of this traffic ban. The street becomes an extended communal parlor, "a society poised still in the attitudes that characterized us all, before the machine came to shift our rhythms," as Jan Morris observed about Spain's old ways.

In addition to its fine walls, gates, towers, and superb views of Rioja Alavesa's vineyards, Laguardia has the ruins of a tenth-century castle; a Gothic church, **Santa María de los Reyes**, with an exceptional 15th-century porch richly decorated with polychrome figures; **San Juan Bautista**, an old church with 13th-century Romanesque roots; the birthplace of fabulist Felix Samaniego, a mansion that is now the Casa del Vino, the official Basque government offices and laboratory for the Alavesa wine industry; and a number of fine old houses, most of which have a wine cellar and/or stables cut into the limestone rock beneath them.

Laguardia's fiesta, June 27–29 (if you have any energy left after Haro's Battle of Wine on the 29th, you might want to try Laguardia's celebration in the afternoon), features a running of the bulls, an amateur bullfight, and dancing in the streets. The festival is famous for the *zurracapote,* the custom that obliges a native of Laguardia to offer a glass of mulled wine to strangers during fiesta.

Laguardia's two best-known wineries are Bodegas Alavesas, producers of Solar de Samaniego, and Bodegas Palacio, which produces a fine *reserva* called Glorioso. Marixa, just outside the walls of Laguardia and across the street from the village *frontón* court, is a very good restaurant serving Rioja regional cuisine—*pochas,* lamb chops, game dishes, potatoes with *chorizo,* and so on.

Just outside Laguardia's walls to the north is the **Poblado de la Hoya**, an important archaeological dig and museum on the site of an Iron Age village. A few kilometers farther is **El Villar**, site of the largest dolmens found in the entire Pyrenean region.

A short excursion south of Laguardia on the road to Elciego (and back to Cenicero) offers the most spectacular views of Laguardia. On clear days Laguardia catches the evening light from the setting sun and shines like a golden kingdom dramatically contrasted against the awesome backdrop of the blue-gray Cantabrian mountains. A few kilometers south of Laguardia, **Elciego** is a picturesque town that is home to Bodegas Domecq and the famous Marqués de Riscal, Rioja's oldest winery, founded in 1860. At the southern edge of Elciego, the road to Cenicero passes through Riscal's property, so don't be surprised if you have to stop for a winery worker rolling a barrel across the road; the *bodega* has the right-of-way.

You can return to Logroño via Cenicero, turning east on the southern branch of N 232 there or returning to the *autopista* for a faster return, or via Laguardia 15 km (9 miles) on northern N 232, which runs along the Ebro, for views of old Logroño that cannot be obtained from other approaches.

The Camino de Santiago and the Monasteries of Southern Rioja

Compared to Navarra's wealth of Camino de Santiago shrines, La Rioja has relatively few sites, because the main route went farther north through the Basque Country for many years until a southern road through the valley of the Ebro was deemed safe enough from Moorish attacks. What the Rioja lacks in number, however, it makes up in importance.

Off the N 111 Logroño–Soria road 12 km (7.5 miles) south of Logroño, high in the hills overlooking the city and the río Iregua, itself a trout stream of considerable importance, stands the historic **castle of Clavijo**, where legend tells us Saint James appeared in 844 on a mighty white stallion to turn the tide against the Moors. The Castilians had gone to war over the yearly tribute of 100 virgins demanded by the invaders from Africa. After the battle, in which Saint James supposedly killed 70,000 of the enemy, he became known as Santiago Matamoros (the Moorslayer), which is the way he is seen astride his mighty horse on the façade of Santiago el Real in Logroño. The appearance of Santiago at Clavijo was a great boost to Castilian morale; it became the spiritual counterpoint to the arm of Mohammed that the Moors carried into battle. On one of the castle towers you can see the outline of a stylized red cross in the shape of a sword, the warrior symbol of Santiago Matamoros and the Order of the Knights of Santiago.

Starting at Nájera, 26 km (16 miles) west of Logroño via N 120, is a day tour of exceptional churches, monasteries, and Camino de Santiago shrines, which ends with the options of returning to Logroño, staying in Santo Domingo de la Calzada (see below), or continuing on west to Burgos in Old Castile.

Nájera is the site of one of the famous battles of *English* Medieval history. Edward, the Black Prince, was an ally of Pedro the Cruel in a bloody battle (according to contemporary accounts, the río Najerilla ran red) against Pedro's brother-in-law, Henry of Trastamara, and Henry's French allies led by du Guesclin. The English troops, "the best fighting men on earth," carried the day on a plain northeast of Nájera. As a reward, Pedro presented the Black Prince with the great ruby that is the main jewel in the crown of England. It was to be a poor reward, since the treacherous Pedro reneged on his other financial promises to Edward. The Black Prince was unable to pay his troops, who then rebelled against him, leading to his eventual ruin. The Battle of Nájera is also known as the Battle of Navarrete because some of the bloodiest fighting took place at the Puente de Navarrete (the bridge over the Najerilla on the road to Navarrete), not because it was fought near Navarrete, 16 km to the northeast.

The great attraction in Nájera is the **monastery of Santa María la Real**, pantheon of a number of the kings of Navarra and several members of the Castilian aristocracy of the Middle Ages. The counts of Haro, the Rioja's greatest aristocratic family, are also buried here. One of the counts, Pedro Fernández de Velasco, once threw a lavish Medieval celebration in honor of Doña Blanca de Navarra (who is buried here). The fiesta's centerpiece was a silver fountain splashing a continuous supply of Rioja wine for the celebrants.

The monastery of Santa María la Real has a splendid early-15th-century Gothic **cloister**, with airy, filigree-like tracery filling the arches, and a magnificent late-15th-century choir, whose stalls are credited to Jewish wood-carvers. During the last half of July a sound-and-light show representing the history of Nájera and Santa María la Real takes place in the cloisters of the monastery.

The great monasteries of San Millán de Suso and San

Millán de Yuso are located in the mountains 12 km (7.5 miles) southwest of Nájera at San Millán de la Cogolla (from Nájera take C 113 5 km/3 miles south, then look for a road to the right with signs pointing to San Millán). In church lore from the sixth century, San Millán duplicated Christ's miracle of the Sermon on the Mount, quenching the thirst of the multitudes with a small measure of wine. The original monastery, **San Millán de Suso**, dates from a Visigothic church founded in 537, but the building we see today is an early-tenth-century gem that was built against a rock into which three chapels were hewn. The nave has several lovely Mozarabic horseshoe arches. Suso also houses the original tomb of San Millán, a splendid Romanesque sarcophagus carved in pale green alabaster.

It is the generally accepted belief that the written Castilian language first began to take shape here in the southern hills of the Rioja at San Millán de Suso. Early in the 13th century a Benedictine monk named Gonzalo de Berceo (from Berceo, a nearby village) first decided to write his poetry in the evolving vernacular of the day, because, he claimed, he was simply not up to writing in Latin. He further discounted his effort, saying that, if nothing else, he hoped his writing would be worth "a glass of *bon vino,*" then went on to create the earliest surviving literature by a known author in the Spanish language—a long metaphorical poem about the Virgin.

The Augustinian **monastery of San Millán de Yuso** (just down the hill below Suso) is a much larger, less interesting 16th-century church, often called the Escorial of the Rioja. The great attraction of San Millán de Yuso is its **treasury**, which contains exquisite ivory carvings depicting scenes from the lives of San Millán and San Felices. As a set they were once considered "among the earliest and finest examples of Christian carving in Western Europe," according to Walter Starkie. Many of them were stolen, like so many of northern Spain's art treasures, by Napoleon's troops retreating as Wellington's army drove them from Spain. The remaining panels—the others are scattered among museums around the world—have been reset in a modern reliquary containing the remains of San Millán.

Southeast of San Millán, and due south of Nájera on route C 113, is **Anguiano** (45 km/30 miles south of Logroño), where the Fiesta de Santa Magdalena is held on July 22 each year. This folkloric festival features daring male acrobatic dancers who wear colorful skirted costumes and perform on stilts.

Southwest of Anguiano, in the mountains off route C 113, is the **Abadía de Valvanera**, a monastery that has 29 inexpensive rooms for rent (and a restaurant serving monastic fare). Here you will find the 11th-century Romanesque statue, the Virgin of Valvanera, patroness of the Rioja and a much-venerated figure in Spain and, especially, in Spanish America. Some experts say that since Isabella la Católica spent eight days here praying to the Virgin during the Reconquest and subsequently bestowed an annual gift of 30,000 *maravedis* on the monastery, the claim that Columbus's ship was actually called Santa María de Valvanera has validity.

Return to Nájera on C 113 from Valvanera to catch N 120 for a 21-km (13-mile) drive to one of the most famous towns on the Camino de Santiago, **Santo Domingo de la Calzada.** The narrow pilgrims' road still passes through the center of the old part of town. Santo Domingo retains many important vestiges of its Medieval glory: sections of the defensive walls, including watchtowers, built during the reign of Pedro the Cruel; mansions emblazoned with coats of arms; an ancient, much-renovated bridge originally built over río Glera by Santo Domingo himself; the pilgrims' hospital, also built by Santo Domingo; and the fine cathedral, whose bell towers dominate the profile of the town from far away.

Santo Domingo was a hermit who lived in the 11th century and devoted his life to helping travellers along the Camino de Santiago and to keeping the *calzada,* or roadbeds, in a passable state of repair. Thus, the village where he lived came to be known as Santo Domingo de la Calzada.

It was in Santo Domingo that one of the most remarkable incidents in Medieval Christian lore is said to have taken place. A young man was making the pilgrimage to Santiago with his parents. They chanced to stop for the night at an inn in Santo Domingo. The innkeeper's daughter took an immediate liking to the young, weary traveller and, as one 16th-century writer put it, "would have had him medyll with her carnally." However, the young man resisted her advances. Thus infuriated, she took revenge by hiding a silver wine goblet belonging to her father in the young innocent's knapsack as he slept. The next morning, as the boy and his parents were preparing to leave, the spurned girl reported the silver cup missing. The young traveller was caught with the goods, dragged before the local magistrate, and sentenced to hang. Miraculously, though hanged from the gallows, he did not die. The boy's father and mother went to the home of the judge who had sentenced him to offer the miracle as divine evidence of their son's innocence. The magistrate, who was preparing to dine on a pair of chickens, a cock and a hen, rejected the family's appeal, claiming that if the boy were innocent, those roasted chickens were alive. At that point the chickens rose and flew away.

This event is reenacted every May 12 with a white rooster and a hen, which are kept in an elaborate and colorful lighted cage high above the floor of the **cathedral of Santo Domingo de la Calzada.** Modern-day pilgrims stop at the cathedral, hoping to hear the rooster crow and to come away with a white feather as a souvenir. The cathedral, which still has some Romanesque vestiges in the apse, was completed as a Gothic church in the late 13th century, making it one of the first Gothic churches in Spain. The tower is 18th-century Baroque.

The **Parador Nacional de Santo Domingo de la Calzada,** next to the cathedral, is installed in the restored remains of the 12th-century pilgrims' hospice and hospital, which was supposed to have been built by Santo Domingo himself. This is a wonderful old hospice, with its vaulted ceilings, antique furniture, period decorations, suits of armor, and a stylized high-relief map of the Camino de Santiago on a stone wall. The tolling of the cathedral bells to mark the hours each night enhances the spirit of Medieval times that this old town evokes. The parador restaurant serves the regional cuisine of the Rioja, but **Mesón El Peregrino,** avenida de Calahorra 17, just east of the cathedral and the parador on the pilgrims' route, is just as good and considerably less expensive. El Peregrino (the pilgrim) has a big, comfortable dining room entered through a bar, where you can have *tapas* before dinner, and serves typical *riojano* dishes such as *alubias con chorizo, menestra,* roast lamb, and so on. The wine list offers a good selection of Riojas. **El Corregidor,** Zumalacárregui 14–16, is a new, comfortable hotel, affiliated with El Peregrino restaurant, that is the best choice if the parador is full.

The best bet for dining in this entire region is **Hostal Echaurren,** Héroes de Alcázar 2 (Tel: 35-40-47) in Ezcaray, only 12 km (7.5 miles) south of Santo Domingo in the foothills of the Sierra de la Demanda, a region becoming popular with hunters and skiers. In this unlikely, out-of-the-way spot, at a renovated *posada* and post house on the old coach road, Marisa Sanchez, the chef and owner, along with her husband, Félix, runs a kitchen of such excellence that she was awarded the national gastronomy prize in 1987, joining the ranks of such celebrity chefs as Juan Mari Arzak and Pedro Subijana from the Basque Country. Echaurren serves the quintessential dishes of the Rioja based on regional products and taken from traditional recipes—*patatas a la Riojana, menestra, chuletillas de cordero,* and *pimientos rellenos de bacalao*—along with homemade pâté with truffles, endives with prawns and salmon, and other outstanding creations from this talented and, until recently, little-known chef. Echaurren has a good wine list and offers a Rioja grower's wine as house wine for 300 pesetas. Best of all, for a great restaurant, Echaurren is not expensive; expect to spend 3,000 pesetas or less per person, depending on what you order. Hostal Echaurren also has 29 renovated rooms and a few apartments for rent. The restaurant and hostal are closed in November.

Hunting and fishing are excellent in the wild mountains of southern Rioja, especially near Ezcaray, south of San Millán de la Cogolla, and in the Iregua river valley. Quail, partridge, wild boar, and deer are especially plentiful, and the rivers there are well stocked with trout (check with the National Tourist Office of Spain for licensing requirements and seasons).

Rioja Baja

On your way east to Calahorra and Rioja Baja from Logroño, try to visit the winery and museum of marqués de Murrieta, just 3 km (2 miles) outside Logroño on the highway to Calahorra, N 232. The marqués de Murrieta was responsible for establishing French winemaking techniques in the Rioja. The winery, which dates from 1872, is one of the most picturesque in the Rioja and still makes some of the region's best (and most expensive) wines. They may even send you away from the *bodega*'s archives with one of their fine old *reserva* wines, many of which are over 50 years old, providing you are willing to make a sizable donation to the Graham Greene Foundation, a pet project of Murrieta's owner, Vicente Cebrián (count of Creixel), to promote cultural relations between England and Spain.

Southeast of Logroño, in the warmer Mediterranean-influenced climate of La Rioja Baja, vines and olive trees grow side by side. Like the Ribera Baja of neighboring Navarra, this area is known for its agricultural products, and is a center of asparagus, pimiento, and artichoke production.

The first town you will encounter after the Murrieta estate on N 232 is **Ausejo**, whose ruined 13th-century castle overlooks the vineyards of this Rioja Baja wine-producing town. The hill on which Ausejo sits is a warren of underground wine cellars. Just after the harvest you can get a whiff of the fermenting wine as you explore the steep streets of Ausejo.

About 7 km (4 miles) from Ausejo on N 232 at El Villar de Arnedo, turn south to **Arnedo**, a town that used to be an important crossroads during the Roman occupation and was also a strategic town during Moorish times. Its strange, eroded red sandstone hills are honeycombed with man-made caves that were once inhabited. Burrowed into a hillside in what was once an old *bodega* is one of the most unusual restaurants in the Rioja, **Sopitas**, Carrera 4, (Tel: 38-02-66), where you can sample regional specialties such as local *alcachofas* (artichokes), *espárragos blancos* (white asparagus), and *setas* (mushrooms); *perdices* (partridge) and *codornices* (quail) and *cabrito asado* (roast kid), along with the stout, high-alcohol wines of the Rioja Baja. In late September Arnedo has five days of fiesta, including *encierros* (runnings of the bulls through the streets), *gigantes y cabezudos,* top bullfights, *jota*-singing competitions, and fireworks à la Pamplona; it's an authentic country-town fiesta without the tourists.

A drive of about 20 km (12.5 miles) east on C 115 will take you through asparagus and pimiento country (you will often see rows of pimientos hung up to dry on the façades of village houses), past strange towns such as Quel, a village huddled up against a hill topped by the ruins of a once-strategic castle, and Autol, whose two odd tower-like rocks, El Picuezo and La Picueza, eroded by ancient waters and the wind, are a geological curiosity. Just beyond Aldeanueva de Ebro C 115 joins N 232, where you turn right for Alfaro, 8 km (5 miles) to the southeast.

Alfaro, where centuries ago the Phoenicians had a lighthouse on río Ebro, is a dusty, sandstone-colored town whose official boundaries encompass almost 200 square kilometers, making it the third-largest municipality in Spain. The town had Celtic-Iberian roots, was named Graccurris by the Romans, and became Alfaro when the Moors took over.

Alfaro is located scant kilometers from the border with Navarra, and not much farther from the line with Aragón and Soria. As a strategic crossroads and fortress town, it became known as the "key to Castile" during Medieval times. Even today, Alfaro has far more in common with Navarrese Tudela and the villages of western Aragón than with Logroño, the provincial capital.

Alfaro is an important fruit- and vegetable-producing town with a major canning industry, and it is also known for some of the best wines in the Rioja Baja.

The best winery in this region is Palacios Remondo, located on N 232 at the northwestern (Logroño) entrance to town. Antonio Palacios, a progressive young winemaker who was trained in Bordeaux, produces a wine with considerable finesse from this warm climate, where the high-alcohol-producing Grenache is the major grape. While demolishing the remains of their ancestral home, the Palacios Remondo family found six bottles wrapped in a parchment will that was written in 1651. The winery now uses a facsimile of the parchment to wrap each bottle of their best wines, the Herencia Remondo reds. The winery has its offices at their Logroño facility, so it is best to call ahead to arrange a visit to the *bodegas* in Alfaro; Tel: (941) 23-71-77.

Hotel Palacios and **Tirachinas Restaurant**, Carretera Zaragoza 6 (Tel: 18-01-00), and an interesting wine museum, all owned by the Palacios family, are located next door between the winery and the bullring. Here is the place to try such local specialties as *menestra de verduras,* white asparagus, *pimientos rellenos,* roast goat, and local artichokes cooked with duck sweetbreads, all washed down, of course, with a bottle of Palacios Remondo wine.

After Alfaro you can head northwest back to Logroño 21 km (13 miles) away on N 232 via Calahorra, perhaps stopping near **Funes** (in Navarra, actually a few miles southeast of Calahorra on the Rioja border) to see the remains of the Roman winery mentioned in the Navarra chapter. Turn north on C 115 at Rincón de Soto; the Funes winery site is just a few hundred yards north of the Ebro, so near Peralta that you may want to continue north for about 10 km (6 miles) to Peralta to sample the cuisine at Atalaya restaurant (see the Navarra chapter). In fact, you may want to tie southern Navarra and the Rioja Baja together and, depending on the direction in which you are heading, end up in either Logroño, Pamplona, or Zaragoza.

The Romans left their impact on this whole area, but especially on **Calahorra**, the major town in the region. Sertorius drew the wrath of Pompey by defending the rights of the native population of Calagurris (modern Calahorra). Pompey laid siege to Calagurris, whose inhabitants held out for four years until they were reduced to cannabalism and finally starved. For their courage and stubborn refusal to surrender, the people of Calagurris became legendary (the event was known as *fames Calagurritana*) in ancient Rome, just as they had earlier to the Carthaginians, when Hannibal had besieged the town with much the same result. From these events rose the grisly legend of La Matrona, one of the last survivors of the siege, who wandered the streets each night lighting fires all over town to trick the enemy into believing that many defenders remained to fight. When the Romans finally entered the town, they found La Matrona gnawing on a human arm.

The great Roman rhetorician and scholar Quintilian (c. A.D. 35–100) and the poet Prudentius were both born at Calahorra. Almost 20 centuries later, Quintilian, who was the greatest educator of his age and the first man in Europe ever to be paid by the state for teaching, is celebrated as an *hijo del pueblo,* a true son of Calahorra. His statue stands in the center of town, and the comfortable, modern **Parador Marco Fabio Quintiliano** is named after him. The parador's restaurant serves good, typical Rioja fare—after the legend of La Matrona, the many vegetarian dishes from this rich agricultural area are welcome—but, alas, for those who want to try the wines of the Rioja Baja, the restaurant's selection is almost nonexistent.

The touristic points of interest here are the Neoclassical church of Santiago, which often has a family of storks residing in the belfry; the gate of Planillo de San Andrés, the old gate to the Roman city; and the important cathedral of Calahorra (Calahorra has been the site of a bishopric since the fifth century), originally built in the 12th century but rebuilt during the 15th to 17th centuries in the Gothic style, then given a Neoclassical façade in the 18th century. The old quarter, built on the original Roman site, is a lively collection of little plazas and steep labyrinthine streets well worth exploring on foot.

Calahorra has several good restaurants, including **La Taberna de la Cuarta Esquina**, Cuatro Esquinas 16 (in the old quarter), which serves such dishes as scrambled eggs with green garlic shoots and *angulas,* artichokes with clams, and fresh *pochas* in season, along with a house wine from a grower in nearby Tudelilla; the homey, inexpensive, and venerable **Casa Mateo**, Quintiliano 15, which is famous for its regional dishes such as the ubiquitous *menestra de verduras, pochas con chorizo,* and *conejo* (stewed rabbit); **Monserrat-2**, Manuel de Falla 7, for *mariscos* (shellfish); and, for fancier versions of Riojan, Navarrese, and Basque dishes, **Chef Nino**, Basconia 1.

GETTING AROUND

The usual route to the Rioja is to take N I from Madrid to Burgos. From Burgos to the Rioja you can take the four-lane toll roads A 1 and A 68, or take N 120 from Burgos to Santo

Domingo de la Calzada for a more leisurely, picturesque entrance into Spain's greatest wine region.

There is train and bus service to Logroño from several northern capitals, but many lines require changes. Zaragoza, Irún, Bilbao, and Madrid (via Burgos) are served by trains to and from the Logroño RENFE station at the plaza de Europa, located four blocks southeast of the Gran Vía along General Vara del Rey and the avenida de España, where the bus station is located. There is regular daily bus service to most of the major towns in the region.

ACCOMMODATIONS REFERENCE

The telephone area code for the Rioja is 941. When calling from outside the country, drop the 9.

► **Abadía de Valvanera.** Monasterio de Valvanera, 26322 **Anguiano.** Tel: 37-70-44.

► **Hotel Los Augustinos.** San Agustín 2, 26200 **Haro.** Tel: 31-13-08.

► **Carlton Rioja.** Gran Vía 5, 26002 **Logroño.** Tel: 24-21-00; Telex: 37295.

► **El Corregidor.** Zumalacárregui 14–16, 26250 **Santo Domingo de la Calzada.** Tel: 34-22-47.

► **Echaurren.** Héroes del Alcázar 2, 26280 **Ezcaray.** Tel: 35-40-47.

► **Parador Marco Fabio Quintiliano.** 26500 **Calahorra.** Tel: 13-03-58; Fax: 13-51-39.

► **Palacios.** Carretera de Zaragoza (N 232), 26540 **Alfaro.** Tel: 18-01-00; Fax: 18-30-66; Telex: 37003.

► **Parador Nacional de Santo Domingo de la Calzada.** Plaza del Santo 3, 26250 **Santo Domingo de la Calzada.** Tel: 34-03-00.

NAVARRA

By Gerry Dawes

From the green rugged Pyrenees in the north bordering France to the tawny hills and fertile river plains in the south bordering Rioja and Aragón, Navarra has some of the most varied geography and beautiful scenery in Spain. The terrain runs the gamut from snowy peaks soaring above pine- and beech-covered slopes and pristine green valleys to wild, awesome canyons, terraced vineyard land, and shimmering, heat-baked southern hills overlooking near-deserts and lush, green truck gardens irrigated by the río Ebro. Gracing this strikingly beautiful land are a number of dramatically situated villages, important historical sites, Medieval castles, and major shrines along the Camino de Santiago, the Pilgrims' Way to Santiago de Compostela.

For almost three centuries (1234–1512), Navarra (Navarre to the French) was a powerful kingdom, as French as it was Spanish, even counting the city of Bordeaux among its dominions. Basque, Roman, Visigothic, French, Aragonese, Castilian, Moorish, and Jewish influences formed the culture of this province and left behind an amazing number of superb monuments and works of art. Here the visitor will see some of the finest Romanesque and Gothic architecture in Spain.

Part of the charm of inland Navarra lies in the fact that it is relatively isolated because of its mountainous terrain and dearth of straight, fast roads for getting there. This has kept mass tourism away from this ancient province of northern Spain; if it were not for the international fame brought to the Fiestas de San Fermín by Ernest Hemingway, Navarra would hardly be discovered at all, but there is so much to see in this province that you should consider it a destination, not a stopover.

And, ever present, as you explore Navarra, is the enticing

thought that even some of the smaller towns have excellent restaurants where you can enjoy Navarra's exceptional cuisine and excellent wines.

MAJOR INTEREST

Wines of Navarra
Navarrese cuisine and restaurants

Pamplona
Fiestas de San Fermín: Running of the bulls and bullfights

El Camino de Santiago
Leyre, Javier, and Sangüesa
Roncesvalles and the Pyrenean villages
Puente la Reina's Romanesque bridge
Beautiful Medieval town of Estella

Southern Navarra
Olite: Medieval castle town
Tudela

The Food and Wines of Navarra

Navarra's cuisine, restaurants, and master chefs rank among the best in Spain. Fresh fish and shellfish from the nearby Atlantic; quail, partridge, and rabbit from the mountains; trout from the cold, clear mountain streams; lamb from all across the province; and succulent vegetables from the Ribera region of southern Navarra provide the ingredients for scores of memorable dishes. Navarrese culinary specialties include *pochas,* a legendary bean dish cooked with chorizo sausages and quail; *espárragos blancos,* fat white asparagus served with homemade mayonnaise; *trucha a la Navarra,* trout cooked with a slice of mountain ham; *pimientos rellenos,* stuffed peppers; and *menestra de verduras,* a melange of young vegetables.

Navarra produces some of Spain's most underrated wines: excellent reds and whites and especially *rosados,* which are unequivocally among the best rosé wines in the world. Navarra *rosados* are dry, fresh, balanced, and endowed with a beautiful classic onion-skin color, and are wonderful to drink with a wide variety of foods. As Hemingway's chroniclers A. E. Hotchner and Carlos Baker would attest, Don Ernesto loved the *rosados* of Navarra so much that he not only drank them in Navarra, he carried iced-down bottles of Las Campanas Rosado all over Spain with him during the

Navarra
0 miles 10
0 km 10
to San Sebastián
N 1
N 240
N 240
to Vitoria
N 1
N 111
Monasterio de Iranzu
Puente la Reina
N 111
Estella
Cirauqui
C 132
N 111
Mañeru
Eunate
Monasterio de Irache
Cerco de Artajona
C 132
Los Arcos
Torres del Río
Viana
Logroño
Río Ega
Río Arga
Río Ebro
to Bilbao, Burgos
A 68
N 111
N 232
Peralta
Funes
Calahorra
LA RIOJA
Rincón de Soto
to Zaragoza, Barcelona

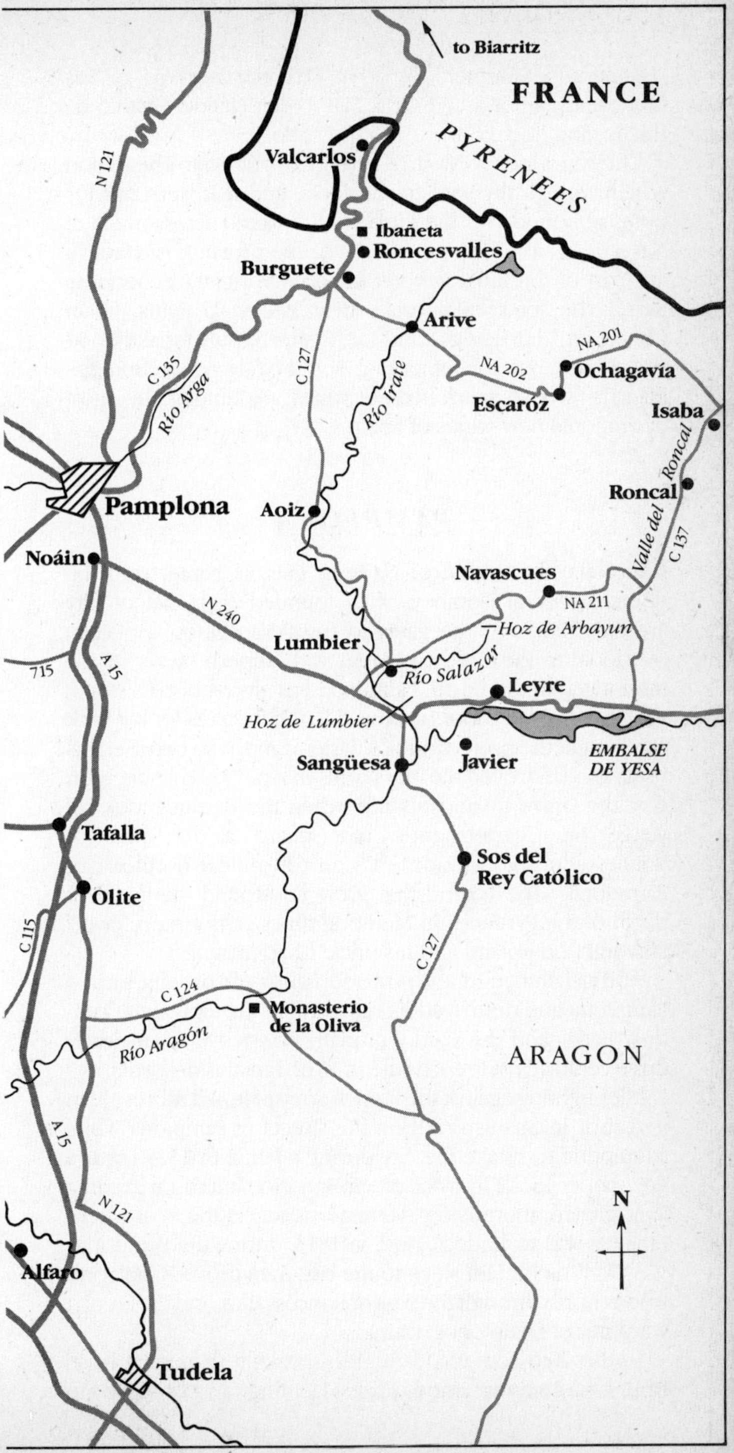

to Biarritz
FRANCE
PYRENEES
Valcarlos
Ibañeta
Roncesvalles
Burguete
N 121
Arive
NA 201
Ochagavía
NA 202
Escaróz
Isaba
C 135
Río Arga
C 127
Río Irate
Valle del Roncal
Roncal
Pamplona
Aoiz
C 137
Noáin
Navascues
NA 211
N 240
Hoz de Arbayun
Lumbier
Río Salazar
715
A 15
Leyre
Hoz de Lumbier
Sangüesa
Javier
EMBALSE DE YESA
Tafalla
Sos del Rey Católico
Olite
C 115
C 127
C 124
Monasterio de la Oliva
Río Aragón
ARAGON
A 15
N 121
N
Alfaro
Tudela

"Dangerous Summer" of 1959. Try the *rosados* of Las Campanas, Señoría de Sarría, Malón de Echaide, Castillo de Irache, and Julián Chivite's Gran Feudo.

The red wines of Navarra have great potential. The region is climatologically wed to the Rioja, and if it were not for political boundaries the Rioja would extend across much of Navarra (as it is, several villages in the province of Navarra are part of the Rioja *denominación de origen*). Señoría de Sarría, the spectacular estate near Puente la Reina, Julián Chivite in Cintruenigo, and Las Campanas also make good red wines, but the emerging star of Navarra is Bodegas Magaña, whose merlot-based wines are among the most exceptional new wines of Spain.

PAMPLONA

Pamplona, the capital of Navarra, gets its name from the Roman general Pompey, who founded this ancient city around 75 B.C. At the gates to the Pyrenees on a plateau overlooking the little río Arga, with superb views of the mountains to the north, Pamplona has always been a strategic city. After the Moors captured it, the Basques took it back and sought the protection of Charlemagne, who betrayed his hosts and destroyed the city's walls in A.D. 778. That decision cost the brave Roland his life, when the Basques took revenge on Charlemagne's rear guard at the pass of Roncesvalles (Roncevaux), 47 km (29 miles) northeast of Pamplona. (The legend that grew up around this incident north of the Pyrenees in Medieval times casts a more favorable light on Roland and his uncle Charlemagne.)

Abd ar-Rahman III, the powerful caliph of Córdoba, sacked Pamplona and destroyed its cathedral in the early tenth century. Ferdinand the Catholic finally wrested it from nearly three centuries of French rule in 1512. Ignatius of Loyola, as a soldier fighting against the French army of Jean d'Albret (Juan de Labrit in Spanish) fell on the streets of Pamplona while attempting to retake the city during a battle in 1521 (near a newspaper kiosk in front of San Ignacio church on avenida San Ignacio, there is a pavement marker at the spot where Ignatius was wounded). And, in 1813, during the Peninsular War, Wellington laid siege to the city, then drove Napoleon's troops north through the pass of Roncesvalles, and the French were out of Spain once again.

In the 20th century, to English-speaking readers at least, Pamplona owes its fame to Ernest Hemingway, whose glorification of Pamplona and its Fiestas de San Fermín in *The Sun Also Rises* has attracted millions of visitors to this mystical northern city for more than 60 years. The charming, sleepy old provincial capital that Hemingway discovered in the 1920s is now surrounded by modern high-rise suburbs, and the population has nearly tripled since 1950.

Despite the veneration of the old core city by the foreign *pamplonicas* who flock here every July, Pamplona is not as rich in fine old churches, museums, and distinguished Medieval architecture as many other cities in Spain. And, like San Sebastián and the rest of the Basque country, Iruña, as Pamplona is known by its large Basque population, has had more than its share of terrorism and major political problems. However, besides the Fiestas de San Fermín, one of the world's greatest, noisiest, and most colorful parties, there is much to recommend in Pamplona, even when it is not *en fiesta*.

As a base for exploring the undersung beauty, charm, and antiquity of Navarra and for sampling the cuisine of one of Spain's greatest culinary regions, Pamplona will reward even lengthy stays. It is a city of shaded streets, fountains, and plazas; interesting shops and boutiques featuring a wide variety of regional and national products; and the richest collection of good restaurants, outdoor cafés, backstreet bars, and pubs of any city its size in Spain, with the possible exception of San Sebastián.

The major items of architectural and historic interest in Pamplona are the cathedral, the old walls of the city, the Museum of Navarra, the Ciudadela fortress and adjacent Parque de la Taconera, the church of San Saturnino, the plaza del Castillo, and the delightful façade of the Ayuntamiento (City Hall). The fact that most of Pamplona's attractions are concentrated in the relatively compact older part of the city and easily reachable on foot from any of the major hotels contributes greatly to Pamplona's appeal.

Standing in the northeast corner of old Pamplona is the 14th- and 15th-century **cathedral**, which James Michener called "the ugliest beautiful church in existence" because the 18th-century Neoclassical façade by Ventura Rodríguez "is a Greco-Roman horror that makes the once gracious building look like the courthouse of Deaf Smith County, Texas." The façade replaced the last remnants of Pamplona's Romanesque cathedral. The beauty Michener refers to is the cathedral's French Gothic interior, which contains one of the finest and most elegant Gothic **cloisters** in the world. Among the cathedral's other attractions are the superb alabaster tomb of Charles III, El Noble (1387–1425), and his queen, Leonor de Trastamara, under whose reign the church was built; the Sala de la Preciosa, an ornate Gothic doorway of intricately carved stone; and the **Diocesan Museum**, in which are displayed polychrome sculpture, paintings, custodials, and religious objects from Navarrese churches, plus an unusual lectern decorated with scenes from a unicorn chase. The museum is in the former refectory and kitchens used by Augustinian monks for almost 800 years (the 11th to the 19th centuries).

Just behind the cathedral are the **ramparts**, whose remaining stone walls still mark the northern and eastern limits of the old fortress city. You can walk along substantial stretches of these old walls overlooking the Arga river for fine views of the Pyrenees. To the west the fortress walls end at the green belt encompassing Taconera Park and the **Ciudadela**, a 16th-century stone fortress built during the reign of Philip II and patterned on the one at Antwerp.

The Navarrese are great music lovers. Both the Ciudadela and Taconera Park are often used as open-air theaters in summer during the Festivales de Navarra, one of Spain's finest cultural events. The Festivales de Navarra feature sophisticated programs of music, dance, theatre, and folkloric music by the finest national and international performers. The Ronda de Otoño, in autumn, is a series of performances and art exhibitions. Pamplona's superb choral group, La Agrupación Coral de Cámara de Pamplona, is world famous, and the colorful municipal band La Pamplonesa is the pride of the city. The famed tenor Julián Gayarre, actually from Roncal to the northeast, and Pablo Sarasate, the 19th-century virtuoso violinist who dazzled the world playing his 1724 Stradivarius, were from Navarra, and both are honored by monuments in Pamplona. Teatro Gayarre is Pamplona's principal theater, and paseo de Sarasate is a major street.

The Navarros and the Vascos (Basques) are great sports enthusiasts. Besides bullrunning, which takes place not only in Pamplona but also in most Navarrese towns during their annual fiestas, the local bloods revel in weightlifting contests (200-kilo stones), woodchopping competitions, musical chairs on horseback, and the ubiquitous *frontón* (whose rectangular two-walled courts—sometimes a wall of the church—can be seen in every village) for jai alai. You can see most of these events in Pamplona and other Navarrese towns during *fiesta.* Outside of *fiesta* you see and bet on professional jai alai every Thursday, Saturday, Sunday, and most holidays at Frontón Euskai-Jai Berri, 6 km (4 miles) northeast of Pamplona on the Roncesvalles road in suburban Huarte.

The **Museo de Navarra**, at the foot of calle Santo Domingo, overlooks the corrals where the bulls are kept before the *encierro* (the running of the bulls) each morning during San Fermín. Located in the 16th-century building that once housed the charity hospital of Misericórdia, the museum contains Roman mosaics, some distinguished Romanesque capitals from the original cloister of the cathedral, fragments from the ninth-century mosque of Tudela, and an interesting collection of Medieval mural paintings taken from different churches in Navarra.

If the plaza del Castillo (see below) is the heart of Pamplona, the charming Ayuntamiento (City Hall), a few blocks to the northwest, must be the soul of the city. Every year on July 6 at noon thousands of people converge on the plaza in front of City Hall to watch the city fathers fire the *chupinazo,* the rocket announcing the beginning of the Fiestas of San Fermín. Then in the afternoon they return in droves to dance the famous *riau-riau* and watch the huge papier-mâché *gigantes y cabezudos* (giants and bigheads) lead the throng out of the plaza and through the streets for hours in the equivalent of a monumental conga line.

Even without the celebrants, the 18th-century storybook Baroque façade of the Ayuntamiento (the rest of the building is modern) is one of Spain's most wonderful civic buildings. The three-story structure is adorned with four pairs of matched columns on each story, each set capped by different matching capitals—one story Doric, another Ionic, and a third Corinthian. The second and third stories each have three matched sets of louvred wooden doors that open onto beautiful wrought-iron balconies decorated with pairs of gilt-painted lions. Pedestaled statues of Prudence and Justice guard the main portal, an archway capped with more filigree wrought iron and another pair of gold lions. Above the third story is an attic with a clock and a balustrade flanked by two statues of Hercules. Capping the whole thing is a pair of stone lions guarding the Pamplonan coats of arms, which are topped with huge crowns; in the middle, looking like a bored Roman eunuch, is a huge statue of Fame, one arm cocked on his hip and the other holding what looks like a primitive trombone poised at his lips.

Just west of the Ayuntamiento, at the beginning of calle Mayor, is the church of San Saturnino with its Romanesque towers and a 13th-century Gothic doorway. Note the brass letters of a pavement marker in front of the church, where, as local lore has it, San Saturnino baptized 40,000 pagans from a well. One block southwest of San Saturnino, on Ansoleaga, is the Cámara de Comptos, an interesting 14th-century Gothic building that served for more than 400 years as a mint.

At the western end of calle Mayor, where it meets the Ciudadela, is the Neoclassical church of San Lorenzo, home of the much-venerated, silver-bedecked, dark-faced statue of San Fermín. Navarra's patron saint is said to be able to descend with a cape and come to the aid of any fallen *mozo,* or bullrunner, in the *encierro.*

A few short blocks southeast of the Ayuntamiento is the arcaded **plaza del Castillo**, with its shops, sidewalk cafés, park benches, shade trees, and bandstand. It is indeed the heart of Pamplona, and during San Fermín it is the place to be. Hemingway, Orson Welles, Kenneth Tynan, James Michener, and many of the foreign regulars used to hold court during fiesta at the **Bar Txoco** ("choko"), just steps from the southeastern corner of the square, where Hotel Quintana (Hotel Montoya in *The Sun Also Rises*) was located. The late Juanito Quintana, the proprietor and Hemingway's great friend, was the prototype for Montoya, Jake Barnes's bullfight mentor. (Now the foreign regulars have migrated to the outdoor cafés in front of Hotel Perla in the northeast corner of the square.) The venerable **Cafe Iruña**, across the square, still replaces its regular tables and chairs at fiesta time with less attractive, but more durable, outdoor furniture.

The Fiestas de San Fermín

In 1926 Ernest Hemingway described the opening of the Fiestas de San Fermín in his immortal novel of Pamplona and the Lost Generation: "At noon on Sunday, the 6th of July, the fiesta exploded. There is no other way to describe it."

Every year at noon on July 6 mobs of people still gather from all over the province of Navarra, the rest of Spain, and—since Hemingway—the world, at the Ayuntamiento to see the *chupinazo* signalling the beginning of the Fiestas de San Fermín. As the rocket streaks into the sky above Pamplona, thousands shout *!Viva San Fermín!,* put on the red neckerchiefs that are the symbol of the fiesta, and begin singing, dancing, and doing some journeyman drinking (their apprenticeship, just as Hemingway observed more than 50 years ago, takes place in the cheaper bars of the old quarter all morning long). Within minutes the plaza del Castillo and the streets surrounding it are filled with the cacophony of flutes, drums, horns, shouts, and exploding fireworks as the red-and-white clad throng dances to the music of Navarra.

The fiesta also features bullfights, jai alai matches, Basque woodchopping contests, *jota* singing competitions, spectacular fireworks, a first-rate international circus and carnival, and, of course, the *encierro,* the running of the bulls. Every morning from July 7 to July 14, brave men wearing white shirts and trousers, red sashes and neckerchiefs, and rope-soled *alpargatas* run with the fighting bulls through the streets of the city for what Hemingway called "a morning's pleasure."

San Fermín is a wild, bacchanalian affair—not for the faint of heart or the abstemious—that goes on in the streets for eight days, subsiding briefly, but never fully, during the wee hours of the morning. Bands begin playing in the streets at 6:00 A.M., virtually assuring that a good night's sleep in Pamplona during fiesta is as rare as a sober celebrant. Adding an international flavor to all this are the thousands of foreigners, many of whom have not missed the fiesta in years. Everyone—from bootblacks to duchesses—joins the party.

Finally, on the night of July 14, the fiesta begins to wind down as the celebrants light candles and walk through Pamplona, alternately singing the bittersweet lament "*Pobre de mi, se han acabado las Fiestas de San Fermín*" (Woe is me, San Fermín is over) and another song (*"Uno de enero, dos de febrero, . . . siete de julio, !San Fermín!"*—First of January, second of February, . . . seventh of July, !San Fermín!) that is the countdown to next year's fiesta.

Running the Bulls

If you are young, brave, foolish, or drunk—it helps if you are all four—you may want to try the *encierro:* running the bulls. This is a dangerous stunt for "a morning's pleasure." A fighting bull can outrun a racehorse for the first 100 yards and can run the half-mile uphill *encierro* course in less than three minutes. If you begin running at the Ayuntamiento after the bulls are released in the streets, they will pass you before you get to the bullring. The greatest danger here, however, is the likelihood of being trampled by a wild-eyed sophomore from an American university. Imagine being in a crowded auditorium when someone yells "Fire!" and you find six or seven fighting bulls, several massive steers, and hundreds of hell-bent runners racing for the only exit.

To get an idea of the layout of the *encierro* route, which is barricaded with a double line of heavy timbers each morning before the run, start at the bottom of the hill on Santo Domingo, where the bulls are corraled the night before. Walk up Santo Domingo and follow the rows of square postholes past the Ayuntamiento to the famous canyon-like Estafeta street and to its end at teléfonos corner, where the run doglegs left down a chute and through a narrow tunnel into the bullring.

To watch the *encierro,* which begins at 8:00 A.M., you must get to the barricades by 6:00 A.M. to get a place to stand. Santo Domingo hill, the Ayuntamiento, and the teléfonos dogleg near the bullring are the best places to see the action. If you get to the ticket windows by 6:30, you can buy an inexpensive ticket to see the climax of the *encierro* from a bullring seat, available only on a first-come, first-served basis. There's also wonderful music from a band parading around the ring, and an amateur bullfight, which features young heifers wreaking havoc on those foolish enough to get in their way.

If you do run the bulls, and if they come within reasonable proximity of you during the *encierro,* check the windows of local photography shops around the plaza del Castillo's side streets. Photographers stationed along the *encierro* route take dozens of snapshots each day. If you find yourself in one, you can purchase a unique personal souvenir of your San Fermín adventure.

Bullfights in Pamplona

Tickets are expensive and very difficult to come by, but a bullfight at Pamplona—for the strong at heart, at least—is an incredible experience. You can try the bullring ticket windows on the day of the fight, but they will probably be sold out. Then check with the scalpers, who will ask a fortune depending on the location (get a seat in the shade; the sun seats are rough territory).

Colorful rowdy *peñas* (social clubs), each led by a noisy band and packing enough wine and food for an army, parade through the streets to the bullring each afternoon with their ribald and politically oriented cartoon banners held high. The *peñas* are fun to watch, but under no circumstances should you buy a ticket to the bullfight in Tendidos 5 or 6, where they sit; it is a war zone. As a foreigner you will be a choice target for ice water, sacks of flour, and any leftover food and cheap wine they may throw at you.

To reach the bullring, walk from Bar Txoco in the plaza

del Castillo south along Espoz y Mina for two blocks, then look to your left. At the corner of paseo Hemingway and calle Amaya is a statue of Ernest Hemingway, dedicated to him by the people of Pamplona in the 1960s. Every year on July 6 someone ties a red kerchief around Don Ernesto's neck, where it remains until the end of the fiesta.

Staying in Pamplona

During San Fermín hotel reservations in Pamplona are almost impossible to get. Most people have to rent rooms in private homes. The Tourist Office at Duque de Ahumada 3 (around the corner from the plaza del Castillo on the way to the bullring) will help you find such rooms for rent.

Pamplona's top-rated hotel, the **Tres Reyes**, is located in Taconera Park and has a swimming pool. Adequate accommodations are available at the centrally located, modern **Maisonnave** near the Ayuntamiento; at the **Orhi**, across from the bullring; and at the bullfighter's hotel, the aging **Yoldi**, a few blocks south of the plaza del Castillo on avenida San Ignacio. The **Eslava**, whose owner Jose Luis Eslava is the director of Pamplona's famous choral group, is located in a plaza on the Ramparts several blocks from the center of town, and offers some relief from the all-night revelry during fiesta, if you can get in.

Caveat: For fiesta the prices of hotel rooms can legally be raised to more than double the normal rate, so expect a hefty supplement if you do get a room. Also try to avoid paying by credit card, which can be subject to exchange-rate manipulation.

Dining in Pamplona

If you are an aficionado of great restaurants, you will find plenty of them in Pamplona. At **Hartza**, Juan de Labrit 19 (across the street from the bullring), sisters Mari, Manoli, and Julia serve some of Pamplona's best food in the elegant dining rooms of a renovated old house decorated with antiques, oil paintings, and beamed ceilings. Hartza is famous for traditional Navarrese and Basque dishes made from seasonal ingredients. Mari or Manoli will recite the dishes of the day—*alubias de Tolosa* (red beans); baked fresh fish like hake, turbot, or sea bream; *almejas a la marinera* (a clam casserole). Take their suggestions and be prepared to pay 5,000–6,000 pesetas per person with wine, dessert, coffee, tax, and tip.

Las Pocholas (Hostal del Rey Noble), paseo de Sarasate 6, was a favorite of Hemingway, who frequented it during the "Dangerous Summer" of 1959. Pamplona's longest-established top-category restaurant is a fading star, some say, but for traditional dishes and specialties such as *ajoarriero con langosta* (codfish with lobster), others swear by Las Pocholas (The Sweethearts), as the long-time owners, the Guerendiain sisters, have been known for more than 30 years.

La Olla, avenida Roncesvalles 2, recently opened by the owner of Maitena, a Pamplona favorite in the plaza del Castillo in the 1960s and '70s, serves a range of unpretentious classic Navarrese dishes—*ajoarriero, pimientos rellenos* (stuffed peppers), and *cordero asado,* (roast lamb).

Sarasate, García Castañón 12, has recently changed its menu to feature dishes based on *cocina nueva,* a culinary trend with French influences now revolutionizing the way the best Spanish chefs cook, but it is also a great restaurant for traditional Navarrese cuisine.

Many San Fermín regulars swear by **Europa**, Espoz y Mina 11, whose rich and often heavy fare and copious portions are offset somewhat by the fact that it is located only steps from the plaza del Castillo in one direction and the bullring in the other. At festival time the crowds seem impenetrable.

Dining at fancy restaurants, with their straitlaced, solemn, formal service, runs counter to the spirit of San Fermín, with its casual, raucous style. Best left for a time when there is no fiesta are highly rated **Josetxo**, plaza Príncipe de Viana 1 (near Hotel Yoldi), with luxurious dining rooms, impeccable service, and beautifully presented, classic Navarrese dishes, and **Rodero**, Arrieta 3 (behind the bullring facing Media Luna park), whose *alta cocina* is a bit precious in concept (duck with grapefruit and honey sauce; asparagus with shellfish).

For authentic Navarrese cooking at moderate prices there are **Casa Luis**, plaza Calatayud 11; **San Fermín**, calle San Nicholas 44; and **Shanti**, Castillo de Maya 39. The great old tavern, **Mauleón**, Amaya 4, near the bullring is a must, especially for *alubias con chorizo* (white beans with sausage), *pimientos rellenos,* the house wine, and the *ambiente*—wine barrels, hustling waiters, *jota*-singing customers, and the joy of it all.

Marceliano, calle Mercado (behind City Hall), is a rowdy old tavern frequented by many Pamplona regulars. It used to be a favorite of both Hemingway and Michener and is today frequented by inveterate fiesta-goers, primarily the stout-hearted, who like the music (impromptu *jotas;* street bands stop at the bar), the *pochas,* the free-flowing *clarete,* and the occasional fistfight.

THE CAMINO DE SANTIAGO

Navarra has some of the richest and most revered shrines on the Pilgrims' Way, the Camino de Santiago, and it also has the distinction of having two branches of the great pilgrimage road within its borders. One enters from France via Aragón through Leyre and Sangüesa in Navarra, and the other, more famous, route begins at the French border at Valcarlos and comes down through the Pyrenees via Roncesvalles to Pamplona. Both routes converge at Puente la Reina, 24 km (15 miles) southwest of Pamplona. From Puente la Reina the Camino passes westward through the Navarrese towns of Mañeru, Cirauqui, Estella, Los Arcos, Torres del Rio, and Viana before entering La Rioja. (For more on the Camino de Santiago, see the chapters on Aragón, La Rioja, Old Castile, and—for the object of the pilgrimage, Santiago de Compostela—Asturias and Galicia.)

Leyre and Sangüesa

Approximately 50 km (31 miles) southeast of Pamplona, by way of route N 240, are Leyre, Javier, and Sangüesa—all exceptionally rich in history and architecture and, except for Javier, important shrines on the Camino de Santiago. The **monastery of San Salvador de Leyre** overlooks the huge Yesa reservoir in the dramatically beautiful Sierra de Leyre. First mentioned as a monastery in documents from A.D. 848, and claimed to have Visigothic roots dating to the sixth century, Leyre became the most powerful and spiritually important abbey in Navarra under the Cistercians. It counted San Sebastián in its dominions and was the pantheon of the first kings of Navarra. The primitive 11th-century Romanesque crypt and the late-11th-century naves and tower were built on the ruins of a sixth-century Visigothic church. In 1954 Benedictine monks from Santo Domingo de Silos repopulated the then-decaying monastery and restored the 17th- and 18th-century buildings for use as a hostal, the **Hospederia de Leyre**, where travellers can spend the night and perhaps, in the monastery, hear the brothers in Gregorian chant.

Javier, 8 km (5 miles) south of Leyre, is the birthplace of

Saint Francis Xavier, one of the founders of the Jesuits and the famous apostle to the Indies, who established missions and converted thousands to Roman Catholicism in India and Japan. The 13th-century **Castillo de Javier** was partially demolished in the 16th century by order of Cardinal Cisneros. While interesting, the castle suffers a bit from the sterility of latter-day restoration. There is a sound-and-light show at the castle on summer weekends.

Sangüesa, 12 km (7.5 miles) southwest of Javier, whose "modern" history—old Sangüesa was Sancossa, a Roman town nearby, then a Visigothic town, then the Navarrese Rocaforte, a castle-fortress hill town, whose ruins can be seen 5 km (3 miles) north—began in 1211 when Alfonso I of Aragón, the Warrior, granted *fueros,* or special rights and privileges, to the people of Rocaforte to get them to move down to the plain, and to European merchants and craftsmen so that they would settle in this area. Alfonso also built a castle to defend Sangüesa against attacks from the Moors and to make the bridge over the río Aragón safe for pilgrims to Santiago.

Sangüesa has one of the most important Romanesque churches in Spain, the 12th-century Cistercian **Santa María la Real**, a national monument. The splendid south portal is decorated in stone with a multitude of figures. Animals, birds, griffins, musicians and blacksmiths, saints and sinners, all vie for the eye's attention in this magnificent rendition of the Last Judgment by a pair of Medieval artists. The church's octagonal tower and spire and odd, silo-like cylindrical staircase on the outside of the tower are a bit incongruous, rising above the splendid intricacies of the grand portal, but they are an interesting ensemble and a distinctive Sangüesa landmark.

A wealth of other monuments and mansions built by prosperous merchants grace Sangüesa, making this small town (population 4,600) a rewarding place to visit. The **Iglesia de Santiago** is 12th-century transitional Romanesque-Gothic with a crenellated bell tower. The tympanum of the church's portal has a large single stone statue of Santiago (discovered in 1965 under some floorboards in the church) standing on a large shell, his garment and hat covered with scallop shells. **San Salvador**, a 14th-century Gothic church, preserves its earlier Romanesque portal and contains a fine set of 16th-century choir stalls originally from the monastery of Leyre. The Warrior Alfonso's castle, now the **Palacio del Príncipe de Viana**, was added to in the 13th century and converted into a palace in the 14th, but kept its crenellated towers, which we see today. An arcaded section of the palace done in Renaissance style is now used as the city hall. Located near Santa María la Real are two mansions of note: the 15th-century Gothic **Palacio del Duque de Granada** on rua Mayor, the original pilgrim route through the city, and, on calle Alfonso el Batallador, the Baroque **Palacio de Vallesantoro** (now Casa de Cultura). On the carved wooden eaves of the latter are some rather grotesque but amusing figures of serpents and mythical creatures.

Also near Sangüesa are two spectacular gorges: the Foz de Lumbier on the río Irati, just a few kilometers north of Sangüesa near the town of Lumbier, and the Foz de Arbayún (6 km long, with vertical drops of up to 400 meters), on río Salazar. The latter can best be seen from the Iso pass between Lumbier and Navascués. A lovely little 12th-century *ermita* (hermitage), San Adrián de Vadoluengo, is located between Sangüesa and **Sos del Rey Católico**, 13 km (8 miles) southeast of Sangüesa, across the provincial boundary. Sos del Rey Católico has excellent accommodations in the modern **Parador Fernando de Aragón**, whose architecture blends harmoniously with the historic buildings in this old town.

We will diverge from the Camino de Santiago here and travel through part of the Pyrenees before meeting the western branch of the Camino at Burguete near Roncesvalles, explore that region, then pick up the main trail again south of Pamplona at Puente la Reina.

The Pyrenean Villages

After a night at Leyre or Sos del Rey Católico, a spectacular drive of 40 km (25 miles) to the northeast on C 137 will take you into the heart of the Pyrenees, where rivers rush out of the high mountains through mystical stands of beech trees into deep-green valleys that shelter some of the least-spoiled villages in Spain.

The isolated **Roncal valley** is famous for its bucolic villages, splendid mountain scenery, colorful folklore including distinctive regional dress, and excellent cheese, *queso Roncal.* The first Spanish cheese to be given an official *denominación de origen* (like wine), Roncal is reminiscent of Italian Parmesan, but milder and softer. Twenty-five years ago it was not uncommon to find some Roncalese wearing regional dress; you can still see their colorful costumes during celebrations. The great tenor Julián Gayarre (1844–

1890) was from Roncal, which also claims some of the great *jota* singers of Navarra. Gayarre's funeral monument in the village cemetery is by Mariano Benlliure (1862–1947), the Valencian sculptor who did the equestrian statue of Alfonso XII in Madrid's Retiro Park and the great *torero* Joselito's funeral monument in Seville.

North of Roncal, at the eastern end of the Navarrese Pyrenees, is the beautiful village of **Isaba**, located in a green valley below the rugged peaks that culminate in the **Mesa de los Tres Reyes** (Three Kings' Table), Navarra's highest mountain (7,984 feet). Every year on the first Sunday in July a colorful *romeria* (pilgrimage cum picnic), where everyone dresses in regional costume, takes place at the nearby hermitage of Idoya. On July 13 the seven mayors of the villages of the valley turn out in typical regional dress to receive the Tribute of the Three Cows from their French neighbors from the Baretous (Bearn) valley. This event, dating from the Middle Ages, is now a fiesta drawing thousands of people each year. The government of Navarra owns the modern 50-room **Hotel Isaba** (renovated in 1986), a good base for those who want to spend quiet days exploring these beautiful mountains or skiing (no lifts) in winter. A few kilometers north of Isaba in the mountain pass of Belagua is the restaurant **Venta de Juan Pito** (closed during the week in winter), a refuge where you can have grilled lamb chops.

From Isaba it is just over 60 km (37 miles) northwest to Roncesvalles, and light-years away from the trappings of modern life. If you have the time, the driving skills, and (most important) the good weather, you may want to take the splendidly picturesque regional mountain roads instead of doubling back on the main roads to Pamplona. You might even want to stay in a *hostal* or pension in one of these mountain towns (besides Isaba, Ochagavía and Burguete have livable accommodations for the adventurous).

About 23 km (14 miles) east of Isaba, across the Portillo de Lazar pass, is Ochagavía, the main village of the Salazar river valley. The 15 villages of this valley retain a Medieval air, and tradition has it that there are witches here. A 42-km (26-mile) road north to Irati passes through the **Selva de Irati**, an enchanting forest of unusually tall beech trees haunted by the ghost of the poisoned queen, Juana de Labrit. The road then runs down the Irati river valley, which Hemingway hiked a considerable distance from Burguete to fish, to the village of Arive. The more direct route is from Ochagavía via Escaroz to Arive (25 km/15.5 miles), where you can choose between turning south to Pamplona via Aoiz or continuing another 9 km (5.6 miles) northeast via Burguete to Roncesvalles.

The western branch of the Camino de Santiago coming from St. Jean-Pied-de-Port crosses the French border at Valcarlos, 65 km (40 miles) northwest of Pamplona (route C 135). Between Valcarlos and Roncesvalles is an important stop on the Camino de Santiago, the former site of **San Salvador de Ibañeta monastery**, where once there were thousands of crosses left by French pilgrims in memory of Charlemagne and in particular of Roland, who died in these hills above Roncesvalles and was immortalized in the great, and first, French epic poem, *Chanson de Roland.* All that remains now is a modern stone monument to Roldan, as Roland is known in Spanish, and a modern hermitage that houses the bell that was tolled to guide lost pilgrims through the night and the thick fogs that often shroud the approaches to the Ibañeta pass.

Between Ibañeta and Roncesvalles (a few kilometers south) is a deep green, mossy forest laced with icy rivulets where you can cool your wines, melons, and other picnic items for an al fresco luncheon such as the one James Michener describes in this setting in *Iberia:* ". . . in a glade so quiet, so softly green that it seemed as if defeated knights might have slept in it the evening before, we spread our blankets and prepared the meal." These woods are a mystical place, haunted by the spirit of Roland's band and the millions of Santiago-bound pilgrims who have walked this holy ground.

The **monastery of Roncesvalles**, which dates to the 12th century, is rather disappointing after the buildup of the legend. Fires, neglect, and overzealous and ill-advised restoration, including the unfortunate choice of a metal roof, have reduced this important monastery to a ghost of its former self. Once a proud hospital and hospice for pilgrims, renowned for its hospitality (good food, real beds, and a cobbler to mend shoes), the monastery now, as Edwin Mullins puts it in *The Pilgrimage to Santiago,* "has the feel of a run-down boarding-school of spartan character . . . an unloved, secular-looking place." Of interest here is the 13th-century **Virgin of Roncesvalles**, a restored Gothic **cloister**, the Gothic pantheon containing the life-size tomb of the giant King Sancho VII the Strong of Navarra, and the treasury, which contains several venerated objects of colorful, but somewhat dubious, heritage.

Several scenes in *The Sun Also Rises* are set in the tiny village of **Burguete**, 3 km (1.9 miles) south of Roncesvalles.

Hemingway's trout fishing expeditions to the río Irati east of Burguete inspired him to write some of the best descriptive passages in literature about fishing and the camaraderie of sportsmen. In keeping with the spirit of the treasury of Roncesvalles, so far as authenticity is concerned, the **Hostal Burguete**, where Hemingway stayed, will show you the piano that the Bill Gorton character supposedly played. Lift the top to see a newspaper picture of Don Ernesto and the name "E. Heminway" (sic) scratched in the wood. If you are in a romantic mood and don't mind roughing it just a bit, Hostal Burguete is still much the way it was in style and comfort, or lack thereof, when Hemingway stayed there in the 1920s. Take warm night clothes even in July.

In the *hostal*'s dining room you can order a good salad, excellent *pochas,* trout, lamb chops with potatoes, and a bottle of Navarra wine. If it is July and you have had the foresight to pick a handful of wild strawberries along the road from Roncesvalles, you can sprinkle them over ice cream for dessert. From Burguete the road C 135 twists south through several small villages to Pamplona.

Puente la Reina

The two great gateway branches of the Camino de Santiago converge 20 km (12.4 miles) southwest of Pamplona on route N 111 at Puente la Reina, whose 12th-century, six-arched **Romanesque bridge** over the Arga is one of the loveliest bridges in the world. The view of the bridge and village mirrored in the waters of the river on a still day is a composition of exquisite beauty. The Pilgrims' Way still follows its original path along the rua Mayor through the center of Puente la Reina, which in its day was an important market town and home to many foreign merchants, who offered fine goods from France and Italy to the steady flow of pilgrims. The **Iglesia del Crucifijo** contains one of Spain's most exceptional crucifixes—an image of Christ, thought to be of German origin, with his arms raised high on a St. Andrew's cross. The 12th-century **Iglesia de Santiago** contains a superb 14th-century wooden statue of Santiago dressed as a "foot-slogger," as Walter Starkie called those pilgrims who walked the Jacobean route, the way of St. James.

Six km (3.7 miles) northwest of Puente La Reina, near the village of Obanos, is the strange, roofless cloister and the beautiful 12th-century octagonal chapel at **Eunate**, thought to be inspired by the Holy Sepulcher in Jerusalem. The church is closely related in style to the Vera Cruz church of the Knights Templar at Segovia and the Holy Sepulcher church at Torres del Río, between Estella and Logroño.

At the northern edge of Puente la Reina is the entrance to **Señorío de Sarría**, a huge estate resembling a feudal village. Some of the finest wines of Navarra, including a wonderful dry *rosado,* are made here. Call ahead to arrange a visit; Tel: (948) 26-75-62. Just one km north of town, where the two Santiago routes actually converge, is a fine modern statue of a pilgrim and the **Mesón del Peregrino**, a good restaurant and hotel decorated in the rustic style of a pilgrims' inn.

A few kilometers west of Puente la Reina on C 111 is the Medieval village of **Mañeru**, and a few kilometers farther is **Cirauqui**. The original pilgrims' road passes through an archway at Cirauqui and up the hill to a 13th-century Romanesque church; a few feet farther on the village ends abruptly, but the cobblestone remains of the old foot trail, a uniform five meters wide—like the bridge at Puente la Reina and most of the old sections of the Camino—heads down the hill to a ruined but still walkable one-arch bridge of ancient heritage, now used by the occasional foot pilgrim intent on retracing the original route and by a Basque shepherd—wearing the traditional beret—with his flock and dog.

Estella

"Estella, la bella" goes the popular rhyme first used in the Middle Ages to describe this historic old town. And beautiful indeed is Estella's striking setting on the río Ega, 20 km (12.4 miles) west of Puente la Reina on N 111, in a valley surrounded by hills and cliffs. Many of Estella's 13,000 inhabitants are descended from rabid Carlists (a 19th-century movement, culminating in civil war in the North, to enthrone Carlos, brother of King Fernando VII, who died without a male heir in 1833). The town's streets are stacked along the hillside and graced with some of the finest Medieval monuments in northern Spain.

Aymery Picaud, a French Cluniac priest who wrote perhaps the world's first travel book in the 12th century—the fifth book of the *Codex Calixtinus*—as a guide to the Camino de Santiago, also praised Estella highly for its sweet water, good bread, excellent wine, and its "meat and fish abundant." The town became an important pilgrim stop in the 11th century, when *franco* (European, or Frankish) and Jewish merchants and artisans were enticed with tax-free status and special privileges (franking privileges!) to populate the area around the ancient Navarrese village of Lizarra, thus helping buttress the Christian frontier against the Moors.

Estella still retains vestiges of this mix of cultures in its many Medieval monuments. The *barrio franco* and the Jewish quarter were originally in the area south of the río Ega around the plaza de San Martín, where the 12th-century **Palacio de los Reyes de Navarra**, one of the oldest secular buildings in Spain, is located. The famous Romanesque capital showing Roland slaying the giant Ferragut caps a column on this building.

Also in this area, below the hill where a once-mighty castle stood until Phillip II—afraid that it might be used against his troops by the Navarros—ordered it destroyed in 1572, is a remarkable church, the 12th- and 13th-century **San Pedro de la Rua**. San Pedro is Romanesque, with Romanesque-Gothic transitional elements and a lovely Romanesque half cloister (the other half was destroyed when the castle walls came crashing down), where pilgrims who died in Estella were buried. Some of the beautifully carved capitals are worthy of note; the four twisted columns that are highly reminiscent of the great cloister of Santo Domingo de Silos (Burgos) are superb.

It is the **north portal** at the top of a long flight of stone steps, however, that really captures the imagination and illustrates how closely the brilliant, often warring, cultures of the Middle Ages were intertwined and how deeply they influenced one another. Here you will find the workmanship and designs of the Morisco, the Moor living under Christian rule: Geometric, nonrepresentational design, instead of a plethora of human and mystical creatures as in Christian style, decorates the monochrome rainbow of archivolts, and a scalloped Moorish archway worthy of Córdoba caps the doorway of this important pilgrim church.

Contrast San Pedro de la Rua with the famous jewel of 12th-century Romanesque art, the doorway of the **Iglesia de San Miguel Arcangel** across the river in the old Navarrese "Christian" quarter of the same name. Built by native Lizarra descendants to show up the foreigners, whom they despised because of their special privileges, San Miguel has a portal covered with scores of detailed stone carvings of symbolic religious and biblical scenes. In Navarra it ranks with the portals of Sangüesa and Tudela for the excellence of its carving and profusion of characters.

After a pogrom in the mid-13th century, the Jews built their ghetto below the eastern side of the castle hill and fortified it. The Santa María Jus del Castillo church in this area was once a synagogue.

Every Thursday Estella has market day in the plaza de los Fueros. In early August, during fiesta, women are allowed to run with the bulls. Two restaurants in the center of town serving good Navarrese food are **Navarra**, Gustavo de Maeztu 16, and the venerable **La Cepa**, plaza de los Fueros 18, on the second floor overlooking the square.

Yet another important stop on the Camino de Santiago is the **monastery of Irache**, 3 km (2 miles) south of Estella just off N 111 at Ayegui. Irache, believed to have its roots in the Visigothic period, was one of the earliest Benedictine monasteries and one of the first pilgrim hospitals on the Spanish portion of the road to Santiago. The massive building incorporates a blend of architectural styles accumulated over the centuries, including a 12th-century Romanesque apse, a Renaissance cloister, and a Herreran-styled tower patterned after the Escorial. Next to the monastery is a wine museum at the Castillo de Irache winery, whose *rosado* is one of the best in Navarra.

Seven km (4 miles) north of Estella, on a branch of N 111 that takes you to San Sebastián over tough but beautiful mountain roads, is the village of Abárzuza. Just northwest of the village in the hills of the Sierra de Andia is the restored **monastery of Iranzu**, which was begun in the 12th century by the Cistercians and finished in the 14th century. The lovely cloister here combines fine elements of both Romanesque and Gothic styles.

If you wish to stay near Estella, the only choice is the modern multistoried **Hotel Irache**, with a swimming pool and tennis courts, located just a kilometer west of Irache.

Toward La Rioja

Between Estella and, to the southwest, Logroño, the capital of La Rioja, there are three more towns of interest on N 111 (return to the main Pamplona–Logroño road) and the Camino de Santiago. **Los Arcos** has a 16th-century church, **La Asunción**, so crammed with Baroque gilt retables, religious statues, and paintings that almost no space is left undecorated. La Asunción's beautiful Gothic cloister, somewhat reminiscent of the cloister of Pamplona's cathedral, was built in the 15th century.

At **Torres del Río**, a few kilometers southwest, is the interesting 13th-century Romanesque **church of the Holy Sepulcher**, believed to be related to the church at Eunate.

The octagonal tower has an exceptional ribbed cupola forming an eight-pointed star on the ceiling.

The last stop on N 111 before Logroño is **Viana**, which is one of several towns in Navarra allowed to sell their wines as Rioja. Viana's 13th- and 14th-century cathedral-sized Gothic church, **Santa María**, is famous as the burial place of Cesare Borgia, who was killed in a minor skirmish near Viana in 1507. Ironically, Borgia's since-profaned tomb is outside the door of the church, and the faithful step on it as they enter. The stylized 16th-century Renaissance south portal of Santa María by Juan de Soyaz, while Plateresque, borders on Baroque; in fact, it was the inspiration for many artists in this area during the Baroque period of the 17th and 18th centuries.

A relatively new restaurant, open just a few years, is **Borgia**, in Viana at Serapio Urra—Tel: (948) 64-57-81—whose highly personalized cuisine, especially dishes based on fowl and gamebirds—duck, goose, woodcock, quail, partridge, and squab—and exceptional wine list have earned it high acclaim.

SOUTHERN NAVARRA

Olite is a splendid, beautifully restored castle town straight out of a Medieval fairy tale. About 40 km (25 miles) south of Pamplona, it can be reached on either the A 15 *autopista,* a toll road, or on N 121. Olite is one of those rare, compact, working villages that maintains its ancient atmosphere, is not overly commercialized, and is not yet so overrun by tourism that its character has changed.

This enclosed village can only be entered through a few ancient arched gateways. In addition to the wonderful, multiturreted, early-15th-century **castle of the Kings of Navarra**, Olite has two Medieval churches: the 12th-century church of San Pedro, with an unusual missile-shaped Gothic tower from a later date, and the 13th-century Santa María la Real, with its later Gothic façade and cloister abutting the castle. In the summer some of the music programs of the Festivales de Navarra are held in the plaza, with the dramatically lit castle as a backdrop.

The **Parador Príncipe de Viana**, in a restored section of the castle decorated with suits of armor, period furniture, and other trappings from a bygone age, is an excellent, comfortable base for exploring Olite and the surrounding area. An alternative, just 3 km (2 miles) north of Olite on

N 121, is the modern **Hostal Tafalla**, which looks like a big truck stop from the outside, but is a good hotel. One of its attractions is an excellent, elegant restaurant, one of the best in Navarra, run by Jesus Martinez Arellano and his family, including the octogenarian matriarch, whose flower arrangements are splendid.

The cuisine is sophisticated—you will see plenty of French touches—but it is based on seasonal ingredients of the region: a salad of tender young lettuce hearts from Tudela with superb prawns in a mustard vinaigrette; scrambled eggs and *perretxicos* (highly prized tiny spring mushrooms) with asparagus and truffles; local red peppers (*pimientos del pico*) stuffed with shellfish; and rabbit stuffed with young vegetables and served with mushroom raviolis. Try the superlative wines of Bodegas Magaña from nearby Tudela, whose merlot and merlot/cabernet sauvignon, made from vines brought from France in the 1970s, are among the best of Spain's new wines and go perfectly with this elegant food.

La Oliva, one of the earliest and most important French Cistercian monasteries in Spain, is located 23 km (14 miles) southeast of Olite (south on N 121, east on C 124) near the village of Carcastillo. The unadorned church, with its Latin cross and pointed arches, is believed to be the earliest piece of Gothic architecture in Spain. The apse is pure 12th-century Cistercian Romanesque, and the delicate, almost filigreed cloister is 15th-century Gothic.

Eighteen km (11 miles) northwest of Olite (and 11 km/7 miles northwest of Tafalla on the road to Puente la Reina) are the considerable remains of **El Cerco de Artajona**, an impressive 12th-century Templar fortress town looking somewhat like a smaller, square-towered Avila.

One of Navarra's greatest restaurants, **Atalaya**, Dabán 11, is located in the town of **Peralta**, about 20 km (12 miles) southwest of Olite on C 115. Entered through an unassuming village bar on the ground floor, Atalaya occupies the upper floors of a building overlooking the town square. All Navarra (and parts of Rioja), even during San Fermín, make the trip to Peralta to eat in Pilar Ibáñez's elegantly run dining room. The classic food of Navarra, again based on fresh, seasonal, and regional ingredients—fat, white asparagus from the Ribera region, served with fresh homemade mayonnaise, baby lamb chops, plump stuffed red peppers, artichokes, *pochas,* partridge, trout, Cantabrian fish, and perfectly cooked fresh vegetables—alternate with rabbit in tarragon sauce and other sophisticated dishes with the chef's own personal touch.

To whet your appetite for Atalaya, you can do a little sightseeing in the vicinity of Peralta. Just north and west of Peralta off C 115, a few kilometers along a country road, is the 15th-century brick castle of **Marcilla**. South of Peralta on C 115—just off the road to the left a few hundred yards before the río Ebro crossing into La Rioja at Rincón de Soto—near the village of Funes are the remains of a sizable Roman winery, complete with in-ground, stone fermentation vats. Back in Peralta you might want to taste, if not accompany a meal with, the town's powerful (15 percent) *rosado,* a gladiator's drink if there ever was one.

Tudela

Ancient Tudela, located on the Ebro 54 km (34 miles) south of Olite and 94 km (58 miles) south of Pamplona, just off the A 68 toll *autopista* that runs northwest from Barcelona to Zaragoza and on up to Logroño, Bilbao, and Burgos, is Navarra's second city (population 25,000), after Pamplona. It is the capital of the fertile (irrigated) garden, the Ribera de Navarra, which produces white asparagus, artichokes, young green garlic shoots, pimientos, and a cornucopia of other superb vegetables and fruits that distinguish the cuisine of Navarra.

Tudela is entered by a long bridge over the Ebro, some of whose 17 arches date from the 13th century. The city was once ruled by the Andalusian caliphate of Córdoba, and remained under Moorish influence longer (from the eighth to the 16th centuries) than any other place in Navarra. (Moriscos, or Moors converted to Christianity, were not expelled from Spain until the early 17th century.) Tudela had the most important Moorish and Jewish quarters in the kingdom, parts of which are still preserved in the narrow, labyrinthine streets of the Morería, the old quarter, lending the air of a Medieval warren to this section of town just southeast of the bridge. Benjámin de Tudela, the famous wandering Jew who traveled all over the Mediterranean world, was born here in the 12th century.

Tudela's **cathedral**, built on the site of a former mosque (of which it retains some vestiges), is a 12th- and 13th-century Romanesque-Gothic transitional church. The fine Romanesque cloister, whose capitals are interesting though somewhat deteriorated, dates from the 12th century. The jewel of this church is the Romanesque **Last Judgment doorway**, which rivals the doorways of Sangüesa and San Miguel in Estella in the profusion and quality of its stone-carved biblical figures. To photograph the entire doorway with its hundreds of carved figures, you will need an ultrawide-angle lens (20mm or below), since it is hemmed in by other buildings crowding the narrow streets of the old quarter.

The **Morase Hotel**, paseo de Invierno 2, is modern, functional, and close to the old quarter. It's a reasonably comfortable place to stay if you plan an extensive exploration of Tudela and the surrounding countryside. Most people drive down from the parador in Olite. The best restaurants in Tudela, both serving typical fare, including excellent local vegetable dishes like *menestra de la Mejana* (a melange of cooked vegetables from Tudela's La Mejana *huerta,* the irrigated garden plots along the Ebro), are **El Choko**, plaza de los Fueros 5, and **Mesón Julián**, La Merced 9.

GETTING AROUND

Pamplona is located 385 km (240 miles) northeast of Madrid. The usual route to Pamplona by car from the capital is to take National Route 1 (N I) from Madrid to Burgos. From Burgos to Rioja you can take the four-lane toll roads A 1 and A 68, which are fast but circuitous and expensive. If you prefer a more leisurely and pleasant drive, you can take N 120 from Burgos through Santo Domingo de la Calzada to Logroño, the capital of La Rioja, then N 111 through Estella to Pamplona.

The only direct *autopista* connection with a major capital, the A 15 to A 68 combination (of recent vintage), is to the east via Zaragoza to Barcelona, 437 km (271.5 miles) away.

If you are coming from San Sebastián, the narrow roads twist alongside rushing trout rivers through scenic valleys, over mountain passes, and through canyons; the route is scenic but slow. The other roads entering Navarra—from the Basque country to the north and west, from France to the north, from Logroño and La Rioja (and thus, from Madrid) to the southwest—are for the most part twisting mountain roads. Resign yourself to taking such drives at a slow pace, both for safety and for the exceptional number of picturesque views and sightseeing opportunities they offer. In fact, on these roads and throughout the Pyrenees of Navarra, night driving and winter driving should be undertaken with extreme caution.

Be forewarned: The parking situation in Pamplona during fiesta is chaotic, and under no circumstances should you leave anything of value in your car in Pamplona—or anywhere else in Spain, for that matter.

Pamplona has an airport at Noáin, a few kilometers from

town, which is served by daily flights from Madrid, Barcelona, and Santander. Hertz, Avis, and the Spanish car agency, Atesa, have offices in Pamplona and will arrange to deliver a car to the airport. The bus station is near the Ciudadela, only a few blocks southwest of the plaza del Castillo. The railway station, with connections to Madrid, Irún, Zaragoza, and other major cities, is a five-minute taxi ride from the center of town.

It can be very hot in Pamplona during fiesta, but it can also get very cold and rainy; the climate is Atlantic Pyrenean. Along with light summer clothing, take a warm sweater, an impermeable jacket, an umbrella, and, of course, a white shirt and white pants, if you want to look like a real *pamplonica*.

ACCOMMODATIONS REFERENCE

When dialing telephone numbers in Spain from outside the country, drop the 9 in the area code.

► **Hostal Burguete**. Unica 51, 31640 **Burguete** (Navarra). Tel: (948) 76-00-05.

► **Eslava**. Plaza Virgen de la O 7, 31001 **Pamplona**. Tel: (948) 22-22-70.

► **Parador Fernando de Aragón**. 50680 **Sos del Rey Católico** (Zaragoza, Aragón). Tel: (948) 88-80-11.

► **Irache**. Carretera de Logroño km 43, 31200 **Estella** (Ayegui). Tel: (948) 55-11-50; Fax: (948) 55-47-54.

► **Isaba**. 31417 **Isaba**. Tel: (948) 89-30-00.

► **Hospederia de Leyre**. Monastery of Leyre, 31410 **Yesa**. Tel: (948) 88-41-00.

► **Maisonnave**. Nueva 20, 31001 **Pamplona**. Tel: (948) 22-26-00; Telex: 37994.

► **Mesón del Peregrino**. Carretera Pamplona-Logroño km 23, 31100 **Puente la Reina**. Tel: (948) 34-00-75.

► **Morase**. Paseo de Invierno 2, 31500 **Tudela**. Tel: (948) 82-17-00.

► **Orhi**. Leyre 7, 31002 **Pamplona**. Tel: (948) 22-85-00.

► **Parador Príncipe de Viana**. Plaza de los Teobaldos 2, 31390 **Olite**. Tel: (948) 74-00-00.

► **Hostal Tafalla**. Carretera de Zaragoza km 38, 31300 **Tafalla**. Tel: (948) 70-03-00.

► **Tres Reyes**. Jardines de la Taconera, 31001 **Pamplona**. Tel: (948) 22-66-00; Telex: 37720.

► **Yoldi**. Avenida San Ignacio 11, 31002 **Pamplona**. Tel: (948) 22-48-00.

ARAGON

By Frank Shiell

Frank Shiell, a New York writer, is a graduate of the University of Madrid. He is fluent in Spanish and travels frequently throughout Spain.

Aragón covers about one-tenth of Spain's land—1,815 square miles—but is home to just 1.2 million, or only about 3 percent, of its inhabitants.

In the past few decades thousands of Aragonese have emigrated to industrial Catalonia to seek a more prosperous life, leaving some areas, especially the southern province of Teruel, sparsely populated. With Spain's 1976 constitutional reorganization of the country into 17 "autonomous communities," Aragón comprises three inland provinces in northeastern Spain, spreading south from the Pyrenees: north to south, they are Huesca, Zaragoza, and Teruel. To the east Aragón borders the regions of Catalonia and Valencia; to the west, the regions of Navarra, La Rioja, and Castilla-León.

Unlike their neighbors in Catalonia, the Aragonese speak Castilian Spanish. Characteristic of the region is the charming and unusual way the people use the diminutive *ico* instead of *ito*—for example, *un momentico* instead of *un momentito.* Aragón could be considered a world in itself; that's the way the Aragonese, or Maños, as they call themselves, feel about it.

The Aragonese are known for their heartiness, exemplified by their energetic and truly strenuous regional dance, *la jota.* Accompanying the dance are songs that are melodic, nostalgic, and energetic. Also potent are the famed wines from the *bodegas* of the town of Cariñena, just 50 km (30 miles) southeast of the city of Zaragoza.

In general, the people are somewhat reserved, yet trustworthy and sincere, and, as many of them say, "We, unlike the Catalans, expect nothing in return."

In the 12th century, when the Kingdom of Aragón became a great Mediterranean power, its capital was the thriving seaport of Barcelona, and its territories encompassed Catalonia and Valencia, spreading as far south as Murcia. The kingdom controlled the Balearic Islands, and even colonized as far east as Sardinia, Naples, and Sicily.

Aragón expanded even more in the 15th century, when it was united with the central region of Castile as a result of the marriage of Fernando de Aragón and Isabel la Católica, known subsequently as the Catholic Monarchs. (Their daughter, Catherine of Aragón, married England's King Henry VIII and soon gave birth to a child who became Queen Mary I ["Bloody Mary"]).

After Spain discovered the New World, most commerce shifted from the then Aragonese capital of Barcelona to Spain's Atlantic coast. Over time, the Kingdom of Aragón lost much of its influence and, over the years, most of its territory.

Today, Aragón is a region of extremely varied landscapes—the Pyrenees of Huesca province, vast plains, the fertile Ebro valley of Zaragoza, and the rugged, verdant southern province of Teruel. Agriculture is important to Aragón. The province of Zaragoza is Spain's largest grower of corn. There are, as well, vast fields of wheat, barley, oats, sunflowers, and such spices as rosemary, chamomile, thyme, and *lavanda,* from which cologne is made.

MAJOR INTEREST

Zaragoza city
Basílica de Nuestra Señora del Pilar
"La Seo" cathedral
Roman ruins
Iglesia de Santa María Magdalena
Public market
El Tubo district
Museo Camón Aznar
Aljafería palace
Sástago palace

Goya's house in Fuendetodos

Holy Week festival in Calanda

Parque Nacional de Ordesa for hiking

The town of Teruel

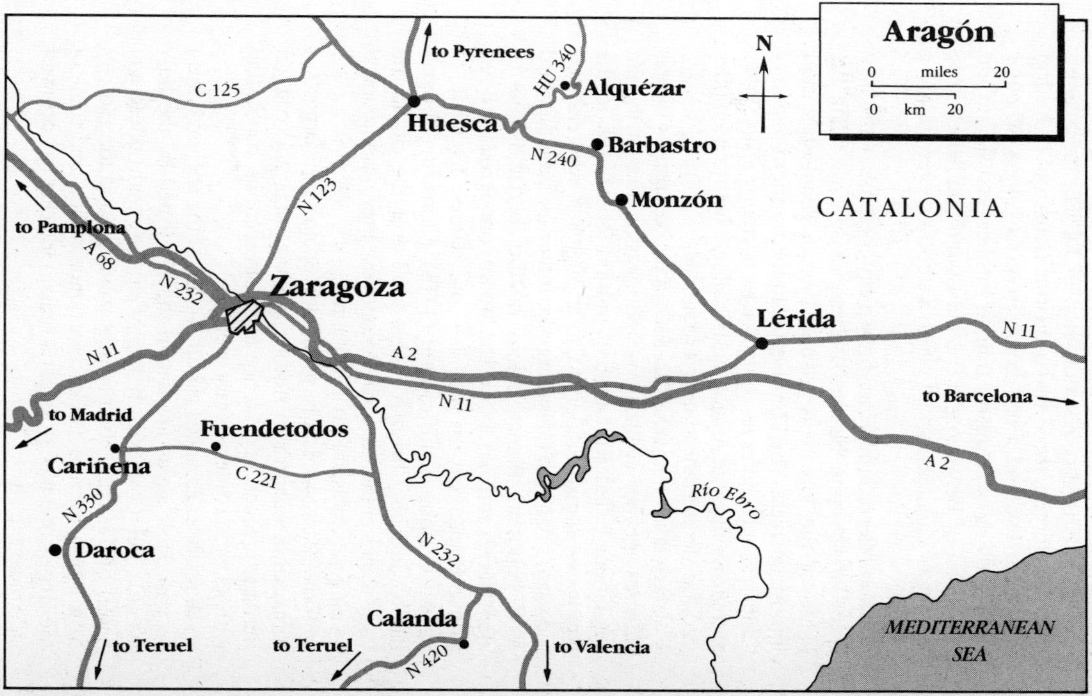
Aragón
0 miles 20
0 km 20
N
CATALONIA
to Pyrenees
HU 340
Alquézar
Huesca
Barbastro
N 240
Monzón
C 125
N 123
to Pamplona
A 68
N 232
Zaragoza
Lérida
N 11
A 2
N 11
to Barcelona
to Madrid
Fuendetodos
Cariñena
C 221
A 2
N 330
Río Ebro
Daroca
N 232
Calanda
to Teruel
to Teruel
N 420
to Valencia
MEDITERRANEAN SEA

The City of Zaragoza

Aragón's capital city, Zaragoza, is almost in the center of the region, halfway between Madrid and Barcelona along highway N II. It is also a station stop of RENFE, the Spanish national railroad, three and a quarter hours out of Madrid and about two and a half hours from Barcelona. Whether you're driving or taking the train or bus between Madrid and Barcelona or between the Basque Country and Barcelona, the city of Zaragoza is well worth a stopover, even for just a night.

Often referred to as the "brown city" because of the dark color of its stone buildings, Zaragoza spreads along the banks of the Ebro, one of the Iberian Peninsula's most important rivers. The Ebro begins in the northern region of Cantabria and, along its route across northern Spain, flows and grows through Aragón and Catalonia before it empties into the Mediterranean near Tarragona.

Zaragoza is often called La Señora de las Cuatro Culturas (mistress of four civilizations). She was an ancient Iberian settlement called Sálduba and around 24 B.C. fell to the legions of Roman Emperor Caesar Augustus, who changed the town's name to Caesaraugusta. It then became the third most important Roman colony on the Iberian Peninsula, after Mérida and Tarragona. The Moors conquered the flourishing Roman city in A.D. 714 and altered its name to Sarakusta. Four centuries later (1118), Alfonso I, "El Batallador," and his Christian troops took over the city in the early stages of the Christian Reconquest; they repronounced its name to Zaragoza (thar-a-GO-tha).

Today, Zaragoza is a bustling city (Spain's fifth largest). A remarkable mixture of historic, architectural, and cultural heritage is much in evidence in its old sections, contrasting with its wide contemporary avenues.

The core of Zaragoza is built on top of the ancient Roman section. Most sights are within the U formed by the busy avenida del Coso, which begins at the south side (right bank) of the Ebro, then swings south around the old city. Now a busy avenue, El Coso was once walled, and some of the large stone-block ramparts remain intact at its northwest side, near the river.

When you arrive, the first thing to head for is the **Basílica de Nuestra Señora del Pilar**, named for the holy patroness of Spain. This immense 17th-century Baroque extravaganza, alongside the river and fronting the plaza del Pilar, is the colossal protagonist of the city. If you arrive in Zaragoza at

9:00 A.M., noon, or 8:00 P.M., just follow the sound of the woman's voice calling the faithful to mass, broadcast over a loudspeaker from the basilica and heard practically all over town. (For the best view of the basilica and its countless spires intermingled with a dozen gigantic, mosaic-covered domes, cross to the far side of either of two nearby bridges, the Puente de Santiago and the Puente Piedra.)

Legend has it that in A.D. 40 the Virgin appeared on a pillar (hence her name) to Saint James (Santiago), who happened to be visiting Zaragoza at the time. Even today, the basilica is one of the two most important pilgrimages in all Spain. (The other is the cathedral in Santiago de Compostela in the northwestern region of Galicia.) Each receives hundreds of thousands of religious visitors a year.

The center of attention in Zaragoza's gigantic basilica is the surprisingly small statue of the Virgen del Pilar, only about three feet high. She stands on a brown Carrara marble pillar on the right side of the altar of her own chapel. Her elaborate cone-shaped dress (*manta*) is changed daily from a wardrobe that numbers in the hundreds. Directly behind her chapel is a small silver-rimmed oval hole through which devotees can kiss or touch an exposed part of the marble pillar itself.

There are many legends about the section of the río Ebro that slides beside the basilica. Locals say it flows as quietly as possible so as not to disturb El Pilar. Once a bus fell off the bridge and is said to have disappeared into Zaragoza's version of the Bermuda Triangle. It is said, too, that despite its obvious course the river also flows to the Mediterranean through another channel deep underground.

On the second and twelfth days of each month—the Virgen del Pilar appeared to Santiago on the second and her Saint's day is October 12—her *manta* is removed to reveal the pillar upon which she stands. October 12, the anniversary of Christopher Columbus's discovery of the New World, is Zaragoza's most important annual celebration. Festivities overwhelm the city and its visitors. In Spain this holiday is known as El Día de la Hispanidad (Hispanic Day). This joint celebration is all the more important to the citizens of Zaragoza because Columbus took a small chunk of the Virgin's marble pillar along with him as a good luck charm on his successful voyage of discovery.

Goya (Francisco de Goya y Lucientes), a native of the nearby village of Fuendetodos (see below), was commissioned to paint the cupolas of the basilica. First, in 1771, he painted a fresco in the section of the high ceiling on the far east side, in front of the giant organ. Then in 1777 he painted one cupola, called *Regina Martyrum,* in the center of the north nave. After a quarrel with the bishop, Goya abandoned his work and, leaving the other cupolas blank, travelled to Madrid and took up his post as court painter.

In the far left rear (northeast) corner of the basilica, you can board an elevator for an ascent to the top of a turret. From there, a climb up quite a few spiral stairs brings you to a wonderful view of the complicated rooftop of the basilica, the río Ebro, and the city of Zaragoza.

Just across the street east of the basilica is a small building, El Templete, that houses one of the city's tourist information offices. One block farther east, on the other side of one of the city's main streets, Don Jaime I, is Zaragoza's **Cathedral del Salvador**, known as La Seo, which combines Gothic, Churrigueresque, and Mudejar design. It is presently closed for restoration, scheduled for completion by Spain's momentous year of 1992 (the fifth centennial of the discovery of the Americas).

Curiously, in 1988 during construction of the new **Via Romana Hotel** (almost adjacent to La Seo), excavators discovered a **Roman forum**. The site is about a thousand square feet in area and evidently extends farther to underground parts unknown. (That's why the hotel couldn't construct underground parking facilities.) The Roman forum is now viewable and is in the process of restoration, also scheduled for inauguration in 1992.

A little farther east of La Seo is the **Iglesia de Santa María Magdalena**, a 14th-century Mudejar architectural masterpiece, with an imposing square tower that is intricately decorated with green, white, and blue tiles. It is known as the church of the rooster because of its weathervane. In the nearby plaza de Lanuza, just southwest of the plaza del Pilar, is the lively and lovely **Mercado Central de Lanuza**, a public market put up in 1904 with a flourish of Eiffel-like wrought iron. During the mornings it is thronged with butchers, fishmongers, and every other kind of vendor, as well as the residents who come to buy here.

If you walk south just a few blocks from the basilica, you will enter a labyrinth of tiny pedestrian streets known as **El Tubo**, the oldest section of Zaragoza, which is well worth a meander day or night. Among the the countless side-by-side shops, restaurants, *tascas* (taverns), and *tapas* bars is a famous and fun café cantante, **El Plata**. It's one of Zaragoza's oldest cafés (more than a hundred years). Traditional nightclub revues are still performed, with *paso doble* dancing and singers performing lyrical, timeless, and piquant songs of yesteryear, as well as contemporary numbers with humorous lyrics. The more Spanish you know, the more kick you'll get out of it; nevertheless, the place is fun and congenial, and open until the wee hours.

The **Museo Camón Aznar** is housed in a splendid Renaissance building in El Tubo, at Espoz y Mina 23. Aznar, who died in the 1970s, was a famous art historian who was considered to be the world's top authority on Goya. Included in the permanent art collection here are works of Goya and Velázquez and other masterpieces Aznar received as gifts or was able to purchase at low prices because of his stature in the art world.

Walking just out of the south side of El Tubo and crossing avenida del Coso, you emerge into another world—that of the broad **plaza de España** and the elegant tree-lined avenue called la Independencia, with its fancy boutiques, department stores, restaurants, and residences.

La Independencia stretches about six long blocks to the plaza de Aragón traffic circle. Along the segment of avenida César Augusto that runs parallel to la Independencia to the west are more good stores, cafés, and the large, modern convention-style **Meliá Zaragoza Corona Hotel.** (Don't be confused by the fact that the streets change both names and personalities on either side of la Independencia.)

From la Independencia, a block before the plaza de Aragón, turn left (east) onto Joaquín Costa and walk a few blocks until you reach the small tree-shaded plaza de los Sitios. Tranquil today, this was a site of bloody battles in 1808 and 1809 when Zaragozanos defended their city against Napoleon's invading troops. A statue in the center of the plaza commemorates the fallen heroes. Just before the plaza de los Sitios, you will come to the belle-epoque **Gran Hotel Zaragoza.** Declared a historic monument, this is the city's aristocrat of hotels; if you don't stay here, it merits at least a visit for cocktails or tea, or just to see the elegant lobby.

West of El Tubo is one of Zaragoza's biggest surprises: the well-restored 11th-century **Aljafería**, residence of the ruling caliphs when Zaragoza was the Moorish capital of northern Spain. This astounding example of Moorish architecture, with its elaborate geometric and intricate honeycomb fantasy designs, its arches, and its patio, fountains, pools, and orange trees, is in a way comparable to the Alhambra in Granada. In the 15th century the Catholic Monarchs built a palace on the second floor. Its remarkable coffered ceiling has a pineapple motif recalling the pineapples brought back from America.

On El Coso near the plaza de España is the **Casa de los Condes de Sástago**, a splendid example of Aragonese Renaissance architecture restored in 1989. Built in the 16th century by the count of Sástago, viceroy of Aragón (whose houseguests included King Philip II), it is now a center for art exhibits and theatrical performances. The building itself is a sight to see, with its tapestries, lavishly painted ceiling in the second-floor throne room, and walls richly decorated with tiles from the Zaragozan provincial town of Muel. Windows on the right side of the façade are bordered in bright blue as a remembrance of ancient tradition and superstition in the mountains of Aragón, where until recently farmers painted blue stripes over the whitewashed walls of the stables in order to keep insects and bad spirits away from the farm animals. A section of the building houses the provincial government of Zaragoza, with a marvelous marble statue in its lobby of George slaying the dragon.

The Aragonese Pyrenees

Jaca, 140 km (85 miles) north of Zaragoza on route N 330, is most often visited as a jumping-off point for excursions into the nearby mountains. The busy tourist office on paseo Calvo Sotelo provides bus schedules to outlying villages and ski resorts and maps of nearby hiking trails. Those wishing to enjoy nature by day but to return to civilization by night can do no better than the very civilized **Gran Hotel**, in the center of town and with amenities that include a swimming pool.

Before you set out for the wilderness, though, take time to explore Jaca's 11th-century cathedral, one of the oldest in Spain and the first to be constructed in the Romanesque style. The grandness of this religious edifice befits Jaca, whose Christian citizenry valiantly fought off the Moors occupying their town in 761, centuries before they were banished from the rest of the peninsula. Modern-day Jaca commemorates the feat with a lively procession on the first Friday of May.

Some of the best hiking in the region—in fact, in all of Spain—is to be had on the trails of the **Parque Nacional de Ordesa**. The main park office is just outside the village of Torla, about 60 km (37 miles) east of Jaca. The most spectacular path is the Circo Soasa, which takes you on a seven-hour circuit of the park—along the ridges of dizzingly high canyons, past waterfalls, and around the base of the Sierra de las Cutas.

Several mountain villages within an easy drive of Jaca provide a refreshing combination of Old World charm and breathtaking scenery. **Benasque**, on the eastern side of the park about 100 km (62 miles) from Jaca, is very pretty and a good base for walks along the río Esera. **Hecho**, 50 km (30 miles) northwest of Jaca and connected by daily bus service, is surrounded by beautiful mountain scenery. What many skiers consider to be the best slopes in the Pyrenees are just 30 km (18 miles) north of Jaca in Astun/Candanchu, actually two neighboring resorts with all facilities. These include, in Candanchu, a charming mountain hotel appropriately called the **Edelweiss.**

Another lovely mountain village is **Alquézar**, 44 km (27 miles) east of the rather dull little city of Huesca. Alquézar's narrow lanes open to magnificent valley views, and its 16th-century church is surrounded in part by the ruined walls of the chapel that Christians built when they recaptured the village from the Moors in the 10th century.

South of Zaragoza

A nice trip to make from Zaragoza is the one to the tiny, tranquil, and picturesque country town of **Fuendetodos** (about 40 km/25 miles south of the city). The great painter Goya was born here, in 1746, and his house is maintained as it was when he lived and worked in it as a youth. Just down the street in an old country house is a new museum that displays 80 of his etchings.

Another famous son of the province of Zaragoza is the film director Luis Buñuel, who died in 1983. Buñuel was a native of **Calanda.** This rather ugly little place, about 100 km (60 miles) southeast of the city of Zaragoza, celebrates one of the strangest festivals in Spain: During Holy Week, beginning Thursday at midnight, teams of drummers parade the streets, drumming nonstop until the following Saturday; by then, their fingers are bleeding all over their drums. The only decent place to stay in town is the 34-room **Balfagón.**

Teruel, 184 km (110 miles) south of Zaragoza and three hours away by twice-daily train service, is the unofficial capital of lower Aragón. It is well worth a visit to see its majestic 13th-century cathedral, Mudejar towers, and centuries-old houses. Teruel's ancient streets and plazas have been the scene of some of Spain's most ardent battles. The town was sacked by the Romans, conquered, with bloody opposition, by the Moors, and locked in battle during the Civil War. It is also the setting of a tragic love story played out by Spain's own Romeo and Juliet, two 13th-century youths named Isabel de Segura and Diego de Marcilla. You can see the doomed young lovers, who died of grief when her father forced her to marry a rich suitor, through the glass front of the tomb they share in the funerary chapel of the Iglesia de San Pedro. The government-run **Parador Nacional de Teruel**—a modern hotel surrounded by lovely gardens—is by far the best place in town to spend the night or to have a meal. It is located just north of the center on route N 234.

GETTING AROUND

Aragón's only airport is in its capital city of Zaragoza, with service by Aviaco (Spain's domestic airline) from Madrid, Barcelona, and Jerez de la Frontera. It is about a 20-minute ride from the airport to the city center.

RENFE (the Spanish national railroad system), on its Madrid–Barcelona route, makes a stop at Zaragoza's Estación in the center of the city.

The best way to get around the old and most interesting part of Zaragoza is by walking; in fact, within El Tubo it's the only way. A car is a nuisance in the city. The best solution is to garage it while you're there. (Local taxis and buses are plentiful.)

However, the best way to travel around the region of Aragón is by rental car. Roads are good, ranging from four-lane superhighways to narrow but well-paved two-lane roads, and there are plenty of picturesque small towns to visit.

It's important to know that with major car-rental companies, such as Avis and Hertz, the rates are about half if you make your reservations by phone from outside of Spain with two days advance notice, rather than making your reservations while you are already in Spain. If you're driving one way, there is usually no drop-off charge.

ACCOMMODATIONS REFERENCE

When dialing telephone numbers from outside the country, drop the 9 in the area code.

► **Balfagón.** Carretera Alcolea a Tarragona 404, 44570 **Calanda** (Teruel). Tel: (974) 84-63-12.

► **Edelweiss.** Candanchu, 22889 **Huesca.** Tel: (974) 37-32-00.

► **Gran Hotel.** Paseo del Generalíssimo Franco 1, 22700 **Jaca.** Tel: (974) 36-09-00.

► **Gran Hotel Zaragoza.** Joaquín Costa 5, 50001 **Zaragoza.** Tel: (976) 22-19-01.

► **Meliá Zaragoza Corona.** Avenida César Augusto 13, 50004 **Zaragoza.** Tel: (976) 43-01-00.

► **Parador Nacional de Teruel.** 44000 **Teruel.** Tel: (974) 60-18-00.

► **Via Romana Hotel.** Don Jaime I 54-56, 50001 **Zaragoza.** Tel: (976) 39-82-15.

BARCELONA

By Stephen O'Shea

Stephen O'Shea is a Paris-based writer who often travels to Spain. He is a contributor to The Penguin Guide to France.

Over the last ten years the word has spread: Barcelona, the booming industrial metropolis of a newly democratic Spain, is currently outstripping its rivals in urban renewal, artistic innovation, and, above all else, exuberance. A sprawling port of 1.75 million inhabitants, the City of the Counts has emerged from the inhibiting years of Franco's rule to move to center stage in Europe's cultural life. Still passionately attached to its distinct Catalan identity and language, the city teems with cosmopolitan influences, all the while displaying a local tradition that encompasses a wide breadth of museums, galleries, and public art projects, as well as a striking architectural heritage that ranges from accomplished Gothic to the inspired madness of Antoni Gaudí. Visitors in search of somnolent folklore here are in for a rude awakening. A great city too long overlooked, Barcelona has come to emulate that quintessential Catalan, Salvador Dalí: In the packed streets, trendy nightspots, and refurbished neighborhoods, the residents of Catalonia's capital are now unabashedly strutting their stuff.

MAJOR INTEREST

Neighborhoods
Barri Gòtic
Eixample
The Ramblas

Museums
Museu d'Art de Catalunya

Museu Picasso
Fundació Joan Miró

Churches
Cathedral
Santa Maria del Mar
Sagrada Família

Secular architecture
Palau de la Música Catalana
La Pedrera
"Manzana de la Discòrdia"

Parks
Parc Güell
Montjuïc
Parc de la Ciutadella

At Barcelona's harbor front stands a tall column crowned by a statue of Christopher Columbus staring intently out to sea. Although there is some historical justification for the monument—after Columbus's first voyage to the New World, he sailed back to Barcelona in order to report his findings to Ferdinand and Isabella—the statue has a touch of the absurd, too, for Columbus is gazing eastward, out over the well-explored waters of the Mediterranean toward Italy. Add to that the injustice dealt to the seafaring merchants of Catalonia by the Castilian Queen Isabella, whose will specified that they be barred from the lucrative trade with the New World (a prohibition that remained in effect until 1778), and it's a wonder that Columbus is given pride of place anywhere in the city.

But that would be to underestimate the Catalan capacity for living with contradictions. Observers such as Alastair Boyd, in his *Essence of Catalonia,* have often praised Barcelona's knack for wedding opposites in compromise, claiming that it reflects the fight in the national soul between the Catalan notions of *seny,* the commonsensical, business-like side of a merchant people, and *rauxa,* their anarchic, Dionysian impulse to have fun. Indeed, both culture and history have made Barcelona a forum of conflicting influences that goes far beyond erecting a statue to someone whose discoveries led indirectly to a two-century economic downturn.

Long the most sophisticated city on the Iberian Peninsula, the most "European" in its outlook, and the most self-assured in its commercial might, for much of its history Barcelona has been a political dwarf, the capital of a stateless nation with little power over its own destiny. Despite a palpable pride in past victories, the national anthem of Catalonia—"Els Segadors" (the reapers)—is almost Celtic in its reminder of past disasters, having first been sung during a doomed 17th-century revolt against the Castilian ascendancy.

That long-standing conflict—Castile versus Catalonia—runs like a leitmotiv through the history of the city and provides a fillip to Catalan nationalism. Distinct from their fellow Iberians in being resolutely Mediterranean—indeed, the Catalan language is more closely related to the Provençal of France's coast than to the Castilian of Spain's interior—the Catalans, now about six million strong, have long considered themselves a people apart. Once an autonomous ally of the kingdom of Aragón, Catalonia ruled a Medieval maritime empire that overshadowed those of Genoa and Venice. The Catalan flag, four red bars on a field of yellow, dates from the 11th century and is Europe's oldest national banner. When dynastic politics of the 15th century led to the region's absorption into a Castile-dominated federation, Catalan self-government, which included a protoparliament of 100 Barcelona notables known as the Consell del Cent, went into a long eclipse.

That misfortune, however, failed to diminish national feeling, as might have happened to people less endowed with the survival schizophrenia of *seny* and *rauxa*. Instead, subject Barcelona looked upon imperial Madrid as a loutish upstart, and "provincial" Catalonia remained the most cosmopolitan of all Spain's diverse regions, Castile included. The Catalan language, despite attempts by the Bourbons (in 1716) and Franco (in the 1940s) to stamp it out, remains a potent vehicle for regional identity. Today most official business here is conducted in Catalan, though this should not trouble visitors to Barcelona. As Catalan is a Romance language, unlike the mysterious tongue of the neighboring Basques, it abounds in cognates to French and Spanish, making menu-reading and sign-deciphering fairly easy. In addition, all Catalans can speak, however reluctantly, Castilian Spanish, and many have a good knowledge of French and English. (In this chapter we use Catalan place names, as they are more likely to be found on signs and maps.)

Added to the region's linguistic and nationalist contrasts, which many Catalans compare to Quebec's particularities within the Canadian federation, are the surprising contradictions to be found in Barcelona's urban landscape.

Known throughout Spain as the city of wily merchants and cool-headed capitalists, Barcelona is nonetheless the site of some of the wildest architectural extravagances in Europe, and has been a breeding ground for radical ideology and avant-garde art. And, in yet another contradiction, the source of Barcelona's wealth—its link to the sea—seems to have been studiously ignored in civic culture and planning until recently, when thoughtful urbanists began reclaiming the waterfront for the citizens.

Perhaps the contrast first noticed by visitors to Barcelona lies in the way the city is physically organized. Nature made the narrow plain that slopes up to the foot of the Sierra de Collcerola from the sea, but it was man who built two distinctive towns there. The oldest part of the city, called the Barri Gòtic (the Gothic quarter), occupies a small rise once known as Monte Taber, a few hundred yards from the shore. Originally a Carthaginian settlement, founded by the prominent Barca family of Hannibal's day, it later fell under the sway of the Romans, becoming a minor provincial town with a grandiose name, Colonia Julia Augusta Paterna Faventia Barcino. Successive waves of conquest—by the Visigoths, the Moors, the Franks—swept over the bustling port, but the Roman enclosure of cyclopean walls, the remnants of which can still be seen, kept the unity of the city.

Barcelona's golden age of independence and pan-Mediterranean influence (its political reach stretched as far as Athens in the 1300s) lent the impetus to expand the city. Two successive Medieval ramparts were built to contain the burgeoning town, stretching from the present-day avinguda del Paral-lel, in the south, to the northern limit marked by the Parc de la Ciutadella. All of this is easily discernible, for the extensive Ciutat Vella, or old town, is unmistakably preindustrial, a warren of tiny streets bordered by lines of balconies from which lush green plants hang down to seek the shafts of noonday sunlight. Yet, just a few blocks inland, the intimacy of the old town gives way to the Eixample (enlargement), an enormous grid of 19th-century boulevards laid out in a fit of rationality by Ildefons Cerdà. It's as if two cultures alien to each other happened to build on the same coastal plain, for the Eixample is as airy and expansive as the old town is cramped and quaint.

To make sense of Barcelona, it's best to visit the old town first, starting at the central plaça de Catalunya and making your way east (seaward) along the entertaining pedestrian thoroughfare known as Las Ramblas. To the south of Las Ramblas, in the old town, which runs to the foot of the seaside prominence called Montjuïc, lies a scruffy neighborhood of sinuous streets and unpretentious charm. Just north of Las Ramblas the old town becomes a maze of small shops and

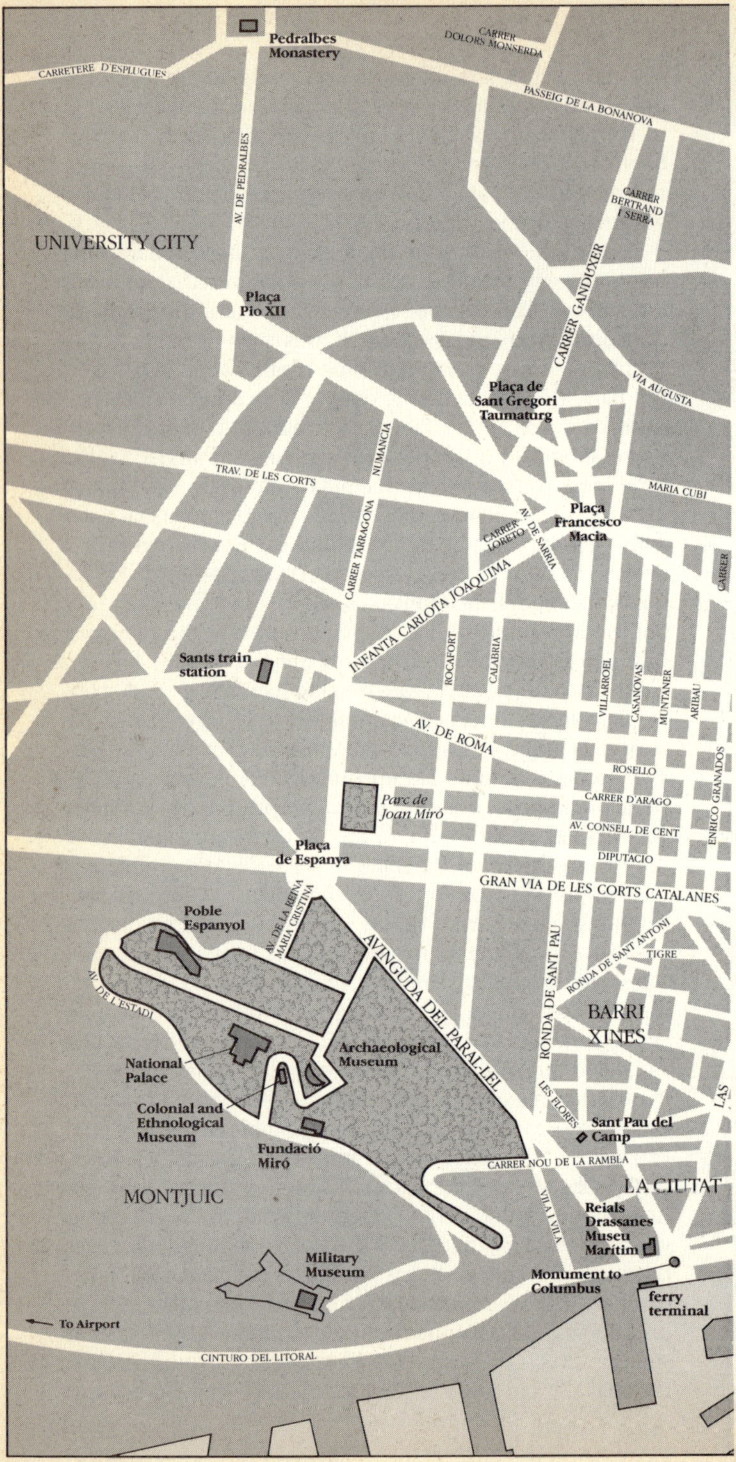

Pedralbes Monastery
CARRER DOLORS MONSERDA
CARRETERE D'ESPLUGUES
PASSEIG DE LA BONANOVA
AV. DE PEDRALBES
CARRER BERTRAND I SERRA
UNIVERSITY CITY
CARRER GANDUXER
Plaça Pio XII
VIA AUGUSTA
Plaça de Sant Gregori Taumaturg
NUMANCIA
TRAV. DE LES CORTS
MARIA CUBI
Plaça Francesco Macia
CARRER LORETO
AV. DE SARRIA
CARRER TARRAGONA
INFANTA CARLOTA JOAQUIMA
CARRER
Sants train station
ROCAFORT
CALABRIA
VILLARROEL
CASANOVAS
MUNTANER
ARIBAU
AV. DE ROMA
ROSELLO
Parc de Joan Miró
CARRER D'ARAGO
AV. CONSELL DE CENT
ENRICO GRANADOS
Plaça de Espanya
DIPUTACIO
GRAN VIA DE LES CORTS CATALANES
Poble Espanyol
AV. DE LA REINA MARIA CRISTINA
AVINGUDA DEL PARAL-LEL
RONDA DE SANT PAU
RONDA DE SANT ANTONI
TIGRE
AV. DE L'ESTADI
BARRI XINES
National Palace
Archaeological Museum
Colonial and Ethnological Museum
LES FLORES
LAS
Sant Pau del Camp
Fundació Miró
CARRER NOU DE LA RAMBLA
MONTJUIC
LA CIUTAT
VILA I VILA
Reials Drassanes Museu Marítim
Military Museum
Monument to Columbus
ferry terminal
To Airport
CINTURO DEL LITORAL

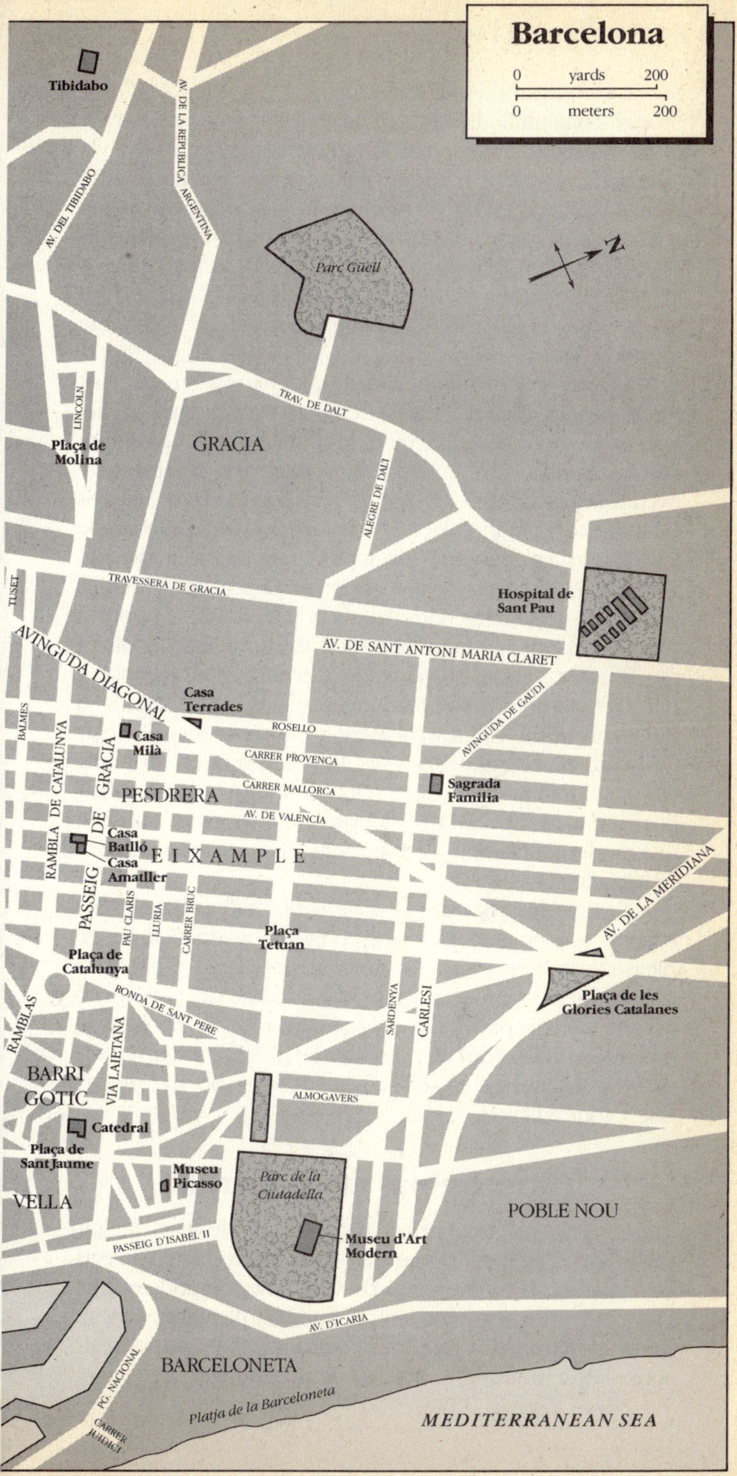
Barcelona
0 yards 200
0 meters 200
N
Tibidabo
AV. DE LA REPUBLICA ARGENTINA
AV. DEL TIBIDABO
Parc Güell
TRAV. DE DALT
LINCOLN
Plaça de Molina
GRACIA
ALEGRE DE DALT
TUSET
TRAVESSERA DE GRACIA
Hospital de Sant Pau
AV. DE SANT ANTONI MARIA CLARET
AVINGUDA DIAGONAL
Casa Terrades
BALMES
Casa Milà
ROSELLO
AVINGUDA DE GAUDI
CARRER PROVENCA
RAMBLA DE CATALUNYA
PASSEIG DE GRACIA
Sagrada Familia
CARRER MALLORCA
PESDRERA
AV. DE VALENCIA
Casa Batlló
Casa Amatller
EIXAMPLE
PAU CLARIS
LLURIA
CARRER BRUC
Plaça Tetuan
AV. DE LA MERIDIANA
Plaça de Catalunya
RONDA DE SANT PERE
Plaça de les Glories Catalanes
SARDENYA
CARLESI
RAMBLAS
BARRI GOTIC
VIA LAIETANA
ALMOGAVERS
Catedral
Plaça de Sant Jaume
Museu Picasso
Parc de la Ciutadella
VELLA
POBLE NOU
Museu d'Art Modern
PASSEIG D'ISABEL II
AV. D'ICARIA
BARCELONETA
PG. NACIONAL
Platja de la Barceloneta
MEDITERRANEAN SEA
CARRER JUDICI

busy commercial alleyways, its crowning glory the Barri Gòtic proper, containing the city's secular Gothic wonders as well as its imposing cathedral. Still farther north, across the vía Laietana, a modern boulevard with an ancient name (the Laietana were the Bronze Age people who first settled the coastal plain), stands the last third of the old town, its down-to-earth marketplaces and humble streets sharing pride of place with a soaring ecclesiastical masterpiece (the church of Santa Maria del Mar) and a treasure house of modern art (the Museu Picasso).

After this walk through picturesque, narrow streets, visit the Eixample, especially if you enjoy luxury shopping, bars and cafés for the well-heeled, and the turn-of-the-century fantasy of Modernist architecture. A huge grid of streets cut by the avinguda de la Diagonal and bounded on the east (just inland from the plaça de Catalunya) by the Gran Vía de les Corts Catalanes, the Eixample stretches from the old town to the foothills of the Sierra de Collcerola. The hills themselves hold attractions that show Barcelona's capacity to surprise: Gaudí's strange Parc Güell, the towering lookout of the Tibidabo, and the lovely monastery of Pedralbes. Yet the hill that will occupy you the longest stands by the seaside to the south of the old town—Montjuïc, a repository of richly endowed museums. This wooded hill also offers stunning views of Barcelona as it spreads from its industrial harborfront west through the old town, and westward still past the modern Eixample to the limits of the rugged Catalan hinterland.

A final section of our coverage is devoted to Barcelona's harbor, a long-neglected area now being opened up to pleasure-seekers from the densely populated plain. Like Christopher Columbus staring out to sea, the city now seems poised to look beyond itself, ready to receive the creative and the curious from all points of the globe. That, given the city's long history of self-sufficiency, may be Barcelona's finest contradiction.

The Ramblas and Environs

The chaotic meeting place of the Eixample and the old town—and the heart of the city—is an appropriately irregular expanse called the **plaça de Catalunya**. Remodeled several times over the past century and still pleasantly lacking the cold dignity that usually accompanies the status of main square of a metropolis, the loud and bustling plaça is lined with banks, outdoor cafés, and the inevitable Corte Inglés department store. In the large, pigeon-filled central plaza, visitors brave enough to drink from the monumental fountains are said to become honorary citizens of Barcelona. Together with the Ramblas, a series of shaded walkways leading from it, the plaça de Catalunya is the center of Barcelona life. No political gathering of any importance and no outpouring of popular rage or joy takes place anywhere else but in this slightly ungainly plaza. In recent years hundreds of thousands have gathered here to celebrate the passing of a dictator (the death of Generalíssimo Francisco Franco on November 20, 1975) and the return of Catalan leader Josep Tarradellas (October 23, 1977) from exile in Mexico.

If the plaça de Catalunya is the setting for extraordinary events in the life of the city, then the Ramblas perform the same function for everyday existence in Barcelona. The end-to-end avenues—respectively, from west to east: rambla Canaletes, dels Estudis, de Sant Josep, dels Caputxins, and de Santa Mónica—form a single thoroughfare almost a mile long that runs along the trace of a Medieval rampart from the plaça de Catalunya to the Columbus monument at the waterfront. It gives the people of Barcelona an ideal place to enact the Iberian ritual of *paseo,* the sunset stroll before the late-evening meal. This tree-lined avenue, with its wide pedestrian area in the middle (there are narrow service streets running along each side), is one of the most entertaining urban environments in southern Europe, rewarding the observant with an effortless study of Barcelona society. Black-clad trendies afflicted with post-modernismo fashion notions jostle for space with quarreling family groups, while sailors on shore leave hungrily walk up from the port past the ubiquitous young couples of Barcelona, the girls in short skirts and the boys with long eyelashes.

Heading from the plaça de Catalunya down the Ramblas, the stroller encounters flower stalls, bird-sellers, fortune-tellers, outdoor cafés, and a succession of huge book and newspaper kiosks hawking everything from the daily newspapers of Helsinki and Tokyo to elaborately erotic comic strips (a post-Franco Barcelona specialty). The booksellers and flower merchants do a particularly booming business on April 23, the feast day of Catalonia's patron saint, Jordi (George), when Catalan custom calls for lovers to exchange roses and books. Visitors will find themselves drawn again and again to the daily spectacle of the Barcelona *paseo,* for it is the best way to get a feel for the city. The Ramblas represent, in short, what all urban planners dream of achieving when they design a pedestrian mall.

The area in and around the Ramblas is a testament to the many faces of Barcelona: patrician, proletarian, bourgeois, revolutionary, and religious. Where the rambla dels Estudis gives way to the rambla de Sant Josep, evidence of the city's past prosperity can be seen in the Baroque standoff between Esglesía de Betlem (the church of Bethlehem) to the south and the Palau (palace) Moya to the north. Farther on from the church is the **Palau Virreina**, an 18th-century mansion built by the viceroy of Peru, which houses a rich decorative-arts museum, showing the ingenuity of local craftsmen up to the present day. Also in the Virreina is the art collection of Francesc Cambó, a turn-of-the-century Catalan leader who tried to unite Barcelona business and labor in a common struggle against the central government in Madrid. Small but distinguished, the Cambó bequest includes works by Botticelli, Gainsborough, Tintoretto, and Titian.

But the Palau Virreina, a refined oasis on the rambla de Sant Josep, is quickly forgotten in the earthy charm of its immediate neighbor, a wrought-iron market building known popularly as **La Boquería**. Unwilling to repeat the mistakes made by Paris and London in moving their central food markets from traditional neighborhoods, Barcelona has wisely kept its beloved Boquería in the center of town, ensuring a constant flow of voluble homemakers past the tarot-card readers and the sculpture of an oversized red pepper set up in the small entranceway off the Ramblas. Once inside, visitors may fall victim to the cornucopia of nuts and candies immediately confronting them or decide to venture farther into the din and try their luck at handling the produce before purchasing it.

Directly to the south, behind the clamor of the Boquería, stands the tranquil Gothic complex of the **Hospital de la Santa Creu** (Holy Cross). Although no longer a hospital—its graceful 15th-century buildings, the entrances decorated with tiles, along with its quiet cloister and garden, now house the Institute of Catalan Studies and the Biblioteca de Catalunya (national library of Catalonia)—Santa Creu attests to the period when this quarter of the old city stood outside the first Medieval perimeter (that is, where the Ramblas now run) and became an area of monastic estates and charity houses. As Catalonia once straddled the Pyrenees, the great waves of monasticism sweeping France in the early Middle Ages, notably the Cluny Benedictines and the Cistercians, also affected Barcelona.

A few sinuous streets away from Santa Creu to the south lies even more striking proof of this neighborhood's Christian pedigree: **Sant Pau del Camp** (St. Paul in the fields), by common agreement the oldest church in the city, even if no one is sure exactly how old it is (a tomb inside dates from 912). What makes Sant Pau remarkable is its **Romanesque cloister** adjoining the abbot's residence, the shamrock-shaped arches, called trilobate, unique in this type of architecture and long an object of curiosity. Pablo Picasso, during his sojourn in the city, executed several studies of them, which can be seen in Barcelona's Picasso museum.

The other giant of 20th century art connected to Barcelona is Joan Miró. Fittingly, in one of his last commissioned works, Miró became just another sidewalk artist on the Ramblas, installing a multicolored pavement mosaic at the busy meeting place of the rambla de Sant Josep and the rambla dels Caputxins. Although the promenade turns slightly seedier at this point—the area between the Ramblas and Sant Pau del Camp trades daytime sightseeing for nighttime red lights—the rambla dels Caputxins makes up the most interesting section of the walk from plaça de Catalunya toward the seafront.

Off its north side, just below the carrer de Ferran (the main north-south axis of the old town), stands a beautiful 19th-century square, the **plaça Reial** (royal square). After the Spanish state confiscated church holdings under the Disentailment Act of 1835, the disused Capuchin monastery that occupied this spot was demolished to create an arcaded enclosure dotted with palm trees, a fountain of the Three Graces, and lamp standards designed by Gaudí. Nowadays it is an ideal spot to wash down *tapas* in the brilliant sunshine and be horrified or bemused—depending on your view of life—by the antics of the drifters who congregate here. On weekend mornings a picturesque coin and stamp market is held in the plaça Reial, although at night the conspicuously vulnerable visitor to the city should take care not to be mugged—Barcelona is, after all, a port. This warning, in fact, should be kept in mind at all times on the lower reaches of the Ramblas, and at night in the narrow streets to the north (the Barri Gòtic) and perhaps especially to the south.

When the 19th-century bourgeois classes of Barcelona commissioned the building of the plaça Reial, they were responding to the wealth that industrialization and colonial trade had brought them. Along with Piedmont and Lombardy, Catalonia was the only other southern European region to experience the Industrial Revolution at the same time as areas in the north of the continent—this despite the chaos that the French occupation of Catalonia caused in the Napoleonic era. Even before the Eixample opened up the city to imaginative (and immensely profitable) real-estate development in the latter half of the 19th century, the merchants of Barcelona began creating an urban environment suited to their aspirations. Primary among these was a movement of cultural self-affirmation that went by the name of Renaixença (renaissance), a celebration of Catalan identity and urban sophistication that had long been suppressed by a centralizing Castilian monarchy. Because little sympathy for cultural life in Barcelona was ever evinced by the authorities in Madrid, the wealthy classes of the city banded together, as private Catalan businesses do even today, to subsidize the arts.

Foremost among these institutions is the **Gran Teatre del Liceo**, the opera house of Barcelona built entirely through private subscriptions. Although the façade giving onto the rambla dels Caputxins near the Miró mosaic looks rather undistinguished, the interior of the Liceo (lyceum) is pointedly Renaissance in inspiration and has hosted many great lyric and orchestral artists since its inception in 1847. Its winter season still draws the elite of Barcelona (that is, those fortunate enough to obtain hard-to-get tickets) for elegant operatic evenings and de rigueur drinks at the pricey Café de l'Opéra. Among the 20 or so operas it presents every season, the Liceu frequently features works by Catalonia's adopted idol, Richard Wagner. The affinity between the unbridled power of the composer from Bayreuth and the ostentatious wealth of Barcelona's propertied classes was especially strong in the opening years of this century, when the latter were constructing magnificent homes throughout the city.

A showy example of this building craze can be visited nearby, just a few blocks southeast from the Gran Teatre del Liceo on the narrower carrer Nou de la Rambla. Eusebi Güell, a textile manufacturer and patron of the arts, commissioned Gaudí to construct a residence worthy of his prominent position in Barcelona society. The resulting **Palau Güell** is Medieval in spirit, recalling the days when great lords had fortified townhouses erected in the heart of the city. The municipality has since turned Güell's imposing folly into a theater museum, although the exhibits are dwarfed by the grandiose, if somewhat weirdly vegetal, ornamentation and the large central well of the house.

The fortress aspect of the Palau Güell became singularly appropriate toward the turn of the century, when the struggle between Barcelona's plutocrats and proletarians turned spectacularly violent and the Ramblas became the scene of clashes that mixed class and regional consciousness. In a phenomenon peculiar to the region, prosperous conservatives and liberals alike opted for vocal Catalonian nationalism after growing disgusted with the bumbling foreign policy of the Madrid government—the disastrous war with the United States in 1898 led to the loss of Spain's lucrative colonial connections. Barcelona's working classes, still subjected to naked capitalism at the time (child labor was outlawed only in 1907), were interested less in political than in economic justice and felt strongly pulled toward the internationalist positions of socialism and anarchism.

The streets around the Ramblas, now so peaceful, were witness to bloody incidents, as successive strikes degenerated into mayhem and Barcelona started the new century with the unflattering nickname of "Bomb City." In one infamous incident in 1893, an anarchist lobbed two bombs from the balcony of the Liceo, killing 20 operagoers—one device was a dud and now sits demurely on display in the city's history museum—and ensuring redoubled repression by the authorities. The darkest days occurred in 1909, after a radicalized populace refused to be conscripted to fight in Spanish-held Morocco. The popular uprising turned anticlerical and anticapitalist, with scores of buildings in the city falling prey to arson before a ferocious army was called in to suppress the revolt. Barcelona's Setmana Tràgica (tragic week) ended with more than 100 dead.

Thus, it should be no surprise that George Orwell could write in his memoir of the Spanish Civil War, *Homage to Catalonia:* "Barcelona is a town with a long history of street-fighting. In such places things happen quickly, the factions are ready-made, everyone knows the local geography, and when the guns begin to shoot people take their places almost as in a fire-drill." Although Orwell set down the events of 1937, his remark is evidence of Barcelona's revolutionary reputation among earlier generations. During the 1936–1939 conflict Barcelona was the strongest redoubt of Republican forces, holding out to the very end and, in defeat, suffering severe anti-Catalan measures from the wrathful victor, Francisco Franco. But even Orwell's tremendous gifts—he gives a masterful account of an internecine

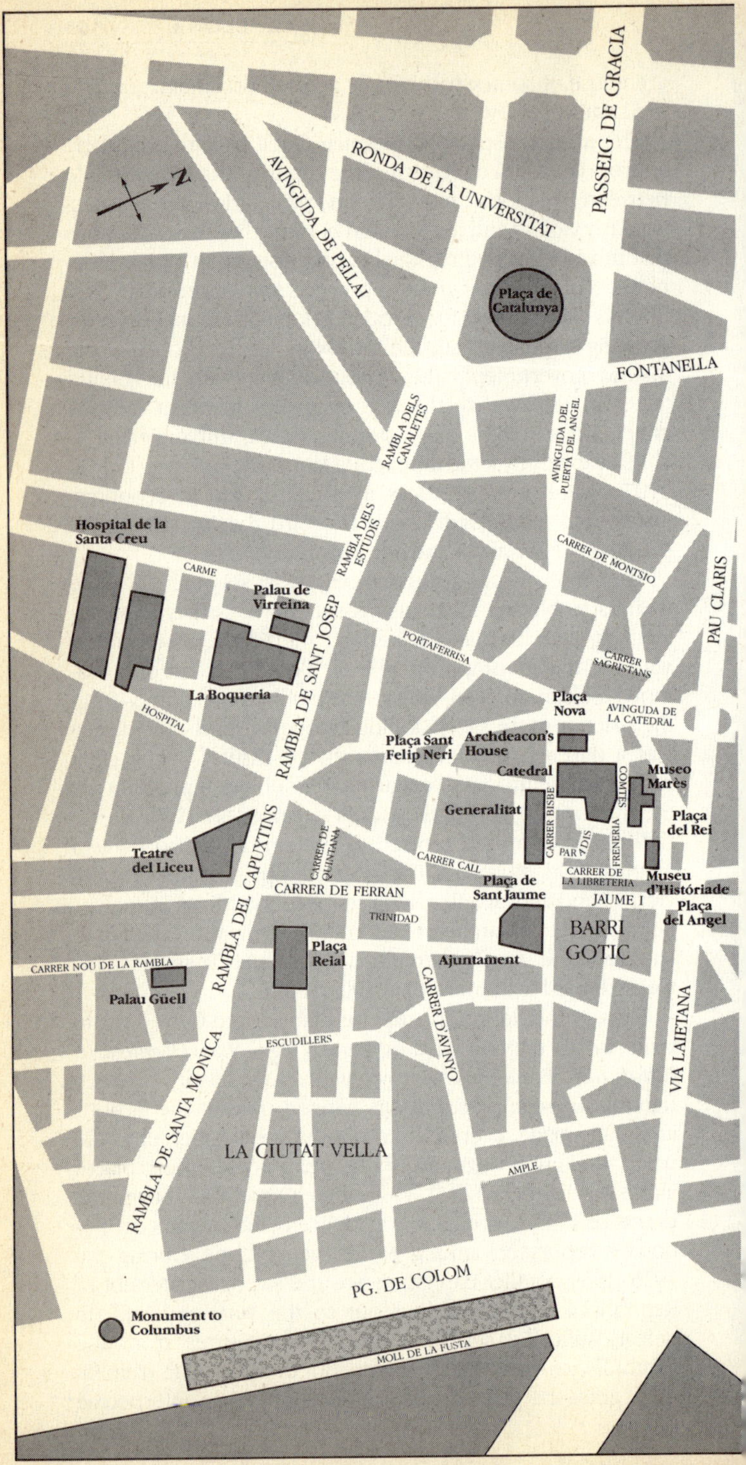

N
RONDA DE LA UNIVERSITAT
PASSEIG DE GRACIA
AVINGUDA DE PELLAI
Plaça de Catalunya
FONTANELLA
RAMBLA DELS CANALETES
AVINGUDA DEL PUERTA DEL ANGEL
RAMBLA DELS ESTUDIS
CARRER DE MONTSIO
PAU CLARIS
Hospital de la Santa Creu
CARME
Palau de Virreina
PORTAFERRISA
CARRER SAGRISTANS
La Boqueria
RAMBLA DE SANT JOSEP
Plaça Nova
AVINGUDA DE LA CATEDRAL
HOSPITAL
Plaça Sant Felip Neri
Archdeacon's House
Catedral
COMTES
Museo Marès
Generalitat
CARRER BISBE
Plaça del Rei
CARRER DE QUINTANA
PARADIS
FRENERIA
Teatre del Liceu
RAMBLA DEL CAPUXTINS
CARRER CALL
CARRER DE LA LIBRETERIA
CARRER DE FERRAN
Plaça de Sant Jaume
JAUME I
Museu d'Históriade
Plaça del Angel
TRINIDAD
BARRI GOTIC
Plaça Reial
Ajuntament
CARRER NOU DE LA RAMBLA
Palau Güell
CARRER D'AVINYO
VIA LAIETANA
ESCUDILLERS
RAMBLA DE SANTA MONICA
LA CIUTAT VELLA
AMPLE
PG. DE COLOM
Monument to Columbus
MOLL DE LA FUSTA

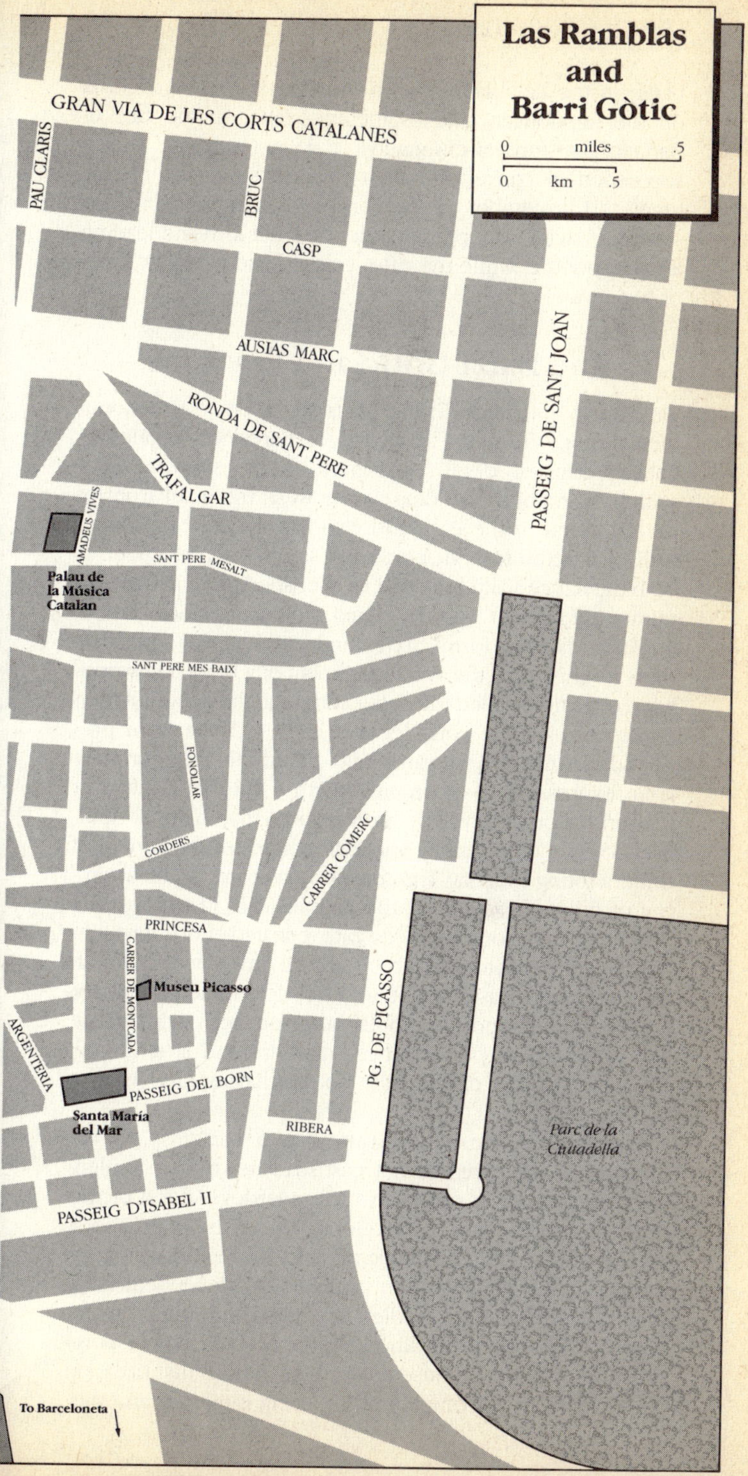
Las Ramblas
and
Barri Gòtic
0 miles .5
0 km .5
GRAN VIA DE LES CORTS CATALANES
PAU CLARIS
BRUC
CASP
AUSIAS MARC
RONDA DE SANT PERE
PASSEIG DE SANT JOAN
TRAFALGAR
AMADEUS VIVES
SANT PERE MESALT
Palau de
la Música
Catalan
SANT PERE MES BAIX
FONOLLAR
CORDERS
CARRER COMERC
PRINCESA
CARRER DE MONTCADA
Museu Picasso
ARGENTERIA
PG. DE PICASSO
PASSEIG DEL BORN
Santa María
del Mar
RIBERA
Parc de la
Ciutadella
PASSEIG D'ISABEL II
To Barceloneta

battle in the Ramblas between Communists and anarchists on the Republican side—sometimes falter in the face of Barcelona's sturdy irrationality: "I do not suppose I have succeeded in conveying much of the strangeness of that time. . . . I remember the fashionably-dressed woman I saw strolling. . .with a shopping-basket over her arm and leading a white poodle, while the rifles cracked and roared a street or two away."

The Barri Gòtic and Environs

On Sunday mornings in the **plaça Nova**, down the monumental steps from the cathedral of Barcelona, groups of Catalan dancers of all ages perform the *sardana*. The setting—a modern building to the west, the great front of the cathedral to the east, and remnants of the old **Roman wall of Barcino** to both north and south—is a reminder of both the dance's antiquity and its cherished place in contemporary Catalonian culture. Arms aloft and hands joined, *sardana* dancers form circles and execute slow, intricate steps in unison, to the accompaniment of a brass and woodwind ensemble called the *cobla*. Although the dance's origin is disputed—some consider it a harvest dance from pre-Christian times—there can be little doubt that the *sardana* is an expression of community. With a little knowledge of Catalan history, the visitor soon realizes that this folk tradition is not another quaint spectacle staged for the benefit of camera-toting tourists: The *sardana* has come to be a symbol of quiet resistance, of the people's will to survive as a distinct Catalan community despite repeated efforts throughout the centuries to quash the regional diversity of Spain. In the very recent past, Catalonia's most determined adversary, Franco, understood the emotional resonance of this dance and outlawed its performance anywhere and at any time. Thus, the dancers of today are not just having fun—they're making a statement.

The Barri Gòtic, which serves as a backdrop to the *sardana* dancers, recalls not past struggles but past splendors. Catalonia was not always an underdog: After a picturesquely named count of Barcelona, Wilfred the Hairy, shook off the yolk of the Carolingian Franks in the ninth century, the seafaring Catalan nation became an independent kingdom during the High Middle Ages, allied with the crown of Aragón. That time of political supremacy and power is recalled in the various museums and institutions that make up the Barri Gòtic, a complex of imposing buildings and narrow streets that, especially at night, preserves the atmosphere of the Medieval city. Stretching from plaça Nova to just east of plaça de Sant Jaume, the Barri Gòtic is the oldest section of the old town. The Ramblas are nearby to the south, as is yet another old quarter centered around carrer de la Princesa to the north.

Although its flamboyant façade dates only from the 19th century, the **cathedral**, which dominates this quarter, is far older, construction having begun in 1298. The dimly lit interior, remarkable for the decorative overkill in the radiating chapels, usually buzzes with crowds of worshipers and visitors, the former being drawn to the crypt of the church's patroness, Saint Eulalia, and the latter attracted to a magnificently carved enclosure in the choir. It was here, in the early 16th century, that the young Holy Roman Emperor Charles V tried to establish the Order of the Golden Fleece, a confraternity of such free-spending Renaissance monarchs as Henry VIII of Britain and Francis I of France. The aptly named order did not survive long, but the *coro,* with its rich wood carvings and sheer size, attests to the wealth of the canons of Barcelona's cathedral.

Further proof of spiritual worldliness can be seen in the capacious **cloister** hugging the south flank of the sanctuary. Although cloisters are usually oases of quietude suggesting the contemplative life, this enclosure is a noisy Gothic atrium frequently filled by neighborhood residents who find an ideal place to exchange gossip underneath its shaded arcades and palm trees. Adding to the occasional uproar are the raucous cries of the geese that make their home around the central fountain—settled there, it is said, in imitation of the Capitoline geese of antiquity. A cool and beautiful place to escape the hot sun of the Mediterranean summer, the cloister is the cathedral's most attractive and memorable feature. While it is true that traces of extravagant Iberian Catholicism can be found in the cloister's southwestern corner, where a chapel given over to the cult of Saint Lucy often overflows with the devout, most of the vaulted ambulatory itself, completed in 1448, seems resolutely—and loudly—down to earth.

Much of the Barri Gòtic is marked by the same informality. At the nearby plaça de Sant Felip Neri, which can be reached from the cathedral via the narrow carrer del Bisbe Irurita, children play handball against the façade of a Baroque church (Sant Felip Neri) and lovers come to snuggle at night by the lone tree in the center of the tiny square. Across the street from the cloister's chapel of Saint Lucy, the courtyard of the old **archdeacon's house** (Casa de l'Ardiaca) is open for public inspection, the single jet of its lovely Gothic fountain sometimes supporting a Ping-Pong ball left there by the irreverent.

Throughout this quarter be on the lookout for gargoyles, small shrines, and other hints at the antiquity of the buildings; doorways crowned by solid stone arches characteristic of Gothic domestic architecture usually deserve surreptitious entry. Inside many of these buildings, now occupied by government bodies, beautifully restored patios can be seen, with a single flight of stone stairs leading to a gallery adorned with a graceful colonnade. In one such place, hidden in the carrer de Paradis behind the cathedral and identified as the Centre Excursionista de Catalunya, the Medieval courtyard shelters four pillars from a Roman temple to Augustus.

On the cathedral's northern flank is the narrow carrer dels Comtes de Barcelona, which, as its name suggests, once played host to the aristocratic rulers of Barcelona. If the cathedral and the area directly south of it are reminders of the power of the Medieval Catalan church, this part of the Barri Gòtic suggests the splendor of its secular elite. On this narrow street the Gothic mansion that once belonged to Barcelona's counts is now a treasure trove for art lovers, holding the collection of Frederic Marés, a 20th-century Catalan artist who combined aesthetics and eccentricity. The cellar and first two floors of the **Museu Marés** house a beautiful display of Romanesque and Gothic polychrome wood sculpture, as well as sculptural works from other periods. On the top floor, however, fancy takes over from refinement in Marés's "sentimental" collection. Evidently a man with an inexhaustible appetite for baubles and curios from flea markets and auction rooms throughout Europe, Marés hoarded everything from hat pins to snuffboxes. This may be the only museum in a Gothic setting with an extensive cigar band collection.

Less anachronistic are the attractions in the **plaça del Rei**, just a few steps northeast of the rear of the cathedral. The spacious square (not to be confused with the Ramblas's plaça Reial), a complex of stately Medieval buildings that includes a five-story tower constructed in the early 15th century, lends dignity to even the most bedraggled itinerant musician. Its western end contains the impressive **Salo del Tinell**, the grand Gothic hall in which Columbus announced his news to Ferdinand and Isabella on his first return from the New World (June 1493). An enormous chamber with remnants of martial frescoes on the wall, it looks as solid as the Barcelona counts once believed their dynasty to be. At right angles to this immense reminder of past glory is another large hall, the **chapel of Saint Agatha**. Spare and evocative of Medieval piety, its stone walls and carved wood ceiling are supported by the work of an earlier ruling class: The chapel sits squarely on the city walls built by the Romans.

More evidence of the Romans appears in the archaeological dig beneath **Museu d'Història de la Ciutat** (the city's history museum), located on the east side of the plaça del Rei in the Clariana-Padellás house. Although frustrating because of its unilingual explanatory notes and signing, the dig gives a good idea of the extent of Roman Barcino, while the museum's upper floors show the locals' considerable pride in the Medieval might of Barcelona. Maps and models are used in an instructive display that reveals how the city has changed over the centuries. Fittingly, the Clariana-Padellás mansion is the best example of these changes, having been moved stone by stone to the plaça del Rei to save it from boulevard builders earlier in this century.

Just as the cathedral and plaça del Rei represent the Church and Crown in the city's past, the **plaça de Sant Jaume**, a hundred yards or so to the southeast (take the carrer del Bisbe Irurita from the cathedral), recalls another powerful element in Medieval Barcelona society: the prosperous burghers and minor aristocracy. The two buildings on this remarkable square, despite their anachronistic façades, house institutions that are direct descendants of age-old councils: the **Ajuntament de Barcelona** (city hall) and the **Palau de la Generalitat** (regional government). Parliamentary in nature, both bodies wrung concessions from successive monarchs, just as today they are the linchpin of Catalonia's autonomous status within Spain. They are also rivals for local prestige. The Ajuntament prides itself on its 14th-century chamber for the Consell de Cent, the hundred grandees who ran the city. A stunning Medieval hall with a Renaissance entrance, the room is a delight to the eye: powerful arches, coffered ceiling, and chandeliers. Across the square, on its western side, the Generalitat (open to visitors only on Sunday mornings) possesses a grand staircase leading to a Gothic arcade. Aside from a series of stirring historical murals, the building's first-floor orange courtyard and Medieval chapel usually leave the visitor convinced of Catalonia's wealth in the Middle Ages.

These two institutions stand for the stubborn Catalan tendency to refuse government by fiat. As early as 1064 prominent families forced Count Ramón Berenguer I to limit their feudal obligations under a landmark agreement known as the Usatges de Barcelona. Throughout the Middle Ages, the Consell de Cent gradually whittled away regal prerogative in matters of taxation, and the city's merchant class grew so influential that its Consulat del Mar (1258) came to govern international maritime law well into the Renaissance.

After these halcyon days of civic independence, the power of the city's merchants began to wane. Difficult, querulous subjects of the centralizing Castilian dynasty that began with the union of Ferdinand and Isabella, the burghers of Barcelona reacted with even greater alarm when that royal line eventually died out and an absolutist Louis XIV of France proposed his grandson for the vacant throne of Spain. In the ensuing War of the Spanish Succession that drew in all of Europe, Barcelona backed the wrong horse (that is, the Hapsburg pretender) and paid dearly for it. Taking a page from his grandfather's book, Philip V, the Bourbon victor, promulgated the Decree of Nova Planta in 1716, abolishing the troublesome civic intermediaries of Catalonia as well as forbidding the use of the Catalan language in the conduct of public business. As always, Barcelona outlived its oppressors. Now, in the plaça de Sant Jaume, the celebrations of the Festa Major d'Estiu, a mid-September religious festival, have powerful Catalan nationalist overtones. In front of the Generalitat, teams from competing Catalan towns build sturdy *castells* (human pyramids) in a custom no less symbolic than the *sardana.* Whereas the dance suggests harmony, the *castell,* by its improbable, acrobatic nature, involves defiance, a trait the political bodies of Barcelona—Generalitat, Ajuntament, and their ancestors—have long displayed toward the powerful.

To the north of the Barri Gòtic proper, across vía Laietana, lies the final third of the old town, a surprising mix of the Medieval and the modern. By leaving the plaça de Sant Jaume by the carrer de Jaume I, the visitor goes out of the original Roman enclosure of Barcino. To the northeast, down a small shopping street called carrer Argenteria, the tall octagonal towers of **Santa Maria del Mar** can be seen stretching skyward. This church, raised by the wealthy merchants of the city beside what was, in the 14th century, the harbor of Barcelona, is considered by many to be the most beautiful example of Catalan Gothic architecture in the old town. The cathedral seems cluttered when compared to its contemporary, Santa Maria, an edifice that had most of its decorative elements consumed in a fire in 1936. That disaster created an interesting side effect: The great Gothic lines of the cavernous church can now be viewed without devotional distractions. A stroll around Santa Maria's ambulatory is a peaceful respite from the teeming liveliness of the neighborhood surrounding the church.

Directly behind Santa Maria is the **Born district**, a hodgepodge of cafés and bars leading north to a 19th-century market building recently converted into an attractive display space for exhibitions of contemporary art. This anachronistic vocation for the Medieval neighborhood becomes even more evident in the tiny **carrer Montcada**, which starts to the west of the Santa Maria's choir. Jammed with tourists in the summer months, the street beckons not only because of its fine Gothic townhouses—Montcada was a fashionable street well into the Renaissance—but also for its art galleries (including a Maeght print gallery), crafts shops, *tapas* bars, and, yes, souvenir stalls. These attractions, however, are secondary to the street's principal crowd-pleaser, the **Museu Picasso.** In a gracious gesture to the Andalusian interloper, Catalan cultural authorities created a museum for the modern master in the 14th-century palace of Berenguer de Aguilar. As in Paris, Picasso's works marry well with Medieval surroundings.

The collection, a legacy from the artist's secretary, Jaume Sabartés, coupled with further donations by the artist, is the largest of its kind in the world. It is, however, far from comprehensive: Picasso's early Blue Period and the work of his old age predominate. Still, the museum is the city's fitting homage to the genius who lived in the neighborhood from 1895 to 1904. The long arm of Montmartre reached out to influence him—and eventually pluck him away—but the memory of Barcelona was to remain with him for many years. It is said that the remembered prostitutes on carrer d'Avinyó, which lies between the plaça de Sant Jaume and the Ramblas, served as models for his later masterpiece *Les Demoiselles d'Avignon.*

A slightly more salubrious place connected with Picasso is **Els Quatre Gats** (four cats) café, in the neighborhood between the Barri Gòtic and the Eixample. Founded in 1897, the café is still open for business on the tiny carrer de Montsió near the plaça de Catalunya. Its creators—admirers and imitators of Montmartre's Le Chat Noir—made the café a meeting place for the young artists who sought to work away from academicism in painting and sculpture. Their frequent sojourns in Paris opened them up to the visual revolution being wrought in the French capital and, in one case, resulted in the conception of a baby whose Catalan surname would belie his Gallic upbringing: Maurice Utrillo. Yet the flowering of Barcelona's bohemia was short-lived—though a brief revival took place in the neutral city during World War I—for the very simple reason that, like Picasso, most of the group elected to move to Paris.

In a neat dovetailing of artistic movements, Els Quatre Gats is housed in the Casa Martí, an edifice designed by architect Josep Puig i Cadafalch, one of the foremost exponents of what Catalans call Modernisme. In addition to being a center of bohemia, Barcelona became a major testing ground for the explosion of architecture and decorative arts that transformed cities throughout Europe at the turn of the century. Modernism, a contemporary of Paris's Art Nouveau and Vienna's Secessionist movements, is the most lasting and spectacular outgrowth of the 19th-century Catalan Renaixença. Influenced as well by the Arts and Crafts school in Britain and the Gothic revival, Modernist architects sought to create a distinctive, national style that would unite fin-de-siècle aesthetics with a triumphant pride in Catalan craftsmanship. Thus, brick, ceramics, tile, and glass were lavished on the new buildings, many of which were designed by architects who doubled as political leaders—Josep Puig i Cadafalch and Lluís Domènech i Montaner are the most prominent examples. It is their buildings, along with those of the more reclusive Gaudí, that give Barcelona its extravagant architectural heritage.

Although Modernist works are usually associated with the Eixample, the old city possesses the best exemplar of the cultural politics of that time. On a side street (Amadeus Vives) off vía Laietana rises the **Palau de la Música Catalana**, a concert hall erected in 1908 by Domènech. In keeping with the tenets of the mature Renaixença, Domènech used every traditional material Catalan craftsmen could provide to construct a Modernist masterpiece that is so heterogeneous and outrageous that it transcends taste. Outside, swirling, multicolored columns compete for attention with marble busts on the red-brick façade and pseudo-Moorish arches; inside, a huge bas-relief of the cavalcade of the Valkyries comes charging out of walls covered with tiles and head-sized ceramic roses, as a stained-glass ceiling, complete with an enormous central bulb, spreads indirect light over the hall. The best way to see this amazing building is to attend a concert here. Even if the performance is mediocre—which is unlikely in a venue where Catalan Pau (Pablo) Casals first set the standards—the permanent spectacle of the Palau is enough to keep you in your seat.

The Eixample

When Barcelona began bursting at the seams in the middle of the 19th century, town planners were asked to submit projects for the enlargement (*eixample*) of the city. Ildefons Cerdà, winner of the contest judged by the central government in Madrid, opted for a rigid, if spacious, grid, slashed diagonally by one predictably named thoroughfare—the Diagonal. Although the project called for numerous green spaces, real-estate developers soon transformed the Eixample into an unrelieved residential and commercial district, possessing few trees and even fewer parks. Despite these signal disadvantages, the Eixample—especially the section directly west of the old town—has become an agreeable urban environment that exhibits the full-blown fantasy of Modernist architecture and the present-day exuberance of Catalan culture. Deceptively repetitive, like much of Manhattan, the grid nonetheless contains enough arresting sights to keep visitors blinking in disbelief.

Named after the now-trendy urban village to the west that it links to the plaça de Catalunya, the **passeig de Gràcia** is the most prestigious avenue of the city. Civic boosters who compare it to the Champs-Elysées inadvertently do it a disservice—Gràcia is far more elegant and interesting. Gaudí's magnificently silly lamp standards, each one targeted for restoration by private business as part of the pre-Olympic sprucing up of the city, adorn the lower reaches of the thoroughfare, in a foretaste of the supreme architectural playfulness to be found on Gràcia between Consell de Cent and Aragó. Here, banks and stolid office buildings done in uninspired Victorian pastiche give way to what local punsters have labeled "La Manzana de la Discòrdia" (*manzana* means both "apple" and "block of houses" in Spanish). Three apartment buildings designed by the unholy trinity of Modernist architects—Domènech, Puig, and Gaudí—stand close together on one city block. Domènech's **Casa Lleó Morera** (at number 35), although its ground floor has been shamefully disfigured by a leather-goods store, exhibits a fanciful façade that draws its inspiration from Hispano-Moorish architecture. However compelling the exterior, the building's true appeal lies inside, where the second-floor apartments (European first floor), now occupied by the offices of a tourist board, display a riot of ceramics, woodwork, stained glass, and statuary. Although these suites are not officially open to the public, try your luck toward the end of the day (after 4:00 P.M.) by flashing this guide and saying that you'd like to take a quick peek at the place. Prepare to be dazzled.

Farther up the block, Puig's **Casa Amatller** looks like a gabled Amsterdam edifice mysteriously transported to the Mediterranean. The families who commissioned such follies were fabulously wealthy. Many had made their fortunes in Spain's colonies and, when forced home by the Spanish-American War, were determined to make a splash in Barcelona society. Above the fireplace in the main room of the Amatller clan's apartments, an elaborate stone allegory of Europe and America makes plain the trading routes on which the family's wealth was based. Again, this building is not a museum, but the scholars studying in the art institute housed on the second floor are usually happy to show around anyone who takes an interest in the peculiar allegorical mantelpiece. Next door, the blue-green waves of ceramics on the façade of Gaudí's **Casa Batlló** can be profitably gawked at for hours—a bench has been set up for just that purpose.

Gaudí's most celebrated apartment building, which art critic Robert Hughes has described indelicately—and, we must assume, intuitively—as "an elephant's erotic dream," stands a few blocks away at number 92. The **Casa Milà,** nicknamed La Pedrera (the quarry), is remarkable both inside and out, stamped with the architect's flowing, organic aesthetic. Hourly tours through the lobby, stairwells, and a few of the luxury flats in the Pedrera are well worth the wait: However conservative the Barcelona establishment was at the turn of the century, it certainly does not show in its taste in decorators. Gaudí, himself a traditionalist in his Catholic faith and his regional allegiance (he refused to speak Castilian), resigned in disgust as the project neared completion because sponsors forbade him to use religious motifs in the seaweed-like outer balconies. Fearful of provoking an anticlerical populace in the wake of the Setmana Tràgica of 1909, the financial backers of La Pedrera preferred their revolutions to remain architectural.

This flamboyant creative tradition in the Eixample, Barcelona's business district, has been revived in the past two decades. In the years prior to Franco's departure, the district was the haunt of Barcelona's "divine left," the group of artists and intellectuals determined to keep abreast of developments in European and American thought—even if that meant nothing more than hopping over to Perpignan every other weekend to browse in the bookshops and attend such forbidden films as *Last Tango in Paris.* On the **Diagonal,** editors and agents brought the work of Latin American "magical realists" to a wider European reading public, despite the cultural deep freeze into which 30 years of Franco had plunged the rest of the country. The creators of contemporary Barcelona and their camp followers, no longer a shadowy group needing divine adjectives, now comfortably coexist with businessmen in the designer bars that dot the Eixample. Daytime activity is concentrated around the upmarket **rambla de Catalunya**, parallel to passeig de Gràcia on the south, where collectors fresh from the galleries on Consell de Cent gather to discuss the latest works of such Barcelona artists as Miguel Barceló. An institute for the living giant of Catalan art, Antoni Tàpies, is now being planned for the nearby carrer de Aragó.

Although slightly disdainful of their fellow Iberians, the denizens of the rambla de Catalunya do not take themselves too seriously: At the eastern end of the mile-long promenade, a statue of a bull doing a passable imitation of Rodin's *The Thinker* surveys the scene; at its Diagonal end a horse in *Playmate* posture lounges suggestively on a pedestal. At the base of the latter, a discreet plaque embedded in the sidewalk carries a bilingual manifesto—in Catalan and English—for the continued exercise of freedom of expression.

Beyond the Diagonal a few blocks to the northwest, the lure of Modernist architecture takes hold once again. The turrets and spires of Puig's **Casa Terrades**, popularly known as Casa de les Punxes (house of the spikes), at the corner of the Diagonal and carrer Roselló, foreshadows the gigantic delirium to be found a mile or so distant: Gaudí's **Templo de la Sagrada Família** (temple of the holy family). By walking the few blocks north of the Diagonal to the famous structure, either along Roselló or Provença, you get a good sense of Barcelona's enduring legacy of Modernist touches: wrought-iron balconies, curved window bays, and colorful casement windows. Although the neighborhood becomes distinctly less affluent than the area around the passeig de Gràcia, its buildings display ornamentation pleasing to all lovers of Modernism.

The Sagrada Família, begun in 1882, is Barcelona's postcard image to the world. Easily the most ridiculous sight on any cultural grand tour of the Mediterranean, the unfinished sanctuary, with its twin sets of four transept spires rocketing skyward, has earned mixed reviews ever since Gaudí's death in 1926 left the cathedral builders bereft of blueprints. In his later years, the great Modernist architect preferred to work in the mysticism of improvisation, thus leaving few firm indications of how he wanted construction to continue—except for a planned, but as yet unstarted, central spire that would point a whopping 500 feet into the air.

Lovers of vertigo can console themselves by scrambling on walkways across the void between the wildly decorated bell towers, even if walking around the structure remains the safest way to be flabbergasted. Although Orwell proclaimed the Sagrada Família "one of the most hideous buildings in the world," indulgent opinion usually sides with contemporary French journalist Paul-Jean Franceschini, who dubbed the church "Our Lady of the Smurfs." For those hooked on the excess of Modernist buildings, further enjoyment lies down avinguda de Gaudí, which runs northwest from the Sagrada Família to the **Hospital de Sant Pau**. The latter, executed by Domènech, is remarkably multicolored and decorative, although this may escape notice after the numbing sight at the other end of the avenue.

The Hills

Montjuïc—the hill "of Jove" or "of the Jews," depending on whose etymology you accept—dominates the southern quarter of the city and overlooks the harbor from a commanding height. The set piece for a burst of Barcelona-boosting, the hill played host to the successful World's Fair of 1929. That event gave the wooded prominence a clutch of varied attractions, which should become even more eclectic after the 1992 Olympics have passed this way. Unlike the old city it rises above, Montjuïc is verdant, calm, and, in some places, majestic. It is also home to the best art galleries in Catalonia.

Not that this could be guessed from the unfortunately pompous main approach to the hill. This ceremonial entrance begins on the Gran Vía de les Corts Catalanes at the plaça de Espanya, a roaring traffic circle with a flame-topped neo-Baroque fountain in its middle. The bombast continues with two tall red-brick campaniles that flank the beginning of the broad avinguda de la Reina Maria Cristina, which leads in turn to a grand staircase. Here, a series of fountains, the largest of which is the scene of spectacular nighttime sound and light shows, usher the visitor up to the Palau Nacional (national palace). But before making the climb to this uninspiring survivor of the 1929 fair, make a small detour to the right of the central fountain. There, amid the abundant proof of the 1929 organizers' lack of a clear-cut aesthetic vision, stands the elegantly spare German pavilion designed by Mies van der Rohe. Partially hidden by the bunker that serves as the headquarters of the Barcelona Olympics committee, the building exemplifies what is best in Bauhaus.

Beyond the German pavilion, to the south a hundred yards or so, stands an attraction that contrasts with the cosmopolitan style of Bauhaus and celebrates all things Spanish. Constructed for the 1929 fair, the **Poble Espanyol** (Spanish village) is an amusing hodgepodge of the ersatz: Buildings in various traditional Iberian styles (Andalusian, Castilian, Galician, among others) crowd the narrow streets in an arresting display of diversity. Although it was long derided as a kitsch tourist trap by Barcelona sophisticates, the recent refurbishing of the Poble and its pleasant outdoor jazz concerts have increased its popularity in recent years.

Farther up the hill, at the top of the monumental staircase, stands the **Palau Nacional**. Despite its unprepossessing appearance, this building houses the spectacular **Museu d'Art de Catalunya**, a treasure-house of painting, sculpture, and ceramics from the last 1,000 years. The gallery prides itself on the section devoted to Romanesque art, a breathtaking collection that is the largest of its kind in the world. Scores of Romanesque murals were transferred here as a hedge against theft and deterioration in the early decades of this century, and the resulting procession of rooms with glorious, Byzantine-style devotional work makes up Barcelona's most prestigious museum. This priceless survey of religious art—murals were removed here from remote hermitages in the Catalan Pyrenees—is supplemented by a large collection of Gothic works, as well as a section devoted to the Renaissance and such masters as El Greco, Velázquez, and Zurbarán. A cultural institution of the first order, the Museu d'Art de Catalunya is now undergoing an extensive renovation program supervised by Gae Aulenti, the innovative Italian architect who transformed a Parisian train station into the Musée d'Orsay.

For lovers of more contemporary art, the **Fundació Joan Miró** lies farther up the hill past the national palace. Opened in 1983, this handsome white villa (designed by Catalan Josep Lluís Sert, the architect of the Maeght foundation in Saint Paul-de-Vence, France) displays a representative selection of the works of Joan Miró, the Catalan artist especially revered here. Admirably organized, the collection spans all aspects of Miró's long creative life, from his early days in the international avant-garde to his final years as Olympian artist uncowed by the authorities in Madrid. A further honor to the artist can be seen near the foot of Montjuïc, just west of the plaça de Espanya, where a pleasantly landscaped park has been named for him. In it stands *Donna i Ocella* (woman and bird), a gigantic but playful work from Miró's later years.

Aside from two small but interesting museums near the Fundació Joan Miró—one devoted to classical archaeology (with artwork from the Greco-Roman ruin of Empúries farther up the Costa Brava), the other to Latin American ethnography—this flank of Montjuïc takes on a distinctly populist flavor. A noisy amusement park draws crowds throughout the year, as does the Transbordador Aeri, an aerial cable car that sweeps from the hill and out over the harbor, depositing its fearless passengers in the maritime suburb of Barceloneta (see below). A far less nerve-racking way to get a panoramic view of the city is to take a shorter aerial excursion by means of the funicular, which can be boarded near the fun fair. It takes sightseers directly over a roller coaster—a curious sensation—and up to the summit of Montjuïc, which is crowned by a citadel that now houses a military museum. From the ramparts of this impeccably restored fortress, all of Barcelona can be seen spreading out over the coastal plain toward the tall hills in the west. The view is well worth the ascent.

The other three hillside vantage points of the city look back toward the sea from the western side of town. The northernmost is the **Parc Güell**, a remarkable green space fashioned by the ever-present Gaudí. (It is best reached by taxi from the center of town or, more appropriately, from the Sagrada Família.) Although originally commissioned to create a subdivision of Modernist houses, Gaudí completed only two characteristically striking—that is, weird—pavilions before financing for the project fell through and before his death. Still, his original notions of landscaping remain: serpentine walkways supported by columns at seemingly impossible angles, and a central plaza—or *mirador*—that is encircled by a magnificent, undulating bench decorated with broken tiles and ceramics. A perennial Barcelona favorite, the Parc Güell is Gaudí's most user-friendly contribution to the city he loved. In the architect's house, to the north of the *mirador,* his curvilinear design for furniture and fixtures can be seen in all its glory.

The most distant—and tallest—lookout over Barcelona is the mountain of **Tibidabo**, which looms more than 1,500 feet over the northern and western reaches of the city. You can reach it from the plaça de Catalunya in three stages: Take the subway to avinguda del Tibidabo, then the tramway through a neighborhood of fanciful villas to the funicular, which runs up the wooded slopes to the summit. Adorned by a large, if graceless, church erected by a 19th-century Catalan saint, Joan Bosco, Tibidabo nonetheless takes its name from words attributed to the devil in the gospel of Saint Matthew: "Haec omnia tibi dabo si cades adoraberis me" ("All this I will give to you if you will but adore me"). Scan the mountains to the northwest for the monastery of Montserrat, and, of course, look to the east for a commanding view of the city and the Mediterranean.

The last of Barcelona's scattered hill sights stands at the foot of the Sierra del Collcerola to the south, near the university district at the beginning of the Diagonal. The **Monestir de Pedralbes** is a highlight for any visitor interested in the art and architecture of the High Middle Ages. Open from 10:00 A.M.–1:00 P.M. and 4:00–6:00 P.M. on weekdays, except Mondays when it is closed, and on Sundays from 9:00 A.M.–1:00 P.M. (and best reached by taxi or from the Reina Elisenda subway station), the monastery is a well-preserved reminder of 14th-century spirituality. Among its finer elements: a vaulted chapter house, a three-story cloister, and an ornate chapel with beautiful stained-glass windows. The impressive ceramics collections formerly housed in the Palau Nacional on Montjuïc is now at Pedralbes as well.

To end a visit to this section of the city, it is best to walk down to the Diagonal by the avinguda de Pedralbes. There, at the bottom on the right, stands yet another photogenic Gaudí attraction: a fanciful wrought-iron gate in the shape of a dragon.

The 1992 Olympics

On October 17, 1986, Barcelona was notified that its bid for the Games of the XXVth Olympiad had been accepted. A citywide party erupted when the news broke, for Barcelona, three times unsuccessful in soliciting the Games (1924, 1936, 1972), would now get a chance to display its new found dynamism to a world audience.

Thus, visitors to the city in the next few years should expect to see signs of Olympic fever everywhere. In addition to the appearance of the mascot, a dog called Cobi who can already be seen smiling from thousands of tee shirts, an orgy of sandblasting, tree-planting, and general urban renewal is well underway. As part of the "Cultural Olympiad," the years prior to the Games have been designated for an accelerated cycle of exhibitions and festivals. Organizers of the performing arts' Festivals de Tardor, held in the autumn, hope to make it a peer of such prestigious European festivals as those of Edinburgh and Avignon.

What clinched victory for Barcelona's Olympic bid was the proximity of the sporting facilities to the city center. Fortunately, this does not mean that there is a forest of construction cranes at every turning. There are four principal sites: Montjuïc, between the national palace and the Castell; Vall d'Hebron, a western suburb; Parc de Mar, a formerly dingy industrial district on the sea, north of the Parc de la Ciutadella; and the Diagonal, the stadia and university complex at the southern extremity of the great thoroughfare, where the 120,000-seat Nou Camp, home to Barcelona's passionately supported football club, is located.

People planning on going to Barcelona should remember that the Olympic Games will take place from July 25 to August 9, 1992. Those who dislike crowds should stay away; those who enjoy the two Barcelona specialties of spectacle and excess will no doubt be delighted.

The Waterfront and the Parc de la Ciutadella

In recent years Barcelona has been trying to repair an injustice in its urban planning: the neglect of its waterfront. Not that the port is idle—it is, in fact, one of the busiest facilities on the Mediterranean and the most active harbor in Spain. However, the citizenry of Barcelona has traditionally been denied the advantages of the city's seaside location. Once the foot of the Ramblas was reached, the roar of trucks and the bustle of docks yielded no quarter to the pleasure seeker.

This has changed slightly. **Reials Drassanes Museu Maritim** (the maritime museum) is no longer the city's best-kept secret. Housed in the most extensive Medieval shipyard in Europe, just south of the Columbus monument at the waterfront end of the Ramblas, Drassanes's vaulted halls are filled with replicas of ships that were once the pride of Barcelona. Special attention is showered on Roger de Flor, the 14th-century pirate-envoy whose tales of official banditry are relished in Catalonia with the same sly pride Englishmen reserve for Francis Drake. Flor, an adventurer who responded to Byzantium's appeals for help, ended up subduing Athens, Neopatria, Sardinia, and other Mediterranean lands, much to the delight and profit of the canny merchants on the Consell de Cent. Also given a place of honor are

Barcelona shipwrights, who built over half the fleet that defeated the Turks at Lepanto in 1571 (including a full-size replica of *La Real,* Don Juan of Austria's galley), and Amerigo Vespucci's map of the New World.

A more far-reaching event is commemorated in the harbor across the street from Drassanes. Moored permanently at the wharf, a full-scale replica of Christopher Columbus's *Santa Maria* awaits inspection. As with many historical ships, the vessel seems frighteningly tiny to have navigated an ocean. Alongside the *Santa Maria,* equally small tour boats—called *golondrinas* (gulls)—depart every 15 minutes for a brief cruise to the end of the long breakwater that protects the central harbor of Barcelona. There is admittedly little to see on this short tour, but it is a pleasant respite from the heat and noise of the city. The observant will immediately pick out local residents on the cruise: Their laps are weighed down by radios and cassette players prudently removed from their cars.

Other than this flutter of history and tourism by the seaside, the waterfront of Barcelona offers few amenities to the visitor. As part of the pre-Olympic cleanup, a stretch of dockside has been covered with paving stones and scattered with park benches, and the passeig de Colom, the central section of the busy coastal roadway, now runs partially below ground level. However, the thunder of traffic can still be heard at this gentrified dock, which may be why the area's smartest restaurant-bar—which sports a smiling crayfish statue on its roof—plays loud music on its outdoor patios.

Nearby, east of the old town, stands a far quieter haven, the seaside suburb of **Barceloneta.** In this triangular grid of narrow streets, the only sound likely to be heard is the occasional domestic spat wafting out of the colorfully painted windows hung with the morning's wash. The antithesis of the Eixample, downmarket Barceloneta hums with passing BMWs and Mercedes only at dusk, when its excellent seafood restaurants open for business. Beyond them lies the municipal beach of Barcelona, a rather grimy affair that at night looks much better, if more threatening, than it does in the unforgiving light of day (swimmers should stick to the resorts on the nearby Costa Brava and Costa Daurada). As in much of Barcelona, the only nature worth observing in Barceloneta is of the human variety.

There is an exception to this rule, however, in the neighboring **Parc de la Ciutadella,** where a botanical garden and a zoo long ago replaced the citadel that gave the park its name. That fortification, bankrolled by a vengeful Philip V to make sure the anti-Catalan decrees of his Nova Planta were enforced, was built at the expense of an old quarter that once stood on the spot (Barceloneta was constructed to house the displaced). In the 19th century the city received authorization to pull down the hated symbol of Madrid rule. The World's Fair of 1888, held in the Parc, became a matter of civic pride, giving the people of Barcelona a chance to let other countries know of their city's eagerness to set foot on the world stage. An arch of triumph, celebrating victories as yet unrecorded, was duly erected on the boulevard approaching the park from the Eixample. The other vestige of that fair, apart from the park itself, is the pavilion that now houses a modest zoological museum. Far more attractive to the contemplative visitor than that, though, is the museum's immediate neighbor, a tranquil **conservatory**, which can be stunningly beautiful when the late afternoon light filters through the slatted roof onto the tropical vegetation within. At the eastern end of the park there is also a zoo.

For those interested in artistic development in turn-of-the-century Barcelona, an admirable art museum can be visited nearby. It shares a building with the Catalan parliament. Although the parliament—the deliberative body of the Generalitat—has made noises (in the self-important manner of legislators and bureaucrats the world over) about evicting its cultural companion, the **Museu d'Art Modern** has renewed its lease in the center of the Parc de la Ciutadella for the next few years at least. Its collections, which display the work of Catalan artists of the last 150 years, take on an international flavor in the rooms given over to the Barcelona bohemians of the 1890s. The portraits executed by Ramón Casas—particularly of Erik Satie in Montmartre and a very young Pablo Picasso—are touching reminders of a long-vanished avant-garde.

GETTING AROUND

For even the inexperienced traveller, finding one's way around Barcelona is relatively effortless. Those anxious about their unfamiliarity with the Catalan language needn't worry: It is a Latin-based language, and most of the essential words you will see on signposts and the like have unmistakable cognates in Spanish or French. Few people expect foreigners to speak Catalan—in any event, an ever-growing number of Catalans have a smattering of English, and Castilian Spanish is understood by everyone.

The airport, El Prat de Llobregat, is located along the

coast, south of the city, and is currently being expanded to handle increased passenger traffic. Cab fare to town runs to 1,500 pesetas, although an inexpensive (about 200 pesetas) rail shuttle, which leaves every 15 minutes for the central Sants train station (west of plaça de Espanya along carrer Tarragono), might keep you out of rush-hour traffic. The *Puente Aereo* is an hourly shuttle service between Madrid and Barcelona. No reservations are accepted; tickets may be bought at the airport. In addition to good air and rail connections, Barcelona can be reached—or left—by sea; ferries, which leave from the port near the Columbus column, link it to the Balearic Islands and a few French ports of call.

Public transit is cheap and efficient. Tickets for both bus and subway may be purchased at kiosks and in banks. As the Eixample is sinfully easy to understand, there is no difficulty in determining bus routes from even the most cursory glance at a map. The subway, which has five lines, is just as effortless to master. The lines are color-coded and called by the names of their termini. A "T-2" ticket, good for ten rides, can be picked up in any station for about 350 pesetas. Call for more information about public transit; Tel: 336-0000. (The central tourist office, always useful for answering questions, is located at Gran Vía de les Corts Catalanes 658; Tel: 301-7443.)

The simplest way to get around is by taxi. Barcelona has a large fleet, which makes for very short waits for a cab. Fares are very low—300 to 400 pesetas for most rides—by New York or London standards. Distinctively black and yellow, the cabs display a green light that flashes *Lliure* (*Libre,* in Castilian) when looking for customers.

Driving in Barcelona is much like the city itself: schizophrenic. The old town is a nightmare; the Eixample, a dream. In the latter, speeding does not seem to constitute an infraction. If you are looking for an unfamiliar street from one of the bigger avenues (for example, the Diagonal), it's best to drive down the sedate service lanes at the sides. Catalans on their broad boulevards do not suffer hesitant drivers easily. The result is a horn-honking symphony during peak hours. Sadly, like many other car-crazy cities in Spain, Barcelona is frequently blanketed in smog.

When walking around Barcelona, take care to secure cameras, purses, and wallets. Although it is not the den of thieves other Spaniards would have you believe, the city is far from angelic. Especially in the old town near the port, keep your wits about you.

ACCOMMODATIONS

Considering its importance, vigor, and enterprising spirit, Barcelona lacks deluxe hotels in the quantity that a city of its caliber deserves. If the number of its first-rate hotels rivaled its restaurants, visitors would be blessed indeed. As it is, there are six categorized as "the tops" in the Spanish government's official hotel guide, and only one of them (the Ritz) has the elegant poshness that such a category suggests. The room rates run the gamut, with some of the top six charging more than twice as much as the others and some of the city's next-highest-rated establishments outcharging their betters. There are three dozen or so good hotels, also varying widely in price. More modest digs are much less expensive, but vary so erratically they aren't worth mentioning. In considering a Barcelona hotel, you would best be guided by location.

Note: With the 1992 Olympics already much more than a gleam in its organizers' eye, a round dozen new hotels are projected, in the works, or due to open within months, most of them centrally located.

The telephone area code for Barcelona is 93; when dialing from outside the country, drop the 9.

Central

Let's assume sightseeing is your major goal. This means you'll be well served by a hotel in or near the old Barri Gòtic, because so much of this area and its border streets are walkable. Most such hotels tend to be old; the more modern, high-rise hotels are generally located farther from the heart of the city. The good news is that there are many hotels located in this central location. The bad news: Only one of them is the Ritz.

Only the **Hotel Ritz** is really luxurious, especially since its recent facelift. It's the only Barcelona hotel that merits a *gran lujo* (deluxe) rating and now looks as it must have back in 1919 when it was built in the grand belle-epoque style, with an exuberance of flourishes, such as crystal chandeliers, handsome carpeting, gilded mirrors, and a plethora of fresh flowers. The hotel's location on one of the busiest thoroughfares in town makes you grateful for the double-glazed windows. It also puts you within easy walking distance of almost anywhere you'll want to go in the city. Rooms are spacious, many with marble fireplaces and Roman-style baths decorated with *sevillano* tiles. There's now a health and fitness center. A garden restaurant and patio bar and the first-rate **Diana Restaurant** add to the Ritz's great convenience. The staff—from top to bottom—is obliging and well-trained, and the concierges are among the best in the business. A member of Leading Hotels of the World.

Gran Vía de les Corts Catalanes 668, between carrers Lloria and Bruc. Tel: 318-5200; in U.S., (800) 223-6800; in New York State, (212) 838-3110, collect.

On the same major avenue is the **Avenida Palace**, around the corner from passeig de Gràcia—good news for anyone with shopping in mind. Built after World War II but in the grand prewar manner, with a sweeping double staircase, marble columns, and antique-style furniture, the hotel seems oddly pretentious, yet its guest rooms are sizable and comfortable, and the location is prime.

Gran Vía de les Corts Catalanes 605; Tel: 301-9600.

Also convenient for both shopping and sights is the **Diplomatic**, which makes up in comfort what it lacks in charm. Its color-coordinated guest rooms are more attractive than the rather ostentatious glass-and-marble lobby. The location's another winner, though.

Pau Claris 122; Tel: 317-3100.

A favorite of many visitors, and deservedly so, is the **Hotel Colón**, with its front rooms (and tiny balconies) overlooking the cathedral, a great place to position yourself for watching the *sardanas* danced in the cathedral plaza. It doesn't hurt to request a front room. While the fin-de-siècle furnishings have become a bit neglected (especially noticeable in the rooms and baths), this is a trade-off for the front-row center convenience. Here, too, the concierges are superior. Tea or drinks in the lounge off the lobby can be a pleasant experience.

Avinguda de la Catedral 7; Tel: 301-1404.

Behind the Colón is its modest relation, **Regencia Colón**, a useful backup hotel choice. It lacks the closeup cathedral views, but is just a block away from the Barri Gòtic. The first hotel built after World War II, it isn't showing its age. Accoutrements have a handcrafted simplicity and are well maintained. And it's peaceful at night. Attractive in a low-key way—and a relative bargain.

Carrer Sagristans 13; Tel: 318-9858.

Another sleeper, and handy to both the old quarter and the bustling Eixample district, is the **Regente**. Unlike so many Barcelona hotels, no matter what the category, the Regente has a certain *je ne c'est quoi*. Public areas have an Art Nouveau flavor, in keeping with the city's landmarks. This is no accident; this jewel was a private mansion from 1895 to 1964. Rooms are small, with minute balconies. There's also a pint-size rooftop with swimming pool and sundeck.

Rambla de Catalunya 76 (corner of Valencia); Tel: 215-2570.

Along the lower Ramblas there are many modestly priced hotels, with much to be modest about. One, though, that can be recommended, even if it is longer on charm than on creature comforts, is **Hotel Oriente**. Facing the entrance to the plaça Reial, the Oriente dates back to the mid-19th century, and its handsome public rooms still evoke a bygone era. Guest rooms are plain and simple. The location is handy by day, somewhat seedy at night.

Ramblas 45-47; Tel: 302-2558.

For simple digs in a superconvenient location, you might also consider **Hotel Suizo**, just off busy (and noisy) vía Laietana on the northern edge of the Barri Gòtic. Rooms are clean, modest, and well-kept in this business-like place that is a mainstay of budget travellers. Comfortable lounge and bar.

Plaça del Angel 12; Tel: 315-4111.

The Shopping Area

The fashionable residential and shopping streets west of Gran Vía to avinguda de la Diagonal have a number of hotels, giving visitors easy access to many of the city's best restaurants and shops, with the Barri Gòtic still within walking distance.

The major large hotel in this area is the **Meliá Barcelona Sarriá**, just off the Diagonal. Now part of the Sol chain, this huge property (22 floors) has recently had a much-needed renovation. Spacious rooms with king-size beds and super service make up for the rather charmless modernity and the prevalence of business and tour groups.

Avinguda de Sarriá 50; Tel: 410-6060.

A small, comfortable, and attractive hotel, right in the center of the shopping action on the busy corner of València and passeig de Gràcia, Barcelona's equivalent of New York's Fifth Avenue, is the **Majestic**. Despite the noisy location, double-glazed windows keep the ample front guest rooms peaceful (there are breathtakingly drab back rooms). A full set of amenities, including attractive furnishings and a rooftop pool, make this hostelry an excellent value.

Passeig de Gràcia 70; Tel: 215-4512.

On the same lively shopping street is the **Condes de Barcelona**, a small, 100-room Art Nouveau gem, currently very "in," handy to shops and restaurants. The rooms are of ample size, with all the normal amenities: minibar, hair dryer, color TV, direct-dial phone, and the like.

Passeig de Gràcia 75; Tel: 215-0616.

Another small hotel with some personality is the **Derby**, on a short, quiet, tree-shaded, semi-residential street between the Diagonal and avinguda de Sarriá. Rooms are modern, well-designed, and fully equipped, with a pleasing coordinated look. A few rooms on the top floor have front and rear terraces. Unlike so many Barcelona hotels, the Derby is contemporary in design without being garish. The lounge is an attractive room with comfortable chairs and original prints on the walls. An English-style pub offers Guinness on tap, along with a selection of *tapas*. Derby is a very good value.

Carrer Loreto 21; Tel: 322-3215.

The **Presidente** is a comfortable place, with a handy location that is a springboard for shopping and for visits to the Barri Gòtic. This modern high-rise hotel earns a high official rating, and it certainly is well equipped with all the essentials, though you might not think so if you judged only by the small lobby. A lounge, one flight up, offers good cross-views of the busy street. The spacious guest rooms are well lighted, with attractive color-coordinated linens and decor. There's even a swimming pool. This is an efficient, well-run, if somewhat characterless hotel.

Avinguda de la Diagonal 570 (corner of Muntaner); Tel: 200-2111.

By the time you read this, the brand-new 290-room **Barcelona Hilton International** will have opened its deluxe doors, on the Diagonal, just north of Numencia, with all kinds of features geared to international visitors, especially those headed here for the 1992 Olympics. Look for the usual Hilton amenities, plus executive floors, a business center, health club, drugstore, and jewelry shop.

Avinguda de la Diagonal 589-595. Tel: 419-2233.

A moderate-price hotel in Barcelona's stylish areas is a find indeed. Such is the somewhat staid **Hotel Wilson**, situated where carrer Muntaner crosses the Diagonal (across from the Presidente). Attractive guest rooms add to the value.

Avinguda de la Diagonal 568; Tel: 209-2511.

Another good value is **Hotel Covadonga**, on the Diagonal just south of plaça Francesc Macià. Fairly standard, as local hotels go, this has adequately furnished (if unexciting), sizable rooms and a fine location.

Avinguda de la Diagonal 596; Tel: 209-5511.

A word or two might be said about the **Hotel Princesa Sofía**, even though it is outside the geographic areas of the hotels mentioned above. The only real problem for travellers is its slightly remote university city location (in the southwest). Aside from that, it boasts all the away-from-home comforts of any large international-style hotel: gym, sauna, indoor pool, two bars with live music, and a dining room with good city views. All that's lacking is old-fashioned charm.

Plaça de Pio XII 5; Tel: 330-7111.

—*Patricia Brooks*

DINING

Catalans have a reputation for no-nonsense hard work. But you have only to watch them in their local restaurants to discover that they play hard, too. And the prevalence of excellent restaurants in Barcelona and throughout Catalonia is argument enough that Catalans recognize the good life when they see it and can afford to enjoy it.

Barcelona's geography has helped define its cuisine, which is best described as a marriage between the fruits of the Mediterranean and the harvest of a southern landscape—tomatoes, garlic, mushrooms, olives, onions, sweet red peppers, rice, olive oil, and aromatic herbs—and the Pyrenees, prolific with game, freshwater fish from mountain streams, and wild mushrooms. The French are comfortable dining in Barcelona, as well they might be: It evokes memories of Provence.

Today's Catalan cooking divides fairly easily into two styles, traditional and *nueva cócina,* both owing more than a nod to France. An easy hand with seafood and fresh produce has given Catalan cooks a natural affinity for the best elements of *nouvelle cuisine* Catalan-style. Barcelona chefs often combine the techniques and ingredients of their classical cuisine with the light touch and "painterly" arrangements of the *nouvelle* style.

Barcelona restaurants tend to follow one of two divergent paths: They are either cheerfully folkloric, with whitewashed walls, lots of ceramic tiles, and rows of garlic and peppers strung from walls, or smoothly sophisticated, as stylishly understated as comparable establishments in New York, London, or Paris. Their common denominator is excellent service, where a warm welcome is nothing extra, just part of a usually flawless professionalism. As a rule, the more folkloric and traditional the place, the more moderate the price.

There are a few dishes that are constants—you'll find them in traditional restaurants and, with some modern adaptations, in the *nueva cocina* ones as well. Rice is the base for many dishes, as in *paella a la Parellada* (made with deboned fish, shellfish, chicken, and meat). Other dishes to look for are *zarzuela* (a succulent fish soup) and its variation, *opera,* when a half-lobster is added; *suquet de peix,* a sort of bouillabaise; and *brandada de bacalao* (codfish with truffles). And be sure to sample Catalan sausages—*butifarra, salchichon,* and *longaniza,* among others—delicious just grilled.

Dining hours are similar to those in Madrid and elsewhere in Spain—late (beginning around 10:00–10:30 P.M.). Visitors accustomed to Madrid dining will find a slight edge of greater formality in Barcelona, in both restaurant style and customer attire, at least in the local temples of haute cuisine. Advance reservations are recommended. As in most cities, you can eat heartily but inexpensively at a rustic, pub-like neighborhood eatery, but fashionable restaurants are not cheap. It should be said, though, that while the cost of dining out in style has been escalating rapidly in Barcelona, as in Madrid, there is still more value received than at comparable restaurants in other major cities of Europe and North America.

Stylish and/or Nueva Cocina Catalunya

As in Madrid, new restaurant openings have become a Barcelona "given" over the past ten years. In the rush to try the new, the tried-and-true reliables sometimes get overlooked.

That may be why **Reno**, a landmark at Tuset 27 (an extension of Enrique Granados, just north of the Diagonal), now offers a dual menu, with both international and *nueva Catalan* dishes that should keep everyone happy. Reno's owner José Julia is Catalan-born, and his consistently high standards, like his father's before him, make this restaurant a pleasure to visit—and revisit. It's a favorite lunch place for businessmen, who undoubtedly feel at home in the handsome, wood-paneled setting so reminiscent of a private club. Try the *cazuelita de arroz con chipirones,* a light version of paella made with squid, or perhaps sole in puff pastry with sauce Aurore. Note also the fine selection of Spanish and French wines. Tel: 200-9129.

Indisputably one of the city's best restaurants is **Neichel**, at avinguda de Pedralbes 16, on the ground floor of an apartment complex out near the Pedralbes monastery (between plaça de Pio XII and Manuel Girona). It should certainly be on any serious diner's short list of places to try in Barcelona. Alsatian chef-owner Jean-Luis Neichel, who was chef at the excellent El Bulli in Roses on the Costa Brava, walks a delicate line between classic cooking and *nouvelle* presentations. His touch is as light and understated as his restaurant's quietly elegant, fresh-flower-accented pastel decor. The duck in a cassis and wild mushroom sauce is memorable, but try the prix fixe *menu de degustación* to get a true sampling of Neichel's skills. And don't miss dessert, one of his hallmarks. Tel: 203-8408.

Agut d'Avignon is deceptive. It looks traditional, with its whitewashed walls, huge, exposed overhead beams, and rush-seated ladder-back chairs, but the rusticity has a sophisticated edge, and so does the food in this urbane Catalan restaurant located on five different levels in a hard-to-find cul-de-sac at carrer de la Trinidad 3 (corner of Avinyó in the Barri Gòtic). The small menu is unusual, with many dishes underscoring the Catalan custom of combining meat or game with fruit, as in goose with pears or duck with figs. Strong suits are the fish and game dishes, mussels in a garlic cream sauce as a starter, trout Navarra-style stuffed with ham, rabbit simmered with red pepper and tomatoes, punctuated, perhaps, by a dessert of *fresas del bosco* (tiny wild strawberries) with whipped cream or of *lionesas* (little cream puffs with chocolate sauce). Pricey it is, as all the deluxe Barcelona restaurants are, but worth every peseta. Tel: 302-6034.

Most critics agree that the Basque **Ama-Lur** is probably the prettiest restaurant in the city. Whether it's as good as it looks is another question. Even its entrance sign—a tiny brass plaque at the entrance to the building at Mallorca 275 (between passeig de Gràcia and Pau Claris)—is discreetly elegant. There's a two-pronged entrance procedure: Ring, and once inside, ring again (like the old speakeasy days). But within the restaurant confines the waiting area is as light, airy, well-furnished, and as full of cut-flower arrangements as a mansion's living room, which it has been outfitted to resemble. The dining rooms are equally spacious and inviting, with smiling waitresses in Mary Petty uniforms ready to pamper guests outrageously. While the food—hake in garlic sauce, veal steak in wine sauce, and other robust entrees—is often very good, it's rarely up to the mystique induced by the staff and surroundings. The menu changes frequently. Desserts, it must be said, *always* live up to expectations: lemon and honey crepes, plum ice cream with Armagnac, and the like. If you want a different, memorable dining experience, and are willing to pay for it, Ama-Lur could be it. Tel: 215-3024.

Another restaurant that's much touted in fashionable Barcelona circles and frequented by local socialites, politicians, and theater people, is **Jaume de Provença**, Provença 88, where it crosses Rocafort, one block north of avinguda de

Roma. Chef-owner Jaume Bargues adds a touch of French expertise to his *nueva cocina* dishes. His isn't flashy cooking, but it's very good, noticeably in dishes such as asparagus mousse (made with tender stalks of fresh baby asparagus) in a mousseline sauce, spinach cannoli in Champagne sauce, and sole in a dry vermouth sauce. The prices are expectedly high, but service, in the series of small dining rooms and alcoves, is usually flawless. A tasting menu is available and is a good way to sample the restaurant's range. A fine wine list includes both Spanish and French selections. Tel: 230-0029.

A useful tip for budget watchers: Nearby at Provença 98 is **Racó d'en Jaume**, the original version of Jaume de Provença, where you can enjoy real "down home" Catalan cooking at a fraction of the price of the upscale model. Tel: 239-7861.

Art Nouveau is the look at **Vía Veneto**, Ganduxer 10, north of plaça Sant Gregori Taumaturg above the Diagonal, with its color-coordinated dark-brown leather banquettes, *café au lait* wood paneling and columns, even elegant Art Nouveau plates. Fortunately, the food lives up to the same high standards. Specialties, a blend of French and Catalan, include mussels with spinach purée, hake in Champagne sauce, and roasted red pepper stuffed with seafood in a subtle garlic sauce. The four-course tasting menu is good value. The wine list is a good one, too, and the wine steward unusually friendly and helpful. Tel: 200-7244 or 200-7024.

Azulete, vía Augusta 281 (north of the Diagonal, below plaça Molina), boasts a romantic setting inside the glass walls of a garden-*con*-pool, and well-made *nueva cocina* concoctions. The setting could hardly be more inviting, especially in good weather. This is a restaurant that seems to be getting better year by year. While the cooking doesn't send up flares, it is delicate and relies on fresh, seasonal ingredients. Favorites of the trendsetting regulars are prawns in Champagne sauce, prawn and vegetable pie, and a *surtido de mar* made with prawns, angler fish, and red mullet. Desserts are ambrosial too, especially the nougat ice with a bitter hot-chocolate sauce. Tel: 203-5943.

Popular **Florián**, at Bertrand i Serra 20 between Ganduxer and Mandri in the north, melds Catalan, French, and Italian influences, creating a delectable bouillabaisse of original dishes. It's a small place (12 tables), but very fashionable because of the freshness of ingredients and the light, dexterous variations on familiar themes, as in the preparation of *angulas* and endive salad, hake with seaweed sauce, and tripe with *chorizo*. A well-chosen wine list tilts toward Rioja reservas and French selections. Tel: 212-4627.

A good place to eat on Sunday, if your pocketbook is expandable, is **Finisterre**, centrally situated at avinguda de la Diagonal 469 (between Villaroel and Casanovas). It's one of the few fancy places open on Sundays and major holidays, and is usually packed with an eclectic mix of local businessmen, stylish-looking three-generation family groups, artists who have "arrived" (otherwise they couldn't afford it), and the city's prominent jocks. In short, a good mix to ensure lots of noisy, easy camaraderie and a spirit of *gemütlichkeit*. The food rises to the occasion, for the most part, especially in the Spanish dishes, such as *arroz abanda* (rice with fish), duck with sweet-sour sauce, and veal with mushrooms. The international dishes are well prepared too, but a bit more *pro forma*. Tel: 239-5576.

Since one of the Costa Brava's best restaurants, **Eldorado Petit**, took up residence in Barcelona several years ago, it has more than proved it can hack it in the big leagues. If you can find it, in a handsome fin-de-siècle house at Dolors Monserdá 7, you're in for a panoply of Catalan-*con-nueva-cocina* inventions, such as turbot in sea urchin sauce or duck breast in vinegar-scallion sauce. They have a way with sauces, as well as a well-stocked wine cellar. While you won't exactly need a second mortgage to finance a meal here, like most of Barcelona's more fashionable restaurants, it is pricey. Tel: 204-5153.

Another establishment familiar to diners in Seville and Madrid is **La Dorada**, the excellent upscale Andalusian seafood house whose Barcelona branch is at Travessera 44–46 between Muntaner and Aribau (one block north of the Diagonal). If you're surfeited with Catalan dishes, this is the place to enjoy *angulas* (baby eels) from Galicia, as well as the famous crisply fried fish dishes of the south, among many regional marine specialties. Seafood from other regions is flown in by private plane daily. Just get your bank loan and sally forth. Tel: 200-6322.

If you want a sea change from Catalan fare, **Guría**, at Casanova 97, between Aragó and València, is a longtime standby for traditional Basque cooking. Look for hake prepared a number of ways, *bacalao,* veal chops, and other familiar northern dishes, along with a decent wine list, heavy on the Riojas. Tel: 253-1038.

Traditional Catalan

Many traditional restaurants border the Barri Xinès (Chinese quarter) on carrer Escudellers. The reasons for the quarter's name are now obscure, but this rundown area east of

Escudellers down to passeig de Colom, which continues across Las Ramblas to the south, has long been seedy. However, it has become so unsavory and unsafe (because of purse-snatching) that it is best avoided day *and* night, unless you travel by cab.

One of the best traditional establishments is **Siete Puertas** (seven doors), located very near the waterfront at passeig d'Isabel II 14. Year in, year out, it keeps its homey flavor and family atmosphere. In a long rambling building, its several dining rooms, with dark wood banquettes, blue-and-white-tile wall paneling, and mirrors, create a pleasant backdrop for enjoying many fine seafood standards. Try the sailor's soup, paella fixed three different ways, *zarzuela,* or *bullabesa.* For dessert, this might be the place to try a *crema catalana,* a richer, sweeter, eggier version of *creme caramel.* Prices are moderate for reliable, nothing-fancy, real Catalan consistency. Yes, tourists go, but so do locals, in loving twosomes or huge family outings, and the decibel level can get high at peak times. It's quieter at night and starts serving early by Barcelona standards—but taxi there. Tel: 319-3033.

Font del Gat restaurant, passeig de Santa Madrona, is a delightful lunch or dinner stop when you are visiting Montjuïc, especially the Fundació Joan Miró. Sit outside in the courtyard if weather permits, enjoying the grilled meat and fish and Catalan specialties at this attractive, medium-priced, tree-shaded place. The restaurant is named for a fountain on the site that was designed by Puig i Cadafalch. Tel: 424-0224.

Simpler, but kind of funky in its perverse plainness, is **Casa Costa**, facing the water on carrer Judici in the waterfront section, Barceloneta. Chic Catalans enjoy the inverse snobbery of eating the freshest possible fish in minimalist paper-tablecloth surroundings. The grilled shrimp with *romescu* sauce (a Tarragona specialty made with tomatoes, chile peppers, garlic, hazelnuts, and olive oil) is a house specialty and is especially tasty. Otherwise, go with the simple grilled fish. Tel: 319-5028.

Also in the traditional and moderate-price category is **Los Caracoles** (the snails), at Escudellers 14, just east of the lower part of the Ramblas. It is best visited at lunchtime, as the neighborhood, as noted earlier, is borderline. While the restaurant has had a long run (since 1835), its snail dishes, paella, and *bullabesa* are still up to par, but the noisy confusion, masses of tourists (both Spanish and foreign), and labyrinthine passages leading from one small room to the next are more than some visitors want to handle. There's an overblown stage-set aspect to the "cutesy" folkloric decor, which is either off-putting or charming, depending on your taste. Tel: 302-3185.

In the Barri Gòtic and popular with fast-track youngish locals is **Café de l'Academia**, carrer Lledo 1, near the town hall. Located in a 16th-century building that was once a stable, this is a moderately priced place for an ample Catalan-style late breakfast or lunch. No dinner. Tel: 315-0026.

On a day spent roaming the Barri Gòtic, a handy place for a lunch break is **Restaurante del Tinell**, carrer Freneria 8, next to the cathedral to the north. Nothing fancy, mind you, but in a cheerful, *faux*-folkloric setting of brick floor, exposed-beam ceiling, and wrought-iron chandelier, you can enjoy a simple lunch of grilled sausages or giltfish sautéed with thyme, tomato, garlic, and onions. Service can be slow, but the old quarter grinds to a mid-day halt anyway. Tel: 315-4604.

Not to be confused with del Tinell is **El Túnel**, located just west of passeig de Colom at Ample 33. This is Barri Xinès territory, so take care. But for moderate prices, old-time Catalan specialties, and a homey style, it is a long-time local favorite. Tel: 315-2759.

Another old-timer, known for its reasonable prices and reliable fare, is **Casa Culleretes**, Quintana 5 (the hard-to-find entrance is on carrer Fernan Boquería), just off the Ramblas. Despite the celebrity photos lining the walls, Culleretes is a favorite of Barcelona family groups, and is just the ticket for sampling such Catalan dishes as *zarzuela marinera* or *costillas de cordero*. Tel: 317-6485.

For a light meal, **Flash-Flash**, at La Granada 25, is popular for its omelets, and serves more than 70 different kinds, as well as various salads and even some meat dishes. But it's the omelets that star. Tel: 228-5567.

West of the Ramblas, just off avinguda del Paral-lel, is a local artists-and-writers' hangout, **Casa Isidre**, Les Flors 12 (in another of those dubious go-by-taxi-only neighborhoods). Among the well-priced, imaginative specialties are *ensalada de marisco, bacalao gratinado al perfume de ajos,* and *las mollejas con alcachofas*. There is also a fine wine cellar. Tel: 241-1139.

—*Patricia Brooks*

CAFES, BARS, NIGHTLIFE

Barcelona has won a formidable reputation among Europeans over the last 15 years for being a city that stays alive long into the night. Along with Berlin and—even Catalans now admit—Madrid, Barcelona is a capital of nocturnal adventures, its lively café society switching to the bars and nightclubs at about midnight.

The Ramblas

For café life, the most compelling spot is the Ramblas. At the **Café Bar Zurich** (plaça de Catalunya), an ever-crowded terrace collects trendies and other people-watchers all year long, making this 1930s establishment a pillar of Catalan lounging. Of the watering holes on the Ramblas themselves, the most enjoyable are the **Café Viena** (rambla dels Estudis 70), a turn-of-the-century spot, and the breathtaking **Café de l'Opéra** (rambla dels Caputxines 74), unchanged since the heyday of Modernism and Art Nouveau. Nearby, at rambla 41, **La Castellana** serves delicious smoked-fish snacks with drinks. **Ambos Mundos** ranks as the plaça Reial's best *tapas*-munching and drifter-watching place.

The Waterfront

The revitalized waterfront has several chic bar-restaurants, the most popular being **Gamberinus** on the Moll de la Fusta. Easily recognizable by the grinning crayfish on its roof (designed by the same fellow who dreamed up Cobi, the Olympic mascot), it can be a pleasant escape from the enforced sobriety of sightseeing. Farther inland, behind the church of Santa Maria del Mar, the **passeig Born** has recently sprouted bars and cafés by the score. Fairly prosperous in comparison to most of its neighborhood, the gentrified Born is peppered with *xampanerías* (bars specializing in Catalan "champagne") and relaxed establishments that peddle everything from *horchata de fruta* (a local concoction tasting of almond) to such imported elixirs as Guinness and Jack Daniel's. **Miramelindo**, as its name suggests, is a particularly good-looking bar, although a brief stroll up this street is all that's needed to find a spot suitable to your tippling pretensions.

The Eixample

The bars of the Eixample, on the other hand, make no claim to being unpretentious. In the past decade here a large number of entrepreneurs have waged what could be called the designer bar wars. Beautifully appointed in keeping with the dictates of minimalist chic, the establishments of the Eixample try to outdo their rivals in wowing the customers. Despite their showiness, they are not frequented only by the hip—there are simply not enough trendy people to go around—but welcome adults of all ages and fashion affiliations. The wisest thing to take along on a late-night expedition to the Eixample is the *Guía del Ocio,* the weekly entertainment guide that faithfully lists the addresses of all the bars in the city. Barhopping from one designer wonderland to the next requires you to give exact instructions to successive taxi drivers.

Nick Havanna (Roselló 208), a bar that features a pendulum, banks of videos, and glass partitions, is the dean of Eixample nightspots, having launched the unrelenting struggle to be trendier-than-thou. Nearby, the **Velvet** (Balmes 61) outshines its neighbors in studied 1950s retro-kitsch, while the best bars of the Diagonal continue to draw *pijos* (rich kids) and other assorted Barcelona night owls. **Soho** (Diagonal 612) aims for lovers of antiseptic cool, **Boliches** (Diagonal 508) has a bowling alley, and **SiSiSi** (Diagonal 442) is for those who like to be tickled by laser beams. All are near the university district. Other perennials are **La Fira** (Provença 1717), a warehouse filled with antique fun-fair rides, and **Universal** (Maria Cubi 182), a two-level affair with a mercifully relaxed upper floor. The latter, close to the Diagonal's plaça Francesc Macià, enjoys the distinct advantage of being in a neighborhood warren of trendy bars. If you simply can't get enough of loud music and astonishing design ideas, you should ask fellow customers for the name of this week's Barcelona bar sensation.

Nightclubs and Music Halls

The three kingpins among the city's enormous nightclubs are **KGB** (Alegre de Dalt 55), **Otto Zutzz** (Lincoln 15), and **Zeleste** (Almogàvers 122). All are crowded and cosmopolitan after 2:00 in the morning. Zeleste, the farthest from the center—it's located in the Poble Nou district far to the north—occupies a former textile factory, its layout a surprising combination of concert halls, rooftop walkways, and plush bars. Major pop groups perform here.

For people unattracted by glitzy nightlife, a visit to the timeless music halls in the avinguda del Paral-lel might be the perfect antidote to the prevailing trendiness. Seedy but charming, such old-fashioned venues as **El Molino** (Vila i Vila 99) put on cabaret-style revues, and dusty performance halls welcome flamenco and tango troupes. **La Paloma** (Tigre 27), hidden in a small street between the Paral-lel and the Ramblas, is one of a vanishing breed: a picturesque, down-to-earth, and inexpensive European dance hall.

—*Stephen O'Shea*

SHOPPING

Barcelona calls itself a city of *botiguers* (shopkeepers), and shopping here is as brisk, cosmopolitan, and exciting as in any major city. Among the inevitable individual "discoveries," you'll find the latest designs in fashion, furniture, and art, along with antiques and handcrafted items.

New, Fashionable, and Trendy

Most fashionable shopping is in the district known as the Eixample, especially such streets as rambla de Catalunya and passeig de Gràcia, the northern (upper) end of Muntaner, and along the long Diagonal. Here you'll find all the big international names—Yves Saint Laurent, Pierre Cardin, and the like—as well as the best of the new Barcelona boutiques, designer showrooms, and galleries. A branch of **Loewe**, famous for its top-quality (and top-priced) Spanish leather goods, is at Diagonal 570: fabulous suits, coats, jackets, handbags, and other accessories. **Gonzalo Comella**, with fashionable clothes for men and women, is at the corner of the Diagonal and vía Augusta. Carrer Tuset, a small street that goes north from the Diagonal, is popular with the young crowd, both for its discos and its many small boutiques with offbeat youth fashions. A famous building, Gaudí's Casa Milà, on passeig de Gràcia, houses **Parera**, a fashionable clothing boutique.

While on passeig de Gràcia, look at **E. Furest**, at number 12–14 (also at Diagonal 468), for men's custom-tailored clothing; **Carlos Torrents**, number 95, for stylish menswear; **Yanko**, number 100, for elegant styling in Spanish leather—handbags, shoes, belts; and **A. Gratacos**, number 108, for a wide assortment of fine fabrics.

The inveterate shopper will want to browse among the clothes and gift shops that are chock-a-block in the streets between plaça de Catalunya and Fernando.

At the frenetically busy and bustling plaça de Catalunya is a branch of Spain's largest department store chain, **El Corte Inglés**, and on a nearby street, puerta del Angel, is another department store, **Galerías Preciados**.

For the cutting edge in contemporary Spanish, especially Catalan, design, turn to **BD Ediciones de Diseno**, carrer Mallorca 291, a showroom run by a group of local architects called Studio Per, featuring furniture by modern designers Javier Mariscal, Pepe Cortes, Pep Bonet, Cristian Cirici, Mireia Riera, and others. Just as intriguing are the excellent limited editions of painstakingly exact reproductions of famous works by Antoni Gaudí, Le Corbusier, Aalto, and other designers and architects of the past. Among the items reproduced are 1920s furniture by the Scottish architect Charles Rennie Mackintosh and the Italian rationalist architect Guiseppe Terragni, and rugs from designs by Cubist painter Juan Gris, Eileen Gray, and others. There's an extra kick at BD Ediciones because the showroom is in a landmark building by one of the most important Catalan architects of the late-19th and early-20th centuries, Lluis Domènech i Montaner.

Another intriguing shop is **Sala Vincon**, passeig de Gràcia 96, for the latest in furniture and decorative objects for the home. Savvy proprietor Fernando Amat seems always to be among the first with new functional objects and furniture.

In the Padrera area, a little grid of streets from the Diagonal east to carrer de Aragó, and from passeig de Gràcia north to carrer Bruc, are many new little shops with contemporary pottery, porcelain, glass, and basketware.

Art and Antiques

Along rambla de Catalunya, passeig de Gràcia, and carrer Consell de Cent are a number of art galleries with works by contemporary Catalan painters and sculptors. **Galeria Joan Prats**, rambla de Catalunya 54, is one of the better-known galleries, featuring contemporary works. **Sala Gaspar**, carrer Consell de Cent 323, at the corner of Balmes, is famous for its contemporary paintings and sculpture by big-name artists. **Serie Disseny**, Ganduxer 28, features small sculptures in limited editions.

Along carrer Moncada near the Picasso museum you will find **Galeria Maeght** (at number 25), a branch of the Paris atelier, with many graphics by international names. Farther along the same street is **Galeria Dalí** with Salvador Dalí etchings and his other graphics for sale.

At the Fundació Joan Miró on Montjuïc there is a **bookshop** with posters, reproductions, slides, and a good assortment of contemporary art books.

A first stop for antiques should be El Boulevard Rosa, a shopping center at rambla de Catalunya 65, between carrers de Aragó and València, where more than 60 antiques dealers have shops and you can browse in a leisurely plant-and-tree-shaded setting. Another central antiques emporium is **Centro de Anticuarios** at passeig de Gràcia 55, with more than 75 dealer shops. Other notable dealers are **Arturo Ramón**, carrer de la Palla 25 (heading west from the plaça de Sant Jaume), and **Santiago Marti**, Provença 243 (between rambla de Catalunya and passeig de Gràcia).

The oldest antiques market is held every Thursday (10:00 A.M. to 8:00 P.M.) in plaça Nueva, in front of the cathedral, but you will find antiques shops throughout the Gothic quarter, especially on carrer Call (leading from plaça de Sant Jaume), carrer de la Palla, and carrer del Banys Nous. **Antiguedades Maria Esclasans**, carrer de la Piedad 8 (a small street behind the cathedral), has a wide selection of *objets*.

Antique jewelry is a Barcelona "find," with especially good buys still available in Art Nouveau pieces. You might look especially at **L'Ancien Bijou**, in Centro de Anticuarios, passeig de Gràcia 55, and **Novecento**, nearby at number 75.

Auction houses are another excellent source of antiques, not just art and vintage furniture, but books, antique ceramics, jewelry, and bibelots. Look for **Balcli's**, Roselló 227 (between Balmes and rambla de Catalunya); **Brok**, Pau Claris 167 (between València and Mallorca); **Prestige**, València 277 (corner of Pau Claris); and **Subarna**, Provença 257 (corner of passeig de Gràcia).

Handmade Crafts and Gifts

Barcelona has two government-run **Artespaña** handicraft shops, one at rambla de Catalunya 121, the other at Diagonal 419, with crafts from all over Spain, but especially Catalan crafts. If you want a *précis* of Spanish handicrafts, a useful stop might be at the **Poble Espanyol** (Spanish village), avinguda del Marqués de Comillas, at the northern edge of Parc de Montjuïc. Almost every region's handicrafts are for sale in 35 craft shops in this exhibition area held over from the 1929 World's Fair. It's touristy, and you'll find few bargains, but for the visitor with limited time for shopping, it can be a gift problem-solver. Carved wooden bowls, fans, lace mantillas, regional ceramics, silk-screened tee shirts—the range extends from tasteful to tacky.

A narrow street just outside the old Gothic quarter, carrer Montcada has two delightful little handicraft shops: **1741** at number 2, with a big collection of pottery, and **Populart**, at number 33, with ceramics, handblown glassware, and folk art.

In fact, the Barri Gòtic itself is a good place for serendipitous browsing through old books and maps, souvenirs, and leather, especially along carrers Ferràn, Portaferrisa, and Freneria. Side by side on Freneria are **La Caixa de Frang**, for earthen casseroles, folk pottery, and well-made kitchen accessories, and **Grafiques El Tinell**, with hand-colored woodcuts and other prints made from antique blocks, as well as old maps and engravings. If you hanker for lace, either antique or modern work, **L'Arca de l'Avia**, Banys Nous 20, has exquisite tablecloths, christening clothes, nightgowns, and blouses. At **Papirum**, Baixada de la Llibreteria 2, you'll find antique, handmade, and hand-colored papers and end papers.

After watching the *sardana* danced, you may want a pair of espadrilles, those traditional shoes with coiled rope soles and canvas tops that Catalan men and women wear for dancing. You can buy espadrilles in many places, but an especially reliable shop is **La Manual Alppargatera**, carrer d'Avinyó, just off carrer Ferràn, connecting plaça de Sant Jaume with the Ramblas. The shoes are handmade, and there's a great selection from all over Catalonia.

Fine old and rare books and the art of bookbinding are Barcelona specialties. Among the best-known bookshops are **Librería Balague**, carrer de la Palla 13–15; **Puvill**, also on Palla at number 29; **Diego Gomez Flores**, carrer Banys Nous; and the bookbinder **Santiago Brugalla**, Aribau 7 (corner of Diputació).

You can browse for old (not necessarily valuable) books at the permanent stalls on carrer Diputació between Aribau and Balmes.

In a music-loving city in a music-loving country, you can expect to find many shops selling musical instruments, records, and cassettes. Some are located in the Ramblas and Gran Vía de les Corts Catalanes, others (especially for guitars) on carrer Ample near the cathedral. A very complete selection of musical instruments (including classical guitars) and early and current sheet music is at **Musical Emporium**, rambla Canaletes 129. Record and video shops are mostly in the Eixample, especially between plaça de Catalunya and the Diagonal. **Vidosa**, Balmes 335–343 (north of the Diagonal, where Balmes crosses Corinto) has an extensive record, cassette, and video collection.

Markets

Food markets are a lively part of Barcelona life. As a visitor, you might enjoy looking in at **La Boquería** (the handiest, off the Ramblas), **El Ninot** (on carrer Mallorca) or **Santa Caterina** (on avinguda de la Catedral). Other good shops for food, wine, and picnic items are **Colmado Quilez** on the rambla de Catalunya at Consell de Cent, and **Montequerias Leonesas**, rambla de Catalunya 5, which has an unusually large deli, wine, and liquor section and a neat little bar in the rear.

Fans of flea markets will find one, **Els Encants**, in plaça de les Glòries Catalanes (eight blocks north of plaça de Tetuàn on Gran Vía de les Corts Catalanes) every Monday, Wednesday, Friday, and Saturday, dawn to dusk.

A **stamp and coin market** sets up every Sunday morning on the plaça Reial, and also on Sundays you will find bargains in old books, stamps, coins, engravings, cassettes, videos, and myriad other goods in the **San Antonio market**, where carrers Urgell and Tamarit meet.

—Patricia Brooks

CATALONIA

By Ellen Hoffman

Ellen Hoffman is a freelance writer whose work has appeared in the Washington Post *and the* Los Angeles Times, *among other publications. Hoffman received a prize from the Spanish government for her writing about the country. She spends several months each year on the island of Minorca.*

Geographically speaking, Catalonia is a shadow of its former self. Today the region shares a border with France along the Pyrenees and occupies about 6 percent of Spain's total land area, including some 250 miles of Mediterranean coast. At its height in the 15th century, the Catalan empire included—in addition to the land within the borders of the modern state—Perpignan and what are now the French Pyrenees; Sicily, Sardinia, and Naples; and Valencia and the Balearic Islands. The empire was defined not merely by geography, but also by the creation of political institutions such as the Consell de Cent (council of one hundred), a participatory system developed in the 13th century for governing its capital, Barcelona. Common language and customs were other factors.

Catalan, a 1,000-year-old Romance language whose origins can be traced to the songs and legends of the Medieval troubadors, appeared as a written language in the 11th century. It has a rich literary tradition that is generally dated from the fiction and scientific works of Ramón Llull, the 12th-century Franciscan priest. It includes the public poetry contests that spurred the 19th-century "Catalan Renaissance," and the works of such 20th-century Catalans as Llorenç Villalonga, Josep M. de Sagarra, and Salvador Espriu. In this section we have used the Catalan spellings of place names, which are most common on signposts and in local guidebooks, followed by the Castilian names in parentheses where there is a significant difference. The section title is the Anglicized "Catalonia" rather than the Catalan "Catalunya" or the Castilian "Cataluña."

Many of Spain's rulers—including the Bourbons in the 18th century and Generalíssimo Francisco Franco in the 20th century—have denied Catalans the right to function as a political entity, to speak their language, or even to observe their own cultural traditions. Neither the loss of territory nor the repression of language and traditions, however, has diminished the core of pride and cultural identity that makes Catalonia one of the most interesting places in Spain.

Since the end of the Franco era in 1975, the Catalan nation, as it calls itself, has been an "autonomous region," or state, within the Spanish political system. Working within this framework, Catalans have undertaken an effort to recoup the language and cultural traditions forced underground for some 40 years. These efforts have been boosted by the selection of Barcelona as host of the 1992 Olympics, seen as an opportunity to educate both the current generation of Catalans and the rest of the world about Catalan culture and history.

Signs of the enthusiasm and commitment to rediscovering and breathing new life into ancient traditions can be seen by the visitor to Catalonia.

The profusion of bookstores and newspaper kiosks vending Catalan-language publications (including two daily newspapers, *Avui* and *Diari de Barcelona*), the omnipresent television sets in bars and cafés with their dials set to TV-3, the Catalan-language channel—to say nothing of the thousands of adults and children who are studying the language and its literature—all testify to the renaissance of the ancient language, which only 20 years ago was a forbidden tongue.

From grandparents to young children, joyful groups of Catalans now perform the lilting Catalan national dance, the *sardana*—previously outlawed—in public squares. Thousands of adults who learned Catalan at home but not in school now attend night school to learn how to write and speak their native language properly, and the unmistakable brilliant red and yellow stripes of the Catalan flag appear on public buildings as well as on lapel pins and bumper stickers.

The more modern Catalan artistic traditions that have nurtured and spawned artists such as cellist Pau (Pablo) Casals and opera singer Montserrat Caballe, Picasso, Miró, Dalí, and architect Antoni Gaudí—these tend to be concentrated in the Catalonian capital, Barcelona. But this in no way

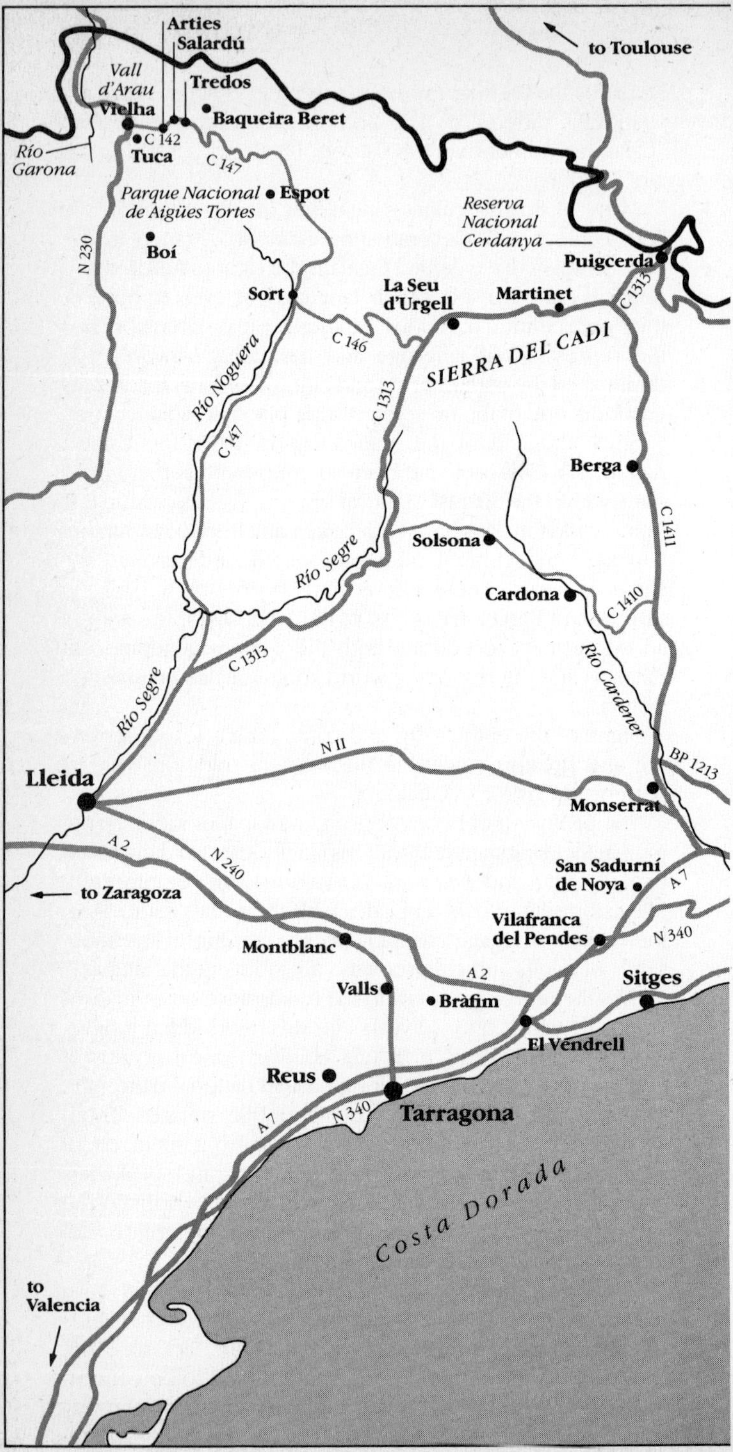

Arties
Salardú
to Toulouse
Vall d'Arau
Tredos
Vielha
Baqueira Beret
C 142
Río Garona
Tuca
C 147
Parque Nacional de Aigües Tortes
Espot
Reserva Nacional Cerdanya
N 230
Boí
Puigcerda
Sort
La Seu d'Urgell
Martinet
C 1313
C 146
SIERRA DEL CADI
Río Noguera
C 1313
C 147
Berga
C 1411
Solsona
Río Segre
Cardona
C 1410
C 1313
Río Cardener
Río Segre
N II
BP 1213
Lleida
Monserrat
A 2
N 240
San Sadurní de Noya
A 7
to Zaragoza
Vilafranca del Pendes
N 340
Montblanc
A 2
Sitges
Valls
Bràfim
El Vendrell
Reus
Tarragona
A 7
N 340
Costa Dorada
to Valencia

Perpignan
FRANCE
PYRENEES
A7
La Jonquera
El Port de la Selva
Cabo de Creus
C 252
GE 614
Portligat
Figueres
Roses
Cadaqués
C 252
Babía de Roses
Ripoli
C 150
Olot
Empúries
Río Fluvia
Banyoles
L'Escala
N 152
Verges
Ullatsret
Girona
Pals
C 255
Aiguablava
Río Ter
Vic
C 250
C 253
S'Agaró
Vidreras
GE 682
GE 681
Sant Feliu de Guíxols
Tossa de Mar
Blanes
A7
N II
Argentona
A 18
A 19
Costa Brava
Alella
Barcelona
N
Catalonia
0
miles
20
0
km
20

detracts from the fact that Catalonia outside Barcelona offers a treasure trove of historical and cultural attractions as well as scenic ones: the Pyrenees mountain range; the pine forests, the steep, salmon-colored cliffs and coasts of the Mediterranean Costa Brava between Barcelona and France; and the gentler agricultural regions around Lleida (Lérida) and Girona (Gerona).

MAJOR INTEREST

Architecture—Romanesque and Modernist
Medieval towns and cities
Roman ruins
Folklore and fiestas
Outdoor sports—skiing, hiking, water sports
Beach scenery and activities
Eating and drinking
20th-century art
The Costa Brava
The Pyrenees

The use of the term "nation" when referring to Catalonia is not an accident. For Catalan nationalists—from shopkeepers to the separatists who continue to fight to sever Catalonia's political links to Spain—this is the preferred term. At times, Catalonia does seem to act like an independent nation, dispatching its president and cultural officials around the globe, the former to make business deals, the latter to disseminate Catalan culture everywhere from the United States to Japan.

The travelling and trading of Catalans, too, has a history. For better or for worse, Catalans have been known since Medieval times—when the vibrant Jewish communities of Barcelona, Girona, and neighboring towns contributed significantly to the growth of commerce—as effective businesspeople. The economic base the Catalans built enabled the region to harness the advances of the Industrial Revolution and become, along with the Basque Country, the economic powerhouse of Spain. As onc Catalan writer observed during World War I, "While the Europeans were torturing each other at Verdun, the Catalans, thanks to Spain's neutrality, devoted themselves to doing business with the contenders. In this way, vast sums of money were accumulated." This active commercial life has endowed Catalans with a cosmopolitanism reflected in, among other things, multilingualism among much of the population.

But more than any other factor, it is the Catalan language that integrates the Iberian, Greek, Roman, Medieval, and, in modern times, tourist influences that have formed contemporary Catalonia. A Romance language with sounds and words that evoke French, Castilian Spanish, or Italian, depending on the moment and the context, Catalan, along with Castilian, became one of the region's two official languages after Franco's death.

In major tourist destinations—such as the Costa Brava—signs and menus appear in several languages, including English, Castilian Spanish, and Catalan. But in more rural areas the lingua franca is Catalan, although residents can speak Castilian as well.

The variety of themes and circuits that can be devised for travel through Catalonia illustrates the diversity and intensity of the region's historic and artistic legacy. It is possible, for example, to base a trip on visits to some of the hundreds of Romanesque churches—dating back to the early days of the Catalan empire—that dot the hills and valleys and mountains; or to visit only the largest monasteries, such as those at Poblet, Montserrat, Ripoll, and La Seu d'Urgell.

In Catalonia, in fact, religious monuments come with the territory, no matter what the theme of your trip. Unless you are an enthusiast of Medieval architecture and history, however, it is possible to overdose. Some may prefer instead to plot a pilgrimage to the monuments of Modernist architecture—products of the turn-of-the-century movement regarded as the Spanish equivalent of Art Nouveau—or to the unique, fantastic Salvador Dalí museum in Figueres; others may pass many days exploring Roman ruins.

You can even plot a tour around dining experiences, because Catalonia has lots of excellent restaurants, especially along the Costa Brava and in the mountains near the French border. The rich gastronomic bounty of traditional cuisine is based on local ingredients such as wild mushrooms and game from the forests and seafood from the Costa Brava—often prepared with a French touch. Catalonia also offers numerous wine-tasting opportunities, which can be exploited either at your daily dinner table or by touring and tasting at the wineries of Penedès or the cava vineyards of Sant Sadurní d'Anoia (in Penedès), capital of Spain's sparkling-wine production.

Catalonia's impressive, varied natural beauty is another reason to schedule a trip here. Depending on the direction you choose, less than an hour outside of Barcelona you begin to encounter long, sandy beaches that give way to dramatic, umber seaside cliffs, tiny coves for swimming and picnicking, and pine forests; or rocky foothills that lead into imposing mountain ranges, dense forests, pristine natural parks with snow-capped mountains; or gently rolling hills covered with almond and fruit orchards.

The calendar offers a large selection of holidays and folkloric activities from which to choose as well. They range from the creation of *castellers* (human pyramids), of which the most famous can be seen during the September fiesta in the town of Valls in Tarragona province; the "dance of death," performed by dancers clad in skeleton suits during the Easter processions in Verges, near the Costa Brava; processions of elaborately costumed "giants" and "dwarfs" in local fiesta celebrations; and the bonfires lit on the eve of San Juan, June 23, throughout the region.

The most important tradition, however, is probably the performance of the *sardana* circle dance to the accompaniment of an 11-person orchestra of winds and bass. The *sardana* is regarded as the Catalan national dance, because, as one book on Catalan culture explains, it is a "community-based, participatory activity and its evolution . . . has followed that of Catalan society." In towns where the *sardana* is performed regularly, usually on Sunday—such as in Besalú, not far from Girona—it is customary to post the schedule in the main square.

The Wines of Catalonia

Somewhat reminiscent of Condrieu in France's Rhône Valley, **Alella** is a tiny *denominación de origen* (DO) whose fame comes from its white wines, which have been made in this area since the Greeks first planted vines here. Four-fifths of Alella's production is white, the best of which is made from Xarel-lo and Pansa Blanca grapes grown on granite slopes a few miles north of Barcelona, in an area rapidly being encroached upon by the city's suburbs. Alella white wines can be lovely, pale, lightly perfumed, off-dry wines of great charm. Marqués de Alella produces the region's best wines.

Empordà (Ampurdán), on the Costa Brava south of Figueres, is an area of the foothills of the Pyrenees near the border with France. The mountains greatly influence Empordà's climate; the average rainfall is quite high, but tempered by the *tramontana,* a strong wind that blows through the region most of the year. Empordà produces sparkling wines, some *petillant* whites, Vi Novell (a Beaujolais Nouveau-style red), and some powerful, low-acid, oak-aged reds of 12 to 13 percent alcohol, but 70 percent of its wines are fruity rosés made from Garnacha and Cariñena grapes. Castillo de Perelada is the brand you are most likely to encounter in Spain. Their Blanc de Pescador white and Cazador red have their admirers. Oliveda makes a good Vi Novell.

Penedès, southwest of Barcelona, is one of the most important wine-producing areas in Spain. Not only does Penedès produce some fine table wines, it is one of the world's biggest producers of *methode champenoise* sparkling wines (see below).

Excellent red, white, and rosé table wines for everyday drinking are produced at lower altitudes along the Mediterranean coast from a variety of high-quality grapes: Parellada, Macabeo (Viura), and Xarel-lo for the whites; Ull de Llebre (Tempranillo), Monastrell, Garnacha, and Cariñena for the reds. Vineyards at higher altitudes in Penedès are planted with Cabernet Sauvignon, Cabernet Franc, Pinot Noir, Chardonnay, Sauvignon Blanc, and other varietals, as well as the best native wines.

Penedès wines have won international wine competitions, and in the course of doing so have dramatically altered the face of winemaking in Spain, the wine consumption habits and attitudes of the Spanish consumer, and the overall image of Spanish wines abroad. Penedès might best be described as the California of Europe. The great producers of this region are Torres and Jean Leon.

Priorato, located in the province of Tarragona, along the coast below Barcelona, is a harsh, rugged land of ancient villages and picturesque vineyards. Artisan winemakers tend old, low-yielding vines growing on impossibly steep terrain composed of volcanic soil and slate. The grapes, usually Garnacha and Cariñena, are brought down from the vineyards by mule and burro to be crafted into massive, powerful (14 to 18 percent!), black-red, oak-aged wines, some of which exhibit a lush fruit bouquet suggestive of blackberries. Look for Masiá Barril and Scala Dei.

Tarragona produces a variety of wines, most of which are destined for export, usually in bulk. In the subregions of Campo de Tarragona and Ribera del Ebro, most of the vineyards, which in recent years have been giving way to almond and hazelnut orchards, are planted with Macabeo, Xarel-lo, and Parellada grapes that yield full-bodied white wines low in acid. Falset produces wines similar to those of Priorato from Cariñena and Garnacha grapes.

Tarragona also produces some excellent sweet dessert wines, especially Moscatels, by the *solera* system (explained in the chapter on Andalusia, in the Jerez section). But Tarragona's chief claim to fame is as the largest supplier of *vinos de misa* (altar wines) to the Catholic Church, whose standards for the preparation of these wines are far stricter than those of any *consejo regulador,* the ruling body that controls the *denominaciones.*

The Spanish designation **cava** is used to denote sparkling wines made by the *methode champenoise* in Penedès and a few other designated areas in Catalonia, La Rioja, Navarra, and Aragón. Cava is a *denominación específica* (DE), which refers to the method of producing the wine, and is subject to both the regulatory councils of the DE and of the DO in which it is located. Cavas are fermented in the bottle like French Champagne. Production is strictly controlled by law, from pressing and fermentation through disgorging, recorking, and bottling.

By far the best cavas are made from Xarel-lo, Macabeo, and Parellada grapes at Sant Sadurní d'Anoia in Penedès, which accounts for 90 percent of Spain's cava production. One firm at Sant Sadurní d'Anoia is the largest producer of sparkling wines in the world.

Cavas are produced in Brut Nature (extra dry), Brut (dry), Seco (slightly off-dry), and Semi-seco (off-dry to sweet) styles. Those labeled Cremant or Extra are generally off-dry or sweet. Some good dry *rosado* (rosé) cavas are also made. Vintage cava, like vintage Champagne, is made only in very good years.

Regulations prohibit cava producers from making or marketing under the same label any sparkling wines that are not made strictly by the *methode champenoise.* Only cava wines can use the name "cava" on the label and place the cava symbol, a four-pointed star, on the cork.

The best cava wines from Penedès have shown very well in blind tastings against French Champagnes and California "champagnes," and many distinguished restaurants pour cava as their house sparkling wine.

Vilafranca del Penedès, capital of the Penedès wine district, has one of the finest wine museums in the world—and you don't have to be a wine nut to enjoy it. It has wonderful dioramas depicting winemaking techniques from the ancient world to Roman Spain to today; an excellent collection of old wine equipment, including Roman amphoras and wine presses; unusual wine utensils and paraphernalia; and a picture gallery. This exceptional museum is perhaps the best of several truly wonderful Catalan wine museums, including the one at Codorníu winery and the superb collection in the castle at Ampurdán.

One of the joys of visiting Catalonia is sampling cavas at one of the many *xampanerías* (Champagne bars) that have become the rage in the past few years. A visit to **Sant Sadurní d'Anoia,** the main cava-producing town, located 44 km (27 miles) southwest of Barcelona, for a Sunday trencherman's lunch is a Catalan institution. Carloads, and even busloads, of day-trippers on family, club, or company outings come out from Barcelona for a typical Catalan feast of grilled food. Here, and in several villages around Sant Sadurní, several restaurants have *servicio barbacoa.* These grill houses, sometimes concessions at cava wineries, either charge patrons a fee for using huge grills for roasting food they have brought—sausages, lamb chops, large mushrooms, *calçots* (green onions), and eggplant, red peppers, onions, etc., for *escalivada,* a typical Catalan dish of roasted vegetables—or they let patrons grill free of charge if they purchase the meats and/or the wine and cava from the establishment.

In addition, the restaurant usually serves full meals in a regular dining room. Here's where you come in. In the dining room, you can order most of the same dishes the *Catalanes* are cooking in the bourgeois barbecue madhouse of picnic tables and grills outside. Plates of *pa amb tomaquet* (Catalan tomato bread), grilled sausages, lamb chops, and rabbit with side dishes of white beans, chickpeas, grilled wild mushrooms, *ali-oli* (garlic mayonnaise), *escalivada,* and salad, all washed down with glasses of cava and *porrones* (glass beakers with drinking spouts) of red Penedès wine, will duplicate the feast nicely in slightly more tranquil surroundings. One such place, which has its own palatable cava and has no pretensions, except for its ability to serve prodigious amounts of home-cooked Catalan specialties, is **Canals y Munne**, plaça Pau Casals 6, in Sant Sadurní.

Cavas can be found on almost every wine list in Spain. The giant cava producers, Codorníu and Freixenet, make a wide range of very good sparkling wines, and Mont Marcal, Ferret, Roger Goulart, Raimat, Segura Viudas, and Juve et Camps (whose Ermita d'Espiells still wine is excellent) all make first-rate cavas.

If you can visit only one winery in Catalonia, make it Codorníu at Sant Sadurní d'Anoia. This huge cava winery, with so many miles of underground aging cellars that it has to be visited in a special train, is in a 19th-century building designed by the Catalan Modernist architect Puig i Cadafalch. The main building, which contains an excellent wine museum, has been declared a national monument. Codorníu is open from Monday through Thursday, but closed at lunch.

—*Gerry Dawes*

Despite the natural barriers posed by the rocky Mediterranean coast and the Pyrenees, modern highways and tunnels have made it possible to tour Catalonia quite efficiently—if you avoid the *salida* (exit) periods (Friday and Sunday afternoons) and the holidays, especially Holy Week, Christmas, and Reyes (Kings, observed January 6), when monumental traffic jams on the highways around Barcelona make what should be a two-hour trip into one that takes four, six, or eight hours.

We offer four approaches to exploring some of Catalonia's most important sights: a route along the Costa Brava; a circuit of Figueres, the city of Girona, and the surrounding region inland of the Costa Brava; an itinerary from Barcelona to the Cerdanya and on to the Vall d'Aran in the Pyrenees; and a series of suggestions for short excursions to a variety of sights southwest of Barcelona, including Tarragona.

Each approach can originate in and/or return to Barcelona, by far the most important gateway to the region. Figueres, Girona, and access to the Costa Brava lie along the route to Perpignan in Roussillon (France); the Pyrenees itinerary could continue on into France below Toulouse; and Tarragona is on the way to Valencia to the south and near the major route west to Lleida and on to Zaragoza in Aragón.

THE·COSTA BRAVA

The Costa Brava (wild coast), a 130-mile strip of Mediterranean beaches, cliffs, coves, and resorts, starts at Blanes, about 60 km (37 miles) north of Barcelona. To avoid traffic congestion and some of the more crowded, commercial, tourist destinations, take A 7 or N II from Barcelona, exit at Vidreras, and head for **Tossa de Mar**, a beach town with something more than beach: the tastefully restored remains of narrow streets and stone houses of a 12th-century town, the **Vila Vella**, surrounded by a thick wall and dominated by a round tower that overlooks the beach.

The twisting, cliffside coast road to the north of Tossa de Mar offers, alternatively, vistas of the turquoise, aqua, deep-blue, and purple waters of highly swimmable coves and sandy beaches, and garish, overdeveloped camping and resort areas that overflow with tourists during the summer.

Sant Feliu de Guíxols, on the coast 23 km (14 miles) northeast of Tossa, developed into a city in the 12th century as the result of the Benedictine monastery there, now being renovated. The town gained fame and economic strength with the discovery of the properties of cork—harvested from the local cork oak trees—for preserving wine. Tourism now dominates the town, which has a pleasant, tree-lined promenade along the beach and several good examples of Modernist architecture, the most prominent of which is the turn-of-the-century Casino dels Nois on the passeig del Mar.

Whether or not you explore Sant Feliu, stop for a meal at **Eldorado Petit**, one of the Costa Brava's top restaurants, sister to the restaurant of the same name operated by the same owner in Barcelona.

Catalan specialties, such as the *suquet* (fish stew) and crayfish *canalones* (ravioli) with a wild mushroom sauce, prevail on the menu of the small, attractive dining room on the rambla Vidal. But the local secret is that the food served in the unpretentious bar on the other side of the kitchen is prepared by the same chefs who serve the customers ordering from the more expensive menu; at lunchtime, laborers fill the tables to dine on hearty portions of delectable dishes such as fish soup or chicken with garlic and other herbs, all at a very affordable price.

North of Sant Feliu along the coast, a brief detour to the left leads to the **Curhotel Hipócrates**, a spa that offers regimens and therapies for disorders ranging from chronic fatigue to weight problems.

Even more effective in addressing the disorders of modern life might be a stay at **La Gavina** in **S'Agaró**, a few minutes' drive up the coast from Sant Feliu. No luxury is lacking in this elegant resort hotel, with its antiques-filled bedrooms, highly regarded restaurant, manicured gardens, and swimming and sunning complex with a magnificent view of the sea. Just in front of the hotel is a public walking path that affords excellent views of the coast. Removed from the tourist hubbub along the beach, the hotel is part of an exclusive preserve of spacious villas—many with a sea view—secluded from intruders by high walls and pine forests.

A few beach towns up the coast from S'Agaró is the modern, clifftop **Parador Nacional de la Costa Brava** at **Aiguablava**. The parador offers both a tranquil retreat from the traffic and congestion of the resort towns, and excellent views of the cliffs and water below—especially if you get a room with a balcony.

Empúries

From Aiguablava it's a 35-km (22-mile) drive north to Empúries to visit the extensive remains of a Roman city (Emporion) built on a site first inhabited by early Iberian tribes, then colonized by the Greeks in the sixth century B.C. On a clear day, this drive toward Empúries offers a vista of snowcapped mountains to the west and cultivated fields and the coast to the east. If time is no deterrent, you can pay a brief visit en route to the restored Medieval town of Pals or to **Ullastret**, a town where a Romanesque church and Medieval walls were built on the ruins of an Umbrian settlement. A small museum about a mile from the village displays finds from excavations of the ancient town.

Located on the outskirts of the modern fishing village of **L' Escala**, the Empúries ruins overlook the sea and several attractive sandy beaches fringed with pines—a good place for a picnic and a swim.

Grapes and olives were introduced to the area by the Greeks, and Empúries conducted lively and profitable trade—mostly in agricultural products—with Greece, even minting its own money, known as the *em,* which preceded the drachma.

The arrival of Roman soldiers to fight the Carthaginians during the Punic War in the third century B.C., however, marked the decline of Greek influence and the beginning of the influence of Roman language and law, which became the underpinnings of Catalan culture. By the first century A.D. the city had become Romanized, and it eventually came under the political control of Tarragona (then Tarraco, a coastal city south of Barcelona and capital of the Roman Empire in Spain).

Although the museum at Empúries contains Greek pottery, coins, and other objects found on the site, most of the houses, temples, and other structures to be seen at Empúries are Roman. (Buy the English guidebook from the shop at the museum entrance unless you read Castilian or Catalan.) A posted itinerary guides the visitor past the Cyclopean gates of the Greek city—so called because of the huge rocks from which they were constructed—into the grid of the ancient streets of the Roman city. A stroll through these streets, past the remains of the marketplace, the broken pillars of the forum, and the stone walls of the shops and houses, evokes a tangible sense of the daily life in ancient Empúries—in contrast to visiting the ruins of Tarragona, which are also impressive but which have been integrated into the modern city.

Cabo de Creus Peninsula

After Empúries the coast road turns inland to Castelló d'Empúries, site of the imposing 14th-century Gothic Santa Maria church, famous for the 15th-century carved alabaster altar in its apse. Then the road swings back to the coast and the Cabo de Creus peninsula. If it's close to sunset, stop briefly in **Roses**, a fishing village at the northeast head of the Bahía de Roses—the perfect place to catch the sun's last rays reflected off the water. At this time of day the fishing docks bustle with activity, with boats arriving and yellow- and orange-slickered fishermen unloading the day's catch onto waiting trucks. While in this area don't miss **Hacienda el Bulli**, an Alsatian-run restaurant serving haute cuisine in a hillside dining room overlooking the bay. The food and the views are equally alluring.

From Roses take the road east out on the peninsula to **Cadaqués**, a half-hour drive over a sinuous mountain road. This affords you first a view of the sweeping Bahía de Roses, then, on the northern coast of the peninsula, which appears from above as a string of tiny white sand beaches, of the tiny white houses of El Port de la Selva.

The fame of Cadaqués, a fishing village turned artists' colony, derives as much as anything from the fact that the adjacent nook on the seacoast, known as Port Lligat, was the home of Salvador Dalí. Other artists who are said to have visited and been inspired by the town's narrow, curving streets, its seaside park, and its setting along a pebbly beach at the base of the foothills include Picasso, Utrillo, Duchamp, and Catalan artists Tàpies and Rusiñol. Although some artists live here year-round, in the winter their work is more visible on the walls of the bars and cafés than in the museums and galleries, because the most important of the former, the **Museu Municipal**, on carrer Monturiol, containing works by Brueghel, Rubens, Fortuny, Toulouse-Lautrec, and many others, is open only during the summer. The **Hotel Playa del Sol**, facing the water, offers a good base from which to inhale the sea breezes and the street life.

Worthwhile scenic excursions from Cadaqués include exploring the nooks and crannies of the coast toward Cabo de Creus and ascending to the 11th-century Romanesque monastery **Sant Pere de Rodes**, nestled into the mountainside facing the sea north of Roses, with views of the entire peninsula.

Figueres, site of the Dalí museum, and Girona—both discussed in the next section—can also be reached by a short drive inland from all these places on the Costa Brava.

GIRONA AND ENVIRONS

The name Girona applies both to the region of Catalonia that encompasses the Costa Brava—the agricultural plain inland from the coast, and a portion of the territory from the Catalan Pyrenees to the French border—and to the modern city about 40 miles inland from Cadaqués.

Girona is about 100 km (62 miles) northeast of Barcelona on the A 7, and **Figueres** is 30 km (19 miles) beyond that. Then it's another 25 km (15.5 miles) or so to the French border, a geographical fact that has had a positive effect on the cuisine of the area. The **Hotel Ampurdán** on N II, just north of Figueres, has comfortable lodgings and a simply decorated, but excellent, restaurant where you can choose from the French and Catalan dishes for which it is widely known and highly regarded. Choices include local fish and seafood in either style, Catalan roast partridge with pears, and an excellent crudités plate. Try a pleasing local Ampurdán wine, such as the red Gran Recosund, vintage 1983, at a very reasonable price.

Figueres, a small, pleasant town, serves as a sort of geographical bridge between the modern art community of Cadaqués and Girona, and the main attraction here is the **Teatre-Museu Dalí**, a tour-de-force that has to be seen even if you've never liked Dalí's work. From the small central plaza known as the Rambla, it's only a couple of blocks to the museum, which from the back resembles a pink box, its roof adorned with rows of huge white eggs and its walls dotted with what look like loaves of spiral-shaped bread. Nearby is the building where Dalí lived for a number of years before his death in 1989. Inside, the atrium structure creates a cocoon-like environment that you can explore by climbing to the top and descending through a series of almost-round galleries.

Every window, every corner offers another perspective on a wide range of Dalí styles and structures. Paintings of melting watches are in a tiny minority here. Instead, the visitor is treated to a stunning range of artistic styles and media: a sculpted sofa; a monumental sculpture of Mae West's face; paintings of human figures fashioned from rocks and pebbles; nude female mannequins, each with arms extended in a different direction, Shiva-style; and much more.

Souvenir hunters who find the museum's postcard and poster supply lacking can find a more complete selection of Dalí memorabilia at Distribucións d'Art Surrealiste, a shop across the plaza from the museum entrance.

If you're not tired of Dalí yet, walk a few blocks to the **Hotel Durán** to view the Catalan artist's paintings displayed in the lobby and dine at the restaurant, a rather formal, well-regarded establishment known for its offerings of regional cuisine.

The City of Girona

About a quarter of the way (30 km/19 miles) south from Figueres toward Barcelona, Girona is a modern city built around a Medieval core, which itself was built over the Roman fortress of Gerunda. The Medieval center is self-contained and of a size that allows for an interesting half-day walking tour of its dark, labyrinthine streets and important monuments.

Entering the city from N II, you'll see signs to the plaça de la Independencia on the west bank of the rather murky ríu Onyar, which divides the Medieval city from the new. Walking under the arcades along rambla de la Llibertat on the riverbank, you'll encounter a bridge that offers both a view of the umber- and mustard-colored, restored Medieval houses that line the east bank, and a footbridge that takes you into the old quarter.

Restaurant Cal Ros, almost hidden along the wall behind the dim arches at Cort Real 9, offers such typical dishes as a country-style Spanish omelet with vegetables, in a homey dining room perfumed by the lingering odor of smoke from wood burning in the fireplace.

Continuing straight a couple of short blocks to carrer de la Força, then left about two more blocks through the dim streets, brings you to the plaça de la Catedral, the center of the Medieval town. Here is the **Catedral de Santa Maria**, which has the largest nave of any Gothic cathedral in the world. An admission fee entitles you to climb the Romanesque bell tower, which offers a good view of the city; to tour the cloister, which is enclosed by graceful arches adorned with Romanesque carvings of animals; and to tour the church treasury.

The most unusual piece in the treasury—where most of the displays are of ornate, gilded, church art—is the *Tapestry of the Creation,* a 12th-century embroidery with flat but vivid representations of Adam and Eve and Noah's animals.

Emerging from the cathedral, descend to the plaza and turn right onto carrer Ferràn el Catolic. A few steps ahead and on your left you'll encounter the entrance to the 12th-century **Arab baths**, where you can visit the *frigidarium,* with its central pool wreathed by eight columns, and other salons for tepid, hot, and steam baths.

As you exit from the baths, take a left into the plaça del Jurats and cross the bridge over the ríu Galligants to visit the Benedictine monastery of Sant Pere de Galligants, in existence since 992 and now the site of the **Museu Arqueològic**. Notable architectural features include the 11th-century door, decorated with plants and animal-like creatures, and the cloister, with columns on which are sculpted depictions of New Testament stories. The museum displays prehistoric and Iberian items, as well as finds from ancient Emporion, the Roman town on the coast (see section on Empúries, above).

From the ninth to the 15th centuries the city had a large Jewish community, some of whose members were executed by the Inquisition before the rest were banished from Spain, along with all other Jews, in 1492. A pamphlet available from the tourist office in the plaça del Vi outlines a walking tour of the dark, narrow streets of the *call* (ghetto), although there are no outward signs or references to the area's Jewish heritage. The tourist office can also provide a pamphlet outlining a walking tour of other Medieval monuments.

Eighteen kilometers (10 miles) northwest of Girona, the lakeside town of **Banyoles** serves as a gateway to a series of charming small towns and, ultimately, to the rugged mountains of the Pyrenees. A circuit of the lake in Banyoles—which will be the site of rowing and canoeing events in the 1992 Olympics—takes you to a tiny, Romanesque, lakeside chapel known as **Santa Maria de Porqueres**. The most notable features of this 12th-century church are the arches over the outside door and the animal carvings on the capitals of the columns inside.

Besalú, a Medieval town 13 km (8 miles) northwest of Banyoles that's a sort of Girona in miniature, has a superbly restored Romanesque arched bridge across the ríu Fluvià. The best views are from the highway and from the terrace of the **Café Can Quei**, which is built into the ancient stone walls in the town center. An important Romanesque church here, part of the 12th-century Benedictine monastery of Sant Pere, is closed to the public.

From Besalú the road west enters more mountainous terrain, passing through the "volcanic zone" of **Olot**, where ancient craters are now carpeted with forests.

From here you can choose from at least two travel strategies: One is to continue west toward Ripoll and the Pyrenees (see below); the other is to return to Barcelona by heading south from Olot or from Ripoll through **Vic**, where you could make a lunch stop at the parador, a modern stone structure built in the style of a Catalan farmhouse.

If you go through Vic, consider pausing to enjoy the local attractions, which include a bustling, arcaded town square; the Catedral de Sant Pere, which was constructed in the late-18th century over the remains of a Romanesque structure (the original bell tower remains); and the reconstruction of a 2nd-century Roman temple discovered in 1882.

THE PYRENEES OF CATALONIA

Another alternative—whether you get there by highway C 1411 through the Túnel del Cadí, north from Barcelona via Berga (about a two-hour trip), or from another direction—is to explore Ripoll, La Seu d'Urgell, and the scenic ski and trout-fishing areas of the Cerdanya from the **Hotel Boix** in **Martinet** on route C 1313, west after the tunnel. Request a room overlooking the fast-running stream next to the hotel, and plan to eat as many meals as possible in the excellent hotel restaurant presided over by owner/chef José Maria Boix.

The restaurant, decked out with a plant on every table, overlooks the stream. A meal starts with an appetizer of tiny, herbed *arbequines,* wonderfully tangy olives from a town near Lleida. Most dishes are based on such local ingredients as wild mushrooms, game, fresh river trout, and river crabs. The pearl onions in a sauce of cream and thyme are exquisite; all breads and pastries—including novelties such as olive bread—are made in the kitchen; and the long, crisp, tile-shaped almond cookie, or *teja,* served to all diners, is a delectable regional treat. The wine list offers the opportunity to try some of Catalonia's best, including the Raimat Cabernet Sauvignon, Reserva 1985.

If you want to explore close to the hotel, the management will provide you with a map of mountain walking trails. Other nearby sports diversions include the Puigcerdà golf course and the town of Puigcerdà, a ski center next to the French border.

A bit farther afield, but easy one-day excursions from Martinet, are **Ripoll** to the east and La Seu d'Urgell to the west, both famous for their Romanesque structures. In Ripoll it's the monastery, with a huge, elaborately carved façade depicting Biblical scenes. (Don't be tempted to spend a night in Ripoll, even if it seems to make sense in terms of your itinerary. It lacks a decent hotel, and the stench from the local paper factory will make you want your stay there to be as short as possible.)

The major attraction in **La Seu d'Urgell** is the cathedral, seat of the largest diocese in Catalonia, also known for the collection of Romanesque and Gothic paintings and sculptures in the **Museu Diocesà** nearby. The old quarter, adjacent to the cathedral on the eastern edge of town, retains the ambience of a Medieval market center; the upper stories of some ancient houses almost touch each other over the narrow streets. The **Parador de la Seu d'Urgell**, diagonally across from the entrance to the cathedral, is a modern hotel with an atrium built around the ancient cloister of the former convent of Santo Domingo.

On the outskirts of La Seu, the **Hotel El Castell**, a member of the Relais & Châteaux network, offers bedrooms with satin bedspreads, an excellent restaurant overlooking the valley, and a swimming pool—all located under the shadow of the remains of an ancient stone fortress, right on the grounds.

Exploring the Pyrenees

The road out of La Seu, west through Sort, through 6,200-foot-high **Puerta de la Bonaigua**—often closed in the winter—and into the Vall d'Aran, offers some of Spain's most spectacular mountain scenery. The going is slow and tortuous, on a road that is unpaved in some spots and often under construction in others. It snakes along the edge of steep mountains, climbing ever higher through dense pine forests toward the snowy peaks around the pass.

Hikers and others who savor the silent isolation of the mountains may want to schedule a few days in the **Parc Nacional de Aigües Tortes**, which has refuges for hikers and is accessible from lodgings in nearby towns, including Boí and Espot.

Approaching Bonaigua pass, the road climbs through a landscape littered with immense boulders. The air becomes purer and more bracing and, as you arrive at the pass, the slate roofs of the houses in the **Vall d'Aran** along riú Garona suddenly come into view.

The valley, a narrow strip of towns surrounded by mountains as high as 12,000 feet, was cut off by snow from the rest of Spain for more than half of each year until 1948, when a tunnel was opened to provide access from the south as an alternate to going over the pass. Until then the local residents—whose language, Aranese, resembles Catalan—maintained a tranquil rural existence in their gray stone houses with deeply sloped slate roofs.

Now the valley has become a modern ski center (the main ski complexes are **Baqueira Beret** and **Tuca**); pizza parlors and high-rise apartment buildings are taking over the landscape. About the only way to make contact with traditional culture is to view some of the small Romanesque churches—only from the outside, because they're usually locked—in towns such as Salardú and Tredòs, or the small museum—open only in late afternoon—in **Vielha**, the capital of the region.

A scrap of history may be encountered by visiting the **Parador Nacional Don Gaspar de Portolá**, in Arties, a short drive east of Vielha. The parador, built in the style of a ski lodge with sloping roof and rustic furnishings, is adjacent to the home of the Catalan explorer of the same name who served as governor of lower California in the 18th century and is credited with founding a number of missions in California. If you ask at the reception desk, a member of the staff may be willing to show you the inside of the Portolá family chapel and the family home, which features window-like glass compartments in the walls, one housing a beehive, others designed to protect birds from winter cold.

If you prefer hiking to skiing, visit in the warmer months, when the mountain trails are open—the tourist office in Vielha can provide you with a map of these—and the crowds smaller or nonexistent.

For a quick return to Barcelona or to explore points of interest in southern Catalonia, exit from Vielha due south through the tunnel (instead of east back through the Bonaigua pass) in the direction of Lleida.

Another option—also convenient if you want to return from La Seu d'Urgell to Barcelona—is to follow the ríu Segre south to Bassella and then east to **Solsona**, to visit the **Museu Diocesà**, a treasure trove of Romanesque and Gothic art from churches in the region; and the Catedral de Santa Maria, with the Romanesque sculpture *Virgin of the Cloister.*

From Solsona it's only 21 km (13 miles) east on route C 1410 to the **Parador Duques de Cardona**, situated in a Medieval fortress castle on top of a hill. If you've ever wanted to know how it feels to be a feudal lord, spend a night under the high ceilings inside the immense, thick walls—or at least stop for a meal on the way back to Barcelona.

If you have the time and the inclination to make another major stop en route back to Barcelona, you can plan a visit to Montserrat, about 52 km (32 miles) northwest of the city on C 1411. Montserrat is actually the name of the mountains—a distinctive range of jagged, gray fingers of rock reaching upward more than 3,500 feet—that have given their name to the **monastery of Montserrat**, one of Catalonia's best-known and most-visited tourist attractions.

The main attraction at the monastery—unlike some of the other Catalan monasteries, which are renowned for their architecture—is the statue *La Moreneta* (black Madonna), which sits on the altar in the basilica. Because the black Madonna is the patron saint of Catalonia and the object of many pilgrimages, be prepared to encounter mass tourism, complete with buses and trash, on this visit. The 12th-century Romanesque door survives, although much of the church was destroyed by Napoleon's troops. The Escolanía (a boys' choir) of Montserrat performs daily at church services.

In addition to the church, there is the **Museu de Montserrat**, on the plaça Santa Maria. One part of the museum houses a collection of art by Caravaggio, El Greco, and other Italian, Flemish, and Spanish painters, and the modern section holds works by Picasso, Dalí, Rusiñol, and others. The cave of the Virgin—where the statue of the Virgin was said to have been found in the year 880—can be reached by a 20-minute walk from the monastery.

SOUTHERN CATALONIA

Barcelona serves as a good base from which to make forays into the Roman and Medieval precincts of southern Catalonia, as well as to enjoy the Mediterranean coast and tour the wine and cava country. Any of the following suggested destinations can be visited on a one-day trip from Barcelona—although it would be best to stay overnight if you are going to Tarragona—or by a circuit you can easily devise by picking and choosing. Because these destinations are quite close to Barcelona, choose your travel days with care; on the weekends the highways are inevitably clogged and very slow.

Vilafranca del Penedès and **Sant Sadurní d'Anoia** are, respectively, the wine and cava capitals of Catalonia, and Sant Sadurní is, in fact, the cava capital of Spain (see The Wines of Catalonia, above).

The Museu dei Vi (wine museum) in Vilafranca, 38 km (24 miles) west of Barcelona, provides an excellent introduction to winemaking in general through its recreation of a wine cellar and displays of the huge wooden presses and other tools used to cultivate and harvest grapes and make wine. Local vintners take turns as hosts for the tasting room, where you can sample their products at the end of the museum visit. The Torres vineyard in Vilafranca welcomes visitors for tours and tasting.

In Sant Sadurní, 11 km (7 miles) northeast of Vilafranca, every road sign seems to point to a cava-making establishment. This town is a showplace of turn-of-the-century Catalan Modernist architecture, and a visit to the Codorníu cava winery offers an opportunity to see the town's most important examples of the Modernist style—the family home and the cellars, with their vaulted ceilings and stained-glass windows—as well as to observe production of the bubbly.

The **Santa Maria de Poblet monastery**, some 89 km (55 miles) almost directly west of Barcelona near Montblanc, was the home of a Cistercian order and the religious center of the kings of Catalonia and Aragón from the 12th century through 1835, when it was closed by the Order. Subsequently sacked and destroyed, the monastery—in which the tombs of the monarchs may be seen—now offers visitors a tour of the restored library, kitchen, and other facilities used by the monks, as well as the church and a museum.

Montblanc, a few minutes east of Poblet, is a Medieval town surrounded by thick 14th-century walls punctuated with 17 towers, and is a pleasant place to stroll and visit the Friday morning market in the square.

While driving in this area and toward Tarragona, consider stopping to taste the typical *calçotada,* (braised tender onions) offered at numerous roadside restaurants. The town of **Valls**, between Montblanc and Tarragona, is famous for this dish, as well as for its *castellers* who form human pyramids by climbing on each other's shoulders at fiesta time.

Aficionados of church architecture may want to visit the **Santes Creus Cistercian monastery**, 30 km (19 miles) northeast of Tarragona. From Barcelona, you can reach it by turning west off the A 7 *autopista,* before El Vendrell, to take the fork of A 2 to the Bràfi turnoff, following the signs. (At El Vendrell, at carrer Guipzcoa 12, there is a museum and archive dedicated to the Catalan musician Pablo Casals, who is revered in Catalonia not only for his ability as a cellist, but also as a conductor and for making music available to the general public.)

The street approaching the monastery is lined with buildings that were once a part of it but are now private residences. The monastery has a Gothic cloister whose delicate columns are adorned with sculptures of flowers and animals; the cross-shaped church contains the tombs of the 13th- and 14th-century Catalan monarchs Pedro II and Jaime II.

Sitges, one of the most popular and most charming beach towns on the Costa Daurada, about 40 km (24 miles) southwest of Barcelona, has been a center of Catalan painting, music, Modernist architecture, and other arts since painter Santiago Rusiñol made it his home at the end of the 19th century. (The Costa Daurada is the stretch between Barcelona and the Valencia area to the south.) Two private, Modernist-style residences, the **Romàntic** and **La Renaixença**, offer comfortable but simple lodgings—some rooms have balconies—and the use of a leafy private garden.

The town, a major destination for gay travellers, has several important museums and sponsors an annual theater festival in the spring and a horror-film festival in the fall; it is also known for its displays of "carpets of flowers" during the Corpus Christi festival in June.

Tarragona

While you visit this modern seaside city about 105 km (65 miles) southwest of Barcelona, it's almost impossible to forget that Tarragona once controlled all of Roman Spain; fragments of Roman columns and walls seem to sprout from the traffic-filled streets. The **Museu Arqueològic**—whose cellars are formed from Roman walls—houses an important collection of mosaics, sculptures, a sarcophagus, and other objects from the local Roman sites.

It's certainly worth braving the heavy traffic and deceptively modern buildings that you encounter before seeing the ample swath of Mediterranean beach and blue water, which is probably what attracted the Romans to the location.

The **balcó del Mediteranni**, an elevated seaside promenade that intersects with the rambla Nova, is a good spot from which to orient yourself for sightseeing. Below and slightly to the north you can see the remains of the **Roman amphitheater.** From the balcó you can walk a sightseeing circuit, heading north a couple of blocks to the Museu Arqueològic on the passeig de Sant Antoni, then entering the old section of Tarragona to the north to visit the cathedral and the passeig Arqueològic—a path along the ancient wall on the north side of the cathedral—and the remains of the provincial forum, and then returning to rambla Vella to circle back to the balcó.

While it is the extensive Roman monuments that most distinguish Tarragona from many other Catalan cities, you might also want to tour the **Catedral de Santa Tecla**, the largest one in Catalonia, noted for its arcaded cloister and the rows of carved figures of the apostles on the façade.

Another important site, the Museu Paleocristià and necropolis, is a mile or so south of the balcó, on the passeig de la Independencia. The **Imperial Tarraco** and the **Lauria**, the accommodations recommended in Tarragona, are both centrally located.

For a view of one last Roman ruin before leaving the area, take the A 7 toward Barcelona and watch carefully to the north for the two-level Roman aqueduct known locally as "the devil's bridge." (In the other direction, of course, the A 7 heads south to Valencia.)

The **rambla Nova**, a promenade that bisects the modern city, is a good place for a stroll and a view of the pink-brick Modernist convent of Las Teresianes. The Mediterranean is visible from the overlook at the end of the strip.

For an excellent meal of fresh seafood in an unpretentious setting, descend to **Restaurant La Puda** on the Moll de Pescadors, across the street from the pavilion where the fisherman dock. (A siren signals the beginning of an auction of the catch around 3:30 or 4:00 P.M.) Good choices here include the *arrosejat,* similar to a paella, made with noodles instead of rice; the house fish soup; and the appetizer platter of the day's fresh seafood.

The city of **Lleida** (Lérida), capital of the Catalonian province of the same name, is a logical stopping-off point if you're going west from Tarragona to Zaragoza in Aragón.

Although modern Lleida is an industrial center, the old quarter known as Canyeret comprises several Medieval monuments, including the old cathedral, or **Seu Vella** (not to be confused with the 18th-century "new" cathedral), built on the site of a former Roman temple and a mosque, and which represents the transition from Romanesque to Gothic architectural style. Other important historic and cultural sites here are the Zuda, a Moorish fortress of which only a few walls survived a siege by the French in the 19th century; and an **archaeological museum**—featuring finds from digs in the area—located in the 15th-century Catalan Gothic Hospital de Santa Maria.

GETTING AROUND

Barcelona is the transportation center of Catalonia. It has a major international airport, El Prat de Llobregat, which is connected to London and New York by daily nonstop flights, and to other cities in the United Kingdom on a less-frequent schedule. Flights from all over Spain on Iberia and Aviaco, the domestic airline, land at El Prat. The *Puente Aereo* is an hourly shuttle service between Madrid and Barcelona. No reservations are accepted; tickets may be bought at the airport. The airports at Girona and Reus (outside Tarragona) do not handle commercial flights.

Catalonia may also be entered from France by train, car, or ferry. The most common point of entry by car is La Jonquera, near Perpignan, which connects with the A 7 and N II to Barcelona. However, there are several border points in the Pyrenees, including Puigcerdà and Collado d'Ares.

The best way to tour Catalonia is by car, although, if your only destination is the Costa Brava beaches, it is possible to get there using public transportation.

Catalonia's major highways fan out of Barcelona in every direction. In some cases—such as to Girona and to Tarragona—there are fast toll roads virtually paralleled by slower, regular highways that pass through towns and carry a lot of truck traffic. Tolls on the *autopista* can be expensive.

RENFE trains from the Sants station, a few blocks northwest of Barcelona's plaça de Espanya, serve the Costa Brava north to La Jonquera at the French border, and the Costa Daurada to the south. (To the north the train stops are somewhat inland, requiring a bus connection to the beach.) There is also train service from Barcelona to the Pyrenees, going through Vic, Ripoll, Puigcerdà, and to the French border. Other train routes include Barcelona through Lleida to Huesca in Aragón to the west; and Barcelona-Tarragona-Zaragoza (the latter also in Aragón).

There is also an extensive network of local buses that can be used to get to and around most parts of the region.

In the summer, Cruceros Costa Brava offers ferry service among various points on the coast, including Sant Feliu and Blanes.

ACCOMMODATIONS REFERENCE

When dialing telephone numbers from outside the country, drop the 9 in the area code.

Costa Brava Area

► **Hotel Ampurdán.** Carretera N II, at km 763, 17600 **Figueres.** Tel: (972) 50-05-62; Telex: 57032.

► **Hotel Durán.** Lasauca 5, 17600 **Figueres.** Tel: (972) 50-12-50.

► **La Gavina.** Plaça de Rosaleda, 17248 **S'Agaró.** Tel: (972) 32-11-00.

► **Curhotel Hipócrates.** Carretera de Sant Pol 229, 17220 **Sant Feliu de Guíxols.** Tel: (972) 32-06-62.

► **Parador Nacional de la Costa Brava.** 17255 **Playa de Aiguablava.** Tel: (972) 62-21-62; Fax: (972) 62-21-66.

► **Hotel Playa del Sol.** Platja Pianch 3, 17488 **Cadaqués.** Tel: (972) 25-81-00.

The Pyrenees and Environs

► **Hotel Boix.** Carretera Lleida-Puigcerdà, at km 154, 25724 **Martinet.** Tel: (973) 51-50-50.

► **Hotel El Castell.** Carretera C 1313, 25710 **La Seu d'Urgell.** Tel: (973) 35-07-04; Fax: (973) 35-15-74.

► **Parador Duques de Cardona.** 08261 **Cardona.** Tel: (93) 869-1275; Fax: (93) 869-1636.

► **Parador Nacional Don Gaspar de Portolá.** Carretera de Baqueira–Beret, 25599 **Arties.** Tel: (973) 64-08-01; Fax: (973) 64-10-01.

► **Parador de la Seu d'Urgell.** 25700 **La Seu d'Urgell.** Tel: (973) 35-20-00; Fax: (973) 35-23-09.

South of Barcelona

► **Imperial Tarraco.** Passeig Palmeras, 43003 **Tarragona.** Tel: (977) 23-30-40.

► **Lauria.** Rambla Nova 20, 43004 **Tarragona.** Tel: (977) 23-67-12.

► **Renaixença.** Isla de Cuba 13, 08001 **Sitges.** Tel: (93) 894-0643.

► **Romàntic.** Sant Isidro 23, 08001 **Sitges.** Tel: (93) 894-0643.

THE BALEARIC ISLANDS

MINORCA, MAJORCA, IBIZA

By Ellen Hoffman

The Balearic Islands share the turquoise and blue waters of the Mediterranean, meteorologically benign latitudes, and isolation from the life and culture of mainland Spain. And for centuries, despite the isolation geographic accident has dealt them, the islands have received both welcome and unwelcome visitors—from Romans and Arabs to pirates, George Sand, and Frédéric Chopin.

Three-thousand-year-old stone monuments, Medieval cathedrals, and finely worked Phoenician sculptures and jewelry are only a few of the surviving clues to the rich and varied history of Minorca, Majorca, and Ibiza—each less than a half-hour plane trip from Barcelona.

These days the great majority of visitors to the Balearics (pronounced bahl-eh-ARE-ics) arrive from northern Europe, and they head here in search of beaches and the jovial hullabaloo of pizza parlors and discotheques that inevitably spring up in resorts catering to mass tourism.

Yet by scheduling a visit outside the high season (which is July and August, plus Easter, Christmas, and New Year's) and by studying the map a bit, it is surprisingly easy to circumvent the crowds and penetrate to the islands' traditional core of natural and man-made attractions.

August—when the Spanish as well as foreigners take their

vacations—is the primary vacation month in the Balearics, and if you go at this time there will be crowds everywhere except on the most isolated beaches. Sunny days appropriate for basking or picnicking can occur in almost any month, but for all but the most robust travellers the Mediterranean swimming season runs from late May into October. April and May—when flowers carpet the islands—are good times for sightseeing, as is all of September and much of October. Winter brings some wet, windy weather to all of the islands, but Minorca gets the brunt of it, while Ibiza remains milder.

If you don't like crowds, and your goal is to experience the "real" Balearics—as opposed to the façade constructed for tourists—avoid August and aim for the months on either side of it. Ideally, a visitor to the Balearics would spend several weeks exploring and discovering the uniqueness of *each* island. Shorter-term visitors, however, should consider several factors when trying to decide on an itinerary.

Minorca offers lots of archaeological sites, a wide selection of beaches, the Medieval town and fishing port of Ciudadela, and a relative lack of mass tourism compared to Majorca and Ibiza.

Majorca, the largest island (about 60 miles east to west and 45 miles north to south), is the only one with a major historic city—Palma—as well as two mountain ranges, including the Tramuntana to the west, which offers dramatic vistas of cliffs and sea. The island is a mecca for artistic and literary expatriates but also has numerous resorts that cater almost exclusively to the package tourist trade, which operates all year but is most obvious during the summer.

Tiny—only 25 miles from one end to the other—Ibiza's whitewashed villages and scenic coves and beaches have been inundated by a wave of cosmopolitan tourists and expatriates ranging from the jet set to colorful dropouts who ply their craftsy wares on the streets and in the boutiques. The fortress-like Dalt Vila (old city) serves as a backdrop to sophisticated, even frenetic nightlife in the summer (and, to a lesser degree, in the winter). But the cliffs and coves of the coast, the postage-stamp-sized, African-looking white towns inland, and the finely crafted jewelry and other Phoenician artifacts in the Puig des Molins museum are best savored outside the summer months, when the traffic has subsided on the island's roads, which are few and narrow.

When plotting your wanderings around the Balearics, keep two things in mind: The islands are smaller than you think, and distances can be covered very rapidly. Although it's not recommended, you could probably visit every town on Ibiza or Minorca by car easily in two days. Majorca is larger, but from Palma to Alcudia on the north coast—"the other side of the island"—is only about 50 km (31 miles).

And although Castilian Spanish is generally understood, each island has its own language derived from Catalan. Street and highway signs may be in Castilian, the local language, or both—and this can be more than a bit confusing. The capital of Minorca, for example, is Mahón in Castilian and Maó in Menorquín. Some militant local-language-only proponents block out or destroy signs in Castilian, so it's not uncommon to encounter defaced or even unreadable road markers and other signs.

MAJOR INTEREST

More than 600 miles of coastline
Seaside cliffs and mountains
Beaches—sandy, rocky, isolated, pristine
Inland, rural landscapes and villages
Archaeological sites
Medieval monuments and towns
Traditional culture and food

Minorca
Prehistoric talayotic stone monuments and towns
Port of Mahón
Ciudadela, a Medieval town
Beaches
View from Monte Toro

Majorca
Cathedral and Bellver castle in Palma
Tramuntana mountain range along north coast
Cabo de Formentor
Valldemossa—Chopin-George Sand apartment at monastery
Sa Calobra and Torrent de Pareis beach, gorge

Ibiza
Dalt Vila
Puig des Molins museum of Phoenician artifacts
Beaches and coast
Side trip to Formentera Island

The beauty and variety of the islands' scenery—from isolated coves with crystalline waters such as Macarelleta on Minorca to the wild and windy pine-covered mountains of Cabo de Formentor on Majorca—is the most compelling reason for a visit. The Balearics offer endless opportunities for picnics, for hikes and excursions to beaches, forests, archaeological monuments, and the countryside, and for vistas of the sea.

Since James the Conquerer (Jaime I) came from the mainland to capture Majorca from the Moors in the 13th century and founded a kingdom that embraced the islands—plus Roussillon and Montpelier in France—Catalan language and culture have dominated daily life in the Balearics. But the perceptive visitor can still identify traces of invaders who came both before and after. Names with the prefix *Bini* or *Ben,* Arabic for "son of"; the Roman theater and other ruins in Alcúdia, Majorca; the cylindrical stone defensive towers constructed along the coasts to spot pirates who cruised the Mediterranean during the Middle Ages; the two gin factories in Minorca's port of Mahón, a reminder that the British occupied that island twice (for a total of 67 years) in the 18th century—all serve as clues to the islands' past.

Medieval monuments—including the graceful cathedral that appears to be levitating above the port—abound in Palma, a city of more than 300,000 that is the capital of Majorca and of the island group. In the much smaller town of Ciudadela on Minorca, many residents live in 500-year-old houses that can be identified on a Medieval map in the town museum. And the old city of Ibiza, a modern tourism mecca, is to this day encircled by the imposing stone walls constructed in the 16th century as a defense against Turkish invaders.

The legacy of these crosscurrents of history is nonetheless a common Balearic culture—apart from that of the mainland—which at the same time endows each island with its own unique traditions as well. Traditional dancing and singing can be enjoyed, especially in the summer months, at hotels and plazas on all of the islands. In Minorca the accompaniment is likely to be guitars; in Ibiza the flute and drum are more usual. The traditional costumes of Minorca and Majorca consist of long skirts and headdresses for women and knickers for men, but Ibizan traditional dress, said to be influenced by the proximity of North Africa, favors more voluminous skirts, dresses, and, for the men, pants, with accents of heavy gold or silver lockets and coils of necklaces.

The Food of the Balearics

The island cuisines are based on the usual Mediterranean natural ingredients, including olives and olive oil, and on an agrarian tradition that includes a lot of pork, especially the typical *sobrasada* sausage; vegetables such as eggplant and zucchini stuffed with ground meat or seafood; and the use of figs and almonds as condiments.

Legend has it that mayonnaise was created in Minorca (where a Mahones is a person who lives in Mahón, the capital), and discovered there by the duke of Richelieu during the brief French occupation in the 19th century. Either mayonnaise or its garlic-flavored sister, *ali-oli,* shows up commonly here as a complement to fish dishes or even as a spread for bread before the meal. Minorca is also famous for its *queso de payes* (Mahón cheese), and for its ice cream.

The spiral-shaped Majorcan pastry *ensaimada* has been adopted throughout the Balearics. The Mediterranean spiny lobster—increasingly rare and ever more expensive—also forms the base of traditional dishes on all of the islands. Special drinks run the gamut from the Minorcan *pomada,* made of lemonade and gin and imbibed during the San Juan fiesta in June, to the *hierbas* liqueur, made of local Ibizan herbs.

The Wines of the Balearic Islands

The islands have no *denominación de origen,* but they have about 10,000 acres under vine, including two wine areas on Majorca, **Felanitx** and **Binissalem**, which produce some especially interesting red wines and rosados from the native Manto Negro, Callet, and Fogoneu grapes. If you are visiting Majorca, try the wines of Bodegas José L. Ferrer and Vins D'Or.

—*Gerry Dawes*

Proceeding from Barcelona, the closest mainland jumping-off point to the Balearics, we cover the islands from east to west; first Minorca and then Majorca, Ibiza, and, just off Ibiza, Formentera. Although each island has its own special places and personality, the three main islands share an unusual ancient legacy—prehistoric talayotic monuments.

Talayotic Monuments

Although excavations on all three islands are exposing more ancient sites all the time, Minorca is the island with the largest number of excavated and accessible ones. Some pre-talayotic structures date back to 2000 B.C., but the more sophisticated forms are believed to date from about 1100 B.C. until the first century A.D., when the Romans came to Minorca.

The stone monuments take three major forms: the *talayot,* a conical tower, perhaps used for defensive purposes; the *naveta,* a structure resembling an upside-down ship's hull, which may have been used for burials as well as for habitation; and the *taula,* a striking, T-shaped construction of two huge slabs of rock whose significance—probably religious—is still debated in archaeological circles.

The Minorcan landscape is strewn with these monuments, although the majority are on the more salubrious southern half, which is protected from the winds. Two *poblados* (towns)—Torre d'en Gaumes, on the road from Alayor to Son Bou, and Son Catlar, south of Ciudadela—offer the visitor an opportunity to view a mixture of all of these forms, as well as caves and the remains of other stone dwellings.

Visiting the monuments is a treat, both because they lack the usual frustrations of waiting in line, entrance fees, and erratic opening and closing hours, and because many are in the fields of private farm residences and offer you an opportunity to get to know the countryside.

The "archaeological map" of Minorca, available in many shops, and a good pair of walking shoes for crossing fields and scaling stone walls are the only equipment you'll need. Local mores require the following courtesies: When entering private property, request permission (it will not be refused); and always close the gates you have opened (to keep the livestock from wandering away).

MINORCA

Ask a Minorcan what's special about the island and the answer will almost always be "the tranquillity." For those natives who may feel geographically—as well as socially and economically—isolated from the *movida* of modern Spain, this may be a damning assessment. But for most residents, as for the more tasteful visitors, all the connotations of "tranquil" are positive.

Minorca remains the least "touristy" of the Balearics but, at the moment, the most conflicted. The traditional shoe and

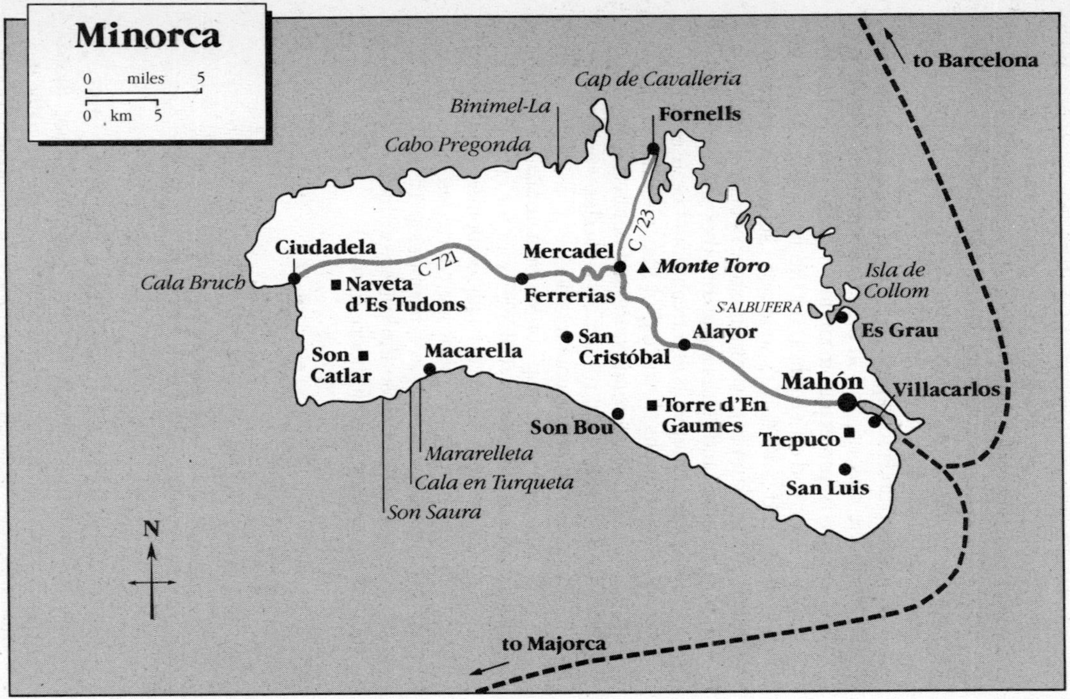
Minorca
0 miles 5
0 km 5
to Barcelona
Cap de Cavalleria
Binimel-La
Fornells
Cabo Pregonda
C 723
Ciudadela
Mercadel
C 721
Monte Toro
Cala Bruch
Naveta d'Es Tudons
Ferrerias
Isla de Collom
S'ALBUFERA
Es Grau
San Cristóbal
Alayor
Son Catlar
Macarella
Mahón
Villacarlos
Torre d'En Gaumes
Son Bou
Trepuco
Mararelleta
Cala en Turqueta
San Luis
Son Saura
N
to Majorca

costume-jewelry industries have declined, and, despite the outcry from environmentalists, economic need is spurring the island to ever-increasing development—and pollution—of some of its loveliest natural areas. Most beach resorts cater to mass tourism; if you want to avoid this it would be best to use Mahón or Ciudadela—the two largest towns, one on each end of the island—as a base from which to make daily excursions to the more isolated areas. Mahón and Ciudadela account for two-thirds of Minorca's entire population of about 60,000, which means that the island's other towns are so small that you can tour the entire center of each on foot in a few minutes.

Mahón is close to the airport and is the nucleus of the English-speaking expatriate community. Ciudadela, a 45-minute drive or an hour's bus ride to the west, offers the visitor the atmosphere of a Medieval city as well as access to some spectacular swimming beaches on the southern coast. The island's one major highway, the 47-km (28-mile) C 721, crosses the island from east to west, from Mahón, passing through Minorca's other main towns—Alayor, Mercadel, and Ferrerias.

Gas stations are scarce in Minorca, and most are closed on Sunday. But you'll find one or more along the main road in the main towns—Mahón, Alayor, Mercadal, Ferrerias, and Ciudadela. The few others are a bit off the beaten track, such as one on the Mahón-Fornells road. As with pharmacies and bakeries, there is a system of "turns" for opening gas stations on the island on holidays and weekends. The list is published each week in the local newspaper, *Menorca,* and in the English-language magazine, *Roqueta,* which is published during the summer. There may be only three or four stations on the whole island open on Sunday, so check your tank before you set out.

MAHON

About 22,000 people—a third of the island's population—live in the quiet, pleasant capital city of Mahón on the eastern end of the island. A five-minute drive from the airport, Mahón sprawls above and atop a cliff overlooking the port—a three-mile-long deep-water harbor with three islands formerly used as military and quarantine facilities—the city's most striking and interesting feature.

Almost everything of interest in this small capital city can be seen in a leisurely couple of hours' walk through a series of geographical "levels"—starting at the **plaça d'Esplanada,** with its cafés, park, and parking lot; descending on Orfila through the pedestrian shopping area that emerges to the right and through the plaça de la Conquista with the church of Santa Maria and the 17th-century town hall to the left; then down the curving road or stairway of carrer Abundancia to the port.

Don't try to tour the center of Mahón by car—narrow, one-way streets make this a nightmare. Leave the car at plaça d'Esplanada. You may, however, want to use it to drive to some of the restaurants at the far eastern end of the port.

Although the port of Mahón was a major commercial and strategic thoroughfare in Carthaginian and Roman times, the city retains virtually no evidence of this early history. The tone set by the neat rowhouses that line the web of streets in the center is more evocative of the 18th century, when the British acquired Minorca (along with Gibraltar) by the Treaty of Utrecht and moved the island's capital there from Ciudadela. Except for a mid-century interlude of some seven years when the French controlled Minorca, the island was under British rule until it was ceded to Spain in 1802.

Vestiges of the British dominance include the Neoclassical façade of the **Santa Maria church** (note the 19th-century organ with 3,000 pipes), originally built in the 13th century; and an English clock, donated by Governor Sir Richard Kane, at the town hall. (Kane is perhaps best known as the governor responsible for construction of "Kane's Road," the first to cross the island from east to west, where the highway is now.)

Also in the plaça de la Conquista is the archaeological museum, potentially the most interesting cultural attraction on the island because of its extensive collection of artifacts from Minorca's prehistoric talayotic period, but it has been closed for years due to lack of funds, and there are no plans to reopen it.

Mahón's two gin distilleries, both located in the port, a couple of minutes' walk west of the stairway on Abundancia, are other vestiges of the British reign. One of them, Son Xoriguer, offers boat tours of the port and is also a good source of souvenirs and gift items, including the local gin and liqueurs and paraphernalia such as shot glasses and aprons. Also in this western area of the port are the ferry terminal; the turn-of-the-century-style **Baixamar** café, where you can get coffee, a drink, and *tapas,* and sometimes see an art show; and several bars.

From the south bank of the port you'll see a series of rocky hills—some of which have been tapped for "urbanization," or clusters of houses—that line the north bank of the port. A good way to get an impression of the immense size of the port is to drive to the eastern end, or mouth of the port, and ascend the hills on the north bank opposite the city.

To the east of the stairway Abundancia, the quay along the port continues for about a mile and is lined with numerous restaurants and bars. **Jagaró**, a greenery-filled house at the eastern end of the port, is a good choice for a fish or seafood meal with touches of *nouvelle cuisine.* Although many restaurants and bars in the port close for the winter, the **Club Marítimo** and a few others remain open all year.

The **Port Mahón Hotel**, an old-fashioned, English-style establishment near the center of town, provides good views of the port, as well as easy access to it on foot. A good urban base for travellers who want to explore the eastern end of the island, it's also within walking distance of the **American Bar**, popular with expatriates, in plaça General Mola; the market (located in the cloister of the Carmelite church); restaurants; bars; and shopping.

Mahón offers the island's largest selection of shopping and services—boutiques, banks, travel agencies, and news kiosks—all concentrated in the pedestrian-only streets. Although the industry is falling on bad times due to global competition, Minorca (especially Ciudadela) is still a major shoe-manufacturing center. **Patrícia**, Poeta G. Roca 1, sells the elegant, expensive shoes, handbags, skirts, and other leather goods made (and also sold) at the factory in Ciudadela. Generally less expensive shoes are sold in numerous shops downtown, and the rope-soled sandals, *alpargatas,* can be bought not only in shoe stores but in hardware, houseware, and gift shops.

If you want to sample traditional Minorcan cuisine, one of the best restaurants on the island is **Pilar**, in the center of town on carrer Orfila. Among the specialties are chicken with shrimp and the peasant soup, *oliaigua,* made with tomatoes and figs. For cultural and historical monuments as well as scenery, however, there are much more interesting places to see on Minorca than Mahón.

Around Mahón

A convenient small hotel on the outskirts of Mahón is **Del Almirante**, once occupied by a British admiral. Located on the highway that leads east from Mahón to Villacarlos, it's accessible by frequent bus service.

From Mahón it's a ten-minute drive to **Villacarlos**, a pretty seaside fishing village where many British expatriates live. Here you can dine outdoors in restaurants crafted from caves formerly used to store fishermen's gear, overlooking the deep blue waters of the port and a bobbing fleet of tiny white fishing boats. You'll find a gaggle of foreign food establishments serving the likes of pizza and crepes, but you can also dine well on fresh local fish and seafood at **Café Trebol**, next to the water on Cales Fonts.

In **Calacorb**, a tiny inlet about a 10-minute walk west, Minorcans and tourists alike hold forth nightly to the accompaniment of live guitar music in the cave-bar known as **C'an Pau**.

For an introduction to talayotic monuments, pay a brief visit to nearby **Trepucó** to see its 13-foot-high taula, the tallest on the island, and other remains of a talayotic village.

North from Mahón

The road northwest from Mahón to Fornells on the northern coast leads to a bird sanctuary, fishing villages, beaches, and some of the island's best eating spots. **S'Albufera**, the only freshwater lake on the island and a protected refuge for hundreds of species of birds, can be reached by turning right on the road to Es Grau shortly after leaving the Mahón port, then left at the sign for the Shangri-La development.

The main road also leads to the tiny fishing village of **Es Grau** on the coast just above Mahón. From Es Grau you can take a ten-minute motorboat trip to the **Isla de Collom**, a tiny uninhabited island with two small beaches—and nothing else—that is visible from the shore. The boat only runs during the summer, and only in good weather. Inquire at the bar Ca'n Bernat at carrer de S'Arribada 18.

Unless a short walk will be a problem for you, or you want to devote your time to learning to wind surf at the school there, don't settle for the rather unappealing beach to the left as you enter Es Grau. Instead, walk through the beach and keep walking along the coast. In five or ten minutes you'll encounter a series of cleaner alternatives. If you hike over the cliff where the first beaches end, you'll find even more pristine swimming spots—virtually always empty—with views of the Isla de Collom. These beaches don't have any facilities, so take food and drink along.

Fornells on the north coast, approached from the same road northwest from Mahón—is a somewhat larger, more touristy fishing village known for its seafood restaurants, its cube-shaped white fishermen's houses, and its picturesque setting on a fjord. The most famous restaurant is **Es Pla** on the water's edge, known to be a favorite of King Juan Carlos and Queen Sofía (who visit Minorca on their yacht). The specialty here is *caldereta de langosta,* a two-course lobster meal of a rich soup followed by lobster meat. Count on spending 5,500 pesetas or more per person if you choose to eat here. Locals opt more often for the less-expensive **Ca'n Miguel** or **S'Ancora**, across the street, or **Es Cranc**, in the village, which they consider just as good.

A sunset visit to the lighthouse of **Cap de Cavalleria**, perched high on a cliff over the sea a few miles beyond Fornells, provides a scenic aperitif for an evening of dining in a nearby town.

Also on the north coast, paved roads and then a decent unpaved road lead to the broad, sandy beach of **Binimel-la.** From here along the coast to the west the physically fit may tramp through some of Minorca's most spectacular coastal scenery—cliffs, beaches, and coves—to **Cala Pregonda**, regarded by many natives as the most beautiful spot on the island because of the craggy, cinnamon-colored rock formations that protrude from and are reflected in the water. The seaside cluster of a half-dozen private houses here has a guard to prevent entry from the road you'll see on the map, but in Spain the beaches belong to the people, and hikers cannot be stopped from walking along the coast to this beach, with its crystal-clear waters. Be sure to wear sneakers or other comfortable shoes for walking on rocks and cliffs. None of the beaches in the area has facilities, so take along lunch and beverages.

THE CENTER OF THE ISLAND

Miles of handcrafted stone fences; undulating hills that sprout brilliant green grasses and carpets of poppies and other flowers in the spring; white farmhouses with arched entrances; knobby, bentwood gates; and grazing cows whose milk will become the famous Minorcan cheese or ice cream—these are the charms of the interior of the island.

Monte Toro, at more than 1,000 feet the island's highest point and the site of a small monastery (with a snack bar), offers a view of the entire island if the day is at all clear. A little more than a mile away from Fornells, it can be reached via that steadily ascending main highway out of Fornells (or from the center of Mercadal) in just a few minutes.

Mercadal, a typical town of white houses and narrow streets that is just about in the exact center of the island, has spawned several good restaurants specializing in Minorcan food. **Ca'n Aguedet**, Lepanto 23, is the most formal, with lace curtains and white table linen. It is *de rigueur* to enter the kitchen to check out the fresh fish or poke your nose into the *caldera* (soup pot) before making a selection. Local specialties on the menu include stuffed eggplant or squash as well as quail, partridge, and fish soup.

Ca'n Olga, a few blocks down the street, offers revolving art exhibits and a pleasant garden as well as good food. **El Molino**, informal and even boisterous, is housed in a windmill visible from the highway after you pass the Mercadal turnoff going west. There the focus is on local dishes such as grilled rabbit, served at wooden tables or on an outdoor terrace overlooking the road. About 6 km (4 miles) south of Mercadal, in the hamlet of San Cristóbal, is **Restaurant S'Engolidor**, perhaps the top contender for best typical Minorcan restaurant. Situated in a traditional house, it also seats diners on a flower-filled terrace in the summer. The restaurant offers the best of island food and ambience—along with attentive and friendly service—at moderate prices. It's closed part of the winter and the schedule is erratic, so call ahead.

From San Cristóbal it's a five-minute ride south to what was once a tranquil, long, sandy beach. However, the beach is eroding and the tranquillity is being shattered as a result of rapid construction of extensive tourist facilities. Nevertheless, any one of the cafés along the water is a good point from which to view the sunset.

CIUDADELA

Capital of the island until the British came to Minorca in the 18th century, Ciudadela, at the western end of the island, retains a large portion of its Medieval streets, residences, and monuments. Old women dressed in black doze or peel potatoes in their doorways on the cobblestoned streets of the old quarter; Sunday mass is at a 14th-century cathedral; local residents line up to draw water from a public well in the flower garden of a 17th-century seminary; and visitors and residents alike stream through the narrow main street to shop in the stores framed by a series of arches known as Los Arcos in Castilian or Ses Voltes in the Minorcan language.

As you enter Ciudadela from Mahón or the airport, the island's only highway, C 721, runs into a dead end at plaça

Alfonso III just after passing the recommended **Alfonso III Hotel** on the left. Another modest, well-kept hostelry, the **Hostal Residencia Ciudadela,** is located on San Eloy, the street that exits from the square to the south, at number 10.

Because the highway is lined with touristy souvenir shops that sell costume jewelry and leather goods, and because large sections of the old city are inaccessible by car, your first views of Ciudadela may present a deceptively modern ambience.

The old, traditional city lies inside the avenue (colloquially, the "Contramurada") that curves north and south from plaça Alfonso III, tracing the no-longer-visible walls of the old city. Although this street changes its name—to the right or north, it's Constitución; to the left, it's first Conquistador, then Negrete—because this is Ciudadela's main traffic artery you'll have no trouble staying on it. (Pedestrians should simply continue across the plaça Alfonso III to the west to enter the pedestrian center of town on Virgen Carmen.)

However, if you're driving, turn left and follow the traffic flow several blocks to the pine-tree-filled park at plaça Colón; turn right and look for parking there or to your right in the plaça d'Es Borne.

Residents and tourists mingle in the main centers of Ciudadela life. These are the **plaça d'Es Borne** (known locally as El Borne, pronounced "BOR-nay"), where the Ayuntamiento is located; the fishing and recreational port below; and Los Arcos (the arches), which run along Josep Maria Quadrado between plaça d'Es Borne and plaça Nova. El Borne, dominated by the arched façade and turrets of the Moorish-looking Ayuntamiento (built on the remains of a Moorish fortress), is probably the town's most important gathering place. The sidewalk along the north side of the square, atop the city's ancient ramparts, offers excellent views of the port, which is used by yachts and fishing boats alike, and is the center of the town's nightlife. The café-bar on top of the Ayuntamiento is a good vantage point for views of the port, the open sea to the west, and the old city wall, which is festooned with wild caper plants.

The Washington Monument look-alike in the middle of the pląca d'Es Borne was constructed in memory of the natives' (losing) battle against an assault by the Turks in 1558. On the east side of the plaza are three Medieval palaces, still privately owned, which house a series of shops, bars, and an English-style tea room, **Es Palau**, on the street level.

Mayor Borne, the street that exits east from the square

across from the Ayuntamiento, leads one block past the palaces into plaça Pio XII, where the 14th-century Gothic **Santa Maria cathedral** is located. Built on the site of a former mosque, the cathedral has undergone various alterations, which have endowed it with a Neoclassical façade. To the left of the cathedral's main entrance on carrer Obispo Torres is the **bishop's palace**, with a flower-adorned courtyard complete with well, which can usually be glimpsed through the gate; and at the end of the street is another palace, owned by the Squella family, with a sculptured cameo of a woman's face carved on the façade.

To experience Ciudadela's Medieval quarter to its fullest, take an immediate left turn at the Palacio del Squella and then a right on San Miguel or on San Sebastian, which will bring you to the narrow, convoluted streets, many of them cobblestoned, of the old residential neighborhoods. The three- and four-story Medieval townhouses along these streets—mostly painted white or a light color on top and gray or brown or green on the bottom—are still inhabited, and although it's highly illegal to keep them in town, you might even hear a rooster crowing from a concealed interior garden. During the San Juan festival some of the horses and riders actually prance into the hallways of these houses.

Don't be concerned about losing your way in these streets. The town is very small, and anyone can direct you back to the cathedral. Proceeding west from the cathedral on Josep Maria Quadrado, enter the narrow pedestrian precinct of **Los Arcos**. This strip, which leads to the colorful, café-filled plaça Nova two blocks away, is Ciudadela's main tourist shopping area, where you can buy anything from an ice-cream cone to *alpargatas,* the locally made sandals.

A right turn at carrer Obispo Vila takes you into a network of tiny streets (take the second left, then first right) that lead to the local food market. Monday's a slow market day, but Tuesday through Saturday the locals arrive before 8:00 A.M. to get the best of the fresh fish, seafood, and produce. Best buys vary with the season, but be sure to go for the fresh figs in the summer. Always available in the butcher shops and other small shops lining the outdoor market are the excellent local cheese, *queso de Mahón* (*queso de payes*), and the local *sobrasada* sausage.

On Obispo Vila, just past the turnoff to the market, is a 17th-century seminary with a flower-filled courtyard where an excellent summer classical music concert series is presented. Across the street from it is the **Paradis** bar and restaurant, one of the few appealing places to hang out on an off-season night.

For more serious shopping, go through the plaça Nova up to plaça Alfonso III (where you entered town), which intersects with the road out of town to Mahón and, to your right and left, the series of main streets that border the old city. Along these streets, especially Conquistador, then Negrete, to the right, you'll find many shops, mostly selling clothing and household goods.

As a major shoe-manufacturing center, Ciudadela has traditionally produced everything from slippers to high-fashion women's pumps and then sold them in factory stores, boutiques, and the front hallways of the families who produce them at home. If you're looking for high-quality shoes, such as some marketed under the Bally label—other places to try—besides those on Conquistador and Negrete—are **Torres**, on Calvo Sotelo, the street that goes west from plaça Alfonso III and leads to Mahón, and the **Patricía factory store** on the road to Santandria south of Ciudadela (which also sells leather jackets and skirts and other leather items).

A nice walk out of Ciudadela's center less than 15 minutes one way takes you along the broad, tree-lined **passeig de San Nicolas** straight west from El Borne to the coast. Along the route you'll also pass some of Ciudadela's hotels, including the **Patrícia**, at number 92, which opened in 1988 to serve business and other well-off travellers to Ciudadela. A sleek, modern, but small establishment, it's the only hotel of its class in town. To the left just before you reach the coast is the **Esmeralda**, a larger, moderately priced hotel catering to the package tourist trade, but with the only swimming pool in town.

Once at the coast you can't miss the statue of American Admiral David Farragut, son of a Ciudadela man who emigrated to the United States. His triumphant visit to his father's hometown in 1867, when he held the rank of admiral and was in charge of the U.S. European Squadron, remains a topic of animated conversation among the locals. From the coast—where there's a crumbling defense tower—the fastest way to return is by the passeig de San Nicolas. Scenic but slower alternatives include taking a right to the passeig del Puerto, which brings you to the port, or a left along a coast road dotted with cliffs and rocks, ending at the tiny and oddly named playa Grande (large beach).

Playa Grande and the streets on the other side of the

beach are the site of several modest, reasonably priced hostels, including the **Mar Blava**, which has a terrace overlooking the water.

The Port

When you've tired of touring, head for the Ciudadela port, home to a small fishing fleet and host to hundreds of yachts in the course of the summer season. It's also the major evening gathering place for everyone from international yachtsmen to punk rockers. From June until early September—but especially in August—it is thronged nightly with visitors from all over Spain and the rest of the world, as well as Ciudadela residents. Dining, bar hopping, disco dancing, and people watching are the favored activities here.

You can descend directly to the port from carrer Cuesta in El Borne next to the Ayuntamiento (stopping to sample the excellent homemade ice cream—flavors include fresh fig, gin, and hazelnut—at **Baixamar**, on the left); or from a stairway (known locally by the Spanish word for it, La Escalera) that intersects with carrer Brecha above the port. Although there may be times when you can navigate the obstacle course of traffic rules legally, driving a car into the port is not worth the trouble. Leave it in El Borne.

Once you've arrived at water's edge, the whole port area is visible. Because the area is so small, restaurants and bars located here do not have specific addresses, so if you can't see your destination, ask directions. From the bottom of the stairway to your left is a strip of waterside restaurants and bars where you can dine or drink inside or out; to your right across the small bridge, then to the left, is another strip: Here you'll find two of the best places to dine.

Dragos, Ciudadela's most cosmopolitan restaurant, offers diners a view of the port while they dine on trendy dishes such as duck breast with wild blackberries and raspberries or one of several Minorcan specialties offered each day. **Mare Nostrum**, next door on the port level, offers excellent, no-nonsense fish and seafood. The *parillada,* a grill of the day's catch, and the typical *caldereta de langosta,* a two-course lobster meal, are good choices here.

Although the area retains its charm—and some may prefer the tranquillity to the crowds—life in the Ciudadela port slows down considerably from October 15 until the beginning of June. Many restaurants and bars close down completely, and some open only on weekends. However, it's always possible to find a place to sip coffee or a glass of wine and take in the view, which reveals a long, narrow channel that meets the Mediterranean at a cliff-lined coast.

Excursions from Ciudadela

The **Naveta d'Es Tudons**, the best-preserved megalithic monument on the island, is easily reached from the highway about three miles east of Ciudadela. Its interior can be explored by anyone willing to crawl in on hands and knees.

The coasts north and south of Ciudadela offer picturesque and unusual vistas of high, rugged, gray cliffs, roadsides lined with bright flowers in the spring, tiny coves and swimming beaches, and private residential areas where summer homes are nestled in niches in the rock at water's edge.

At plaça Alfonso III, where the highway from Mahón enters Ciudadela, following the main road and the signs around to the right will bring you to the north coast, including **Cala Bruch**, a "beach" of terraced rocks where you can sun and swim without getting sandy, and where on a windy day the surf beats on the rock walls of the cove with thundering force. Cala Bruch has a restaurant with an outdoor café that is open all day and in the evening during the summer.

To explore the coast south of Ciudadela, turn left (west) from the plaça Alfonso III and follow the Contramurada, or main avenue, to the end, where you must turn left on carrer Majorca. This will lead you past playa Grande toward Santandria, a beach with some cafés, and to points south. In general, however, shun the overused, often polluted beaches close to Ciudadela—including Santandria. Head instead for the south-coast beaches such as **Son Saura**, a long, crescent-shaped sandy strip with pine forest just behind the beach (the monuments of Son Catlar are a short detour on the way); **Cala en Turqueta**; and **Macarella** (once there, climb over the cliff to the right to **Macarelleta**, a white-sand beach frequented by those who prefer to bathe in the buff). Good walkers or hikers should consider using the trails among these and many other coves to explore the south coast on foot.

These beaches—and most of the island's best—are too far to reach on foot. You'll need either a car or a motorcycle for the trip across a network of unmarked, unpaved, sometimes downright rocky roads that, in some cases, cross private property. Before you go, ask at your hotel or another local source for directions. Be prepared to encounter gates leading to private property on your way. Always leave gates as you find them.

During the summer, excursion boats depart from the

Ciudadela port to tour either the north or the south coast, with stops for a swim and lunch on the way. But because of the generally clear, clean aquamarine water and the range of unusual rock formations, cliffs, and fauna, all of Minorca's coast and beaches merit a visit even if it's too cool for a dip.

Ciudadela at Fiesta Time

A good time to experience what some would characterize as the "true" spirit of Ciudadela is during the San Juan festival, June 23–24, when some 100 horses and riders course through the Medieval streets—even entering some houses—as they reenact ancient rites whose now-murky origins are Christian, Moorish, and pagan. As with the running of the bulls in Pamplona, the fiesta attracts thousands of revelers, many of whom participate by thrusting themselves under the prancing horses' hoofs, challenging the equestrians to prove their mastery of the art.

The daily (except Sunday and Monday) outdoor morning market in Ciudadela is a good place to absorb local color—at fiesta time, the fishmongers sing traditional songs in voices that are anything but *sotto*—as well as to pick up picnic supplies.

MAJORCA

The largest island in the Balearics, and by far the most visited, Majorca was also the first to lure modern-day travellers and expatriates to its shores.

"One of the most beautiful landscapes in the world and one of the most unknown . . . tortured, bent-over, sapless trees; terrible bramble bushes, magnificent flowers, carpets of lawn and reeds; spiny caper plants. . . ." rhapsodized French novelist George Sand in *Winter in Mallorca,* based on her 1838–1839 visit here with her lover, Frédéric Chopin. The scenery alone wasn't enough to convince the pair to stay, though. They left three months after their arrival on the island, besieged by bad weather, Chopin's affliction with tuberculosis, and the indignities inflicted on them by what they saw as a combination of crude peasants and haughty local society.

But other luminaries continued to arrive. One was Arch-

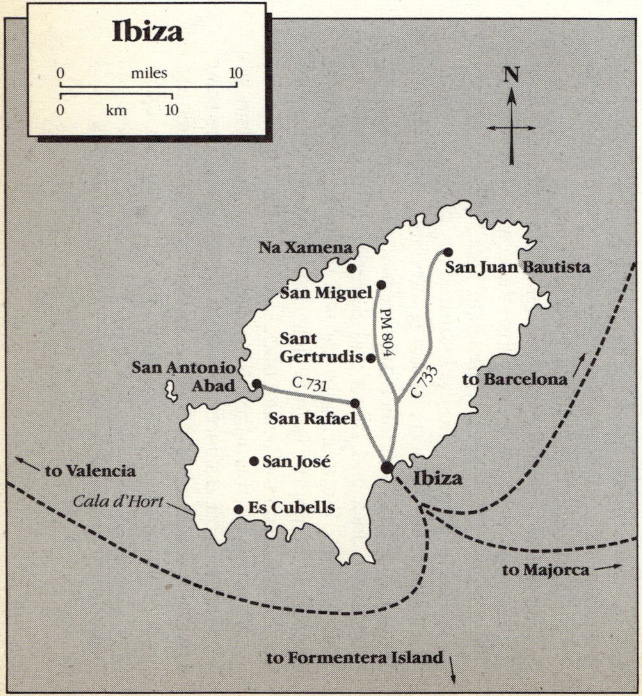
Ibiza
0 miles 10
0 km 10
N
Na Xamena
San Miguel
PM 804
San Juan Bautista
Sant
Gertrudis
San Antonio
Abad
C 731
C 733
to Barcelona
San Rafael
San José
Ibiza
to Valencia
Cala d'Hort
Es Cubells
to Majorca
to Formentera Island

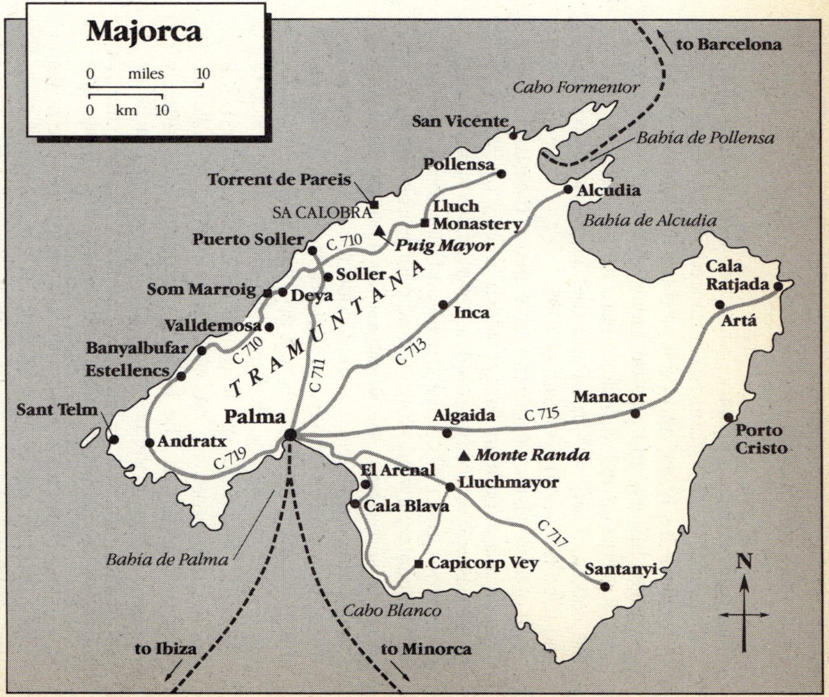
Majorca
0 miles 10
0 km 10
to Barcelona
Cabo Formentor
San Vicente
Bahía de Pollensa
Pollensa
Torrent de Pareis
Alcudia
SA CALOBRA
Lluch
Monastery
Bahía de Alcudia
Puerto Soller
C 710
Puig Mayor
Soller
Som Marroig
Deya
TRAMUNTANA
Inca
Cala
Ratjada
Artá
Valldemosa
Banyalbufar
Estellencs
C 710
C 711
C 713
Sant Telm
Palma
Manacor
Algaida
C 715
Porto
Cristo
Andratx
C 719
Monte Randa
El Arenal
Lluchmayor
Cala Blava
C 717
Bahía de Palma
Capicorp Vey
Santanyi
N
Cabo Blanco
to Ibiza
to Minorca

duke Luis Salvador of Austria, who came to Majorca in 1867 at the age of 19 and became so entranced with the island that he made it his home and dedicated his life to studying its language, history, and natural environment. Another was poet Robert Graves, who came here in the 1920s, became the center of an ever-growing artists' and writers' colony, and lived here until his death in 1985.

All of these visitors chose the same area of the island—the **Tramuntana mountain range**, which snakes up Majorca's west coast to the north through a series of tiny sandy coves, precipitous gray cliffs, olive groves, and pine forest to Cabo de Formentor, a wind-blown ten-mile-long promontory.

The island, whose shape suggests an amoebic form with pods oozing tentatively into the Mediterranean, measures 45 miles from north to south and 60 miles from east to west. Its main geographical features are two bays and a mountain range. The Bahía (bay) de Palma, on the southwest side of the island, is the site of the capital city. It is separated by a small promontory on the west from Bahía de Pollença, another resort area. The Bahía de Alcúdia, almost directly opposite Palma on the northeast coast, has a long beach that is the main attraction for sun-worshiping tourists from northern Europe. The Tramuntanas, rising almost parallel to and just inland of the west coast of the island, feature nine peaks over 1,000 feet, the highest of which is Puig Mayor at more than 4,300 feet.

The eastern side of the island is defined by a smaller mountain range, whose most scenic features are the rocky coastal cliffs where it culminates north of Artà.

The center of Majorca is an almost flat agricultural area—for the most part less touristy than the coasts—whose notable features include the Binissalem area, where Majorcan wines are produced, and the industrial city of Inca.

Bus service connects major resorts and towns on the island, and excursion trains run several times a day between Palma and Inca and Palma and Sóller to its north in the Tramuntanas, but touring by car will give you much more freedom to enjoy the island's sights at your own pace as well as to explore off the beaten track.

Even though this island is considerably bigger than Minorca and Ibiza, distances are still relatively short. The route you take makes a big difference in the duration of your trip. From Palma straight across the island to Alcúdia, for example, is a straight 60-mile trip. But if you want to explore and savor the Tramuntanas and the coast—as you should—a drive from Palma to Alcúdia should take you several days with overnight stops.

Palma, which is well-endowed with hotels, makes a convenient base for exploring any other part of Majorca because *all* the main highways emanate from the city. But unless you're especially partial to big, busy cities we recommend that you devote a couple of days to seeing the sights in Palma—with a possible excursion or two to the east—and then head west and base yourself in Banyalbufar, Deya, at the Hotel Formentor, or some other destination closer to the coast and the Tramuntanas. From these bases it is easy to make numerous excursions, or just rest on the coast and contemplate the views of the sea and rugged cliffs.

PALMA

Like George Sand and Chopin, who travelled 18 hours on a steamboat to get there, virtually all modern visitors to Majorca set foot first in Palma, the capital and—with a population of more than 300,000—the largest and most cosmopolitan city of the Balearic Islands.

Palma presents many faces to the visitor: the seaside, palm-lined passeig Marítim open to the Mediterranean's breezes; the dark, twisting streets of the centuries-old Arab and Gothic quarters that flank the modern main street, the passeig d'Es Borne; honky-tonk nightclubs and modern apartment blocks; and the sophisticated boutiques along the arcaded avinguda Rei Jaime III.

But what makes the city worth a stop are its Medieval monuments, the two most impressive of which can both be seen by the visitor arriving by water, and often by the airplane traveller as well: the cathedral, known locally as La Seu, and Bellver castle.

From the coast of the ample bay on the southwest end of the island, Palma spreads inland toward the north, east, and west. If you're fortunate, your landing at the airport, about a ten-minute ride east of the city, will offer views of El Jonquer, a farming area dotted with windmills, and of the cathedral.

Entering town from the airport you'll approach from ronda Litoral, an avenue that traces the sea on the left and passes below the cathedral and the Medieval quarter on the right. Just past the monuments, the ronda intersects with avinguda Antoni Maura to the right and the passeig Marítim curving around to the left or west along the river.

Antoni Maura penetrates to the city center, passing the Medieval quarter, with the cathedral and the Almudaina on the right, merging into the lively passeig d'Es Borne and at plaça Pio XII intersecting with the Rei Jaime III, a major shopping street to the west.

The passeig Marítim, which continues along the water past a yacht basin, also passes by the 15th-century Gothic restored commodity exchange, Sa Llonja, and becomes a sort of tourist strip, the site of several major hotels as well as restaurants and bars, and at its western end runs below—but within sight of—the Medieval Castell de Bellver, one of the city's most impressive monuments.

Castell de Bellver

Even if your stay in Palma is very limited, leave time for a visit to the hilltop castle, about a mile and a half from the city center. Because one of the main attractions of the castle is its 360-degree view of the city and its environs, this excursion is a good way to start a day of touring. Bellver can be reached on foot, but it's a long, tiring walk, so a trip by taxi or bus is recommended.

During the 300 years in which the subsequent kings of Majorca carried out the cathedral construction started by Jaime I in 1230, they also managed (in the 14th century) to erect Bellver castle as a summer residence. From outside, the castle appears to be a forbidding military fortress surrounded by a moat, but a step inside reveals a graceful circular interior court open to the sky. On the first floor of the castle there's a city museum featuring exhibits of ceramics and other finds from the island's prehistoric archaeological sites. A stairway to the right as the castle is entered leads to the roof, which offers a view of the sea, the Palma skyline, and the hills that rise behind the city. Like the cathedral, the castle is illuminated at night.

Casco Antiguo

To tour the old quarter of Palma, the Casco Antiguo, return to the city center and turn east from Antoni Maura, following the signs to the **Almudaina**—a palace for the kings of Majorca built on the site of a former Moorish fortress—which gives onto plaça Almoina, where you'll find the entrance to the cathedral.

Situated just above the port of the sweeping Bahía de Palma, the **cathedral**—Gothic and graceful—seems to float above a forest of sailboat masts. Comparisons document its impressive dimensions. The great nave is larger than those of the cathedrals of Milan, Chartres, Cologne, and Reims, as are the lateral naves, some of which are some 90 feet high. The rose window, which has a diameter of 17½ feet, is the largest in the world.

Inside, what is most impressive is the immense distance from the main chapel and altar to the main door at the back—made all the more remarkable by the unusual placement of the choir in front by the chancel, instead of in the middle where it would truncate the space. The chapel of the Holy Trinity, beyond the choir, houses the tombs of Majorcan kings Jaime II and Jaime III. A crown-shaped wrought-iron canopy designed by Catalan architect Antoni Gaudí hangs over the chancel. It features Christ on the cross, adorned by the ceramic mosaics that characterize Gaudí's work; 35 bell-shaped hanging lamps said to represent the faithful; and representations of grain and grapes for sacrifice.

The juxtaposition of the modern Gaudí work with the cathedral's Medieval structure attests to the fact that since Jaime I (known as "The Conqueror," and buried in the cathedral) took the island from the Moors in the mid-13th century and ordered the construction of the cathedral, Majorca has retained Catalan culture at its core.

After touring the interior of the cathedral, be sure to exit to plaça Almirante Moreno on the south side for a good view of the Bahía de Palma. (While in this area you may also want to walk by the graceful **Llonja**, with its arched ceilings and fluted columns, on passeig Sagrera across from the sea just west of Antoni Maura. However, the building is open to the public only when there's an art exhibition.)

From the cathedral it's easy—many signs mark the routes to historical monuments—to tour the Casco Antiguo on foot. A logical itinerary for a couple of hours of strolling and sightseeing would take you through the narrow streets to the **Arab baths** at calle Serra 13; to the **Església de San Francisco** with its 14th-century Gothic façade and the tomb of 13th-century philosopher and native son Ramón Llull, at plaça San Francisco 6; then through the old streets lined with imposing mansions to the inviting **plaça Santa Eulalia**, adorned by plane trees and enlivened by cafés. This is a good place for an energizing cup of coffee or snack, as in the nearby **Xicara Xocolatería** (a dark local bar that specializes in hot chocolate) on carrer Morey, which intersects with the plaza to the south.

Once on Morey, it's a few steps northwest to the hoary

Almudaina arch on Victoria Almudaina. Along with the Arab baths—both are believed to date from about the tenth century—it's the only significant remaining physical evidence of Palma's Moorish period. Continuing on Victoria Almudaina, you'll arrive shortly at plaça Cort, dominated by the town hall. The stairway on Quintana across the street from the town hall descends into a labyrinth of pedestrian shopping streets offering distractions that range from the tempting chocolates in the window at **Pajarita Bonbonera** on San Nicolas to Cacharel, Stefanel, and other stylish boutiques on adjacent streets.

From here it's a short descent to the passeig d'Es Borne, where one option is to buy a newspaper at the kiosk and call it a day.

A second option is to head north on San Jaime to the plaça Obispo Berenguer de Palau 8 and **Celler Sa Premsa**, a wine cellar converted into an informal restaurant where you'll rub elbows with an animated crowd of locals who patronize it for the typical dishes such as the hearty Majorcan vegetable soup, accompanied by Majorcan Binissalem wine.

A third option is to turn west from the passeig d'Es Borne at the plaça Pio XII where it intersects with Rei Jaime III. The city tourist office is at number 10, sandwiched in a row of boutiques and department stores. (You can get information about travelling in all of the Balearic Islands here.) Places to shop include **Majorica**, at number 11, which vends the cultured pearls for which Majorca is famous; **Galerías Preciados** department store, which sells everything from clothing to kitchenware; and more shoe stores—most of their wares are high-fashion and expensive—than you could ever imagine on one street. **Artespaña**, at passeig Mallorca 17, at the intersection with the west end of Rei Jaime III, is a good place to search for handicrafts and home furnishings such as hand-embroidered table linens.

The quarter bounded by Jaime III to the north, passeig d'Es Borne to the east, and the sea to the south includes a network of streets that can seem quaint by day and seedy by night. The passeig Marítim, which edges the sea, leads on the west to the **Hotel Meliá Victoria**, a modern high-rise hotel with rooms overlooking the harbor; to the **plaça Gomila**, a center of discos, bars, and other nightlife also to the west; and, to the east, to the recommended **Portixol** seafood restaurant at the seaside about three-and-a-half miles from the center, at Sirena 27.

Palma does have an international flavor, and one way to exploit this is to dine at **Xoriguer** restaurant, Fabrica 60 (about a ten-minute taxi ride west of the center) where the cuisine is French. Another is to treat yourself to lodgings (and pool, gymnasium, garden, discotheque, and more) at the luxurious **Son Vida Sheraton** resort, about three miles north of Palma on a hill overlooking the countryside.

EXCURSIONS FROM PALMA

By far the most interesting and scenic region of Majorca is the Tramuntana range and the cliffs, towns, coves, and forests that cling to it as it weaves its way up the west coast. A tour of this region—along with a day or two in Palma—is the main draw of Majorca. (See the West Coast section below.)

However, if you have time and itchy feet there are other side trips that will take you through pleasing coastal and country scenery and offer perspectives on historical figures, including Medieval philosopher Ramón Llull and Father Junipero Serra, who is credited with—among other things—the discovery of San Francisco Bay.

The east coast, where the rocky cliffs, coves, and tiny beaches are endowed with considerable natural beauty, has been overdeveloped into a series of resorts for the northern European package trade; although some sights of intrinsic interest remain, tourist buses, heavy traffic, high-rise hotels, and shopping centers detract from the experience considerably.

Suggested destinations are divided into two groups: those south and southeast of Palma and those along or close to the east coast. To see all of these sites it would be best to devote a day each to the south and the east. However, by picking and choosing (for example, skipping La Marina and Capicorp Vey and proceeding right to Lluchmayor) you may be able to see most of these in one long day, returning to Palma at night. (Although this section is organized as a car trip, you can visit virtually all of these destinations by taking local buses from Palma or joining organized tours offered by travel agencies there.)

South of Palma

Follow directions to the airport and follow signs to the C 717, which can be picked up heading south just beyond the airport. From here you can visit **La Marina**, a nature preserve famous for the cormorants, peregrine falcons, and many other bird species that nest around the 100-foot-high cliffs of Cabo Enderrocat, Cabo Blanco, and other coves along the coast. (After 1.5 km/1 mile turn right off C 717 to El Arenal and pick up the unnumbered coast road toward Cala Blava. The nature area stretches for more than 20 km/12 miles along the coast.)

Capicorp Vey, a Bronze Age archaeological site, is reached from Cabo Blanco by taking the road that leads inland toward the north. The site is 5 km (3 miles) from the lighthouse. The pottery, tools, and other finds from the excavations here are important and have been put in the Museu Arqueológico in Barcelona. A key to the locked site—where you can still see two stone cylindrical defense towers (talayots) and other stone remains of the town—is available at the farmhouse across the road along with a short pamphlet about the site . . . if somebody's home, that is.

By continuing north on the road from Capicorp Vey for 13 km (8 miles) to the intersection with C 717, you'll reach Lluchmayor, which has a small windmill museum in a windmill on the highway just before the west entrance to the town.

Above nearby Randa is perched the **Santuario de Cura**, a Franciscan monastery 1,800 feet above sea level on the spine of Monte Randa. Famous for its views of most of the island, the monastery—which has a library containing manuscripts, music books, and prayerbooks of his era—was used as a retreat by the monastery's founder, 13th-century Catalan philosopher Ramón Llull. (This Franciscan missionary to the Near East and Africa—where he was tortured for his faith—was the author of the *Ars Magna,* one of the oddest works of the Scholastic period. In it he attempted to show that the Church's doctrines comprised the entire world, arguing without recourse to dogma, using Leibniz-like truth tables and logic circles. According to philosopher Etienne Gilson, who thinks Llull's life would make an excellent subject for a novel, "It is by no means certain that the project of Ramón Lull is dead.") To get to the monastery, take PM 501 north out of Lluchmayor about 4 km (2.5 miles) and then turn east toward Randa.

Petra, about 4 km (2.5 miles) northeast of Randa, is the birthplace of Father Junipero Serra, the Franciscan missionary-explorer whose 18th-century expeditions from San Diego up the coast of California were responsible for the creation of several missions, including the one at San Luis Obispo. Here at Petra you can visit his modest family home—where maps and other mementos of his life are displayed—at Es Barracar Alt 6 (ask for the key at number 15); the San Bernardino convent where he lived for many years; and the Bonany sanctuary where he preached his last sermon (4 km/2.5 miles from the center, reached by following signs to the road back to Palma).

The East Coast

Unless you want to make the stops to the south just outlined, take C 715 toward Son Ferriol and Algaida east out of Palma and aim for Artà, 78 km (48 miles) north. There are several interesting sights to see along the way—and beyond Artà to the north toward Cala Ratjada, after which you can make your way through a network of roads along the east coast back to Palma.

At Manacor, 47 km (29 miles) east of Palma, you can visit and buy souvenirs at the Majorica cultured pearl factory and tour the **Museu Arqueológico Municipal** (visits must be arranged ahead; Tel: 55-33-12, ext. 45), which houses an ample collection of mosaics and sarcophagi from the fourth-century Basílica de Son Pereto as well as artifacts from settlements from the prehistoric and subsequent periods.

Ses Païsses, a well-marked site of prehistoric talayots, is on the east side of C 715 about 1 kilometer (½ mile) before you reach Artà.

Artà itself—its most famous attractions are the caves of the same name, which are on the coast (see below), not in the town—is a Medieval village whose most interesting features include the Betlem hermitage on a hill north of town, which offers views as far west as Cabo de Formentor and southwest to the Colonia of San Pedro; the Museu Arqueológico, which includes finds from Ses Païsses and other sites; and the Església de San Salvador, located in the Almudaina, a former Moorish fortress.

A former fishing village, now a center of German tourism, Cala Ratjada offers good swimming, as does Cala Guya, a 15-minute walk north on the coast. For more tranquillity, privacy, and views of the cliffs and the clear waters popular with snorkelers, hire a fishing boat in Cala Ratjada to take you north along the coast; or hike—it will take more than an hour from Cala Guya—past Coll marina to the **playa Cala Mesquida.** (If it's time for a serious lunch try the French cuisine—on the terrace if it's a nice day—at **Ses Rotges** on Alcedo. Like many restaurants and hotels in Majorca's tourist areas, it closes for several months during the winter; Tel: 56-31-08.)

About 13 km (8 miles) and 25 km (15 miles) south of Cala

Ratjada on the coast, respectively, Cuevas de Artà and Cuevas del Drach are extensive networks of limestone caves, and among Majorca's top tourist attractions. The **Cuevas de Artà** are noted for their height and the height of the stalagmites (one column is 72 feet high) and stalactites and for the "organ" and other formations created by the action of water on the rock. Highlights of a visit to the **Cuevas del Drach** include sitting in an underground auditorium that can fit more than 3,000 people and viewing a sound and light show on Martel lake (a 500-foot-long body of water named after the French geologist who explored the caves in the 19th century). Be prepared for long lines, traffic, and crowds if you visit the caves in the summer.

From Porto Cristo, where the Cuevas del Drach are located, it's 13 km (8 miles) back to Manacor and then another 50 km (31 miles) on the C 715 to Palma. If lunch is on your agenda, in Porto Cristo try **Ses Comes**, avinguda de los Pinos 50 (Tel: 57-04-57), where the house specialty is lobster.

THE WEST COAST

Nearly six million visitors arrive in Palma every year, an enormous tourist influx considering the size of the island. Many of them arrive on charter flights and most of them head for northeast-coast seaside resorts that cater to mass tourism. Probably due to the lack of large beaches, the west coast of Majorca has suffered the least from this plague of high-rise hotels, pizzerias, junky souvenir shops, pubs, and German beer halls.

This is precisely the area chosen by Sand, Chopin, Robert Graves, and other discerning visitors for its scenery and tranquillity, and for the experienced traveller it probably remains the place to aim for on Majorca.

Distances are small on the island, and it's possible to complete a relatively satisfactory driving tour of this coast in one very long day or two shorter ones. The better way to absorb the essence of the region is to choose a hotel as a base and make leisurely forays to an appealing variety of both natural and cultural attractions. Banyalbufar, Deya, and Cabo de Formentor are three locations—at varying distances from Palma—from which this can be accomplished.

If you stay in Deya, the most central of these locations, you will be able to make one-day excursions to all of the points recommended here. But from Banyalbufar to Formentor—or vice versa—requires quite a bit of mountain driving in one day. A compromise might be to spend a few nights in each location.

Palma to Deya

The road to the coast from Palma that goes around the southwest coast, C 719, passes through the small, traditional town of Andratx, with its shuttered houses, into a region of citrus groves and pine forests. A brief detour to Sant Telm offers a view of the transparent coastal waters washing over the rocks, and of La Dragonera, the rocky offshore island whose only current residents are birds and lizards. Archaeologists have found remains of a prehistoric necropolis there, and the island also has a place in history as the point from which Jaime I conquered Majorca; it has also been known as a pirate refuge.

The C 719, which becomes C 710, the main road north from Andratx toward Valldemossa, then takes you through tiny towns such as Estellencs and Banyalbufar, where stone houses and terraces of olive, almond, and citrus trees cling to the mountainside overlooking the sea.

From its vantage point on a cliff the **Hostal Mar i Vent** in **Banyalbufar** offers a modest, homey perch from which to contemplate the sea. A terrace and dining room with sea views, a grandfather clock in the reception hall, and salons with comfortable armchairs contribute to its atmosphere.

Valldemossa, the town where Sand and Chopin spent their much-publicized winter, is all she said it was: with the stone houses, the graceful gardens, and the mountain views from the cells of the Caufujan, the Carthusian-monastery-turned-private-property where they rented three former monks' cells in which to live.

Ironically, the town whose society shunned the lovers during their lives has become a virtual Sand-Chopin shrine. Souvenir stands line the streets and have overflowed into virtually every room of the monastery, which serves both as city museum and a sort of voyeur's peephole into the lives of the two famous artists. Museum exhibits include fragments of Sand's manuscripts and the preludes Chopin wrote here, as well as the musician's pianos and other mementos. But in the midst of all the commercialism the most affecting sight today is what most attracted Sand and Chopin 150 years ago: the tiny garden behind each cell, and the view of the valley and mountain beyond. A good lunch stop is **C'an Pedro**, located in a house on carrer Archduke Luis Salvador.

It's only a few miles down the road to **Son Marroig**, the

Austrian archduke's seaside villa *cum* garden. In the garden is an ethereal white, Neoclassical, domed kiosk that offers a view of the cliffs and the sea. The small museum inside the villa displays personal effects ranging from Berber rugs to Majorca seascapes by native painter Antoni Ribas (hijo); there's even an antique photograph of the yachts of the archduke and his cousin, Austrian Empress Elizabeth, floating in a limpid sea. In the summer the villa is used for a public concert series.

Next comes **Deya**, an expatriates' colony made famous by Robert Graves—who lived there for many years until his death in 1985—and numerous other artists and writers who have lived or visited there.

This tiny mountainside town has to be one of the most beautiful in the Balearics, with its sandy-colored, red-tiled houses enlivened by cascades of flowers and vines. The houses, however, tend to be walled to guard against intrusion by the numerous tourists who come to browse in the art galleries, quaff a beer in one of the cafés, or visit the archaeological museum located in the area of town below the main road, which contains finds from local excavations of Bronze Age sites. (At press time it was closed for renovation but is expected to reopen soon.)

The **Hotel La Residencia** here offers a superb combination of elegance and tranquillity at a price commensurate with the quality, and is one of the best choices you can make for lodgings in this area. Located on 30 acres of orchards and farmland, the natural stone buildings house guest rooms furnished with antiques and public rooms that serve as a gallery for paintings by local artists. With this hotel's gardens, terrace bar, swimming pool, and one of the best restaurants on the island—**El Olivo**—there's never a need to leave the grounds.

Deya to Formentor

Because of the cliffs, it is difficult to gain access to the coast in this region. For a rewarding peek at the waters and the cliffs, as well as a good meal, exit from Deya on C 719 toward Sóller and turn left at the sign for **Bens d'Avall restaurant**, where the road curves sharply to the right after kilometer 56. Signs lead to a pleasant establishment with an outdoor terrace—abloom with flowers in season—overlooking the water. The focus here is on fish and seafood of good quality at a fair price.

After Deya the main road twists and turns to reveal myriad perspectives on the gray whale of a mountain, Puig Mayor,

Majorca's tallest. The town of Sóller suddenly emerges in a valley of olive, citrus, and almond groves, and the coast appears again on the descent to **Puerto de Sóller**, a pleasant port shared by fishermen and tourists and lined with cafés.

In addition to the picturesque port, the town's main claim to fame is an antique orange trolley whose open-sided cars are lined with wooden benches. The cars transport visitors from the town of Sóller to the port below.

From Sóller to the northeast the road oozes through about 30 tortuous km (18 miles) of mountains, pine forest, and reservoirs unmarred by traces of civilization, to the turnoff for the scenic coastal area known as Sa Calobra and the Torrent de Pareis. The descent from the mountains to the coast unravels along 18 km (11 miles) of hairpin curves and plunging ramps, where the only signs of life are olive trees, large tufts of dry grasses, and grazing sheep.

After passing through a tiny space between two huge vertical rock slabs, the road runs through cork and citrus orchards to the **Sa Calobra cove**. Walking to the right through two tunnels in the rock, you arrive at the **Torrent de Pareis**, where a stream emerges between the rock walls and makes its way to the sea at a confluence of smoothly pebbled "beach," white-sand beach, and translucent Mediterranean waters.

Leaving Sa Calobra and getting back on the C 710, about 10 km (6 miles) toward Cabo de Formentor you can visit the **Lluch monastery**, just off the highway toward the coast. It is the spiritual home of Majorcans, who come to worship the 13th-century Gothic carved, black Virgin and Child known as the Morenata.

Lluch has been a holy site since the Virgin reputedly appeared here to a shepherd in the 13th century. However, the church—which dates from the 17th century—was rebuilt in the 19th century by several architects including Gaudí, who was also responsible for the Stations of the Cross here.

From Lluch it's about 20 km (12 miles) on C 710 through stark, rocky mountains to the town of Pollença and its bay. Follow the signs through town to begin your exploration of **Cabo de Formentor**, the long, narrow, feather-shaped promontory that protrudes from Majorca's north coast into the Mediterranean. The farther you drive on the twisting 19-km (12-mile) road along Formentor's mountainous spine, the narrower the road becomes and the more sparse the low vegetation. At the end there's a lighthouse (with a small parking lot) and a panoramic view of the sea.

At the beginning of the cape you'll see signs for the

turnoff to the **Hotel Formentor**, whose formal seaside gardens, pine forests, and facilities—including tennis courts, swimming pool, discotheque, and riding trails—sprawl just inland from a long strip of sandy beach. More than a hotel, this is a resort—frequented by Spanish nobility as well as political and literary figures—where most guests take the full pension and settle in for a long stay. It's a bit on the formal side: For the men, no tie, no dinner.

Returning to Palma

The most extensive traces of Roman civilization in Majorca are the remains of the ancient city of Pollentia, at the modern town of **Alcúdia**, 8.5 km (5 miles) from Puerto de Pollença on Bahía de Pollença at the base of Formentor. For the archaeology buff who wants to see anything and everything Roman, the relatively small, ill-maintained remains of the city and the Roman theater—plus the Museu Arqueológico, which displays finds from the excavations—may be worth a detour; for those who have only a passing interest, probably not.

The inland route back to Palma, C 713, while not as scenic as the coast, is much faster and passes through pleasant citrus and olive groves and vineyards. If you choose it, consider stopping for lunch at **Celler Ca'n Amer** at Pau 39 in Inca, an industrial city known for its production of shoes and pottery. This former wine cellar where dark wooden wine casks line the walls and strings of garlic and peppers dangle above the bar—popular with locals for business lunches—exudes traditional atmosphere. To pique the appetite, a pitcher of red wine, bread, and a plate of garlicky Majorcan olives are served when you arrive. To follow you can choose traditional dishes such as *tumbet* (vegetable casserole), hearty soups, and fresh fish.

IBIZA

Ibiza is a mecca for the jet set and a refuge for one of the world's largest remaining colonies of true 1960s hippies. And either or both of these factors may be reason enough for those who avoid rather than seek out discotheques and funky boutiques to stay away from Ibiza, even if they're tempted by the beaches and the scenic coast.

But there are some very good reasons to visit Ibiza: to experience its imposing Dalt Vila, whose Medieval walls encircle an area that was populated by Phoenicians, Romans, Arabs, or Christians since the seventh century B.C., and to be introduced to the treasure trove of sculpture, ceramics, jewelry, and other finds extracted from the tombs of a Phoenician necropolis found right in Ibiza City. A drive along the small roads on the island's interior, through groves of olives and citrus and tiny white towns, is another motive for a visit.

Whether viewed from land or sea, Ibiza's most prominent landmark is walled Ibiza City, nestled high above the port on the southeast side of the island. All of Ibiza's main roads fan out from Ibiza City. A nine-mile highway to the west connects it with San Antonio Abad, an uncomfortably dense tourist resort on the coast. About five miles south of San Antonio, Monte Atalaya, the island's highest point, rises more than 1,400 feet, overlooking a craggy coastline made more interesting by several offshore islands—really just chunks of rock that protrude from the water. Much of the island's coastline features cliffs that hang over the water, and tiny sandy beaches, many unfortunately overdeveloped with vacation villages and abominations such as water slides.

If you're exploring Ibiza by car, watch for signs to your destination. Many roads have no name or number, but there's almost always a sign pointing to the restaurant or beach you're seeking. If you insist on visiting Ibiza in August, be prepared to experience monumental traffic jams; the road system is just not adequate to the pressures of the season.

As on the other Balearic islands, the discerning visitor should avoid lodging in a hotel or area that caters to mass tourism. Because the island is so small—it's easy to explore by car or bus from almost any base—the main decision on lodgings is whether to opt for a base in Ibiza City, where the nightlife is virtually on your doorstep, or for a more tranquil, isolated hostelry on the coast.

IBIZA CITY

The city of Ibiza is a tapestry of historical threads. **La Marina**, the water's-edge seamen's quarter dating from the 15th century—now a center of nightlife—merges through the

Portal de les Tables into the stolid 16th-century walls and gates built to shield the city from attacks by the Turks. The walls enclose a maze of tiny streets lined with flat-roofed, blocky white houses, many of which are occupied by restaurants, bars, and shops.

The city wraps around Ibiza's harbor. The modern quarters lie to the northeast and the older La Marina and Sa Penya quarters lie inland—opposite the quay for ferries to and from the island of Formentera—to the south. It's just a few blocks' walk inland toward the always-visible ancient walls to the base of the Dalt Vila, the historic core of Ibiza occupied in turn by Phoenicians, Romans, Arabs, and Christians. This is the part of town that—for its history, its monuments, and its street life—has the most to offer a visitor.

If it weren't so vertical, a walking tour of the **Dalt Vila** could be accomplished in a very few minutes. But the verticality also enhances the charm—the glimpses of the sea and the wall-to-wall old, mostly white houses and shops, restaurants, and bars beckoning you to browse or pause for a drink—as you climb through the cobblestone streets to the cathedral overlooking the harbor and the nearby Ibiza archaeological museum, one of two archaeological museums in the city.

The best place to start your ascent is at the Portal de les Tables—one of three entrances to the Dalt Vila—in La Marina.

An excellent in-town hotel choice, **La Ventana** is located on Sa Carrossa, the street opposite the entrance to the contemporary art museum. Situated on the way to the top in what was formerly an old house, this spotless, cheerful hotel offers views of Ibiza City's rooftops from its second-floor rooms and of the sea from the third-floor rooms. For breakfast there are croissants and coffee on a self-service honor system. The hotel's street-level restaurant—worth a visit even if you're not staying there—features an international menu (lasagna with fish, featuring a rich, creamy white-wine sauce, and the homemade desserts are recommended).

The high point of the Dalt Vila is dominated by the cathedral, which, like the contemporary art museum you'll pass as you climb, was at press time closed indefinitely. Once you've attained the summit of Dalt Vila, you'll have a fine view of Ibiza's tile rooftops, the sea, and beaches from the balustrades. Open all day, the balustrades are reached by walking through a gate to the right of the cathedral. But there are even better views from the terrace and windows of the **Ibiza archaeological museum** at plaça de la Catedral 3, open only in the morning. This museum contains ceramics and other finds from Phoenician and prehistoric sites all over the island. Among its main attractions are three sculpted Roman figures.

However, if you only have the time or interest for one archaeological museum, definitely choose the **Puig des Molins museum** at vía Romana 31 in the modern city below. Devoted to the finds from the Punic necropolis of the same name (which is where the museum is located), Puig des Molins displays objects from Phoenician tombs located on the site, which is believed to have served as a cemetery from 654 B.C. to the first century A.D.

The undisputed star attraction is a terra-cotta bust of a woman thought to be the goddess Tamit. Deeply etched reddish hair, topped by a pillbox headdress, sweeps back from a serene, full face with an enigmatic gaze. The fact that the face is reproduced thousands of times on postcards, posters, and ceramic imitations sold all over the island does not detract from the beauty of the real thing.

Another novelty of the museum is the collection of delicate ostrich eggs—most are on display in room II—painted with simple patterns of flowers or scarabs or with abstractions. Their exact significance is not known, but one theory is that they were placed in the tombs as a symbol of resurrection. Room IV houses a collection of small, finely worked objects including medical instruments, tiny scarabs, gold rings and earrings, amulets representing Egyptian gods, and necklaces of many-toned glass beads. Room IV also has a model of a side view of the necropolis, and many of the other museum rooms contain groupings of items found together, tomb by tomb. Several museum rooms display some of the hundreds of terra-cotta statues found in the tombs, of interest because they depict figures dressed in the garments, headgear, and jewelry of their time.

In addition to the Puig des Molins museum, the main attractions outside the Dalt Vila revolve around the high-fashion, often expensive shops in La Marina; the afternoon and evening handicrafts market staged by local artisans and hippies in the passeig Vara del Rey plaza, which intersects with carrer Ramón y Tur a couple of blocks inland from the port; and passing time with friends—new or old—in hangouts such as the **Teatro Pereya**, conde Rosselón in La Marina, noted for its live jazz performances.

The **Royal Plaza**, a well-run and well-appointed modern hotel on plaça Frances, a five-minute walk from the passeig Vara de Rei, makes a good base for business and other upscale travellers.

OUT ON IBIZA ISLAND

As on Minorca, some of the best beaches can be approached only by unpaved roads through the pine groves that inspired the Greeks to call Ibiza and neighboring Formentera the Pitiüses (pine-covered) islands. One worthwhile excursion takes you north along the east coast from Ibiza City to Cala Mastella, Cala Boix (a *cala* is a cove), and the views of the coast in between.

Reason enough to make the trip is to eat lunch at the **Chringuito de Joan Ferrer** at Cala Mastella. A drive down a twisting, unpaved road to the sea reveals fisherman Ferrer's small white boat and roofed but otherwise open-air restaurant on the rocks right at the water's edge. This is a family business. Ferrer arrives at the dock and lugs in a plastic bucket of fish. Then the women cook them over logs in a huge open fireplace.

The menu—it never changes—is the traditional fish stew, *bullit de peix,* served in two courses to diners seated on benches at wooden picnic tables overlooking the water. First comes a brilliant yellow melange of potato chunks and the day's catch. Next comes a huge bowl of soupy yellow rice, rather tangy and garnished with bright-red crab's legs. This place may seem terribly out of the way, but it's popular, and in the summer it's necessary to make reservations two or three days in advance for lunch—Ferrer's is not open for dinner. There's no phone, so the only way to make reservations is to go there in person.

For a very different but equally worthwhile view of the Ibiza coast, take C 733 north out of Ibiza City through Santa Gertrudis and San Miguel and follow the signs to the **Hotel Hacienda** in the Na Xamena urbanization, an isolated, elegant aerie ensconced in a cliff-top pine forest overlooking a pinkish rock promontory over the sea. If you value tranquillity and can afford the considerable tab, this is the place to stay on the island.

There's no beach here, but the outdoor swimming pool and terrace around it are ample; the rooms overlook the sea. The traditional white architecture, complemented by greenery, makes the hotel a tranquil and beautiful choice. And its restaurant, which attracts diners from around the island, sometimes offers a special menu of fourth-century B.C. Phoenician dishes such as partridge with dates.

Inland towns such as San José, San Miguel, and San Rafael all have bright, white houses, some with brightly colored trim, and small churches with bell towers. **Balafi**, a tiny, enclosed compound of a few houses and a cylindrical defensive tower surrounded by a wall, can be approached from a turnoff on the road from Ibiza to San Juan. Leave the car at the edge of the road and take the footpath to examine this curious colony more closely, but be aware that the residents keep large dogs that tend to growl a lot to keep unwanted visitors from getting too close.

One house that welcomes visitors with open arms is **La Masía d'En Sord**, at kilometer 1, carretera a San Miguel, outside Ibiza City, a huge, traditional farmhouse converted into a restaurant-gallery by artist-owner Nieves Puente. The menu is Continental with local touches such as rabbit grilled over an open fire. Diners may sit inside on banquettes piled comfortably with pillows, or at tables in the garden. The large house feels intimate because there are several small dining rooms rather than one cavernous one. The walls—on which are displayed everything from drawings of Ibizan women in traditional dress to abstract oils—bear testimony to the changing artistic moods of the owner and her daughter.

FORMENTERA ISLAND

Connected to the rest of Spain only by ferries and sightseeing boats, Formentera is the fourth-largest Balearic island, with a population of about 4,500.

Best-known for its beaches—where nude bathing is as much an attraction as the sand and clear water—Formentera suffers from a lack of fresh water that has slowed the tourist trade. Although the island is a popular destination for day trips, most of the accommodations are small hostels, many of which are booked ahead of time by groups.

Playa Mitjorn, on the south coast, is an excellent long, almost undeveloped bathing beach. Here stand two rather upscale hotels, each with over 300 rooms, swimming pools, and other facilities: **Club La Mola** and the **Formentera Plaza**.

You can take a ferry from Estación Marítim at the foot of avinguda Bartolomé Roselló—they depart and return several times a day—for the one-hour, often-rough sea passage from Ibiza City to Formentera's port, La Savina, where you can rent a car, bicycle, or moped for touring. Tour boats depart from Ibiza from the port at San Antonio Abad.

GETTING AROUND

Iberia flies from London to Palma, but this is the only scheduled air connection between an international departure point and the Balearics. Therefore most air travellers who are not taking charter flights will have to approach the islands from a point—most likely Madrid or Barcelona—on the Spanish mainland.

The Iberia Airlines "Visit Spain" pass, which allows travellers who are crossing the Atlantic on Iberia to travel throughout Spain for 60 days for a special low fare, allows you to stop at each of the islands (in addition to points on the mainland) if you plan the itinerary so that it's not necessary to double back on your route.

Both air and sea transportation schedules between mainland Spain and the Balearics, as well as from one island to another, change several times a year—sometimes radically. If you plan to travel during the summer, at Christmas, Easter, or any Spanish holiday, or on a weekend, it may be hard to get last-minute plane reservations. And although boat travel has its charms, travelling this way increases the length of your journey considerably (see below).

You can safely assume that there will be daily service on Iberia or on Aviaco, the Spanish domestic airline, from Madrid and Barcelona to Ibiza, Majorca, and Minorca. (No other airlines fly these routes.) Barcelona, about a half-hour flight from each of the islands, is the closest jumping-off point. Flights from Madrid are about an hour.

In planning your trip, try to reserve ahead, because flights are usually heavily booked: during the winter months (from about October to Easter) because there often are not enough to meet the normal demand from island residents; and during the summer months—even though flights are added—because of the influx of tourists. (And unless you can tolerate a delay, always book and confirm your return to the mainland well ahead of time.) There are some flights to the islands from Valencia—it's only a half-hour to Ibiza—but they are not always daily and schedules are always subject to change. Frequent strikes and threats of strikes make flying even more of a lottery in Spain than in most other countries.

Trasmediterránea Lines runs ferries from the mainland and among the islands two or three times a week during the winter, more often in the summer (starting in June). From Barcelona to any of the three islands directly is an eight-hour trip, sometimes overnight. The ferry—which has staterooms as well as armchairs—carries cars and is also equipped with restaurants, bars, television, game rooms, and an outdoor pool. While the trip can be pleasant on a warm summer day, in the winter the Mediterranean can be quite rough.

The Trasmediterránea ferries also connect Minorca, Majorca, and Ibiza. The company can be reached in Barcelona at vía Laietana 2 (Tel: 319-9612 or 319-8212) and in Valencia at Manuel Soto 19 (Tel: 367-6512).

In the islands, Trasmediterránea offices are located in Mahón (Minorca) at Nuevo Muelle Comercial, Tel: 36-29-50; Palma (Majorca) on passeig Muelle Viejo, Tel: 72-67-40; and in Ibiza City (Ibiza) on avinguda Bartolomé Vicente Ramó 2, Tel: 30-16-50.

Another ferry company, Flebasa, offers year-round service from Denia, about halfway between Valencia and Alicante on the southern coast of Spain, to Ibiza. They have offices in Denia (Tel: 78-41-00), Madrid (Tel: 473-2055) and Ibiza (Tel: 34-28-71).

Each of the islands has some bus service, although it is not adequate for exploring the more isolated beaches and monuments. Bus schedules are available from local tourist offices. The only trains on the islands are on Majorca. There are two lines—one between Palma and Sóller, the other between Palma and Inca—which offer service several times a day from the plaça España in Palma.

The Spanish company Atesa, as well as Avis and Hertz, offers car rentals on all three major islands. Each island also has several—in the case of Majorca, numerous—other agencies. Sometimes the best car rental rates, especially if you need the vehicle for a week or more, can be secured as part of a vacation package. If you'll only need a car for an occasional excursion, unless you're visiting in August, at Christmas time, or during Holy Week, you may get the best deal by postponing your car-rental decision until you actually arrive on one of the islands. Bicycles, motorcycles, and motorbikes are also widely available for rental, and serve well for many excursions.

ACCOMMODATIONS REFERENCE

When dialing telephone numbers from outside the country, drop the 9 in the area code.

Minorca

▸ **Alfonso III Hotel.** Cami de Mao 53, 07701 **Ciudadela**, Minorca. Tel: (971) 38-01-50.

▸ **Del Almirante.** Fonduco Puerto de Mahón, 07701 **Villacarlos**, Minorca. Tel: (971) 36-27-00.

▸ **Hostal Residencia Ciudadela.** San Eloy 10, 07701 **Ciudadela,** Minorca. Tel: (971) 38-34-62.

▸ **Esmeralda.** Passeig de San Nicolas 171, 07701 **Ciudadela,** Minorca. Tel: (971) 38-02-50.

▸ **Hostal Mar Blava.** Urbanización Son Oleo, 07701 **Ciudadela,** Minorca. Tel: (971) 38-00-15.

▸ **Hotel Patrícia.** Passeig de San Nicolas 92, 07701 **Ciudadela,** Minorca. Tel: (971) 38-55-11.

▸ **Port Mahón Hotel.** Avinguda Fort de l'Eau, 07701 **Mahón,** Minorca. Tel: (971) 36-26-00.

Majorca

▸ **Hotel Formentor.** Playa de Formentor, 07470 **Cabo de Formentor,** Majorca. Tel: (971) 53-13-00.

▸ **Hostal Mar i Vent.** José Antonio 49, 07191 **Banyalbufar,** Majorca. Tel: (971) 61-00-25.

▸ **Hotel Meliá Victoria.** Avinguda Joan Miró 21, 07014 **Palma,** Majorca. Tel: (971) 23-25-42.

▸ **Hotel La Residencia.** Finca Son Canals, 07179 **Deya,** Majorca. Tel: (971) 63-90-11.

▸ **Son Vida Sheraton.** Urbanización Son Vida, 07013 **Palma,** Majorca. Tel: (971) 45-10-11.

Ibiza

▸ **Hotel Hacienda.** Na Xamena Urbanización, 07080 **San Miguel,** Ibiza. Tel: (971) 33-30-46.

▸ **Royal Plaza.** Pedro Frances 27, 07800 **Ibiza,** Ibiza. Tel: (971) 31-00-00.

▸ **La Ventana.** Sa Carrossa 13, 07800 **Ibiza,** Ibiza. Tel: (971) 30-25-48.

Formentera

▸ **Formentera Plaza.** 07871 **Playa Mitjorn,** Formentera. Tel: (971) 32-00-00.

▸ **Club La Mola.** Apartado San Francisco 23, 07871 **Playa Mitjorn,** Formentera. Tel: (971) 32-00-75.

VALENCIA

AND ALICANTE

By Patricia Brooks

Although Valencia is famed in song and in kitchen, it is left off most visitors' itineraries. As Spain's third largest city and capital of the Mediterranean province of the same name, Valencia is oddly uncharismatic at first sight—a huge port and major industrial-agricultural hub that fell victim to high-rises and urban sprawl. A visitor driving through its flat geography may see only the ugly signs of shipping and industry, assume that's all there is, and take the turnoff skirting the city, going north to Tarragona and Barcelona, south to the Costa del Sol, or west to Madrid, and completely missing Valencia's center.

Yet there are many reasons why this would be a mistake, many things to recommend a stop in Valencia: three rich, important museums; a cathedral with several unusual treasures; a lively covered market that is a photographer's dream; a clutch of interesting churches; streets pocketed with handsome 15th- to 19th-century mansions and public buildings; a graceful location spanning both banks (but mostly the south one) of the río Turia; and more than its share of colorful history.

To cover its major sights will take two very full days, but the city has so many additional charms that grow on you—gentle climate, a languid sidewalk-café lifestyle, gardens, fountains, unexpected outdoor sculptures, serendipitous discoveries—that a third or even a fourth day will be rewarding.

Alicante, 177 km (111 miles) farther south, is less important historically, but its balmy weather, seaside charm, and wide swath of palm-fringed seafront promenade are instant crowd pleasers. Being a springboard to the resorts of Benidorm, Denia, and other points both north and south along the **Costa Blanca**, as the coast here is called, doesn't hurt either. A day or two in Alicante is well spent.

Linking the two cities, in an area sometimes called the Levante, is a coastline as different and appealing in its own way as any in Spain. Fertile flatlands, bordered by a barrier of mountains on one side and the Mediterranean on the other, provide an unusual landscape. And, as elsewhere in this wildly diverse country, the scenery changes frequently, as the road climbs from sand dune–protected lagoons to cypress-spiked cliffs and wild promontories high above rock-edged bays, then quickly down again to sandy inlets and boat-filled harbors.

MAJOR INTEREST

The ruins at Sagunto

Valencia
Cathedral
Lonja Gothic silk exchange
Central market
Museo Provincial de Bellas Artes, a major international institution
Colegio del Patriarca Renaissance building and art museum
The city's plazas
Instituto Valenciano de Arte Moderno (IVAM)

Manises ceramics

Gandía and Játiva, ancient towns of the Borgias

Alicante
Explanada de España harbor promenade
Museo Colección Arte de Siglo XX
Castillo de Santa Bárbara

Elche palm forest town

The Foods of Valencia and the Levante

When you think of Valencia and food, one word pops into mind: *paella.* The rice-based, saffron-tinted stew known as *paella Valenciana* is certainly Valencia's glory dish, and nowhere in Spain—in the entire world, for that matter—is it prepared with the same élan. The true, traditional *paella*

Valenciana consists of rice, small snails (usually periwinkles or sea snails), rabbit or chicken, and green vegetables—foods abundant in the region. Eels and land snails, also found in the area, are considered Valencian "originals" as well. Needless to say, there are as many *paella* variations as there are chefs. From the *Moros y Cristanos* (Moors and Christians, or rice with black beans) version to rice with squid, to lamb and chickpeas, to zucchini and other vegetables, to Cuban-style with bananas and fried eggs, sampling different *paellas* is part of the pleasure of a visit to this area.

It is believed that the word *paella* comes from *patella,* Latin for pan, referring to the flat round metal pan (*paellera* in Spanish) in which the rice is cooked. Using the proper shallow, open pan is considered essential to a good *paella,* for the nature of the pan ensures even cooking and "finishing," without steaming.

One given of "eastern," or Levantine, cooking is that *arroz* (rice)—abundant, flat-grained Valencian rice—will be the base of so many of the dishes served. You might encounter *arroz con costra al estilo de Elche* (Elche style), made with chick-peas, pork, *blanquillos* (small Levante sausages), chicken, and the black Catalan *butifarra* pork sausage. *Arroz con pollo a la Alicante* consists of rice, chicken, green peppers, tomatoes, and artichokes, and *arroz a banda* has a seafood broth. *Arroz con pollo* (with chicken) is found in almost every restaurant in the area.

The produce garden of Spain, the Levante is a harvest of fresh fruits and vegetables, widely evident in the cuisine. No vegetable is more widely used than the artichoke. A delicacy elsewhere in the world, artichokes in Valencia and along the coast are common and are often served as a first course—a plethora of tiny chokes seasoned with bits of ham. Delicious! Imaginative use of vegetables, such as zucchini, eggplant, and potatoes stuffed with ground meat, enveloped by an almond (another native crop), herb, and garlic sauce, is a Valencian trademark.

Other Levantine dishes include *cocas,* a pie made of sweet red peppers, tomatoes, anchovies, and *toyina* (salted tuna), and *pastel de Villena,* a pork loin stuffed with ham, *butifarra,* bacon, and vegetables, and then covered with a minced meat paste and baked.

Sweets are popular, too, and you'll want to look for Valencian sweet bread (*pan quemado*), Valencian flan (made with oranges and lemons), rice and apricot pudding, *tarta Huerto del Cura* (orange cream cake), and, above all, the almond-honey nougat candy known as *turrón* of Jijona and Alicante, which you will find also served in turrón-flavored ice cream, sherbet, and in sweet sauces. Candied almonds, available all over Spain, are especially prevalent in Valencia, Alicante, and along the coast. And don't miss the refreshing, creamy drink *horchata,* made of a tuber called *chufa,* or earth almond, which, when processed, tastes like an elusive cross between almond and coconut.

Wines of Valencia and Murcia

The warm, dry Mediterranean regions of Valencia (Valencia, Alicante, and Castellón de la Plana) and Murcia (the region south of the Valencia region) contain five *denominaciones de origen*—Alicante, Utiel-Requena, Valencia, Jumilla, and Yecla—all primarily engaged in the production of powerful bulk wines for blending. In this endeavor the Levante is second only to La Mancha. Recently a number of top producers have begun reinvesting money in their wineries and vineyards with an eye toward producing better-quality bottled wines. Modern temperature-controlled fermentation techniques have led to some improvement in the quality of a few table wines, but the region is still far from being a bastion of quality.

Alicante produces full-bodied reds and *rosados* from 90 percent Monastrell grapes. The vineyards are located in the highlands above the Mediterranean beach towns of the Costa Blanca. This area was one of the last occupied by the Moors, and so, prohibitions from the Koran aside, a sweet-tooth legacy remains in some luscious dessert wines, especially Moscatel.

Most of Utiel-Requena's (Valencia) vineyards grow the black Bobal, which produces powerful red wines, but new vineyards are being planted with Tempranillo and Garnacha. Because Utiel-Requena's summers are milder than those nearer the Mediterranean, the area is able to produce some good lighter, fresh *rosados.*

Valencia also produces medium-bodied white table wines from Merserguera grapes, large quantities of low-acid, high-alcohol red table wines of 14 to 15 percent, and some delicious Moscatels. Some of the huge firms specializing in bulk wines are also making some interesting new quality wines for sale in bottle.

In Jumilla (Murcia) 90 percent of the vineyards grow Monastrell, which yields thick, black wines of up to 18 percent alcohol. Recently Jumilla has begun to produce some lighter, very well-made oak-aged table wines.

Valencia/
Alicante
0 miles 20
0 km 20
N
to Tarragona
and Barcelona
Tortosa
Benicarló
N 340
E 15
Costa del Azahar
Castelló
de la Plana
Río Palencia
Sagunto
Río Turia
Gulf
of
Valencia
Manises
Valencia
N 11 E 901
to Madrid
El Saler
La Albufera
N 332
to Balearic Islands
Játiva
Monte
Bernisa
Gandía
N 430
Denia
Cabo de San Antonio
Jávea
Cabo de la Nao
Alcoy
N 340
Peñon de Ifach
N 330
E 15
Jijona
Benidorm
Villajoyosa
Río Vinalopo
Elche
Alicante
N 340
to Murcia
and Costa del Sol
Costa Blanca

Yecla (Murcia), which is completely surrounded by the Jumilla and Alicante districts, makes not only traditionally robust reds from Monastrell grapes, but also some big, smooth red wines and *claretes* from Monastrell and Garnacha.

A notable feature of the Levante's vineyards is their high proportion of ungrafted vines. The chalky soil and dry climate are not hospitable to aphids, so the vineyards in the Levante were not destroyed during the phylloxera epidemic at the turn of the century.

The Levante's greatest dish, *paella,* is often accompanied by a red wine.

—*Gerry Dawes*

EN ROUTE TO VALENCIA

While you can drive to Valencia from three different major destinations (Madrid, the Andalusian Costa del Sol, or Barcelona), it's more logical to fly (a 35-minute plane ride from Madrid) or to make the drive as an add-on to a Tarragona visit, coming down through southern Catalonia from Barcelona. This is the way we cover Valencia province here. Just 259 km (155 miles) south of Tarragona via the superfast *autopista* E 15, the route eventually leads over terrain you won't encounter elsewhere in Spain—flat as the proverbial pancake, with wet, languid marshlands and incredibly fertile soil. This is the area known as the Levante, with the level fields and farms of La Huerta (the irrigated region or garden).

It was the Romans who built the elaborate irrigation systems (developed further by the Moors) that have made La Huerta into the most productive land in Spain. La Huerta consists of field after field of artichokes, tomatoes, and melons, and orchards of apricot, fig, and almond trees. Most dominant are the orange trees, stretching in orderly rows farther than the eye can see and giving this section of Mediterranean landscape (from just south of Tarragona to Jávea) its name—the **Costa del Azahar** (orange-blossom coast).

Allow time as you drive south to Valencia for a few interesting stops along the way. About 48 km (30 miles) south of **Tortosa**, which has a 14th-century Gothic church with a cloister and a Moorish tower, is the small coastal town of Benicarlo. Near the beach at the edge of town is the modern **Parador Costa del Azahar**, an attractive lunch stop, with good regional seafood and rice dishes and a swimming pool and beach where you might have a preprandial dip.

Farther along, about 25 km (16 miles) north of the city of Valencia, you will encounter **Sagunto** (with some 55,000 inhabitants), which is about where La Huerta begins in the north. It was in this area that Hannibal was wounded during the eight-month siege in 218 B.C. that triggered the start of the Second Punic War. When the Carthaginians attacked the little seaport the natives sought help from Rome—but it never came. Rather than surrender, the women, children, and elderly threw themselves into a furnace, while the men resisted bravely but hopelessly, and were killed. Follow the winding road that leads up to the hilltop behind the town to **Castillo de Sagunto**, to see scores of Iberian, Carthaginian, and Roman ruins and enjoy some splendid views of La Huerta and the sea. Halfway up the hill is the town's most important sight, the surprisingly well-preserved **Roman theater**, where 8,000 spectators once sat. It is a gem.

THE CITY OF VALENCIA

Valencia has seen more than a little bit of history since the Romans founded it around 138 B.C. on the site of a former Greek colony. The Romans, and later the Visigoths, Moors, and Christians, set their sights on this strategic port city and its agricultural riches, but it was El Cid who provided its most romantic legends. After a siege of 20 months, the famous warrior entered Valencia in 1094, wrested the city from the Moors (who had held it for more than 300 years), and ruled until his death in 1099. The Moors returned, however, in 1102, and they held this rich port again until 1238, when Jaime el Conquistador (James I) of Aragón seized it once and for all.

History has left its scars on Valencia. The city was on the losing side all too often: in the War of the Spanish Succession early in the 18th century, and a hundred years later when it suffered serious reprisals after rebelling from and then losing to Napoleon's forces under Marshal Suchet in 1812. In the Civil War, Valencia was the last outpost of the Republican forces in Catalonia, finally falling (after Madrid) to Franco's troops on March 30, 1939.

Modern Valencia, victim of high-rises, exhaust fumes, and general urban sprawl, does not, at first glance, inspire lingering. But your feelings begin to change once you reach the inner core of this flat-as-a-tortilla city straddling the río Turia, which snakes its way east to the port of El Grao and the Mediterranean. The streets that border the southern side of the river's bend have a particular grace, and other parts of the old center are dotted with tree-shaded plazas and enough architectural surprises to delight any traveller.

Summer here is almost insufferably humid, so, if possible, a visit would best be made during any of the other three seasons. The liveliest time is during the explosive (literally) Fallas de Valencia, March 15–19, held in honor of San José (Saint Joseph), the patron saint of carpenters and other artisans. Started in the Middle Ages when the carpenters celebrated Saint Joseph's Day by burning their wood shavings, Fallas today is one of the major festivals in Spain, a citywide extravaganza of gigantic wood, cloth, and papier mâché *ninots* (caricatures) displayed in satirical, mocking floats or tableaus visible at every street corner and plaza. After a series of seemingly nonstop parades, fairs, dances, bullfights, performances by bands of musicians (as many as 4,000 in all), and fireworks comes the finale. At midnight of the final night of the *fallas* (bonfires), the *ninots* are strung with firecrackers and set afire. Anyone with sensitive ears might choose another time to visit and be content to enjoy seeing some of the most colorful *ninot* heads at the Fallas Museum, plaza de Monteolivete 4, where the most inspired, prize-winning ones are rescued each year from cremation and put on permanent display.

The City Center

Large as Valencia is, its center, south of the river, is manageable and forms a loose semicircle along tree-lined calle de Guillem de Castro (the street's name changes to Jativa and then to Colón), cutting a wide swath from calle Blanquerias on the west side to calle Ciudadela on the east. Between Guillem de Castro and the Turia are many labyrinthine streets lined with old palaces, houses, and government and commercial buildings that echo with the city's cultural and political history and accomplishments. This is the area where you will spend most of your time—with a brief foray north across the river. The center is walkable (or taxiable).

Before you begin to roam the old city on foot, you might deposit your luggage and car at a hotel. A convenient choice is the **Astoria Palace**, a comfortable, stately establishment on plaza Rodrigo Botet, a delightful, quiet, tree-shaded plaza just two blocks north of plaza del País Valenciano, which itself is near the southern edge of the city's center, but still close enough for you to walk to virtually everything you'll want to see. The Astoria Palace is arguably the best hotel (and the priciest) in town; the rooms are comfortable, with full amenities, if somewhat small baths. A fine restaurant, popular with locals, and a lively disco, **La Bruja**, add to the hotel's amenable aspects.

Another centrally located hotel is the recently spruced up **Reina Victoria**, just off the plaza del País Valenciano. The hotel's public rooms have always had a Neoclassical elegance, but lately the guest rooms and baths have been redone too, and there is a good restaurant with local specialties and a friendly place for drinks, **Bar Inglés**. The wrought-iron balconies of some guest rooms overlook the beautiful plaza, but those rooms get the traffic noise as well. Even so, this is a delightful, convenient place to stay.

Two other smaller, and also more moderately priced, hotels that are equally central are the **Bristol**, a charming old-fashioned hotel near the Iglesia de San Martin, just off calle San Vicente, and **Hotel Inglés**, which generates considerable *fin-de-siècle* character and faces the Museo Nacional de Cerámica on Marqués de Dos Aguas.

If you'd rather be away from city noise, just 10 km (6 miles) south of the city, on El Saler Beach, are two other options: the **Sidi Saler Palace-Sol**, a large, modern resort hotel with many amenities, garden, pool, tennis, and a wonderful beach, which helps compensate for the hotel's lack of charm, and **Parador Luis Vives**, a modern member of the government-run parador chain, with beach, pool, and golf course. Both are on El Saler beach and are geared for the holiday traveler. If your plan is to visit Valencia for Fallas, either of these two modern, somewhat impersonal hotels would assure more sleep than one in the city.

Back in the city for its sights: **Plaza del País Valenciano**, a large, graceful square with fountain and gardens, is faced by two monumental buildings opposite one another; the 19th-century Ayuntamiento (City Hall) on the west stares directly across at the General Post Office. The plaza crosses calle San Vicente Martin, then leads into avenida María Cristina, which takes you to plaza Mercado, but more of that later.

Instead, turn north (right) up San Vicente, where you will pass, on the right, the 14th-century **Iglesia de San Martin**, with an admirable bronze statue of the saint on the façade. Then it is just a short block to the **plaza de la Virgen**, with the **Iglesia de Santa Catalina** and its adjoining 17th-century hexagonal Baroque tower of golden stone on the left, and the cathedral (which Valencians call La Seo) looming directly ahead. If you're thirsty, pause along plaza Santa Catalina at a

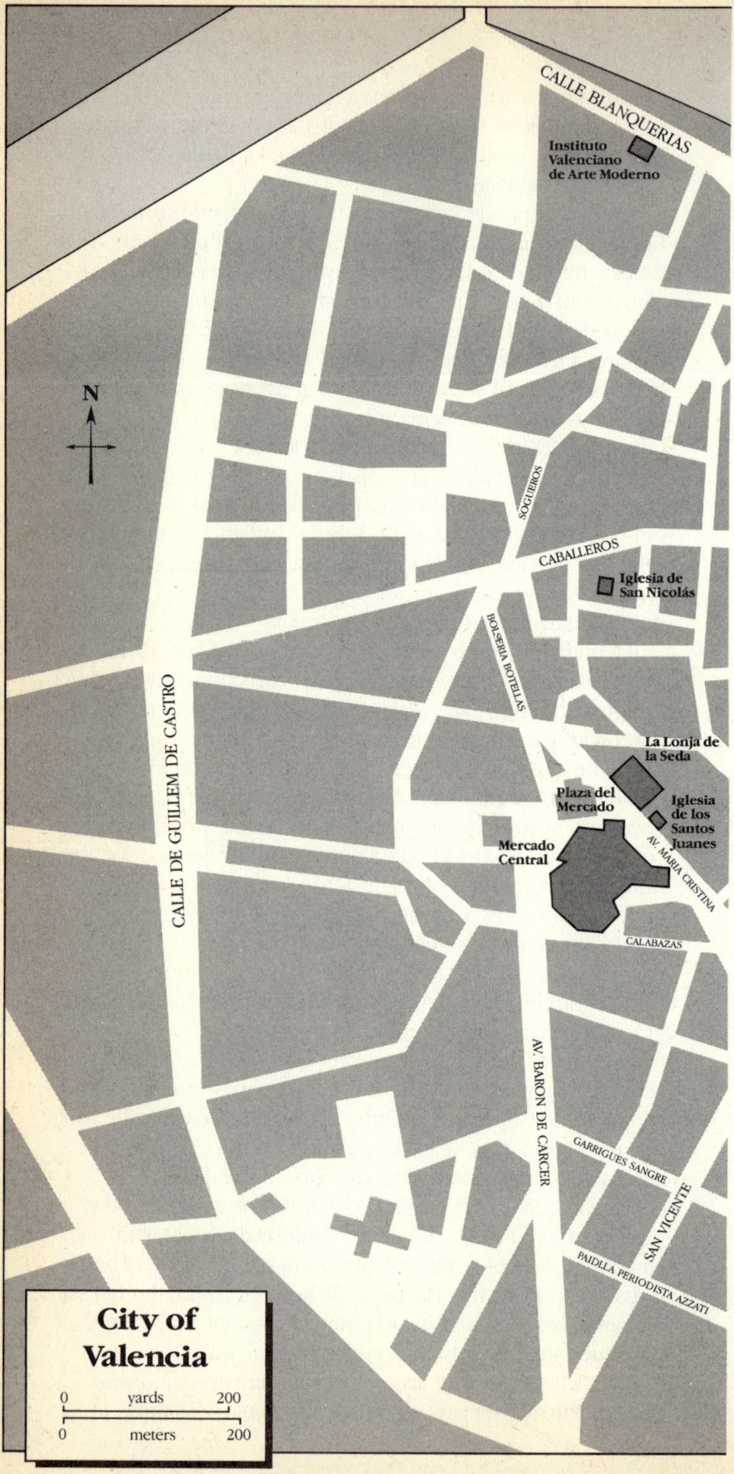
CALLE BLANQUERIAS
Instituto
Valenciano
de Arte Moderno
N
SOGUEROS
CABALLEROS
Iglesia de
San Nicolás
BOLSERIA BOTELLAS
La Lonja de
la Seda
Plaza del
Mercado
Iglesia
de los
Santos
Juanes
Mercado
Central
AV. MARIA CRISTINA
CALABAZAS
CALLE DE GUILLEM DE CASTRO
AV. BARON DE CARCER
GARRIGUES SANGRE
SAN VICENTE
PAIDLLA PERIODISTA AZZATI
City of
Valencia
0 yards 200
0 meters 200

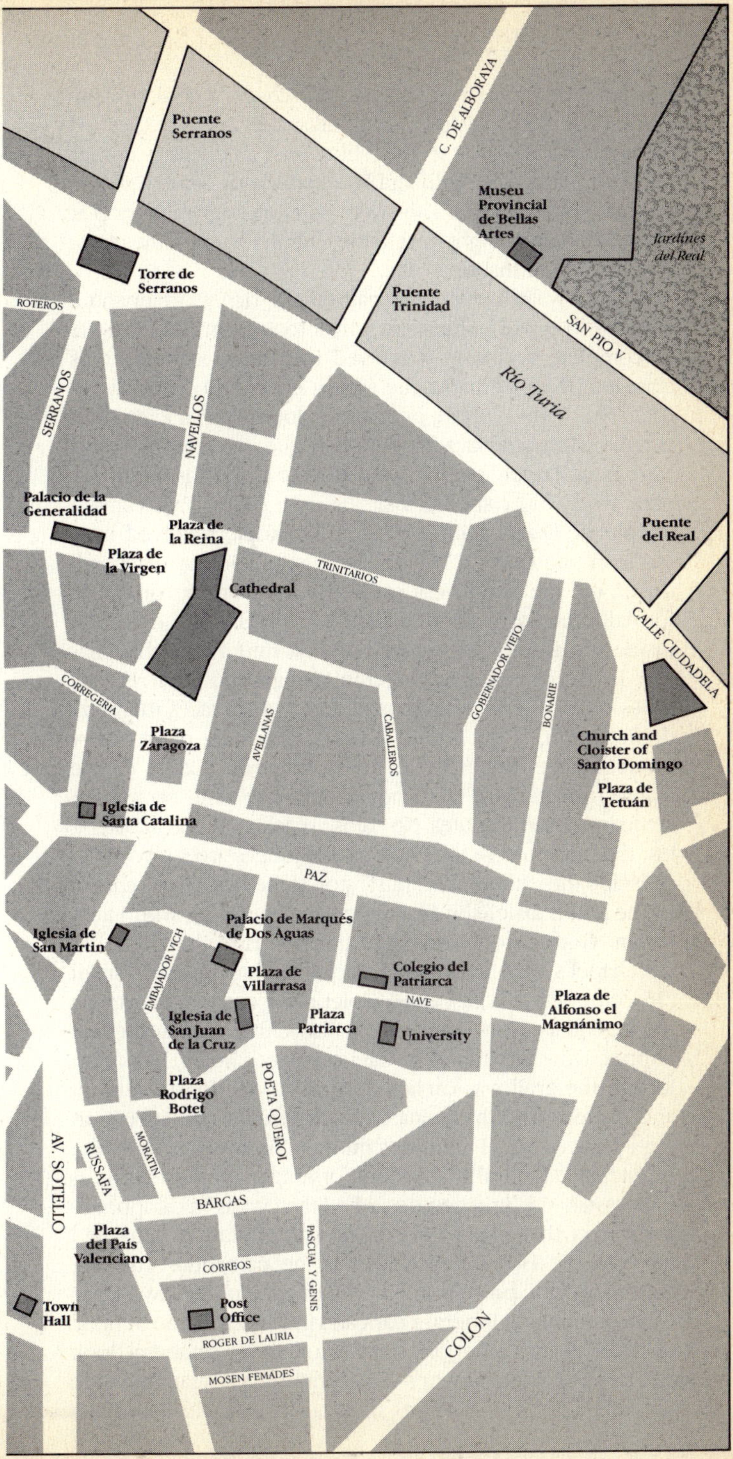

Puente Serranos
C. DE ALBORAYA
Museu Provincial de Bellas Artes
Jardines del Real
Torre de Serranos
ROTEROS
Puente Trinidad
SAN PIO V
Río Turia
SERRANOS
NAVELLOS
Palacio de la Generalidad
Plaza de la Reina
Plaza de la Virgen
Cathedral
TRINITARIOS
Puente del Real
CALLE CIUDADELA
GOBERNADOR VIEJO
BONAIRE
CORREGERIA
Plaza Zaragoza
AVELLANAS
CABALLEROS
Church and Cloister of Santo Domingo
Plaza de Tetuán
Iglesia de Santa Catalina
PAZ
Palacio de Marqués de Dos Aguas
Iglesia de San Martin
EMBAJADOR VICH
Plaza de Villarrasa
Colegio del Patriarca
NAVE
Plaza de Alfonso el Magnánimo
Iglesia de San Juan de la Cruz
Plaza Patriarca
University
POETA QUEROL
Plaza Rodrigo Botet
AV. SOTELLO
RUSSAFA
MORATIN
BARCAS
PASCUAL Y GENIS
Plaza del País Valenciano
CORREOS
Town Hall
Post Office
COLON
ROGER DE LAURIA
MOSEN FEMADES

horchateria, where you can try a *horchata,* a cool, creamy drink with the consistency of a milkshake, made of crushed ice and *chufas* that is so refreshing on a Valencian summer day. **Horchateria El Siglo** and **Horchateria de Santa Catalina** are both old reliables. The sweet of tooth might also stop at **Turrones Ramos,** right next to the church tower on the plaza, for a turrón or marzipan "fix."

As you walk around the **cathedral**'s richly ornamented exterior, you will understand why it took from 1262 to 1482 to complete and why it evolved in that time, as fashions changed, from Romanesque (south door, called Puerta del Palau) to Gothic (north, or Apostle, door), with a later 18th-century Baroque façade. The Baroque interior elements have been largely peeled away, leaving Gothic as the dominant style. The cathedral's site is even older: First came a temple of Diana, then a Visigothic church, followed by a Moorish mosque. The tall, Flamboyant Gothic octagonal tower on the southwest corner is the Micalet, or, more formally, the Torre del Miguelete, so named because the bell inside the tower chimed for the first time on Michaelmas Day 1418. For centuries the chimes regulated the irrigation times of La Huerta. The Apostle door, which faces the plaza de la Virgen, is the site of a famous meeting place. Every Thursday the Tribunal de los Acequieros (Court of the Waters) meets, as it has since at least the tenth century, to settle irrigation disputes. No oaths are taken or records kept, but the decisions of the eight farmer-judges are irrevocable.

Inside the cathedral a "must" stop is the **Holy Grail chapel** in the south aisle (the first right after entering), with Flamboyant Gothic stone tracery as delicate as feathers. Behind the chapel's altar in a glass-protected Gothic niche is a small (15 centimeters high), deep violet agate cup reputed to be the legendary Holy Grail, the chalice Christ used at the Last Supper. How did it land in Valencia? According to Valencian legend the grail was carried to Spain in the fourth century and protected in the monasterio de San Juan de la Peña in the Pyrenees for 11 centuries more, until it was given to the Valencian cathedral by the King of Aragón. Not everyone is impressed. V. S. Pritchett described the cup as "a disappointing object that might have come from Tiffany's." Reached through the Holy Grail chapel is the **cathedral museum**, with many fine polychromed religious sculptures, two large Goya paintings, a Ribera, a dark and murky Zurbarán in need of cleaning, and other paintings. While in the cathedral, look also at the **Capilla Mayor**'s 15th-century high altar with side panels painted by students of Leonardo da Vinci; the alabaster windows in the splendid Flamboyant Gothic lantern; and the fine 17th-century choir stalls, among other gems.

Leaving the cathedral by the north door, you'll enter **plaza de la Reina**, a cynosure of the city's open-air life, graced with an elaborate 19th-century fountain, a reclining, white marble Neoclassic Colossus ringed by obsequious stone nymphets, pink-and-gray marble pavement, old-fashioned gas streetlights, sidewalk cafés, and rows of fragrant orange trees.

Half a block west on calle de Caballeros is the grand 15th- to 16th-century Gothic **Palacio de la Generalidad**, sometimes called Audiencia, where the Valencia Cortes used to meet and general taxes were collected. Peek inside to admire the coffered ceiling and *azulejos* (tile) frieze around the Grand Council Chamber, and the *artesanado* ceilings in the attached 17th-century tower. There are a number of fine old manors and Gothic patios on this street. Four short blocks farther west is the **Iglesia de San Nicolás**, one of the city's oldest churches, redone in exuberant Churrigueresque style, and itself a repository of Valencian art and treasures, the most notable being the altarpiece by Juan de Juanes in the chapel to the left of the main entrance.

The Marketplace

If you go south (left) just beyond San Nicolás, it is just a three-block walk to another cluster of Valencia's treasures in the noisy, bustling plaza del Mercado. The pulse of Valencian life, the plaza was once the scene of exhibitions, bullfights, even executions, but it is now a great, bubbling explosion of a flea market and food market. The centerpiece of all the action is the covered Mercado Central, which looks like a 19th-century fantasy of vividly colored tiles and glass-domed cupolas; it was actually built in 1928 on the site of an earlier market. There are some 1,300 market stalls arranged in two separate sections: the produce and meat section under an orange-tile-decorated dome above which sprouts a bronze cockatoo weathervane, and the seafood section, beneath a fish weathervane, whose interior tile designs are scallop shells.

Across from the market is the **Iglesia de los Santos Juanes** (church of the Saint Johns), with an effusive Churrigueresque façade. The interior was badly damaged during the Civil War but has been somewhat restored. (Valencia, the last holdout of the Republican government, suffered extensive damage.)

On the northeast side of the plaza is **La Lonja de la Seda**

(Silk Exchange), a remarkable 15th-century, gargoyle-ornamented Flamboyant Gothic edifice with tower, built on the site of a Moorish *alcázar* (fortress). You can climb the tower for first-rate views of the city; be sure also to see the 15th-century sculpted ceiling in the Salon de Consular del Mar (Maritime Court), the orange-tree court, and the curved slender columns of the high-ceilinged great hall.

The 15th century was Valencia's heyday, a period of great commercial success and the flowering of the arts. As you stroll through the old city, you'll see numerous remnants of the Flamboyant Gothic style so popular then. The painters Jacomart, the Orsonas (father and son), Juan Reixach, and Luis Dalmau all flourished at this time (you'll see their work in the Museo Provincial de Bellas Artes), as did artisans who brought the crafts of ceramics, gold- and silversmithing, wrought-iron mongering, and embroidery to a pinnacle of artistic development. Their mastery is evident in churches and public buildings throughout Valencia.

Behind La Lonja is a little street, calle Corregeria, that is lined with book and stamp shops. One of the most engaging is **Libreria de Viejo**, a tiny shop full of old volumes and antique toys. A branch of the government-run **Artespaña**, with fine handicrafts from the region and all over Spain, is on another street behind La Lonja, at Poeta Querol 1.

Plaza de País Valenciano

If you stroll southeast along avenida María Cristina from plaza del Mercado, you will return to plaza del País Valenciano. By now, a lunch break might be in order, perhaps at **Ateneo**, on the plaza. The menu includes excellent local rice-based dishes and fish, such as sea bass with fennel, served in either a casual or a more formal setting. Ateneo's only drawback: a not-always-ingratiating staff. Also on the plaza, and a handy, inexpensive place for a quick *bocadillo* (sandwich) or *tapas* lunch, is **Barrachina**, a block-long glorified deli/café.

Alternatively, you might go a few blocks beyond the General Post Office building to Mosén Femades, a narrow street to the east with a number of satisfactory restaurants and *tapas* bars. **Río Sil**, at number 10, serves a nifty *paella Valenciana* in a setting that mixes the rustic tavern with the sea, with ship figureheads along the wood-paneled wall and cabinets full of pewter, ceramics, and ship models. **Alcázar**, at number 12, also produces quality *paella* in various styles, and you can enjoy it at an outside table, weather permitting (and it usually is). Mosén Femades ends at calle Pascual y Genis, and if you turn right and continue several blocks you'll come to another commendable restaurant, **Mesón del Marisquero**, calle Félix Pizcueta 7 (an extension of Pascual y Genis). Also atmospheric, the Mesón specializes in seafood soups and casseroles, as well as in hearty meat dishes, kebabs, roasts, and the like.

A visitor interested in bullfight lore and memorabilia ought to walk two blocks south of Mosén Femades, to the semicircular boulevard called calle de Jativa, to see the plaza de Toros and, next to it, on pasaje Dr. Serra, the **Museo Taurino**. One of Spain's oldest and most complete bullfight museums, it is full of artifacts relating to the sport.

Museo Nacional de Cerámica

If you retrace your steps back up calle Pascual y Genis, in six blocks or so you will find yourself in another grouping of handsome buildings near one another: the Palacio del Marqués de Dos Aguas, facing plaza de Villarrasa; the Iglesia de San Juan de la Cruz (sometimes called San Andres; a 17th-century brick building with Baroque portal and white-and-gilded Baroque interior faced with ceramic tiles) next door, but facing calle Poeta Querol; Colegio del Patriarca, fronting on the **plaza Patriarca**; and the old university directly across from it (the university's library contains a copy of the first book of any consequence printed in Spain, *Les Trobes*).

"Unique" is a treacherous word, but the 18th-century Baroque mansion called the **Palacio del Marqués de Dos Aguas** (Palace of the Marquis of Two Waters) deserves it for its remarkable, sensuous three-dimensional portal, a Baroque fantasia in white alabaster, carved by sculptor Ignacio Vergara, showing two crouching giants pouring water from amphorae to illustrate the marqués's name. Only traces remain of the frescoes that Vergara had originally painted all over the façade. The ornately splendid rooms now form a handsome backdrop for the **Museo Nacional de Cerámica** collection. This is no small collection, but three floors and some 5,000 pieces of mostly Spanish ceramics from Iberian times to Picasso. You don't have to have a passion for pottery to make this a major stop on your Valencia visit. Note the 13th-century Paterna and 14th-century Manises lustreware, the delightful all-tile (including the stove and chimney) kitchen covered with culinary scenes painted on tile (top floor), the Picasso gallery (top floor), the magnificent double stairway lined with ceramic panels, and the gilded glory of an 18th-century coach that Vergara created for the Dos Aguas family (ground floor). A room on the top floor is devoted to artifacts of the Valencian novelist Vicente Blasco Ibáñez.

Allow time also for the **Colegio del Patriarca**, a real standout. This 16th–17th century structure (built as a seminary) has a graceful two-story Renaissance patio and a museum with some choice works by Caravaggio, Van der Weyden, Juan de Juanes, El Greco, Ribalta, Dirk Bouts, and many 15th- to 17th-century Valencian artists, as well as some excellent Brussels tapestries. There are also six fine 16th-century Flemish tapestries in the Capilla de la Concepción. In the southwest corner of the colegio is the **Iglesia de Corpus Christi**, richly ornamented with frescoes and a splendid *Last Supper* by Ribalta above the main altar.

A small street between the colegio and the 19th-century university building, calle de la Nave, is lined with fashionable shops and boutiques. The street leads to the imposing orange tree–lined plaza de Alfonso el Magnánimo, whose center is occupied by a triumphant equestrian bronze statue of El Cid, the work of American sculptor Anna Hyatt Huntington. At the south end of the plaza is an El Corte Inglés department store.

Museo Provincial de Bellas Artes

It will take a full second day to explore Valencia's major remaining art treasures. You might begin by walking or taking a taxi from the plaza del País Valenciano neighborhood northeast toward **plaza de Tetuán** and the river. Facing plaza de Tetuán is the mammoth presence of the **church and cloister of Santo Domingo.** A student of Roman Catholic history might find the Capilla del Capitullo—where Saint Vincent Ferrer took his vows as a Dominican—of interest. Just a block south is the house (now a small museum) where the saint-missionary was born, number 61, at the corner of calle del Maria and calle de Maria Carbonell.

Proceeding across the Puente del Real, a delightful 17th-century bridge with tiny religious shrines built in niches midway, and then to the left at the end of the bridge, you arrive at the Jardines del Real. Sometimes called Viveros, this is Valencia's largest city park, with formal gardens, an abundance of roses, walkways favored by lovers, an excellent restaurant, and even a small zoo in the garden's center. For those who love the Puente del Real, the 16th-century Puente del Mar to the east has even more ornate shrines built in and is also a pleasure to walk across.

A long block, following the edge of the gardens, brings you to the **Museo Provincial de Bellas Artes**, a prime reason for your visit to Valencia as well as to this part of town. (Aside from the museum and the park, there is little to interest a visitor on this northern side of the river, where university and government buildings dominate.) Inside this Baroque former convent is one of Spain's most important museums, with four floors and more than 50 rooms of treasures. At the entrance level are many Iberian-Roman-Moorish archaeological finds, such as a large Roman floor mosaic of the second-to-fourth centuries, as well as 16th- to 17th-century polychrome religious sculptures. The first floor (or what North Americans would call the second) is the most exhilarating, with gallery after gallery full of choice Medieval, Renaissance, and 15th- to 19th-century paintings.

A major surprise for visitors is the richness of the 15th-century school of Valencian primitives typified by Jacomart and Reixach. Valencia's three most famous painters—José de Ribera, Francisco de Ribalta, and Bartolomé Estéban Murillo—are also well represented. In room 30 is a stunning triptych, *Los Improperios* (The Mocking of Christ), by Hieronymus Bosch; one room is a harvest of Goya paintings and drawings; and next door in an alcove a Velázquez self-portrait hangs in solitary seclusion. There are works by El Greco, Juan de Juanes, and scores of others. The second floor is devoted to 19th- and 20th-century works, the most interesting of which are the contemporary paintings of Eusebio Sempere, Valencian-born Manolo Mompo, Juan Genoves, Equipo Cronica (a marvelous spoof of Velázquez called *El Alambique*), and other post-World-War-II Spanish artists in room 68.

After a morning in the museum, an elegant, if expensive, place for lunch is right next door in Jardines del Real at **Viveros**. Most locals agree this is Valencian dining at its most graceful, surrounded by gold-brocaded walls, comfortable padded chairs, handsome silver, tablewear and flowers, and an attentive staff. If the food can't quite live up to all this, well, nobody's perfect. Stay with the *paella Valenciana, arroz con langosta, arroz con marescos,* or other rice dishes and you'll do fine. And don't miss the orange soufflé for dessert. Another excellent dining choice is back across the river: **La Hacienda**, Navarro Reverter 12, several blocks southeast of plaza de Tetuán. In a flower-decked patio you'll lunch *nueva cocina*-style on regional dishes and fresh fish. Desserts here are noteworthy too, especially the lemon and orange tarts, and there's a good wine list, strong on Riojas.

Later, after seeing the Museo Provincial de Bellas Artes, if you have lunched at Viveros, you can recross the river, via Puente Trinidad, just west of the museum. Two blocks west of the bridge back on the south side of the river is the **Torres de Serranos**, a fortified 14th-century gate, restored in this century, with fine city views from the top and a small maritime museum inside. Five short blocks farther west is the city's latest attraction, the dramatic new **Instituto Valenciano de Arte Moderno**, known as IVAM. Just opened in 1989, it consists of two buildings: the brand-new modern Julio González Center, with nine exhibition halls and galleries, named for the contemporary Spanish artist whose works are the nucleus of IVAM's permanent collection; and the Centro del Carme, a 13th-century Carmelite convent, with well-restored 14th-century Gothic and 16th-century Renaissance cloisters, refectory, and chapter house, all of which now form three exhibition halls featuring changing exhibits of international art.

From there you can head south along a honeycomb of streets that will eventually bring you back to the plaza Mercado.

While in Valencia you will see many examples of the attractive blue-and-white pottery of **Manises**, a village whose metallic lustreware was famous in Moorish times. Many Valencian shops carry the distinctive blue-and-white Manises plates, bowls, platters, and pitchers, or you can make the very short drive 8 km (5 miles) west of town, via avenida del Cid, to Manises to browse for yourself at the various pottery factory showrooms. Another Valencian product is the internationally known and collected Lladró porcelain ware. You can buy the famous Lladró figurines at many Valencia shops, or can even visit the Lladró factory in Tabernes Blanques, just 5 km (3¼ miles) north of town.

THE ROUTE TO ALICANTE

South of Valencia City, on the road to Alicante, you'll pass through an area called La Albufera, mile after mile of lagoons and watery rice fields, the source of the rice for much of that delicious *paella.* Fed by the Turia and the Acequia Real, Albufera is known for its vast stretch of sandy beach.

Farther along this coastal road, 68 km (42 miles) south of Valencia, is **Gandía**, the little town that was the Duchy of the Borgias (Borjas in Spanish), including the infamous Pope Alexander VI, father of Cesare and Lucrezia and grandfather of Spain's San Francisco Borjas (who was born in Gandía). The former **Borja Palacio de los Duques** is now a Jesuit college, but anyone interested in viewing the ornate rooms, state apartments with coffered ceilings and marble floors, a small museum, and the Patio de Armas (a special beauty, lined with coats of arms) can take an hour-long tour. Gandía also boasts miles of golden-sand beach, the most productive and fertile *huertas,* and a good restaurant, **Gamba**, playa de Gandía, east of town on the Nazaret-Oliva road, with excellent fish and *abanda* (rice-in-broth) dishes.

About 30 km (19 miles) inland from Gambía, on the north side of Monte Bernisa, which is covered with towering cypress trees, is **Játiva**, birthplace of two 15th-century popes (Calixtus III and Alexander VI) and the 17th-century painter José de Ribera. Called Xàtiva by the Moors (until they lost it to Jaime el Conquistador in 1244), Játiva was old even when the Romans developed it from Phoenician origins. Castles dominate the mountain peaks, and the town is a delight for wandering, to see the many splendid old mansions and fountains along calle Moncada, the 16th-century **Iglesia de Colegiata**, and the cluster of excellent paintings by Valencian primitives in the hillside Gothic **Ermita de San Félix**. Cresting all are the imposing, well-defined ruins of the **Castillo**, whose foundations were Iberian and Roman, and within whose walls Cesare Borgia was once imprisoned. The vistas from here are sensational, stretching all the way to the Mediterranean.

From Játiva you have two ways to approach Alicante: via the inland road (N 340) south through Alcoy, a slower but more scenic route, or by going back east to Gandía, then continuing south on the coast-hugging *autopista* E 15. This latter drive is scenic, too, and fast, skirting most of the high-rise development horror of the sea resorts along the way. After Denia, whose ancient origins and history have long been obscured by tourist hotels and condos, the road dips deeply down to Jávea, in a sheltered location between two capes, Cabo de San Antonio and Cabo de la Nao. This makes a good lunch stop, at the modern, resort-like **Parador de la Costa Blanca**, which serves decent, if unexciting, regional meals. It is also a good place, if need be, to spend the night. Right at the water's edge, this four-story parador is better from the inside looking out. Inside, it's a bit sterile, but the views from the large bedrooms—of the sea, canal, and a well-manicured garden full of palm trees—are lovely. This parador offers good value for a resort area.

Some 12 km (7.5 miles) farther southeast is one of the coastline's most dramatic sights: the 1,089-foot-high **Peñón de Ifach**, a huge rock formation jutting from the sea. After a series of scalloped turns in the road you'll pass Miami-like Benidorm, with a long, heavenly beach (if you can find it through the canyons of concrete high-rises). Then, 11 km (7 miles) farther, you will reach **Villajoyosa**, which, despite being a resort, still retains a bit of the feeling of an old Spanish town. A delightful, dazzlingly white Moorish-style hotel, **Montíboli**, built on a hillside overlooking the sea, is an excellent, if dear, choice for those who want to linger a bit on this coast. Quietly luxurious, it has a fine restaurant, access to the beach, golf, and riding stables. Alicante is just a short hop south, as the gulls fly.

ALICANTE

Some cities have "it," others don't. Alicante telegraphs charm the minute you catch sight of its 2,100-foot-long, black, red, and white tessellated tile-paved **Explanada de España**, a palm-lined promenade that follows the harbor. A breezily balmy climate most of the year (even in winter), with skies as clear and blue as a Murillo heaven, adds considerably to Alicante's natural appeal. Its level location, embraced between two hills and spread before a wide bay and natural harbor, makes it an ideal port, which it has been since Roman times.

There are few major sites in Alicante to remind you that this was once the major stronghold of the kingdom of Valencia. It is a city that is simply fun to be in, to join the families and lovers strolling along the Explanada at twilight, to sip a *fino* at a sidewalk café, to stop for tea or ice cream at **Slika**, a tiny tearoom on rambla Méndez Nuñez, to stroll along old-fashioned calle Mayor, with its marble sidewalks lined with fancy candy shops, or to browse the narrow streets of **Barrio Santa Cruz**, the oldest part of town. Later, overlooking the Explanada and the harbor in the upstairs dining room of **El Delfín**, at Explanada de España 12, you can enjoy trout pie (the house specialty), baked bass, or other fresh seafood, finishing perhaps with ice cream topped with a flourish of turrón de Jijona (nougat sauce). Jijona, where so much of the best turrón is made, is just a few kilometers northwest of Alicante on N 340, so it's no wonder Alicante is rife with candy shops. In short, Alicante is as much a city of the senses as you'll find in Spain. The surprise is that, in spite of the foreigners who have "captured" this coast, Alicante remains essentially a Spanish town.

A determined sightseer will ride the elevator from the paseo de Gomis (above the playa del Postiguet) to the top of rambling **Castillo de Santa Bárbara** for wide-angle views of the town beach below, the sea, harbor, and surrounding countryside. The castle dates from the 13th to the 16th centuries, but is believed to have Carthaginian foundations.

Four streets west of the elevator entrance is the Ayuntamiento (City Hall), a 17th- to 18th-century Churrigueresque building on plaza 18 de Julio. The large collection at the **Museo Colección Arte de Siglo XX** (Museum of 20th-Century Art), nearby on calle de Villavieja, diagonally across from Iglesia Santa María on plaza de Santa María, belonged to the late Eusebio Sempere, a post-World-War-II modernist painter who was an Alicante native, though a Madrid resident. On three floors of an old building you'll find works by Miro, Dali, Picasso, Saura, Tàpies, Manrique, Sempere, and other Spanish painters and sculptors, along with such international artists as Arp, Braque, Vasarely, Kandinsky, Tamayo, Calder, and Bacon.

Mostly, though, Alicante is to be enjoyed passively, the pause that refreshes on a whirling sightseeing tour.

The city's big festival is held on Saint John's Day, June 23. This is a day of parades, street dancing, and fireworks, ending not with a whimper but a bang: a *nit de foc* (night of fire) when caricatures in wood and paper are torched in spectacular bonfires.

For your Alicante stay, consider the convenient **Gran Sol Hotel**, a handy high-rise in the center of town, just one block from Explanada and the harbor, with comfortable rooms and great views from the snack bar on top. But parking is a problem. If you prefer a quieter spot, there is the **Sidi San Juan Sol**, just east of town at Cabo la Huerta. All bedrooms face the beach in this large, comfortable resort hotel with many amenities and rooms with large closets and terraces. The pseudo–*fin de siècle* decor and ponderous reproductions may seem off-putting in a beach setting, but Spanish guests and tour groups seem to take it all in stride.

Excursions from Alicante

A pleasant day trip southwest of Alicante about 24 km (14 miles) on N 340 is to palm-forested **Elche**, a Moorish-looking town of flat-roofed, white-washed houses that straddles both sides of the river Vinalopó. Elche has the unenviable luck to be in one of the hottest spots in Spain, a fate assuaged by the oasis-like effect of all those swaying palm trees that surround the town on three sides. Dates are the major crop, as quickly becomes evident from the number of shops and stalls selling the local product as well as baskets made from palm fronds. The *ramilletes* (fronds) hung from houses all over Spain after Palm Sunday originate in Elche.

Elche's main attraction, **Palmeral de Europa**, just east of town, is a date-palm forest of more than 100,000 trees, believed to have been planted by the Phoenicians but cultivated by the Moors: the only date-producing palms in Europe. A tour of the forest takes about two hours but is recommended for early morning before the heat rises. Afterward there should be time before lunch to visit **Basílica Santa María**, an imposing 17th-century church with a Baroque façade and portal by Nicolás de Bari. The church is the setting of an annual 13th-century mystery play about the Assumption of the Virgin, held in August.

Plan to lunch at the notable **Els Capellans**, just a 15-minute walk from the plaza Mayor, inside the Huerto del Cura (Garden of the Priest), at Federico Garcia Sanchiz 14. Surrounded by palm trees, you might lunch on *arroz con costra,* an Elche specialty of rice cooked with white sausage, chicken, rabbit, and two other types of sausage. Then wander through the Huerto del Cura, a well-kept garden distinguished by its venerable 150-to-200-year-old Imperial Palm.

South of Elche 2 km (about a mile) on the secondary road to Dolores is **La Alcudia de Elche**, an excavation site where the famous *Dama de Elche* was unearthed in 1897. This mysterious, evocative bust of a woman is believed to be Iberian, dating from the 5th or 4th century B.C. The original is in the Museo Arqueológico Nacional in Madrid, but you can see a copy, along with other Iberian and Roman artifacts, in a small museum on the La Alcudia site.

Southwest of Elche on N 340 is the city of Murcia, and beyond that the city of Almería at the eastern end of the Costa del Sol (for the latter, see the chapter on Andalusia). **Murcia,** while the capital of the province of Murcia, has little to recommend it to a traveller, although a determined gourmet might go out of the way to eat at **El Rincón de Pepe**, at Aposteles 34, long considered one of the finest regional restaurants in Spain, with an excellent wine list. Murcia's other claim to fame is an especially moving procession during Holy Week. Movie fans might find it of interest that many

of the "spaghetti" westerns and epic films produced in Spain in the past ten to 20 years were made among the rough-hewn cliffs and hillsides of the Murcian countryside, which resembles the American Southwest.

Alcoy, north of Alicante about 40 km (25 miles) on N 340, is a small town known for its annual Moros y Cristianos (Moors and Christians) celebration around Saint George's Day (April 23), when two armies of "Moors" and "Christians" slug it out in mock combat, until "Saint George" intervenes at the end to help the Christians triumph. There are many such mock battles in towns in this area, so wracked throughout the Reconquest by real conflicts. Alcoy's fiesta is the most famous, perhaps because Alcoy residents believe they won their real battle against the Moors in 1276 only because of the saint's intercession.

While in Alcoy, have a look at the **Museo Arqueológico**'s sizable collection of Iberian pottery and Greek artifacts, and then stop to see the attractive 18th-century tiles in the churches of Santa María and Santo Sepulchro. And don't miss the local specialty, *peladillas*—sugared almonds.

Alcoy's contemporary claim to fame is **Venta del Pilar**, a delightful restaurant ensconced in a 200-year-old country house on carretera de Valencia. Good regional dishes, lots of fresh seafood, and the house specialty—almond, orange, and chestnut tarts—make this a worthy meal stop.

GETTING AROUND

The speedy *autopista* consists of 622 km (386 miles) of superhighway, running from Gerona in Catalonia in the northeast all the way south to Alicante. A luxurious TER train follows the coast from Port-Bou in Catalonia down to Murcia. Long-distance motor coach lines also make a regular coastal run. In addition, there are daily flights from Madrid and Barcelona to Valencia and Alicante. Still, the best way to sightsee and explore the countryside is by car.

ACCOMMODATIONS REFERENCE

When dialing telephone numbers from outside the country, drop the 9 in the area code.

▸ **Astoria Palace**. Plaza Rodrigo Botet 5, 46002 **Valencia**. Tel: (96) 352-67-37.

▸ **Bristol**. Abadía San Martín 3, 46002 **Valencia**. Tel: (96) 352-11-76.

▸ **Parador Costa del Azahar**. Avenida Papa Luna 3, 12580 **Benicarlo**. Tel: (964) 47-01-00; Fax: (964) 47-09-34.

► **Parador de la Costa Blanca.** Playa del Arenal 2, 03730 **Jávea.** Tel: (96) 579-02-00.

► **Gran Sol.** Rambla Méndez Núñez 3, 03002 **Alicante.** Tel: (96) 520-30-00.

► **Hotel Inglés.** Marqués de Dos Aguas, 46002 **Valencia.** Tel: (96) 351-64-26.

► **Parador Luis Vives.** Carretera Alicante, 46011 **Valencia.** Tel: (96) 328-68-50.

► **Montíboli.** Apartado 8, Carretera N 332, 03570 **Villajoyosa.** Tel: (96) 589-02-50; Telex: 68288 HMON E.

► **Reina Victoria.** Barcas 4, 46002 **Valencia.** Tel: (96) 352-04-87; Telex: 64755 HRV E.

► **Sidi Saler Palace-Sol.** Playa del Saler, 46002 **Valencia.** Tel: (96) 161-04-11.

► **Sidi San Juan Sol.** Playa de San Juan de Alicante, 8 km (5 miles) east of the city center, 03002 **Alicante.** Tel: (96) 565-13-00.

LA MANCHA

By Patricia Brooks

Many regions of Spain have clear-cut identities. There is a unity of sorts to Andalusia, to Catalonia, to Galicia. But La Mancha, the region arrayed more or less around the south and east of the Madrid area, exists in the shadow of Castile like an appendage, so it is probably natural that it now has a new name, the hyphenated Castilla–La Mancha. As such, it is Spain's largest region, encompassing five provinces (Albacete, Ciudad Real, Cuenca, Guadalajara, and Toledo).

The image many visitors have of La Mancha is of a parched, arid landscape, and, indeed, the name in Arabic—*Manxa*—means "dry earth." That is just the broad stroke of the La Mancha picture, however. Olive trees, grapevines, blood-red wild poppies, wheat and purple-blooming saffron fields, mountains that are home to wild boar, bear, buck, deer, and roebuck, a natural park, and shimmering lagoons also constitute La Mancha. So do the many towns and villages—sleepy and off the beaten track—that nonetheless shelter some extraordinary sights. Toledo and Cuenca, skirting the edges of La Mancha, are famous, but most visitors aren't aware of the marvels that loom behind the names Almagro, Sigüenza, Pastrana, and Viso del Marqués. Like almost every other region in Spain, La Mancha has its share of mysteries and surprises.

MAJOR INTEREST

Rugged landscape, with windmills, castles
Foods of La Mancha

Illescas (between Madrid and Toledo)
Hospital de la Caridad (El Greco paintings)

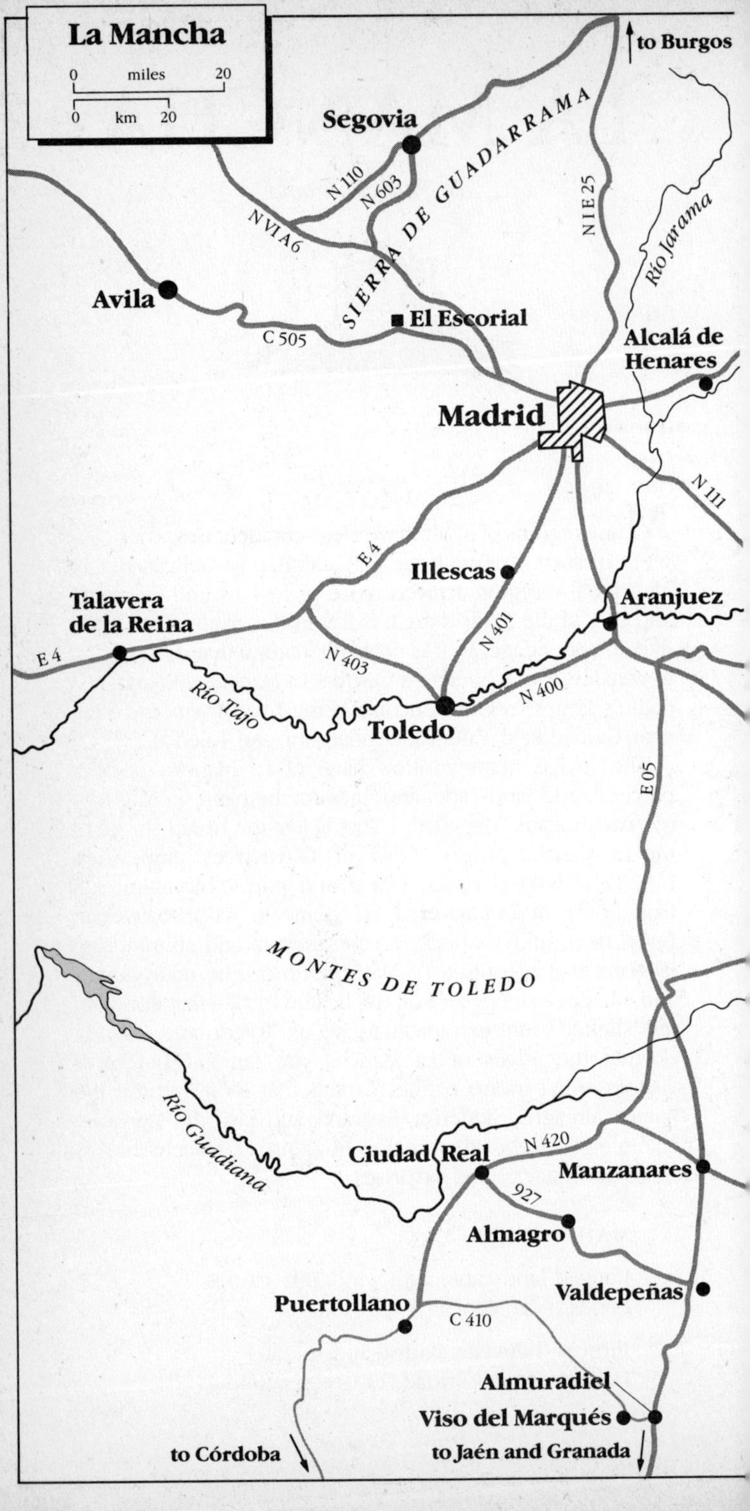

La Mancha
0 miles 20
0 km 20
to Burgos
Segovia
SIERRA DE GUADARRAMA
N 110
N 603
N VI A 6
N I E 25
Río Jarama
Avila
El Escorial
C 505
Alcalá de Henares
Madrid
N 111
E 4
Illescas
Talavera de la Reina
Aranjuez
N 401
N 403
E 4
Río Tajo
Toledo
N 400
E 05
MONTES DE TOLEDO
Río Guadiana
Ciudad Real
N 420
Manzanares
927
Almagro
Valdepeñas
Puertollano
C 410
Almuradiel
Viso del Marqués
to Córdoba
to Jaén and Granada

to Zaragoza
Sigüenza
C 204
Río Henares
N II
Guadalajara
N 320
MAR DE CASTILLA
Pastrana
SERRANIA DE CUENCA
Ciudad Encantada
Río Tajo
C 200
CU 921
CU 912
Cuenca
Río Huécar
N 400
Tarancón
N 400
N 420
N 320
Río Zancara
N 301
EMBALSE DE ALARCON
N 420
Belmonte
N 111
Alarcón
Mota del Cuervo
to Valencia
Campo de Criptana
Alcázar de San Juan
N 301
Río Júcar
N 430
Albacete
N

Toledo
Museo de los Concilios y de la Cultura Visigoda
Sinagoga del Tránsito
Sinagoga de Santa María la Blanca
Casa y Museo del Greco
Iglesia de Santo Tomé
Museo de Santa Cruz
Gothic cathedral

Pottery shops of Talavera de la Reina

Almagro
Plaza Mayor
Corral de las Comedias

Viso del Marqués
Renaissance palace

Cuenca
Casas Colgadas, including the Museo de Arte Abstracto
Diocesan Museum
Rock formations at Ciudad Encantada

Alarcón
La Trinidad church

Pastrana
Colegiata and tapestries

Sigüenza
Catedral de Santa María

A Man of La Mancha

Few writers have put their stamp on an entire region as thoroughly as Miguel de Cervantes did on La Mancha, an area that sweeps from Toledo to Ciudad Real and Almagro in the south, east to Cuenca, and northeast past Guadalajara to Sigüenza.

Cervantes didn't invent his terrain, as William Faulkner did Yoknapatawpha County, but instead peopled a real terra cognita—an austere yet beautiful land with harsh climate and clear, crisp air—with his own unforgettable characters. *Toda la espaciosa y triste Espana* ("All the space and sadness of Spain") is how native son Luis de León described it. You have only to drive through the craggy landscape, punctuated with the occasional castle and windmill, to realize this *had* to be the land of Don Quixote and Sancho Panza. Ever since

Cervantes created them, they have represented La Mancha's (and Spain's) extremes: Quixote, the idealistic, ascetic dreamer; Panza, the earthy, pragmatic peasant.

Miguel de Cervantes Saavedra was born just beyond the fringe of La Mancha, east of Madrid in Alcalá de Henares, and nothing in his humble background, as the son of an unlicensed itinerant doctor with seven children, would have presaged that he would write one of the great novels of all times, a book translated into more languages than any other except the Bible. Nor did his early life suggest that he would one day be acclaimed as the major poet of Spain's *siglo de oro* (golden age; 1519–1609), a period that also included the playwrights Lope de Vega and Pedro Calderón de la Barca.

In fact, Cervantes's soap opera of a life was marked with ironies. Born in a university town at the height of its intellectual prestige, he was educated only in the college of life. After 58 years of struggle, poverty, and hopelessness, he created the *comic* novel, *The Life and Adventures of the Renowned Don Quixote de la Mancha* (1605). This cheerful tale was written in prison (tradition tells us), when Cervantes was in the depths of despair. Before the author could complete the second part and begin to enjoy his life, a false version by an unidentified rogue was sprung upon the public, forcing Cervantes to rush the real sequel to print in 1615. He died a year later. Perhaps the final irony is that Spain's decline, set in motion partly by the defeat of the Armada in 1588, was under way when its greatest novel arose, and that this work, the first modern novel, influenced England—through writers like Fielding, Smollett, Sterne, Scott, and Dickens—in ways that Philip II's military power never could.

The Food of La Mancha

The impoverished image *Don Quixote* evokes of La Mancha is not noticeable at table in the region today. Because of the abundance of game in the mountains and fish in the mountain streams and rivers, pheasant, partridge, hare, trout, and river crab are commonly served.

While dishes here lack the grace and subtlety of those of certain other regions, the operative words are abundant and hearty in such specialties as *pisto manchego* (a tasty and firmer, denser form of ratatouille), *gazpacho manchego* (a chilled soup with hare, partridge, ham, and chicken), *sopa de ajo* (garlic soup), *cordero a la caldereta* (lamb ragout), *perdiz* (partridge) served *estofada* (stewed) or *escabechada* (preserved or pickled), *cabrito asado con ajillo* (roast kid with garlic), and *cangrejos asados a la plancha* (grilled crab).

Variations of a dish mentioned in *Don Quixote, olla podrida* ("rotten pot"), consist of a heavy, one-dish stew of meat and vegetables simmered together in a special, wide-mouthed pot called an *olla.* This is a *manchego* (that is, of La Mancha) staple whose antecedent is an ancient Jewish dish known as *adafina.* A Toledan version, made with lamb, is called *chanfana. Migas pastor,* or savory sautéed bread crumbs (much better than it sounds), is as popular and widely enjoyed in La Mancha as in Castile.

Manchego cheese, or *queso manchego,* now widely produced elsewhere as well, is unquestionably the king of Spanish table cheeses, milder than cheddar, with a similar but smoother texture.

Alaju, a popular Arab-accented dessert, is made of rosemary-scented honey, walnuts, and bread crumbs; *melindres* (honey fritters) from Yepes are also enjoyed in Toledo. *Churros,* crisp, golden "fingers" of fried dough, are enjoyed throughout the region, as in Castile, at breakfast or as a midmorning snack, sprinkled with sugar or dunked in hot chocolate.

The Wines of La Mancha

The land of Don Quixote is the largest *denominación de origen* in Spain, with more than a million acres of vines. Even though La Mancha is better known for its reds and *claretes,* 90 percent of the grapes grown there are Airén, a white-wine grape. Manchegan red wines are made by fermenting Airén musts with the red wine grapes, Cencibel (the Tempranillo of Rioja) and Garnacha, in huge earthenware vats called *tinajas* or, increasingly, in temperature-controlled stainless-steel vats. Most La Mancha wine is sold in bulk for blending, to be used for sangría or as house wines in the cafés of Madrid.

Valdepeñas is located in southern La Mancha just north of Despeñaperros, the mountainous entrance to Andalusia. In the 19th century Alexandre Dumas wrote, ". . . at last we enjoyed the real Valdepeñas, sharp yet exciting to the palate." Ernest Hemingway swore that Valdepeñas produced the best house wines in the world, and Frank Prial of *The New York Times* once wrote that it was "probably the best jug wine in the world." (See South of Toledo, below.)

Genuine Valdepeñas is an excellent young *clarete*-style wine made from the white grape Airén mixed with a minimum of 20 percent Cencibel. Some estate-bottled Valdepeñas are made from 100 percent Cencibel and age as nicely as a *petit château* Bordeaux. As ubiquitous in the bars and restaurants of Spain as Beaujolais is in France, Valdepeñas has become almost a generic name synonymous with pleasant, light-red house wine, so much so that very little of what is served as Valdepeñas is authentic. If you want to try real Valdepeñas, you will have to buy it by the bottle. Don't be surprised if your red Valdepeñas arrives chilled; the Spanish often prefer it that way.

Castilla–La Mancha has two other *denominación de origen* wine regions, Almansa and Mentrida, which produce undistinguished wines used mostly for blending.

—*Gerry Dawes*

TOLEDO

Toledo is often cited as a day trip from Madrid, and indeed it is easily reached by car or bus in less than two hours, 70 km (43 miles) south via N 401, and by train in about two hours, landing you at a charming, pseudo-Moorish train station that sets the table for your Toledo feast.

But a mere day in Toledo would be as sacrilegious as allotting only one day to Bath or Florence or any other city laden with treasures that need to be savored slowly. Toledo, *the* city to choose if you have only one option outside Madrid, is perched above, and seemingly stitched into, a rough-hewn bluff that is surrounded on three sides by the deep gorge of the río Tagus, which flows westward across Spain and Portugal, past Lisbon and into the Atlantic.

Cervantes called Toledo "that rocky gravity, glory of Spain and light of her cities." Playwright Tirso de Molina (1584–1648) described his native city as "the heart of Spain." But it was El Greco, Toledo's adopted son, who captured it best—on canvas—and his *View of Toledo* is yours, as recognizable today as when he painted it more than 400 years ago. Tan buildings gleaming golden in the sunshine, with red terra-cotta roofs, spilling almost on top of one another, on streets that twist, curve, and fold back on themselves, spiraling ever upward: These give this former Castilian capital its high profile by day.

But by night Toledo assumes a completely different persona—which is one more reason why you should spend at least one night here, preferably two, and ideally three or four. Soft amber lights, highlighting the town's most famous buildings, cast a glow on Toledo's twisting, corkscrew, cobbled passageways and narrow streets, evoking a spirit so hidden, eerie, and Medieval that it can best be captured only at the times of day before the tour buses clamber into town and after the daytime crowds leave. It is nighttime when Toledo's many legends and ghost stories seem especially believable.

Toledo is one of those rare cities that is even more than the sum of its parts, and its parts—a profusion of churches, museums, ancient portals, gardens hidden behind solid sheltering walls, tiny plazas—are pretty spectacular. The entire town has been declared a national treasure, and all its new buildings must conform to the style of those from the 12th to 15th century. This produces a harmonious whole and gives Toledo a rare unity, though its history is much more diverse than its golden profile suggests.

The Cathedral

There are many gates leading into town, but a traditional way to enter, if you are driving south from Madrid, is via the new (meaning mid-16th century) Bisagra gate. On the right, a short distance before the gate, you will pass the Hospital de Tavera, a 16th-century Renaissance complex built by Cardinal Tavera that is worth a brief stop in order to see several marvelous paintings by El Greco (especially his *Holy Family,* a preview of what awaits you in Toledo itself) and others by Zurbarán, Tintoretto, and Ribera.

Continue on the road past the Bisagra gate through the Puerta del Sol (with a 12th-century Mudejar gatehouse) and then right to the **plaza del Zocodover**, Toledo's beehive of a main square, described by Cervantes (who once lodged nearby) in his book *Novelas Ejemplares.* At dusk the Zoco, as it is usually called, is the liveliest scene in town, where the nightly *paseo,* or walkabout, takes place, and the town's residents are out in full force. The word *Zocodover* is derived from the Arab word *sük ed-dawabb* ("horse market"), and this introduces you to the first of Toledo's many Moorish influences. While in the Zoco you might want to have coffee at one of the surrounding bars, then sample the favorite Toledan sweet, *mazapán,* a sweeter version of marzipan—another Moorish gift, which remains a local cottage industry. You can buy some at the Santo Tomé pastry shop in the plaza.

From the Zoco walk south a few steps along cuesta del Alcázar to the **Alcázar**, the highest point in town, facing the river on the east. The Alcázar itself is worth visiting, mostly for its commanding views of the city and countryside, but it is easily skipped if time runs short—unless you are a Spanish Civil War buff. The original Moorish fortress (which El Cid once commanded), built on the site of a Roman fort, was later converted (by Alonso de Covarrubias first, then Juan de Herrera) to a royal palace for Charles V, then was almost completely demolished during an eight-week siege in the Civil War, and was later reconstructed to look as it did for Charles V.

Back in the Zoco, if you follow calle de Comercio (off the west side of the square) upward, it brings you in short order to the **cathedral.** Built in installments (1227–1493) on the site of the Great Mosque, which in turn had been constructed over a Visigothic church, the cathedral demonstrates the rich layering of Toledo's cultural influences. Only one tower of the original plan was built: It is half-Moorish in the style of the Giralda in Seville, with similar elegance. The second tower (finished in the 17th century) has a dome designed by El Greco's son. Thus in these two towers can be seen the two most powerful imprints to be found throughout Toledo: those of the Moors and El Greco.

The cathedral is considered the finest Gothic masterpiece in Spain, next to that of Burgos. Though conceived in the French Gothic style, by the time it was finished it had become instantly Spanish, with many Flamboyant and Plateresque touches. A Spanish proverb says, "Toledo has the richest of our cathedrals, Oviedo the holiest, Salamanca the strongest, León the most beautiful."

Few would argue. Among many notable architectural elements are the three Gothic doorways on the west front; the elaborately decorated central doorway, Puerta del Perdón, by Juan Alemán; the Sala Capitular with a fine paneled ceiling; and the north tower with its famous Campana Gorda (fat bell). Covarrubias's Plateresque Capilla de los Reyes Nuevos (New Kings Chapel) contains the tombs of Henry III and his wife Catherine of Lancaster, daughter of England's John of Gaunt.

The man most responsible for the accumulation of the cathedral's treasures was Francisco Jimenez de Cisneros, archbishop of Toledo and adviser to Queen Isabella. Inside the poorly lighted cathedral, look in the sacristy for El Greco's *Disrobing of Christ* (1579) over the altar, Goya's *Betrayal of Christ* (1788), 16 El Greco paintings of Apostles, and paintings by Titian, Rubens, Van Dyck, and others. In the Capilla Mayor (main chapel) is a magnificent Plateresque *reja* (grille) and a gilded Gothic retable with four tiers of life-size figures in New Testament scenes. The walnut *sillerias* (choir stalls) have superbly carved scenes by the talented German immigrant Rodrigo Alemán.

Behind the sanctuary is 18th-century artist Narciso Tomé's *Transparente,* an island of angels and life-size sculptures surrounding a Madonna and Child and a Last Supper. A focal point of the treasury is a ten-foot-high, 400-pound monstrance by Enrique de Arfe (1506–1562) that is a triumph of silver and precious gems, filigreed angels, bells, flowers, and turrets.

During the late-spring feast of Corpus Christi (the date depends on Easter), *the* place to be, if you like pageantry, is Toledo. Gold-threaded tapestries are hung on the cathedral's exterior walls, the streets are strewn with wild thyme, and marchers in Medieval costumes toss rose petals along the procession path. The centerpiece of the procession is the Arfe monstrance. When it is returned to the cathedral, jubilant explosions of rockets and a rendition of the national anthem punctuate the event. Spanish celebrations are never desultory.

Moorish-Jewish Toledo

Two themes are interwoven throughout Toledo, as in the two towers of the cathedral: Following them can form the guidelines for your visit, and from the cathedral you can play, or follow, both themes with ease. First there are the loose threads of the 12th through 15th century, the city's golden era, when Moslems, Jews, and Christians coexisted more or less harmoniously, creating a cultural and artistic climate unparalleled elsewhere at any time in Spain and rare anywhere in the world.

Then there is the Toledo of El Greco, who left behind—in churches, museums, and the cathedral—a legacy of works that can keep you roaming for several days through the hilly but compact town, seeking them out. Both Toledo themes overlap, so that you can enjoy them almost simultaneously, as with the cathedral.

Toledo's superb location, nestled above a bend of the Tagus, shielded by protective hills, made it a natural site for, first, the seat of Visigothic kings after the collapse of Rome, then Moslem emirs, and finally the Christian kings of León and Castile, who designated Toledo their capital. The city is a textural overlay of cultures. The Romans provided the name, Toletum, and left remains of a Roman circus in the public gardens north of town. Visigoths left even more, according to the Moors who routed them in 711 and then extolled the architectural treasures they left behind. But as conquerors are wont to do, the Moors first destroyed them, then incorporated Visigothic elements into their own buildings, such as the capitals in the minuscule 10th-century mosque that still later became the 12th-century Romanesque **Iglesia de Santo Cristo de la Luz** (with fine fresco remains on the walls). It is tucked into a hillside below the steep cuesta del Seminario at the north edge of town. Other Visigothic fragments, columns, and incised stones can be seen in the **Museo de los Concilios y de la Cultura Visigoda** (Visigoth museum) located in the tiny 13th-century **Iglesia San Román**, a former mosque. It is just three blocks or so northwest of the cathedral on calle San Román (few blocks are straight in Toledo; they are usually a series of quick left-right-left turns). Note the Arabic tower and horseshoe arches and the 16th-century cupola by Covarrubias.

The Moors spent four centuries in Toledo—half the time they dominated most of southern Spain. They left handprints all over town, in the local addiction to the use of brick in walls, the underpinnings of many churches, several bridges, and the town gates. Later, if you break for lunch at the Hostal Cardenal (more about it below) in the northern part of town, notice especially the nearby **Puerto de Alfonso VI** (the ninth-century old Bisagra gate), through which King Alfonso VI and El Cid passed in their 1085 conquest of the city.

When the rule of the Moors ended, they left behind many artisans, builders, and scholars. Most Moorish traces in Toledo date from this period, the 12th through the 15th century, and developed into the architectural and decorative style known as Mudejar, signifying traditional Moorish work done by Moslems living under Christian rule. ("Mozarabic," another word frequently encountered in Spain, refers to Christian work executed in Moorish style.)

Mudejar Toledo is ubiquitous: You will see examples of it in the Christian churches of San Miguel (south of the Alcázar), El Cristo de la Vega (just outside the west walls on Paseo de los Canonigos), and Santiago del Arrabal (just uphill from the old Bisagra gate), where Vicente Ferrer, who was later made a saint, preached conversion of the Jews so vociferously that his followers reportedly threw those Jews who failed to convert to Christianity off nearby cliffs.

In ecumenical times, before the Inquisition changed Spain's sociopolitical climate, Jews were part of Toledo's glory. The **Sinagoga del Tránsito** (1366), on paseo del Tránsito (southwest of the cathedral), is a handsome small building decorated in Mudejar designs with polychromed stucco-work and Hebrew wall inscriptions that praise God, King Pedro the Cruel, and Samuel Ha-Levi (the king's treasurer and synagogue founder). Levi was later tortured and killed by the king, and there are those who insist the red-bearded financier still haunts the area where he once lived. (El Greco's house, one block east, is on land that was part of Levi's estate.) The synagogue became a church, El Tránsito, after the Jewish expulsion from Spain in 1492. Part of El Tránsito is the **Museo Sefardí**, which houses maps, tombs, and memorabilia from Sephardic Jewish life in Medieval Spain.

A block north on calle de los Reyes Católicos, in what was the old Judería (Jewish quarter), is **Sinagoga de Santa María la Blanca** (1180), the main synagogue in 12th-century Toledo. This tiny architectural gem, with a restored interior that is a forest of 24 richly ornamented octagonal columns and Arabic arches, was seized by Vicente Ferrer's followers in 1405 and underwent numerous metamorphoses. Viewed in juxtaposition with El Tránsito, it offers an even deeper insight into the Medieval Jewish world.

If you follow the same street a block or so farther north, you will come to another major Toledo treasure, the majestic Isabeline **Iglesia de San Juan de los Reyes**, part of a Franciscan monastery that was built by the Catholic kings after their victory over the Portuguese at Toro (before the conquest of Granada). They intended it to be their burial place (but later opted for Granada), and the escutcheons and symbols of Aragón and Castile are evident throughout. The northwest façade was begun by Covarrubias in 1553 and finally finished in 1610. Note the walls of the apse, hung with chains of Christian prisoners of the Moors, who were released by Ferdinand and Isabella's army.

El Greco's Toledo

It has been more than 400 years since Doménikos Theotokópoulos (1541–1614) arrived in Toledo, but his legacy remains everywhere. The Crete-born painter, dubbed El Greco, had studied with Titian and absorbed the works of Michelangelo in Rome and then wandered the Mediterranean region. He "found himself," so to speak, in this prosperous Castilian hilltown, where he hoped to benefit from Hapsburg patronage. But Philip II didn't like El Greco's startling new style, derived from Italian and Byzantine influences, and the king never hung the single altarpiece he commissioned.

El Greco found other patrons among the city's nobility and clergy, and he stayed in town during the last 35 years of his life, painting most of his finest pictures. When he arrived in Toledo the city of 55,000 was in its prime. It had been Charles V's "Imperial City" (1519–1558), and it was (and still is) the seat of the primate of Spain. After Philip II made Madrid the capital of Spain in 1561, Toledo declined; by the time Alexandre Dumas visited in 1846 there were fewer than 12,000 residents. Today's tourism has brought it almost up to its 15th-century level.

An aside: If you are coming to Toledo from Madrid by car in pursuit primarily of El Grecos, plan to stop briefly en route at **Illescas**, a small town just off the main road N 401, to see the five El Grecos at the modest convent church of **Hospital de la Caridad**. *San Ildefonso* is an acknowledged masterpiece, but two other knockouts are in the sacristy to the left of the altar: the soaring *Coronation of the Virgin* and the *Nativity,* in which Christ in the manger is viewed from the surprising perspective of a cow's horns.

Once in Toledo, you will meander southwest from the cathedral to calle de Tránsito and the **Casa y Museo del Greco** (El Greco House and Museum), a much-rebuilt 16th-century house whose period furniture and wood-paneled rooms form a logical backdrop for the 20 paintings displayed. Among them is the magnetic *View of Toledo.* The private chapel of the house has a Mudejar ceiling encrusted with stars. The house name is a bit misleading; El Greco actually lived nearby, with the same sweeping view of the Tagus, in 24 rooms of the long-gone palace of the marqués de Villena. The Casa y Museo del Greco and El Tránsito are, along with the cathedral, the most visited of Toledo sights.

Almost as popular, and just as important, is the **Iglesia de Santo Tomé**, a zigzaggy two blocks or so north of the El Greco house. Here you will see a major Greco masterpiece, *El Entierro de Conde de Orgaz* (The Burial of the Count Orgaz). This superlative painting joins the natural and supernatural worlds on a single canvas. It includes portraits of Greco contemporaries: Philip II, though alive at the time, looks down from heaven; Cervantes, Lope de Vega, and the artist himself are in the crowd of onlookers. Here again Moorish Toledo joins El Greco's "trail": Note the Mudejar influences in Santo Tomé's tower.

There are also 22 El Grecos in the **Museo de Santa Cruz**, a sometimes overlooked treasure trove of mostly 16th- and 17th-century Spanish art. A former hospital, just a block or so east of plaza del Zocodover, the museum is a richly ornamented Plateresque delight, the creation of architect Enrique de Egas, who built the royal chapel in Granada, and Alonso de Covarrubias.

In addition to all the El Grecos, the museum contains paintings by Goya, Veronese, and Ribera; 16th-century Flemish tapestries; a fine altarpiece by Pedro Berruguete; primitive sculptures and paintings; and a room full of Emperor Charles V's artifacts. In the attached cloister you'll find a marvelous caprice of Plateresque "embroidered" arches, as well as a small archaeological museum and a gallery of ceramics and *azulejos* (glazed tiles).

Much enjoyable time in Toledo can be spent just making discoveries of your own, looking at the old city gates (the Mudejar Puerta del Sol on the north) and the ancient bridges (especially the pedestrian ones, de Alcántara to the east and San Martín, southwest).

Dining, Staying, and Shopping in Toledo

Considering its riches of sights and the hordes of tourists who come to see them, Toledo is surprisingly short of first-rate restaurants. There are three, however, and all of them are hotels, too, that make excellent overnight places. Two of the most romantic and historic border the city, making it easy to leave your car there and travel around in Toledo by foot. **Hostal del Cardenal**, built into the city walls, is an 18th-century archbishop's palace with serviceable rooms, a restful garden, and a scenic location next to the historic Puerto de Alfonso VI. Its restaurant (operated by the owners of Botín in Madrid) has wonderfully hearty specialties such as game, especially *perdiz,* venison ragout, or wild boar. Almost an even match is the newer (1986) **María Cristina**, nearby, just outside the north gate. Once a 15th-century church (Hospital San Lázaro), this small, moderately priced hotel has been beautifully restored and charmingly furnished. The Imperial Suite is the dome of the original church. The restaurant, **El Abside** (the apse), inside the central arch, is decorated in Mudejar style and features regional and international dishes.

If you don't mind driving (or taxiing) across the river, the **Parador Conde de Orgaz**, located on cerro del Emperador (Emperor's Hill), is especially pleasant for lunch, because from its terrace you have a broad view of Toledo. Constructed to resemble an old Toledo building, this modern brick-and-glass hotel has comfortable rooms, a large lounge, a patio, and a competent restaurant. Try such regional dishes as *sopa de ajo* (garlic soup) and roast lamb here.

Shopping in Toledo runs the gamut from touristic junk to respectable crafts, often bunched together in the same souvenir shops. The most famous Toledo craft, an Arab legacy, is damascene ware—steel etched with silver, gold, or copper thread, made by hand with great precision. Unfortunately, unless you shop carefully, you may end up with a machine-made product in tin and inferior metals. The famous Toledo knives, prized for many centuries, have been trivialized to letter openers. There are two dozen or more authentic damascene workshops in Toledo, but finding their output isn't always easy. A reliable source is **Artespaña**, calle Samuel Levi 2.

You will also find many shops full of the famous hand-painted Talavera ceramics in Toledo. But if you have a serious interest and time, head for the source, **Talavera de la Reina** itself, a pottery-producing town about 100 km (62 miles) west of Toledo. There you can browse through many ceramic studios and workshops where the famous decorative ware, which is now made in yellow, blue, and green, has been produced for eight centuries. The largest producer is **Artesanía Talaverana**, avenida de Portugal 32.

SOUTH OF TOLEDO

A rich lode of La Mancha is south of Toledo along the western environs of the Madrid–Jaén (Andalusia) road, E 05. Coming south from Madrid and Aranjuez, the road leads past undistinguished Manzanares and past **Valdepeñas**, where the various *bodegas* and cellars might tempt you to stop to sample the region's light, refreshing red wine (see Wines, above). On the main highway in Manzanares is the **Parador de Manzanares**, a good place to break your drive with a hearty La Mancha lunch of game, *migas pastor,* and local cheeses and wines.

Almagro

A more significant stop should be northwest from Valdepeñas 15 km (9.5 miles) on 927 to Almagro, often bypassed because it is off the main north-south highway, but one of the smaller (population 9,000) joys of La Mancha. The cheek-to-jowl abundance of handsome mansions, churches, and chapels may puzzle the casual visitor, as 20th-century Almagro seems the proverbial "town that time forgot." But in its heyday, the 16th century, it was a bustling commercial center where the king's banker, Jakobo Fucar (Fugger in Flemish), kept his storehouses of silver and mercury, which were mined at Almaden to the west.

Almagro was a religious center as well, with convents established by all the major religious orders of the Catholic church. In 1574, under a royal grant from Philip II, the University of Almagro was established in **El Monasterio del Nuestra Señora del Rosario** (Monastery of Our Lady of the Rosary) and flourished until its demise in 1828. You can see its façade at the corner of ronda de Santa Domingo and calle de Colegio.

But Almagro's glory days began even earlier. From the early years of the Moslem invasion of Spain, the small Roman town was one of those frontier outposts that passed back and forth from Christians to Moors until it became a stronghold of the powerful and prosperous Order of the Knights of Calatrava. In 1214, two years before the knights made it their official seat, the town was settled by 70 noble Christian families at the order of the archbishop of Toledo. By the time Alfonso X, El Sabio (the Wise), convened his parliament here in 1273, Almagro was thriving.

Amid a cluster of graceful Renaissance and Plateresque façades, colleges, convents, churches, and cobbled streets, there are two standout sights, the first of which is the oblong **plaza Mayor.** Lined lengthwise with rare block-long Flemish-style, glassed-in arcades projecting above solid-stone columns, the plaza Mayor is the best spot to find the intricate, traditional lacework Almagro is famous for. Continuing from the plaza, you can reach the second sight, a restored 16th-century theater, the **Corral de las Comedias.** Built with a stage at one end and stalls around an open courtyard and reminiscent of Elizabethan theaters of the same era, the Corral evokes images of Lope de Vega and Pedro Calderón. In fact, their plays are still performed in this national monument during a festival of classical drama and comedy held annually the last two weeks of September. The **Convent of the Knights of Calatrava** (also called La Asunción) is worthy of a stop, at the eastern edge of town on camino de Calatrava. Note its splendid carved stone Renaissance stairway and two-story Plateresque cloister.

The old Convento de San Francisco has been rebuilt as the **Parador de Almagro**, one of the handsomest hostelries in the government-run chain. This famous monastery, built around 16 patios, each with its own character, now boasts fountains, gardens, large rooms (simply decorated with antiques, tapestries, crafts), and a swimming pool. It is a marvelous place to spend the night or just to have lunch if you are making the drive from Madrid down to Granada. Castilian garlic soup, rabbit in wine sauce, white beans with quail, ragout of spring lamb *manchego,* and hake with cider are some of the excellent specialties. As paradors go, the food here is among the best.

Viso del Marqués

Ciudad Real, a few miles northwest of Almagro, may have been "the seat of the god of smiles" to Cervantes, but today it is relatively inconsequential to tourists. A few sights of interest include the 14th-century Puerta de Toledo, an old Mudejar-style town gate; a notable Gothic cathedral with fine choir stalls; and the Gothic Iglesia de San Pedro, with Mudejar and Gothic doorways, a Flamboyant Gothic rose window, and a Baroque retable. Far more interesting than Ciudad Real, however, is the little-known Viso del Marqués, about 25 km (15 miles) south of Valdepeñas, just 8 km (5 miles) west of the main road; make the turnoff at Almuradiel.

The centerpiece of this minute village is an Italianate Renaissance palace (1564–1585) built for Alvaro de Bazán, marqués de Santa Cruz, an intrepid naval commander under Philip II. The palace would be a dazzler anywhere, but sitting as it does on this isolated patch of the dusty La Mancha plain it seems all the more remarkable. Of course, Viso wasn't always so remote; it was once on the main route for all traffic heading north or south.

Believed to be the work of a Genoese painter-architect, Giovanni Battista Castello, who worked on El Escorial, the palace's origins are still an enigma. What isn't a mystery is its full-fledged Renaissance beauty, with proportions that take the breath away: Doric columns, elegant patios and courtyards, a magnificent barrel-vaulted stairwell, and, throughout, lavishly decorated walls, ceilings, and archways embellished with themes that illustrate the marqués's brilliant career and successful battles. The Spanish still debate whether the outcome of the Armada in 1588 would have been different if he had lived to take command.

If you want lunch, you'll have to go back to Almuradiel for some roast lamb or *pisto manchego* at **Los Podencos** in the Hotel Podencos, carretera de Andalucía.

Unless you are heading south to Andalusia through the dramatic, narrow mountain gorge called Despeñaperros (overthrow of the dogs), where bandits once ambushed travellers, your best bet for seeing Viso del Marqués is to make it a day trip from Almagro, the prime place in the area for bedding down for a night or two, at the parador.

Almagro makes a good base for exploring the Don Quixote villages of La Mancha, if that is your pleasure. Keep in mind, of course, that following the good don's "trail" is like pursuing Romeo and Juliet in Italy; we are talking about fictional characters and events. One place where fiction and reality blend is **Argamasilla de Alba,** just a few miles northeast of Manzanares. It was here that Cervantes was imprisoned and reputedly began writing *Don Quixote.* The prison, rebuilt, can be seen at the whitewashed, cave-like Casa de Medrano. In the local parish church is a painting of Don Rodrígo de Pacheco, a local bigwig believed to have been the inspiration for the "knight of the rueful countenance."

CUENCA

Much of the drive east from Madrid to Cuenca, 164 km (102 miles) away via N III, then left at Tarancón onto N 400, is like a lunar landscape. Then suddenly you are confronted with a grove of giant poplars and cypress, etched against ocher bluffs, and the silhouette of a town at the top.

Cuenca is literally a cliff-hanger. Houses, some dating back to the 12th century, are sculpted into and dramatically overhang the cliffs above a deep gorge. Some 600 feet below, the Júcar (HOO-char) and Huécar (WAY-cahr) rivers converge near the newer, lower part of town. The Júcar flows on toward Valencia; the Huécar ends at Cuenca's feet.

Like many Castilian hill towns, Cuenca consists of a busy but dull lower modern town and an upper vintage one, with a cathedral, a town hall built into the gateway to the upper town, and ancient buildings. Cuenca made an ideal lookout, as the Moors discovered in the ninth century. From the top you can see for miles into Castile, yet the cliffs themselves act as a natural, impenetrable fortress, with the rivers forming a moat on three sides. No wonder the earlier Romans and Visigoths valued it too.

In the 12th century Moslems and Christians had a tug-of-war over Cuenca, alternately capturing and losing it. In 1177, after a nine-month siege, the Christian king Alfonso VIII, borrowing strategy from *The Odyssey,* supposedly sent two supporters, crouching and covered by sheepskins, past the Moslem gatekeeper. Once inside they slew the guard and opened the gate to Alfonso's army. From then on the town was a Christian outpost, and later it became the headquarters of the Knights of Santiago. In honor of Alfonso's ingenuity, Concuenses, as Cuenca people call themselves, still burn a light at night at Cuenca's lower gate.

Casas Colgadas

To explore Cuenca's upper town, drive up the corkscrew road through the 18th-century gate (supporting the town hall above it), and park in the small plaza Mayor just below the cathedral. The only way to see all the narrow streets and overhanging vistas of this area is on foot.

What brings most outsiders to Cuenca these days is Las Casas Colgadas, three adjoining 15th-century houses whose balconies are cantilevered from the steepest cliff above the Huécar. In the early 1960s an affluent Madrid painter, the late Fernando Zóbel, persuaded Cuenca authorities to let him convert the picturesque but decaying buildings (which once functioned as the town hall) into a museum, in exchange for renovating the buildings.

With impeccable taste Zóbel and fellow artists Gustavo Tornér and Gerardo Rueda, all members of the 1960s new wave of Spanish artists, peeled away plaster (and discovered a hidden Gothic stairway and arches), whitewashed the interior walls, and turned two of the attached buildings into a stunning **Museo de Arte Abstracto**, a showcase for Antoni Tàpies, Luis Feito, Eduardo Chillida, Manolo Millares, Antonio Saura, and some 60 others of the post–Picasso-Miró generation.

In the third building is a charming restaurant, **Mesón Casas Colgadas**, the best in town by far, where local specialties include *trucha Figón* (trout from the Júcar), Huécar *cangrejos* (crabs), grilled wild mushrooms, *conejo escabechado* (pickled rabbit), and excellent desserts such as *alaju* and *helado con nueces cantonesas* (ice cream with walnuts). The Spanish enjoy a postprandial digestive; try the local *resoli* (coffee liqueur). Another restaurant in the lower town, **Figón de Pedro**, Cervantes 15, has the same ownership and similar menu but lacks the vista. Balconies in both the restaurant and the museum have stunning views of the river below and the textured, craggy cliffs on the opposite side. Down the hill a short distance to the left of the Casas Colgadas is the San Pablo footbridge, a scary, shaky passage over the Huécar that leads to the convent of San Pablo on the opposite cliff.

Zóbel died in 1984, but the museum's future is secure because it is now part of the Madrid-based Fundación Juan March. Because of the museum and Cuenca's windswept prospect, many Madrid artists have made some of the ancient upper-town buildings their weekend homes as respite from the hot, dry Castilian summers. Winter here is another story—a chiller.

Elsewhere in Cuenca

In the years since the museum opened, Cuenca has metamorphosed from a withered town whose future was past to an increasingly prosperous one. Even the early Gothic **cathedral** up a few steps in the plaza Mayor, which you pass on the way along the cobbled side street to the museum, has been scrubbed down. Don't be put off by its eclectic exterior; the interior is light enough in the morning to reveal some fine treasures, including rare (for Spain) Anglo-Norman influences in the nave (1208–1250). Also special are several superb *rejas* by Hernando de Arenas, a local 16th-century master; a Madonna by sculptor Pedro de Mena; a treasury with a lovely Baroque ceiling; and an ornate Plateresque portal leading to the Sala Capitular.

Around the corner from the cathedral (to the right if you are facing the cathedral), on the way to the Museum of Spanish Abstract Art but easy to miss, is a new Cuenca sight: the **Diocesan Museum**, installed in a 16th-century archbishop's palace, with numerous treasures from Cuenca churches and the cathedral handsomely displayed without an inch of clutter. A first-rate Gérard David *Crucifixion,* two fine El Greco paintings, a choice Byzantine diptych of the Virgin Mary, and numerous santos, altar rugs, and tapestries are among the surprises.

Semana Santa (Holy Week), celebrated with elaborate processions in many Spanish cities, is at its most awesome in Cuenca, as candle-carrying multitudes slowly wend their way up the narrow lanes along the cliffside, looking in the darkness like elongated ribbons of flickering lights.

Just below the plaza Mayor is another likable restaurant, with views facing the opposite direction across the valleys from those of Mesón Casas Colgadas. It is **Los Arcos**, and while it doesn't measure up to Cuenca's other restaurants, it serves up splendid vistas and decent *pisto manchego, gazpacho pastor,* and other regional dishes.

As for places to stay, your very best bet is **Hotel Cueva del Fraile**. Though 7 km (4.5 miles) outside Cuenca, it is worth the drive for the mountain views, pleasant rustic Spanish flavor, tennis courts, and swimming pool. A distant second, at the edge of the lower town, is **Hotel Torremangana**. Though officially categorized a four-star hotel, the amenities are less than the stars suggest. It is central Cuenca's best—with modestly furnished, serviceable rooms.

Excursions from Cuenca

It is a scenic twisting mountain drive 35 km (22 miles) north of Cuenca to **Ciudad Encantada** (Enchanted City), a series of spectacular rock formations that you can walk through, under, and around. Names like El Tobogán (a roller-coaster walk through a narrow passage of steep boulders), Hongo (Mushroom), Las Barcas (Ships), and Elefante y Cocodrilo (Elephant and Crocodile) telegraph the shapes of the boulders. It's an eerie, wonderful sight—but you have to enjoy walking.

Alarcón, 82 km (51 miles) south of Cuenca on N 320/111, built on a rocky ledge that rises from a Júcar river gorge, boasts the quintessential "castle in Spain," a 14th-century fortress, now turned into a premier, though off-the-track, parador, **Parador Marqués de Villena**. Its dining room has some of the best regional dishes in the area, including a local specialty, a spicy pâté called *moteruelo*. The village also has four fine churches, mostly in a ruined state, and a well-restored 13th- to 15th-century church, **La Trinidad**.

Another castle, considered one of the most "typical" in Spain, is at **Belmonte**, 70 or so km (44 miles) southwest of Cuenca on N 420. Built in 1456 for Juan Pacheco, the marqués de Villena, the hexagonal castle is dramatically sited. It was abandoned, then restored in the 19th century, and is now open to view. The furnishings are long gone, but the Mudejar ceilings are worth seeing. Fray Luis de León (1528–1591), scholar-poet-professor at the University of Salamanca, was born in the village.

Should you continue on N 420 southwest toward Ciudad Real and Córdoba, you'll pass through **Mota del Cuervo** and then **Campo de Criptana**, both classic Manchego villages noted for their Quixote-style windmills.

PASTRANA

Like most Spanish towns, Pastrana, just east of Madrid and some 100 km (62 miles) from Cuenca (west on N 400, then north on the road to Guadalajara), has its share of serendipitous artistic surprises. Pastrana's are inside the **Colegiata**, a small Gothic church with a Romanesque portal. It would be sufficient to discover the imposing retable with ten paintings by Juan de Borgoña, the fine choir stalls, and the tomb of the powerful and mysterious Ana Mendoza de la Cerda, known through time as the one-eyed Princess of Eboli. But that's merely a prelude.

In the treasury, through doors with artful bas-reliefs, there are rooms full of reliquaries, santos, antique chests, silver and gold chalices, and vestments. But the raison d'être of a visit consists of four richly detailed Gothic tapestries, some of which date to the 15th century. In sweeping form, they depict the 1471 conquest of Tangier and Arzila in Morocco by Alfonso V of Portugal (El Africano) and are thought to be the work of the great Portuguese artist Nuno Gonçalves. They were supposedly a gift of Philip II to the princess, who bequeathed them to Pastrana.

SIGUENZA

Sigüenza, 135 km (85 miles) northeast of Madrid, is the northeastern outpost of Castilla–La Mancha, often overlooked (more's the pity) by foreign visitors, unless they are en route from Madrid to Zaragoza and Barcelona via **Guadalajara**. The last, badly bombed during the Civil War, is worth a very quick stop largely for its **Palacio del Infantado**, the Plateresque palace (1461–1492) of the Mendozas, with a totally restored diamond-pointed façade and graceful patio with a double gallery of columns.

Sigüenza is something else: a thoroughly Medieval town on the Henares, with sloping streets that climb in layers up to a castle-fortress, which evolved from a Visigothic castle to a Moorish *alcazaba* (a fortified residence). From 1124, after the Christians captured Sigüenza, the castle was much rebuilt to double as a bishop's residence (Ferdinand, Isabella, and Juana la Loca were among its royal visitors), and now, finally, as a hostelry, **Parador Castillo de Sigüenza**. Luxurious as paradores go, Sigüenza's spacious rooms with either courtyard or mountain view and its grand public *salas* have kept their historic character, as well as many paintings, ceramics, and antiques from time past. A grilled window inside the parador overlooks the castle's nicely decorated Romanesque chapel.

From the parador, a short walk down cobbled calle Mayor brings you to the lower town and the graceful, though restored, plaza Mayor, surrounded by porticoes and balconies and, on one side, the **Catedral de Santa María**. The cathedral was begun in 1150 but was considerably altered in the 13th century and later. Its Romanesque-Gothic-Renaissance façade has a French flavor, but its interior is completely Spain. An expansive sweep of elongated Gothic arches with towering vaulted ceilings is a major delight, but so are the beautiful rose window (13th century), an ornate Neoclassical 16th-century retable above the main altar, a multitiered lacy valentine of an altarpiece (called Retablo de Santa Librada, after Sigüenza's patron saint), and many intriguing side chapels. As in many Spanish cathedrals, there is little light. To see the numerous and eclectic delights here, you need to look for the custodian in charge of light and keys.

To the right of the main altar is the 16th-century chapel of the Arce family, with its pièce de résistance, a delicately sculpted reclining alabaster figure of a youthful knight, dreamily lounging through eternity. He is El Doncel (The Young Knight) de Sigüenza, Martín Vázquez de Arce, Queen Isabella's page, who was killed in 1486 at the gates of Granada.

The cathedral's tour de force is inside the 16th-century **Sacrista de las Cabezas** (Sacristy of the Heads): the work of Plateresque architect Alonso de Covarrubias. Carved in high relief on medallions that completely cover the barrel-vaulted ceiling are 300 heads of bishops, scholars, soldiers, and other notables. Like a Chinese treasure box, the sacristy opens into the **Capella Espiritu Sanctu**, with its *Annunciation* by El Greco, Titian's *Descent from the Cross,* and other paintings. From the late-Gothic cloisters you enter a salon of tapestries, with so many 17th-century Flemish tapestries that they have to be hung from rods like carpets displayed in a showroom. The cathedral, like Sigüenza's many other churches and monuments, has a blue-and-white ceramic plaque attached to its façade, delineating the major treasures inside, a helpful précis for visitors in a hurry.

The sights in the town itself are plentiful, beginning with the **Diocesan Museum** diagonally across from the cathedral, lodged in a Neoclassical 18th-century building. Its prize is Francisco Zurbarán's *Immaculada,* painted with great clarity. Unfortunately, many of the museum's vast assemblage of

Romanesque sculptures have been crudely repainted, and the museum looks as though it is in need of funds for upkeep.

Much of the lower town has an old-fashioned 1950s look. Time did not, despite the looks, stand still here: Sigüenza was a Nationalist stronghold throughout the Civil War, and the battle damage was considerable. It is worth a walk to see the various early churches (in varying states of repair). **Artesanía de Sigüenza**, calle Mayor 17, is a tiny shop with attractive local crafts, mirrors, ceramics, and wooden chests.

A modest local gathering place, **Hostal-Restaurante El Doncel**, calle General Mola 3, serves solid regional dishes like *migas castillana* (bread crumbs, ham, chorizo, and fried egg) and *cabrito asado con ajillo*. For more stylish, and pricier, dining (in alcoves ringed by antique stone arches) the choice here is the parador. Try the *cabrito asado en cazuela* (in casserole), and save room for a special honeyed dessert cake, *borrachitos Seguntinos*.

GETTING AROUND

There is frequent train service (15 trains a day) from Madrid's Atocha Station to Toledo, a one-and-a-half-hour trip, and good bus service from the main Madrid station. From Madrid to Cuenca is a three-hour train (five a day) or bus (four daily) ride; Sigüenza is on the Madrid–Zaragoza train route, with ten trains a day, taking one and a half to two and a half hours. To visit the other towns requires changing at major junctions, such as Toledo, Ciudad Real, or Cuenca. You *can* get there from here—but it takes time. As elsewhere in Spain, there are discoveries to be made at every bend in the road, so a car is unquestionably the way to go if at all possible.

RENFE (Spanish National Railway System) operates two summer (through September) weekend excursion train-bus tours: La Mancha (which includes several villages, Almagro, and an overnight in Valdepeñas) and Ciudad Encantada de Cuenca, as well as a one-day (Saturdays, Sundays, and holidays) guided tour to Sigüenza called Doncel de Sigüenza.

ACCOMMODATIONS REFERENCE

When dialing telephone numbers from outside the country, drop the 9 in the area code.

▸ **Parador de Almagro**. Ronda de San Francisco, 13270 Almagro. Tel: (926) 86-01-00.

▶ **Hostal del Cardenal.** Plazoleta de Alfonso VI, paseo de Recaredo 24, 45003 **Toledo.** Tel: (925) 22-49-00.

▶ **Parador Castillo de Sigüenza.** Plaza del Castillo, 19250 **Sigüenza.** Tel: (911) 39-01-00.

▶ **Parador Conde de Orgaz.** Paseo de los Cigarrales, Circunvalación Carretera, 45000 **Toledo.** Tel: (925) 22-18-50.

▶ **Hotel Cueva del Fraile.** Hoz del Huécar, 16001 **Cuenca.** Tel: (966) 21-15-71.

▶ **María Cristina.** Marqués de Mendigorria 1, 45003 **Toledo.** Tel: (925) 21-32-02.

▶ **Parador Marqués de Villena.** Avenida Amigos de los Castillos, 16213 **Alarcón.** Tel: (966) 33-13-50.

▶ **Hotel Torremangana.** Carrero Blanoc 4, 16002 **Cuenca.** Tel: (966) 22-33-51; Telex: 23400 HTMG-E.

EXTREMADURA

By Carla Hunt

Carla Hunt is a freelance writer and contributor of articles to North American and international newspapers and magazines. Her family has lived in Portugal since 1970, and she travels regularly to the Iberian Peninsula.

According to a recent survey, there are 6,591 stork nests in 31 of Spain's 50 provinces, and a large number of these nests—perched atop church steeples, belfries, spires, towers, turrets, and domes—are in the two provinces that make up Extremadura: Cáceres has 1,687 and Badajoz has 1,333.

There is another interesting statistic regarding Extremadura, the vast, beautiful, and little-visited region called "the cradle of the conquistadores," lying southwest of Madrid along the Portuguese border: This area produced seven of the most famed discoverers/explorers/conquerors of the Americas. Extremadura cannot lay claim to Christopher Columbus, whose discovery of the Americas will be commemorated on its 500th anniversary in 1992, but the area's native sons do include: Hernán Cortés, who marched through Mexico; Francisco Pizarro, who brought down Peru's Inca Empire; Pedro de Alvarado, who did the same to the Maya of Guatemala; Pedro de Valdivia, who founded Santiago but was unable to master the Mapuche Indians of Chile; Vasco Núñez de Balboa, who first sighted the Pacific Ocean; Francisco de Orellana, the first navigator of the Amazon; and Hernando de Soto, discoverer of the Mississippi River and conqueror of Florida.

The roots of this phenomenon lie almost literally in the soil of Extremadura. The ancestors of these conquistadores of the

16th century and of today's rather stolid Extremeños were the veterans of the legions of Emperor Caesar Augustus, who in 23 B.C. gave them land around Mérida to farm upon their retirement from active duty. During the Middle Ages the sons of Extremadura filled the ranks of such Christian corps as the Knights Templar, the Knights of Santiago, and the Knights of Alcántara, who fought the battles of La Reconquista (the Reconquest), which in the 15th century drove the infidel Moors from Spain after an 800-year occupation.

The conquerors came from a land much like those they went to in North and South America: big, open, hard. Extremadura had never been an easy place to earn a living, and many farmers and herdsmen who realized that the future at home was bleak volunteered for service overseas. As James Michener, author of *Iberia,* has said: "Uneducated, despairing villagers conquered the New World [where] their raw Extremaduran courage proved the most valuable commodity carried westward by the Spanish galleons."

The men of Extremadura returned home, using their acquired wealth to build mansions and palaces for themselves, particularly in the city of Cáceres, and rich, though not opulent, churches to the glory of God.

Extremadura still sits near the bottom of Spain's economic ladder, a condition not always apparent to the springtime traveller in particular, who will find the fields blanketed in golden wheat, silvery olive groves, and wildflowers, the city walls and balconied houses buried in roses as big as peonies. Parts of the northern plateau are forested and rather harsh, partly covered by the Montfrague nature park, partly obscured by herds of goats and sheep, which each spring and fall are moved along the sheepherding route between the dramatic Sierra highlands that border the province of Salamanca and the more peaceful hill country around Cáceres. For hundreds of years the finest Merino wool came from these sheep and served as the currency of the realm. Toward the end of May and in September, herds come to market and people to the livestock fairs in Extremadura, the largest taking place in Cáceres.

The local tourist office has borrowed a page from ancient Gaul and divided Extremadura into three parts. Northeast, from roughly Trujillo to the rather inaccessible mountain area of Las Hurdes, is called "green Extremadura." The farther north you go, the more you will think of the most remote parts of America's Appalachia and its natives; those in Las Hurdes are blonde and blue-eyed, reminders of their Celtic and Visigothic ancestors.

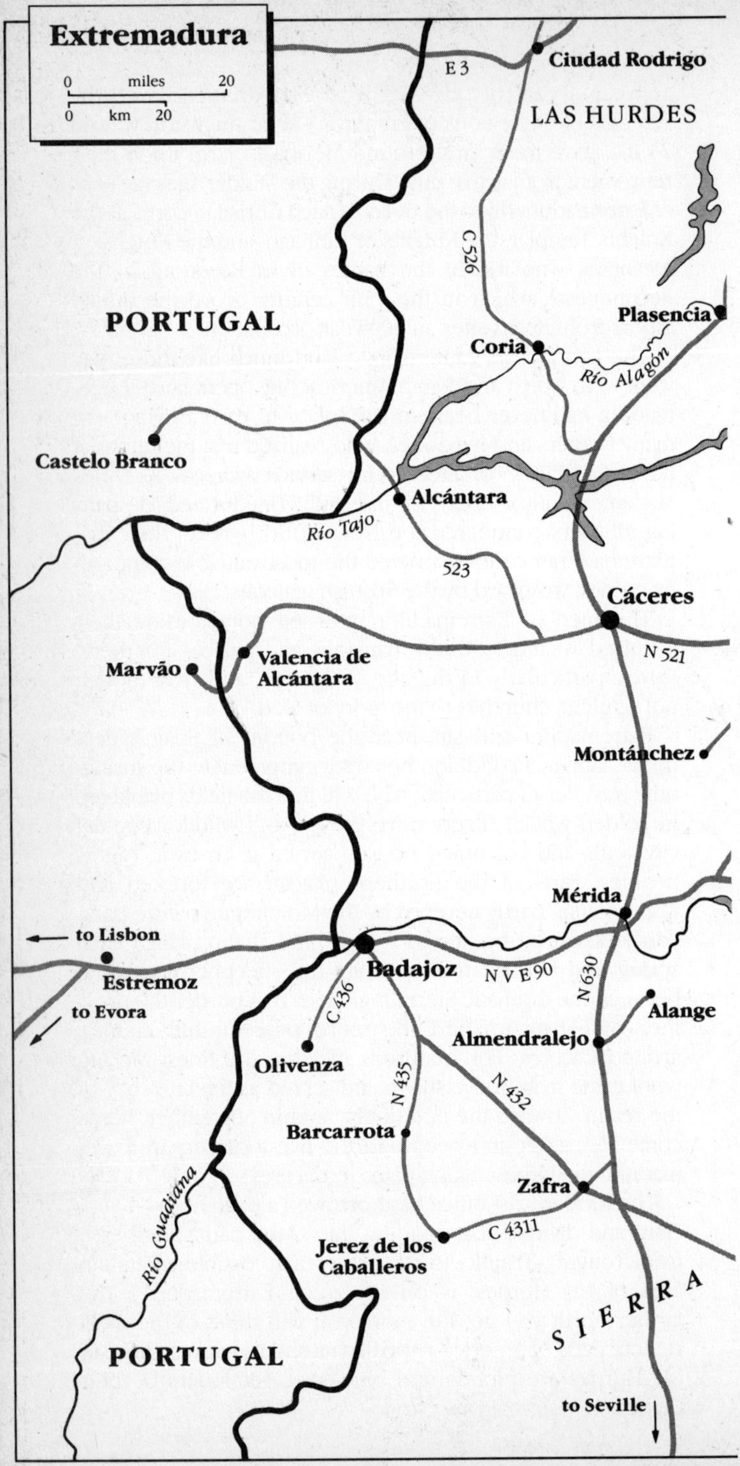
Extremadura
0 miles 20
0 km 20
E 3
Ciudad Rodrigo
LAS HURDES
C 526
PORTUGAL
Plasencia
Coria
Río Alagón
Castelo Branco
Alcántara
Río Tajo
523
Cáceres
N 521
Marvão
Valencia de Alcántara
Montánchez
Mérida
to Lisbon
Estremoz
Badajoz
N V E 90
N 630
to Evora
C 436
Alange
Almendralejo
Olivenza
N 435
N 432
Barcarrota
Zafra
Río Guadiana
C 4311
Jerez de los Caballeros
SIERRA
PORTUGAL
to Seville

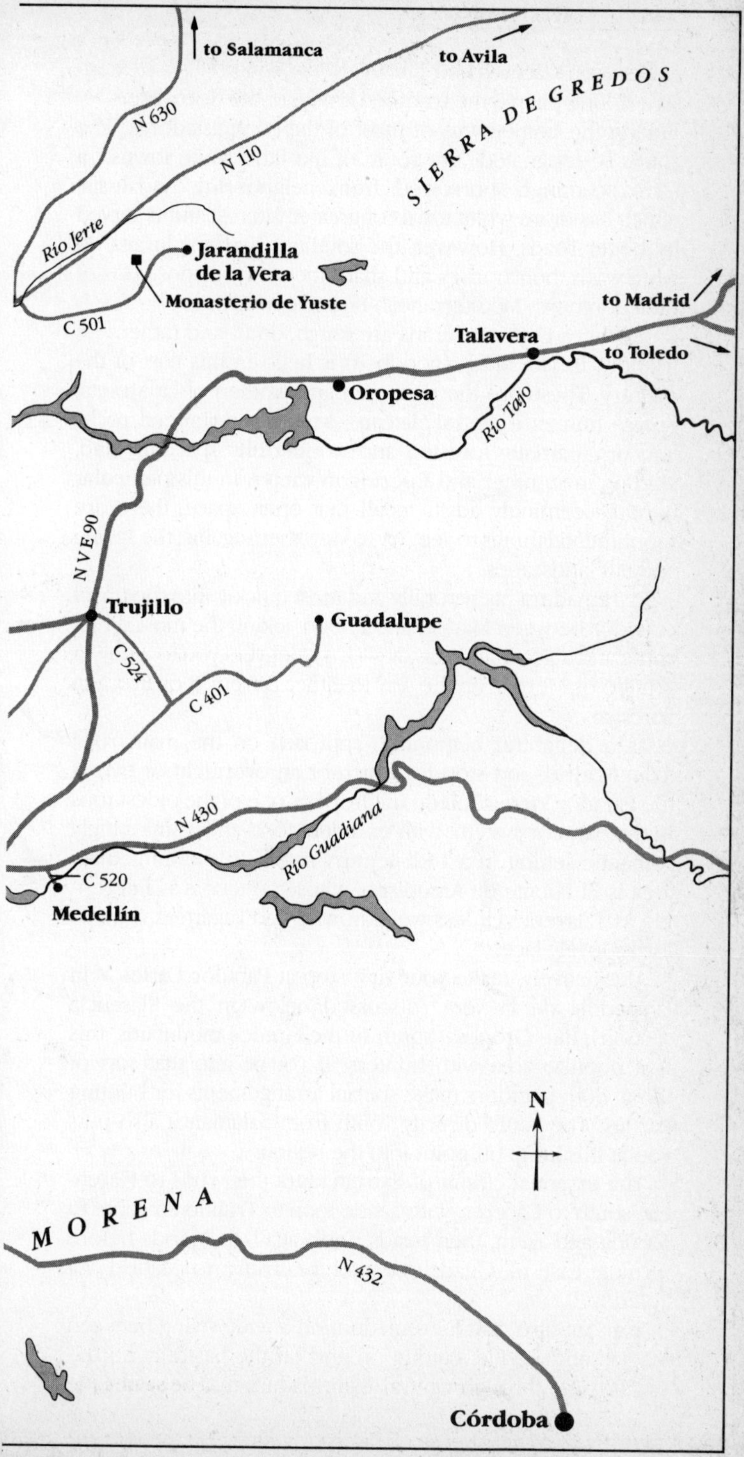

to Salamanca
to Avila
SIERRA DE GREDOS
N 630
N 110
Río Jerte
Jarandilla de la Vera
Monasterio de Yuste
C 501
to Madrid
Talavera
to Toledo
Oropesa
Río Tajo
NVE90
Trujillo
Guadalupe
C 524
C 401
N 430
Río Guadiana
C 520
Medellín
N
MORENA
N 432
Córdoba

Between Cáceres and Mérida to the south falls an extensive rolling plain—the so-called "route of the discoverers"—linking the hometowns of most of the conquistadores. The south is designated "the route of the little white towns," a term seemingly borrowed from neighboring Andalusia, which has more white towns of greater interest and is served by better roads. However, the southern Extremadurans do whitewash their houses and share the sunny dispositions of their southern, Mediterranean-bound countrymen.

Northern Extremadurans are tough, dour, and rather less friendly. In fact *adios* (goodbye) is hello in this part of the country. These are the true men and women of La Meseta, Spain's immense central plateau—a mountain-rimmed, rocky and dry, partially forested and wonderfully spacious land, sizzling in summer and freezing in winter. In this particular corner, seemingly adrift in all that open space, there are monumental things to see. Try to view them against the spring and fall landscapes.

Extremadura fits naturally and most quickly into the travel corridor between Madrid and Lisbon; taking the most direct route and a good highway, N V (E 4), delivers you to a stay in Trujillo or Mérida, on the way to either Estremoz or Evora in Portugal.

As a delightful beginning, approach on the main road from Madrid, and stop for lunch or an overnight or two at the **Parador Virrey Toledo** in Oropesa, one of the oldest inns in the parador system, with excellent food and a smashingly romantic setting in a 14th-century castle. In the immediate area is El Puente de Arzobispo, whose pottery is as interesting as Talavera's (if less well-known), and Lagartera, famous for its lovely lace.

Alternatively, make your first stop at **Parador Carlos V** in Jarrandilla de la Vera (discussed below in the Plasencia section); like Oropesa, south of the Gredos mountains, this is a popular area with hunters. If you're into that sort of thing, both paradors make special arrangements for hunting parties. The route directly south from Salamanca also puts you at this jump-off point into the region.

The essential circuit of Extremadura then runs to Plasencia, south to Cáceres, with a side loop to Trujillo en route to Mérida and Zafra, then heads north again to Mérida before turning east to Guadalupe and returning to Madrid via Toledo.

You can also visit Extremadura on a wide swing between Madrid and Seville, cutting on and off the basically north–south route through central Extremadura that becomes the

Zafra/Seville route. Driving off the beaten path here is time-consuming but not rugged. Unless you are heading, say, down to the Roman baths tucked away in the village of Alange south of Mérida, even two-lane roads are fairly well paved and there is little traffic.

There are not a great many hotels to choose from in Extremaduran towns and cities, but there are six excellent and historic paradors, most with the best dining in town. Itineraries should be planned around them.

MAJOR INTEREST

Cáceres
The monumental old city
Archaeological and ethnographic museum

Plasencia
Cathedral

Coria
Castle
Cathedral

Alcántara
San Benito monastery
Roman bridge

Trujillo
The Pizarro family palace
Plaza Mayor
Arab fortress

Guadalupe
Franciscan monastery

Mérida
Roman theater complex
Roman art museum

Medellín, Cortes's hometown

Zafra
Castle of the dukes of Feria

Jerez de los Caballeros
Castle of the Templars
San Bartolomé church

Olivenza
Santa María Magdalena church

The province is famous for its sharp cheeses, Montánchez ham and sausages, wild game in season, codfish dishes, and gazpacho. You don't come to Extremadura for a gourmet experience, however. You come for a grand and unspoiled countryside, for history as recorded in the remembrances of things past: cave paintings from Paleolithic times (as yet not very accessible), stone dolmens from the Celts, Roman ruins, Mujedar architecture, Romanesque and Gothic churches, hill-top fortresses, quaint Medieval villages, and walled towns.

You should also come with a dictionary. English is most definitely not spoken here. In exchange for the benefits of travelling without crowds and enjoying a most interesting and enchanting region, you have the drawbacks of not being understood and not understanding. There is little material in English at the tourist offices, and no English-speaking guides available to show you around (with a few exceptions, such as at the monastery in Guadalupe).

A second problem in touring Extremadura is that so many places are *cerrado* (closed). The reason given locally is that many art treasures have been stolen from historic civic and religious buildings. The officials do not seem to have jumped to the solution of posting guards, whose salaries could be covered by visitor entrance fees. Sometimes the only way to see a church is to be there for Mass, most generally in the evening, but Mass times are hard to anticipate. Church doors are more likely to be open for religious holidays, on local saints' days, and during the confirmation and wedding seasons in May and June. In tiny villages, often a church neighbor will have a key—the word for it is *clave,* and for open it's *abierto.*

The Wines of Extremadura

Extremadura is a harsh and dry land, and it is tempting to say that Cortés and the rest of the conquistadores left home in search of better food and wine. Most of the area's wine production, centered around the town of Almendralejo, south of Mérida, is distilled into alcohol or sold in bulk to the wineless provinces of the Cantabrian coast. **Tierra de Barros** (Badajoz), which takes its name from the clay earth used to make pottery in this region, is Extremadura's only *denominación de origen.* Located in the western foothills near the Portuguese border, it has long been known by aficionados of regional wines for its powerful, deep-colored reds. Although in the past much of the produce of this area had been distilled to make grape spirits, many *bodegas* are starting to produce quality table wines. Lar de Barros is a noteworthy red wine, made from a blend of Tempranillo, Graciano, and Garnacha grapes.

There are a few other artisan wines, such as Cañamero and Montánchez (Cáceres), that are much admired locally. Cañamero is often cloudy, which its aficionados say proves it is unfiltered, therefore giving it character. Montánchez can seldom be found outside the spectacular village of the same name, about 50 km (30 miles) south of Cáceres. Isolated and ancient, **Montánchez** is resplendent with stunning views and a charming statue of the Virgin in the tiny hermitage chapel that shares the perch above the village with crumbling fortification walls and toppled Roman temple columns. All this makes the trip out to sample its wine and legendary mountain hams well worth the trouble.

Marqués de Cáceres, an excellent Rioja that can be found all over Spain, is not, as suggested by its name and by some writers, from Extremadura.

—Gerry Dawes

Cáceres

Cáceres, (west of Madrid on E 90 to Trujillo, then on from there west on route 521), is capital of its own province and the most important city in northern Extremadura. The city is a treasure trove of historic buildings. Most are enclosed by well-preserved walls dating from Roman, Moorish, and Medieval times; 12 of the original towers protecting the enclosure still stand. The city was founded by the Romans in 28 B.C., but the name goes back only as far as the Moorish Almohad conquest, when it was called Qazris.

There is a certain sameness (or unity, depending on your artistic sense) to the palaces, manor houses, and religious buildings of golden stone and pale brick that flank the narrow streets and tiny plazas. Many manor houses were built with wealth acquired during the conquest of the Americas, and many are still distinguished by the owners' coats of arms over the doors and by particularly beautiful courtyards. The most elegant square is the **plaza de Santa María**, with a fine 16th-century Gothic cathedral of the same name and a lovely bishop's palace.

Another important architectural enclave is grouped around the **plaza San Mateo**, almost at the top of the old town and to the right of the main entrance. If you approach this plaza from the Mérida gate, you will walk along the calle Ancha and, at number 6, find the newly opened

Parador de Cáceres, which occupies the premises of a 14th-century mansion complete with a big square tower, iron balconies, and various coats of arms on the walls, including that of Diego de Ulloa, who was the commander of the city at the time the tower and palace were first used. The interior of this four-star inn is hung with old tapestries and contemporary wall hangings; public areas, as well as the 27 guest rooms, are grouped around a central courtyard. Future plans call for expansion into the neighboring convent to provide an additional 20 guest rooms.

The plaza San Mateo was once the Moorish center of town, and the church, standing tall and very Gothic at the highest point of the city, is built on the site of a former mosque. On the same plaza is the **Palacio de la Cigüeñas** (storks' palace), the only palace left in town with a fortified tower. (In the 15th century Queen Isabella the Catholic got so fed up with the constant family feuding that she ordered all the other towers knocked down.)

Most important on this square is the **Palacio de las Veletas** (weather vane palace), which incorporates part of the Moorish alcázar, and beneath it a splendid cistern whose grand arches reflect in the waters. Best of all, the Veletas houses an excellent museum. Artifacts in the archaeological section date to prehistoric times, when local inhabitants were painting caves and hunting with Stone Age weapons. More current displays are from the Arab and Medieval periods. In the ethnographic section, colorful dioramas document historic costumes and customs of Extremadura.

In the nearby **Casa del Mono** (monkey house) is another museum, this one focusing on provincial paintings, sculpture, and religious art, and outside the ancient walls is **Casa de los Caballos** (house of the horses), which is today's museum of contemporary art. Other than these museums and a few churches, visitors get to see very little of the interiors of Cáceres. The tourist office on plaza General Mola, also outside the walls, has a good city map identifying dozens of historic buildings in the old city quarter by name.

A few miles southeast of the city is the hilltop sanctuary of the city's patron saint, the Mountain Virgin, who shares the site with an enormous statue of Christ. At the end of April, just after the festival of Saint George, who is honored in Cáceres with a parade of costumed Christians and Moors, the faithful make a pilgrimage to the lovely chapel of the Mountain Virgin.

In addition to Parador de Cáceres, the best accommodations available are businessmen's hotels in the new city, the

Alcántara and the **Extremadura**. The hotel food is mediocre, but in the city center there is the pleasant **Atrio** restaurant at avenida de España 30, which also has a fairly good wine cellar. For a bit of the atmosphere of dining in a former palace, try **El Figón de Eustaquio** at plaza San Juan 12. Cheaper choices and cafés are grouped around plaza General Mola.

Plasencia

The storks return to Plasencia from February to July; travellers will enjoy this town, at the bend of the río Jerte 80 km (50 miles) north of Cáceres and not far to the west of Jarandilla de la Vera, in both spring and fall. Here you will find a lovely Medieval bridge with six sturdy arches spanning the river, and aristocratic palaces with heraldic signs and iron balconies on their façades.

The **cathedral**, begun in the 14th century, is the outstanding feature. When it was completely reconstructed in the 16th, the nave and the apse were separated, so it is part Romanesque and part Gothic. The cathedral has an altarpiece decorated with statues by the 17th-century sculptor Gregorio Fernández, and 16th-century choir stalls that were carved by Rodrigo Alemán. The "new" cathedral has lovely **cloisters** with finely worked capitals.

Plasencia is a pleasant place to explore on foot, one you might visit if you are coming into Extremadura from Madrid. About 65 km (40 miles) before arriving here, almost due east on route 501, is a forested preserve around the **Monasterio de Yuste**, located on a smaller, well-marked road. After four decades commanding the Hapsburg Empire, the great Charles V retired here in his final years, painfully burdened by severe attacks of gout. In his apartments, maintained as they were when he died in 1558, visitors taking the tour of the monastery will find his wooden gout chair among the original furnishings. The masterwork paintings and priceless tapestries have gone elsewhere.

While he was waiting for his apartments to be readied, the emperor stayed in the nearby village of **Jarandilla de la Vera**, located in the Tiétar valley below the monastery 15 km (9 miles) to the east on 501. This is a very lovely area, white with cherry blossoms in spring and terraced with vineyards and tobacco fields. The brick, almost Moorish-looking storage barns house the drying tobacco leaves. Travellers coming from Madrid (217 km/135 miles east of Jarandilla) to

Extremadura should do as the emperor did, and stay in the same 15th-century monastery, now converted into the **Parador Carlos V.** The food is very good at the parador, especially the fresh game in season. For a sampling of regional cuisine in Plasencia itself, try the best restaurant in town—the **Alfonso VIII** in the town's top hotel of the same name.

Coria and Alcántara

Due west of Plasencia (32 km/20 miles), and due north of Cáceres, is Coria, overlooking the valley of the río Alagón, a tributary of the grander Tagus. The town is surrounded by solid Roman walls; its bridge also dates from Roman times, while the dramatic castle and cathedral are Medieval. The latter's Gothic edifice is rather interesting, embellished with elegant Plateresque decoration and topped by a Baroque tower. Inside, the single aisle has decorative ribbed vaulting above and stone-slab flooring carved with family crests that cover the tombs of those buried below.

Alcántara, southwest of Coria and almost at the Portuguese border, sits high above an even more dramatic bridge, built in A.D. 105 to span the Tagus. You cross this bridge to climb the steep road into the once-fortified town where the Knights of Alcántara, one of the great orders of chivalry in Spain, presided. They played a major role in the Reconquest (during which they were still called the Knights of Saint Julían Pereiro, changing their name to Alcántara after defending the city against the Moors in the 13th century). The Knights were active as well as in the wars with Portugal and even those of independence against France.

The castle of the Knights is now in ruins, and not much more remains of their 16th-century church. The famous church here now is that of the **San Benito Convent**, with a newly restored Plateresque façade. The favorite local dish is partridge, but there is nary a restaurant to be recommended in town. (When you are on the road in Extremadura, picnic food can play an important role in your midday meal.)

Trujillo

Along a good straight road going 48 km (30 miles) east of Cáceres, set atop a granite hill along the N V (E 4) coming from Madrid, is Trujillo, which has been inhabited by Celts, Romans, Moors, and Christians. Within its ancient walls is a precious legacy of monumental castles and palaces, churches and noble mansions, monuments and towers. Life centers around the old town and the **plaza Mayor**, one of Spain's most beautiful squares, particularly in the evening light. Its shape is unusual, almost three-sided, with different and oddly angled levels linked by wide flights of stairs. The centerpiece of the square is the great bronze equestrian statue of native son Francisco Pizarro, cast in 1927 by American sculptors Mary Harriman and Charles Runsey, who have provided both rider and horse with hats.

Trujillo was the birthplace of the Pizarros, whose family palace, **Palacio de la Conquista**, on the main square, was built by Hernando Pizarro with riches from the New World. Actually both brothers, Francisco and Hernando, sailed for the Americas, but it is Francisco who is "credited" with the destruction of the Inca Empire in Peru. He married an Inca princess, seized and executed the local ruler, occupied his capital, plundered his riches, and was in turn murdered himself. His brother Hernando fared better, marrying his half-Inca niece and returning to Trujillo to live royally ever after as the marqués de la Conquista. Other history-making Trujillo natives are Francisco de Orellana, the first explorer of the Amazon; Francisco de la Casas, who accompanied Cortés to Mexico and founded the city of Trujillo in Honduras; and Diego García de Paredes, founder of Trujillo in Venezuela. Hundreds of other Trujillanos joined in the Americas expeditions, and many Latin American towns bear their names.

Also to note on the plaza Mayor are the Palacio Duques de San Carlos, which is now a convent, and the Iglesia de San Martín, whose 18th-century organ is still in use. Off the square you pass through one of seven entrance gates into the old walled city, a lovely place to wander up and down the narrow, stony streets; make sure to stop at **Santa María**, a Gothic church that is the pantheon of Trujillo's great conquerors. Walk far enough uphill and you come to a massive crenellated wall, reinforced by big square towers and a 12th-century **Arab fortress** called El Castillo. Above the keep stands the 16th-century statue of the Virgen de la Victoria, patron saint of the city.

The **Parador de Trujillo**, occupying part of the restored 16th-century Santa Clara convent, is worth a visit, and it may convince you to stay longer. Many of the 46 rooms with canopied beds and marble baths were once nuns' cells; the Renaissance cloister, with its gardens and fruit trees, is delightful. Breakfast is served in the old refectory, and the vaulted dining room was once a chapel. The specialty of the house is *caldereta extremeña,* a savory stew made with either baby lamb or kid. Accommodations and meals will be less expensive at the **Hostal Pizarro** on the main square; the food is hearty, made with fresh produce, but avoid the house wine.

Guadalupe

An hour east of Trujillo (80 km/50 miles, with the last approaches twisting and winding uphill) is the rather remote pilgrimage town of Guadalupe, whose centerpiece and raison d'être is a gem of a **Franciscan monastery**. It was founded in the 14th century to house the Virgin of Guadalupe's statue, which was discovered by a shepherd shortly before Alfonso XI won his victory over the Moors in 1340. The king built the grandiose shrine for the Hieronymite order of monks in her honor, and over the years the Virgin became (and still is) the object of international pilgrimages. The conquistadores took their Extremaduran saint with them and founded namesake churches of Our Lady of Guadalupe in the Americas. (Her feast day, October 12, is dedicated to all Spanish-speaking countries.)

The monastery continued to be embellished by royalty and the faithful through the 18th century. It is full of art treasures; its façade, bristling with battlements and turrets, is golden and exuberant with Flamboyant Gothic decoration. Guided tours (45 minutes long, which is too short, so do it twice) are the only way to see the treasury rooms and the Mudejar cloisters (daily 9:30 A.M. to 1:00 P.M. and 3:30 to 7:00 P.M.).

The tour includes visits to the chapterhouse and its splendid collection of illuminated books and small Zurbarán paintings; the embroidery museum with superb vestments and reliquaries; and the gold and white sacristy with its eight major Zurbaráns. Above the altar in the little chapel of Saint Jerome in the sacristy is one of Zurbarán's most famous works, *The Apotheosis of St. Jerome*. How nice it is to find a master painter's works hung in the places for which they were actually created!

The climax is a look at the Camarín, a chapel-like room where the Virgin sits on an enamelwork throne, a tiny, richly dressed figure with a little black face.

Guadalupe is known for its pottery, too, which has distinctive colors, and its copperware; there are many small artisans' shops around the monastery square where such local wares can be purchased. Several cafés on the square serve up coffee with honey-and-almond sweets called *muegados*, offering the best seat in the house for a frontal view of Spain's most important shrine to the Virgin Mary, after Montserrat.

Again, hotels provide some important sightseeing in themselves. Across from the monastery is the **Parador Zurbarán**, a 16th-century hospital-convent with pool, gardens, and a patio full of lemon trees. Guadalupe has a fine hotel alternative in the **Hospedería Real Monasterio**, which actually occupies a part of the big monastery and has its bar in the Gothic cloister. Both hotels are charmingly furnished with historic reproductions; the Hospedería has a very good restaurant.

Mérida

To see Roman Spain at its best, you must visit Mérida, on the río Guadiana 65 km (40 miles) due south of Cáceres. Mérida's history began in 23 B.C. when the emperor Augustus authorized the veterans of his fifth and tenth legions to retire from active service and take farms in the area. A bridge—the longest of the period in Spain—was built over the río Guadiana, and Mérida became a primary link in communications between Seville to the south and Salamanca to the north. In imperial times the city was known as Augusta Emerita, and it became the capital of Lusitania, Rome's vast province on the Iberian Peninsula.

Mérida presents a romantic face if you arrive from the south, from Zafra or Seville, via the Roman bridge over the Guadiana. You arrive immediately at the Moorish Alcazaba (citadel), and not far away on this side of town is the famous Roman theater and other monuments. Coming in from the north, you leave the main highway to Badajoz and pick your way through a not overly attractive modern Mérida. But there will always be arrow-shaped signs pointing to the parador on plaza de la Constitución (see below), not only a nice place to stay but a good place to have a drink and get directions to the main ruins of the Roman theater and the museum of Roman art on the southern perimeter of the city. There is a good-size parking lot near the ruins, which are too far to walk to from most hotels.

The Romans left a lavish legacy of monuments around the Roman theater: an immense **Circus Maximus**, where chariot races were held and where flooding permitted boats to stage naval battles; and the **amphitheater**, connected to the main theater by a passageway, which held 15,000 spectators who watched while wild beasts confronted gladiators. Below the main archaeological area is the **Casa Romana del Anfiteatro**, a rich villa from the end of the first century, whose mosaic floor showing people crushing grapes with their feet is in remarkably good condition.

The **Roman theater**, however, one of the most beautiful Roman complexes in Spain, is the gem of the remains, sitting incongruously side by side with modern Mérida. It was built in 24 B.C. by Agrippa, Augustus's son-in-law. A semicircle of stone tiers provided seating for 6,000, and on the rebuilt stage statues of the gods once more stand in their niches among the columns; the chorus area is some 60 feet in diameter. The theater's rear wall is a long, two-story façade with 32 marble columns with Corinthian capitals on tall bases. Behind this are the marble-floored actors' rooms.

Behind the stage is a portico where audiences could stroll during intermission, as they do today during the annual summertime classical drama festival. Greek and Roman comedies and tragedies, as well as ballet and symphony concerts, are presented from the last week in June to the first week in August.

Other sights to see include the **Alcazaba** (fortress) at the end of the 60-arch Roman bridge at the southern entrance to the city. A square building, much longer than a football or soccer field on each side, it was originally built by the Moors and was last used by the Knights of Santiago. Much of the material used in construction came from Roman and Visigothic structures destroyed during the Moslem occupation. The castle has an interesting *aljibe* (water cistern), which over the centuries fed water to Romans, Moors, and Templars in turn.

From the Christian period, the 13th-century **Iglesia de Santa Eulalia**, located in the center of town, is a Romanesque structure that also recycled the stonework of previous occupiers. The church is dedicated to the child martyr Eulalia, who according to legend was cooked in an oven on the site for spitting in the eye of a pagan priest. In front of the church is the little **temple of Mars**, locally called the oven of Santa Eulalia.

Near the ruins complex is the relatively new (opened in 1986) **national museum of Roman art of Mérida**, housing some 32,000 pieces of Roman art and artifacts. The museum itself is a monumental work in pale-brick vaulted interiors, designed by Rafael Moneo, chairman of the department of architecture at the Harvard University Graduate School of Design. Constructed especially for the collection, which is housed on three open levels, the museum is one of the most interesting anywhere. In the process of construction, a Roman road was unearthed and incorporated into the building's basement. Many of the objects in the collection were stored for centuries in the old Iglesia de Santa Clara, and others were gathered from other corners of Spain. The huge mosaics set into walls and floors are the most exquisite displays, but the statuary, religious pieces, coins, jewelry, and everyday objects are all excellent.

Once again, here is an Extremaduran town with a parador to visit as well as to stay in. Called the **Parador Vía de la Plata**, this inn was once a convent, itself built on the site of a palace that housed the Pretorian Guard in Roman times. The historic mix shows interestingly in the decor, which incorporates many antiquities in its furnishings and is even rather Andalusian in feeling. Rooms have lovely amenities such as embroidered pillows on the bedsteads and balconies over the convent garden. The food, stressing regional cuisine, is among the best of the paradors. Another good hotel with a history is the **Emperatriz**, right on the main square, the plaza de España. It occupies a 16th-century seignorial mansion with a central patio garden. Just outside of town is the big, modern, comfortable, and new **Hotel Las Lomas**.

Alange is a little town, about a 20-minute drive south of Mérida on back roads, that is rather intriguing. It is a spa, one of three in the region, where people come for a long list of cures. The waters, rich in calcium, magnesium, and sodium bicarbonate, bubble up from ancient springs. People come here to drink from, bathe in, and spray themselves with the same waters and in the same actual baths enjoyed by the Romans. There are two large indoor pools, covered with cupolas and resembling the public baths in Istanbul—without the fine mosaics. The spa occupies a small, former Arab castle, which became a retreat for the Knights of Santiago. Taking the cure in a historically landmarked spa is rather fun; however, non-Spanish-speaking participants may have a hard time following the prescribed recipes and treatments.

Badajoz is worthy of mention if only because it is the last major stop in Spain on the main route from Madrid or Mérida to Estremoz and Lisbon in Portugal. The town occupies a hill on the left bank of the río Guadiana, 6.5 km (4 miles) from the Portuguese border. The bridge over the river, Puente de Palmas, was designed by Juan de Herrera in 1596 and was built on Roman foundations. It is rather grand—1,909 feet long with 32 arches. There are substantial remains of Moorish occupation dotting the surrounding hills.

In town, look for the recently reopened **Museo Arqueológico**, housed in a 16th-century mosque on the plazoleta del Reloj. The exhibits include Roman statues, elaborate mosaics, Visigothic and Islamic artifacts, and cases of stone carvings, silver jewelry, coins, medical instruments, and pottery.

Medellín

Don't consider staying in or going to Medellín, 24 km (15 miles) due east of Mérida, for any other reason than that Hernán Cortés, conquistador par excellence and conqueror of Mexico, came from here. His family was of the minor nobility but, as a younger son, he knew he would receive no inheritance. After studying law, he joined the army and later departed for the New World. There, with his Extremaduran training and a handful of men, he brought down the Aztec Empire and claimed Mexican lands and riches for Spain. His tall bronze statue standing in the village square, with plaques listing his Mexican victories, leaves little doubt that here was a man of unusual arrogance and, undoubtedly, exceptional courage.

There is little else of note to see in tiny, whitewashed Medellín, except the 17th-century bridge over the río Guadiana and the crumbling castle on the hill above town. It is hard to find anyone who knows its history, although it certainly dates to the Middle Ages. The main church—like many in Extremadura—opens only for services, and none seems to follow a schedule except on Sundays.

Zafra

Zafra, rather Andalusian in character, about 60 km (40 miles) due south of Mérida on the way to Seville, is the belle of southern Extremadura. Known as Zafar under the Moors, it was the seat of the dukes of Feria, the first of whom in 1437 built a fortified *alcázar* (castle) with six great round towers. The massive stone structure, right in town, has been converted into the **Parador Hernán Cortés**, complete with its own chapel bearing a splendid golden cupola and a Sala Dorada with a richly carved gold ceiling. The central marble patio is thought to have been designed by Juan de Herrera, Philip II's favorite architect, who was responsible for such works as El Escorial and the cathedral at Valladolid.

You can park at the parador and walk to every place of interest; it's almost next door to the old town plazas. Across from the inn are two artisan stores with a good selection of pottery, baskets, and other crafts that show the Andalusian influence.

Zafra owes its fortified look to the military orders of Santiago and Alcántara, and its artistic legacy to the Ferias, who were as wealthy as they were cultured.

The old town is grouped around the arcaded 18th-century plaza Grande and the 14th-century plaza Chica. These are lovely, arcaded squares, with low white houses and iron-work balconies ablaze with flowers. Just between the two plazas is a granite *vara* column, which served as a measure for length in the Middle Ages when Zafra was a major market town. The city is still known for its cattle fairs, the most important of which is the Feria de San Miguel, held during the first week of October.

The most important religious site in town is the **Iglesia Colegiata de la Candelaria**, built by a duke of Feria in 1546 and identified by its massive red-brick belfry. Inside are altarpieces executed by Zurbarán in a side chapel and by José de Churriguera on the main altar. Lorenzo Suárez de Figueroa, who was the town's benefactor and the first duke of Feria, and his wife are buried in alabaster tombs in the convent of Santa Clara, built in the 15th century.

A short walk from the Parador Hernán Cortés and just outside the wall that forms the parador entrance is a second good hotel, the **Huerta Honda**, which is built in the popular, low architectural style around a central patio with a pool. Its restaurant is one of the most attractive in the region and certainly tops in both food (look forward to the desserts) and wine.

Jerez de los Caballeros

As you drive west from Zafra through the rolling hills of the Sierra del Castellar, after some 48 km (30 miles) the Baroque towers of Jerez de los Caballeros rise out of the Ardila plain. The old market town has the distinction of being the birthplace of Vasco Núñez de Balboa, who first crossed the Darien Isthmus (now Panama) and discovered the Southern Sea (the Pacific Ocean). Hernando de Soto, the first to explore the Mississippi, was born in the nearby town of Barcarrota; he also lived in Jerez in a whitewashed house at Hernando de Soto 1. Anyone in town can lead you to it, although you're not allowed to enter. A visit to Jerez is of interest primarily to those committed to following in the footsteps of the conquistadores.

The 13th-century **castle of the Templars**, perched on the rocks above the town, is built in the shape of a rectangle. In the 14th century, the Knights (*caballeros*) did battle for their lives, and lost, in the Torre Sangrienta (bloody tower). Their order was officially dissolved and the town handed over to the Knights of Santiago, who built many noble mansions, churches, and convents in Jerez. Next to the castle is the Iglesia de Santa María, a Baroque church built on a former Visigothic site.

The **plaza de España** in the center of town is dominated by the massive and richly decorated Torre de San Miguel of the church of the same name. Its outstanding exterior features—more interesting than those in the interior—are two Neoclassical doorways, one carved in granite and the other in white marble.

Another notable tower crowns the **Iglesia de San Bartolomé**; not unlike the Giralda in Seville, it is richly covered with polychrome tiles to match the blue and gold of the church below. Located in the upper part of town, the church houses a magnificent 16th-century tomb containing the remains of Don Vasco de Jerez and his wife. The baptistery, a 15th-century Gothic-style chapel, is the oldest part of the church.

San Bartolomé is the town's patron saint. His feast day, August 24, is marked with festivities and processions.

The history of the Jerez de los Caballeros area goes much further back than the age of the discoverers—all the way to prehistoric times in fact, as evidenced by the megalithic **Dolmen de Toniñuelu**, 5 km (3 miles) northwest of town in a pasture known as La Granja (the farm). Solar symbols carved on the monument suggest its builders were sun-worshippers.

Olivenza

Among the dozens of little towns to explore in Extremadura, one of the few reminders of things not from a Moorish or even Spanish past is Olivenza. Its historic outlook is toward Portugal. In the thirteenth century the town was given to Beatrice of Castile by her brother on the occasion of her marriage to the infante Don Afonso of Portugal; it was subsequently ruled by Afonso's son Dinis. In 1607 it was occupied by the Spanish and in 1801 ceded to Spain during the War of the Oranges. Bloody battles were fought on the same ground by Wellington in 1811.

Just a few miles from the Portuguese border (80 km/50 miles northwest of Zafra and about the same distance southwest of Mérida), and surrounded by olive grove country, Olivenza has remained a part of Spain, but it has a very definite Portuguese look. The tell-tale signs—the elegant, twisting columns that were hallmark architecture during the period of Manuel I at the end of the 15th century—dominate the Baroque sanctuary of Iglesia Santa María Magdalena. The church is said to have been designed by the brothers Diego and Francisco de Arruda, architects of the Hieronymite monastery and Belem tower in Lisbon. This Portuguese design in Spain is unique to Olivenza.

The same hallmark columns decorate the façade of the municipal library, and there is a glorious little chapel in Casa de la Misericordia that is covered in Portuguese *azulejos*. Those blue-and-white tiles also decorate the Hospital de la Caridado. Spain has declared the town a national treasure and installed the **Extremadura ethnographic museum** in the old royal bakery. The museum houses exhibits of local customs, showing methods of agriculture, and crafts such as ceramics, embroidery, and ironwork. There are also some archaeological artifacts.

GETTING AROUND

The best way to navigate about Extremadura is by car—in fact, it's about the only way. There is air service from Madrid to Badajoz, which offers little of interest and is not even a well-located center from which to visit the regional highlights.

The Spanish railways run escorted overnight trips on summer weekends from Madrid to both Mérida and Cáceres, which provide rather nice and inexpensive excursions for a sampling of either city. The programs include rail transport, sightseeing, some meals, and a choice of accommodations.

But most visitors come to Extremadura by road, into the northern area from Madrid and into the southern from Seville. There are many new roads in the region, and the going is just fine when driving on the major red roads and secondary green ones indicated on road maps. Those marked in yellow will usually mean rough riding.

The most direct road to the north leads to Plasencia and Cáceres, via Talavera (160 km/100 miles from Madrid) and Oropesa. The national highway bends at Oropesa, with a right turn north and eventually west to Jarandilla (64 km/40 miles), Plasencia (another 64 km/40 miles), and Cáceres (another 88 km/55 miles). On your way from Madrid, Jarandilla is a good place to stop the first night. The roads into the region are windy and hilly, but perfectly easy to follow.

Another lovely drive—again with twists and turns—into the north of the region is from Salamanca, coming south via Ciudad Rodrigo toward Coria, Alcántara, and Cáceres or from Ciudad Rodrigo to Plasencia.

Trujillo is a straight run east from Cáceres (57 km/36 miles, well under an hour), and Mérida to the south (80 km/50 miles) is an easy hour-or-less drive. Medellín is an hour east of Mérida. From either Mérida or Medellín it is an uphill, twisting, and very scenic run northeast to Guadalupe.

The road from Seville (take N 630) comes up from the south to Zafra and Mérida. En route from Seville, there is a turnoff just past Santa Olalla onto C 434; then at Fregenal de la Sierra take N 435, which leads to Jerez de los Caballeros, via some 80 km (50 miles) on a secondary road. Taking the long way from Seville to include Jerez is a pretty drive, but don't count on going farther than Zafra when coming from Seville. It's an easy 48 km (30 miles) between Zafra and Mérida.

The Alentejo province of Portugal, sitting on Extremadura's western border, offers additional access to the region. The main road comes from Lisbon via Estremoz into Badajoz, which is well worth detouring; go straight to Mérida. Farther north, cars from Castelo Branco can cross the border at Alcántara en route to Cáceres. The last hill town in Portugal, Marvão, is a gem of a place to stay the night, or at least to have lunch, at the small parador; it provides a perfect view of the plain of Spain.

ACCOMMODATIONS REFERENCE

When dialing telephone numbers from outside the country, drop the 9 in the area code.

► **Alcántara.** Virgen de Guadalupe 14, 10001 **Cáceres.** Tel: (927) 22-89-00.

► **Alfonso VIII.** Alfonso VIII 34, 10600 **Plasencia.** Tel: (927) 41-02-50.

► **Parador de Cáceres.** Calle Ancha 6, 10001 **Cáceres.** Tel: (927) 21-17-59.

► **Parador Carlos V.** 10450 **Jarandilla de la Vera.** Tel: (927) 56-01-17.

► **Hotel Emperatriz.** Plaza de España 19, 06800 **Mérida.** Tel: (924) 31-31-11.

► **Extremadura.** Virgen de Guadalupe 5, 10001 **Cáceres.** Tel: (927) 22-16-00.

▸ **Parador Hernán Cortés**, Plaza Corazón de María 7, 06300 **Zafra**. Tel: (924) 55-02-00.

▸ **Hotel Huerta Honda.** López Azme 30, 06300 **Zafra**. Tel: (924) 55-08-00.

▸ **Hotel Las Lomas.** Carretera Madrid km 338, 06800 **Mérida**. Tel: (924) 31-10-11.

▸ **Hostal Pizarro.** Plaza Mayor 13, 10200 **Trujillo**. Tel: (927) 32-02-55.

▸ **Hospedería Real Monasterio.** Plaza Juan Carlos I, 10140 **Guadalupe**. Tel: (927) 36-70-00.

▸ **Parador de Trujillo.** Plaza de Santa Clara, 10200 **Trujillo**. Tel: (927) 32-13-50.

▸ **Parador Virrey Toledo.** 45460 **Oropesa**. Tel: (925) 43-00-00.

▸ **Parador Vía de la Plata.** Plaza de la Constitución 3, 06800 **Mérida**. Tel: (924) 31-38-00.

▸ **Parador Zurbarán.** Marqués de la Romana 10, 10140 **Guadalupe**. Tel: (927) 36-70-75.

ANDALUSIA

By Robert Packard

Robert Packard has written many articles about Spain. His work has been published in the travel section of The New York Times *and the* Philadelphia Inquirer *and in* Connoisseur *and* Travel & Leisure *magazines. He is also the author of a book on writers and places,* Refractions *(1990). A resident of New York City and Maine, he visits Spain frequently.*

"For half the world the image of Spain is the image of Andalusia," writes Jan Morris. Andalusia's climate and culture are distinctive; the language is that of Spain, but the fires are banked differently. Andalusia (pronounced an-da-loo-THEE-a in Spanish) occupies the entire southern portion of the Iberian Peninsula, an area as large as Portugal—and the rest of Spain often finds Andalusia hard to take: too much sunshine, goes the claim, and too little attention paid to the hard currency of life.

The landscape of this Andalusian world includes extensive Mediterranean and Atlantic seacoasts. The terrain—"in variety, strangeness and grandeur, the Spanish landscape is unequalled in Europe," in the words of V. S. Pritchett—boasts mountain areas as diverse as the white Moorish hill-town Baetic range, the snow-capped Sierra Nevadas with Spain's highest continental peak near Granada, and the wild Alpujarras immediately to their south. Scattered about Andalusia like so many architectural jewels are the mosque at Córdoba, the Alhambra at Granada, and the cathedral at Seville.

All those stereotypical "Spanish" images come to life in Andalusia: flamenco, bullfighting, Sherry bodegas, beach cabañas, gazpacho, horse breeding, religious rituals, gypsy music, and fiestas that take over entire communities. Andalusia has forests of dark pine, embankments of sheer rock, flowers of tropical radiance, wildlife sanctuaries, streets lined with orange and lemon trees, whitewashed houses with inner courtyards, black-iron window grilles, mantillas, long flounced dresses, skin-tight dark trousers, Cordoban brimmed hats, fans, guitars, and a climate to swear by.

But Andalusia is not some mindless sun-drenched retreat. The real world intrudes. A particularly haunting Andalusian reminder of the intransigence of fate pervades the atmosphere. Death still comes in the afternoon here, hooded penitents recall unspeakable acts in the name of the Inquisition, and the darkness may carry the spine-tingling wail of the *saeta*—that lament of the faithful during Holy Week. Despite the international high life on the Costa del Sol, Andalusia also continues to have one of the highest unemployment rates in Spain.

From prehistoric times Andalusia has been a center of culture on the Iberian Peninsula. The Phoenician/Punic (Carthaginian) culture was of inestimable importance to the development of pre-Roman Iberian culture (so called) in southern Spain. The Phoenicians set up colonies on the coast near Málaga in the eighth century B.C. Spectacular Phoenician bronze statuettes have been found at Huelva, on the coast near Portugal, for example. Imports of art and other artifacts from Greece and the Greek colonies were a common feature of life in the Phoenician and Carthaginian towns along the coast here from very early times until the Roman occupation. In the fifth and fourth centuries B.C. there was a very prosperous Carthaginian city at Gadir (Cádiz); the Phoenicians from Tyre, ancestors of the Carthaginians, probably had had a flourishing base at Gadir three centuries earlier. Even the oldest parts of the Puerta de Sevilla at Seville have been attributed to the Carthaginians.

The Romans called the area Baetica; the Visigoths, Vandalusia (land of the Vandals); the Moors, Al-Andalus. When for 600 years Spain was part of the Roman Empire, Córdoba served as an administrative hub; when for almost 800 years the Moors were a presence in Spain, Córdoba became one of the intellectual capitals of the entire Medieval world of Europe; during Spain's all-powerful Golden Age Renaissance, Seville was by royal decree the gateway to the Americas. And now, at a time when economic recovery for Spain as a member of the European Community is vital, Andalusia leads the country in annual tourism revenue.

The rest of Spain has rarely looked kindly upon the

people of Andalusia, and foreign observers often add to the abuse. One of the milder derogatory comments came from George Borrow, the classic English writer on Spain, a century and a half ago: "The Andalusians, in all estimable traits of character are . . . as far below the other Spaniards as the country they inhabit is superior in beauty and fertility to the other provinces of Spain." But Andalusians tolerate the disapproval of others: They attribute it to ungovernable envy.

"Andalusia is *sol y sombra* both—sun on one side of the street, shadow on the other: a mirror both of Spain's delight and of her poverty," writes Jan Morris. But Andalusia does not fall so easily into bullring classification. For Spaniards the shadowed *sombra* is both the more desirable and the more expensive of seats; it is the gringos who want to sit in the sun.

MAJOR INTEREST FOR THE SEVILLE-CORDOBA-GRANADA TRIANGLE

Seville
Cathedral, Patio de los Naranjos, and Giralda
Alcázar
Gardens and parks
Hospital de la Caridad
Casa de Pilato
Museo de Bellas Artes
Barrio de Santa Cruz
Archivo General de Indias
University
Itálica and the Museo Arqueológico Provincial
Shopping
Festivals

Córdoba
The Mezquita-Catedral
The Roman bridge
La Judería (the Jewish quarter)
Cordoban leather
Museo Arqueológico
Palacio del Marqués de Viana
May Festival
The Medina Azahara

The Andalusian Northeast
Ubeda
Baeza
Cazorla

Cazorla national park
Jaén

Granada
The Alcazaba
The Alhambra
Palacio de Charles V
The Generalife
La Cartuja
The cathedral
The royal chapel
The Sierra Nevada and Alpujarras mountains

MAJOR INTEREST FOR THE ANDALUSIAN COAST

Western Costa de la Luz

Doñana national park
Palos de la Frontera

Moguer

Jerez de la Frontera
Sherry bodegas

Cádiz

The White Towns
Arcos de la Frontera
Ronda

Málaga
Picasso in Málaga
Museo de Bellas Artes
The Alcazaba
The Roman amphitheater
The cathedral

The Costa del Sol East of Málaga
Nerja
Almería

The Costa del Sol West of Málaga
Torremolinos
Mijas
Marbella
Casares

Music and dance seem indigenous to Andalusia. Even the most ardent northerner will acknowledge that flamenco developed principally in the region of Andalusia. The roots of *cante* (Spanish song) lie in stylistic traits common to Arabic, Jewish, Byzantine, and even Hindu music: the repetition of a single note and the use of pitches not found in Western scales. Certainly Andalusia has been the chosen home of Arabs, Jews, Byzantines, and gypsies of Indian heritage. The *soleares* and other song forms are said to have sprung from the Triana gypsy quarter of Seville. Even the names of songs evoke Andalusia: *rondena* (Ronda), *malagueña* (Málaga), *granadinas* (Granada). Beneath the haunting surface of all that Spanish music lies a strain of melancholy, a characteristic motif that links it forever, say the Andalusians, to their region.

In the 1840s *cafés cantantes* began to open in Seville, Cádiz, Jerez, and other Andalusian cities, creating a home for performances of flamenco song and dance as well as flamenco guitar playing. Purists will tell you that most of today's public presentations are on a degraded commercial level and that the art of flamenco is rarely honored in its true sense. Finding performances of first-rate flamenco dancers, singers, and guitarists is difficult, but even those of a secondary level can provide a festive evening. Ask your hotel concierge for recommendations. There is a varied selection of flamenco clubs in Granada's Sacramonte section; in the villages around Córdoba; and among Seville's flamenco "halls" or theater-nightclubs. During the summer Cádiz, Jerez, and Seville have flamenco competitions. Jerez offers a summer course on Flamenco Art, organized by the Catedra de Flamencologia. Many of the nightclubs in the Costa del Sol's Torremolinos and Marbella area offer flamenco shows.

The Food of Andalusia

Food experts complain that every section of Spain lays claim to national dishes that turn out to have originated in other parts of the country. Gazpacho, however, seems legitimately Andalusian; probably of African origin, it usually contains tomatoes, bread, olive oil, garlic, and pepper, but there are many regional variations. Andalusia claims the best ham in the country, the Jabugo of Huelva, although Granadians maintain that their Trevélez rivals it. Deep-fried fish is probably the most frequently served dish of Andalusia; on the Atlantic coast, Cádiz often fries different species (sole, mullet, whiting) in the same pan; Málaga on the Mediterranean fries fresh baby anchovies. Every variety of shellfish appears on Andalusian tables. Garlic soup, especially in

Málaga, often has an egg floating on top and white grapes resting on the bottom.

A rather special Andalusian dish beloved of Granada is the *tortilla Sacramonte,* an omelet whose ingredients (fried and breaded brain together with veal and lamb sweetbreads) makes it not for every taste. Córdoba loves ox-tail stew, and Seville has a special fondness for stew with tripe. Veal chops anywhere in Andalusia are close to incorruptible. Fresh fruit, vegetables, crusty bread, and, of course, local Sherries and wines are also special treats in Andalusia. *Tapas* are best found, according to Spanish food expert Penelope Casas, "where they originated—in Andalusia. Seville in particular is *tapas* heaven." Nonetheless, according to Somerset Maugham, "in Andalusia you eat romantically rather than to the satisfaction of your palate."

The Wines of Andalusia

Andalusia is home to four *denominaciones de origen*—Condado de Huelva, Málaga, Montilla-Moriles, and Jerez-Xeres-Sherry—all primarily engaged in producing fortified wines.

Condado de Huelva wines are the descendants of the wines of Lepe mentioned by Chaucer in "The Pardoner's Tale." Huelva's Atlantic climate produces light dry wines of the fino and amontillado family from the native Zalema grape and the Palomino of Jerez, but here these *solera*-system wines are called *condado pálido* (pale). *Condados viejos* (old) can run the spectrum from dry to sweet. Some light, fresh, dry white table wines are also made from Zalema grapes.

The wines of this area could receive a great deal of attention in 1992 during the huge celebrations to commemorate the 500th anniversary of the discovery of the Americas. In all probability, Christopher Columbus provisioned his ships with Condado wines when he sailed from the Huelva port of Palos on his first voyage.

Mentioned in literature since Roman times, **Málaga** wines come from mountain vineyards north and east of the capital of the famous Costa del Sol. Málaga is an intensely sweet, rich, raisiny, walnut-colored wine made from Pedro Ximénez and Moscatel grapes. The wines of Málaga improve with age almost indefinitely. Lagrima, which Richard Ford called "ruby tears," is a rare Málaga made from the essence of sun-concentrated grapes pressed by their own weight. Sip Málaga or pour it over ice cream. Like cream

Sherry, it goes exceptionally well with coffee. For those with a sweet tooth, Scholtz Hermanos or López Hermanos are brands to look for.

Considered by Frank Schoonmaker to be "one of the best aperitif wines in the world," **Montilla-Moriles** wines come from the hill country near Córdoba. In the heat of Córdoba's scorching summer the Pedro Ximénez grape achieves wines of 15.5 percent alcohol naturally, so Montilla finos are not generally fortified with grape spirits. Consequently they are lighter, finer, and more delicate than many Sherries, and greatly admired in many parts of Andalusia. Montilla wines are fermented in huge earthenware *tinajas* and then enter a *solera* system (see the Sherry section below). Montilla produces a range of finos, amontillados (a name derived from Montilla), olorosos, and creams, plus incredibly rich Pedro Ximénez wines. Look for Alvear Fino.

(The wines of Jerez are discussed in that section.)

—Gerry Dawes

Holy Week

Celebrations of Semana Santa (Holy Week), from Palm Sunday to Easter, lead all other spectacles in Spain. Not surprisingly, those in Andalusia top those of the rest of the country. Seville, in turn, outdoes her Andalusian neighbors. In almost every community, no matter how small, there are observances that recall the trials of Christ and the tears of the Virgin.

Holy Week processions profoundly alter the routine of daily life, and you will find that travel is radically changed with respect to freedom of movement, business hours (or days!) for shops, restaurants, and offices of all kinds, and securing hotel reservations. But Holy Week is a major aspect of Spain's culture, and regardless of your religious or ethnic background, you will witness a unique and extravagant spectacle.

Many Andalusian cities and towns have distinctive Holy Week rituals: In Arcos there is a running of the bulls on Easter Sunday; in Málaga (a close second in pageantry to Seville) parishioners go directly from Easter Mass to the season's first corrida in the bullring; on Good Friday in Córdoba a full symphony orchestra and chorus occupy the cathedral within the mosque; in Granada the ladies dress in black, with mantillas and jewelry, and walk along with the religious floats.

On Palm Sunday everywhere the church ornaments are

draped in black; parishioners take home blessed palm branches to adorn every balcony. Every day of Holy Week is marked by regalia of different color: The sound of "thunder" fills the Seville cathedral on Wednesday, and again on Saturday, when every bell in the city is tolled. No city in Spain surpasses Seville when it comes to processions; there may be 30 or more in a 24-hour period. *Pasos* (floats) carry startlingly life-like polychrome figures depicting the scenes of the Passion: the Last Supper, the Garden of Olives, the Descent from the Cross. Many processioners wear long robes and *capuchones* (pointed hoods that cover their faces except for two eye slits), evoking the Spanish Inquisition and, for Americans, the Ku Klux Klan. Many, barefoot as a testament to humility and suffering, carry yard-long candles; some carry crosses to atone for sins.

The streets are darkened, melancholy wails of the *saeta* rend the air. The Christ figures are startlingly realistic, with blood from wounds and expressions of intense agony. Each parish displays its particular Virgin, crowned, extravagantly garbed and bejewelled, but always with crystal tears on her sanctified, innocent cheeks.

Hotel reservations must be made well in advance (at least a year in Seville), and rates everywhere are substantially higher. Holy Week in Andalusia has no equal: an extraordinary fusion of religious intensity, civic competitiveness, atavistic ritual, and high drama.

Bullfighting

Once an activity of the upper classes, bullfighting evolved from such lofty social beginnings to become a popular spectacle. For centuries the nobility bred the bulls, then fought them in front of the king and his court. But with the advent of the Bourbon dynasty in the 18th century and Philip V's disdain for the activity, bullfighting became what is surely one of Spain's great expressions of popular enthusiasm.

The first professional bullfighter is said to have been Andalusian, Pedro Romero of Ronda, who in the late 1700s reputedly killed over 5,000 bulls without any injury to himself. An inscription in the Ronda bullring museum states that in 1771, at the age of 17, he killed his first bull.

Bullfighting was then at its most primitive: The object was simply to kill the bull. Today the spectacle is a pageant, with so many intricate appurtenances that it has become an art form. As in life, a bullfight has spectators who sit in the torrid sun (*sol*) and those who sit in the cool shade (*sombra*); seats in the sun are (surprise!) cheaper and more numerous. The bullfight season in Spain opens in March and ends on October 12. Virtually every town in Andalusia, celebrating local fiestas, offers a bullfight in its own bullring.

Andalusia's immense size—just a bit smaller than Portugal—seems at first glance to hinder a coherent plan for visiting major points of interest, but in fact the eight provinces (Huelva, Cádiz, Seville, Córdoba, Jaén, Granada, Málaga, and Almería) are readily accessible by car over mostly good, if sometimes mountainous, roads. And the road signs are excellent. But if you do get lost, the worst tactic is to produce a map, an artifact that will stimulate avid interest and no recognition. The name of the nearest large town on your route, on the other hand, spoken in a vigorous tone, invariably results in directional assistance, sometimes accompanied by an offer of personal guidance. Málaga has the largest international airport in Andalusia, and Seville will soon double the size of its air facilities. Trains connect all but inland mountain towns. Bus service is available everywhere, but it varies from ultramodern to primitive.

First we cover the Seville-Córdoba-Granada triangle, for which Seville is the air gateway. Córdoba is a possible—though rushed—day trip from Seville by train; Granada, though linked to Seville by rail, is not. East of Córdoba and north of Granada, on the way to Madrid, are the historic towns of northeastern Andalusia, among them Jaén and Ubeda. South of Granada—and usually visible from town—is the Sierra Nevada mountain range.

The second main area covered in Andalusia is the coast: south along the Atlantic and the Mediterranean, separated by Gibraltar.

We start on the coast at the Costa de la Luz, with Jerez and Cádiz southwest of Seville, and nearby Doñana national park and other places on the Atlantic west toward Portugal's Algarve. After them we move east of Jerez inland through the Moorish white towns, starting with Arcos de la Frontera and ending at Ronda (and even farther east, if you are driving to Granada, at the inland resort of La Bobadilla).

Málaga is next, due south of La Bobadilla (and of Córdoba farther to the north). Málaga is the central city—and the major air gateway—for the Mediterranean's Costa del Sol. After Málaga we go first to the east and Almería, the less-developed part of the coast, then west through the famous resorts of Torremolinos and Marbella, to finish past Gibraltar

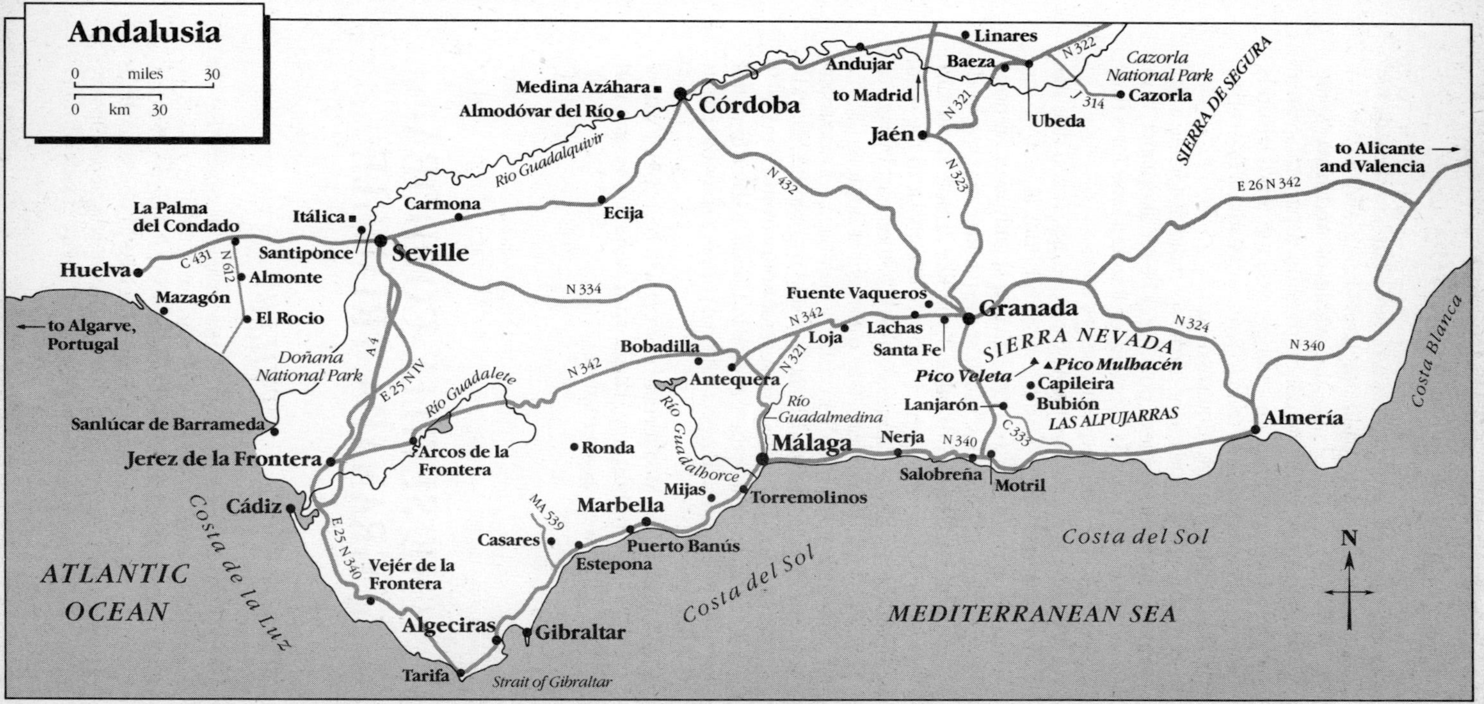
Andalusia
0 miles 30
0 km 30
Medina Azáhara
Almodóvar del Río
Córdoba
Andujar
to Madrid
Linares
Baeza
Ubeda
N 322
Cazorla
National Park
J 314
Cazorla
SIERRA DE SEGURA
Jaén
N 321
N 323
to Alicante
and Valencia
E 26 N 342
Río Guadalquivir
N 432
La Palma
del Condado
Itálica
Carmona
Ecija
Santiponce
Seville
Huelva
C 431
N 612
Almonte
Mazagón
El Rocio
to Algarve,
Portugal
Doñana
National Park
N 334
A 4
E 25 N IV
Fuente Vaqueros
Granada
N 342
Lachas
Loja
Santa Fe
N 324
N 340
SIERRA NEVADA
Pico Veleta
Pico Mulbacén
Capileira
Bubión
LAS ALPUJARRAS
Lanjarón
C 333
Bobadilla
Antequera
N 321
Río
Guadalmedina
Río Guadalhorce
Río Guadalete
Sanlúcar de Barrameda
Jerez de la Frontera
Arcos de la
Frontera
Ronda
Málaga
Nerja
N 340
Salobreña
Motril
Almería
Costa Blanca
Cádiz
Mijas
Torremolinos
MA 539
Marbella
Casares
Puerto Banús
Estepona
E 25 N 340
Vejér de la
Frontera
Algeciras
Gibraltar
Tarifa
Strait of Gibraltar
Costa de la Luz
ATLANTIC
OCEAN
Costa del Sol
Costa del Sol
MEDITERRANEAN SEA
N

on the eastern end of the Costa de la Luz, on the Atlantic coast, almost back to Cádiz and Jerez.

While we cover almost the whole of Andalusia, some travellers may prefer to concentrate on a particular area. Using Seville as a base, for example, you can make leisurely day-long visits by car or train to Jerez and Cádiz; a day trip to Doñana national park requires a car.

The Moorish white towns are so splendid that while a day trip by car from Seville is possible, a better alternative is to make Jerez, Arcos de la Frontera, or Ronda a base for a two-day visit to these infrequently visited spots.

Granada is also a fine locale for side trips. If you find the snow-peaked Sierra Nevadas an irresistible aspect of the Alhambra panorama, you can drive in slightly over an hour to the peaks themselves, lunch at the parador, and, depending on the season, ski or hike. If you like remote mountain towns and don't mind the narrow roads, a visit to the wild Alpujarras (south of Granada on N 323, then east by way of Lanjarón) will delight you. Stay overnight at Bubión.

Although many travellers visit the Jaén-Baeza-Ubeda triangle of northeastern Andalusia as a side trip on the Madrid–Costa del Sol drive, they are several hours from Granada; if you stay overnight at the parador in Ubeda, a day trip to the scenically beautiful Cazorla national park is a splendid possibility.

Visitors to the Mediterranean coast will be happier with a base outside of bustling Málaga, with Nerja to the east and Mijas to the west as alternatives.

THE SEVILLE-CORDOBA-GRANADA TRIANGLE

SEVILLE

While Andalusia may not be the image of Spain, Seville certainly seems to epitomize Andalusia. Seville makes an effort to play the starring role in every Andalusian production. Other Andalusian cities look upon Seville as one who grabs the best parts and then graciously asks for assistance. Observers are fond of playing a *yin* and *yang* game with Seville and neighboring Córdoba, 60 miles up río Guadalquivir. Seville emerges as flirtatious, beguiling, theatrical, and given on occasion to the kind of exaggerated piety that foreshadows unrestrained revelry. Córdoba, on the other hand, comes off as handsome, unaffected, intellectual, and sere to the point of aridity.

Even the most sanguine Sevillano would acknowledge that the annual *pasos* and penitents of Holy Week (mile after mile of floats of religious figures accompanied by funeral dirges wailed in the candlelit darkness), followed by the annual Feria (fair week) of dancing, costumes, horses, bulls, music, song, and not a little vino, represent a more than passing flair for public display. Civic reticence has never been a Sevillian attribute, and nature bedecked the city appropriately: The streets and boulevards are lined with orange trees, the parks lush with exotic blooms, the hours of sunshine unsurpassed.

Unlikely as it seems, the spirit that pervades and motivates Seville today stems from the city's victory over the Moors in 1248. For Seville, the Reconquest was quite simply a triumph of Christ over Mohammed; the Catholic Church ultimately conferred sainthood on the conqueror, Ferdinand III, who chose to live in Seville during his lifetime. Seville's gigantic Gothic cathedral, its obsession with Christian ritual, its uninhibited expressions of grief and joy—all are in nature lineal from the Reconquest.

In the flush of Spain's Golden Age Seville became the country's leading city. The Guadalquivir (more navigable then than today) brought, by royal decree, America's wealth to her docks. Under Philip II in the 16th century, Seville had worldwide political importance, reflecting its overseas trade monopoly as Spain's most important port. The city's subsequent fall from prominence mirrors the decline of Spain itself after the Renaissance. No industries were created; banking and commerce fell into the hands of foreigners; war debts ruined the economy.

Seville came to know dark days: four years of occupation by the French during the Napoleonic Wars; a Civil War period as a fascist base in Andalusia. But on the positive side, the inauguration of the annual Feria in 1847 heralded the touristic invasion of Seville, and the Ibero-American Exposition of 1929 brought worldwide attention to the city.

For today's visitors a cautionary note, struck with some insistence, warns that petty crime in Seville is on a par with

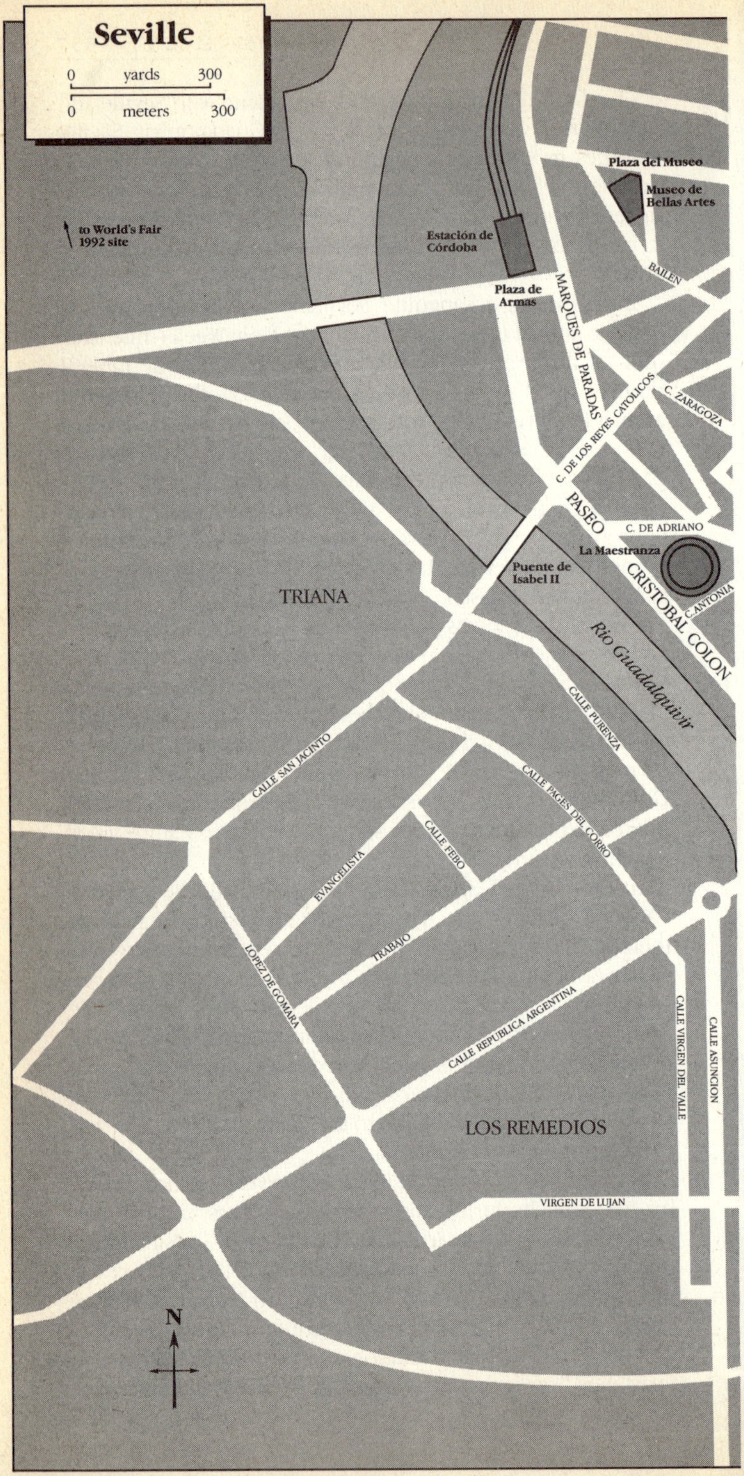

Seville
0 yards 300
0 meters 300
Plaza del Museo
Museo de Bellas Artes
to World's Fair 1992 site
Estación de Córdoba
Plaza de Armas
MARQUES DE PARADAS
BAILEN
C. DE LOS REYES CATOLICOS
C. ZARAGOZA
PASEO
C. DE ADRIANO
La Maestranza
CRISTOBAL COLON
Puente de Isabel II
C. ANTONIA
TRIANA
Rio Guadalquivir
CALLE PURENZA
CALLE SAN JACINTO
CALLE PAGES DEL CORRO
CALLE FEBO
EVANGELISTA
TRABAJO
LOPEZ DE GOMARA
CALLE REPUBLICA ARGENTINA
CALLE VIRGEN DEL VALLE
CALLE ASUNCION
LOS REMEDIOS
VIRGEN DE LUJAN
N

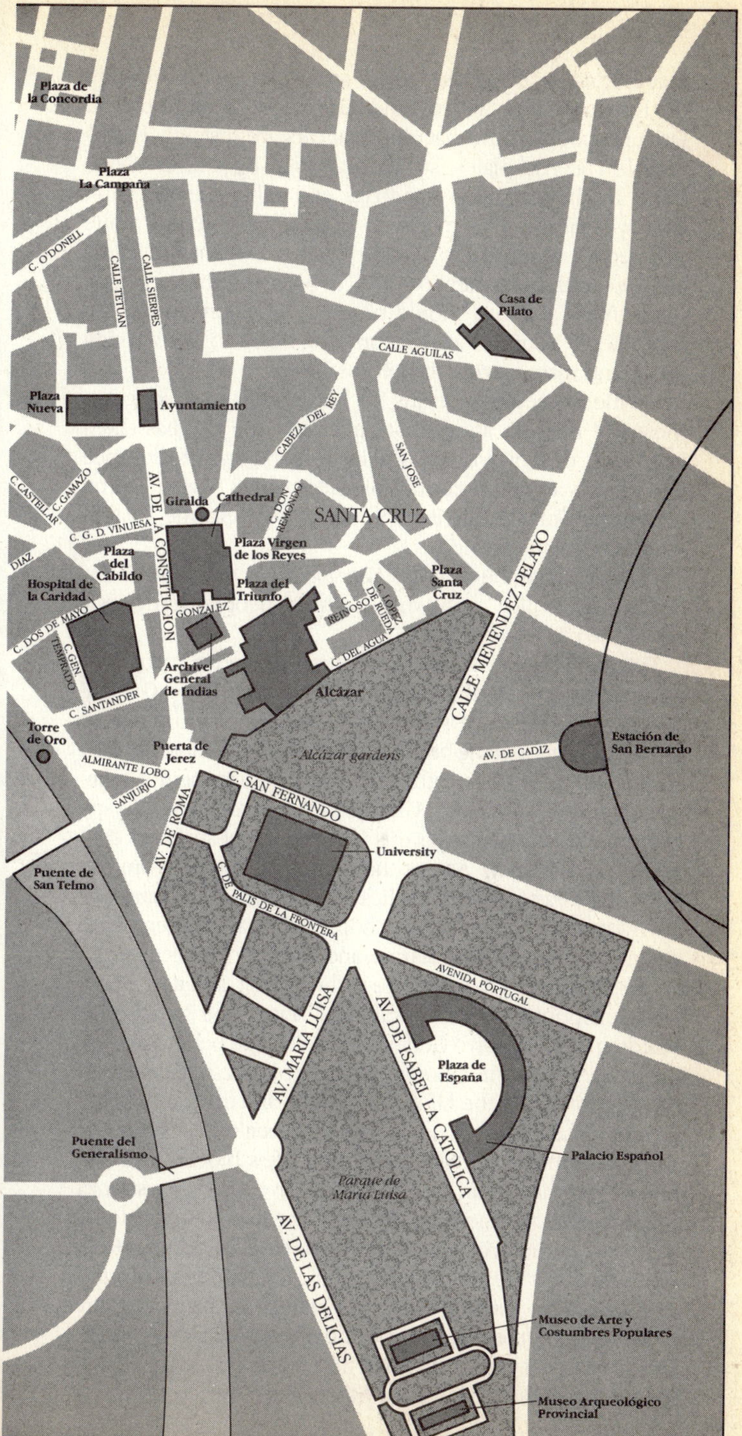
Plaza de la Concordia
Plaza La Campaña
C. O'DONELL
CALLE TETUAN
CALLE SIERPES
Casa de Pilato
CALLE AGUILAS
Plaza Nueva
Ayuntamiento
CABEZA DEL REY
SAN JOSE
C. CASTELLAR
C. GAMAZO
AV. DE LA CONSTITUCION
Giralda
Cathedral
C. DON REMONDO
SANTA CRUZ
C. G. D. VINUESA
DIAZ
Plaza del Cabildo
Plaza Virgen de los Reyes
Hospital de la Caridad
Plaza del Triunfo
Plaza Santa Cruz
C. REINOSO
C. LOPEZ DE RUEDA
CALLE MENENDEZ PELAYO
GONZALEZ
C. DOS DE MAYO
C. GEN TEMPRADO
C. DEL AGUA
Archive General de Indias
Alcázar
C. SANTANDER
Torre de Oro
Puerta de Jerez
Alcázar gardens
AV. DE CADIZ
Estación de San Bernardo
ALMIRANTE LOBO
SANJURJO
C. SAN FERNANDO
AV. DE ROMA
University
Puente de San Telmo
C. DE PALIS DE LA FRONTERA
AVENIDA PORTUGAL
AV. MARIA LUISA
AV. DE ISABEL LA CATOLICA
Plaza de España
Palacio Español
Puente del Generalísmo
Parque de Maria Luisa
AV. DE LAS DELICIAS
Museo de Arte y Costumbres Populares
Museo Arqueológico Provincial

that in Rome and Naples; you are advised to keep a firm grip on handbags and wallets, and leave nothing in your car. Drivers should know that all rental cars are instantly recognizable (license plates, stickers) as such by thieves. Don't drive in the city with handbags and other valuables on display—cars are sometimes broken into even while stopped for traffic lights. Garage your car at night. Travellers are recognizable when on foot as well (clothes, camera, demeanor), and you should be especially alert during the long siesta hours when visitors are likely to be walking about and most citizens are off the streets.

Seville sometimes seems to be producing a long-run theatrical hit with appropriate matinees; the city has taken hold of its destiny with just the instinct and lack of reticence that attracts an enthusiastic audience. In 1992 Seville will be hosting a World's Fair and preparing to welcome visitors from around the world.

"I can't remember," writes *Newsweek* photographer Peter Turnley of Seville, "a city where so many people were happy about the place they live in."

For visitors, Seville's main focus of interest, centering around the cathedral, lies immediately east of río Guadalquivir where it is crossed by the Puente San Telmo. Just four blocks northeast of the bridge with its guardian Torre del Oro stands the enormous cathedral. Within the cathedral compound, the 322-foot-high Giralda tower (which you can spy from almost anywhere in this beautiful level-surfaced city) serves as a beacon. Across the plaza del Triunfo from the cathedral's eastern entrance lies the delightful old quarter of Barrio de Santa Cruz, with its shops, restaurants (often open-air, in the quarter's little plazas), and *tapas* bars; directly south across the plaza is the entrance to the Alcázar, and its gardens beyond; opposite the cathedral's south face is the Renaissance building of the Archivo General de Indias, and behind that the Museo de Arte Contemporaneo. Three blocks south, on calle San Fernando, are the Alfonso XIII hotel and the university (a former cigar factory); south of them begin the extensive gardens of the Parque de María Luisa. A few blocks northeast in this compact urban area, facing the river, is La Maestranza (Plaza de Toros); the Hospital de la Caridad is three blocks northeast of the bridge on Temprano. Three blocks north of the cathedral's western doorway on avenida de la Constitución (avenidas José Antonio and Queipo de Llano on many older maps) is the plaza Nueva, the Ayuntamiento (city hall), and the shopping district. Across the bridge, on the west bank, stretches the Barrio de Tiana with its gypsy heritage.

The Cathedral

The builders of Seville's enormous cathedral, begun in 1402, declared their intention of creating a structure so large that men would look at it and think them mad. They succeeded. Underlying their probably apocryphal assertion is a singular concern with how God would look at it. Their building, hardly accidentally, renders man insignificant: The edifice has five naves, each the size of a city street; the main altar stands at a huge crossing; the reredos, an ornamental screen behind the altar, is the largest in all Christendom. The immensity of the interior is said to be outdone only by St. Peter's in Rome and St. Paul's in London.

Built on the ruins of Seville's great mosque, which in turn had replaced a Visigoth church (and it, probably, a Roman temple), the cathedral faces west. The great main doors—today in sad need of cleaning—open only for ceremonial occasions; the public enters from an eastern door (there are nine portals in all) leading into the altar area of the building.

Nearby is the **royal chapel**, the crown and axial of a series of radiating chapels. Here, on the altar, is the silver and gold catafalque of Saint Ferdinand, the conqueror of Seville. Above the latter, surrounded by surprisingly muscular cherubs, stands the Virgin, smiling faintly and holding in her arms a doll-like Child, richly robed and crowned. She leaves this chapel every August 15 and is carried throughout the city before adoring throngs; Ferdinand even took this 13th-century Romanesque figure with him into battle. The chapel has a stunning Renaissance dome, rimmed in a series of martyr's heads in decreasing circles toward its distant center. The tombs, on either side of the pews, look toward the altar: On the left is buried Alfonso X (Ferdinand's son), young and handsome; opposite him is his mother, Beatrice, who appears not only beautiful but considerably younger than her son. Both marble heads are adorned with gold crowns.

One way to grasp the daunting architectural space within the cathedral is to walk to the extreme western end of the interior and turn around. Before you are massive column shafts, supporting huge arches, rising to a distant ceiling. The stone floor is bare. Light shines through the Flemish stained-glass windows. One single aisle is as large as the entire nave and choir of Westminster Abbey.

From this principal doorway (Puerta Mayor), you see that two immense enclosures break the long axis of the building (384 feet). The first is the *coro* (choir), now undergoing extensive restoration, almost directly in the center of the nave, with a superb grille by Francisco de Salamanca; the choir stalls, with more than 100 seats, are splendidly carved. Jan Morris suggests that in Spanish cathedrals the *coro* provides the intellectual focus of the whole building.

Beyond this choir area, at the extreme eastern point of the nave, is the *capilla mayor* (altar), the centerpiece of the entire cathedral. On three sides are gilded 16th-century screens. A huge late-Gothic retable (75 feet high) has more than 1,000 figures grouped in scenes from the lives of Jesus and Mary. This altarpiece was designed by Pieter Dancart, a late-15th-century Flemish sculptor; the side wings were added later.

The cathedral has more than a dozen chapels lining its north and south sides. Most of them have ceiling-high protective iron grilles, and many of them are so dark that their interiors, often coated with layers of dust, are impenetrable. One exception is the San Antonio chapel, or baptistry, on the north side, with Murillo's *San Antonio de Padua* and his *Christ's Baptism.* Near the entrance to the Patio de los Naranjos (more on this later) is Cano's *Mary,* at the altar of the Virgin of Bethlehem. On the south side, the San José chapel has paintings by Valdés Leal and Lucas Jordan, and in the San Hermenegildo chapel is a stunning Gothic alabaster tomb by Lorenzo Mercadente: The stone head of the mitered deceased rests on three alabaster cushions that seem to be sinking under the weight.

The transept contains a monument to Columbus, supported by four giant figures, and beyond it in the Sacristía de los Cálices is a treasure trove of paintings by Murillo, Goya, Cano, Pacheco, Valdés Leal, and Titian. Here there is an unusual amenity for the cathedral, a chart that identifies the paintings. Next door, as it were, is the **Sacristía Mayor,** decorated in exuberant Plateresque style with a wonderful dome and beautiful stone carving, which houses the cathedral treasures, mostly from the 16th century, of silver, bronze, and ivory.

The spacious open-air **Patio de los Naranjos** (court of orange trees) extends along the entire northern face of the cathedral. This purification court of the former mosque has been altered little. In the center of the quadrangle stands an octagonal alabaster fountain basin said to have come from the original Visigoth church; from it radiates a patterned grid of 66 orange trees. A beautiful, horseshoe-shaped Moorish archway leads to this orange court from calle Almanes (no access). Today the patio has a patterned brick floor with four knee-high marble fountains at the corners. When the trees are in blossom or laden with fruit the court is a tranquil retreat just a step away from the site of the unremitting human flow that characterizes the interior of the cathedral.

The Giralda

Sevillanos are enormously attached to the Giralda, the slender 322-foot-high tower directly adjacent to the northeast corner of the cathedral. Built as a minaret in 1184 with disciplined Arabic decorative motifs in its yellow brick and stone paneling, it was amended four centuries later by Hernán Ruiz. He added a belfry (with 24 deafening bells) and capped it with a weather vane. For the people of today's Seville the Giralda rings out the time, signals the weather, and serves as a beacon, as indeed it does for visitors, often orienting those lost in a maze of Medieval streets. It looks not unlike an outsize early Italian Renaissance campanile.

You can ascend a ramp that winds upward as it follows the interior of the rectangular carapace. Through slits in the walls, which give some light to your progress, you can view increasingly rewarding panoramas of Seville. A warning posted to the effect that persons should not ascend singly lest they succumb to suicidal impulses casts a chill often exacerbated at the top by the every-quarter-hour explosive clamor of the bells. But the view from the summit is a knockout.

The flat-roofed nave of the enormous cathedral with its triple flying buttresses has beyond it to the west the Guadalquivir and the bridges, to the south the Alcázar and the María Luisa gardens. To the west lies a city of white, highlighted by that splendid Seville landmark La Maestranza and, across the river, the Triana (gypsy) district, then modern high-rise apartments and the hills. In the immediate foreground to the north lie the old city, the distant suburbs, and the oil refineries. Close to the east is the Santa Cruz section, a labyrinth of passageways, and farther away the startling contrast of modern Seville with its tall buildings.

The Alcázar

Only a few steps south of the cathedral across the plaza del Triumfo stands the extensive royal palace known as the Alcázar, built by Peter the Cruel, who ruled Castile and León from 1350 to 1369. Originally a 12th-century Arabic Almohaden fortress, this fascinating building has undergone many architectural transformations; it even incorporates stylistic elements as recent as the 19th century. Nevertheless, the overall impression suggests the strength and delicacy of Mudejar (Moorish artisans and styles under Christian rule) architecture. The influence of Granada's Alhambra is unmistakable—in the courtyards, in the arches and the stucco ornamentation, in the ceilings and fenestration—copied with flair and imagination.

The Alcázar contains superb Flemish tapestries of the 17th and 18th centuries; tilework of rare beauty from the 14th century; and beyond the marvelously decorative ambassador's hall, a frieze of portraits of Spanish rulers dating from the time of Philip II. Visitors are particularly taken by the harem or living quarters (guides tell the same joke about eunuchs to each successive tour group), where the capitals of the columns are mostly from Córdoba and its nearby Medina Azahara. Within this huge Alcázar complex are Christian altars, a display of exquisite Spanish fans, and 12 Flemish tapestries depicting the 1535 Tunisian campaign of Charles V. Part of the building dates from reconstruction after the earthquake of 1744.

Visitors are likely to leave Seville's Alcázar (usually through a stable-like area housing antique carriages) with a confused chronological sense of its architectural and decorative components. But even with this striking lack of conformity and continuity—and the sometimes jarring incongruities—the Alcázar offers many individual rewards of artistry.

The Gardens of Seville

Before exiting the Alcázar structure, however, you can pass directly to the **Alcázar gardens**, so extensive that several hours can be spent under their seductive spell. They incorporate as many stylistically diverse elements as the fortress-palace itself: Moorish, Renaissance, 19th century, and contemporary. The landscape architecture here gives a new meaning to the word "eclectic." A grotto wall, part colonnade, part unsightly stone encrustrations, divides the garden. On the formal side is a large pool with a jarring orange-colored background wall; throughout the garden are fountains and the welcome sound and sight, dear to the Moors, of falling water; in the center is a mid-16th-century gazebo, a creation of Charles V, with superb tiling. The sound of Seville's traffic comes from beyond the high crenellated brick walls. On the informal side of the gardens are long walkways and an abundance of blooms, fruit trees, and palms. The climate of Seville means that flowers are gloriously in bloom here in all seasons. These Alcázar gardens recall, as well, the Generalife gardens of the Alhambra (although the latter has the crushing advantage of location), but the feline population of Seville outranks that of Grenada by as many as two to one. Some of Seville's Alcázar garden ponds have goldfish, others have ducks, creatures unthinkable in the elegant ambiance of the Alhambra.

"We drove through the Parque de María Luisa and down the Paseo de las Delicias, names that breathe or whisper of the tall acacias, the roses, camellias, and orange trees, of what must be the most beautiful park in Europe," writes Sacheverell Sitwell. The **Parque de María Luisa**, running for many acres along the banks of the Guadalquivir south of the Alcázar and then the university, was laid out by the French garden designer Forestier in the 19th century. It was initially English in design, but today its style is distinctly Spanish with its fountains, avenues, tiled benches, and romantic sweeps.

A half-day visit to this beautiful park gives you a sense of what pleasure Sevillanos have in living in their seductive city. The Parque de María Luisa (unlike the Alcázar gardens) is open to the public and they use it extensively. Huge acacia trees with clusters of white or yellow flowers are set off dramatically in contrast to the languorous palm trees and the fragrant pines. Luxuriant roses, with a dazzling range of size and color, complement flowerbeds that become splashes of blue and white, orange and yellow, mauve and deep purple, and here and there an explosive blaze of red. The many fountains throughout the park, in tiles of various shades of blue, ocher, and green, lend another refreshing note of light and color that brings a needed sense of coolness to the hot summer months; somehow these fountains seem particularly "Spanish," and the dominant decorative motif of the park is achieved through this extensive use of *azulejos* (glazed tiles). If a public park can be opulent, the María Luisa, with its ponds, swans, gazebos, and murmuring doves, surely qualifies.

The 1929 Ibero-American Exposition brought great changes to the garden area: A huge semicircular palace, the **Palacio Español**, was built with handsome arcades; in front of it, the vast plaza de España has a kind of moat with bridges under which pass countless small boats manned by what V. S. Pritchett calls "congenitally incompetent rowers." At the south end of the Parque de María Luisa are two large structures: the **Museo de Arte y Costumbres Populares**, and the **Museo Arqueológico Provincial** (for the latter see below).

Seville is particularly rich in open park spaces; the abundance of flowers and softly shaded areas casts an almost irresistible spell over most visitors, and the entire population of the city seems to spend part of each weekend in its parks and gardens.

Hospital de la Caridad

This Baroque charity hospital (seat of a brotherhood, but in this case with an actual hospital off its courtyard) has a church commissioned by Don Miguel de Manara, the reputed model for Don Juan, in 1661. Just two blocks west of the riverbank Torre del Oro, on Temprano, the church (with its magnificent paintings) and the courtyard (with its narrative-pictorial glazed tiles) share a theme: the transitory nature of life and the quality of mercy it presupposes. Two superb allegorical paintings by Valdés Leal face one another across the church entranceways. His subject is grim mortality. On the face of one he has written *in ictu oculi* ("in the blink of an eye"). Close examination of either work is not for the faint of heart. You are most likely to be reassured by the six huge Murillo canvases that adorn the church walls, each representing Biblical acts of mercy. Murillo's style and flesh tones evoke a gentle and even sentimental radiance.

Above the altar stretches an extraordinary three-dimensional work by Pedro Roldán. Created in 1673, *The Burial of Christ* depicts the background of the crucifixion; extending out over the altar area is a sculptured body being borne away. Despite its motif of charity, the church has overpowering Baroque twisted gold columns on either side of the altar, a reminder that glitter was once identified with glorification.

Casa de Pilato

A pleasurable morning excursion could include both the Casa de Pilato and the Museo de Bellas Artes, a short taxi ride away from one another. The former, a superb Renaissance palace built in 1480 by Pedro Enríques de Ribera, is ostensibly fashioned in the style of the Roman villa of Pontius Pilate. The house, with its central grand patio and adjacent gardens of lemon and orange trees, has particularly fine examples of luster tiles. Gothic, Renaissance, and rather pronounced Mudejar styles have been incorporated in a way that transfigures the Roman model, and somehow the integration works handsomely. The two-story mansion—it has one of the very few domed stairways in

Spain—is furnished with countless Roman artifacts: statues, busts, helmets, reclining figures. Some of the elaborate Mudejar ceilings are intricately worked in gold. The Gothic chapel has heavy Mudejar stucco and beautiful azulejos.

The house, on calle Aquilas in the center of Seville, was once the starting point for the annual Holy Week processions. The patio fountain, centered on a tiled surface and enclosed by a gallery of marble pillars supporting Roman arches, suggests the cool spaciousness of symmetrical design that characterizes the Spanish Renaissance at its best.

Museo de Bellas Artes

Some—particularly those who live in Seville—say that the fine arts museum here is second in importance only to Madrid's Prado. Housed in a 17th-century monastery on the plaza del Museo, about a half-mile northwest of the cathedral, and specializing in the Golden Age Renaissance period of Spain, it places emphasis on Seville's illustrious native artists. In the cloisters and adjacent church are a particularly large number of Murillos (room 7 alone has 20 of his works) as well as canvases of Pacheco (the teacher and father-in-law of Velázquez), Ribera, Cano, and some superb Valdés Leals. There is also an El Greco painting of his son, *Portrait of Jorge Manuel.* Zurbarán is shown at his most exceptional in room 6, which houses his famous *Virgin of the Caves.* Velázquez, who was born in Seville but made his career in Madrid, is not penalized for his civic abandonment.

The museum is currently undergoing extensive renovation, presumably with a view toward Seville's 1992 World's Fair, but many paintings are scheduled to be placed on view in 1990 in the adjoining church, which was built in the early 17th century by Juan de Oviedo.

The Barrio de Santa Cruz

No district in Seville has more native flavor than the Barrio de Santa Cruz. This former Jewish quarter begins just east of the cathedral area. Many of its streets are narrow enough to be confined to pedestrians only, and in any event it is an area to wander about on individual voyages of discovery. A car is not only a hindrance, but the driver could well use a police escort in finding the way through the labyrinthine maze.

Almost all the white three-story buildings here have flowers in window boxes, flowers at doorsteps, and flowers and plants in courtyards glimpsed through black-grilled gateways. Little seems to have changed since George Borrow wrote, in 1843, "Nothing is more calculated to interest the stranger as he wanders through Seville than a view of these courts obtained from the street through the iron-grated door. Oft have I stopped to observe them, and as often sighed that my fate did not permit me to reside in such an Eden for the remainder of my days." Such inner courtyards usually have a central fountain, and beyond the abundance of greenery and the ubiquitous geraniums, a dado of Moorish tiles. In summer this retreat, covered with an awning, serves as a family living room.

The Barrio today is an odd mixture of fashionable neighborhood, tourist lure (not yet a trap), craftsmen's shops, low-income dwellings, restaurants, and *tapas* bars. Somehow it has managed, like the Jewish quarter of Córdoba, to retain its distinctive air. Once more, a cautionary note that in such secluded areas it pays to be careful about camera straps, shoulder bags, and other "detachable" personal items.

Travelling is one of life's supreme pleasures, and here in Barrio de Santa Cruz you have a chance to stroll at will, to stare, to pause, to enjoy a drink and *tapas,* to balance the cultural weight of the city's historic sites with a welcome sense of leisure and freedom from itineraries. The elegant narrow streets are cool, comparatively speaking, the little squares are shaded by orange trees and small palms, many of the iron grilles are exquisitely wrought, the craftsmen's workshops are often stimulating to visit, and what visitor can resist the temptation to peer innocently through the entrance of a particularly beautiful flower-filled patio.

Archivo General de Indias

This impressive Renaissance building, adjacent to the cathedral, was designed by El Escorial's Juan de Herrera. Sometimes called the Casa Lonja (exchange house), the archive now holds documents, maps, and charts pertaining to the Americas, and as such it is the repository for Spain in her role as discoverer and empire-builder. The building, infrequently visited by travellers, has an inner courtyard with Doric and Ionic columns. It is a place of consuming interest.

Lining the salon walls of this marble-floored edifice are priceless documents behind protective grilles. A plaque states that on January 1, 1660, the painting and drawing academy founded by Bartolomé Estaban Murillo began its activities in these precincts. Displays on view include copies of letters from Columbus to his son, from Cervantes asking for a job, and from George Washington in 1789 regarding a commercial treaty with the chiefs of the Choctaw nation, as well as priceless original maps.

The archive is open daily; visitors sign in and are free to examine the exhibits.

The University

The 18th-century university building in Seville is the largest in Spain after the Escorial; it is said to have more than 100 courtyards. Once a cigar factory and exchange house, it served as the setting of Bizet's *Carmen* and is rumored to have once employed 10,000 cigar makers.

The building, across calle de San Fernando south of the Alcázar gardens (San Fernando itself has bookshops and, at its eastern end, a comfortable *tapas* bar), has corridors the length of football fields, down which stride a prodigious number of students, all of whom seem to know where they are heading. The coffee shop has the cosmetic overtones of a *tapas* bar, and the classrooms are archaic. What matters here is serious academic pursuit. You get a tangible sense of the youthful energy of Spain today, and the institution provides a sharp and instructive physical contrast with American and English universities.

Itálica and the Museo Arqueológico Provincial

While nothing takes the place of a visit to an archaeological dig, most of the objects and artifacts from the ancient Roman town of Itálica are now in the Museo Arqueológico Provincial in the Parque de María Luisa. Itálica, the birthplace of two Roman emperors, was clearly a provincial city of substance. Its ruins (9 km/6 miles out of the city on N 630) are easily reached today from Seville by local bus, which leaves every half-hour from calle Parades near the Córdoba train station. At Itálica are the impressive remains of an enormous amphitheater (said to have seated 40,000 people) and the grid of an urban complex, the streets clearly outlined, the floors of some of the buildings showing artful and imaginative mosaics. But the city is dead, moribund in the particular way of an archaeological dig whose objects, signifying the life and artistries and energies of its former dwellers, have been moved elsewhere. Smack in the middle of the nearby contemporary town of Santiponce stand the ruins of a Roman theater, and archaeological work is still going on nearby.

Fortunately many treasures from Itálica are on exhibit at the handsome Museo Arqueológico Provincial. This Renaissance pavilion, large and well lighted, allows you to view the exhibits chronologically. The rooms devoted to the Roman period have many statues of Greek inspiration. "Roman cities . . . liked to represent their gods copied from the original Greeks," reads a plaque in Spanish (there are no museum identifications in other languages); nearby statues of Mercury and Hermes attest to this close artistic connection. Particularly valuable and interesting are the magnificent floor mosaics, one of Bacchus from the third century A.D., and a number of stunning mosaics mounted on walls. Busts, funerary inscriptions, numerous amphora, Roman glass, urns, and other objects, mostly from Itálica, bring strength to the collection. A large-scale wall map shows the location and extent of Iberian cities under Roman jurisdiction during the 600 years of occupation.

A display of decorative terra-cotta figures from rooftop drainage-chute gutters reaffirms once more Roman ingenuity in combining the practical with the aesthetically pleasing. In room XXVI a display of elaborate Visigoth jewelry of the post-Roman period is a kind of Andalusian counterpart to the Visigoth jeweled votive crown in Madrid's Museo Arqueológico Nacional. There is also a picture display of the excavations at Munigua, north of Carmona (some 25 miles from Seville), where archaeological work is currently in progress.

Staying in Seville

Seville has a number of international-style hotels indistinguishable from their fellows. But almost everything of major interest is centered around the cathedral-Giralda area, where no transportation other than your feet is needed, and the most satisfying accommodation is in this locality, whereas most of the "international" hotels are a bit removed.

The monarch of Seville's hotels, as it has been for most of this century, it is the *gran-luxe* and decidedly pricey **Alfonso XIII**, where even the maids have maids.

Occupying the most central and expensive real estate in the city, south of the Alcázar gardens and just west of the university, the Alfonso sits there imperturbably, indifferent to its architectural façade—which comes close to parody. It is hard to determine precisely what the architects had in mind in this marriage of pseudo-Moorish and Edwardian. The hotel has a huge open central court (it was built before Seville's summers were made bearable by air-conditioning). The two small elevators have mirrored walls, brocaded benches, carpeted floors, three doors to close before they function, and young, uniformed attendants to ensure that they keep operating. The hotel's three floors above the lobby/dining-salon/bar area are connected by carpeted stairways whose side walls are entirely of decorative tiles, making the choice of walking or taking the lift a difficult one.

Once you enter the spacious bedrooms or suites, all is comfort and modernity, from air-conditioning to mini-bars to huge marbled bathrooms. The windows look out beyond the tops of orange trees to the swimming pool below and the muted traffic of Seville in the distance. Having a drink in the inner courtyard downstairs is an event in itself. The dining room goes well beyond conventional hotel fare and service.

As with all of Seville's hotels, three price ranges exist, reflecting the seasons; the week of the Feria in April has its own extravagant tab.

Also centrally located is the **Doña María**, a superior 64-room residence (no dining room) hotel just east of the Giralda on Don Remondo. The decorating hand has not been unrestrained in some of the rooms, but otherwise the Doña María is ideal for travellers who want to avoid tour groups and conventions. The hotel has a rooftop swimming pool.

The **Inglaterra** is another well-located and highly rated hotel, facing the Ayuntamiento's Plateresque façade from across the plaza Nueva. Its 120 rooms were recently modernized. The terrace dining room overlooks the plaza Nueva, a central gathering place for many of Seville's festivals. An additional boon is garage space here in midtown Seville. The rooms that face the plaza Nueva can be noisy, but all are air-conditioned and comfortably, if unexceptionally, furnished.

The **Apartamentos Murillo**, an apartment hotel with some air-conditioned housekeeping apartments, can be rented by the day, week, or month. Located on one of the narrow streets in the Barrio de Santa Cruz near the Alcázar gardens, the building is best approached from calle Menéndez Pelayo, a block from the plaza Santa Cruz. The apartments are clean and comfortable, if somewhat spartan. They are less than a block away from the inexpensive 60-room

Murillo hotel (run by the same management), a non-air-conditioned little hotel that is pleasant in nonsummer months. The lobby is worth a visit at any time.

Forty-five minutes east of Seville, on the route to Córdoba, the town of **Carmona**—Roman walls, Moorish fortifications, whitewashed houses—has a gem of a parador in the hillside Moorish castle that Pedro the Cruel took over as his palace. It's a bit of a commute to Seville, but you might think of the **Parador Nacional Alcázar del Rey don Pedro** as a fine lunch stop on the Córdoba run.

Dining in Seville

No restaurateur in Seville expects his clients to have souls above food, and one restaurant that serves good fare is **Figón del Cabildo**, across from the cathedral on avenida de la Constitución in the attractive plaza del Cabildo. Although *figón* means "joint" or "cheap eating house," this is neither. The menu has many specialties, such as a rich shellfish soup, and bass "supreme" in a shrimp sauce. Salads tend to be *nueva cocina;* veal is cooked to order and comes with an extra-sharp knife. The Sevillian businesspeople who eat here seem never to arrive for lunch before 2:30 P.M., which means that travellers get the staff's undivided attention at a more conventional hour. The attractive room has a brick fireplace, a beamed ceiling, a tiled fountain at the entrance near the bar. Tel: 22-01-17; closed Sunday afternoons. In the plaza del Cabildo itself are shops (some antiques) of more than general interest.

The **Bodegon Torre del Oro**, a cavernous restaurant near the Torre del Oro, is a large cheerful place with red tablecloths and is informal enough to be comfortable with children and good enough to satisfy adults with its large and varied menu. The room is separated from an extensive bar area, and there is additional space for large parties or tourist groups. The service is quick and attentive in this unpretentious place close to the center of town. The Rioja house wine, served in pitchers, is better than adequate. Open for dinner only. Santander 15; Tel: 21-42-41.

In the immediate cathedral area, **El Giraldillo** (Tel: 21-45-25), with a touristy decor, has a number of tables set out in the plaza Virgen de los Reyes for those who prefer to dine al fresco. Specialties include both Andalusian gazpacho and paella, as well as shrimp in garlic sauce and a shellfish casserole. Not exceptional but wonderfully convenient.

In the Barrio de Santa Cruz, **La Albahaca** offers attentive service and superb food. It is located in a mansion whose ground floor is broken up into intimate dining rooms near the "waiting bar" at the entrance. The decor includes shoulder-high tiles along the walls, crystal candelabras, Murillo copies, and handsome pewter service plates. Through the windows you will glimpse orange trees, white walls, and tiled roofs. Hot pumpkin soup is splendid here, as are sole in orange sauce and salads as decorative as they are edible. The menu lists a "cake of anchovies with mousseline sauce in caviar," and there is a fine wine list. Plaza de Santa Cruz 12; Tel: 22-07-14. Closed Sundays.

Enrique Becerra has so many devoted regulars that it is wise to arrive a little early. A small downstairs dining room has a beamed ceiling and brass carriage lamps, entirely Sevillian in tone and manner. Attentive service prevails in a friendly, informal atmosphere. The extensive menu has daily specials and the wine list is comprehensive. Hot dishes, including soup, are served at the right temperature, as are the cold ones—a not inconsiderable virtue. Specialties include chops and seafood. Gamazo 2, in the plaza Nueva area; Tel: 21-30-49.

Bars and Flamenco Clubs in Seville

In a city that rarely dines before 10:00 P.M., night-time activities tend to begin around midnight. The entire area (once the infamous **Triana** gypsy section) on the west bank of the Guadalquivir between the San Telmo and the Isabel II bridges (across from the Torre del Oro and the plaza de Toro) is taken over nightly by Seville's younger set. Bars, discos, and restaurants vie with sidewalk gatherings to produce a scene of party-time activity, especially on weekends. Triana is not for the conservative fun seeker.

Tablaos (tableaux), or locations where flamenco entertainment is offered, sometimes geared to the tourist trade and rather scorned by purists, include **El Patio Sevillano**, next to the bullring, which features a number of shows during the evening, "depending on the attendance." Paseo Cristóbal Colón 11; Tel: 21-41-20. **Los Gallos** in the plaza de Santa Cruz offers two shows, one at 9:00 P.M. and one from 11:00 P.M. "til dawn." Los Gallos claims to offer the purest flamenco singing and dancing, and many celebrated flamenco artists have performed here. Plaza de Santa Cruz 11; Tel: 21-69-81.

Discos and jazz clubs with live entertainment are best

discovered through on-the-spot schedules available at hotel front desks.

Shops and Shopping in Seville

Shopping in Seville centers around pedestrian-only **calle de Sierpes**, which stretches north from behind the Ayuntamiento at plaza Nuevo, and which has its own character (some famous Holy Week processions come down this street) but which hardly ranks as a place of distinguished or elegant shops. A good selection of ceramics can be found here at **Maritan Ceramics**, Sierpes 76, and at **Sevillarte**, Sierpes 66, both near the plaza Nuevo end of the street. East of the cathedral, near the entrance to the Alcázar, ceramics stores include **Cerámicás Santa Cruz**, **El Azulejo**, and **Cerámica Colón**.

A wide selection of Spanish fans can be seen at **Díaz**, Sierpes 69–71, and some beautiful lace mantillas and tablecloths are on display at **Alvarez Quintero**, Sierpes 52. Seville's **Artespaña** store, one of the chain offering Spanish crafts of quality, is at plaza de la Concordia 2.

Holy Week and the April Fair

No one should visit Seville during either Holy Week or the April Feria (usually from April 18 to April 23, except when these dates conflict with Easter, in which case the fair takes place a week later) unless the express objective of the visit is to be among the celebrants. During these two periods the city is completely given over to celebration, the one somber, the other boisterous. Hotel rates zoom, restaurants are jammed, and streets are impassable.

During Semana Santa (Holy Week) processions of more than 50 brotherhoods take place in every section of the city. Groups of men, sometimes numbering 40 or more, carry on their shoulders *pasos* (floats) with religious figures, elaborately conceived and adorned with flowers. The streets are usually darkened and the *pasos* are accompanied by penitents dressed in long robes and pointed hoods and carrying tall, lighted candles. Dirges and *saetas*—mournful hymns based on flamenco music—fill the air, and fife and drum corps provide the musical accompaniment.

The April Feria is an explosion of dancing—flamenco and Sevillana in particular—wine-drinking, bullfighting, parades of horses and carriages, floodlights, fireworks, picnics, and parties. Men wear leather chaps with scarlet cummerbunds, short jackets, and broad-brimmed hats; the women are spectacularly costumed in full-skirted flamenco dresses, often with vivid polka dots—flowers adorn their hair. The fair began as a rural livestock gathering in 1848, and, while cattle-dealing still goes on, such relatively mundane activities are secondary in this rush of festive excitement and riotous color.

CORDOBA

Contemporary Córdoba, 128 km (80 miles) east-northeast of Seville, may not capture the heart of the casual visitor; the mind is a more likely target. This was, after all, the home of Seneca, Averroës, and Maimonides, and it remains a place where Moslem architecture and decoration vie with their Christian counterparts. But Córdoba in the late 20th century seems content to coast on its illustrious past, an inviting prospect for the visitor, except that in summer the city is a cauldron. The Guadalquivir (once the Roman Baetis) is no longer navigable; indeed, for most of the year it is scarcely a river. Córdoba cannot compare with Seville or Granada in diversity of sights, accommodations, and activities. Romanticists say that underneath modern Córdoba lies a Moorish city, and beneath that a Roman one; realists reply that the surface is what the traveller encounters.

The Arabic Heritage

That Cordoban surface has a mosque fit to dazzle the world, an Arabic-Jewish section of a richly evocative flavor, and, just 4.5 miles away the ruins of a palace, the Medina Azahara, that may once have been unequaled in splendor and opulence.

At the time of the Roman Empire, Augustus chose Córdoba as the capital of the province of Baetica (Andalusia). The importance of Córdoba declined under the Visigoths, but after capturing the city in 711 the Arabs made it the capital of Moorish Spain, in 756. Córdoba became a caliphate in 929 at a time when Moslem Spain was the most advanced country in Europe. In the tenth century Córdoba was the largest, wealthiest, and most cultured city in all of Europe.

Arab historians favor exaggeration, but scholars today believe that Córdoba's population in the tenth century was over half a million. Córdoba had a prodigious number of mosques, public baths, private mansions, and a library with at least a quarter of a million volumes. The city's streets were lighted and paved.

The Medieval Renaissance

Moorish Córdoba was a center for science in the Middle Ages: Medicine, botany, chemistry, physics, mathematics, astronomy, geography, and Greek philosophy were among its chosen disciplines. Algebra and spherical trigonometry were almost entirely inventions of the Moors, who had also introduced Arabic numerals, vastly more adaptable to mathematics than the Roman ones. Córdoba probably had the first real European university in the sense in which we use the term today.

The Arabs changed the sound and the look of Spain. They brought into Europe many musical instruments, including the *shawm* (a forerunner of the oboe), kettle drums, the lute, and the oval guitar; they gave to Spanish music the exotic quality that identifies it today. They introduced paper to Europe, making possible the development of printing. Some say that Córdoba inaugurated European glassmaking, and certainly glass was widely used in Moorish Spain.

The Moors' high level of civilization rested squarely on agriculture. They used waterwheels and dug carefully engineered irrigation ditches. (From the Roman bridge in Córdoba today you can spot an Arab mill 100 yards downstream.) Flowing water was crucial to the Moors for ritual cleansing, to provide aesthetic delight in parks and gardens, and to ensure sufficient produce from fields and orchards to sustain a large urban population.

Christians were initially allowed to retain some churches and use their own schools and libraries, but as the Reconquest in the north of Spain bit ever deeper into the peninsula, Latin was banned and Christian children in Córdoba attended Arabic schools. The Jews, who had been fiercely persecuted by the Visigoths, flourished under the Moors' rule, and many emigrated from the East to settle in Córdoba. As a center of Hebrew learning in the Middle Ages, the city boasted a Talmudic school renowned throughout Europe. Arabic was the official language, but bilingualism in Arabic and Hispano-Roman dialect (the Spanish linguistic equivalent of Middle English) was the norm among the educated classes of all religions.

The city was the birthplace of many celebrated figures: the rhetorician Seneca (55 B.C.–A.D. 39) and his son, Lucius (4 B.C.–A.D. 65); the poet Lucan (39–63); the writers Juan de

Mena (1411–1456) and Luis de Góngora (1561–1627); and the painters Pablo de Céspedes (1538–1608) and Juan Valdés Leal (1631–1691). But it is the philosophers Averroës (in Arabic, Ibn-Rushd; 1126–1198) and Moses Maimonides (1135–1204), both born in Córdoba, who epitomize the importance of the city, and Moorish Andalusia, to Western culture.

It was largely through Andalusia that Aristotle was introduced to Christian Europe, and Averroës—at one time the chief judge of Córdoba—was the commentator on the texts of Aristotle and other Greeks that had been assembled and transmitted across North Africa by the scholars of the Arab world (many of whom were Jews and other peoples). When, after Averroës's death, his commentaries were translated into Latin, there occurred a great burst of emphasis on philosophy in the West. The major problem of how to reconcile the rational aspects of Greek thought with revealed Christian tenets absorbed Peter Abelard, Duns Scotus, Thomas Aquinas, and other celebrated doctors of the church. Averroës's commentaries were part of European university curricula for centuries following his death. Maimonides was concerned with Aristotle as well. All three cultures, in fact—Jewish, Christian, Arabic—shared the common problem of reconciling their individual religious laws with Aristotelian thought.

Arab schools of thought in Spain in the Middle Ages were not necessarily those at the apex of Arab civilization as a whole, but they, and the rest of Arab culture in Spain, were truly dazzling in relation to the Christian West of the time—which they so greatly influenced.

Although Córdoba is a relatively large Andalusian city (population 300,000), the area of interest to visitors is compact and can be seen easily on foot. The Mezquita-Catedral and the Alcázar are on the north bank of the Guadalquivir, near a sharp bend in the river. Two blocks to the west, the park-like Victoria-Cervantes boulevard runs directly north (about 20 blocks) to the railway station. The old town lies to the east of these boulevards and here you have the Judería (the ancient Jewish section), the Museo Arqueológico Provincial, La Sinagoga, the Viana palace, the Plaza de Toros, the Zoco with its shops of leather and silver filigree, a dozen churches and monasteries (Romanesque-Gothic, Baroque, Neoclassical), and, of course, restaurants and hotels. The Mezquita-Catedral is directly north of the old Roman bridge; the Alcázar is a block to the west on the riverbank. Strolling around this exceptional city with its strong Moorish character gives you a sense of Córdoba's outstanding historic and cultural background; it seems little changed from its Medieval-Renaissance days. A suggestion: Walk from the Roman bridge to the Mezquita-Catedral, through the Jewish quarter, and up to the Viana palace.

The Mezquita-Catedral

The term "unforgettable," shredded of meaning by travel chroniclers, needs resuscitation here. No visitor will forget the Mezquita-Catedral (mosque-cathedral) in Córdoba. But the exterior of the enormous building is forbiddingly bleak; one of the first acts of the Christians after conquering Córdoba was to stone up the entrance doors (which gave light and shadow to the interior rows of columns) ranging alongside the building. Today you enter the mosque from the **court of orange trees**, usually by way of the Puerta de Pérdon (pardon door), to come upon a forest of more than 800 pillars dividing the rectangular building (slightly smaller in size than St. Peter's in Rome) into 19 north-to-south and 29 east-to-west aisles. These pillars of marble, jasper, porphyry, and breccia support two tiers of arches with alternating *voussoirs* (wedge-shaped or tapered pieces forming an arch) of white stone and red brick.

These columns and arches inspire a kind of visual exuberance, their delicacy and strength exalting the senses. The double arches produce a lighter and airier effect than single arches could have achieved. The limits of space are deliberately obscured so that you experience it as something fluid, limitless, and mysterious.

Begun in 785 by Emir Abd ar-Rahman I, the original mosque rectangle was enlarged three times, doubling the size of the building. Columns used for interior pillars came from Carthage as well as from Roman and Visigothic buildings in France and Spain. Since their height varied, some columns were buried below the floor level, while others were raised on added bases and topped with Corinthian capitals. The arches trace the famous horseshoe curve.

The mosaic tiles and marble that once covered the floor and interior walls are gone, but in the most sacred chapel the original mosaics remain, gleaming with a delicate and luminous splendor. The *mihrab* (prayer niche), a sacrosanct place, is domed over with a single great block of white marble carved in the form of a shell (it is chained off, preventing a full view from the observer's stance under a magnificent mosaic ceiling).

The mosque at Córdoba is a capsule art history of Andalusia: Carthaginian and Roman pillars, Visigothic columns with fleur-de-lis carvings, Byzantine pillars from Constantinople. The mosque occupies land that once held a Roman temple of Janus, later replaced by the Visigothic Christian church of St. Vincent.

No one who enters the mosque can be unaware that a large Christian cathedral stands within its confines. The inserted cathedral, primarily Plateresque, replaced 63 columns of the mosque. Built in the 16th century, the cathedral has its own rather eclectic architectural distinction, but its superimposition on the artistic singularity of the mosque is an aesthetic desecration. Emperor Charles V (who built the Renaissance palace in the Moors' Alhambra complex at Granada) is said to have remarked (in a suspiciously apocryphal quote that varies with each telling) that the builders of the cathedral had destroyed something unique in order to construct something that might have been erected anywhere. It is only fair to point out that the Moors themselves (after buying it) razed the Visigothic church in order to build the mosque, and we probably should be grateful that the Christians, in the fervor of the Reconquest, did not destroy the mosque entirely. Fortunately, what remains of the mosque encompasses sufficient space that the intrusion—not only the cathedral but shrines and artifacts—can be aesthetically disregarded if scarcely ignored.

The Roman Bridge

One of Córdoba's still heavily trafficked bridges across the Guadalquivir was built by the Romans, refurbished by the Moors, and recently had a much-needed traffic light installed at its northern end. The bridge has 16 arches, although the river that flows beneath it today is a pitiful remnant of the original waterway; a herd of cows regularly grazes part of the riverbed most of the year. At the southern end of the bridge, across the river from the mosque and the Alcázar, stands the **Torre de la Calahorra**, built in 1369 to guard the "entrance" to Córdoba; today the tower is a historical museum, a dividing line—according to a plaque—"between east and west."

Walking north back toward the city across this bridge you get a strong sense of the history and the glory that once was Córdoba. Directly ahead is a monumental arch erected by Philip II and said to have been designed by Juan de Herrera. Slightly to the left is the great Medieval mosque from whose roof rises the incongruous Renaissance cathedral. Farther left, to the west overlooking the river, is the extensive 14th-century **Alcázar** with its fine collection of Roman mosaics. The beautiful adjoining cypress gardens, with their tranquil pools and fountains, date back to Arabic times, as does a vegetable garden, cultivated even now.

The pedestrian walk on the Roman bridge is so narrow that people cannot pass without stepping into the roadway, where vehicles are usually whizzing by; halfway across the bridge is a shrine whose candles are often lit even at high noon. To the right stretches the maze of tiled roofs and white walls of the old Judería. The bridge itself is no-nonsense solid and substantial with its inevitable Roman sense of style, somehow durably reassuring in a Cordoban world of historical evanescence.

The Judería

The Jewish quarter will remind you that Córdoba's Jewish population lived in economic and cultural harmony with the Moors, to their mutual benefit. On calle Judios north of the Alcázar, near a monument to the physician and philosopher Moses Maimonides, is a tiny 14th-century **synagogue** whose Mudejar interior has the traditional women's balcony. The synagogue is as modest in size as the mosque is overwhelming. So close to the mosque-cathedral, the building's architectural reticence disguises its historical significance. A block or so away, on the far side of the crenellated city wall, stands a monument to Maimonides' contemporary, Averroës.

The narrow, twisting streets of the extensive Jewish quarter make walking a delight, as glimpses of courtyards and shaded interiors succeed one another. The inevitable contrast with Seville's analogous area, the Barrio de Santa Cruz, is striking: Here in Córdoba the atmosphere is secret, reclusive—despite the often blinding whiteness of the walls. Seville's area seems by comparison open and free of arcana. Here in Córdoba some of the alleyways turn back on themselves as the city slopes down to the riverbank, and it is easy literally to lose yourself in the fascinating maze. The labyrinth seems to be deserted—but unexpectedly a door opens, a pedestrian turns a corner, a dog yawns as it stretches in the warm sunlight.

Cordoban Leather

Just a few hundred feet from the northeast corner of the mosque's court of orange trees is **calleja de las Flores** (flower alleyway), a charming if self-conscious cobbled passageway whose white walls, flower-bedecked doorways, window boxes, and inner courtyards end in a little courtyard offering a splendid view of the cathedral belfry, which replaced the minaret of the mosque. Halfway along this absurdly narrow alleyway, pale green tiles set flush with the wall advise passersby in Spanish, English, French, Hebrew, Arabic, German, and Japanese that through an adjacent door is the **Meryan** shop and factory specializing in fine leathers.

The Meryan shop sells embossed leather at reasonable prices, one of the few places left in Spain where leather is embossed, not simply stamped. This intricate and demanding art goes back to the Moors, when the name Córdoba became synonymous with fine leatherwork. And the influence of Córdoba and its art is even reflected in other languages: cordovan and cordwainer in English, *cordonnier* (shoemaker) in French, *cordewainer* in Flemish. Although the Moors first introduced hand-tooled and embossed leather to Spain, it was not until after the Reconquest in the 15th century that this Cordoban art flourished. Throughout Europe Cordoban leather, often studded with silver and gold ornaments and painted with embossed designs (called *quadamecil*), was treasured for chair coverings, chests, bedsteads, screens, and frames. In castles and churches large panels of embossed leather often hung as ornamental wall coverings.

Not everything in the Meryan shop is crafted there, and the shop has handsome jewel boxes, attaché cases, and book and folio covers as well as furniture. The proprietors will gladly show you their products, displayed in rooms once used as inner courtyards.

Visitors shopping for leather goods in Córdoba should be wary of the Zoco, at calles Judíos and Averroës, where vendors sometimes sell "embossed" Spanish bags imported from Morocco and machine-stamped billfolds ground out in the factories of Madrid.

Museo Arqueológico and Palacio del Marqués de Viana

Several blocks to the northeast of the mosque-cathedral is the Museo Arqueológico, housed in the Renaissance palace in the plaza de Jerónimo Páez. The museum has artifacts from the Roman, Visigothic, Moorish, and Spanish Renaissance periods. The rooms are light and spacious and contain what some declare to be the best ceramics collection in the world, as well as the largest collection of lead sarcophogi extant. The museum rests on an old Roman foundation. A visit offers a vivid glimpse of Spain's history. Visitors should check in advance, however, as the museum is undergoing renovation.

The extensive Viana palace, just west of the Iglesia de San Agustín and a few blocks southeast of the railway station and plaza Colón, was acquired as a museum in 1981. The charm of the palace lies in its numerous courtyards, which range from the classically formal colonnaded fountain area to a communal neighborhood court complete with potted plants, washtubs, and resident cats. The palace is located in a densely populated area, but within its precincts quiet and calm prevail during a leisurely tour from flower bedecked courtyards to one that has plants (*Boxus sempervirens*) as old as the 17th-century palace itself. Visitors can also visit the furnished rooms on the second floor, but only in the company of a guide; here are Jan Brueghels, Jordaens, Goya tapestries, Mudejar ceilings, fabulous Moorish rugs, tiled walls, rare *azulejos,* and a library of rare books. Of unusual interest in the entranceway area is the old coach room, with its ancient carriages, livery, and equestrian appurtenances.

Throughout the entire month of May the city of Córdoba is bedecked with flowers. The city's parks and squares, private patios and balconies, boulevards and alleyways are all adorned with floral arrangements of spectacular color and diversity (prizes are given for outstanding displays). This a fine time to visit the city.

Staying and Dining in Córdoba

Córdoba has limited hotel accommodations. **Parador Nacional de la Arruzafa**, large and uncharacteristically conventional in style and appointments (for example, it has a swimming pool), is north of the city limits, and you'll need a car to get there. The **Meliá Córdoba**, on paseo de la Victoria, is comfortable, unexceptional, and within walking distance of the mosque.

Two hotels, on streets running adjacent to the mosque, offer comfortable lodgings. The **Ardave**, facing the east side of the mosque, is strikingly handsome if a little overdressed, and gives one a sense of well-being; the **Maimonides**, on the northwest side, is unpretentious and entirely adequate. Both hotels have two-season rates, the higher being from mid-

March to mid-October; both are residential (no dining room, but breakfast served). The Ardave has a large garage.

El Caballo Rojo, at Cardenal Herrero 28, on the mosque's northern boundary, is a delightful, atmospheric restaurant that pampers guests with good food and service, beginning with a dry Sherry fino and hors d'oeuvres on the house. The menu is extensive and imaginative. The emphasis is on seafood. Andalusian gazpacho, here served snow-white, made with almonds and a touch of garlic, along with *rape Mudejar*—fresh fish prepared with raisins, pine nuts, and montilla—are specialties. The restaurant extends for several rooms on the second floor, and its location is supremely convenient for visitors to the mosque. Tel: 47-53-75.

El Churrasco, in the heart of the Judería, has a striking interior with a striped awning overhead to ward off the rays of the courtyard sun. Specialties are grilled-meat dishes (*churrasco*). At Romero 16, Tel: 29-08-19, it's popular and convenient to Córdoba's sites.

The Medina Azahara

Four miles to the west of the city, off route C 431, is a remarkable site: the ruins of the Medina Azahara palace, which dates from 936, when Abd ar-Rahman III undertook to construct not only a royal residence but an entire city for his favorite wife, Zahara. Today this vast ruin gives only a suggestion of how magnificent the completed complex must have been: On three terraced levels were the Alcázar, the gardens and orchards, and the city proper, where the mosque was located.

Arab historians insist that the construction of the Medina Azahara involved 10,000 men, 2,600 mules, and 400 camels over a 25-year period. The columns of marble and jasper, like those in Córdoba's mosque, came from ancient cities. We hear of 12,000 men in garrison, 4,000 servants in the palace, 2,000 horses in the stables. The Medina Azahara had hanging gardens, aviaries, zoos, streams, courts and kiosks, bejeweled gold fountains, and quicksilver pools. In 1010, less than a century after its completion, it was attacked, burned, and pillaged by Berbers who believed themselves politically betrayed by the Al Mansur dynasty.

Visiting the site today, where, in a relative sense, the excavations have just begun, at the very least suggests to the viewer a world of artistic and economic opulence. It is at once depressing—an Ozymandius-like capsule lesson on the ephemeral—and magnificent. The remnants of the palace itself lack the lace-like mural designs, the ground alabaster, and the stucco of Granada's Alhambra. Instead, the Medina Azahara is monumental, with giant blocks of marble intricately carved and said once to have been imbedded with jewels. Some remaining floors are of white marble.

By the time Córdoba fell to the Christians, its place in the European, the Arabic, and the Spanish sun had faded. The conqueror Fernando found Córdoba in 1236 no longer "the capital of a flourishing, civilized state, but a decayed provincial town." The baton had long since passed to Seville, which when captured a mere 12 years later by Ferdinand III of Castile would in turn lose its leading role in Moslem culture to Granada, which remained preeminent for slightly more than 200 years.

THE ANDALUSIAN NORTHEAST

An area of Andalusia frequently bypassed by travellers is the northeast province of Jaén, east of Córdoba and north of Grenada. Here are Ubeda and Baeza, two towns of exceptional interest, and a game preserve, Cazorla, outstanding among Spain's ten national parks. Both Baeza and Ubeda were prosperous Moorish towns—Baeza was a *taifas* (small kingdom) capital—that served as early bases for the Reconquest campaigns of Andalusia. During the Renaissance they became cities of remarkable architectural distinction, and the later shifting of campaign focus left their stunning structures almost untouched.

The city of Jaén, now on the main Granada–Madrid highway (N 323), is beautifully situated, as are Baeza and Ubeda, among vast symmetrical olive groves. They warrant a visit for their own sakes, but can be thought of as an optional side trip of a day or two from Granada, or as a rewarding pause on the route south to the Costa del Sol. Cazorla, infrequently visited, is a gem for sports-minded and nature-loving travellers. Baeza and Ubeda, only a few miles apart, are about 50 km (31 miles) northeast of Jaén on N 321 through agriculturally lush and peaceful countryside.

Ubeda

One single irregularly shaped plaza in Ubeda (plaza Vázquez de Molina) contains the most splendid assemblage of Renaissance buildings in all Spain. Their façades are a uniform gold or sand color (the Spanish call it impure white), and their disciplined lines convey the elegance and simplicity characteristic of Renaissance architecture at its best. And just beyond that plaza are structures within two or three blocks of one another that elsewhere would have individual stellar prominence.

Why does Ubeda have this corner on Renaissance architectural wealth? The Spanish have an expression, "irse por los cerros de Ubeda," which implies "getting off the track" in conversation or just generally wasting time. Literally it means "to go by way of the hills of Ubeda." And Ubeda, along with its handsome neighbor Baeza, is no longer on the route to anywhere. Ubeda was once a direct-line connection between Andalusia and northern Spain. But the establishment of commercial routes by way of the city of Jaén, to the southwest, and the loss of political-military strategic position as both Córdoba and Seville fell to the Reconquest forces, meant that Ubeda ended up off the track despite her great Renaissance holdings. Ironically, this also meant that no political or commercial forces felt the need to disrupt or alter them.

There are at least ten exceptional buildings in Ubeda, variations on a Renaissance theme, serenely confident in their uniformity of line but varying in all sorts of unexpected and sometimes witty quirks of design. The best way to experience Ubeda's architecture is to go first to the tourist office in the plaza de los Caídos for a small brochure, "The Map and Monuments of Ubeda," that offers invaluable line drawings and thumbnail sketches of the most outstanding buildings. The nucleus of masterworks in this small (population 30,000) town of narrow streets is Ubeda's old western section (Zona Monumental y Artesania). Excellent directional signs from N 321 through the more modern section of Ubeda lead you to the focal point, plaza Vázquez de Molina.

Three of the plaza buildings have long Florentine Renaissance façades. One of them is the **Condestable Dávalos,** now a national parador, a 16th-century palace (renovated in the 17th century) that belonged to Fernando Ortega, dean of Málaga; the second oldest of Spain's paradors (opened in 1930), it has a wonderful glass-enclosed courtyard, regal stairways, and high carved ceilings. Another Renaissance gem on this plaza is the **Palacio de las Cadenas** (palace of the chains), designed by Andrés de Vandaelvira with Corinthian orders on the first floor and Ionic on the second. The third building, also by Vandaelvira, is some distance from this treasure trove of

Renaissance structures: the **Hospital de Santiago** on calle de Obispo Cabos, several towers of which have recently had their tile work renovated; the Hospital has the disciplined severity of the Escorial without the grandiosity.

Of the churches in Ubeda, the first in rank is probably the plaza's **Capilla del Salvador**, designed by Vandaelvira and Diego de Siloé; the southern doorway of this chapel was "inspired" by Pedro Machuca, Charles V's Renaissance palace architect at the Alhambra. Directly adjacent to El Salvador's apse is its Hospital de Ancianos ("the Salvador ancients"), strikingly beautiful with its double-tiered classic columns. On plaza Vázquez de Molina is the **Iglesia de Santa María de los Reales Alcazares**, with an extraordinary and oddly shaped cloister, currently undergoing some restoration. A few blocks away is the **Iglesia de San Pablo** on plaza Primero de Mayo, a building that manages to incorporate a Gothic arched doorway within a Renaissance structure of distinction.

Behind the parador on plaza Ayuntamiento, a building to regard with pleasure and edification is the late-16th-century **city hall** with its double loggia: three arches supporting pairs of Corinthian columns, above which is an open façade with six arches. This is a building on which infinite craftsmanship has been lavished.

Of private dwellings, the **Casa de las Torres** (tower mansion), three blocks north of the plaza at the corner of calle Condestable Dávalos, is a Plateresque extravagance of the early 16th century, a detailed decorative morass that verges on the ludicrously excessive but manages to achieve balance. The **Palacio de Vela de los Cobos**, tucked into the corner of the narrow calle María de Molina, is the mid-16th-century mansion of the magistrate of Ubeda. It is a delight to observe, and its unobtrusive single white marble column at the corner balcony wittily mirrors those of the upper floor balcony-colonnade; the building has stonecutter's marks on all its blocks.

The place to stay in Ubeda is clearly the parador, and it is the place to eat as well; the service in the dining room may be the best of all of Spain's paradors.

Baeza

Baeza, only 9 km (5 miles) to the southwest of Ubeda on the way to Jaén, has half the population and suffers quite unfairly from the attention paid to its renowned neighbor. It suffers, too, from a lack of hotel accommodations and restaurants, and visitors usually come over from Ubeda for a quick look at the glories of Baeza and just as quickly depart.

Baeza was once a Roman town, then a prosperous Visigothic city, next the capital of a *taifas* (kingdom) under the Moors, and eventually the first town in Andalusia to fall to (or be rescued by) the Christian Reconquest forces. For a time thereafter, Baeza and Ubeda served as marshalling points for Reconquest forces in their drive south to recapture the rest of Andalusia. A university was founded here in 1595, and a printing press established in 1551, but, like Ubeda, Baeza became a byway and eventually developed into its current mold: that of a quiet town in a rich agricultural area, surrounded by miles of olive groves marching in all directions of the compass.

But this peaceful town of 15,000 has some superb buildings. Along the narrow, winding, almost empty streets are 16th-century structures of rare quality. The tourist office of Baeza may well have the most distinguished housing of any in Spain, a building constructed in the early part of the 16th century. Its Plateresque façade has a small projecting balcony from which the first Mass is said to have been offered after the Reconquest. Once the old civil court, it has six notaries' doorways on the ground floor. Above the doorways are medallions, and the windows of the second floor have railings and pediments.

In the center of the **plaza de los Leones** (lions' square), on which this classic building stands, is a fountain with ancient lion figures said to have been taken from the ruins of a Roman town. The statue has a tall, garbed female figure, whose lineage is reputed to be Iberian-Roman and whose likeness is that of the wife of Hannibal. This square also has a Renaissance building variously called the Old Butcher Shop, the Abattoir, and the **Carnicería**, with a gallery on its upper floor centered by a magnificent coat of arms of Charles V. As if this were not enough, the square has two monumental archways, unevenly crenellated, one of which, the arch of Villalar, was erected in 1526.

Baeza's buildings and monuments are strikingly lacking in military fortifications: Queen Isabella had those all torn down in 1476 to end a kind of Guelph-Ghibelline, Montague-Capulet internecine struggle here between the noble families of Benavides and Carvajales.

Baeza has a small Romanesque church, **Santa Cruz**, so perfect an architectural example of its type that it could serve as a model; constructed after the Reconquest in 1227, it has a Gothic chapel with mural frescoes. Opposite this church, one of Baeza's great houses or palaces, the **Palacio de Jabalquinto** on the cuesta de San Felipe, is a stunner, with its Isabelline façade, whose surprising chromatic effect is the result of the multiplicity of diamond heads and heraldic pinecones. Flanking this façade are two elegant torch-shaped columns that rise to become small balconies. The interior of the building has a relatively simple patio with two lions at the foot of the Baroque stairway.

The **Ayuntamiento** (city hall), off the plaza del Pópulo, is an original and unexpected example of Andalusian Plateresque. Philip II's coat of arms is between the balconies on the upper floor. Facing the plaza is the former corn exchange, with a classic façade of five arches, repeated on the second floor, both with Doric capitals.

A visitor begins to wonder what Renaissance Baeza may have been like at a time when the butcher shop, the jail, and the corn exchange were all deemed worthy of creation as architectural works of art.

The old university, with its spacious patio, became a high school in the late 19th century. Of the churches, the **Catedral de Baeza**, constructed on the site of an old mosque, has a 13th-century "moon" doorway, a 14th-century rose window, and a monumental iron grille by Bartolomé. The interior of the cathedral was remodeled by Vandaelvira in the late 16th century. Just alongside the cathedral is the **Casa Consistoriales**, an elegant building with two beautiful Gothic windows and, on the door, the royal coat of arms of Juana and Philip, the parents of Charles V.

Walking around in Baeza is a delight; the town is quiet and unpretentious, yet endowed with buildings and monuments of true distinction. Baeza has charm and a quality discovered by the few outsiders who have settled here and strive to underplay its rare characteristics. Like its neighbor Ubeda, however, Baeza is scalding hot in midsummer, and its midwinter can be severe. A very pleasant place to sample Andalusian fare here is the **Juanito restaurant**, which takes fine advantage of the prolific produce, game, and meats of the region.

Cazorla

Cazorla is the name of both a town and a national park. The town, 65 km (40 miles) east of Jaén on country roads, has a population of 10,250, and its white houses with umber-tiled roofs have as a backdrop a mammoth rock outcropping topped by the ruins of a Moorish castle and an ancient tower. The old town, clinging to this projection, seems not to have changed much since its days as a Moorish settlement; the new town, sprawling far below it, is very much part of the 20th century. There are two castles, the Moorish one on the heights, the Castillo de la Yedra below. Cazorla was once a practically impregnable Moorish stronghold, and historians claim that "over thirty castles had to be taken" to achieve Christian Reconquest victory in 1248. The old town has three main squares; the plaza de Santa María has a Renaissance fountain whose waters are said to come from río Cerezuelo flowing beneath the square.

Everything about the precipitously hilly town of Cazorla is modest, except its dramatic location. Food and lodging can be had in the town, but no hotels or restaurants are geared for travellers. All the more reason to assure the visitor that this hidden-away mountain town has that hard-to-find stamp of authenticity: The Moorish past and the Spanish present coexist gracefully.

Cazorla National Park

This national park in northeastern Jaén province was established in 1960. Twelve miles northeast of the town of Cazorla, it encompasses a rectangular-shaped area whose mountains surround a deep, fertile valley. This valley is the source of Spain's great río Guadalquivir, which gives life to Córdoba and Seville and empties into the Atlantic in the Cádiz-Jerez marshland of Coto Doñana.

The park is carefully supervised by ICONA (institute for the conservation of nature), and you must pass through a supervised gateway to enter. The park is magnificent: rich in wildlife and scenically beautiful. The roads, however, although paved, are not for the timid, as they are often cut in the rock above precipice-like drops and have many sharp turns.

The wild mountains, peaked with whitish-gray stone, have vast tracts of pine trees. Within the park is a parador, **El Adelantado**, a base for hikers, sportsmen, and vacationers. From the front terrace and garden of the parador you can look out on a valley that rises up to the leveled stone perimeter far above. This vista resembles those in Utah's Bryce Canyon and Zion national parks in the United States.

A day's hike from the parador follows a path directly behind the building that climbs perhaps 1,000 feet, levels off on a narrow but well-defined hiking trail, and carries you along on the top of the mountains, affording exceptional locations for photographing, picnicking, botanizing, and snoozing. One fork of the trail leads eventually down to the town of Cazorla; through a vent in the rocks you can see all the way below to the acres of olive trees lined up like a gigantic army on parade.

Permits for big-game (mountain goat, deer, buck) hunting during an autumn/winter season must be requested from ICONA. Wild boar can be hunted year-round, but a special permit is required. Trout fishing offers abundant opportunities for record catches. Bird watchers are likely to run out of numbers here; of special interest among rare birds is the Quebrantahuesos, or lammergeier, a sort of gigantic falcon with a wing span of ten feet, more powerful by far than the eagle. Botanists will find an exceptional variety of trees, shrubs, and wildflowers; a tiny and extremely rare species of violet called the Andalusian edelweiss is found only in these parts. The scent in the woodland areas permeating this world of nature may persuade you not to return to civilization.

Jaén

The city of Jaén (population 103,000), the capital of Andalusia's northern province of the same name, is on the direct route between Madrid and the Costa del Sol by way of Granada. The city has the classic Andalusian history, from the Carthaginians to the Romans to the Visigoths; under the Moors, it became a *taifas* capital. On its eastern side are miles of olive trees in formal rows; to the west rises Santa Catalina hill, on top of which is a castle built by the Arab king Alhamar and reconstructed in 1246 by Ferdinand III. The national parador **Castillo de Santa Catalina** is adjacent, with its transcendent vista of the Sierra Morena and the surrounding countryside.

Surprisingly, Jaén has less of interest than you might suspect considering its background. The streets are narrow, it is difficult to get around, and the 1525 design of the entrance to the huge cathedral by Vandaelvira succeeds in dwarfing its surroundings at the expense of aesthetics. The cathedral has superb choir stalls from the 15th and 16th centuries; in the chapter chapel there is an altarpiece by Pedro Machuca, Charles V's architect.

An extensive area of 11th-century **Arab baths** lies under the Renaissance **Palacio de Villardompardo** on the plaza Luisa de Marillac. Cold, warm, and hot rooms, a central pool, complex heating devices, beautiful chandeliers, and tiling cover an area so large that the baths are said to be the most important known in Spain. Call the provincial administration (Tel: 26-21-11) for information on available visiting times.

Jaén has two good restaurants, **La Fontana**, on Arquitecto Berges 23, offering a variety of shellfish, and **Los Mariscos**, on Nueva 2, which specializes in Spanish cuisine. The parador has a commendable restaurant and offers the best accommodation in town.

GRANADA

Granada is Andalusia's most rakish city, with a mock-sixties look to many of its pedestrians, perhaps because of the gypsy population and a large tribe of nomadic young backpackers. Granada's midcity traffic is horrendous (and you can't bypass the central city), but, unlike in Jerez, signs here are well posted: high enough that the truck ahead of you does not obscure your vision and cause you to head for Motril when your destination is Madrid.

For most travellers Granada means the Alhambra, and indeed, the city itself, despite its splendid situation geographically, has a limited number of compelling attractions. Had Granada not been the last great stronghold of the Moors, causing Ferdinand and Isabella to mark it as the site of Reconquest triumph and unification of Spain, culturally it would be ranked as a conventional Andalusian city. Should you be passing through Granada with the Alhambra as your only stop, follow signs for the cathedral area; here you will find clear Alhambra signs leading you to the plaza Nueva, where you make a sharp right uphill for the Alhambra promontory.

Much of Granada's urban activity centers around a high traffic density point, the plaza de Isabel la Católica, where calle de los Reyes Católicos meets Gran Vía de Colón. Two blocks north of the plaza on Gran Vía is the entrance to the royal chapel; behind it (one entrance is on calle de la Carcel) rises the enormous cathedral. The colorful, touristy plaza Bibarrambla and the Alcaicería (silk exchange) are a block west of the cathedral. Here you are likely to encounter Granadians from every walk of life and visitors of every nationality. The tackiest of souvenirs are on display here, as well as some fine embroidery, silver, ceramics, and brass.

Two blocks south of this atmospheric locale, calle de los Reyes Católicos runs west to the Puerta Real, an area of traditional old cafés and pastry shops. Stores in the vicinity offer an enormous variety of wares for visitors, including mantillas, shawls, leather goods, blue and green "grenadine" pottery, fans, silver filigree, dolls, woven bedspreads, and lacework.

Between Gran Vía and Elvira, a street running parallel to it one block east, are some inexpensive and savory restaurants. East of here is the plaza Nueva and beyond it the hillside **Albacin section** of Granada, which faces the Alhambra across the puny río Darro. White Moorish houses, some of them tiny, some opulent with high, white-walled enclosures, together with former mosques now converted to Baroque churches, mark this locale as the place where Moors continued to live even after the Reconquest. If you continue east you reach the Sacramonte with its gypsy caves.

Just three blocks east of the plaza de Isabel la Católica is the inconspicuous cuesta de Gomerz leading south from the plaza Nueva. This busy thoroughfare, lined with shops, climbs a steep slope to the Puerta de las Granadas, the archway-entrance to the extensive grounds of the Alhambra. Climbing upward, the road continues through deeply shaded elm tree woods, planted at Wellington's instigation, to the Alhambra promontory, where signs lead you on to the entrance of the Alcazaba-Alhambra compound. Your ticket of admission, purchased at the administration building, includes a visit to the Generalife gardens.

The Alcazaba

Travellers climbing to the summit of the Alcazaba fortress watchtower on the Alhambra promontory are forewarned: They are about to be dazzled by what awaits them. "Nothing in life," a nearby plaque reads, "nothing, is sadder than to be blind in Granada." It's all miraculously here, just as Washington Irving, the brochures, the photographs, the travel books, and all those other travellers promised.

"There is notoriously nothing more to be said on the subject," as Henry James observed of Venice. White Granada spreads out far below you; to the northeast are the Sacromonte hills, honeycombed by gypsy caves, and a ravine. The full sweep of the Alhambra is to the east—its buildings, towers, gardens, and the great defensive wall. And in the distance to the southeast are the snow-clad Sierra Nevadas. As if this were not enough, at sunset Nature often loses control and indulges in a display that defines hyperbolic excess.

On this great promontory above Granada, it is not hard to distinguish between the Alcazaba (fortress), dating back to the ninth century, and the Casa Real, or Alhambra, a series of palaces constructed without any preconceived plan by Yusuf I (1333–1354) and Mohammed V (1354–1391). The Alcazaba is considerably less showy than the Alhambra, but from a standpoint of provenance we have here the original structure in a sense that is not true of the Alhambra.

This ancient fortress has a no-nonsense look of authenticity. It was erected for military purposes, and is entirely independent of the palaces of luxury and refinement on the eastern part of the promontory. These reddish brick and stone façades rise from a base formed by a screen of ramparts. Remnants of small houses, a workshop, a bakery, and a cistern, as well as dungeons for the Christian captives, tell us that the Alcazaba once housed a small settlement. There's something thoroughly utilitarian about it all, a point to keep in mind when touring the palaces; here, outside on these battlements, we see the Moors as fighters and conquerors, tough, ruthless, and determined. Without them the Alhambra would not exist.

The Alhambra

The Alhambra is not a building but a generic term that today, apart from the Alcazaba and the Generalife gardens, describes a hilltop settlement that includes private dwellings, shops, a small post office, a hostal, a Catholic church, a Franciscan convent converted into a parador (more on that below), a restaurant, a mammoth 16th-century Renaissance palace, and an administration that handles more than a million tourists annually.

The focal point for most travellers is the 25-or-so palace interiors and courtyards. You enter at the Mexuar, a former council chamber, and in a vaguely predetermined order pass through the Hall of the Ambassadors, the Court of the Myrtle Trees, the Hall of the Two Sisters, the Court of the Lions with its two adjacent rooms, the Royal Baths on a lower level, and the Daraxa Garden with its mirador overlooking the escarpments.

How authentic is all of this? When Washington Irving arrived in 1829 for his three-month stay, the Alhambra had suffered years of neglect and decay. "The palace of the King" had become "the nesting place of the beggar." The Alhambra, guarded by a handful of invalid soldiers garrisoned nearby, was a riot of unconventional tenancy. Whenever a tower fell to decay, writes Irving, it was seized by "some tatterdemalion family who became joint tenants with the bats and owls of its golden halls and hang their rags, those standards of poverty, out of its windows and loopholes." Eccentrics and one confined maniac were among the cast of characters.

The condition of the walls, the ceilings, and the floors (the numerous palace courtyards are open to the sky) bore the scars of both the elements and the French military occupation of the buildings during the Peninsular War in the early part of the century. When he was not immersing himself in the romantic sensibility of an imagined past, Irving observed that the "beautiful reliefs . . . and Arabic inscriptions" were frequently "scrawled over" and the Alhambra was at the mercy of "the pilferings of the tasteful traveler."

But as hordes of travellers follow one another through the Alhambra today, the palace looks as fresh and inviting as if the Moors had departed just the previous weekend. The overwhelming impression is one of opulence of imagination, design, and craftsmanship.

Three materials predominate: plaster, wood, and tile. Fragile plaster, often in stucco form, was used so extensively that it seems evident that aesthetic satisfaction of the moment was of more interest to the Moors than posthumous architectural recognition. Wood was used as a decorative counterpoint to plaster: the **Hall of the Ambassadors**, a perfect square with some 150 designs stamped in the plaster, has an intricately carved 60-foot domed cedar ceiling. Tiles are set in walls to frame doorways; tiles serve as dadoes to decorate the lower part of a wall; green, black, ocher, and white tiles predominate in the royal baths, adorning the walls and alcoves in geometric patterns.

You pass through the much photographed and beautifully proportioned **Court of the Myrtle Trees**, and enter the pièce de résistance: the **Court of the Lions**. The rectangular court has a fountain at midpoint, supported on the backs of 12 grotesque lions. On close examination (but not too close; they were recently roped off), the lions turn out to be caricatures of savage beasts. Their teeth are bared in burlesque grins, their tails neatly wrapped around their left hindquarters. They are stripped of any dignity by water jets spurting from their mouths.

To the north is the Hall of the Two Sisters; to the west, the Mocarabes Gallery; to the south, the Abencerrajes Gallery. Here you are invited to kneel at the pool to catch the reflection of the entire Court of the Lions. The marble flooring reputedly still carries the bloodstains of some beheadings that took place here.

The palace rooms are stripped bare. The carvings and tracery of the walls and ceilings are mostly bone white. Remnants of the blues and reds and golds of the original are rarely discernible. As with the Parthenon, contemporary viewers get an erroneous sense of the original aesthetic. Here the lamps, the colored glass, the furniture, the rugs, the draperies, the play of interior hues are gone. The tenants have left; the house is empty.

Most of us move unthinkingly back and forth from these chaste interiors to courtyards lush with floral exuberance and the sparkling play of fountains. Such contrast was unknown to the Moors. For them, balance was all. They lived in a world of measured equipoise; we visit only their vacant rooms.

Washington Irving's Quarters

Washington Irving lived for three months in 1829 in a suite of rooms built by Charles V overlooking the Daraxa Garden. Were he to awaken in these apartments today, he would find himself, much as Rip Van Winkle did, in a familiar world whose properties have somehow altered. The condition of this suite in Irving's time reinforced his romanticized view of the Alhambra. The "ruined" apartments had windows "dismantled and open to the weather," and the ceilings were "broken in many places."

These rooms have been refurbished, renovated, and reconstituted. They look like a fashionable decorator's idea of a literary lair. The walls, once "scrawled over with the insignificant names of aspiring travelers," are now pristine. The carved ceilings and the tiled floors are in mint condition. A desk stands ready for Irving to write upon, silk-embroidered chairs for the comfort of his guests, a spinet for musical enjoyment, and on the walls his portrait shares space with those of Ferdinand and Isabella. Beyond the windows, Irving's citron and orange trees have yielded to regal cypresses rising from the garden whose center fountain is surrounded by ten geometric planting areas.

A plaque on the door advises in Spanish that "Washington Irving wrote in these rooms his Tales of the Alhambra in the year 1829." At most, Irving wrote here a handful of the chapters that make up his book published three years later. The door is locked, however. The metamorphosed rooms apparently await Irving's return.

The Palace of Charles V

The Emperor Charles V's immense Renaissance palace in the midst of the Alhambra is as incongruous as the Christian cathedral built with his compliance in the center of the Córdoba mosque. On the one hand the intrusions are aesthetically and culturally offensive, but on the other they call attention to the phenomenon that Reconquest frenzy did not destroy such Moorish treasures in its wake.

Charles V's palace provokes a variety of responses. "An arrogant intruder," wrote Washington Irving; "we pass by it with a feeling almost of scorn." In our own time James Michener in *Iberia* calls it, "hideous . . . that monstrous edifice . . . a bleak . . . brutal cube." "The most beautiful of all Renaissance palaces outside Italy," declares Marino Antequera, a contemporary art historian in his book on the Alhambra.

In 1526 Charles employed as his architect Pedro Machuca, a Spaniard who had studied in Italy under Michelangelo. This square building has a great interior circular court open to the sky; the court has 24 double-tiered Ionic columns, and the ceilings of the colonnades are of carved cedar. The exterior of the lower surface of the building is rusticated masonry as in a Florentine Medici palace.

Unlike Córdoba's cathedral superimposed on its mosque, this is not a religious intrusion but a cultural-political statement on contrasting styles and the power they reflect. This massive palace has a cleanness of line, of symmetry, and of proportion that represents the best of late-Renaissance architecture. On its own terms it is an admirable structure: uncompromising, meticulously crafted, handsome.

The Generalife

Gardens contribute significantly to the splendor of the Alhambra. Beyond the palaces themselves, the Partal Gardens extend from the northern embankment of río Darro up a series of terraces marked off by stone steps. Pools, fountains, and an opulent abundance of flowers make these gardens a place of beauty.

But the great formal garden of the Alhambra promontory is the Generalife (hen-er-al-EE-fay). This long rectangular garden is cut into the hillside at right angles to the Alhambra complex, separated from it by the terraced río Darro ravine. The Generalife, a term derived from the Arabic *Gennat-*

Alarif, meaning "garden of the architect," is ranked by experts as one of Europe's great gardens. Three elements determine such recognition: the vistas offered from vantage points of colonnades, balconies, and promontories; the extensive use of fountains and pools; and the plantings of trees and flowers in a climate that ensures blooms throughout the year.

Only the belvedere and the guardhouse beyond belong to Moorish times. The rest consists of Christian reconstructions and additions. The Generalife was privately owned for some years, tenanted by Spanish nobility (the marquéses de Campotojar). The plantings are contemporary, the pools and fountains extensively realigned, and, apart from some ancient trees, the Generalife is a modern re-creation of an ancient design.

In retrospect, the Alhambra is different from what the traveller anticipates, as adulthood is different from the way we perceive it as children. It is richer, less comprehensive, and more rewarding. "Architecturally the Alhambra Palace has little merit," writes A. C. Calvert in *Southern Spain.* "It is impossible to trace any order in the distribution of its parts. There is nothing imposing about the edifice, nothing stately. Its great charm lies in its decoration, which is wonderful and, in its own line, beyond all praise." On the other hand, Jan Morris sees the Alhambra as "foppish within, tremendous on the outside," and V. S. Pritchett claims that, "except for its massive and splendid outer walls and gates, which are the main beauty of the place, the Alhambra is a gay and flimsy construction."

We owe the revival of interest in Arabic Spain and in the Alhambra to Irving, Chateaubriand, Victor Hugo, and Gautier. But, as H. V. Morton observes in *A Stranger in Spain,* "Anyone who has read [Richard] Ford's grim account of the decay of the Alhambra will wonder how much of the present building is genuine and how much is restoration." The Arabic scholar James Dickie claims that "what confronts us now is but a remnant, the end-product of an uninterrupted process of metamorphosis over five centuries. It were unfair not to add that it was the much-derided Romantics who saved the Alhambra. Through the fame their writings conferred on it, the Alhambra became a household word in every language."

To those of us who visit it today, the Alhambra, however dubious its provenance, rewards us with an insight into the magnificence of Moorish architecture and decoration. What we see now may be a pale, and often inaccurate, reflection of what once was here, but enough remains to inspire us.

La Cartuja

In the northern section of Granada, the Carthusian monastery, known as La Cartuja, has in its church what is sometimes called a Christian response to the Alhambra's decoration. It is hardly that, but here in unrestrained, exuberant Baroque stucco, almost entirely in white, the walls and domed ceilings are set off against doors and cedar furnishings with opalescent and silver decorative motifs. The cloisters of the monastery are unadorned and peaceably inviting; here, as everywhere in Granada, the city's glory is the abundance and beauty of its flowers, with roses, in particular, of exquisite color, shape, and size.

The Cathedral

Below the Alhambra promontory in the city of Granada stands the huge cathedral designed by Diego de Siloé in 1528. But Alfonso Cano is responsible for the façade, with its three tall arcades. The cathedral has five naves and nine chapels. Cano's paintings are here as well, and in the rotunda are twin facing panels, a medallion by Cano, and figures of los Reyes Católicos at prayer by Cano's illustrious pupil Pedro de Mena. The cathedral generally gets bad notices from art historians, however, who have described it as "pretentious" and "the saddest of wasted opportunities."

The Royal Chapel

The royal chapel, right next to the cathedral, was built by the Catholic monarchs (los Reyes Católicos) to hold their mausoleums and later those of their daughter, Juana (the Mad), and her husband, Philip (the Fair). The chapel is an unmitigated tribute to the monarchs in the light of the glorious culminating victory of Christianity after nearly eight centuries of Moorish presence. This Renaissance chapel was designed by Enrique Egas, and the beautiful wrought-iron grille that closes off the transept was created by Master Bartolomé.

Four supine figures lie in state, those of Ferdinand and Isabella carved in white marble by Fancelli, those of Juana and Philip by Bartolomé Ordóñez. In the sacristy are Ferdinand's sword, Isabella's scepter, and a collection of Isabella's fabulous art holdings, significantly non-Spanish, including works by Memling, Van der Weyden, Perugino, Berruguete, and Botticelli. The high altar retable has Renaissance groups and figures against a background of scrollwork and grotesques.

A chilling reminder of mortality as the ultimate equalizer are the four stark sarcophagi under the magnificent tomb itself (you walk down a flight of stairs to gaze at them).

Ferdinand and Isabella have become such legendary figures of glory in Spain that we have to remind ourselves that they represent more than just a royal couple who had a signal victory over the Moors. Under them, in 1479, Spain for the first time became a united country: Castile and Aragón were now one, at least politically. And the defeat of King Boabdil at Granada in 1492 signaled the end of almost 800 years of Moorish occupation in Spain. For Christians this victory symbolized the triumph of Christ over Mohammed. The discovery of the New World in the same year was the beginning of a Golden Age of wealth and international power for Spain; largely forgotten is Isabella's installation of the Inquisition, first in Castile and then on the entire peninsula. She appointed Torquemada as Grand Inquisitor in 1483, and the Moors, Jews, and, later, Protestants became the objects of persecution. In 1492, the Jews in Spain were ordered to convert to Christianity or leave Spain, or be murdered. Most left, a grievous loss of skills and intellect that was to rebound to the country's disadvantage over the following centuries.

Staying and Dining in Granada

By almost any standard, the **Parador Nacional de San Francisco**, in a renovated convent right on the Alhambra promontory (and the location of Queen Isabella's original entombment), is the best bet for lodging and dining. From its terrace you look out on the Generalife garden, and the interior of the inn reflects decorative paradors at their best. Its popularity is such that reservations need to be made many months in advance.

Close by is the venerable **Alhambra Palace**, with service and rooms that are first class. The Alhambra Palace has something of a parking problem, but it is handled with admirable dispatch. The view of the city from the bar terrace is worth the price of several drinks. It's likely to be noisy in public rooms on weekends, when local celebratory functions take place.

Down in the city proper, the **Meliá Granada** on Angel

Ganivet just five blocks east of the plaza Isabel la Católica, and the **Luz Granada** on avenida de la Constitución, which leads to both N 432 (Córdoba) and N 342 (Málaga), are modern and geared to handle many guests.

You will find it simpler to take a taxi to most restaurants in downtown Granada, which is crisscrossed by a labyrinth of streets that follow no perceptible pattern and reflect the Roman-Visigothic-Moorish heritage. The **Baroca**, at Pedro Antonio de Alaron 34, Tel: 26-50-61, closed Sundays and all of August, pleases many customers with both international and Granadian cooking. The **Alcona de las Monjas**, on the plaza Padre Suárez, Tel: 27-08-00, specializes in native dishes, and **Cunini**, at Capuchinas 14, near the northwest corner of the cathedral, Tel: 26-37-01, is known for its seafood; the shellfish are brought up daily from Motril. On the south side of the Alhambra hill, the **Carmen de San Miquel**, at Torres Bermejas 3, Tel: 27-67-33, with a panoramic view from its Andalusian fountain-adorned patio, includes local specialties as part of its larger international menu. For lunch, a number of small and inevitably crowded restaurants in the Alhambra vicinity, most notably down the road from in front of the Alhambra Palace hotel, have their menus and prices conveniently posted.

THE SIERRA NEVADA

The snowcapped peaks in the background of the Alhambra are a mere one hour's drive south from Granada, uphill all the way. The road (46 km/29 miles) rises to a height of 11,148 feet on what road signs declare to be the route to the highest spot in Europe. Here is Andalusia's ski center, providing some of the best skiing in Spain, even, very high up, in midsummer. A cluster of inns and seasonal hotels, such as the **Meliá Sierra Nevada** and the **Meliá Sol y Nieve**, in the ski resort town of Pradollano, as well as a national parador about a mile beyond, provide accommodations. When the road is open to the summit, you can get close to the Veleta and Mulhacen peaks, the highest in continental Spain.

Clearly this can be a day trip with Granada as a base, or you can stay at the comfortable all-seasons **Parador Nacional Sierra Nevada** in the quiet of the Sierra peaks. Some of the vistas are uncommonly fine, and there is something intriguing about their proximity to semi-tropical Granada, often a very hot place in midsummer. In nonwinter months these mountains, with their northern exposure, are rather desolate above the timber line, and there is a decided ski-resort-out-of-season look to the terrain. But hikes for the hearty and a parador menu that emphasizes local dishes make the Sierra Nevada inviting.

The Alpujarras

The Alpujarras mountain range, the southern face of the Sierra Nevada, has long been known as a "wild" and little-travelled part of Andalusia. Moors fled here after the final conquest of Granada in 1492, and were not finally expelled until 1609 by Philip III, giving ample testimony to the remoteness of the area.

A visit to a town high in these mountains between Granada and the Mediterranean is decidedly a matter of temperament: It will test the driver's resilience on what are the most tortuous roads remaining in Spain; it will call for composure and a minimum of advice from the passengers. But gratification that far exceeds mere pleasure in arrival/survival awaits. The mountains are as steep as the valleys are deep. The former are snowcapped well into June; the latter are verdant and dark and act as sluices for rushing water.

One town to visit is **Bubión**, 71 km (44 miles) southeast of Granada, where a few years ago a modest and inviting village compound for travellers was built in the style of the white Moorish row houses of the region. The compound has 24 houses of different sizes, well equipped and comfortably furnished, with fireplaces to ward off the evening chill. Reservations can be made for these travellers' houses by writing or phoning the **Villa Turistica de Bubión** (see Accommodations Reference).

The towns of the Alpujarras resemble the White Towns of the triangular route of southwestern Andalusia, but here they are more starkly Arabic in profile, built on slopes of higher mountain ranges where in winter they are virtually snowbound. Local produce comes from terrace-farming on the inclines. The façades of these Alpujarras houses, with their rounded chimneys, are not interspersed with inviting entrances to courtyards; both climate and politics dictated dwellings that would be protective of their occupants.

Villagers here today weave traditional fabrics whose bright greens, reds, and whites are somehow Alpine in mood. Only the precipitous roads save the Alpujarras from becoming Spain's next great touristic "discovery"; even so, **Capileira**, the town immediately north of Bubión, could become the next century's Mijas (see the Costa del Sol section).

THE ANDALUSIAN COAST

Western Costa de la Luz

Just 60 miles southwest of Seville, where the río Guadalquivir empties into the Atlantic on the western Costa de la Luz, is the **Doñana national park**, a 173,000-acre park containing a mind-numbing diversity of wildlife. The spectacular area itself, with beaches, lagoons, and marshes, to say nothing of forests of juniper, pine, and cork oak, also features shifting sand dunes. A short listing of animals and birds could not begin to suggest the diversity of sightings: A single ornithologist is said to have spotted 1,891 birds of 35 different species in one afternoon. The animals range from lynx to wild boar to weasels and dormice.

From Seville, the best way to reach the park is to turn off the Seville–Huelva highway (N 431) at La Palma del Condado onto a local road leading to Almonte and El Rocio. The park's information office is several miles on the right beyond El Rocio; the 12-minute introductory slide presentation on Doñana's geological history is in Spanish.

Along the shore northwest toward Huelva, at **Mazagón**, is the 23-room **Parador Nacional Cristóbal Colón**, which you can use as a base for exploring. Built on the edge of a cliff, surrounded by acres of pines and scented lavender, and lulled by the distant roar of coastal waves, the parador is one of those tranquil spots whose location you swear you will never reveal to anyone. Visitors are not permitted to tour the park proper on their own: Four-hour safari tours leave twice daily from the reception area, about 11 km (7 miles) beyond the information office, at 8:30 A.M. and 4:30 P.M.; advance reservations should be made through the Nature Conservation Institute at Huelva; Tel: 24-93-09. Try the **Las Dunas restaurant** at Mazagón for its paellas and fresh Atlantic catch.

In light of the 1992 celebrations of the 500th anniversary of Columbus's discovery of the Americas, a splendid side trip can be made from Mazagón to **Palos de la Frontera**, on the Tinto estuary across from Huelva some 12 km (8 miles) to the northwest, from whose harbor Columbus sailed on August 3, 1492.

Using the Parador Cristóbal Colón at Mazagón as your base, you can almost completely avoid Huelva, an uninviting industrial city, while visiting Palos, La Rábida, and Moguer. These towns, a stone's throw from one another, lie at the joint delta of the Odiel and Tinto rivers, which became a principal anchorage for the conquistadores. Thanks to the intervention of Juan Pérez, the prior of the little port of La Rábida, los Reyes Católicos gave Columbus the necessary backing.

Shifting coastal shorelines have silted up the harbor of Palos de la Frontera, the actual point of Columbus's departure. A memorial to him (made by Gertrude Vanderbilt Whitney) and the 14th-century St. George's church are among the other sites of historic interest here. Hernán Cortés, conqueror of Mexico, set out from this port in 1528. In fact, by the 16th century río Tinto was the main point of departure for Spain's explorations to the Americas.

The monastery where Columbus stayed at **La Rábida**, southwest along the Tinto estuary from Palos de la Frontera, is open to the public, and a small museum here contains models of the three celebrated ships of his first voyage, as well as navigation charts and old books. The port of **Moguer**, north of Palos de la Frontera, considered by some to be one of the most dazzling all-white Andalusian towns, was another harbor used by the conquistadores. It is also the birthplace of Nobel Prize–winning poet Juan Ramón Jiménez, whose interesting house you can visit.

JEREZ DE LA FRONTERA

Near the mouth of río Guadalete and the Atlantic, less than two hours southwest of Seville by way of one of Spain's few *autopistas,* the essentially flat town of Jerez physically resembles other towns and cities of southern Andalusia: The buildings are white with tiled roofs, the parks are filled with tropical plants and blooms, and the streets, lined with orange and lemon trees, are infuriatingly hard to maneuver through (they follow an arcane traffic system based on the "disappearing/recurring one-way" school of urban design). With a population of more than 175,000, Jerez is really a small city. It shares its proud "de la Frontera" cognomen with other Andalusian localities—Arcos, Vejér, Chiclana, Jimena, Castellar, Conil—as witness to its role in the Christian Reconquest.

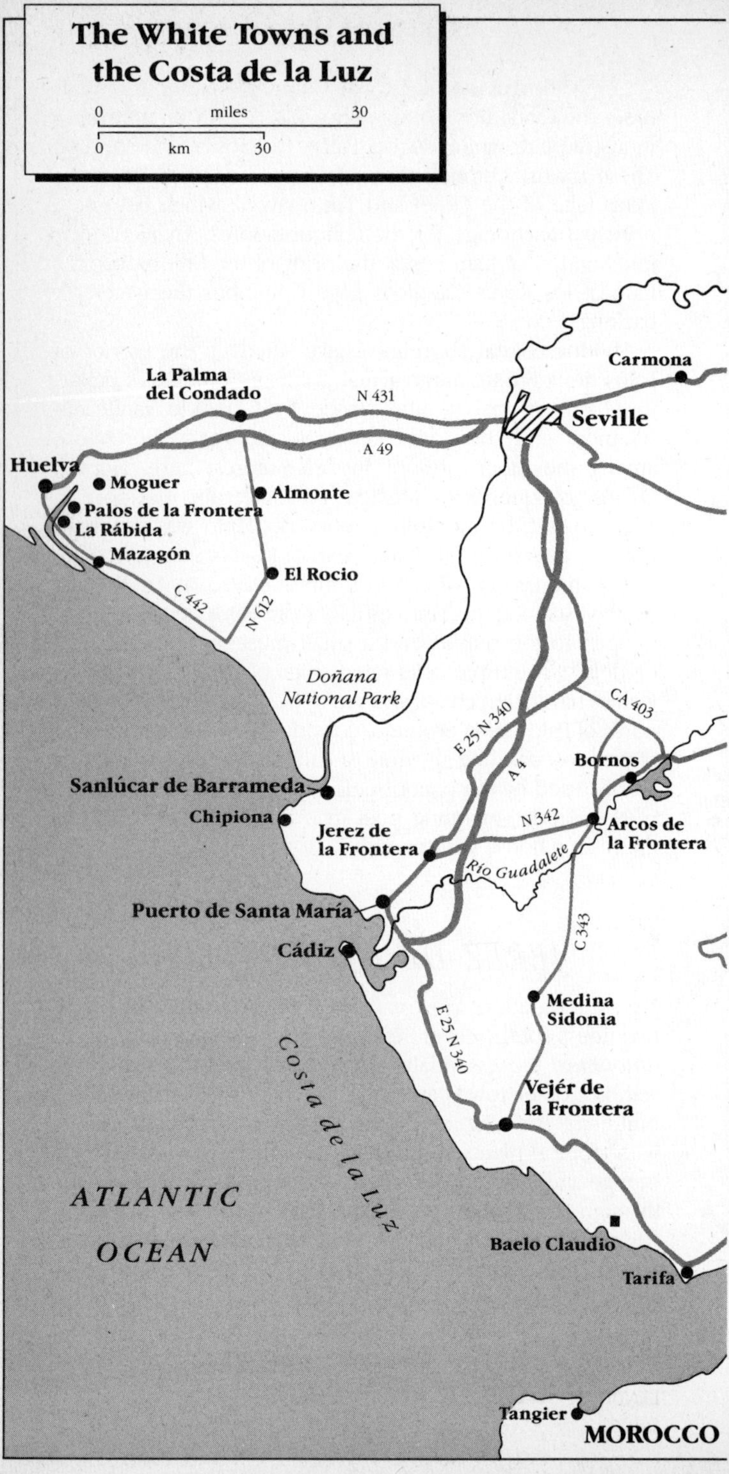
The White Towns and the Costa de la Luz
0
miles
30
0
km
30
Carmona
La Palma
del Condado
N 431
Seville
A 49
Huelva
Moguer
Almonte
Palos de la Frontera
La Rábida
Mazagón
El Rocio
C 442
N 612
Doñana
National Park
CA 403
E 25 N 340
A 4
Bornos
Sanlúcar de Barrameda
Chipiona
N 342
Arcos de
la Frontera
Jerez de
la Frontera
Río Guadalete
Puerto de Santa María
C 343
Cádiz
Medina
Sidonia
E 25 N 340
Costa de la Luz
Vejér de
la Frontera
ATLANTIC
OCEAN
Baelo Claudio
Tarifa
Tangier
MOROCCO

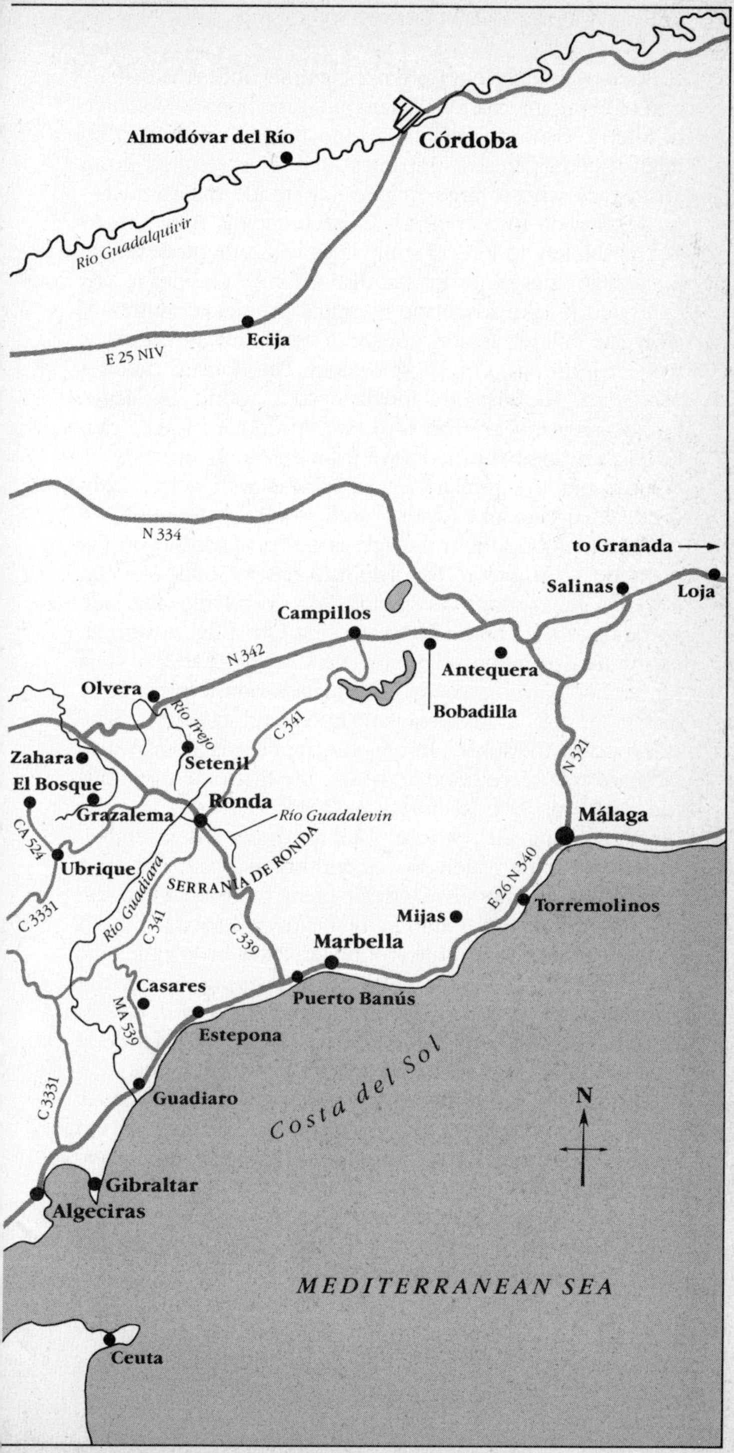
Almodóvar del Río
Córdoba
Río Guadalquivir
Ecija
E 25 NIV
N 334
to Granada
Salinas
Loja
Campillos
Antequera
Bobadilla
N 342
Olvera
Río Trejo
C 341
Setenil
Zahara
El Bosque
Grazalema
Ronda
Río Guadalevin
N 321
Málaga
CA 524
Ubrique
SERRANIA DE RONDA
E 26 N 340
Torremolinos
C 3331
Río Guadiara
C 341
C 339
Mijas
Marbella
Casares
Puerto Banús
MA 539
Estepona
Costa del Sol
N
Guadiaro
C 3331
Gibraltar
Algeciras
MEDITERRANEAN SEA
Ceuta

But Jerez is different from its neighbors. It has the distinction of being internationally famous as the home and source of Sherry. Centuries of Sherry and brandy production by English and Spanish companies here have resulted in an aristocracy whose large ranches, alongside the vast vineyards, provide lush areas for horse breeding. Breeding, in fact, is the key to Jerez. Family lines with inherited wealth, equestrian lines of purity and distinction, plant lines in soil cultivated to take advantage of unique natural conditions—all create in Jerez an atmosphere in which lineage is quality.

Jerez itself has a proud genealogy. The Romans called it Asta Regia. The Visigoths fought fiercely against the Moors for the area in 711. The Christian Reconquest forces captured the walled, fortified town from the Moors in 1264.

Jerez has the remains of an alcázar with a late 12th-century octagonal tower, and several distinguished churches, among them the Iglesia de San Dionisio on the plaza de la Asunción. San Dionisio has a Gothic-Mudejar tower, a fine patio, and a high Rococo retable; the side entrance to the church has a startling Christ figure with an expression of infinite despair. The **Casa del Cabildo Vieja** (an archeological museum-library), also on the plaza de la Asunción, has a Renaissance façade and contains some unexpected treasures. Among the numerous Roman artifacts are two carved Roman heads, the first of a querulous old man, his face acidulous with exasperation, and the other a young girl, whose youthful sweetness is embellished by her intricately woven and braided hair. The most remarkable holding is a Greek helmet, attributed to the seventh century B.C., found in the nearby riverbed.

But it is the countryside around Jerez that brought it fame and that will delight the visitor. In the spring the verdant fields are ablaze with wildflowers: blue, pink, red, yellow, purple. The half-hour drive from Jerez east to Arcos de la Frontera (see The White Towns, below) is a visual treat.

The rare soil for the Sherry vineyards is almost snow white in spring, when it absorbs the rains like a sponge, and then in the blazing heat of summer it hardens into a glass-like armor, deflecting the beating rays, while the vines' lengthy roots feed from the reserves of moisture lying beneath the crust. The ranches, for both horses and breeding of bulls, seem to stretch like endless blankets of deep green. From a distance the huge black bulls look prehistoric. The horses here are among the finest in Europe, and in this aristocratic locale polo fields are as common as tennis courts.

Jerez has three good restaurants, the cuisine in all of them taking advantage of the city's proximity to the sea: **El Bosque**, avenida de Alvaro Domecq 25, Tel: 30-33-33, in a park-like setting, specializes in regional dishes; **Gaitan**, Gaitan 3, Tel: 34-58-59, recently renovated, has a diversified menu; and **La Mesa Redonda**, Manuel de la Quintana 3, Tel: 34-00-69, centrally located near the plaza del Caballo, has a limited but excellent menu. The **Hotel Jerez**, with 120 rooms, is in the residential section of the city, surrounded by tropical gardens; it is comfortable and air-conditioned (especially nice in this city of torrid summer temperatures), and has a swimming pool and a good restaurant.

Sherry

Jerez-Xeres-Sherry claims (Rioja disputes it) to be Spain's oldest *denominación de origen* (DO), the Spanish equivalent of France's *appellation contrôlée*. Jerez de la Frontera, **Puerto de Santa María**, and **Sanlúcar de Barrameda** at the mouth of the Guadalquivir to the northwest, the three great Sherry towns, form what is known as the golden triangle that encompasses the greatest vineyards of the region.

The finest, most delicate wines of Jerez—the dry manzanillas, finos, and amontillados—come from Palomino grapes grown in a white, chalky soil known as *albariza* in vineyards located between Jerez and Sanlúcar. These wines of the fino family are made possible by a unique type of yeast known in the Sherry country as *flor* (flower), which grows in a cream-colored layer on the surface of the wine in barrel. The layer of yeast cells prevents air from reaching the wine, which protects the wine from oxidation during the long periods it spends in wood. *Flor* also consumes any sugar left in the wine and contributes a pleasant, yeasty quality to the wine.

In some wines, primarily from lesser-quality vineyards, the *flor* is weak or does not grow at all. These wines are destined to become olorosos, which are coarser and less delicate than wines of the fino family. Olorosos are fortified by adding grape brandy, which raises the alcohol levels to the 18 to 23 percent range. Olorosos are often sweetened with wine made from Pedro Ximénez grapes, which have been sunned on straw mats to concentrate their sugars and flavors. This blending technique is used to produce sweetened olorosos and cream Sherries. Pedro Ximénez, or PX, as it is often called, and Moscatel are also used to produce intensely sweet dessert wines of the same name.

The Solera System. Sherries are not vintaged wines; they are made by an expensive, labor-intensive process—the *solera* system, which ensures continuity of style and quality in the various types of wines offered by each *bodega.* A *solera* is a complicated network of barrels for blending and aging Sherries until they are ready to be bottled and sold. To ensure maximum freshness, Sherries are never bottled until the *bodega* receives an order.

For each style of wine to be made, rows (called *escalas,* or scales) of 500-liter American oak casks are set up. There may be from three to 14 rows containing from a few up to hundreds of barrels in a single *solera.* The bottom row, or last *escala,* contains the oldest and finest Sherry and is called *solera,* a word that derives from *suelo,* Spanish for floor. The other rows are called *criaderas* (nurseries) and are identified by their row number (#1, #2, #3, etc.).

Wine for shipment is always drawn from the oldest row of casks, the *solera.* To maintain quality, usually no more than one-third (and often less) of the wine is taken from the *solera* scale in any one year. The *solera* scale is replenished with an equal amount of wine from *criadera* row #1; #1 is replenished from *criadera* #2; and so on until the last row is reached. The last row is replenished from wine of the *añada* (current year). This complex, costly fractional blending process (known as "running the scales") requires great expertise and much manual labor. By the time each *añada*'s wine has completed its several-year journey through the scales of the *solera* system, it will have taken on the noble characteristics of the older wines in the system.

Almacenistas. Until recently, only the most dedicated aficionado of fine Sherry, usually armed with knowledge acquired in Spain or in England and living near a wine merchant who cares about such things, had a chance of acquiring a bottle of classic Sherry in good shape. Fortunately for lovers of fine Sherries, the Sherry producers of Jerez are waking up to the fact that the market may be much more receptive to the real thing than to offerings primarily designed to cater to the sweet tooth of mass-market sherry drinkers.

The Jerez firm of Emilio Lustau is the undisputed star of this budding Sherry renaissance. Many of the best wines in the Lustau line come from *almacenistas,* usually professional people or shopkeepers, who invest in small *bodegas* for modest profit but primarily because of their love of Sherry. The custom has been for the large Jerez *bodegas* to go to these smallholders when they have a small order, usually from a British or Dutch importer, for fine amontillado or old oloroso, or when they need some wine from a specialized *solera* to give character to a blend needed for a larger order.

The 1/17, 1/28, and similar notations seen on the labels of some of the *almacenista* Sherries denote the number of barrels (1 through 17, 1 through 28, and so on) in a particular *solera.* A small lot of wine (say, 25 cases) of the oldest average age is drawn from the *solera* and bottled for sale, then the *solera* is replenished from other barrels in the system. These numbers can be taken as an indication of the relative rarity of the wine, but if a particular wine sells out, a new lot with the same characteristics and quality will sometimes be available from the *solera.* The trick to maintaining quality in these small *soleras* is to take only small amounts no more than two or three times per year. An *almacenista*'s stock in trade is quality wines with an average age of two decades or more; there are no shortcuts when it comes to aging. A dedicated *almacenista* will never allow the quality of his *solera* to be diluted by selling too much wine in any given year.

Until Lustau got the idea to bottle the better wines of the *almacenistas* (who had been selling wines to Lustau for the private-label Sherries that make up the bulk of the firm's business in the United Kingdom), names like Cayetano del Pino, Rosario Benítez Girón, Hijos (sons) de Julio Coveñas, and Viuda (widow) de Antonio Borrego could be found only in obscure tomes. As it turns out, these *almacenistas,* most of whom come from Sanlúcar de Barrameda, not Jerez, were the true guardians of great strains of classic unblended amontillados and olorosos. Even though the large *bodegas* will sometimes show important visitors a dazzling sample from a limited "family" *solera,* they seldom have enough of these old treasures to market commercially (Domecq's Sibarita and Venerable are exceptions). Be forewarned, however, that these are not Aunt Lizzie's sweet little sipping wines; they are concentrated wines. A little bit goes a long way, so if you are a fancier of Bristol Cream or Dry Sack on the rocks, you may not find these wines your *copita de Jerez.*

Types of Sherry. Each *bodega* makes several different types of Sherry. Many wine experts consider **manzanilla** the world's greatest aperitif wine. It is a very light, dry, ethereal Sherry that comes only from the wonderful town of Sanlúcar de Barrameda, whose gentle ocean breeze is credited with giving manzanilla its distinctive tangy, taste-of-the-sea quality. One of the greatest experiences in the world of wine is to go down to Bajo de Guia beach at day's end, buy a bottle of iced manzanilla at one of the fishermen's restaurants, and watch the sun sink slowly into the sea. The Sanluqueños say that if you ever have a glass of manzanilla at sunset on Bajo de Guia, you will never drink another glass of manzanilla anywhere in the world without seeing the Sanlúcar sunset in the glass. Manzanilla is especially good with Sanlúcar's sensational fresh shellfish, and it goes beautifully with a wide variety of seafood and *tapas.*

Manzanilla fina, at 15.5 to 16 percent alcohol, is lower in alcohol than any other type of Sherry. Hidalgo's La Gitana is splendid. Fuller bodied and slightly higher in alcohol are the *manzanillas pasadas,* or aged manzanillas. Barbadillo Solear, San León, La Guita, and La Goya are superb *pasadas.*

Fino, the most popular type of dry Sherry, is a light, fresh, pale-gold wine that, while fuller bodied than manzanilla, can be crisp and quite delicate. Its bouquet is slightly reminiscent of almonds. The lightest and most elegant finos come from Sanlúcar de Barrameda and Puerto de Santa María; the more powerful full-bodied ones are aged in Jerez. Because they are fortified wines, they usually contain 16 to 18 percent alcohol. Try Valdespino's rich, full-bodied Inocente, the ubiquitous González-Byass Tío Pepe, Domecq La Ina, the light Osborne Fino Quinta, La Riva Tres Palmas (rare), Diez-Mérito Don Zoilo, and the finos of Emilio Lustau. If you happen into a small *bodega* or tavern with its own Sherry or barrels, ask for the *fino de casa,* house fino. Drink it with shellfish, *tapas,* hors d'oeuvres, and appetizers with vinaigrette.

Amontillados are aged finos. In their natural state they are totally dry, gold to amber in color, have a racy, pungent bouquet, and a long, complex, nutty finish. At 17 to 20 percent, they are higher in alcohol, fuller bodied, and richer than the lighter finos, and can be enjoyed with fried foods, fish, almonds, olives, and *tapas* that require a less delicate wine than fino or manzanilla. They are the classic accompaniment to soups and splendid with powerful cheeses. Many commercial brands are slightly sweetened, and therefore not authentic amontillados. Try one of the sublime *almacenista* amontillados of Emilio Lustau if you want to experience the real thing.

Palo cortado is a very rare, fine, full-bodied Sherry with the nose of an amontillado, and the color, body, and alcohol (17 to 23 percent) of an oloroso. Since most firms, as Jan Read points out, "concoct" these wines by blending amontillado and oloroso, authentic palo cortados are hard to find, but well worth the trouble. Again, you should seek out a palo cortado from one of Lustau's *almacenistas.* Sip it by itself to admire its perfection and complexity.

Oloroso, which means "fragrant" in Spanish, is an aromatic, full-bodied (17 to 24 percent alcohol), dry to medium-dry, mahogany-colored Sherry that is rich and mellow with flavors reminiscent of walnuts. It goes best with a dish of nuts and a good book in front of a fireplace in cool weather. Many of the Lustau *almacenista* olorosos are wonderful for wine connoisseurs, but they are too concentrated and powerful for the palates of many casual wine drinkers, who should be able to satisfy their desires for a dryish oloroso with Domecq's lovely Río Viejo.

A **cream Sherry** is an oloroso sweetened with Pedro Ximénez. Creams can be full, rich wines, and can be particularly good when the oloroso is very fine and judiciously sweetened. They are sipping wines with power (18 to 24 percent alcohol). Try them with desserts; pour a little over ice cream. Creams can be especially good alongside a cup of strong Spanish coffee. For those who prefer their olorosos sweetened, González-Byass Apostoles, Diez-Mérito Don Zoilo Very Rare Sweet, and Sandeman Royal Corregidor are excellent.

Several other excellent dessert wines are made in the Sherry district. Old East India is a unique dessert wine made from Sherry that is aged in casks left in the blazing Jerez sun to simulate the ancient way of making it, which was by lashing it to the decks of ships on a round trip to the Indies.

Incredibly rich, unctuous, and often achingly sweet, pure Pedro Ximénez wines are like liquid raisins. The best, like Lustau's San Emilio, are bursting with ripe, concentrated fruit, coffee, and chocolate flavors. There are also some excellent moscatels from the beach resort of Chipiona just below Sanlúcar.

—*Gerry Dawes*

The Jerez September Wine Festival begins at the collegiate church at Santa María and ends in the streets, bars, and flamenco clubs. The ceremony on the church's unusually handsome steps is presided over by the patron of winegrowers. He receives the new grapes carried on a silver platter by the queen of the fiesta and held high in baskets by the ladies of her court, all wearing Andalusian garb, brightly colored, form-fitted midcalf-length dresses with flounces at the hem and on the elbow-length sleeves. Richly robed church dignitaries offer their blessings. Officials in red uniforms with white-plumed helmets hold back crowds of onlookers, many of them children. The festival also includes a livestock fair, a horse auction, and flamenco dancing. The entire city seems to be in costume.

Most of the great Sherry companies, with some 19 huge *bodegas* located all around the city, will accept visitors for prearranged tours at specified hours. The tours offer detailed explanations of the fairly complex method of producing the four main types of Sherry, with plenty of samples along the way.

Horses are no less important to Jerez than Sherry. At the annual horse show (Feria del Caballo), held in late April or early May, Jerez shows its purebred Carthusians in racing, dressage, and carriage competitions. The city, strung with lights and decorations, is adorned with millions of spring flowers. The streets are filled with riders of horses, women and men alike wearing Cordoban hats, vests, formal shirts, and chaps. Carriages are drawn by two, four, or six horses, their harnesses decorated with garlands of blossoms. Seated within are young women in colorful flamenco dresses. In the formal jumping competitions the riders wear black boots, white breeches, red coats, white ties, and black headgear.

CADIZ

"Cádiz," wrote Lord Byron to his mother in 1809, "sweet Cádiz, is the most delightful town I ever beheld, very different from our English cities in every respect except cleanliness (and it is as clean as London), but still beautiful, and full of the finest women in Spain, the Cádiz belles being the Lancashire witches of their land." "I have quite forgotten to say a word about Cádiz," wrote Benjamin Disraeli to *his* mother in 1830, "which is charming! Brilliant beyond description. 'Fair Florence' is a very dingy affair compared to it. The white houses and the green jalousies sparkle in the sun."

Cádiz today is a good deal less than brilliant, and delightful is not the first adjective that comes to mind. Seen from the water Cádiz is a strip of whitish buildings extending into the sea on the Costa de la Luz southwest of Jerez, the waves of the Atlantic crashing against the protective seawall. Seen from the mainland across the bay as it stretches out on a spit, in the right light (which falls upon it with surprising frequency) Cádiz looks as if it is rising out of the water. But up close you find that time has not dealt kindly with this beldam. The seawall and the beachfront are tacky, the houses weatherbeaten, the traffic impossible, the weight of 20th-century industry and commerce pressed upon it so heavily that Cádiz emerges flattened and bereft of its fabled charm.

The ancient city stands on a five-mile promontory only a mile wide extending into the bay; Cádiz has one of Europe's great natural harbors. The old city, seedy now—even in Richard Ford's time (the 1840s) the cathedral was described by him as "a stranded wreck on a quicksand"—is separated by the Puertas de Tierra at the narrowest point from the utterly uninviting contemporary industrial beachfront area.

You visit Cádiz to celebrate its history. With 3,000 candles on its birthday cake, Cádiz is one of the oldest inhabited cities in the Western world. Variously called Gadir by the Phoenicians possibly as early as 1100 B.C., Gaderia by the Greeks in 500 B.C., and Gades by the Romans, the city became the wealthiest port in Europe with the discovery of America. This wealth made Cádiz a target, particularly for the British: Drake, Essex, Howard at the time of the Armada; Nelson at the time of the Napoleonic Wars. Perhaps Cádiz's finest hour came during the French attack in 1812, when Spanish patriots convened the Cortes (parliament), promulgating a liberal constitution that lasted until Ferdinand VII repudiated it.

The **Museo Provincial de Bellas Artes** (fine arts museum) on plaza Generalíssimo Franco has in its collection 21 fine paintings by Zurbarán; the **Hospital de Nuestra Señora del Carmen** on calle de Obispo Calvo has El Greco's *The Ecstasy of St. Francis* in its chapel; the patio has an 18th-century ceramic *Stations of the Cross.*

For lovers of seafood, the **El Faro** restaurant near the old cathedral facing the Atlantic offers the widest variety of the day's catch. The management claims their fish have "never made the acquaintance of the refrigerator." The **Atlántico** hotel, on the Parque Genovés at the extreme western tip of the promontory facing the sea, has a garden and swimming pool; their restaurant offers better than usual hotel fare, and at lunchtime there is an extensive buffet.

We cover the eastern part of the Costa de la Luz, beyond Cádiz and around to Algeciras, Gibraltar, and the beginning of the Mediterranean Costa del Sol, at the end of this chapter, following the Costa del Sol section.

THE WHITE TOWNS

"The route of the white towns" sounds like a public relations answer to "Follow the Yellow Brick Road," but it provides its own magic in a roughly triangular area that includes the Moorish white towns of southwest Andalusia. Two sides of this inverted triangle follow the Atlantic and Mediterranean coastlines to form an apex at Tarifa on the Strait of Gibraltar; the third side traces the inland route through the mountains from Arcos de la Frontera east to Ronda. Many of the towns in their dramatic settings seem untouched, as if they were still part of the Medieval Moorish world.

Only a traveller with a heart of granite and an eye of glass could remain indifferent to what unfolds while driving these narrow, winding, and almost empty mountain roads. Every few miles a town comes into view, etched white against a rocky embankment or dark green vegetation. The towns, down to the last one, were built by the Moors. The streets are narrow, the houses face inward to their courtyards, the roofs are tiled. And every house is whitewashed.

Many white towns look best from a distance. They are a pleasure to visit, but, like jewels, they benefit from their settings. These white towns have nothing to do with tourism. They rarely offer accommodation except to commercial travellers and sportsmen; in most of them the local bar serves as the place to eat. They have few buildings of architectural distinction; their Christian churches are modest. They seem sufficient unto themselves.

Their dominant element remains their whiteness. Ablaze in the sunlight, spectral at night under moonlit skies, ashen beneath the stars, they look like spring-cleaned North African towns, freshly washed and somehow transported to Mediterranean Europe.

A good way to make these towns part of a coherent travel plan is to concentrate on the northern base of the inverted triangle. On this inland route running east-west very roughly between Ronda and Arcos de la Frontera, the diversified landscape includes vineyards, pine forests, citrus farms, ranches, valley streams, olive groves, mountains both jagged and rounded, and a seven-mile-long lake. Rounding a curve, you spy a white town in the distance and it seems unreal: the setting theatrically conceived, the brilliance suspiciously unblemished.

The Towns

- Arcos de la Frontera
- Bornos
- Zahara de los Membrillos
- Grazalema
- Olvera
- Setenil
- Ubrique
- El Bosque
- Medina Sidonia
- Ronda

Either Arcos de la Frontera, on the western end, or Ronda, on the east, could serve as a base for white town exploration. Ronda is too big (population 32,000) to be considered a representative white town, but Arcos has all the appropriate qualities.

Arcos de la Frontera

Half an hour's drive northeast from Jerez, through countryside that in spring has poppies flaming the roadside, past vineyards and wheat fields and ranches, Arcos first appears as a strip of white atop a narrow rock promontory that falls 500 feet to río Guadalete.

Arcos separates the traveller from the tourist. The town provides no amusements, no shopping, no restaurants, no bars other than the undifferentiated basic type. In Arcos there is nothing to do. But for the traveller Arcos offers a hidden world. The Spanish essayist and journalist Azorín called the town "the most beautiful in all Spain." Even discounting chauvinism, Arcos is something of a knockout.

Arcos looks like a huge ship cresting a green sea, its hull a stone-gray, its superstructure the church towers. On three sides of the town the promontory drops to the river. You enter by way of the fourth, the passage so narrow that it becomes a single ascending street. Soon only one vehicle can proceed in either direction, and even that under the eave of a flying buttress at the rear of the Iglesia de Santa María de la Asunción.

You turn right onto the plaza de España, the town square. On one side is the Iglesia de Santa María de la Asunción, whose façade is a blend of Romanesque, Gothic, and Mudejar; on another the massive Medieval castle of the dukes of Osuna; on the third side is the **Parador Nacional Casa del Corregidor**. Running the full length of the fourth side is a balcony lookout.

This balcony is given an unprintable name by the locals in recognition of the fact that everyone utters the same expletive when standing at the edge of the escarpment, transfixed, looking down at the green farmland by the banks of the river with its two bridges, and beyond that to acres of vineyards, olive groves, ranches, and, on the distant horizon, the notched line of peaks of the Serranía de Ronda range.

At the far end of the promontory, the Iglesía de San Pedro, on the site of a Moorish fortress, has a 16th-century tower you can climb for a transcendent vista after requesting the key from the church caretaker. The Iglesia de Santa María de la Asunción has choir stalls and a main altar of Andalusian Baroque, an *Immaculada* painting by Francisco de Ricci and a *Virgin of Bethlehem* attributed to Alonso Cano.

You can stay right here at the parador, with a room whose balcony mirrors the public one. The parador was recently refurbished and makes a splendid base for a white town tour of a few days. A nearby 17th-century ranch, **Fain**, is an exceptionally fine place to stay for the traveller who is lucky enough to combine a love for beautiful furnishings (in this Andalusian ranch surrounded by hills with olive trees and a swimming pool fed from sparkling spring water) with a relative disregard for expense. Fain has eight luxurious suites. Guests can ramble in the countryside, go hunting or horseback riding, and savor the Andalusian ranch life. You have the strong impression that you are the host here, not a guest. You can dine in your own suite or in the dining room, the impeccable service stemming from Fain's mastery of the kind of understated elegance that refuses to call attention to itself.

Bornos

The first white town on N 342 northeast of Arcos is Bornos, fronting a ten-mile reservoir. Bornos is one of those places that suffers in retrospect; after visits to other white towns, Bornos seems less inviting than it did initially. At its center is the 17th-century Palacio de los Ribera, whose courtyard, with double-tiered arches of Renaissance proportions, now houses what is unfortunately the busiest place in town, the community welfare office.

Zahara de los Membrillos

From Bornos to Zahara de los Membrillos the landscape becomes mountainous. Deep valleys of brick-colored earth and rock peaks replace the earlier flat terrain. Route N 342 follows a pine-bordered stream; you catch a first tantalizing glimpse of Zahara through a cut in the hills. Its white dwellings stand etched against the rocky projection on whose side they are built. If only one white town could be visited, Zahara might well be the choice.

The town's one street zigzags back and forth as you climb the rock face to the small town plaza. From there you can walk up to the Moorish tower at the summit. The tower itself is dark and moldy, but on this summit a 360-degree perspective of quite spectacular beauty takes in the sweep of the wheat fields, meadows, and vineyards, all encircled by a perimeter of mountains. Church bells ring out the hour. An eagle soars, leisurely searching for prey. The roofs of the houses are rust-colored against their white walls. Around you are wildflowers enough to boggle a botanist: pink, purple, yellow, bright red, and blue; strands of wheat among them whose seed has been blown here by the Atlantic winds; cacti with giant leaves; and thistles.

With a population of 2,000, Zahara is neither a village nor a full-fledged town. The occasional donkey is still tethered outside a window. Arabic to its roots, Zahara was a formidable Moorish stronghold (each October a celebration is held to commemorate the 15th-century Christian Reconquest). Zahara de los Membrillos exemplifies the Moorish-Spanish blend that characterizes the best of the white towns. It is not easy to leave.

Grazalema

But when you do, avoid a well-paved, inviting road whose signs direct you to Grazalema. That invitation turns out to be an invitation to torture, to cutting back and forth to reach and cross a mile-high peak called Puerto de las Palomas (port of the doves). Minor car trouble up here becomes a major headache. Instead, from Zahara drive back to your original turnoff point, and take C 339 to Grazalema.

Grazalema is some 3,716 feet above sea level. One of the oldest of the white towns, and one of the most admired by writers, it was called Lacidula by the Romans. Grazalema is built on two levels, and parallel streets extend from one end of the town to the other. Immediately behind the houses are rock projections. The white houses have bright flowers in pots affixed to the outside walls; the patios and balconies are alive with basil, scarlet geraniums, and carnations. A Moorish arch has been incorporated as part of the Iglesia de San Juan. Just outside the town is the Pinzapar forest, nearly 300 acres of a rare species of pine. For centuries Grazalema blankets were carried by the highwaymen of the Serranía de Ronda, and today these blankets are still woven here on large looms. Baskets, mats, and blinds made from esparto grass are also crafted in Grazalema.

Yves Bottineau, in *The Wonders of Spain,* says that Grazalema, "follows the slope of the hills, the tiled roofs of the churches and houses matching the color of the rockface, so that it seems as if earth, men, and town lived in a kind of symbiosis."

Olvera

From a point along N 342, northeast of Grazalema and Zahara, you see the façade of the rather large town of Olvera spread horizontally along the side of the mountain. It is a photographer's best shot. Once in Olvera it is easy to forget that a brochure calls it "a concert of limestone and rock high on a cliff which is presided over by a silhouette of a rocky castle"; Olvera is mostly about livestock. Like Grazalema, Olvera was once the refuge of bandits and cutthroats because of its remoteness.

If you wander along the alleys behind Olvera's church in what the citizens call the Arab quarter, you come upon an extraordinary number of dogs, vaguely greyhound in origin. Pedestrians routinely step over them. The dogs have a world-weary air incongruously at odds with their skinny frames. Like Olvera itself, they look better from a distance. And from such a perspective Olvera looks very good indeed, even ravishing, framed by the dark green countryside. That's the way to view it.

Setenil

From Olvera to Setenil, take the road toward Ronda, passing through Torre Alháquime. Setenil, southeast of Olvera, is more a geological sport than a representative white town. It is built within a mountain that has been sliced through, century after century, by the waters of río Guadalporcúm. Thus, after climbing to reach the town you descend into it. Many of the houses are built into the rocks that serve as bridges over the streets themselves. The housefronts are whitewashed, the windowsills flower-bedecked, but the roofs are monstrous rock slabs. Some streets are partly covered over with rock. More bizarre than unusual, more eccentric than inviting, Setenil's freak-like attraction offers an example of local adaptation to nature's idiosyncrasies.

Ubrique

Ubrique, south of the Arcos-Ronda axis, is a prosperous white town with a population of 17,000. The mammoth rocky promontories in the background, formidable to observe, seem protective rather than threatening. The town is given over to leather crafts. Small factories and shops are hospitable to visits, and you can observe the cutting and stamping procedures. Some handwork by leather artisans is done here as well. A picnic on a rocky ledge outside Ubrique (the shops of Ubrique have all the wine, cheese, bread, pastries, and succulent fresh fruit you could desire) offers a view of this white town, dramatically situated, immaculately clean, its streets lined with orange trees.

El Bosque

Some 17 km (10 miles) northwest of Ubrique is El Bosque (the woods), a town well named: a quiet, bosky retreat whose tranquillity is complemented by the modesty of its surrounding hills and plains. El Bosque (population 2,000) has the southernmost trout preserve in Europe, an ancient bullring, a modern swimming pool, and a handsome inn, **Las Truchas.** This inn (where only Spanish is spoken) could serve as an alternate to the Arcos parador as a base for white town explorations.

Medina Sidonia

From Arcos on a southern route (C 343) toward the Atlantic, Medina Sidonia sits in the middle of a plain, a town of ancient origins—Phoenician, Roman, Visigothic, Moorish. Otherwise unattractive, unkempt, lacking in amenities, it nonetheless bears an illustrious name, that of the powerful and wealthy duke whose unfortunate fate it was to be chosen by Philip II to lead the disastrous Armada attack on England after the death of the original commander, the marqués de Santa Cruz. The town is surrounded by ranches where breeders and bullfighters have their white *cortijos* (farmhouses) close to where the handsome bulls are bred. You can be witness at gatherings at nearby ranches of bullfighters and young aspiring *maletillas* (self-appointed apprentices) preparing for the big season that heralds the start of spring in Andalusia.

The Iglesia de Santa María la Coronada, a good example of Andalusian Gothic, dates back precisely to the time of the Reconquest of Granada (1492) and, as a result, the establishment of the dukedom of Medina Sidonia.

Ronda

Ronda is a paradox. A town on the edge of a thousand-foot cliff, separated from the Mediterranean coastline by mountains that rise 3,652 feet from sea level, famous as a bandit hideout, the very definition of geographic inaccessibility, Ronda seems nevertheless to have been visited by every traveller to southern Spain since the time of the Romans.

Writers have dealt with Ronda so extensively that the subject of its spectacular location has been stripped of the last bromide. The great ravine—you can scarcely avoid an attack of vertigo as you look to its depths—is spanned by three bridges, one built by the Romans, another by the Moors, and the "new" one, finished in the 1780s.

Benjamin Disraeli travelled from Gibraltar to Ronda on horseback in 1830. He characterized Ronda's setting as "a savage mountain district, abounding in the most beautiful scenery and bugs! There are a number of little villages in this Sierra, entirely inhabited by robbers and smugglers." Bug-ridden, bandit-infested Ronda seemed to Disraeli the quintessence of romantic Andalusia.

Today's Ronda is divided by the ravine. The older south side is more compelling, away from the restaurants, souvenir stands, and shops. Here in ancient Ronda is the **Casa del Rey Moro**, the 11th-century palace of the Moorish kings. The rock steps going down to río Guadalevín were supposedly cut by Christian slaves. The **Iglesia de Santa María**, built by order of los Reyes Católicos Ferdinand and Isabella, on the site of an old mosque, is a beautiful example of late Gothic art, furnished with two excellent Baroque altarpieces; Arab traces are preserved in the Mihrab with its stucco decorations, and in two horseshoe arches.

The houses on the steep, curved streets here are more like mansions. Ronda is that most unlikely of white towns, one with a heritage of elegance quite apart from its strategic military position. One example is the **Palacio de Marqués de Salvatierra**, with its fine views from a triple terrace.

Over on the other side of the ravine, however, stands Ronda's small bullring, of classic proportions, the **Plaza de Toros de la Real Maestranza de Caballeria de Ronda**. Ronda claims that it is the oldest bullring in Spain. The bullring's most obvious architectural distinction—a perfect circular shape—is achieved with a harmonious two-tiered perimeter of 68 stone (rather than the usual wood) columns, spaced about eight feet apart. Ronda's bullring looks great: the right size, the right proportions, the right panache.

The bullring museum has a fascinating collection of *taurino* memorabilia, including suits-of-light worn by many famous bullfighters. Pictures, clippings, letters, swords, and footwear are all on display. Many photographs highlight the exhibit: Hemingway is here, of course, with Antonio Ordóñez and Luis Miguel Dominguin, as is Orson Welles, whose ashes were buried at his request at the nearby country place of Ordóñez (between Ronda and Campillos).

King Juan Carlos I said it best on the occasion of a recent visit to Ronda's bullring: "La fiesta de los toros no se debe cuestionar: forma parte de nuesta tradicion y de nuestra cultura." ("The celebration of bullfighting is not open for debate: It is part of our tradition and of our culture.")

In Ronda the best restaurant is the **Don Miguel** on the northwest side of the ravine; many other Ronda restaurants—all with menus and prices conspicuously posted—find it hard to compete with Don Miguel's location. Ronda's famous old hotel, the **Reina Victoria**, perched on the edge of the gorge, is largely given over to groups, but a room with a balcony facing that view makes other matters irrelevant. The room once occupied by Rainer Maria Rilke, a fervent admirer of Ronda, has been preserved (or re-created) by the management. A very pleasant and modest hotel on a side street, the **Polo**, is spanking clean and well run.

East toward Granada

En route from Ronda to Granada, you follow C 341 northeast to Campillos. This 60-km (38-mile) drive rivals any in Spain for the beauty and tranquillity of its pastoral mountain landscape. The road is not much travelled. It has nothing of any great drama, just mile after mile of hills and streams and meadows, of trees and wildflowers, and vineyards and orchards. Here is the best of Spain in the serenity of its singular countryside.

La Bobadilla

At Campillos you join N 342 to head east for Granada. But on 342, past Antequera and the turnoff south to Málaga, and about 17 km (10 miles) before Loja, turning left at Salinas, you will arrive at (Finca) La Bobadilla. La Bobadilla is not a village or a town; it is a resort, pure (in the sense that it has no disguises) and simple (in its dedication to the sybaritic).

La Bobadilla covers an area almost exactly equal to that of Gibraltar. In the conventional sense, this hotel complex has no rooms. It has instead 35 suites, each differently styled, all of them elegant and containing every conceivable amenity. The suites, which range in size and level of luxuriousness, have around-the-clock room service, balconies, and fireplaces, and some have private gardens. Breakfast (if you don't partake of a buffet that practically redefines the word) is set for you at a table in your quarters. La Bobadilla has two restaurants, one of them **La Finca** (*finca* means ranch or plantation), with superb cuisine. Swimming pools, hunting, horseback riding, tennis, a fitness club: All are here to keep you in the physical condition needed to savor the self-indulgence of this Lucullan life.

Advertised as a resort established on a "centuries-old Moorish palace-estate," Bobadilla turns out to be spanking new. Its lobby is a "great hall" of Moorish arches—one of the few serious decorative errors in a place that has more than enough decorative ingenuity—and there is a church (as recent as the complex) with a 30-foot-high organ where concerts are given, and which is the site of fashionable weddings and christenings. That none of this comes inexpensively is hardly a surprise. The only question is whether you believe that you deserve to be pampered in this extravagant manner.

La Bobadilla has nothing historically to do with Bobadil, the young Moorish king who surrendered Granada to Ferdinand and Isabella. *His* civic commemoration is the town of Suspiro del Moro (sigh of the Moor) south of Granada on N 323, where his mother's apocryphal admonition that he shed tears like a woman for what he should have defended like a man suggests the kind of relationship that has made psychoanalysis a lucrative profession. (There is a *town* of Bobadilla off the N 342 between Campillos and Antequera, as well as a major rail junction, Bobadilla Estación, connecting with Málaga, nearby; neither has any connection with or proximity to La Bobadilla resort.)

A slight detour north at Lachas on N 342 en route to Granada takes you to the little town of Fuente Vaqueros, where Federico García Lorca was born. On N 342 itself just west of Granada, the town of Santa Fe is the place where Ferdinand and Isabella encamped while conducting their siege of Granada.

THE COSTA DEL SOL

The Costa del Sol covers approximately 300 km (186 miles) of Mediterranean coastline. The largest city on this seafront, Málaga, with a population of over half a million, somehow serves as a dividing line for travellers. To Málaga's east is an extensive undeveloped and sparsely populated area, but from Málaga southwest to Algeciras and the Strait of Gibraltar the coastline has become unrecognizable from what it was a scant 50 years ago.

Gone forever from the west are the quaint little Andalusian fishing villages and ports, gone are the hidden coves and bathing beaches. Here to stay are the high-rises, the vast complexes of pseudotowns and villages, of restaurants, bars, fast-food outlets, gasoline stations, and vendors of souvenirs. A good many of the permanent residents of the Costa del Sol, after having first tried out the place on vacation, come from England, Scandinavia, France, and Germany. In the ports are yachts and sailing craft flying the flags of many nations. Supermarkets the size of city blocks are frequented by clients whose common denominator is that few speak Spanish.

"Hideous, vulgar, and gimcrack are the new tourist towns of Andalusia," writes Jan Morris, "where Spanish speculators have allied themselves with hordes of shady foreigners to develop the Costa del Sol: forgotten are the old instincts of form and balance, the organic strength of Spanish architecture, the sense of frank and decorous resignation. All is flash and easy profit."

Western Costa del Sol's highway N 340, with more accidents than any comparable roadway in Spain, is currently being widened, with the result that moving by fits and starts is now more of a problem than speeding. It is fair to say that this strip of western Costa del Sol pavement is the least pleasant thoroughfare in all Spain.

The Costa del Sol is no longer nationally identifiable; it has become indistinguishable from similar touristic desecrations in France and Italy, Yugoslavia and Greece. Fortunately you can turn off the highway from time to time, and in a space of only a few miles you can find Andalusia once more.

MALAGA

Málaga is one of those cities whose contemporary reputation rests mostly on its past. Málaga's harbor once made it the cynosure of each succeeding epoch's commercial and military eye: The Iberians settled here, as did the Carthaginians, the Greeks, the Romans, and the Visigoths. Málaga became a major Moorish center. After the Reconquest, the great cathedral, begun in 1528, replaced the central mosque. But during the time of Spain's American empire, the Atlantic ports of Cádiz and (via the Gaudalquivir) Seville gained precedence over Málaga's Mediterranean harbor.

Today's Málaga tends to get mixed notices from visitors. There are those who find it a delightful town with a laid-back feeling, its orange-tree-lined streets, picturesque harbor, and horse-drawn carriages lending just the right air of insouciance for casual sightseeing. Others see the city with its population of half a million, most of them living in what seem to be endless sprawling outreaches, as Marseilles-like tough; it does have one of Spain's highest rates of crime and unemployment. Just as in Seville, when wandering about some of Málaga's beautiful parks and ancient side streets you should keep an eye on your valuables. But almost every visitor agrees that the small central area around the cathedral splendidly combines the historical significance of Málaga's illustrious past with the present blessings of its climate and site. At the turn of the century, well before the development of the Costa del Sol, Málaga was a favored vacation spot, especially for the British. But it is often unjustly overlooked by today's travellers, who see it more as a transportation base from which to light out for some Mediterranean resort.

Running due south through the center of the city, río Guadalmedina empties into the sea immediately west of the great harbor. The paseo del Parque esplanade, with its tropical trees and colorful blooms, divides the harbor area from the city proper. Just three blocks north of this stands the cathedral, the center of the ancient Málaga of prime interest to the visitor. A few blocks directly east of the cathedral are the Alcazaba and the ruins of the Roman theater, and behind them to the northeast is the **Gibalfaro hill** with its castle offering panoramic views of the cityscape. Three blocks west of the cathedral is Málaga's main shopping area on calle del Marqués de Larios.

Picasso in Málaga

At Málaga's plaza de la Merced 15 (off the north end of the short calle Alcazabilla, between the cathedral and the Alcazaba), a plaque erected in 1961 on the occasion of an homage to Velázquez reads simply: "Picasso was born in this house on October 25, 1885." The house is one of six in a double row of houses that makes up the entire north side of this inviting, well-proportioned urban square. Five stories high, they are the comfortably bourgeois, architecturally harmonious dwellings of the middle class. They look more French than Spanish. From this traditional background came the 20th century's most revolutionary artist.

Just two blocks away, in the **Museo de Bellas Artes** (fine arts museum), room XVIII is given over to Málaga's expatriate native son. Picasso is sparingly represented here in oil: two original representative oils painted when he was 14 and 15, respectively: *Pair of Ancients* and *Man with a Shawl.* The latter is signed P. Ruiz Picasso. Otherwise, the collection consists of his lithographs from the 1940s and 1950s.

This former Moorish palace, apart from some early Iberian artifacts, has rather too many "anonymous," "school of," and "workshop" hangings, but there are two paintings by Luis de Morales, one by Ribera, a Murillo, and a fine "school of" Zurbarán. It is no discredit to the Museo de Bellas Artes to say that it suggests why Picasso left Málaga: There is enough here to inspire and not sufficient to gratify.

The Alcazaba

This 11th-century Moorish fortress, built on the foundations of a Roman amphitheater, has been much restored, but enough remains of the original commanding structure, with its view of Málaga's harbor, seacoast, and mountain backdrop, to suggest something of the city's former military, political, and geographical advantages. In this entirely Moorish setting, a museum contains some outstanding Iberian artifacts, as well as some fine Roman statuary and household articles. The site is improved by a phenomenon typical of Málaga: an abundance of flowers—bougainvillaea and giant roses in particular—that seem to grow wherever there is a square foot of soil.

What remains of the seating section of a **Roman theater** stands to the north of the Alcazaba but within its entranceway confines. A model of this theater in the fortress museum suggests that it may well have seated 20,000 people.

The Cathedral

As is customary in Andalusia, an enormous Christian cathedral, begun in the 16th century, replaced the great mosque of the city. Its steeple unfinished, the cathedral has gigantic Corinthian columns that rise to cupolas with a particularly

Malaganian touch—palm fronds, shells, and (perhaps) anchors etched on the vast ceiling. But despite its size, the interior of the cathedral is simple, with three naves and chapels, as well as the royal chapel through whose windows the Málaga sunlight penetrates. Pedro de la Mena, who was given a giant retrospective in the cathedral last year, created some wonderful choir stalls here.

Staying in Málaga

Atop the Gibalfaro, the commanding hill by the harbor, on the northwest side of the Alcazaba, the **Parador Nacional de Gibalfaro** has very limited accommodations but offers a sense of seclusion and, of course, that view. In the center of the city, the **Málaga Palacio** is close to practically everthing: the cathedral, the Alcazaba, the Museo de Bellas Artes, the airport bus stop, a large parking garage, and the port itself.

Some 9.5 km (6 miles) west of downtown on the way to Torremolinos (turn left at the international airport exit on the Cádiz highway), directly on the beach, with two pools, is the **Hotel Guadalmar**, comfortable, unpretentious, noisy on weekends with local celebratory functions, fine for children, and just a three-minute taxi ride from the airport. But without a car you are stuck in Guadalmar-land.

Dining in Málaga

Directly opposite the Museo de Bellas Artes (although you enter from a narrow side street) is the **Tormes**, a modest and entirely gratifying restaurant for lunch; you are likely to be the only non-Malaganian on hand in this well-patronized establishment. The **Café de Paris**, on the paseo Maritimo facing the Malagueta beach, on the other hand, is a rather elegant place to dine, offering a widely diversified menu. In the same menu category are the **Figón de Bonilla**, also in the paseo Marítimo area, and the **Taberna del Pintor**, the latter specializing in roasted meats. All three offer the famous Jabugo ham. The parador offers lunch and dinner; here you are likely to find not a single Malaganian on hand.

THE COSTA DEL SOL EAST OF MALAGA

Although the Costa del Sol officially runs east to La Rábita, the border of Almería province, and the coastline itself runs to Almería, 223 km (140 miles) east of Málaga, most visitors and locals think of this as a technicality: The term has come to signify the *western* strip. To the east relative peace and tranquillity reign.

Nerja

Of particular interest are the wondrous caves near Nerja, 52 km (32 miles) east of Málaga, where some paleolithic discoveries are on exhibit. A path through the lighted, almost surreal caves with their stalagmites and stalactites reveals an eerie world. Concerts and ballet performances are given in the caves in the summer.

The best place to stay in Nerja is the **Parador Nacional de Nerja**, facing the Mediterranean; an elevator takes you down to a beach of fine white sand. Open only for dinner, the **Pepe Rico** restaurant, just off N 340, located in a rustic profusion of flowers and plants, serves diners on the patio in this park-like setting and has a sophisticated menu.

Almería

From the town of Motril, east of Nerja, you can climb directly north to the Alpujarras (and Granada) on N 323, but just before you reach Motril you might take a look at the white coastal town of **Salobreña** between the mountains and the sea.

At Almería, 112 km (70 miles) farther east along the coast from Motril, the ancient Moorish Alcazaba has towers, high walls, and gardens. The cathedral, built in 1524, is a fine example of late Gothic. Despite a population of over 150,000, Almería has a small-town feel, and the Spanish refer to it as if it were on the far side of Mars. V. S. Pritchett likens Almería to one of Chekhov's bright but fading Black Sea towns: "a hot little seaport cooped into a hole below the coastal range." Almería, like Málaga, was a Republican town in the Civil War, as indeed were all Spanish ports, with their sense of the world outside of Spain. Almería has renamed one of its main streets Federico García Lorca and another Pablo Picasso.

On the main street overlooking the port is the comfortable **Gran Hotel Almería**; at the extreme east of the city is the **Hotel Playaluz**, which has a garden and a beachfront setting. One of Almería's better restaurants, close to N 324, the Granada highway, is the **Anfora**, with a diversified menu that emphasizes seafood.

THE COSTA DEL SOL WEST OF MALAGA

Torremolinos

Torremolinos is the classic example of what went wrong with the Costa del Sol. Once a simple fishing town with a pleasant beach, today it frequently looks as if it were in the throes of preparing for a rock concert. Not a square inch of real estate remains vacant. Torremolinos is where contemporary international youth hang out when they don't have quite enough on the ball to go elsewhere. A good many visitors to Torremolinos, however, find precisely what they are seeking.

For those who want to be close by, but still far enough away to play tennis and golf in a more tranquil seaside atmosphere, the **Parador Nacional del Golf**, 9 km (6 miles) west of Málaga and 4 km (2.5 miles) east of Torremolinos, is both comfortable and handsome; the dining service is better than adequate.

Mijas

About 30 km (19 miles) southwest of Málaga on the coastal highway to Cádiz (Carratera de Cádiz–N 340), past Torremolinos, a road to the right leads to the mountain town of Mijas. This hilltop white town, some 9 km (6 miles) from the seacoast, was discovered by travellers many decades ago, but it remains a charmer.

Like the French Riviera's Vence, which it resembles somewhat, its streets are mostly given over to shops, outdoor cafés, and restaurants. But Mijas is brighter and livelier, and the nearby hills are starkly Spanish, not verdant French. They share the same nearby sea (in both cases with scarcely acceptable beaches and discolored water at the shoreline).

Like many spots in this section of the Costa del Sol, Mijas has a colony of British vacationers and expatriates, to the extent that English is routinely spoken here, and many of the bar-cafés list quick-service dishes, all of which seem to end with "... and chips." One Mijas restaurant in the central plaza advertises "pub food."

Near the summit of the town alongside the bullring is a splendid park-*mirador* (lookout), and even if you turned your back to the brilliant Mediterranean panorama your eyes would light upon the white church wall, the tiled roofs, and behind them the mountain peaks.

Mijas is fun to visit, one of those towns where the sense of holiday permeates the atmosphere. To get to one of the restaurants, **El Padrastro**, you either climb 60 steps or take a private elevator near the town square; the food up there, unlike the vista, is unexceptional. The **Hotel Mijas**, on the left just before you enter the main plaza of the town itself, is a very comfortable, thoroughly satisfactory accommodation. Ask for a room with a view, slightly more expensive but worth it. This hotel has a swimming pool, as does virtually every hotel on the Costa del Sol. The Mijas also has an indoor pool, tennis court, riding, and golf nearby.

Just 4 km (2.5 miles) farther west of the Mijas turnoff along the Cádiz highway, another turnoff to the right leads to Mijas-Golf, a splendid location with two 18-hole courses designed by Robert Trent Jones. The **Hotel Byblos Andaluz** here is a luxurious spot catering to fashionable Europeans, none of whom look as if they require the services of the health spa that is an inconspicuous but elaborate part of this hotel's makeup.

Guests at the Byblos Andaluz expect, and get, the ultimate in service and comfort. Encircled by rounded hills and blessed with Mediterranean breezes, the Byblos, facing those emerald fairways, has the Costa del Sol's ultimate luxury: quiet. Luncheon is an elaborate poolside buffet; three restaurants serve dinner, one of them French haute cuisine. The Byblos is an elegant, expensive hotel run with grace and efficiency.

Marbella

Here, west of Torremolinos and Mijas toward Gibraltar, is the Costa del Sol's most fashionable resort. Most of Marbella's numerous luxurious estates and villas are hidden from sight. Available to everyone's eye, however, is the stunning array of yachts and sailing craft that crowd the harbor, their suntanned crews and owners looking as if clouds were forbidden to appear on their personal horizons. Here, and at Puerto Banús just to the west, come people who are unavoidably referred to as rich and famous.

The Costa del Sol now has the largest influx of Arabs since the time of the Reconquest. Marbella has become the playground of countless Saudis and other Middle Easterners. This means new mosques, lavish shops, luxurious hotels, and extravagant restaurants to cater to their needs. Thus the number of expensive venues here far outweighs less affluent locales. In this category, known for its celebrity clientele, is the **Marbella Club**, west of the town, with first-class everything. Among its numerous amenities, the Club has a private beach. Other superdeluxe Marbella hotels are **Los Monteros**, near the Marbella Club, known as "the priciest hotel in Marbella," and the **Puente Romano**, close to Puerto Banús.

In choosing a place to dine, you will find that the **Don Leone**, Tel: 81-77-16, on the Puerto Banús harborfront, serves wonderful Italian food on its terrace. The best restaurants on the Costa del Sol are here, all of them with high tabs. They include the Horcher-owned **La Fonda**, Tel: 77-25-12, on Santo Cristo plaza; the Belgian-run **La Hacienda** (Tel: 83-12-67), 12 km/8 miles east of Marbella on the north side of N 340 in the Las Chapas area; and **La Meridiana**, Tel: 77-61-90, behind the mosque in Las Lomas, near Puerto Banús.

Casares

As you continue west along the Cádiz highway toward Algeciras and the Gibraltar area, the surroundings become industrialized and decidedly nonresort-like. A startling reminder of the exceptional quality of locations along this coastline before exploitative developers took over can be found in Casares, a "white town" just 14 km (9 miles) off the highway. (Look for the turnoff to the right a few miles beyond Estepona.) This uphill road runs through unpopulated farm country, with unexpected turns ending in an explosive view of Casares standing on the summit of a rock promontory, the town topped by a church steeple and a crumbling castle.

In the background of this beautiful Moorish town lies the Mediterranean; in the foreground green hills extend to the base of the village escarpment. The Costa del Sol of Torremolinos and Marbella is a million miles away; Casares is ur-Andalusian to the core of its Moorish-Reconquest being.

Algeciras and Gibraltar

Algeciras, on the west side of the Bay of Algeciras (Gibraltar forms the east side of the bay), has little to offer the traveller except a wonderfully atmospheric turn-of-the-century hotel, the **Reina Cristina**, on a hill at the western end of the city. It's the kind of hotel in which some rooms still have wood-burning fireplaces, where service and attention to detail still count, and the restaurant is better than conventional. To the spacious gardens come local wedding parties to have their pictures taken against the hotel's *grande dame* background (wags have suggested a wedding of Andalusian hotels, with Seville's Alfonso XIII as groom, the Reina Cristina as the bride, and Ronda's Reina Victoria as matron of honor). But beyond the hotel lies a gray, materialistic, charmless city, despite its views of Gibraltar and the distant mountains of Africa. Ferries connecting Algeciras with Cueta and Tangier account for more than a million passengers yearly.

Some 25 km (16 miles) northeast of Algeciras, off N 340 at Guadiaro, the Sotogrande estate between the beach and the Sierra Almenara hills is a sports-lovers haven. Polo, tennis, two golf courses, a yachting marina, swimming pool, disco, and wide sandy beach are part of what the **Hotel Sotogrande** has to offer. This 4,000-acre estate is what the Spanish call an urbanization; the rooms with private patios have views of Gibraltar across the bay.

Gibraltar offers you that most unexpected travel sight: It looks exactly as you had imagined. This limestone rock at the junction of the Mediterranean and the Atlantic has been occupied by the Phoenicians, the Romans, the Visigoths, the Moors, and the Spanish, until 1704 when it became a British colony. A passport and valid car insurance (all Spanish rental cars must have it) is compulsory for a visit, however brief. Visitors usually seek out St. Michael's cave, whose five passages are filled with impressive stalactites and stalagmites. Apes roam freely along the Upper Rock; the main street shops offer goods from around the world.

EASTERN COSTA DE LA LUZ

The Atlantic coastline running from Algeciras-Tarifa northwest to Huelva and the Portuguese border is called the Costa de la Luz, a name honored more in guidebooks and maps than in actual use. The differences between this coastline and its Mediterranean counterpart is immediately discernible. Here there seems always to be a stiff wind, and the beaches, mostly deserted and of much finer sand and greater width than those of the Costa del Sol, have few towns and villages in their immediate vicinity. On weekends and holidays they are crowded with picnickers, but in general tourism has set foot very lightly in this area.

In this section we cover the Costa de la Luz from Tarifa west to Vejér de la Frontera on the way to Cádiz—which is covered as part of the western Costa de la Luz at the beginning of the Andalusian Coast part of the chapter.

Baelo Claudio

Just 20 km (13 miles) west of **Tarifa**—from whose port you can look across to Morocco's Atlas mountain range and on clear days pick out white dwellings there—are the extensive remnants of the Roman fishing town Baelo Claudio. You turn left off N 340 and drive a short distance to the coast itself. There, next to a parking lot for a dozen cars, behind a wire fence, are the ruins of what was once a prosperous Roman town. Founded in the first century A.D. and forgotten for most of the past 15 centuries, Baelo Claudio has unusually well-preserved ruins and few visitors, and it is neglected by almost all guide and reference books. The archaeological work, in any real sense, has only just begun.

In this town, fish (in the spring, tuna swarm into the Gibraltar Strait and enter the Mediterranean to spawn) were cut up, salted, stacked in layers in tanks of brine, and in about three weeks were ready for shipping throughout the Roman world. A Roman delicacy, called *garum,* was a specialty of Baelo Claudio: a fish paste of crushed flesh and roe steeped in smaller tanks, then left in containers in a warm room to evaporate the brine. When the paste cooled, it was sealed in jars and exported to gourmets all over the Mediterranean world. Many of the concrete vats are still here in the "factory" of Baelo Claudio.

This vigorous Roman town, a municipality with what historians estimate was a seasonal population of some 20,000 to 30,000 residents, had all the requisite amenities for urban civilization: a basilica, a forum, a temple, and a theater as well as baths and less conspicuous elements to make the town function efficiently: water supply and drainage, roadways, and industrial and residential zoning.

Baelo Claudio was discovered by archaeologists in 1917, but funding has made only sporadic work possible; at the moment no such work is being carried on. But what the visitor gets is a superb sense of the layout of the town, its streets and theater, and stone walls, arches, and columns. You can tell that the basilica was once a rectangular building with a broad nave ending in an apse, flanked by colonnaded aisles, and probably used as a courtroom and public hall. There is even a monument plaque, erected in the second century in honor of a young man, Quintas Pupio Urbicos, apparently the mayor.

Adjacent to the ruins are a few modest contemporary houses and a cafeteria-bar. Here you can apply for admission to the fenced-in Roman area: It is closed Sunday afternoon and Mondays, otherwise open from 10:00 to 1:15 and 4:00 to 6:15.

Vejér de la Frontera

Vejér de la Frontera is a gem. Halfway between Tarifa and Cádiz, built on a commanding bluff, Vejér—even from a great distance—has that unmistakable, classic "white town" panache; as the road climbs up to this town, it looks better with every twist and turn.

Within the town, the narrow, sharply angled, steeply inclined streets run through banks of white walls, punctuated by black window grilles and doorways leading to courtyards. "Vejér de la Frontera [is] perhaps the most spectacular of all Spanish villages," writes Jan Morris.

Vejér is whitewashed within an inch of its civic well-being. It sits atop these commanding ramparts looking out over miles of Andalusian countryside (it is about ten miles inland from the Atlantic coastline). What remains of an Arab fortress shares a dominant position with the Iglesia de San Salvador, built on the foundations of a mosque. The Jewish quarter, still well preserved, is located near the paseo de las Corbijadas, on one side of the ramparts.

Tourism as such is unknown to Vejér. Over the years, travellers have visited and admired the town, but lack of accommodations made for brief stays. Within the past year, however, a 17th-century monastery has been converted into the **Hotel Hospedería del Convento de San Francisco** (referred to on some signs as Hotel Convento). The hotel has what must be Spain's single most inconvenient and uninviting entranceway: flush on the sidewalk of the minute plaza on which four narrow streets converge. There is no place to park, turn, unload your baggage, or do anything but drive back to the ramparts and return on foot to register.

Nor is the front-desk "lobby" all that inviting, but once on the second floor you know that you have come upon a real find. The monastery's large rooms have been converted handsomely into lounges and a refectory-like dining hall. The bedrooms, former cells, modernized and with adjacent bathrooms, are models of how to take advantage of the best of an ancient and noble building. The hand-carved furniture throughout the hotel was made in Valencia; the headboards reflect the angle of the high arched ceilings.

From Vejér it is 52 km (33 miles) northwest to Cádiz, and from Cádiz and Jerez to its north a straight shot north to Seville on the *autopista* (or, from Jerez, a loop to the east through the White Towns and back down to the Costa del Sol via Ronda).

GETTING AROUND

The best way to travel around Andalusia is by car, although train and/or bus service is available to and from most major locations. The *only* way to travel to some sections of Andalusia, such as the route of the Moorish white towns and the entire wild Alpujarras mountain range, is by car. Andalusia's two major airports are in Málaga (the largest) and Seville (currently being expanded); Córdoba, Granada, and Jerez have smaller airports, mostly for domestic flights. Car rental offices are at all airports, in all major cities, and in every resort on the Costa del Sol.

The best way to see Andalusia's principal cities is on foot. The areas of particular interest for travellers in Seville, Córdoba, Granada, and Málaga are remarkably concentrated for pedestrian viewing.

For travellers who enjoy luxurious train journeys, the Al-Andalus Express offers four- and five-day trips within Andalusia, stopping at five principal cities: Seville, Córdoba, Granada, Málaga, and Jerez de la Frontera. The elegant train combines the glamour of the Orient Express with the decor of the 1920s in the salon, the bar, and the dining cars; the sleeping accommodations and shower facilities are entirely modern. While travelling from city to city, the Al-Andalus offers passengers bar service, games, videos, and, in the evenings, live musical entertainment and dancing. Branches of the National Tourist Office of Spain have information on this train, as do most travel agents.

Seville

A great virtue of Seville is that, as in Florence, almost everything of major interest to the traveller is within a ten-block area. A car can be a liability, and some areas—like the Barrio de Santa Cruz—have many narrow one-way or pedestrian-only streets. Both Seville and Florence, although they bear no physical resemblance to one another, reflect the predominantly Renaissance period of their cultural backgrounds, with a great cathedral as the nucleus. Seville's summer heat is as severe as that of Florence, and although air-conditioning is everywhere, July and August can be punishing.

Seville has two train stations: the Estación Córdoba just north of the Guadalquivir's Isabel II bridge, for northern routes; and the Estación Cádiz, about two blocks directly east of the cathedral-Alcázar gardens area, for southern routes. But check your schedules carefully, as some cities such as Córdoba are serviced by both stations. The international airport, in the process of expansion, is about ten miles east of the city on the road to Córdoba; it is served by both taxis (about 1,000 pesetas to city center) and buses (about 200 pesetas). Within the city, taxis are plentiful and reasonably priced; drivers are courteous and knowledgeable but rarely speak English.

Córdoba

Córdoba is on the main highway (N IV) between Madrid and Seville-Cádiz. By car or rail, you can see much of Córdoba on a day trip from Seville (about two hours one way), or from Granada or Málaga (three to four hours) arriving in Córdoba at lunchtime and returning the next afternoon. The old city is best seen on foot, and in fact many of the fascinating narrow streets leading down to the river are impassable by car. Taxis are plentiful and reasonable; horse-drawn carriages are fun to go about in (check on the fare beforehand—perhaps 1,800 pesetas). If you park your car on the far side of the Roman bridge, be sure to lock it and take all valuables with you. Parking garages are available near the mosque. Córdoba has a small domestic airport to the west of the city on N 431. The city is blazing hot in midsummer, lovely in spring and fall, moderate but chilly at night in midwinter. Directly north of the city on N 342 are fine camping and hiking areas in the scenic Sierra Morena.

Granada

Granada is 430 km (266 miles) directly south of Madrid on N IV and N 323. You can continue south from Granada on N 323 to Motril on the Mediterranean (about an hour) or go west on N 342 and veer south past Loja on N 321 for Málaga (about an hour and three-quarters) and the more frequented parts of the Costa del Sol. Granada to Córdoba on N 432 is 166 km (103 miles) and takes about three hours over an indifferent road; from Granada to Seville on N 342, turning north at Antequera on N 334, is 256 km (160 miles) and takes perhaps four hours.

Granada's small airport is west of the city at Santa Fe; airport buses leave from the plaza Isabel la Católica; a taxi will cost about 1,000 pesetas, but check with the driver before you set out. The railway station is off avenida de la Constitución on the avenida Andaluces; trains connect Granada with all the major cities of Andalusia. Granada's bus station is on camino de Ronda on the west side of the city; there is an extensive local bus system.

You can drive your car from the lower city up to the Alhambra compound, but, in general, if your hotel is not on the Alhambra promontory you are better off using the city's moderately priced taxis, both to go up to the Alhambra and to get around within Granada itself. We live in a world in which almost everyone speaks a little English, but taxi drivers are often the exception; you can avoid misdirections by writing out your destination beforehand. Granada's midtown traffic at rush hour is often anarchic and frustratingly slow.

Walking about the central city is a delight. You *can* walk up to the Alhambra from the plaza Nueva, but it's a long haul, and the entire Alcazaba-Alhambra-Generalife complex must be visited on foot. If your legs are in good shape, walking back down into the city is pleasurable, and you can visit Manuel de Falla's small house on Antequeruela Alta on the way down. Like all Andalusian cities, Granada is torrid and often hazy in midsummer, the time that, ironically, draws the most visitors. Spring in Granada is justly famed for its profusion of beautiful flowers and shrubs; winter can be rainy—with the occasional quirky snowfall—but on sunny days Granada is clear and sparkling.

Málaga

Traffic is heavy in downtown Málaga and parking is limited; the garage next to the Hotel Málaga Palacio in the cathedral quarter is a good bet. The central area of Málaga is best seen on foot. It's best to take a taxi up to the Gibalfaro, but you should negotiate the fare, which includes waiting time, beforehand. The international airport is 8 km (5 miles) west of the city on the Málaga-Cádiz highway. Taxis run about 800 pesetas from the city to the airport; buses to the airport leave from calle Abades between the cathedral and the Hotel Málaga Palacio.

Train service runs west between Málaga and Fuengirola on the Costa del Sol, passing through Torremolinos and Benalmadena, with a stop at the airport; trains run every half-hour from 6:00 A.M. to 11:00 P.M. The Málaga terminal for this train is alongside the principal RENFE railway station on calle Cuarteles, several blocks west of río Guadalmedina in the harbor area. Trains connect Málaga with all the principal cities of Spain. Several ship companies have regular service to Ceuta and Tangiers; for information call the Estación Marítima, Tel: 63-37-06.

ACCOMMODATIONS REFERENCE

When dialing telephone numbers from outside the country, drop the 9 in the area code.

Seville

The telephone code for the Seville area is 954.

▶ **Parador Nacional Alcázar del Rey don Pedro.** 41410 **Carmona.** Tel: 14-10-10. Telex: 92992.

▶ **Hotel Alfonso XIII.** San Fernando 2, 41004 **Seville.** Tel: 22-28-50. Telex: 72725 HAS E.

▶ **Hotel Doña María.** Don Remondo 19, 41004 **Seville.** Tel: 22-49-90.

▶ **Hotel Inglaterra.** Plaza Nueva 7, 41001 **Seville.** Tel: 22-49-70. Telex: 72244 HOTIN.

▶ **Apartamentos Murillo.** Reinoso 6, 41004 **Seville.** Tel: 21-60-95.

▶ **Hotel Murillo.** Lope de Rueda 7, 41004 **Seville.** Tel: 21-60-95.

Córdoba

The telephone code for the Córdoba area is 957.

▶ **Parador Nacional de la Arruzafa.** Avenida de la Arruzafa, 14012 **Córdoba.** Tel: 27-59-00.

▶ **Hotel Ardave.** Magistral Gonzalez Frances 17, 14003 **Córdoba.** Tel: 48-13-37. Telex: 76594 HOMT.

▶ **Hotel Maimónides.** Torrijos 4, 14003 **Córdoba.** Tel: 47-15-00; Telex: 07659 HOTM.

▶ **Hotel Meliá Córdoba.** Paseo de la Victoria, 14002 **Córdoba.** Tel: 29-80-66.

The Andalusian Northeast

The telephone code for this area is 953.

▶ **Parador Nacional El Adelantado. Sierra de Cazorla.** Tel: 72-10-75.

▶ **Parador Nacional Castillo de Santa Catalina.** 23000 **Jaén.** Tel: 26-44-11.

▶ **Parador Nacional Condestable Dávalos.** Plaza Vázquez de Molina 1, 23400 **Ubeda.** Tel: 75-03-45.

Granada/Sierra Nevada
The telephone code for this area is 958.

▶ **Alhambra Palace.** Peña Partida 2, 18009 **Granada.** Tel: (58) 22-14-68.

▶ **Hotel Luz Granada.** Avenida de la Constitución 18, 18012 **Granada.** Tel: (58) 20-40-61.

▶ **Meliá Granada Hotel.** Angel Ganivet 7, 18009 **Granada.** Tel: (58) 22-74-00.

▶ **Hotel Meliá Sierra Nevada.** 18196 **Sierra Nevada-Pradollano.** Tel: 48-40-00. (Open winter only.)

▶ **Hotel Meliá Sol y Nieve.** 18196 **Pradollano.** Tel: 48-03-00. (Open winter only.)

▶ **Parador Nacional de San Francisco.** Recento de la Alhambra, 18009 **Granada.** Tel: (58) 22-14-40.

▶ **Parador Nacional Sierra Nevada.** Carretera Sierra Nevada, km 35, 18196 **Sierra Nevada.** Tel: 48-02-00.

▶ **Villa Turistica de Bubión.** Alpujarras, 18412 **Bubión.** Tel: 76-31-11. Fax: (958) 76-31-36.

Western Costa de la Luz
The telephone code for this area is 956.

▶ **Hotel Atlántico.** Parque Génoves 9, 11002 **Cádiz.** Tel: 21-23-01.

▶ **Parador Nacional Cristóbal Colón.** Carretera Mazagón-Moguer, 21130 **Mazagón.** Tel: 37-60-00.

▶ **Hotel Jerez.** Alvaro Domecq 35, 11405 **Jerez de la Frontera.** Tel: 30-06-00.

The White Towns
The telephone code for this area is 952.

▶ **Hotel La Bobadilla.** Apartado 52, 18006 **Loja.** Tel: 32-18-61.

▶ **Parador Nacional Casa del Corregidor.** Plaza Cabildo, 11630 **Arcos de la Frontera.** Tel: 70-05-00.

▶ **Fain.** Algar Road, 11630 **Arcos de la Frontera.** Tel: U.S. (818) 907-0642. Spain: 70-11-67.

▶ **Hotel Polo.** Mariano Xouviron 9, **Ronda.** Tel: 87-24-47.

▶ **Hotel Reina Victoria.** Doctor Fleming 25, **Ronda.** Tel: 87-13-40.

▶ **Las Truchas.** Avenida Disputación 1, 11670 **El Bosque.** Tel: 71-50-61.

Málaga

The telephone code for the Málaga area is 952.

▶ **Parador Nacional de Gibalfaro.** Atop the Gibalfaro hill, 29016 **Málaga.** Tel: 22-19-02.

▶ **Hotel Guadalmar.** Málaga-Cádiz Highway at airport exit (km 228), 29080 **Málaga.** Tel: 31-90-00.

▶ **Hotel Málaga Palacio.** Cortina de Muelle 1, 29001 **Málaga.** Tel: 21-51-85.

Costa del Sol East of Málaga

The telephone code for this area is 952.

▶ **Gran Hotel Almería.** Avenida Reina Regente 4, 04001 **Almería.** Tel: 23-80-11.

▶ **Parador Nacional de Nerja.** El Tablazo, **Nerja.** Tel: 52-00-50.

▶ **Hotel Playaluz.** Bahia el Palmer 34, 04001 **Almería.** Tel: 34-05-04.

Costa del Sol West of Málaga / Eastern Costa de la Luz

The telephone code for this area is 952.

▶ **Hotel Byblos Andaluz.** 29650 **Mijas-Golf.** Tel: 47-30-50. Telex: 79713 BYANE.

▶ **Hospedería del Convento de San Francisco.** 29620 **Vejér de la Frontera.** Tel: 45-10-01.

▶ **Parador Nacional del Golf. Torremolinos.** Tel: 38-12-55.

▶ **Marbella Club.** Carretera Cádiz-Málaga, km 158, 29600 **Marbella.** Tel: 77-13-00.

▶ **Hotel Mijas.** Urbanización Tamisa, 29650 **Mijas.** Tel: 48-48-00.

▶ **Hotel Los Monteros.** Urbanización Los Monteros, 29600 **Marbella.** Tel: 77-17-00.

▶ **Hotel Puente Romano.** Carretera de Cádiz, km 184, 29600 **Marbella.** Tel: 77-01-00.

▶ **Hotel Reina Cristina.** Plaza de la Conferencia, 11207 **Algeciras.** Tel: 60-26-22.

▶ **Hotel Sotogrande.** Carretera de Cádiz, km 154, **Guadiaro.** Tel: 79-21-00.

THE CANARY ISLANDS

By Patricia Brooks

For northern Europeans the Canaries are their islands in the sun, their winter getaway destination, their fastest escape route (via a short plane ride) to winter warmth. But the seven Spanish islands forming part of an archipelago spanning a distance of some 300 nautical miles out in the North Atlantic 850 miles southwest of Cádiz, 300 miles south of Portugal's Madeira, and only 70 miles from the coast of Africa (southern Morocco) have all the familiarity of, say, Siberia to most other travellers.

"Oh yes, the Canaries . . . they're Portuguese, aren't they?" is a typical comment. Or, "The Canaries? Aren't they somewhere in the Caribbean? Or are those the Caymans?"

Such confusion is nothing new. Both Ptolemy and Plutarch wrote of the Fortunate Islands, yet their descriptions leave some doubt as to whether they were really speaking of the Canaries, rather than the Azores or some other group of North Atlantic islands.

Still, the Canaries *were* known to ancient Greeks, Romans, and other early sea voyagers, and were once called the Garden of the Hesperides. A journey recorded by Pliny in about 40 B.C. speaks of "Canaria, so called from the multitude of dogs of great size." The dogs, or *canis,* are long gone, but the name, adopted by conquering Spaniards centuries later, remains.

Today any winter visitor can understand why the Canaries were dubbed, rightly or wrongly, the Fortunate Islands. Temperatures have no wild swings, but hover year-round between 65 and 86 degrees F (18 and 30 degrees C). Thus the islands—especially Grand Canary, Lanzarote, and

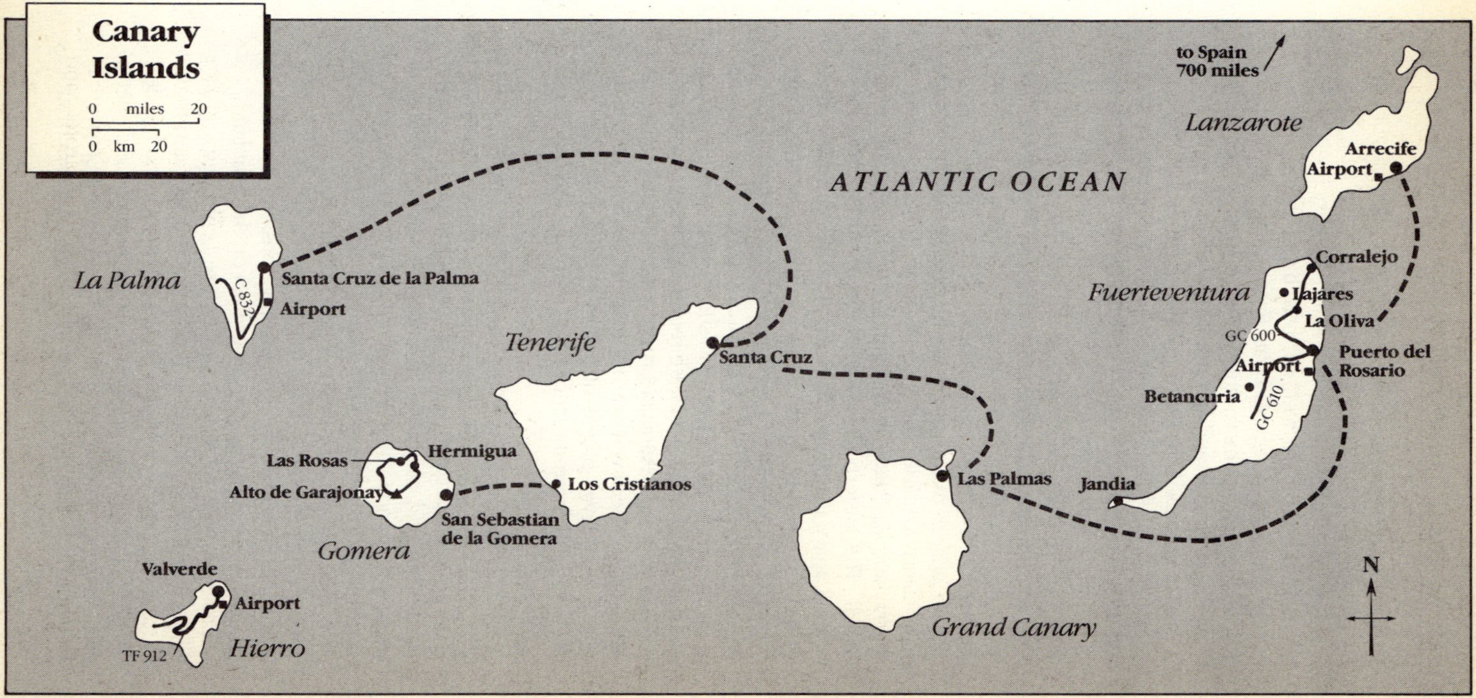
Canary Islands
0 miles 20
0 km 20
to Spain 700 miles
ATLANTIC OCEAN
Lanzarote
Arrecife
Airport
Fuerteventura
Corralejo
Lajares
La Oliva
GC 600
Puerto del Rosario
Airport
Betancuria
GC 610
Jandia
Grand Canary
Las Palmas
Tenerife
Santa Cruz
Los Cristianos
La Palma
Santa Cruz de la Palma
Airport
C 832
Gomera
Hermigua
Las Rosas
Alto de Garajonay
San Sebastian de la Gomera
Hierro
Valverde
Airport
TF 912
N

Tenerife—are strong and steady magnets for vacationing Europeans.

It is believed that in the pre-Spanish days, each island was a kingdom unto itself, with no interchange among them—not so much as a fishing boat. Even today, when island-hopping is easy, many vacationers tend to pick one island, apply suntan lotion, and stay put.

A pity, for each of these volcanic islands has its own personality. If you've seen one, you definitely haven't seen them all. Tiny **Gomera**'s misty green-terraced mountains are as different from **Lanzarote**'s black volcanic fields as the latter are from the wide, white-sand beaches of **Grand Canary** and the acres of banana plantations of **Tenerife**. Island-hopping, by plane or ferry, can only contribute to the charm of a visit.

The Canaries make up two provinces of Spain. Clustered in the western Canaries are the islands of Tenerife, Gomera, Hierra, and La Palma, with Santa Cruz de Tenerife as the capital. The eastern province, closer to Africa, consists of Grand Canary, Fuerteventura, and Lanzarote, with Las Palmas de Gran Canaria in Grand Canary as the provincial capital.

In planning a visit, you should first decide whether it is to be total getaway or a mix-and-match trip blending sightseeing with such leisure activities as sunbathing, swimming, and sports. Even then decisions are required, for getaway islands like **Hierro** and **La Palma** are rustic, with minimal infrastructures, while **Fuerteventura** has recently undergone a burst of touristic development but is essentially still a getaway island. On all three the climate is desirable and the terrain agreeable.

If you want more of a balance between leisure and sights, however, then consider the first four islands. On balance, Tenerife and Lanzarote offer the best matchup between sightseeing and play time. Gomera is a lovely clump of green-tufted mountains dropped into the ocean, but the tourist facilities are limited, the best consisting primarily of a very pleasant parador perched above the harbor. At the opposite extreme is Grand Canary, which is 90 percent tourist development, 10 percent attractions. In all the Canaries, prices are considerably lower than on the mainland.

Carnival, a movable feast just before Lent begins in late winter (usually sometime in February), is celebrated in the Canaries as nowhere else in Spain. In fact, it is no big deal on the mainland. But in Santa Cruz de Tenerife and Puerto de la Cruz on Tenerife and Las Palmas on Grand Canary, it is an explosive, raucous, fun-loving, week-long celebration, marked by fireworks, brass bands, folk dances, and parades of costumed celebrants snaking through the streets to musical accompaniment.

MAJOR INTEREST

Unusual volcanic landscapes, especially on Lanzarote and Tenerife
Miles of sandy beaches and coves, acres of banana plantations on Grand Canary and Tenerife
Fresh seafood and Canarian food specialties

Lanzarote
Montañas del Fuego (Mountains of Fire)
Route of the Volcanoes
Jameos del Agua volcanic cave
Mirador del Río and other scenic look-outs
Museo Internacional de Arte Contemporaneo

Tenerife
Pico del Teide mountain and Las Cañadas National Park
Victorian city of La Orotava
Santa Cruz de Tenerife
The village of Icod de los Vinos with its dragon-tree

Gomera
San Sebastián de la Gomera
Church of the Assumption

Grand Canary
Barrio Vegueta
Casa de Colón
Cathedral
Pozo de las Nieves volcanic mountain
The getaway islands of Hierro, La Palma, and Fuerteventura

In this era of renewed ethnic consciousness and regional autonomy in Spain, you will hear frequently in the Canaries about the **Guanches**. These mysterious people dating from the Stone Age were the only occupants of the islands when the Spaniards arrived. No one is absolutely sure of their origins, except that they were fair-skinned and thought to have come from North Africa. Their bone structure suggests they were of the same racial type as Cro-Magnon man. Similarities in the few Guanche words extant and the Berber language suggest that Guanches may have been Berbers who strayed the short distance west of the North African coast to the islands and then stayed there, never travelling even as far as the next island. Curiously, no excavation has ever unearthed anything resembling a boat on any of the islands. Originally, the term Guanche was applied only to inhabitants of Tenerife, the last holdouts against the Spaniards, but it is now used for the natives of all seven islands.

Nowadays Canarians look and speak like most other Spaniards. Their customs and traditions, after 500 years, have become totally absorbed into Spain's. What remains of the Guanches today can be found mostly in a few indigenous dishes, such as *gofio* (a type of heavy corn-and-wheat bread), *puchero* (a Canarian stew), *mojo* (a spicy red or green sauce made of oil, vinegar, garlic, coriander, peppers, and cumin) used to season meat and fish, and *papas arrugadas* (potatoes boiled in their skins, with a salt crust).

The Wines of the Canary Islands

The Canary Islands produce several types of wine, but have no DO wine-region classification and export little, if any, wine, even to the Spanish mainland. However, the wines of the Canary Islands, especially the Malvasia of Lanzarote, have been known since the 16th century, and are mentioned by Shakespeare, Voltaire, and in accounts of the exploits of Sir Francis Drake.

The best wines of the Canaries are expensive, because they are made under some of the most impossible, but interesting, winemaking conditions in the world. The vines are ungrafted because the phylloxera aphid cannot live in the volcanic soil of these vineyards; there is no rain, so vines must get their water from dew absorbed by porous volcanic stones. Since strong, hot winds can blow from Africa, each vine must be planted in a yard-deep pit or protected individually by a stone wall. Vineyard work and winemaking here is very labor-intensive, but the whole process, from the strikingly picturesque vineyards to the old-fashioned harvesting techniques (the grapes are still pressed by treading), is one of the most unusual in the wine world.

—*Gerry Dawes*

Spain and the Islands

Spain didn't get around to conquering the Canaries until the 15th century. Of course, Spain wasn't Spain, as such, until Ferdinand and Isabella united their kingdoms and finally defeated the Moors in a more widely noted 15th-century event. Arabs had stumbled on the islands in the 12th century; a Genoese navigator, Lanzarotto Malocello, stopped in Lanzarote in the early 14th century and left the island his name but nothing else. Some French ships were driven to the islands by a gale in 1334, and the Portuguese came close—but didn't find the islands—at about the same time.

It was in 1402 that Spanish forces, led by Frenchman Jean de Béthencourt, stepped ashore at Lanzarote, the first island to be taken. For much of the 15th century the islands were claimed and reclaimed by Spain and Portugal. Spanish sovereignty was finally established by a treaty between Portugal and Castile in 1479, but it took until 1496 for the locals on Tenerife to be conquered. To Spain, the islands were a bulwark against, and a possible springboard to, North Africa, and, later, a way of protecting Spanish ships from Barbary pirates.

For centuries after, the islands remained backward, and it was the rare foreigner who found the way there. There were few amenities to encourage them in the way of hotels, roads, or infrastructure. All that changed radically in the mid-1970s when tourists, hungry for new and accessible all-weather vacation sites, discovered the shimmering sand beaches of Grand Canary, and its rapid development began pell-mell.

LANZAROTE

If you had to choose just one Canary to visit, for sheer uniqueness it should be Lanzarote (Lan-zah-RWO-tay), the fourth largest and most easterly island. Much of this 313-square-mile mountainous, treeless, and nearly rainfree "island of the moon" is almost a minimalist study in black and white: one-story white houses (with kelly-green doors) surrounded by black volcanic soil, from which shoots of green plants emerge, counterpoint to the vivid green of the house doors. Even many of the beaches, especially those along the flat northeast coast, are covered with fine black sand. (Most of the golden-sand beaches are in the southwest, at Puerto del Carmen and, even farther west, Playa Blanca at the tip. The rugged, mountainous north, northwest, and western shores of Lanzarote are too dangerous for swimming.) Grapes are grown in the carefully cultivated *picón* (volcanic pebbles), and the vines look like snakes twisted along the ground, instead of growing upright. Camels and donkeys are still used to cultivate the fields.

Grand Canary
0 miles 10
0 km 10
Las Palmas
Arucas
C 810
GC 110
C 811
Artenara
Bandama
Tejeda
Pozo de las Nieves
Airport
GC 1
C 810
Maspalomas
Playa del Ingles
Playa de Maspalomas
N

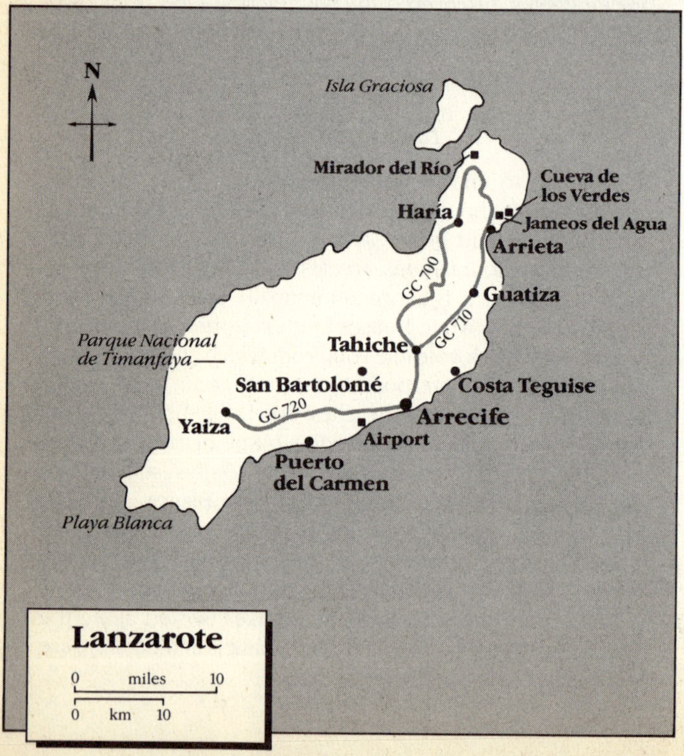

N
Isla Graciosa
Mirador del Río
Cueva de los Verdes
Haría
Jameos del Agua
Arrieta
GC 700
Guatiza
Parque Nacional de Timanfaya
Tahiche
GC 710
San Bartolomé
Costa Teguise
Yaiza
GC 720
Arrecife
Airport
Puerto del Carmen
Playa Blanca
Lanzarote
0 miles 10
0 km 10

In contrast with the touristic overdevelopment of Grand Canary and patches of Tenerife, most of Lanzarote remains relatively pristine. Lanzárote owes its careful development to one man, Cesár Manrique. You can't wander far in Lanzarote without hearing his name or seeing his handprints, so to speak, wherever aesthetics are involved, whether it's the prevention of random construction or preservation of the whitewashed houses that provide the island's signature.

Trained as a painter, Manrique was part of the Spanish abstract movement of the 1960s in Madrid, but in 1968 he returned home to Lanzarote. Since then he has been unofficial custodian of the island's environment (persuading the government to ban billboards) and designer-beautifier of most of the island's man-made attractions. Among his many credits are the cool green airport interior, wall sculptures in two major hotels (the Gran Hotel in Arrecife and Hotel Meliá Salinas Sol), and plans for the development of the island's most elite tourist *urbanizacion* (development project), Costa Teguise. His is a rare legacy, and one can only wonder what will happen to the island when he is gone. There are few places where one person alone can make such a noticeable difference. The island's small size (population 50,000) has probably made this possible.

Visitors to Lanzarote tend to be well-travelled, upscale Europeans in search of something a bit different mixed with their sunshine-and-sea cocktail. Jordan's King Hussein and the actor Omar Sharif are among the international set with vacation homes on the island.

Most visitors arrive by air. At the airport, two miles south of the capital city and ferry port, Arrecife (R-uh-SEE-fay), near the center of the east coast, you should pick up a rental car (essential for touring the island) and head for one of the coastal touristic developments, which have become small cities in themselves.

The most posh and exclusive development is five miles or so northeast of Arrecife on the coast, a well-run resort infrastructure and burgeoning community called **Costa Teguise**. There, after passing through a pancake-flat, arid, and beige landscape, you will suddenly come upon a "created community," clustered near the water's edge, of condominiums for rent, a golf course, shops, *supermercados,* restaurants and other entertainment facilities, avenues bordered with palm trees and greenery, and two excellent hotels.

The edge goes to the more established one, **Meliá Salinas Sol**, which is considered *the* place to stay on the island. It is the quintessential resort: large, with an atrium filled with towering trees, well-kept and palm-fringed grounds, an imaginative Manrique-designed saltwater swimming pool with volcanic bridges you can swim under, many sports facilities, and an attractive restaurant. Guest rooms all have flower-bedecked terraces overlooking the pool, a sandy beach, and the ocean. Topless sunning around the pool is discreet and not discouraged.

A short walk away is the **Teguise Playa Hotel**, a new, comfortable establishment facing the ocean, and also with an atrium lobby. The rooms have balconies with ocean views. Myriad sports facilities are available. Either accommodation makes a comfortable launching pad for exploring the island.

Less pricey and just as convenient are the resort hotels in the other major tourist development area on the island, the more built-up and crowded **Puerto del Carmen**, about 11 km (7 miles) west of Arrecife. There the hands-down hotel choice is **Los Fariones**, a high-rise like all the others, with the usual amenities: golf, tennis, a garden, heated swimming pool, a sheltered private beach, and spacious, well-decorated rooms. Puerto del Carmen, like Costa Teguise, is a totally created-for-tourism community of shops, restaurants, and hotels, but with better natural tawny beaches, bigger, noisier crowds, and more congestion. Each development, like comparable ones on the Costa del Sol on the mainland, has such a support system that a vacation there can be totally self-contained.

If your purpose is a quick here today/gone tomorrow once-over of the island, you might base yourself in **Arrecife** itself, a slightly scruffy, dusty port, noticeably lacking in sidewalks and charm. It does boast one good hotel, however, the **Gran Hotel**, centrally located downtown, facing the water, with a huge swimming pool, right next door to the town beach of golden sand.

Arrecife's main claim to sightseeing fame is the **Museo Internacional de Arte Contemporaneo**, Manrique's collection of mostly Spanish abstract paintings and sculptures, installed in the 18th-century fort, **Castillo de San José**, one of two sturdy fortresses guarding the Arrecife harbor. Included are works of Tapiés, Jose Guerrero, Francisco Ferreras, Millares, Fernando Zóbel, and others of the Spanish abstract school, as well as artists from Germany, France, Argentina, and the United States. The fort's interior is a handsome gallery space: The stone walls and floors, arched ceilings, and staircases make an intriguing contrast with the art.

There's a secondary reason to visit the museum: **Restau-**

rante San José. Located on the lower level of the fort, the restaurant has wide windows that wrap around the sea side of the building, so that diners have a full harbor view as they enjoy *paella*, grilled *mero* fish stuffed with ham, or other fresh seafood.

In the other castle, the 16th-century **Castillo de San Gabriel**, there is a museum of archaeology and anthropology.

Lanzarote, for sightseeing purposes, divides rather neatly into north and south, each different from the other, and a day for each gives ample time to cover the major sights. Although it is possible to scoot from north to south in a single day—the excellent roads are wide and under-trafficked—you would miss the pleasure of frequent stops for vistas and photographs.

Ruta de los Volcanes

What created the stark black landscape of Lanzarote was not one but several volcanic eruptions. The first occurred in the western Timanfaya area in 1730; 30 craters exploded from the earth simultaneously like cannons, with plumes of flame that continued for 19 days, burying 11 villages and one-third of the island. New eruptions continued for six years. Molten lava was layered 33 feet deep and covered 77 square miles. More eruptions followed in 1824, and even today you are aware of roiling life beneath the black lava on the Montañas del Fuego (Mountains of Fire). All told, there are some 300 extinct volcanoes on the island.

The 200 km (120 miles) of that old volcanic zone, known as the Route of the Volcanoes, is now a national park called **Parque Nacional de Timanfaya** about 24 km (15 miles) from Arrecife on the southwestern part of the island. It isn't just tourists who are intrigued by the 30 famed cones and fields of rubble-like lava; American astronauts heading for the moon used the lava landscape to preview what they might face on their moonwalks.

After paying a steep entrance fee at the park, drive along a well-kept one-way road through treeless fields and hillsides of black, gray, and rust-brown lava, devoid of any sign of flora or fauna, to Islote de Hilario. At this central point, park your car and board a free bus for a one-hour tour across desolate craters, through just over six miles of the most dramatic and eerie part of the route, where impassable clumps and swirls of chocolate-colored lava rest motionless, like a surrealistic

Dalí painting. There's a recorded commentary (in several languages) to keep you apprised of what you are seeing.

Afterward, back at Islote de Hilario, guides demonstrate the still-active nature of the seemingly sleeping volcano by throwing cold water into a pipe, causing geysers of steam to spurt forth instantly, and then poking mounds of brush into another hole 20 inches deep and observing the flash fire that quickly erupts. The temperature underground reaches 400°F. The gravelly earth is burning-hot to the touch. Later you may lunch there on meats or chicken grilled over an open hearth fueled by the volcano's heat in an attractive circular restaurant, whose wide glass windows overlook the silent lava-encrusted slopes and valleys.

Near the edge of the park you can arrange a 15-minute camel ride part way up a mountain slope. The reward for a jolting, swaying, disagreeable ride, as several camels are tethered bumpingly together, is a head-on view of a crater.

Eight km (5 miles) south of the Montañas del Fuego, and 5 km (3 miles) from the camel stop, is **Yaiza**, an Arabic-looking town with white buildings whose approach road is lined with vivid orange-blossomed cacti. Many foreign artists have settled in the town's dazzling all-white houses. **Galería Yaiza**, which sells modern local art and photographs, is located in one of these houses.

At the edge of town is **La Era**, one of the island's prettiest restaurants, more notable for its setting in an authentic old Canarian country house than for its hearty, somewhat unsophisticated cooking. Three tiny rustic dining rooms filled with attractive ceramics, baskets, and plants open onto a bougainvillaea-festooned courtyard.

Jameos del Agua

To explore the northern part of the island, take the main road north from Arrecife to Tahiche, and then follow its eastern branch toward Guatiza and Arrieta. Just beyond Arrieta the road branches again, and this time you will take the right road that leads toward two of the major sights in this northern part of the island, Jameos del Agua and Cueva de los Verdes. As you drive along the easy-to-follow route you will notice fields of cacti and vineyards protected by low volcanic-stone walls. As there is so little rainfall and not a single river on the island, the grapevines are grafted to prickly pear cactus, allowing the vines to survive on the cacti's humidity. The north, with its patches of cultivated green fields and more than a few palm trees dotted along the roadside, is a stark contrast to the parched and blackened southwest.

Jameos del Agua is a remarkable natural Lanzarote sight, converted by Manrique into a tasteful and intriguing tourist attraction. On several levels of a *jameos* (volcanic cave) are a nightclub with dance floor, a free-form swimming pool edged by palm trees, a garden of oleander and cacti, and a seawater lagoon in which live thousands of sightless white crabs (*munidopsis polimorpha*), unique to Lanzarote.

Nearby is **Cueva de los Verdes**, 7 km (4 miles) of connecting underground caves, formed when lava streams cooled and hardened into passages. The natives once hid from Barbary pirates in these caves.

At the northern tip of the island is the **Mirador del Río** (*mirador* means lookout), gouged into the top of the cliff overlooking the minuscule isle of **Graciosa** across the narrow El Río sea inlet. (Some Lanzarote hotels offer day swimming excursions to Graciosa and its powdery white-sand beaches, Conchas and Caleta del Sebo.) The views are spectacular from the mirador: You can sit inside a very attractive bar, sip a *café con leche,* admire the view through enormous windows, and watch hawks swoop and hang gliders dip along the craggy cliffs. You have the same view outside along a walkway protected by a guard rail. Upstairs in the mirador is a tiny shop with a good selection of guidebooks, Canarian dolls, and other handicrafts.

Return on the twisty, curving road that loops through the mountains along the western side of the island to Haría, then Teguise, where you will pick up the road south to Tahiche and Arrecife. Pause at **Haría**, a scenic town of low-slung houses, whose glistening whiteness, punctuated by garlands of purple and fuchsia bougainvillaea, has a North African cast. In the modern church are works by two Canarian sculptors: an Assumption of the Virgin by Lujan Perez and Christ by Borges Linares. From the **Mirador de Haría**, 3 km (2 miles) south of town, there are grand views of the Atlantic, the coastline, and the valley.

TENERIFE

Like Lanzarote, Tenerife (Ten-er-EE-fay) was bypassed by Columbus, although as he sailed from Gomera to Grand Canary on his first voyage to the Americas he noted flames spouting from Tenerife's Pico del Teide. With the wisdom of one familiar with volcanoes, he reassured his frightened

Tenerife
0 miles 10
0 km 10
Playa de las Teresitas
Aeropuerto de los Rodeos
Taganana
La Victoria de Acentejo
TF 114
La Laguna
San Andrés
Puerto de la Cruz
TF 5
San Juan de la Rambla
Santa Cruz
C 824
TF 1
Garachico
La
Orotava
Pinar de la Esperanza
Icod de
los Vinos
Candelaria
C 820
C 821
El Portillo
Pico del
Teide
Montaña Blanca
C 823
Las Cañadas National Park
TF 623
Valle de Ucanca
Guía
Puerto de San Juan
Montaña
Colorada
C 822
Vilaflor
N
C 821
TF 1
Playa de las Américas
Los Cristianos
Airport

Spanish crew that it was a function of nature, not a judgment of God.

Centuries later, Miguel de Unamuno described Tenerife and its dominant volcano this way: "And there in the distance . . . stood the island of Tenerife, like a celestial vision, dominated by that gigantic watchtower of Spain, the peak of Teide. . . . One would have said that the island was suspended in the sky."

As the largest Canary, Tenerife has a terrain that is all things to almost all visitors. There you will find plantings at home in both warm and cold climates. As the old saw goes about the weather (wait a minute, it will change): Five miles up a road, the botanical profile of Tenerife might shift from subtropical to temperate, then, within miles, back again.

There are three well-defined vegetation zones on this 792-square-mile island, which is shaped somewhat like a ladle and which climbs from sea level to over 12,000 feet. The first zone lies between Taganana at the northeast "handle" and Bufadero on the west, which extends from the levelest land to some 1,300 feet. It has a climate like Egypt's and plant life that includes date palms, sugar cane, coffee trees, banana trees, orange trees, and cacti. This is the domain of the dragon-tree, a curious spiky-branched, cactus-like tree that seems to "perspire" a bloodlike resin, which was used in the Middle Ages to treat leprosy, and which grows only in the Canaries.

The second, higher, zone, between Candelaria at the eastern base of the "handle" and La Victoria de Acentejo directly north, produces laurel, holly, almond, and beech trees, and such crops as maize, tomatoes, prickly pears, potatoes, and grapes. It has a climate resembling that of Italy and southern France.

As the road escalates upward from San Juan de la Rambla on the north, or top of the "ladle," to Vilaflor south of Pico del Teide, the terrain and temperature change a third time: Above 3,300 feet, heather, gorse, Scotch broom, and pine predominate.

Wild-flower fanciers have a field day on Tenerife, which boasts almost 1,000 wild flowering plants, about 270 of which are found only in the Canaries.

"Settling in" is your first consideration, and there are three major destinations, all on different parts of the island. Tenerife attracts basically two kinds of European sun-seekers: The Germans and Scandinavians, individually and in tour groups, tend to head north (where the "handle" joins the "ladle") to the bustling, built-up coastal town of **Puerto de la**

Cruz, built above scenic volcanic rock formations and with a black-sand beach; the British and other Anglophones, especially families in search of a getaway "do-nothing" holiday, prefer the creamy sand beaches and sprawling Miami Beach–like seaside developments that have sprung up quickly in recent years in **Playa de las Américas** and **Los Cristianos** at the southern bottom of the "ladle," where you catch the ferry to Gomera. A third choice—and best for sightseers, as opposed to "laid back" vacationers—is the lively, less "touristy" port city of **Santa Cruz de Tenerife** (usually shortened to Santa Cruz) near the northeast edge of the island.

To reach any of the three you should rent a car, easily picked up at the airport, which is located near El Médano in the south. A superhighway runs along the coast, beginning at Los Cristianos, north to Santa María del Mar, just outside Santa Cruz, where it becomes an even faster *autopista* that curves inland around the top of the "handle" and over along the north coast as far as Puerto de la Cruz.

Staying on Tenerife

Far and away the most elegant hotel on the island is the **Mencey**, in Santa Cruz. The name meant king or ruler in Guanche times, and the Ciga-run hotel is indeed regal, after having recently undergone a costly renovation. Spacious, deluxe rooms with balconies overlook either the superbly groomed garden, palm-sheltered grounds, and swimming pool, or the city and harbor. The Mencey also boasts one of the island's finest Continental restaurants. To enjoy the beach, however, you have to drive two to three miles along the northeast coast to Playa de las Teresitas (more about that later).

Puerto de la Cruz in the north is literally cheek-by-jowl with high-rise hotels in all prices and categories. They line the hills ringing the little fishing port, stretching right down to the seaside promenade that curves around the black rocky ledges above the swirling sea. The most secluded deluxe choice is the **Meliá Botânico**, cresting a hilltop above town. The hotel is spacious, set on lavish grounds dotted with lush plantings, a swimming pool, and tennis courts overlooking the town and water.

Although the hotel is a quiet sanctuary, the town below is chock-a-block with shops, restaurants, nightclubs, bars, discos, and a casino catering to the masses of European tourists who flock there. Smack in the middle of the action is the **Monopol Hotel**, and while it may be a bit noisy, it has several things going for it: more moderate prices, balconies almost literally over the water, a plant-filled atrium-lobby, a swimming pool, and considerable charm.

Should you choose the southern tip of Tenerife as "home base," once again you have dozens of accommodation choices, all high-rise and large, many self-contained resorts geared to sun-lovers and lotus eaters, where you merely collapse by the pool or beach for days on end. Most such places are long on service and convenience, shorter on charm. **La Siesta Hotel** in Playa de las Américas is a block from the gorgeous beach and comes equipped with two swimming pools, tennis courts, gardens, and the comforts—but not the solitude—of home.

Pico del Teide and Las Cañadas

Casting a figurative shadow over the triangular island is Pico del Teide, or Mount Teide, the highest elevation in Spain, at 12,198 feet, located in the center of the "ladle." Its crater measures 7½ miles in diameter, 42 miles in circumference. That Teide dominates the island (and is its major attraction) is evident even in the island's name: Tenerife in Guanche means snow-capped mountain.

To reach the foot of Teide, there are four roads from the coast through **Las Cañadas National Park**, all of them crossing a terrain that changes in color and character from valley to mountain pass (*cañadas* means ravines).

The most scenically dramatic route, C 821, begins at **La Orotava**, a north-central hill town, known especially for its 18th-century Baroque **Iglesia de la Concepción** and for the typical Canarian houses along calle de San Francisco. Most noted of a group of 17th-century houses with fretted wooden balconies is **Casa de los Balcones**, which now contains an **Artespaña** handicraft showroom. (Curiously, most of the embroideries in the Artespaña are from China.) You'll see similar pine balconies, old and new, all over the island, but few as elaborate and old as these. During the Feast of Corpus Christi the ground of the entire plaza del Ayuntamiento in La Orotava is decorated with fresh flowers and an enormous colored sand-and-stone painting depicting the feast.

The road upward, past valleys of banana plantations, is well marked over the 54 km (34 miles) from La Orotava to the Valle de Ucanca and Las Cañadas, site of an ancient collapsed volcano crater. It is on this plateau that all four roads meet, near Montaña Blanca, where the cable-car station is located. The cable car to Teide's summit is operational on days when there is no wind. If you're feeling adventurous you can walk from the summit terminal at 11,664 feet to the crater's edge. It's a 45-minute walk over loose volcanic rubble and past sulphurous smoke holes. Once there, you will get views that extend all over the island, and on very clear days—typical for Tenerife—you can see the forms of Gomera, La Palma, and Grand Canary in the distance.

In Las Cañadas you can take a coffee or lunch break at the **Parador de las Cañadas del Teide**, a comfortable rustic lodge that is part of the national parador system. Its dining room, with a fire glowing in the hearth much of the year, is a good place to try such Canarian specialties as Canary soup or *cocido canarias* (a stew of chunks of beef, corn cobs, squash, cabbage, green beans, potatoes, carrots, and zucchini, served in gargantuan portions). The parador also has a few modest guest rooms and a heated outdoor swimming pool. Next to the parador is a small hermitage to the Virgen de las Nieves. After lunch you might hike through a landscape that looks like the American West, with cactus, sagebrush, huge lava boulders called Los Roques, and others, Los Azulejos, which glisten and gleam like lustrous ceramic tiles.

To enjoy more of the varied landscape, plan to return by a different route. Almost equally dramatic, but less twisting, is via C 821 to the El Portillo fork to C 824, 58 km (36 miles) toward the northeast through a towering pine forest, Pinar de la Esperanza, to La Laguna, Tenerife's former capital. A third drive, around a pine forest via C 821, over twisting mountain roads and a steep mountain pass, veering around the red-earthed face of another mountain (Montaña Colorada), goes south to **Vilaflora**, a spa with the highest elevation of any town on the island. Much of the bottled water sold on Tenerife comes from Vilaflora, as does a sweet, fresh goat cheese. There is a pleasant, Belgian-run inn at the edge of town, **Tajinaste**, where you can lunch on a quiche on the sun-drenched terrace or even spend the night in a simple guest room. A fourth route to or from Las Cañadas is from Puerto de San Juan on the southwest coast, via Guía on C 823, but scenically it is the least interesting, with fewer startling vistas.

Santa Cruz de Tenerife

Compared to the fast-expanding touristic developments of Los Cristianos and Playa de las Américas on the southern coast, and of Puerto de la Cruz on the north shore (discussed above and below), with all their high-rise hotels, Santa Cruz, the main ferry port, seems so settled and permanent.

In fact, it was a capital-come-lately, not emerging as a major city until the 18th century. Today Santa Cruz looks like many a provincial Spanish city, full of bustle and business. For a pleasant repast there, stop at one of the outdoor cafés in the main **plaza Candelaria**, which faces the harbor, and watch the passersby (always an enjoyable pastime in Spain).

The major sight of interest is **Castillo de Paso Alto**, a former fortress and now a military museum, with uniforms, weapons, and the cannon (called the Tiger) that fired the shot that cost Admiral Horatio Nelson his right arm and the battle when he attacked castle and town on July 24, 1797.

The city has several intriguing modern landmarks. Inside the lushly planted **Parque Municipal García Sanabria**, diagonally across from Hotel Mencey on rambla del General Franco, are a number of contemporary sculptures by Spanish artists, including Amadeo Gabino. Ambling along The Rambla you will encounter a bronze work by Henry Moore, as well as large pieces by various Spanish sculptors. Note the handsome 19th- and early 20th-century mansions lining the north side of The Rambla; many are now foreign consulates.

You will notice in Santa Cruz, and elsewhere in the Canaries, avenues that still bear the names of Generalísimo Franco, José Antonio Primo de Rivera, Calvo Sotelo, and other Falangist heroes—a reminder that these conservative islands were Franco's launching pad for the Nationalist revolution that began the Civil War in 1936.

Seven km (4.5 miles) east of Santa Cruz along the coast is **Playa de las Teresitas**, a lovely expanse of white-sand beach. The sand was imported from the Sahara some years ago, and is in stark contrast with other beaches on the north coast, which are volcanic black sand. Near the beach is the village of **San Andrés**, where there are three or four simple but very good seafood restaurants. The best is **Restaurante Don Antonio**, calle Duque 19, where grilled sole reigns supreme. (Be sure to ask for the piquant *mojo* sauce to go with it.)

The North Coast

From Santa Cruz, on a fast *autopista,* it is just 38 km (24 miles) northwest to **Puerto de la Cruz**, no longer recognizable as the sleepy little fishing village it was just 20 years ago.

Across from the Botânico Sol Hotel on five acres of hillside above the town is the **Jardín Botânico**, begun in the 18th century at the request of Carlos III. The gardens provide a sheltered, refreshing oasis of greenery, with native (and many foreign) plants and trees, orchid houses, and a bizarre-looking rubber plant almost 200 years old.

If you don't mind crowds of fellow visitors clogging the promenade, you might stroll downtown (parking is a terrible problem, so you might just as well leave your car above the town center) and meander along avenida de Colón, the waterfront promenade where everyone congregates to stroll, shop, meet friends, and just observe the passing scene. As you amble, you will pass Lago de Martianez, a novel park, built into a ledge of black lava rocks that jut into the water. Created by Lanzarote artist Cesár Manrique, the park consists of white paths bordered with flowers leading around a series of sculpted sea-fed swimming pools, an artificial lake with five islands, a restaurant, a gigantic nightclub, and a Manrique sculpture, *Homage to the Sea.*

You never have to search for a place to eat in Puerto de la Cruz: You are surrounded by them. Full of plants and character is **Mi Vaca y Yo**, where you'll find fresh grilled seafood at moderate prices. It is on Cruz Verde, something of a "restaurant row," one of the small streets just off avenida de Colón.

West of Puerto de la Cruz 23 km (14 miles) on the coastal road C 820 is **Icod de los Vinos**, a hillside village above the Atlantic, noted for the 1,000-year-old dragon-tree, once believed to have medicinal properties. A remarkable sight, it has a thick trunk that resembles many trunks melded together, and spiky cactuslike branches forming an umbrella overhead. Up a side street from the tree is **Iglesia de San Marcos**, parts of which are 15th century, with a Renaissance portal, a carving by Pedro de Mena, and a gilded Baroque retable. The church faces peaceful, tree-shaded plaza Parque San Lorenzo de Caceras, which leads up a few steps to a plaza framed with old, traditional pine-balconied Canarian houses.

Just below Icod de los Vinos is Playa de San Marcos, a black-sand beach enclosed in a natural harbor. You can enjoy the freshest of grilled sole (and other fish), served with delicious salt-encrusted *papas arrugadas,* for an extremely modest price at **Restaurante San Marcos**, right on the beach.

If you continue along the pleasantly curvaceous coastal drive west you will come to **Garachico**, an almost totally unspoiled town facing a huge rock in the ocean known simply as Roque de Garachico. If you have foregone lunch at

San Marcos, you have a second chance in Garachico at an attractive upstairs restaurant, **Isla Baja**, which overlooks the waterfront promenade and serves a delicious *paella Valenciana.* There's nothing too special about Garachico, which was the capital of Tenerife until devastated by a volcanic eruption in 1716, but there is a craft shop installed in the waterfront fort, **Castillo de San Miguel**, where the Canarian lace and embroideries are very reasonable. From the fort you can walk over a series of connected black volcanic ledges just above the ocean, which splashes just enough water over the rocks to let you know it's there; ladders attached to several of the rocks lead down into the water, making this the local equivalent of a "swimming hole."

GOMERA

The tiny round 146-square-mile mountainous island of Gomera just west of Tenerife sometimes seems ephemeral, as mist hangs like a veil over its vibrant green terraced mountains planted with banana groves and grapevines. Few volcanic traces remain, and Gomera is unusually verdant for the Canaries. The smallest of the seven major islands in terms of population (18,000), it is a little emerald jewel.

While it is possible to rent a car and drive up the mountains by yourself, the turns are so frequent and the steep drops so precipitous that to enjoy the heart-stopping views it is better to leave the driving to another.

The easiest way to see Gomera is by day tour from Tenerife, departing from the ferry dock at Los Cristianos in the southwest, arriving in 40 minutes in the photogenic, snug harbor of **San Sebastián de la Gomera**, the capital on the southeast coast. The tour usually goes by bus up to a tiny hamlet called **Las Rosas**, overhanging a cliff, where you have lunch, and then continues to **Hermigua**, a delightful village of white-walled houses. The 16th-century **Convento de Santo Domingo** has a Baroque altarpiece and Mudejar ceiling. Dominating the island is (4,879-foot) Alto de Garajonay.

There is ample time once back at sea level in San Sebastián to walk to its few significant landmarks. Columbus shuttled between Gomera and Grand Canary, taking on supplies, before setting off from San Sebastián on September 6, 1492, to cross the Atlantic. In the **Church of the Assumption** he heard Mass before sailing, and in the inner courtyard of the Customs House is a well where he supposedly laid in his water supply for the voyage. A good lunch stop is at the **Parador Conde de la Gomera**, on the hill overlooking the town and harbor.

If you are tempted by the do-nothing peacefulness of Gomera—its few foreigners and absence of nightlife and sightseeing agenda—the parador is certainly the place to stay for its tranquillity, superb hilltop vistas, and welcome swimming pool. With a little time, you might even hear some of the islanders' special whistling language called *silbo,* developed in centuries past, when the only way Gomerians could communicate with each other over the mountain ridges was through a complicated form of whistling. A few *silbadores* still practice the art today.

GRAND CANARY

The third largest island, at 592 square miles, Grand Canary, more or less in the center of the Canaries group, resembles a giant clam shell. Dominating the interior is Pozo de las Nieves, an often snow-capped 6,394-foot peak.

Staying on Grand Canary

The south shore is a succession of long golden-sand beaches, most notably San Agustín, Playa del Inglés, Maspalomas, and El Oasis. The beaches are so beautiful and the vast sand dunes so inviting that it was probably inevitable that when development began, this area would be the magnet for the "tourist cities" that have been subsequently built up: streets lined with high-rise hotels, condominiums, stores, restaurants, pubs, churches, everything necessary to keep a vacationing population happy and anxious for a return visit—very much like the Costa del Sol on the Spanish mainland. That Europeans love it can be attested to by the herds of tour groups, families, and singles who pile off charters from Britain, Scandinavia, Germany, and the Netherlands every day throughout the winter months. In fact, the climate is so congenial that many expatriates from the north have made Grand Canary (Tenerife, too) home.

Developed as the area is, it is the logical place for you to stay in order to combine a bit of sun, ocean, and recreation with your sightseeing. The best address is the **Royal Maspalomas Oasis** on Playa de Maspalomas, a large deluxe resort hotel with a grand beach and many sports facilities and amenities, all attended to on spacious, well-kept grounds. Maspalomas, not many years ago just a breathtakingly beautiful beach, with mammoth sand dunes, a palm oasis, and saltwater lagoon, is now a sizable, self-sustained tourist city. Another luxurious property is the **Meliá Tamarindos** resort hotel, facing another gorgeous beach, Playa de San Agustín, 10 km (6 miles) northeast of Maspalomas, a few miles closer to the airport, with lovely gardens, large rooms facing the ocean, a sports center, and things to do to keep you pampered and satisfied.

Las Palmas de Gran Canaria (**Las Palmas** for short), the capital, duty-free port, and largest population center in the Canaries (approximately 300,000) is some 58 km (35 miles) to the north, at the island's northeast tip. It too is crammed with hotels in various categories, but the city's commercial center has become so crowded and jerry-built with stores and shops that it doesn't offer much solitude for reclusive visitors. It does swing, however. The international airport, on the east coast, is just about equidistant from Las Palmas and the south beaches, so picking up a rental car at the airport is advised. You will need it for sightseeing anyhow.

If you opt to stay in Las Palmas, the **Hotel Reina Isabel** on Alfredo L. Jones, just off the main paseo de las Canteras, facing Playa de las Canteras (a superb 16-mile-long tawny-sand beach sheltered by a low reef), offers every imaginable luxury, including a heated swimming pool and a sauna. More moderately priced, but also convenient, is the old-time, pseudo-Moorish **Hotel Santa Catalina**, in the very pretty Parque Doramas, straddling the oldest part of the city and the new. In the park is Pueblo Canario, a compound where Canarian folk dances and songs are performed in costume in the open air every Sunday (11:45 A.M.–1:15 P.M.) and Thursday (5:30–7:00 P.M.).

Around Grand Canary

Scenically, Grand Canary has a good deal of the variety of Tenerife, with an interior volcanic and mountainous core, deep ravines, valleys of banana groves, and a south shore lined with sandy beaches. It is Grand Canary's mountainous interior that shows off the island's diverse and most spectacular landscape. A tortuous winding road will take you southeast from Las Palmas inland. As you climb ever upward to the village of Tejeda, the vegetation and terrain change dramatically the higher you get. A turnoff to the left at Monte Coello takes you to **Pico de Bandama**, where at the Bandama Mirador you can peer into the huge volcanic crater, now green with planted crops. You might even practice your putting at the Golf Club of Grand Canary, poised on the crater's edge. Climbing still farther upward, past clusters of golden broom and pine forests, you reach Cruz de Tejeda, the mountain pass some 4,747 feet high.

The village of **Tejeda,** the most elevated on the island, is set in another crater, which the writer Miguel de Unamuno, who knew the Canaries well, having been exiled to Fuerteventura after the 1923 coup d'état of Primo de Rivera, described as a "petrified tempest; a tempest of fire and lava, rather than of water." Pause at Tejeda for lunch at the government-run **Parador Cruz de Tejeda,** a charming rustic retreat (no rooms) set among almond orchards with spectacular views of Roque Nublo, a jagged basalt spire, and snowcapped Pozo de las Nieves. Signposts will lead you on to Artenara, a village on the edge of a precipice, and Juncallilo, a troglodyte village whose inhabitants live in well-maintained caves created out of lava streams. From there it is possible to continue to **Pinar de Tamadaba,** the stately survivor of a pine forest that once covered the island. At Tamadaba you can walk through the forest to a precipitous cliff, from whose top you'll have a splendid view all along the west coast, and you may even spot Mount Teide on Tenerife.

Another day, another breathtaking drive: This one from Las Palmas leads 22 km (13.5 miles) west to Arucas, a pretty little town near a volcanic cone called **Montaña de Arucas.** From Arucas, the road goes south 10 km (6 miles) through a valley of banana plantations to Teror, a cool summer resort in the interior, bordered by pine woods and ringed with mountains. Teror's real claim to local fame is the Virgen del Pino, patroness of Grand Canary. The statue of the Virgin of the Pines, reportedly found in the branches of a local pine tree in the 15th century, now resides in the Baroque Basilica of Nuestra Señora del Pino. Islanders make a gift-bearing pilgrimage to the shrine on September 8, the Festival of the Virgin of the Pines.

Las Palmas

Sprawling Las Palmas is really two cities, the modern hodgepodge known as **Puerto de la Luz** and **Barrio Vegueta,** to the southwest, which dates back to the Spanish conquest. Much of the modern section is commercial and industrial, but dominating its touristic center is the fantastically long Playa de Las Canteras and a promenade, the tile-surfaced **paseo de**

las Canteras, that shadows it, lined by hotels, cafés, tourist shops, boutiques, and restaurants. The problem with this beach and promenade is that it is the victim of its own success: The beach is almost too crowded for swimming or even tanning, and the promenade at dusk seems as trafficked as Times Square or Shaftesbury Avenue.

Vegueta has been almost swallowed by its larger modern neighbor, yet from a sightseer's point of view it is infinitely more compelling.

When Columbus landed, on August 25, 1492, in search of a replacement for his damaged caravel, Vegueta *was* the city. Its narrow streets, lined with faded pastel houses, lead into a beautiful, elongated square, **plaza de Santa Ana**. On one side is an imposing 19th-century town hall. Opposite is the Gothic **cathedral**, parts of which date back to the 15th century, though the façade is Neoclassical. Inside are a Baroque altar and, in the treasury, a 16th-century monstrance attributed to Benvenuto Cellini.

Around the corner from the cathedral, at calle Colón 1, is the **Casa de Colón**, where Columbus stayed, briefly, in 1502. The house was built for the first Spanish governors and is interesting in itself, with open courtyards and rooms with wooden Mudejar ceilings. While there isn't much there to remind you of Columbus, there are fascinating exhibits relating to his voyages, as well as nautical artifacts of the 15th and 16th centuries: maps, ship models, cannons, navigation instruments, and banners. Two appealing little squares in the old quarter are **plaza de Santo Domingo** and **plaza del Espíritu Santo**.

The big attraction of modern Las Palmas is shopping. As a duty-free port, the city is a bargain-hunter's paradise, with goods from all over the world—but you need to know the particular item's value at home because not everything is a real buy. Especially prevalent are Indian, Arab, and Oriental shops with clothes, fabrics, name-brand electronics, cameras, perfumes, and jewelry. "Negotiating" the price is expected. **Artesania Canaria Taguguy**, Armas 1, across from Casa de Colón, is a shop with local baskets, pottery, and other crafts. **Museo Canario**, near the cathedral, is worth checking out for its Guanche artifacts and idols.

Plan on dinner at **El Acuario**, plaza de la Victoria 3, considered the island's finest restaurant. The accent is French and the seafood marvelous, and the prices, although on the elevated side, are lower than on the mainland.

THE GETAWAY ISLANDS

While Hierro, La Palma, and Fuerteventura are less visited than the islands just discussed, each has something to recommend it.

Tiny **Hierro**, the smallest, most westerly Canary at 167 square miles, with just 7,000 inhabitants, is wooded and mountainous, with cliffs dropping into the sea. The lack of an airport and a dearth of beaches discourage the mass tourism that has afflicted the bigger islands, but the island holds great appeal for naturalists. If you wish to commune with nature, bird watch, and practice your Spanish (the locals are known for their pure Castilian), a good place to base yourself is at the **Parador Nacional de El Hierro**, which has a swimming pool and most conveniences.

Verdant, V-shaped **La Palma**, also on the western side of the Canaries group, north of Hierro, is also a natural wonderland, with grottoes, gorges, lush vegetation, giant ferns, pine groves bordering the island's 17-mile circumference, banana groves, vineyards, several fine beaches, houses with the distinctive Canarian wooden balconies, and the largest volcano crater known, the **Caldera de Taburiente** (known as the Caldron), located in the island's center. The major city of Santa Cruz de la Palma, on the east coast, perches like an amphitheater on a steep slope at the edge of another crater, La Caldereta. A modest but comfortable base for exploring this not-yet-exploited island is the **Parador Nacional Santa Cruz de la Palma** in the capital, a short distance from the airport.

Of the three "getaway" islands, only **Fuerteventura**, the second largest Canary island and the closest to Africa, is undergoing major tourist development. "High time," say beachophiles, who revel in its miles of fabulous sandy shoreline and its clear waters, ideal for snorkeling and diving; "a pity," say lovers of solitude, who fear the island is heading down the overbuilding trail that has plagued Grand Canary. New hotels continue to go up, mostly at Corralejo in the north and Jandía at the southern tip, but there is still a lot of untrampled beach left, and the leaf-shaped island is a fisherman's paradise because it is separated from North Africa by a surging strait that is the favorite racing territory for tuna and swordfish.

The attractive, distinctively Canarian-looking **Parador Nacional de Fuerteventura** is on Playa Blanca, a lovely beach just 2 km (1.25 miles) from the capital, Puerto del Rosario, on the northeast coast and 6 km (3.75 miles) north of the airport. From there by rental car you can scout your favorite beach discoveries and also visit La Oliva in the north, where there are many fine mansions; Lajares, where fine needlework is made, passing the Route of the Windmills along the way; and the old capital Betancuria, located in a small volcano in the center of the island, with some fine old buildings. Another comfortable place to stay is **Tres Islas Sol**, a fine hotel at Playa de Corralejo on the north tip of the island.

GETTING AROUND

It is approximately two hours by air from Madrid to Tenerife—though it's only an hour on your watch because of the time-zone change—via Iberia or its sister airline Aviaco, with six flights a day. Flights from Madrid to Grand Canary are just as frequent and take only a few minutes longer. There are also direct, if fewer, flights from Madrid to Lanzarote, Las Palmas, and Fuerteventura, as well as daily nonstop flights from Barcelona to Tenerife and Grand Canary.

From London's Heathrow, there are three Iberia flights a day to Tenerife and Grand Canary; from New York a daily flight (via Madrid) to both islands.

Once in the Canaries, you can hop via Iberia, Aviaco, or Air Binter to every island except Gomera and Hierro, which have no airports.

Transmediterranea has twice-a-week service from Cádiz to Santa Cruz, Tenerife, and to Arrecife, Lanzarote; the boat leaves at 2:00 P.M., arriving at 8:00 A.M. two days later in Tenerife, another day later in Lanzarote. There is daily ferry service (3½ hours) between Santa Cruz, Tenerife, and Las Palmas, Grand Canary. Thursday through Sunday, ferries travel from Tenerife to Lanzarote, departing at 6 P.M., arriving at noon the next day, stopping at Las Palmas and Fuerteventura. Ferries from Grand Canary to Lanzarote, via Fuerteventura, depart at 11:45 A.M., arriving the next day at noon. Ferries for Gomera leave daily from Los Cristianos, Tenerife.

Once you are on the islands, the best, most expeditious way to travel is by car. Numerous car-rental agencies have offices at the Lanzarote, Tenerife, and Grand Canary airports. Roads on the three islands have excellent two-lane asphalt surfaces; back roads are less well surfaced. Tenerife and Grand Canary also boast fast-moving *autopistas*.

ACCOMMODATIONS REFERENCE

When dialing telephone numbers from outside the country, drop the 9 in the area code.

▸ **Arrecife Gran Hotel.** Avenida Mancomunidad 11, 35500 Arrecife, **Lanzarote.** Tel: (928) 81-12-50.

▸ **Parador Conde de la Gomera.** San Sebastián de la Gomera, 38800 **Gomera.** Tel: (922) 87-10-00.

▸ **Meliá Botânico.** Richard J. Yeoward, 38400 Puerto de la Cruz, **Tenerife.** Tel: (922) 38-14-00; Telex: 92395 HOTA.

▸ **Hotel Los Fariones.** Urbanización Playa Blanca, 35500 Puerto del Carmen, **Lanzarote.** Tel: (928) 82-51-75; Telex: 96351.

▸ **Parador Nacional de Fuerteventura.** Playa Blanca, 35600 Puerto de Rosario, **Fuerteventura.** Tel: (928) 85-11-50.

▸ **Parador Nacional de El Hierro.** 38900 Valverde, **Hierro.** Tel: (922) 55-01-00.

▸ **Meliá Salinas Sol.** Playa de las Cucharas, NE Costa Teguise, **Lanzarote.** Tel: (928) 81-30-40.

▸ **Mencey.** Dr. José Naveiras 38, 38001 Santa Cruz de Tenerife, **Tenerife.** Tel: (922) 27-67-00; Telex: 92034 MCEY E.

▸ **Monopol.** Quintana 15, Puerto de la Cruz, **Tenerife.** Tel: (922) 38-46-11; Telex: 92397 HMLT E.

▸ **Hotel Reina Isabel.** Alfredo L. Jones 40, 35000 Las Palmas, **Grand Canary.** Tel: (928) 26-01-00; Telex: 95103.

▸ **Royal Maspalomas Oasis.** Playa de Maspalomas, Maspalomas, **Grand Canary.** Tel: (928) 76-01-70.

▸ **Hotel Santa Catalina.** Avenida Litoral, 38660 Playa de las Américas, **Tenerife.** Tel: (922) 79-23-40; Telex: 96014.

▸ **Parador Nacional Santa Cruz de la Palma.** 35005 Las Palmas, **Grand Canary.** Tel: (922) 41-23-40.

▸ **La Siesta Hotel.** Avenida Litoral, 38660 Playa de las Américas, **Tenerife.** Tel: (922) 79-23-00; Telex: 91119.

▸ **Meliá Tamarindos.** Retama 3, 35100 Playa de San Agustín. **Grand Canary.** Tel: (928) 76-26-00.

▸ **Teguise Playa.** Urbanización Costa Teguise, **Lanzarote.** Tel: (928) 81-66-54; Telex: 96399 PTGS.

▸ **Hotel Tres Islas Sol.** Playa de Corralejo, 35627 Corralejo, **Fuerteventura.** Tel: (928) 86-60-00.

CHRONOLOGY OF THE HISTORY OF SPAIN

Prehistory

Weapons and charred bones from elephant hunters' camps indicate that Paleolithic man lived in Spain perhaps half a million years ago. The earliest human remains have been uncovered on the Meseta (the high plateau covering much of central Spain) not far from present-day Madrid. Two Neanderthal settlements dating from 200,000 B.C. have been found at Gibraltar.

Paleolithic man left caves on the Iberian Peninsula decorated with remarkable paintings of the "cold-weather" animals they hunted: deer, bison, horses, and wild boar. These masterpieces are said to be more than 12,000 years old. Painted on the ceilings of stone caves, such as those at **Altamira** (near Santander, on the Bay of Biscay in northern Spain), these animal depictions have an unexpected technical perfection. Bones of animals found on the floors of the caves suggest that the paintings were part of a ritual. Discovered in 1879, the Altamira paintings are polychromes of several colors of pigment (ocher, manganese oxides, carbon black, iron oxide). Because some of the figures are over six feet long, and the cave is only five to six feet high, the best way to view the paintings is to lie on your back.

Other cave paintings, showing match-like figures using bows and arrows, have been found near Valencia. These narrative scenes of human beings date from 4000 to 3000 B.C.

The Iberians and the Celts

Spain's earliest well-documented peoples were as distinctive as the regions they occupied. Probably migrating from North Africa between the 13th and sixth centuries B.C. across the Straits of Gibraltar, the Iberians first settled along the

Andalusian coast; then some moved inland beyond the Sierra Morena range. The southern Iberians appear to have lived in walled cities, mined the copper deposits near Almería, and buried their dead in elaborate cave tombs. Some 40 miles west of Granada, constructions from about 2500 B.C. take the form of funerary chambers beneath *tumuli* (mounds). These cromlechs are on the outskirts of the town of Antequera. Less well documented than the Iberian tribes are the Basques, who probably antedate the Iberians but whose origins remain unknown.

Through the rough northern passes of the Pyrenees in about 900 B.C. came Celts from western Europe. Speaking an Indo-European language—the puzzling Basque language is not Indo-European—the fair-skinned Celts tended sheep on the vast plains, built forts, and hired themselves out as mercenaries.

The sculptured polychrome stone head known as *La Dama de Elche* dates from this early Iberian period; it is the pride of Madrid's Museo Arqueológico Nacional.

Throughout its early history seafaring peoples came to Spain: the Phoenicians, the Greeks, and later the Carthaginians (Carthage began as a Phoenician colony in North Africa). The Phoenicians established a trade center at Cádiz (then Gadir) in about 1100 B.C.; the location offered easy access to both the Mediterranean and the Atlantic coastlines of Europe. In the seventh century B.C. the Greeks began colonizing Iberia, establishing a lively and profitable trade in the south. They are said to have introduced what are today regarded as prototypical Spanish staples: the olive and the grape. They may also have brought some form of bullfighting or bullbaiting.

But it was the Carthaginians who first actually gained control over much of the Iberian Peninsula. Using their strategic position on the North African coast, they invaded Iberia in the sixth century B.C. The Greek historian Polybius (second century B.C.) claims that by the fourth century Carthage had established a protectorate over all the Iberian tribes.

Much later (Flaubert's novel *Salammbô* evokes this period) Carthage, in the person of Hamilcar Barca and his son Hannibal, stung by defeat in the First Punic War against Rome in 241 B.C., led huge armies (and those celebrated elephants) on tortuous expeditions that were to end in another defeat in 206 B.C., when Carthage was forced to relinquish the entire Iberian Peninsula to Rome. (But the Barca family name endures as the root of the name Barcelona.)

The Romans

Some 600 years of Roman rule (206 B.C.–A.D. 410) gave Spain a network of roads for military and mercantile purposes, a collection of seaports with docks and lighthouses, and a pattern of proven methods for cultivating mines, agriculture, and trade. Roman law gave Spain concrete evidence that order and prosperity resulted from disciplined administration. And, not least, Rome gave Spain its language.

Spain gave Rome minerals, raw materials, and olive oil, esteemed the finest in the ancient world (used for eating, cooking, lighting, and as a substitute for soap). Spain also gave Rome two emperors, Trajan and Hadrian, both born in Itálica (now Santiponce, near Seville). Born in Spain as well were the rhetorician Quintilian, the epigrammatist Martial, and the poet Lucan. The latter's uncle, Seneca, and Seneca's father (the Elder) were both born in Córdoba. The younger Seneca was the leading intellectual figure in Nero's Rome and an influential politician, and in Renaissance times he was considered a model for dramatists.

Rome's cultural gift to Spain was the homogeneity of aesthetics and practicality. The coupling of architectural styles and engineering skill characterizes the aqueducts of Segovia (still in use), Tarragona, and Mérida. The Roman bridges—often today equipped with traffic lights—with their graceful curved arches and buttresses to stem tides and floods at Córdoba, Salamanca, and Ciudad Rodrigo might all have been designed by the same talented professional. Roman theaters took advantage—as did those of the Greeks before them—of the natural geographical contours, as at Mérida and Tarragona. The mosaics at Itálica and Ampurias trace delicate decorative motifs for such utilitarian elements as floors and walls. Even the dead were well cataloged and handsomely commemorated, as attested to by the extensive class-conscious cemetery at **Carmona**, between Seville and Córdoba.

The ruins of an entire Roman town, now being excavated at **Baelo Claudio** (south of Cádiz on the Costa de la Luz) testify to the municipal role of law, religion, and the arts in a town that was in fact a stinking coastal fish-factory center (even the vats survive).

- **210 B.C.**: Rome's Scipio Africanus captures Carthago Nova (New Carthage, now Cartagena) and forces the Carthaginians out of Gadir (Cádiz) into North Africa.
- **206 B.C.**: Romans occupy most of the Iberian Peninsula despite continued local opposition. Spain be-

comes the first vast area assimilated by the Romans; Hispania, as the Romans called Spain, is divided into two great provinces—west of the Ebro, and east of that river.

- **181 B.C.**: Rome induces Iberian cities to pay taxes and provide auxiliaries for the imperial forces.
- **135 B.C.**: Iberian rebels establish a stronghold settlement at **Numantia**, near the río Duero; in 133 B.C., after eight months of resistance against the Romans, the Numantians set their city and themselves afire; the Romans rebuild Numantia, whose ruins today near Soria, northeast of Madrid, trace a typical Roman provincial town.
- **72 B.C.**: Pompey the Great is sent to Spain to defeat the rebellious Sertorious and returns to Rome boasting that he had conquered 876 cities.
- **45 B.C.**: The struggle between Julius Caesar and the faction of Pompey culminates in the battle of Munda (near Córdoba), with Caesar emerging victorious. Caesar is assassinated in 44.
- **19 B.C.**: The emperor Augustus defeats all tribal opposition in Spain and divides the Iberian Peninsula into three provinces: Baetica (southern Spain), rich and populous, with its capital at Córdoba; Lusitania (roughly modern Portugal), sparsely inhabited but rich in minerals, with its capital at Mérida in present-day Extremadura; and Tarraconensis (all of north, northwest, and central Spain), with its capital at Tarragona on the Mediterranean coast.
- **A.D.74**: Full Roman citizenship is granted to all Iberians under the Edict of Vespasian.
- **93–138**: Successive Roman emperors, Trajan and Hadrian, are born in Itálica, near Seville. Itálica's amphitheater, the fourth largest in the Roman world, is built to hold 30,000.
- **212**: *Civis Romanus Sum:* Every freeborn subject in the Empire is granted Roman citizenship by the Edict of Caracalla.
- **319**: After a lengthy period of dealing with refractory Christian groups, Christianity having reputedly been introduced to Spain by Saint James (Santiago) and a visit by Saint Paul circa 65, the Catholic Church is recognized as a legal institution, sharing rights with other religions.
- **410**: The Visigoths sack Rome and by 500 dominate Spain.

The Visigoths

Despite three centuries in which they ruled the Iberian Peninsula, the Visigoths are generally given short shrift by historians of Spain. They are likely to be grouped with those "barbarian hordes from the north," such as the Vandals, who invaded England, France, and Italy in the wake of the fall of the Roman Empire. In general, however, the Visigoths preserved the Roman administrative organization they found in Spain.

The small stone Arian-Christian Visigothic churches had geometric decorative motifs, anticipating their Moorish successors in Spain with arches shaped like horseshoes. Today, Madrid's Museo Arqueológico has on display a magnificent jeweled votive crown that attests to the Visigoths' predilection for, and talent for creating, sumptuous jewelry. The Gothic language brought by the Visigoths to Iberia was soon subsumed by the Latin-speaking population, while Greek survived as a literary language among the cultivated.

- **505**: The Visigoths establish supremacy on the Iberian Peninsula.
- **554**: The Visigoths make Toledo their capital; ultimately Church councils here will become the main force in Visigothic government.
- **568–586**: The reign of King Leovigild unites the peninsula; he subjugates the Basques, amalgamates the previously independent kingdom of Galicia, and recovers Baetica from the Byzantines, who had controlled it since the emperor Justinian (483–565) had sent an army to win back Spain for Rome.
- **578**: Saint Leander is named Archbishop of Seville; he and his successor, Saint Isidore (560–636), bring Spain much cultural distinction in Europe.
- **584**: King Leovigild's son, Recared, introduces a codified law and a workable tax system modeled on Roman precedents. Converted to Catholicism, Recared oversees the religious unification of Spain, fusing the Visigothic and Hispano-Roman populations.
- **613**: King Sisebut drafts anti-Semitic legislation compelling all Jews in Spain to be baptized or be banished from the peninsula.
- **711**: King Roderick is routed by an army of 12,000 Berbers from North Africa. In three years these "Moors" establish control in almost all parts of the peninsula.

The Moors

Claims that the Moors "occupied" Spain for almost 800 years are misleading on two counts. Over that period the Moors were a steadily decreasing presence as the Christian Reconquest moved southward; in the final 200 years only Andalusia was under Moslem rule, and for the last century and a half Moorish Granada stood alone. But it is incorrect to speak of the Moors in Spain as if they were somehow on a prolonged visit: They were a significant part of Spain for almost twice as long as America has been "occupied" by Europeans. For eight centuries there were Moslem Spaniards and Christian Spaniards and Jewish Spaniards.

As a Moslem caliphate, Córdoba became the cultural center of western Europe. Two Córdoban contemporaries, Averroës (1126–1198) and Maimonides (1135–1204), exemplified that cultural dominance. Averroës brought the teachings of Aristotle to the West and was himself a physicist, an astrologer, a mathematician, a doctor, and a philosopher. Maimonides, the famed Jewish scholar, was a doctor, a theologian, and a philosopher.

"The greatest calamity that ever happened to Spain was its expulsion of the Moors," wrote Samuel Prime in *The Alhambra and the Kremlin* (1873).

The Moors gave the Iberian Peninsula a heritage of decorative and architectural distinction. Long after the Christian Reconquest faded from memory, Moorish artisans employed by Spaniards continued in the Islamic artistic (Mudejar) tradition. Three great Moorish cities of Andalusia highlight distinctive aesthetic characteristics of the Islamic dynasty: in Córdoba (756–1010) the horseshoe-shaped arch of the great mosque; in Seville (1010–1248) the Giralda tower, then a minaret, with its brick construction and wide bands of decorative relief; and in Granada's Alhambra (1248–1492) the use of stucco and ceramics, proportioned fenestration and door panels, and stalactite ceilings.

- **711**: Moslems from North Africa annihilate the Visigoth forces; soon the Moors occupy the entire Iberian Peninsula.
- **722**: Spanish resistance begins at Covadonga (on the northernmost Atlantic coast), marking the opening of the 800-year Christian War of Reconquest.
- **756**: An independent emirate (distinct from Damascus control) is established at Córdoba.

- **785**: Emir Abd ar-Rahman I begins construction of Córdoba's Mezquita (great mosque).
- **778**: Charlemagne invades Spain; he is defeated by the Moors at Zaragoza but keeps Navarra and the "Spanish March," which became Catalonia.
- **929**: The emirate at Córdoba is raised to a caliphate.
- **936**: Abd ar-Rahman III begins the construction of a vast, opulent palace complex, Medina Azahara, on the outskirts of Córdoba.
- **961–976**: The reign of al-Hakem II; Córdoba reaches heights of prominence as the wealthiest, most populated, and most cultured European city.
- **1010**: Córdoba is sacked by Christian forces, thus ending its preeminence in Andalusia.
- **1031**: Division of the caliphate into *taifa* (faction) kingdoms.
- **1094**: El Cid (Rodrigo Díaz de Vivar), the prototypical Castilian chivalric warrior, conquers Valencia; the 12th-century anonymous *El cantar de mío Cid* later becomes the foremost Spanish epic.
- **1184**: A minaret, later converted to the Giralda tower, rises in Seville.
- **1195**: Victory at the battle of Alarcos (in La Mancha) of Almohad horsemen over Spanish Christian forces pushes the lines of the Reconquest back north to the río Tagus.
- **1212**: The battle of Las Navas de Tolosa. Alfonso VIII, with united forces, achieves victory over the Almohades, now limited to Andalusia territory.
- **1236**: Córdoba surrenders to Ferdinand III of Castile.
- **1248**: Seville surrenders to "Saint" Ferdinand.
- **1300**: Juan Ruiz writes *Libro de buen amor,* a fusion of minstrel and learned verse, earning him later comparison with Chaucer and Boccaccio.
- **1334–1391**: The palaces of the Alhambra at Granada are built under the reigns of Yusuf I and Mohammed V.
- **1469**: Ferdinand of Aragón marries Isabella of Castile.
- **1478**: The Inquisition begins.
- **1483**: All Jews are ordered to leave southern Spain.
- **1487**: Málaga is taken by Christian forces.
- **1492**: *January:* Moorish King Boabdil surrenders Granada to Ferdinand and Isabella; the Reconquest of the peninsula is completed. *March:* Expulsion of all Jews who refuse to be baptized (some 150,000),

many of whom go to either the Low Countries or the Levant. These Sephardic Jews have in some instances preserved their Castilian speech, known as Ladino. An estimated 300,000 *conversos* remain in Spain. *October:* Columbus claims newly discovered lands overseas to the west for the Spanish Crown.

- **1494**: Pope Alexander VI publishes a bull dividing the New World between Spain and Portugal.

The Golden Empire

In the 16th and 17th centuries Spain was the most powerful country in the Western world. With vast territories in the Americas and the wealth they produced, and with the European Hapsburgian inheritance (Sicily, Naples, Milan, Sardinia, the Netherlands, Burgundy), Spain was an economic and political force of the first rank. The architecture, painting, literature, and sculpture of the period reflect Spain's self-awareness as a preeminent power.

Two antithetical Renaissance architectural styles—the Plateresque and the Classical—neatly suggest extremes of the Spanish character. The former, an exuberantly elaborate sculptured tracing, is possibly best seen in the entrance façade at the University of Salamanca. The second style, coolly severe and disciplined, was chosen by Holy Roman Emperor Charles V for his palace at the Alhambra and by his son, Philip II, who found in Juan de Herrera the perfect architect for his massive Escorial. A rare example of this style in a private residence still exists in mint condition in a palace built by the marqués de Santa Cruz at **Viso del Marqués** in La Mancha. Madrid's formal plaza Mayor, designed by Juan Gómez de Mora in the late 16th century, shows the Classical style at its urban best.

Literature in the Spanish Renaissance was crowned by *Don Quixote de la Mancha,* and Miguel de Cervantes's timeless classic reflects the national ethos as well as elusive reality. Cervantes, who died the same year as Shakespeare, shared fame in his lifetime with Lope de Vega (1562–1635), whose plays are the cornerstone of today's Spanish theater. Pedro Calderón de la Barca's play *Life's a Dream* may be his most honored work. Luis de Góngora y Argote (1561–1627), whose poetic style, relying on antithesis and parallelism, is the most individual of his era, contrasts sharply with his illustrious predecessor, Garcilaso de la Vega (1503–1536), a poet who is to the Spanish Renaissance what Spenser is to Elizabethan England. The picaresque novel, with its hero travelling from one adventure to another, is best represented (in addition to *Don Quixote*) by the anonymous *Lazarillo de Tormes* (1554) and Mateo Alemán's *Guzmán de Alfarache* (1599).

Tirso de Molina's (d. 1648) seminal drama *Don Juan* was to inspire more than 40 writers, poets, and composers, among them Molière, Byron, Goldoni, Mozart, Shaw, and Brecht, as well as José Zorrilla's drama *Don Juan Tenorio*.

Only two Spanish artists during the Golden Age were well known outside Spain, Bartolomé Esteban Murillo (1617–1682) and José Ribera (1588–1652); and international recognition of El Greco (1541–1614), Diego Velázquez (1599–1660), and Francisco de Zurbarán (1598–1664) began only in the 19th century. Most early Spanish Renaissance painters confined themselves to richly colored and often mystically sentimentalized religious scenes, or to portraits of the nobility. Velázquez, painting almost nothing but secular subjects, is a masterly exception.

Gothic carving developed a purely Spanish style, the Isabelline, with fantastic lace-like surfaces. The interiors of Spanish Renaissance churches offer exquisite carving in both wood and alabaster, particularly in choir stalls, mausoleums, and retables. Crafts of the Renaissance included tapestries, embroideries, embossed leather work, and wrought iron in patios and on the ubiquitous balconies. Massive furniture decorated with wood carving filled Renaissance rooms.

- **1508**: Garci Rodríguez de Montalvo publishes the first novel of chivalry, *Amadís de Gaula*.
- **1512**: Ferdinand V annexes the kingdom of Navarra, completing the unification of Spain.
- **1513**: Juan Ponce de León discovers Florida; Vasco Núñez de Balboa sights the Pacific Ocean.
- **1516**: Charles I (Charles V of the Holy Roman Empire) becomes the first ruling Hapsburg king in Spain.
- **1519**: Hernán Cortés begins the conquest of Mexico.
- **1526**: Pedro Machuca designs Charles V's palace at the Alhambra.
- **1533**: Francisco Pizarro conquers the Inca Empire in Peru.
- **1540**: The Society of Jesus (Jesuits) receives the approval of Pope Paul III; Francis Xavier is one of six members.
- **1554**: The anonymous *Lazarillo de Tormes* introduces the picaresque novel to world literature.

- **1556**: Philip II assumes the throne after the abdication of his father, Charles V, who goes off to live at a monastery in Yuste (Extremadura).
- **1562**: Saint Teresa of Avila begins writing her spiritual autobiography; Philip II's palace-monastery-museum complex, El Escorial, is begun.
- **1580**: Philip II unites Portugal with Spain.
- **1586**: El Greco (Domenicos Theotocopoulos) paints *Burial of the Count of Orgaz* in Toledo.
- **1588**: The defeat of the Spanish Armada by the British fleet heralds Spain's decline as a world power.
- **1600**: El Greco paints his *Saint Jerome,* now in the Frick Collection, New York City.
- **1605**: Cervantes publishes *Don Quixote.*
- **1609**: Lope de Vega writes *The New Art of Writing Plays.* A soldier-priest, the dramatist claimed to have created more than 1,500 works, making Spanish dramatic comedy his province.
- **1624**: Velázquez paints an unadorned portrait of Philip IV.
- **1631**: Francisco Zurbarán paints *Apotheosis of St. Thomas Aquinas.*
- **1640**: Portugal regains independence from Spain.
- **1656**: Velázquez paints *Las Meninas,* his most celebrated work.
- **1665–1700**: The reign of Carlos II.
- **1678**: Murillo paints the prototypical Madonna in his *Immaculate Conception.*
- **1689**: José Churriguera, architect and sculptor, designs his first great work, a catafalque for Queen María Luisa. His ornate variation of the Baroque style—Churrigueresque—is best seen in the sacristry of the **Carthusian monastery** at Granada.

Bourbon Spain

In a century that marked Spain's subjugation to foreign influence—the Bourbons were, after all, French, and Italy also exerted a strong cultural influence—Goya (Francisco José de Goya y Lucientes, 1746–1828) emerges as the great exception in that age of mediocrity and lack of originality. He became court painter in 1786 under Carlos III. His earlier work had centered on popular scenes—bright, free, and charming—and now he offered paintings of notables that were realistic and often unrestrainedly candid. In the years 1790 to 1800 he produced his *Caprichos,* a series of etchings laced with social satire. A later series, *The Disasters of War,* depicts scenes of horror and black despair reflecting the realities of the War of Independence (discussed below).

In music, the *zarzuela* continued the popular Spanish operetta tradition. Italian opera and Italian singers enjoyed court favor under Philip V and Ferdinand VI.

Despite the efforts of reformers in all fields, the 18th century was one of continued cultural decline following the collapse of the Hapsburg economy. Attempts to improve agriculture, stimulate commerce and industry, and establish a better educational system met with limited success. Even Spain's writers seemed drained of originality and expressive power.

- **1700**: Philip V founds the Bourbon dynasty in Spain. His accession to the throne leads to the beginning of the War of the Spanish Succession in 1701.
- **1704**: Gibraltar is taken by the British.
- **1713**: War of the Spanish Succession ends with the recognition of Philip as king of Spain. By the Treaty of Utrecht, however, Spain cedes Gibraltar to the British and loses its Italian possessions—Sicily and Sardinia—as well as Luxembourg and Flanders.
- **1714**: Philip V opens the royal library, said to contain 200,000 volumes, to the public.
- **1746**: Ferdinand VI takes the throne.
- **1752**: Ferdinand VI founds the academy of San Fernando for artists.
- **1759–1788**: Carlos III takes the throne and launches an extensive public works program, completes work on the royal palace in Madrid, and builds the Prado.
- **1786**: Goya paints a portrait of Carlos III as a beak-nosed hunter with dog and musket.
- **1788**: Carlos IV takes the throne.
- **1793**: When Louis XVI of France is guillotined, Spain declares war on France.
- **1800**: Goya paints *Family of Charles IV* (now in the Prado), a depiction of a powerful, bedizened, ridiculous, yet majestic family.

Napoleonic Spain and the War of Independence

Goya captured the horror and passion of the War of Independence in *The Third of May, 1808,* depicting in blazing colors the execution by firing squad of citizens of Madrid who had protested the French presence in Spain.

- **1804**: Napoleon is crowned emperor.
- **1805**: Spain joins with France in a war against England. The Spanish navy, out of Cádiz, is defeated at the battle of Trafalgar.
- **1808**: Napoleon invades Spain and declares his brother, Joseph Bonaparte, king, forcing both Carlos IV and his son, Ferdinand VII, to renounce rights to the Spanish throne. On May 2, the War of Independence (Peninsular War) begins. The Spanish army of 27,000 soldiers is victorious over the French at Bailén. Napoleon takes personal command; British campaigns against the French are led by the duke of Wellington.
- **1809**: The French (who now have close to 400,000 men in Spain) occupy Andalusia, except for Cádiz.
- **1812**: Liberals at Cádiz draft a constitution abolishing the Inquisition, censorship, and serfdom, and making the monarch subordinate to the wishes of the Cortes (parliament). Wellington is victorious at the siege of Ciudad Rodrigo.
- **1814**: Napoleon recalls the French troops; the War of Independence ends; Ferdinand VII takes the throne and repudiates the constitution. During the decade 1810–1820 most of Spain's South American territories gain their independence.

The 19th Century

Despite the fact that Spain was relatively barren aesthetically, French composers born during this century turned to it for inspiration (Ravel for *Boléro;* Bizet for *Carmen;* Lalo for his *Symphonie Espagnole;* Chabrier for his *España*), and Spanish composers established themselves internationally: Albéniz (*Iberia*), Enrique Granados (*Goyescas*), Joaquín Turina (*Seville Symphony*), and Manuel de Falla (*La Vida Breve*).

The three Carlist wars that followed the death of the conservative Ferdinand and the claims of Don Carlos, his brother, as legitimate successor were fundamentally civil wars between liberals and conservatives. The former advocated constitutional government without church interference, and the latter favored an alliance between church and state. In 1875 the Bourbon Alfonso XII, as constitutional monarch, oversaw a period of social and political reforms. But the Spanish-American War late in the century ended with Spain granting independence to Cuba, ceding Puerto Rico to the United States, and selling the Philippines to the United States for $20 million. Spain as an international power had ceased to exist. "Never was a century more disastrous to a nation than the nineteenth century was to Spain," writes Jan Morris.

- **1814–1833**: Ferdinand VII rules as absolute monarch.
- **1821**: Spain accepts the independence of Mexico.
- **1833–1868**: The reign of Isabella II.
- **1833–1874**: Three Carlist wars in which church-supported royalists fight liberal constitutionalists.
- **1870–1873**: The reign of Amadeus, chosen by the Cortes as constitutional monarch. He abdicates in 1873.
- **1873–1875**: The first Spanish republic is established.
- **1883**: Antoni Gaudí begins building his Barcelona church, La Sagrada Família.
- **1886–1912**: After the death of Alfonso XII, Queen María Christina is regent for her son, Alfonso XIII.
- **1898**: The Spanish-American War.

The 20th Century to the Civil War

Celebrated Spanish cultural figures born into this period of crisis in the nation's self-confidence at the turn of the century include: Pablo Picasso (1881–1973), who was born in Málaga, lived most of his life in France, and dominated the world of 20th-century art; José Ortega y Gasset (1883–1955), philosopher, writer, and statesman, best known for *Revolt of the Masses* (1930); Miguel de Unamuno (1864–1936), one of the "Generation of '98," whose *Tragic Sense of Life* is his philosophical credo; Juan Ramón Jiménez (1881–1958), poet and author of the children's classic *Platero y Yo;* Antonio Machado (1875–1939), poet of strength and reflective simplicity and an interpreter of the Castilian landscape; Federico García Lorca (1899–1936), the dramatist and poet whose Civil War assassination gave him a mythic aura; Joan Miró (1893–1983) painter, sculptor, engraver; Juan Gris (1887–1927), celebrated artist member of expatriate group in Paris; architect Antoni Gaudí (1852–1926); and artist Salvador Dalí (1904–1989) and Luis Buñuel (1900–1983), Spain's finest film director, who collaborated on two surrealist films, *Un Chien Andalou* and *L'Age d'Or.*

- **1902**: An anarchic union formed in Barcelona proposes general strikes instead of political action; Alfonso XIII assumes the throne at the age of 16.
- **1909**: A general strike is called in Catalonia; Spain is placed temporarily under martial law.
- **1912**: A railway strike is broken militarily by liberal prime minister José Canalejas, later assassinated.
- **1914–1918**: Spain maintains neutrality in World War I.
- **1917**: Violent strikes in northern Spain.
- **1923**: Barcelona army rebellion; Alfonso XIII approves General Miguel Primo de Rivera's military dictatorship; the constitution is suspended.
- **1926**: Treaty with Italy; Spain adopts fascist administrative policies.
- **1930**: Primo de Rivera resigns after economic failures.
- **1931**: April elections force Alfonso XIII to leave Spain; second Republic proclaimed; liberal constitutionalists installed.
- **1932**: The Agrarian Reform Act expropriates large tracts of land.
- **1933**: Elections find Spain split between leftist liberals and the newly founded fascist Falange party under José Antonio, son of former dictator Miguel Primo de Rivera.

The Civil War and the Franco Regime

Picasso's *Guernica* speaks for this searing period in Spain's history. The bombing by German planes of the ancient Basque town of Guernica on April 26, 1937, a market day, with its killing of more than 2,000 civilians, became the ominous herald of our time. The world saw itself at the mercy of aerial expeditions of destruction.

Picasso submitted the painting he called *Guernica* to the 1937 Paris World's Fair in response to his commission from the Spanish government. *Guernica* is not in itself a painting of a war scene. There is no battle, no opposing factors. Figures in the painting include six human beings and three animals, a table, a horseshoe, a sword, a flower, an arrow and a spear (both broken), and a gas lamp. *Guernica* has no single meaning; it evokes the neurosis of a war-torn age.

Picasso explicitly denied permission for the work to enter Spain until a "stable, democratic government" was installed there. In Picasso's view this did not occur in his lifetime. He died in 1973, Franco two years later. In 1981, on the hundredth anniversary of Picasso's birth, *Guernica* was moved from New York's Museum of Modern Art to Spain, where it was placed in the Casón del Buen Retiro of Madrid's Prado.

- **1936**: Army revolt in Spanish Morocco; General Francisco Franco lands in Spain and Civil War breaks out; the battle of Madrid; government moves to Valencia; Franco is proclaimed generalíssimo and insurgent head of state; Primo de Rivera is executed by the government; Federico García Lorca is shot by Falangists.
- **1937**: Guernica is bombed. Picasso's masterly *Guernica* engenders strong support from the Republican side; Nationalists gain control of northeastern Spain.
- **1937–1938**: The Republican government moves to Barcelona; battle of the Ebro with the loss of 150,000 Republicans.
- **1939**: In January Barcelona falls to Franco's forces, aided by German tanks and planes; a vast number of refugees leave Spain for France; the Civil War ends; England and France recognize the Franco regime; Spain's population is reduced by nearly a million through Civil War deaths and emigration.
- **1939–1945**: Spain is nonbelligerent in World War II but supplies aid to the Axis powers in the early part of the war.
- **1946–1947**: Spain is excluded from both the United Nations and NATO as well as from Marshall Plan aid.
- **1953**: Spain signs a treaty with the United States, exchanging bases on Spanish soil for $226 million in aid.
- **1955**: The United Nations admits Spain; revitalization as well as slackening of dictatorial restrictions begins in industry, housing, social security, and education.
- **1967**: The Religious Liberty Act loosens the grip of the Catholic Church.
- **1968**: The Press Act somewhat lessens press censorship.
- **1969**: Juan Carlos, grandson of Alfonso XIII, is proclaimed heir to the throne.
- **1975**: Franco dies; Juan Carlos I becomes king of Spain.

Spain Today

Since Franco's death in 1975 Spain has undergone a political and cultural transformation. The individual citizen of Spain today lives in a world in which freedom of expression and conduct prevail. The Catholic Church's ability to maintain the illegality of divorce, birth control, adultery, homosexuality, and abortion has been broken. Women's rights, now taken for granted, are only a few decades old. The increasing influx of tourists has given Spain a billion-dollar yearly source of income, and the manners and morals of the visitors have affected the land they chose to visit.

Spain's classic figurative separation from the rest of Europe is now a thing of the past; Spain is an active member of the world of great nations, and the Spanish people have recovered from a civil and political illness that seemed almost terminal. The vaunted pride of the individual Spaniard, once thought a matter of ethnic inheritance, is now a characteristic justified by the courage and energy expended in the last 20 years.

- **1976**: Juan Carlos appoints Adolfo Suárez González as prime minister.
- **1977**: First post-Franco elections; establishment of the ministry of culture.
- **1978**: Spain approves a new national constitution.
- **1981**: Suárez resigns; coup d'état is attempted by the Civil Guards in parliament, but Juan Carlos is successful in dealing with the insurgents; Leopoldo Calvo Sotela y Bustelo becomes prime minister, aligning Spain with NATO.
- **1982**: Felipe González is elected prime minister as the Socialist Party wins elections; Spain joins NATO.
- **1986**: Spain joins the European Community.
- **1988**: One-day general strike protests the inequity of business-boom benefits and workers' salaries; the unemployment rate of 18 percent is the highest in Europe.
- **1989**: Spain assumes the presidency of the European Community; Camilo José Cela wins the Nobel Prize for literature; Felipe González is reelected prime minister.
- **1992**: European Community integration is to be completed; Summer Olympics are to be held in Barcelona; World's Fair is to be held in Seville; 500th anniversary of Columbus's discovery of the Americas.

—Robert Packard

INDEX